ENLIGHTENED

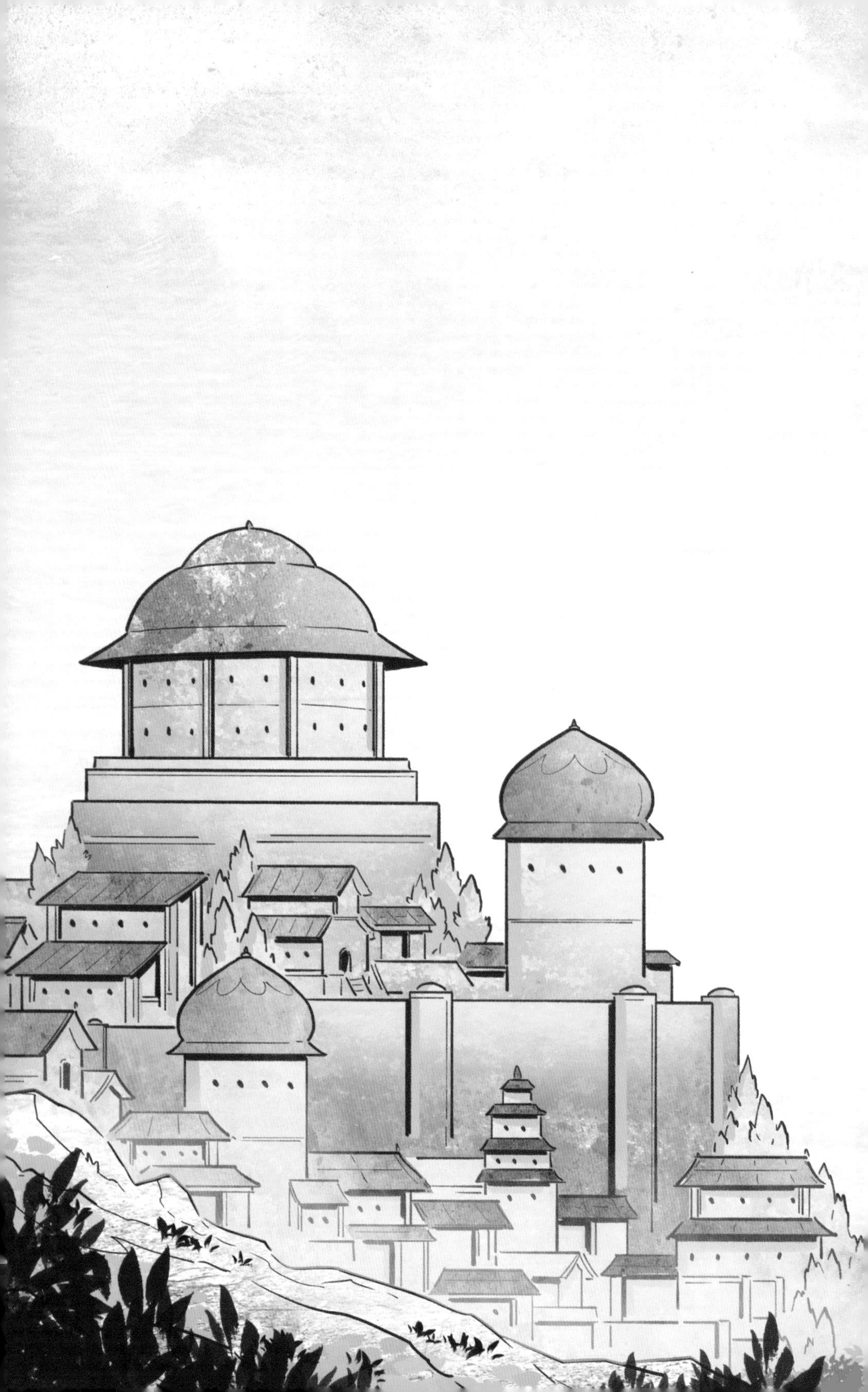

ENLIGHTENED

SACHI EDIRIWEERA

atheneum
New York London Toronto Sydney New Delhi

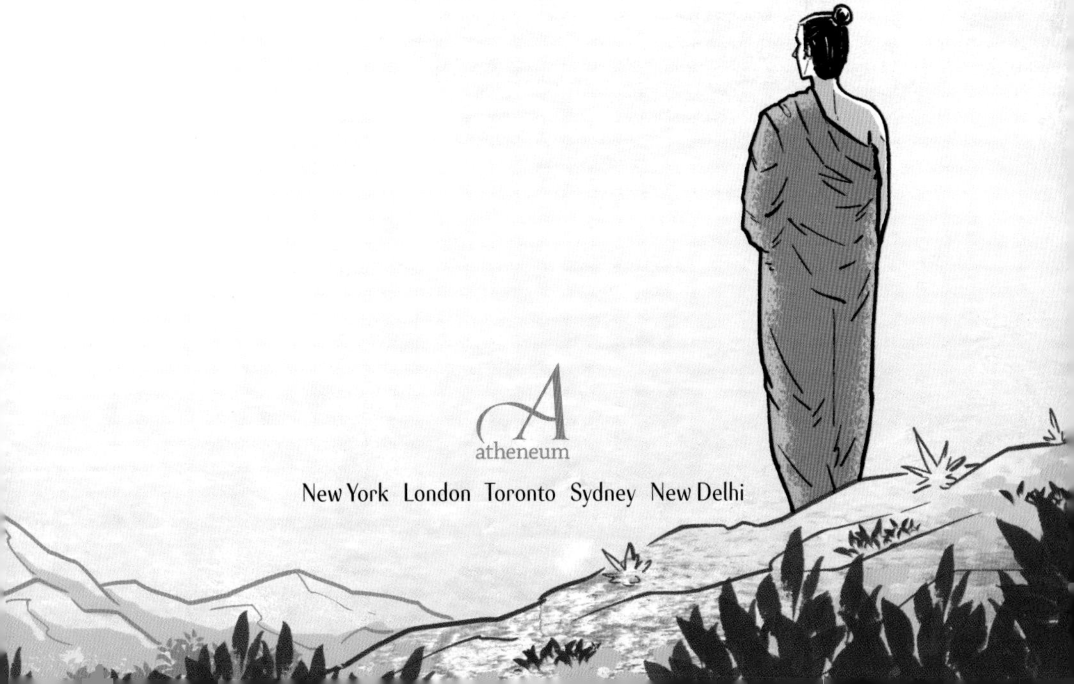

atheneum

An imprint of Simon & Schuster Children's Publishing Division

1230 Avenue of the Americas, New York, New York 10020

© 2023 by Sachi Ediriweera

Book design by Greg Stadnyk © 2023 by Simon & Schuster, Inc.

For information about special discounts for bulk purchases, please contact Simon & Schuster Special Sales at 1-866-506-1949 or business@simonandschuster.com.

The Simon & Schuster Speakers Bureau can bring authors to your live event. For more information or to book an event, contact the Simon & Schuster Speakers Bureau at 1-866-248-3049 or visit our website at www.simonspeakers.com.

The text for this book was set in fonts by Blambot.

The illustrations for this book were rendered digitally.

Manufactured in China

First Edition

2 4 6 8 10 9 7 5 3 1

Library of Congress Cataloging-in-Publication Data

Names: Ediriweera, Sachi, author.

Title: Enlightened / Sachi Ediriweera.

Description: First Atheneum hardcover edition. | New York : Atheneum Books for Young Readers, 2023. | Audience: Ages 12 up | Audience: Grades 7-9. | Summary: "A fictionalized biography of the life of Siddhartha Gautama, better known as the Buddha, the progenitor of Buddhism"— Provided by publisher.

Identifiers: LCCN 2022019272 (print) | LCCN 2022019273 (ebook) | ISBN 9781665903110 (hardcover) | ISBN 9781665903103 (paperback) | ISBN 9781665903127 (ebook)

Subjects: LCSH: Gautama Buddha—Juvenile literature. | CYAC: Gautama Buddha—Fiction. | Graphic novels. | LCGFT: Biographical fiction. | Graphic novels.

Classification: LCC PZ7.1.E275 En 2023 (print) | LCC PZ7.1.E275 (ebook) | DDC 741.5/973—dc23/eng/20220809

LC record available at https://lccn.loc.gov/2022019272

LC ebook record available at https://lccn.loc.gov/2022019273

To all the great teachers.
Thank you for showing us the way.

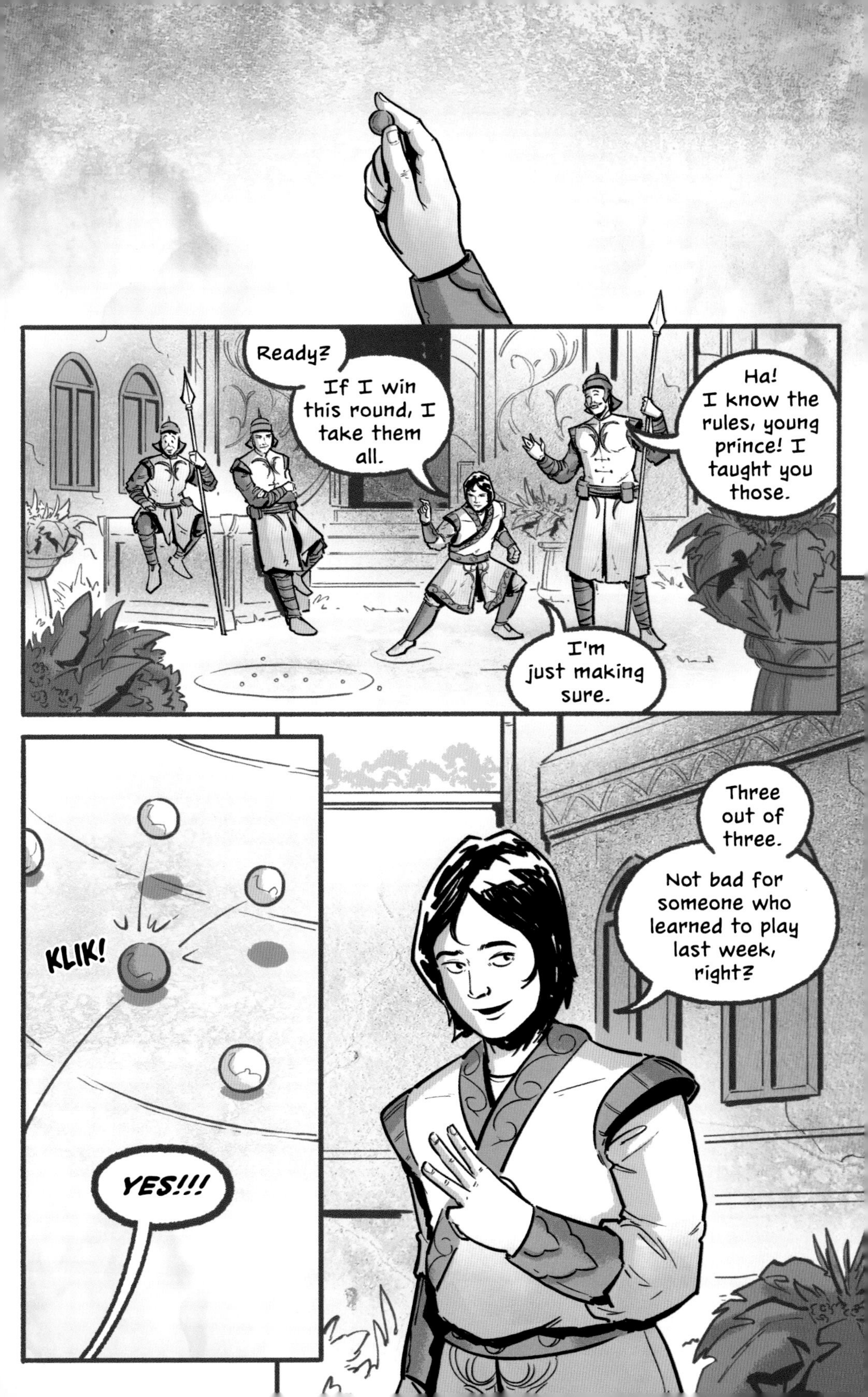
Ready?
If I win this round, I take them all.
Ha! I know the rules, young prince! I taught you those.
I'm just making sure.
KLIK!
YES!!!
Three out of three.
Not bad for someone who learned to play last week, right?

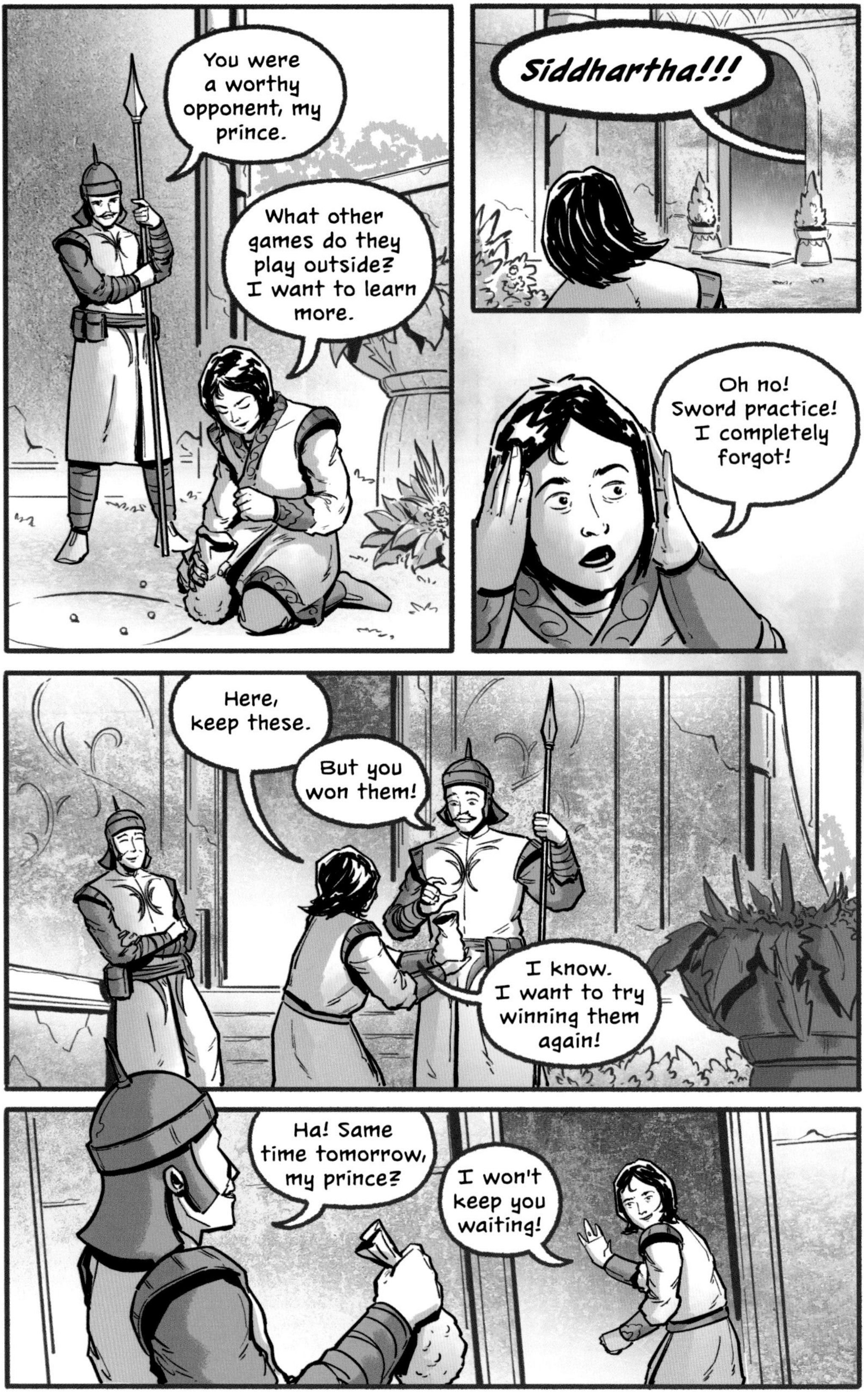
You were a worthy opponent, my prince.
What other games do they play outside? I want to learn more.
Siddhartha!!!
Oh no! Sword practice! I completely forgot!
Here, keep these.
But you won them!
I know. I want to try winning them again!
Ha! Same time tomorrow, my prince?
I won't keep you waiting!

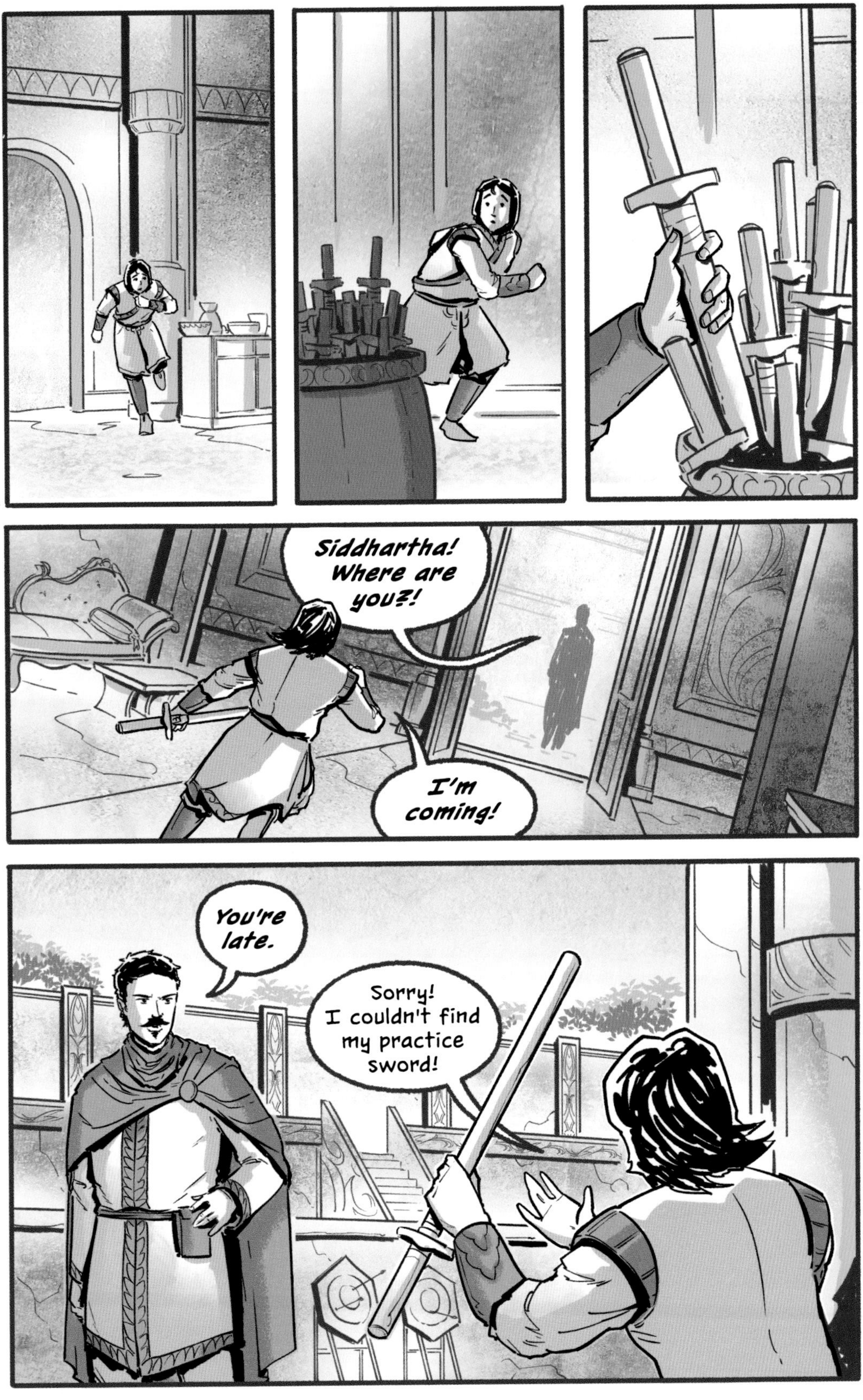
Siddhartha! Where are you?!
I'm coming!
You're late.
Sorry! I couldn't find my practice sword!

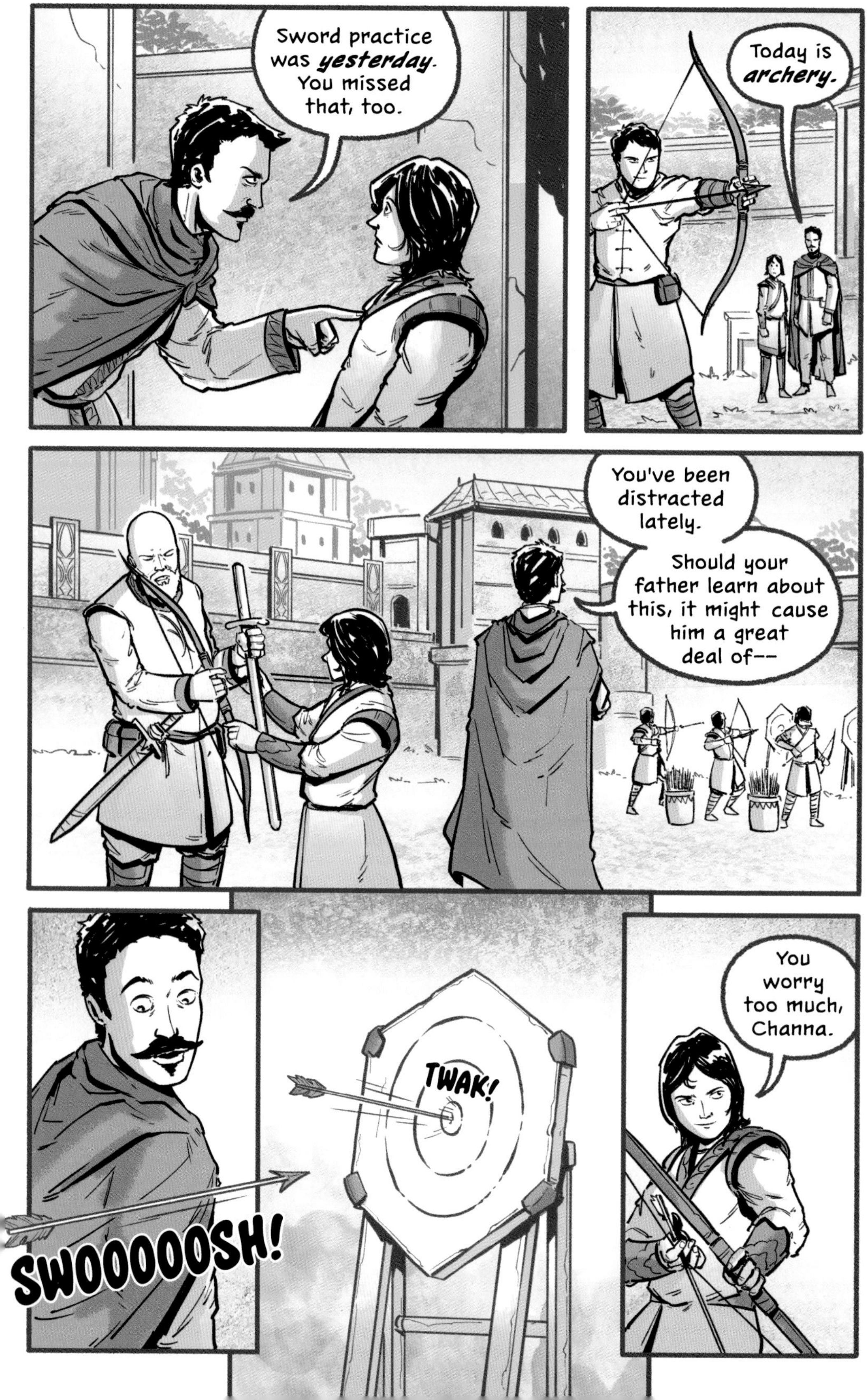
Sword practice was *yesterday*. You missed that, too.
Today is *archery*.
You've been distracted lately.
Should your father learn about this, it might cause him a great deal of--
TWAK!
SWOOOOOSH!
You worry too much, Channa.

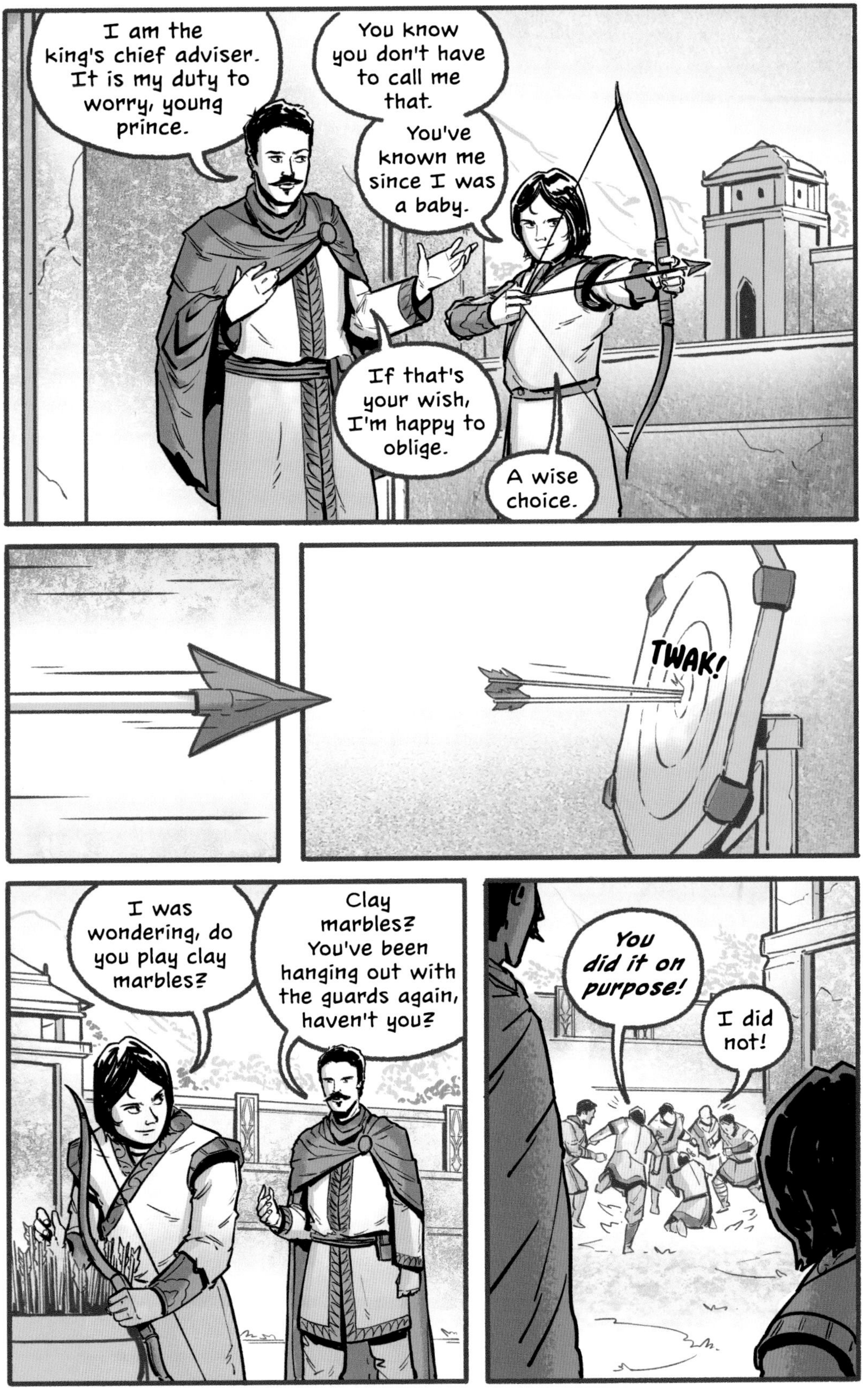
I am the king's chief adviser. It is my duty to worry, young prince.
You know you don't have to call me that.
You've known me since I was a baby.
If that's your wish, I'm happy to oblige.
A wise choice.
TWAK!
I was wondering, do you play clay marbles?
Clay marbles? You've been hanging out with the guards again, haven't you?
You did it on purpose!
I did not!

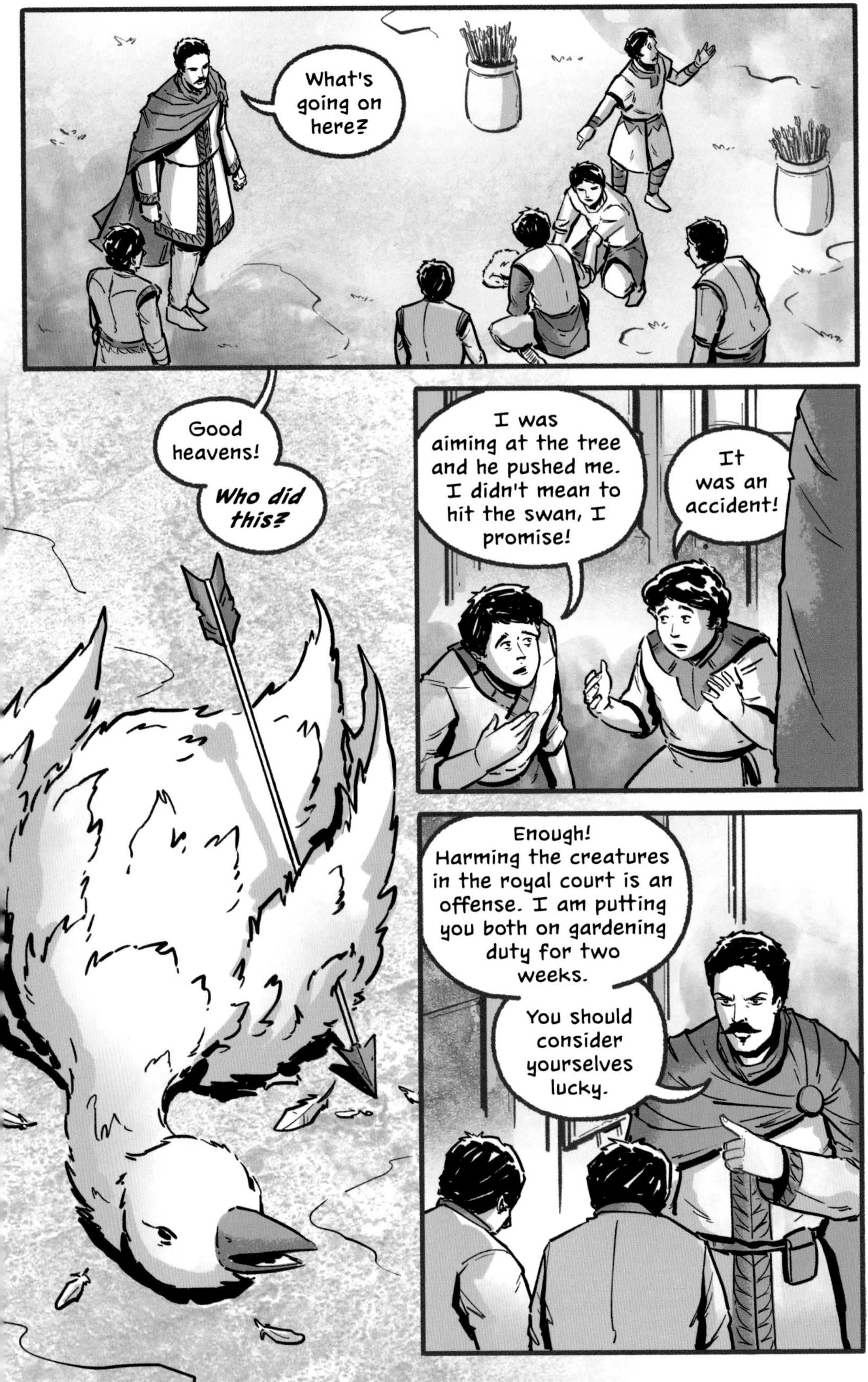
What's going on here?
Good heavens!
Who did this?
I was aiming at the tree and he pushed me. I didn't mean to hit the swan, I promise!
It was an accident!
Enough! Harming the creatures in the royal court is an offense. I am putting you both on gardening duty for two weeks.
You should consider yourselves lucky.

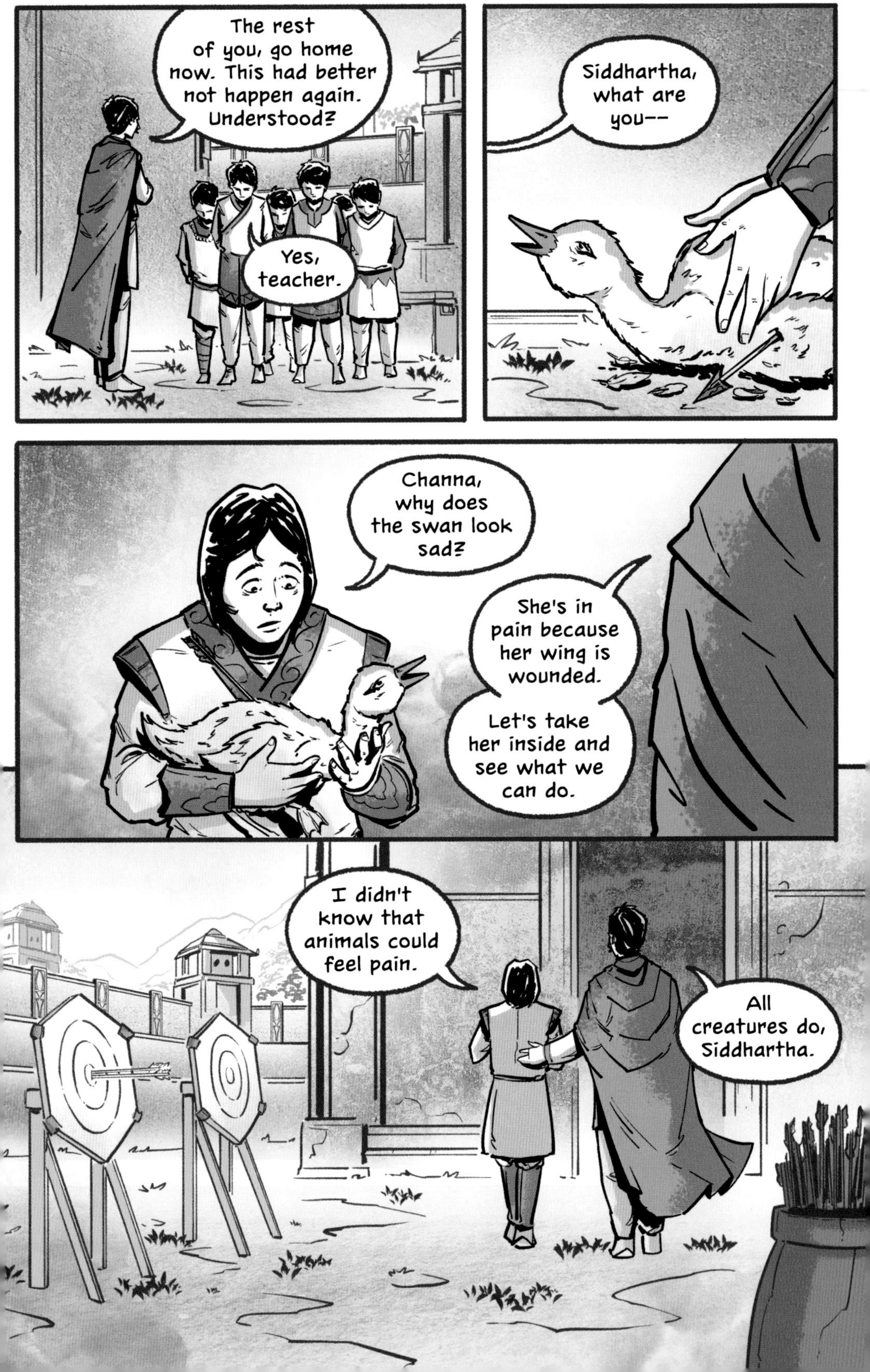
The rest of you, go home now. This had better not happen again. Understood?
Yes, teacher.
Siddhartha, what are you--
Channa, why does the swan look sad?
She's in pain because her wing is wounded.
Let's take her inside and see what we can do.
I didn't know that animals could feel pain.
All creatures do, Siddhartha.

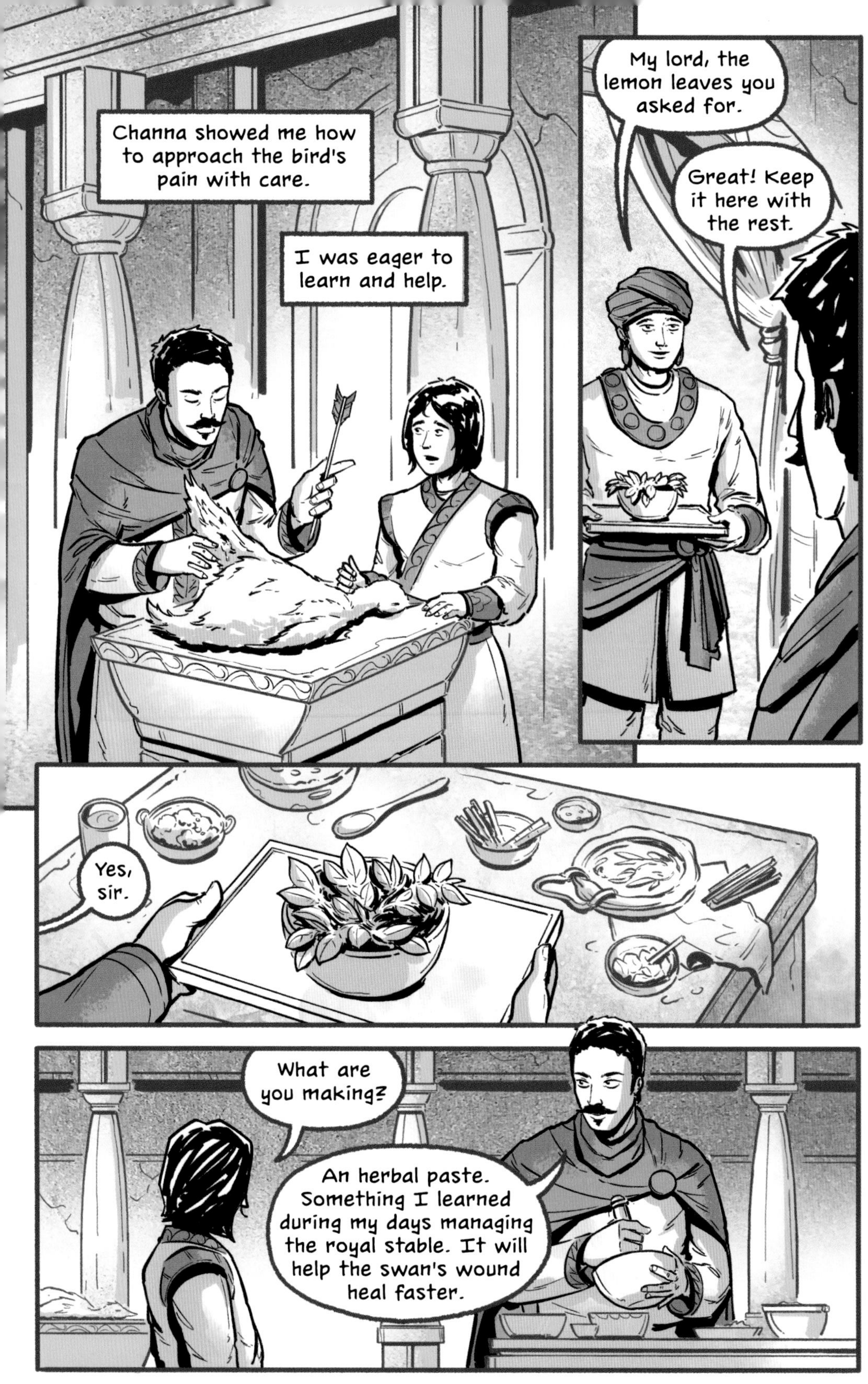
Channa showed me how to approach the bird's pain with care.
I was eager to learn and help.
My lord, the lemon leaves you asked for.
Great! Keep it here with the rest.
Yes, sir.
What are you making?
An herbal paste. Something I learned during my days managing the royal stable. It will help the swan's wound heal faster.

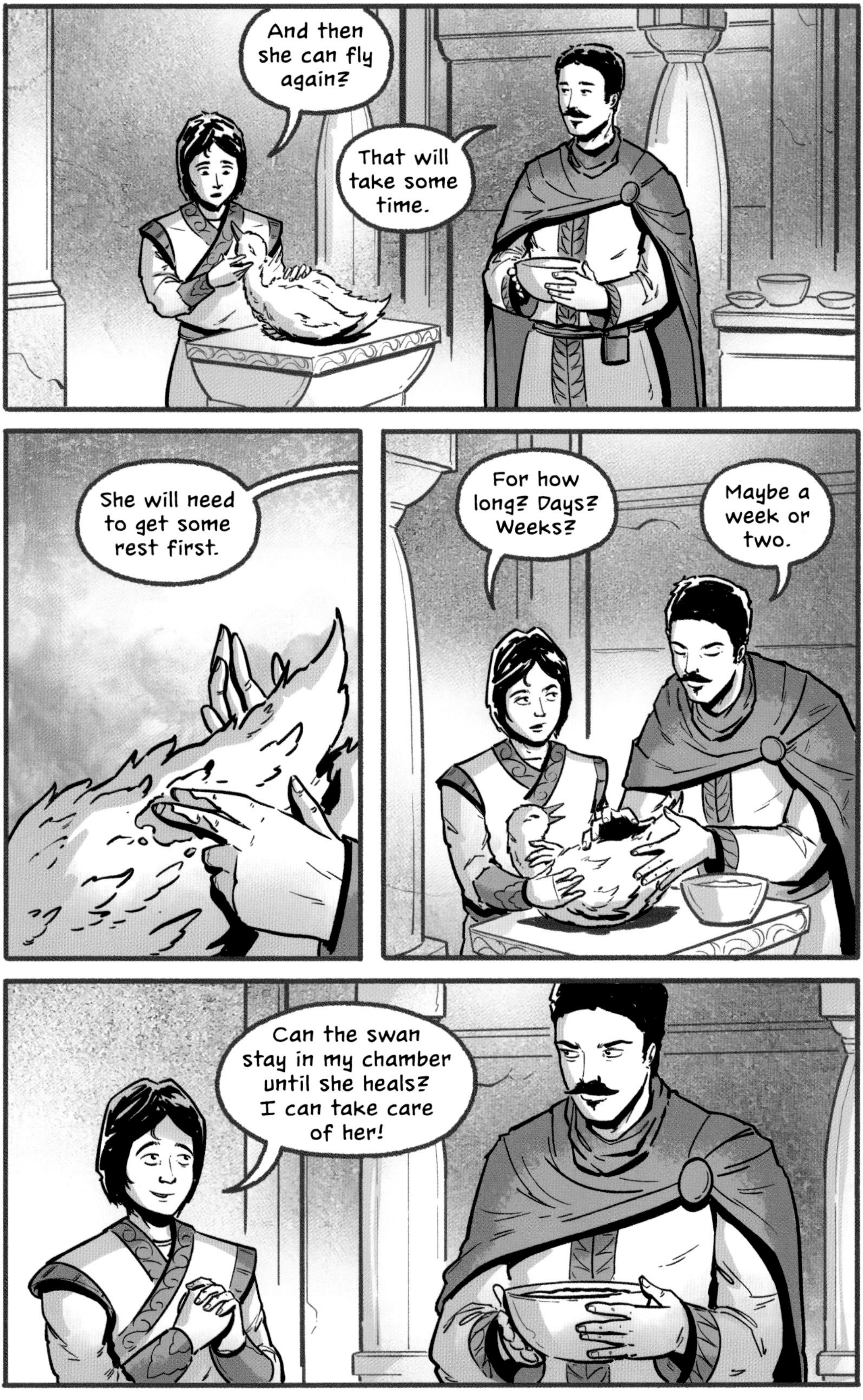
And then she can fly again?
That will take some time.
She will need to get some rest first.
For how long? Days? Weeks?
Maybe a week or two.
Can the swan stay in my chamber until she heals? I can take care of her!

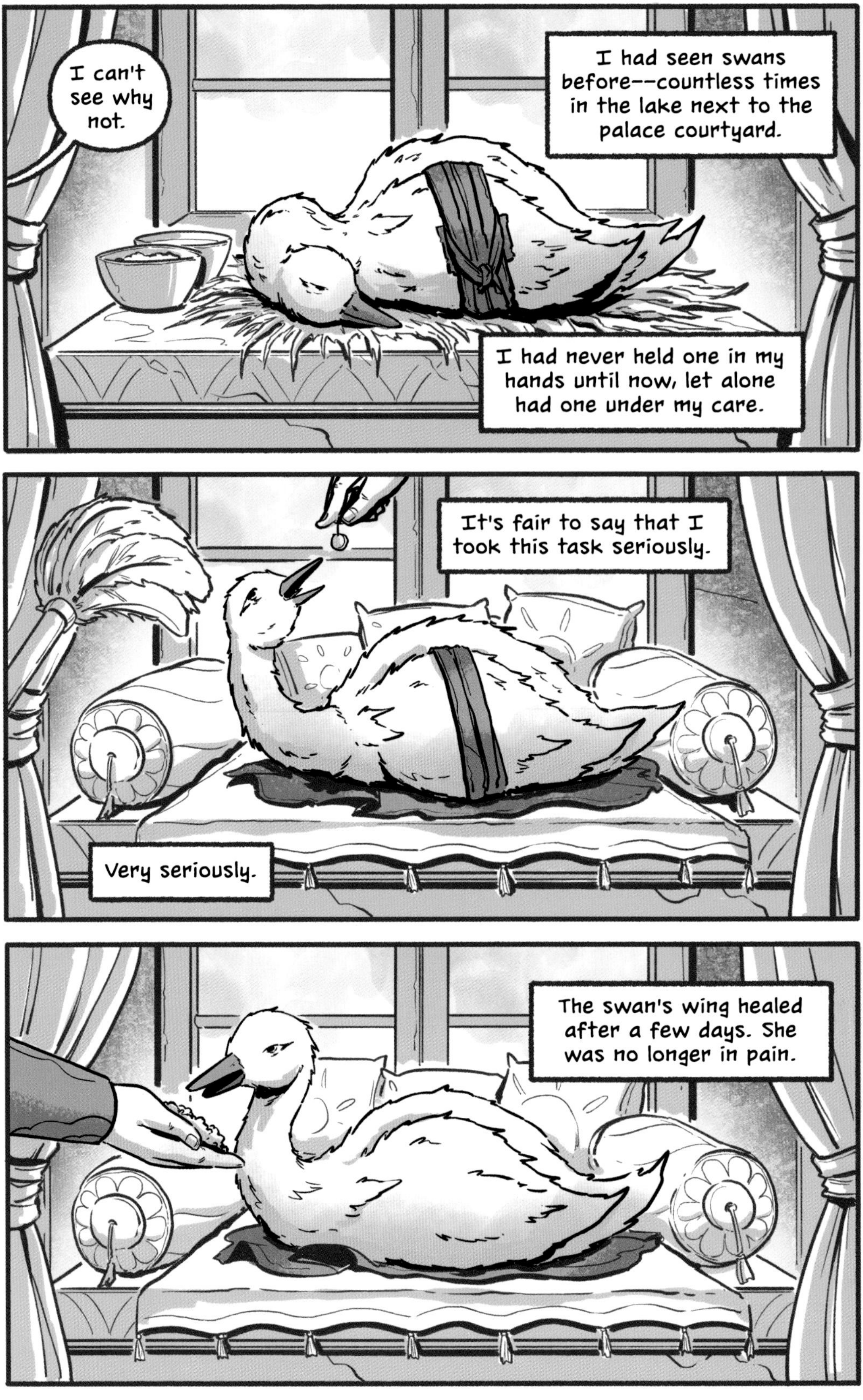
I had seen swans before--countless times in the lake next to the palace courtyard.
I can't see why not.
I had never held one in my hands until now, let alone had one under my care.
It's fair to say that I took this task seriously.
Very seriously.
The swan's wing healed after a few days. She was no longer in pain.

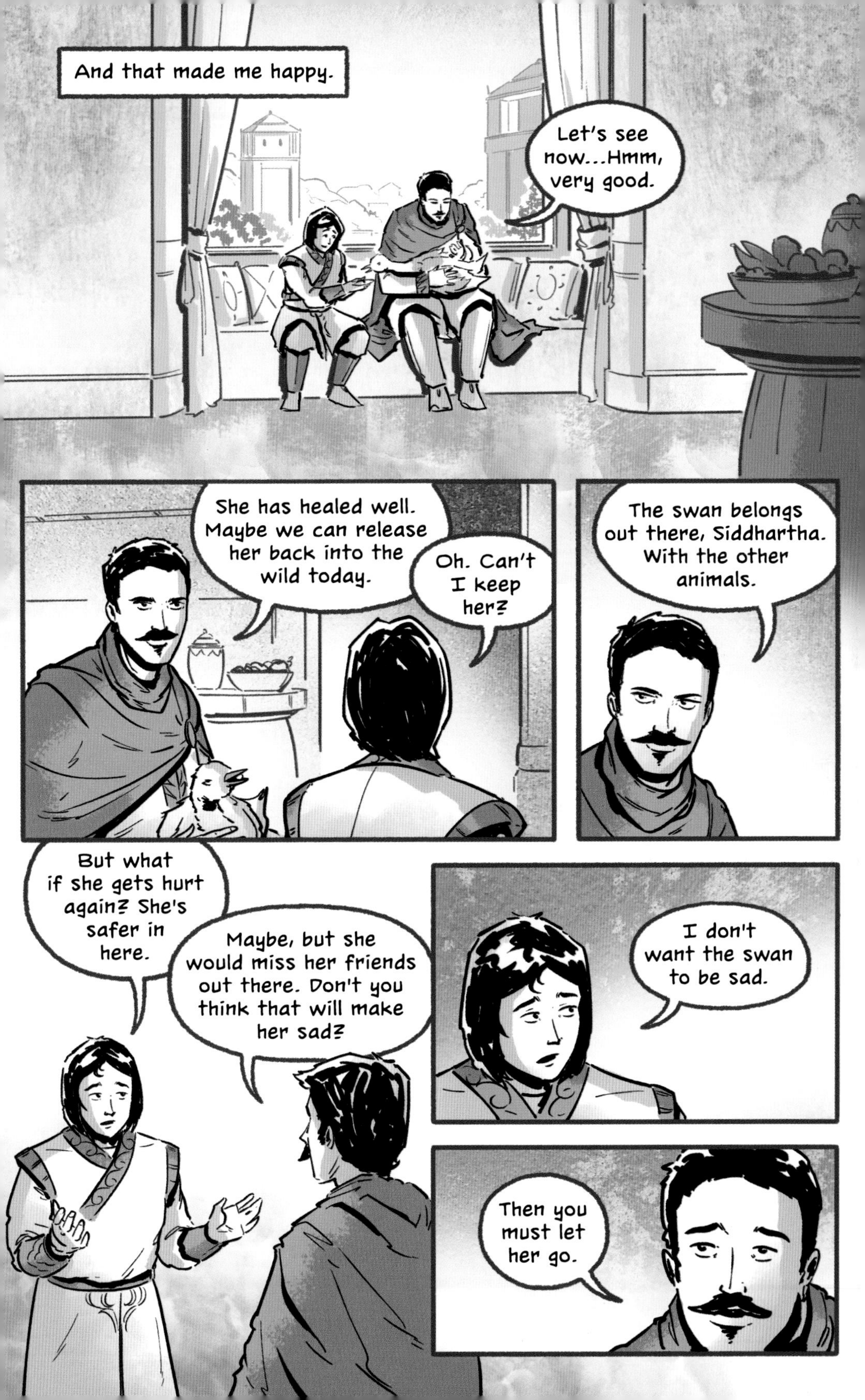

And that made me happy.
Let's see now...Hmm, very good.
She has healed well. Maybe we can release her back into the wild today.
Oh. Can't I keep her?
The swan belongs out there, Siddhartha. With the other animals.
But what if she gets hurt again? She's safer in here.
Maybe, but she would miss her friends out there. Don't you think that will make her sad?
I don't want the swan to be sad.
Then you must let her go.

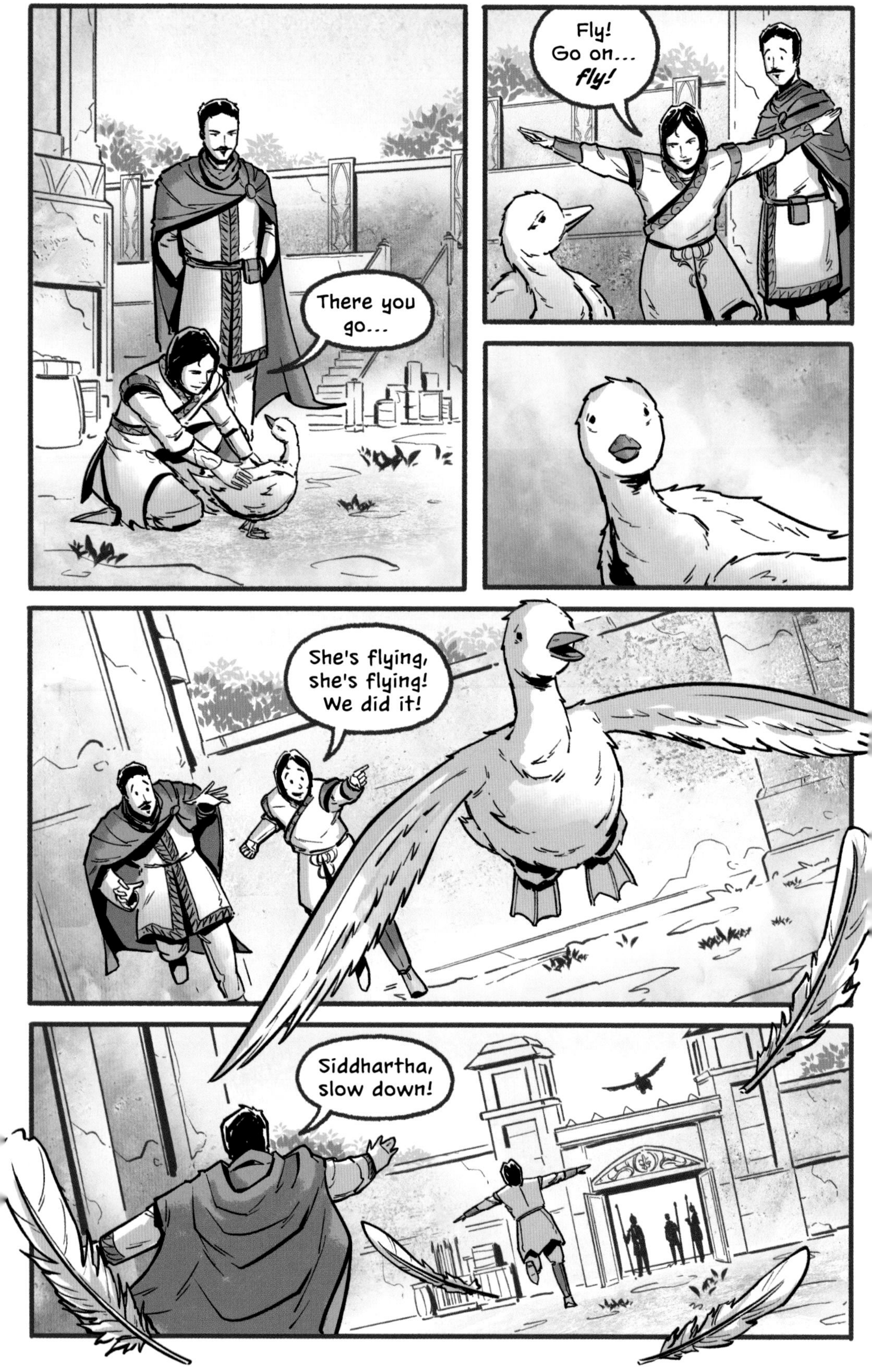
There you go...
Fly! Go on... *fly!*
She's flying, she's flying! We did it!
Siddhartha, slow down!

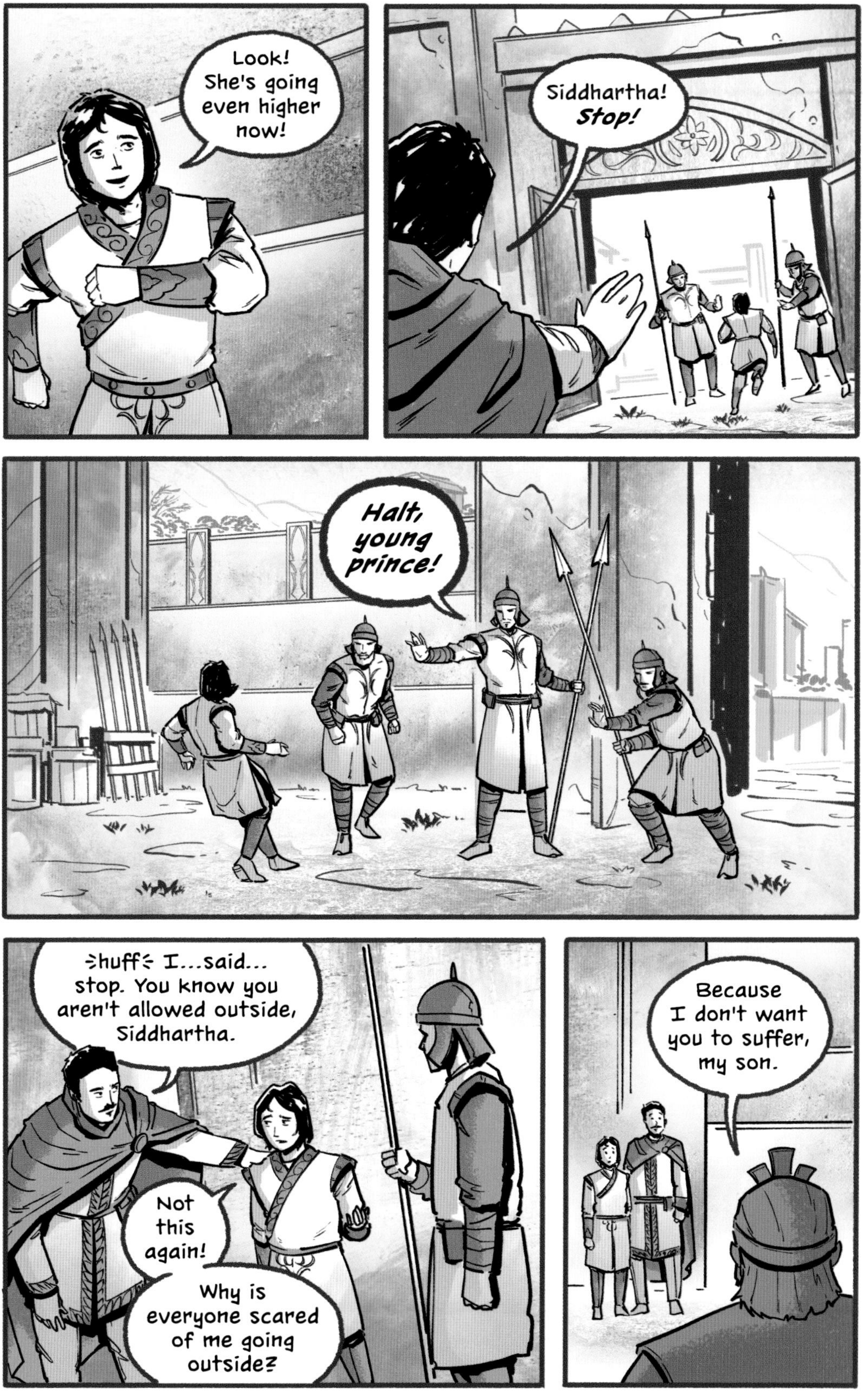
Look! She's going even higher now!
Siddhartha! Stop!
Halt, young prince!
⪢huff⪡ I...said... stop. You know you aren't allowed outside, Siddhartha.
Not this again!
Why is everyone scared of me going outside?
Because I don't want you to suffer, my son.

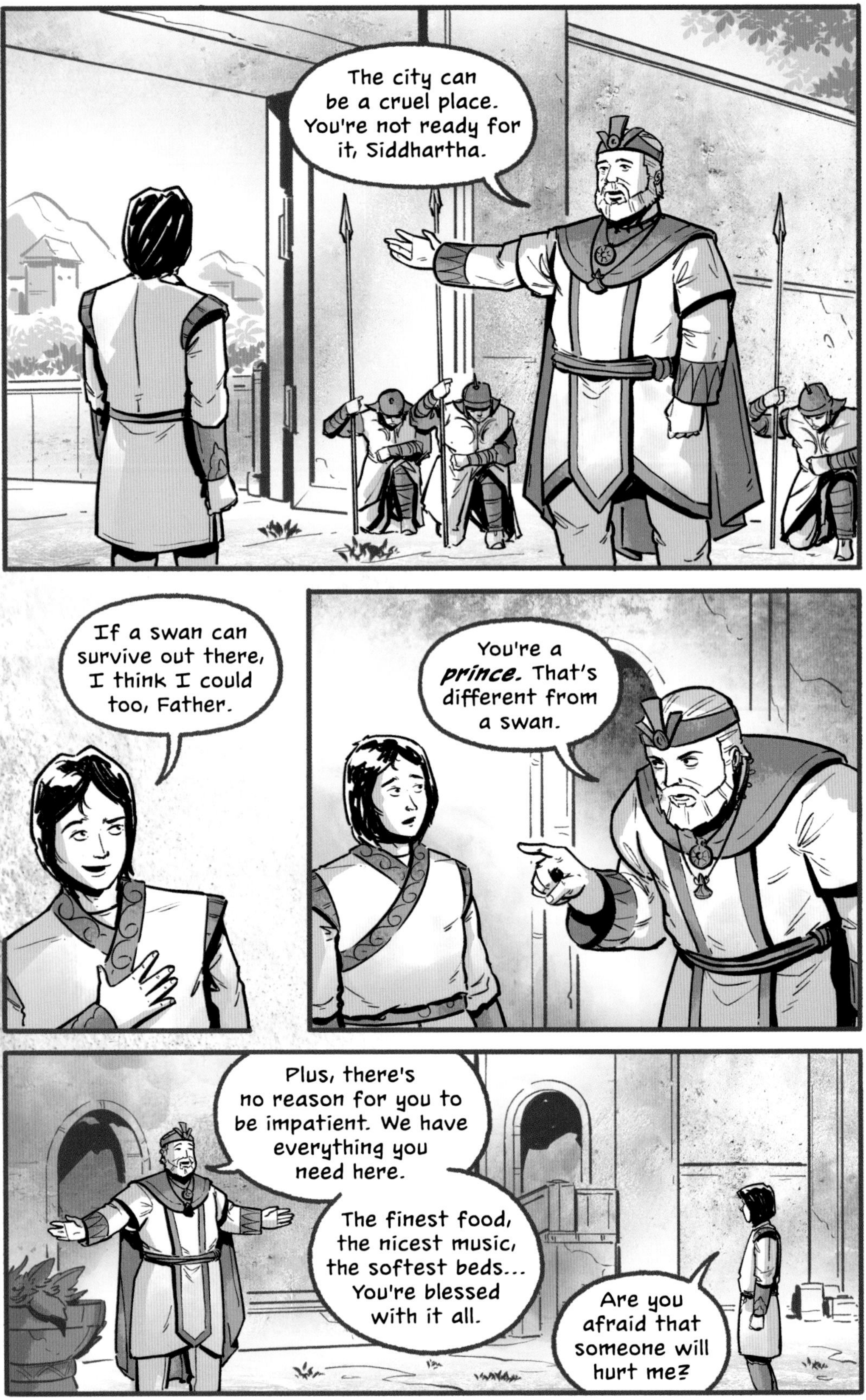
The city can be a cruel place. You're not ready for it, Siddhartha.
If a swan can survive out there, I think I could too, Father.
You're a *prince.* That's different from a swan.
Plus, there's no reason for you to be impatient. We have everything you need here.
The finest food, the nicest music, the softest beds... You're blessed with it all.
Are you afraid that someone will hurt me?

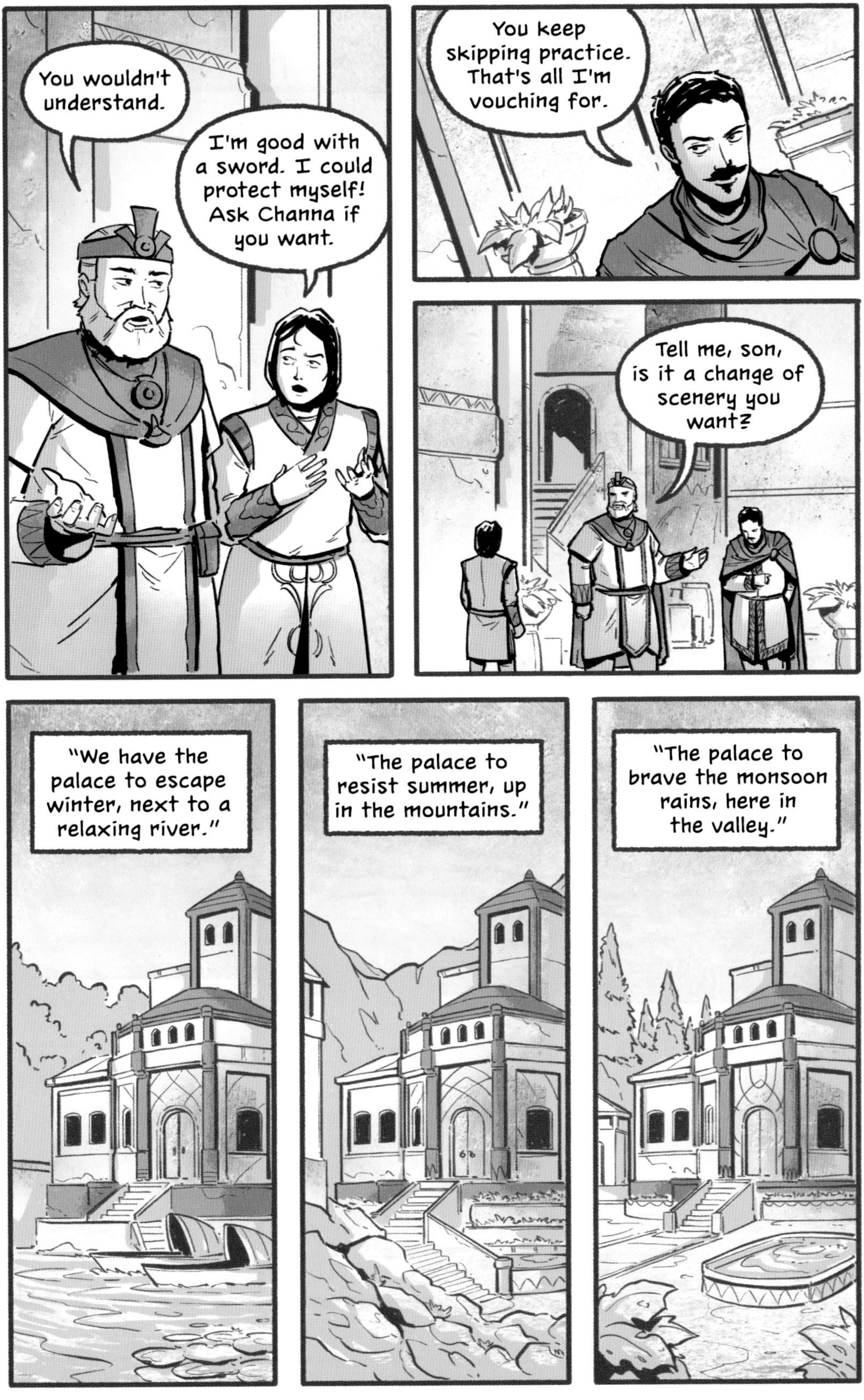
You wouldn't understand.
I'm good with a sword. I could protect myself! Ask Channa if you want.
You keep skipping practice. That's all I'm vouching for.
Tell me, son, is it a change of scenery you want?
"We have the palace to escape winter, next to a relaxing river."
"The palace to resist summer, up in the mountains."
"The palace to brave the monsoon rains, here in the valley."

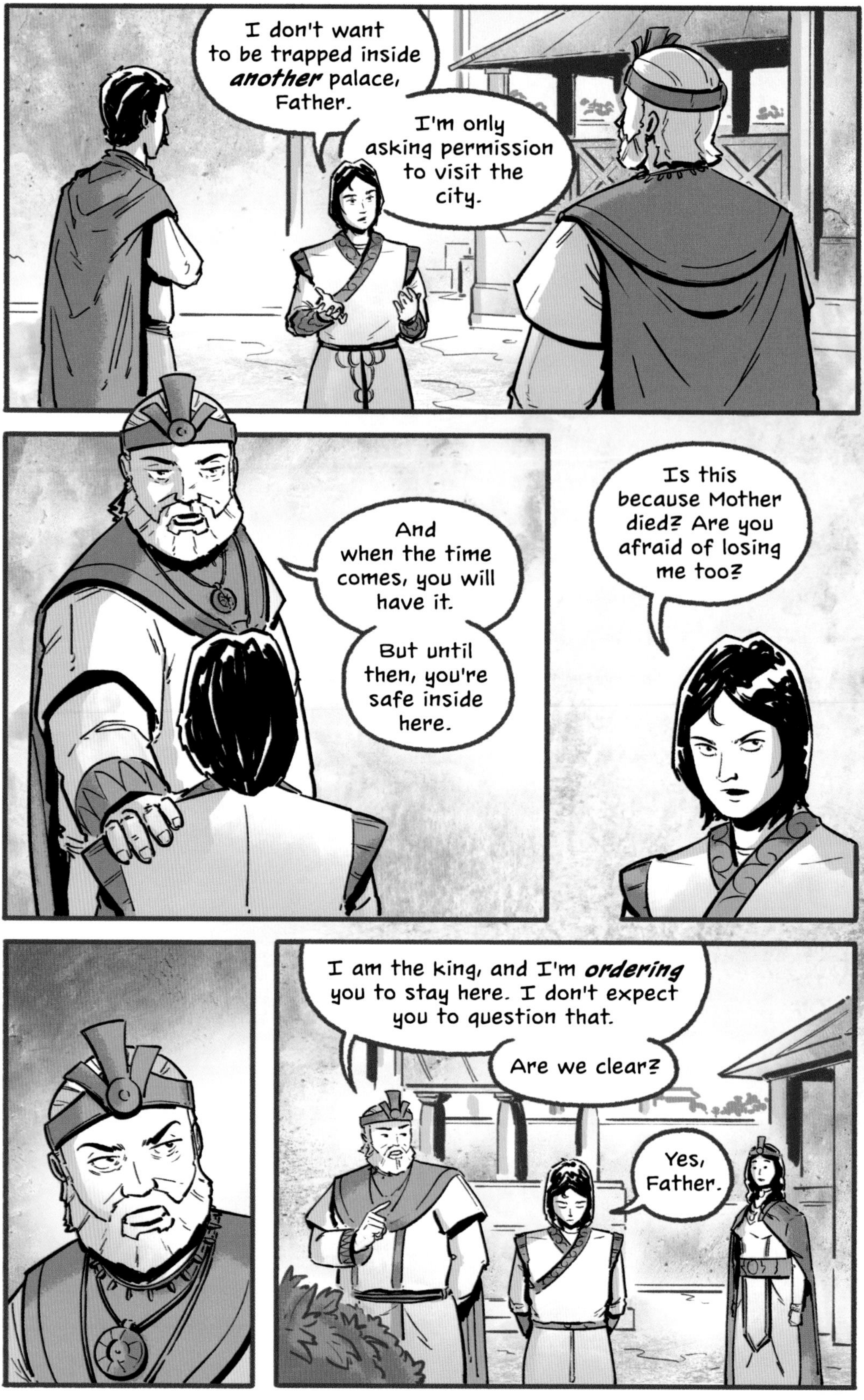
I don't want to be trapped inside *another* palace, Father.
I'm only asking permission to visit the city.
And when the time comes, you will have it.
But until then, you're safe inside here.
Is this because Mother died? Are you afraid of losing me too?
I am the king, and I'm *ordering* you to stay here. I don't expect you to question that.
Are we clear?
Yes, Father.

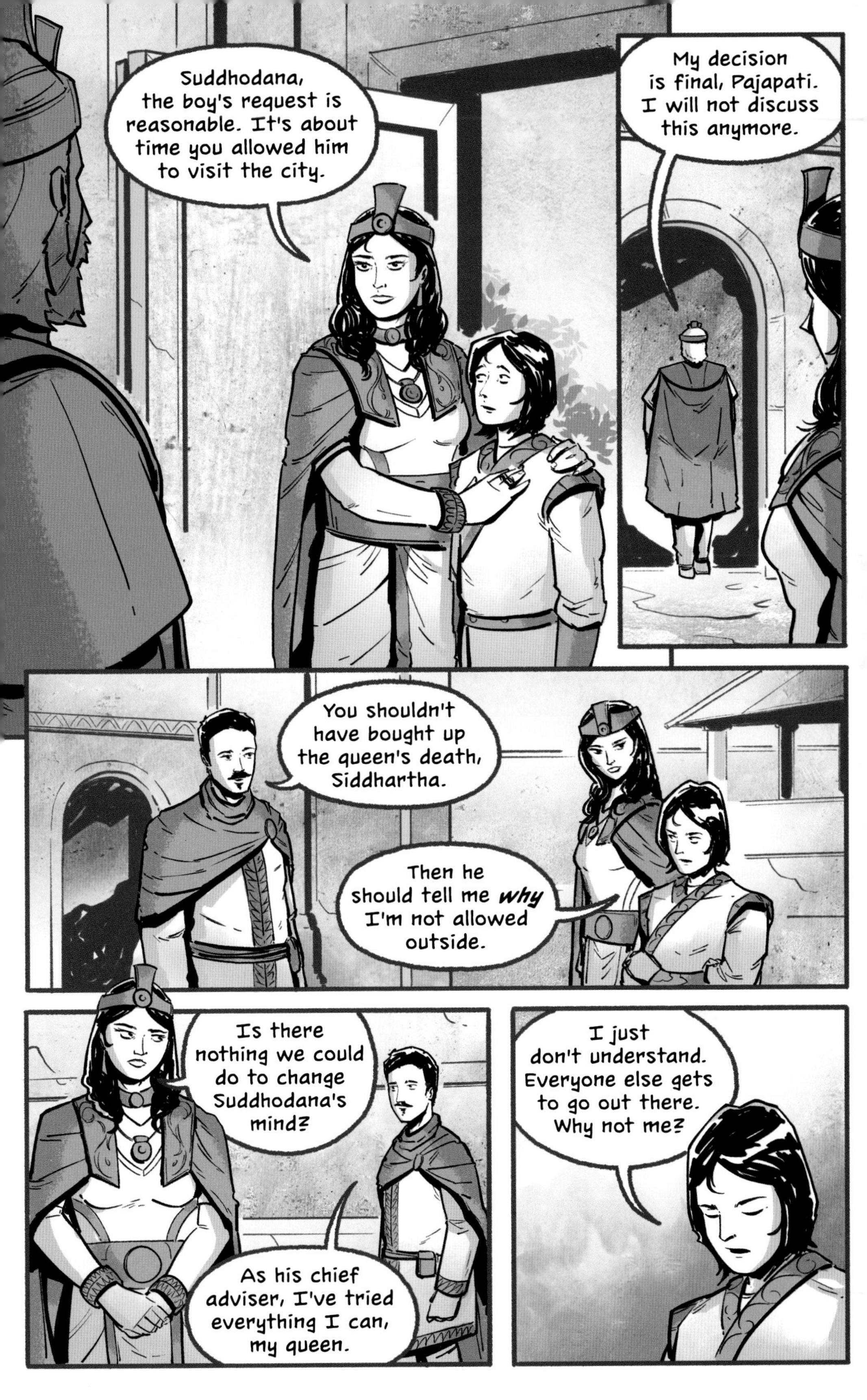
Suddhodana, the boy's request is reasonable. It's about time you allowed him to visit the city.
My decision is final, Pajapati. I will not discuss this anymore.
You shouldn't have bought up the queen's death, Siddhartha.
Then he should tell me *why* I'm not allowed outside.
Is there nothing we could do to change Suddhodana's mind?
As his chief adviser, I've tried everything I can, my queen.
I just don't understand. Everyone else gets to go out there. Why not me?

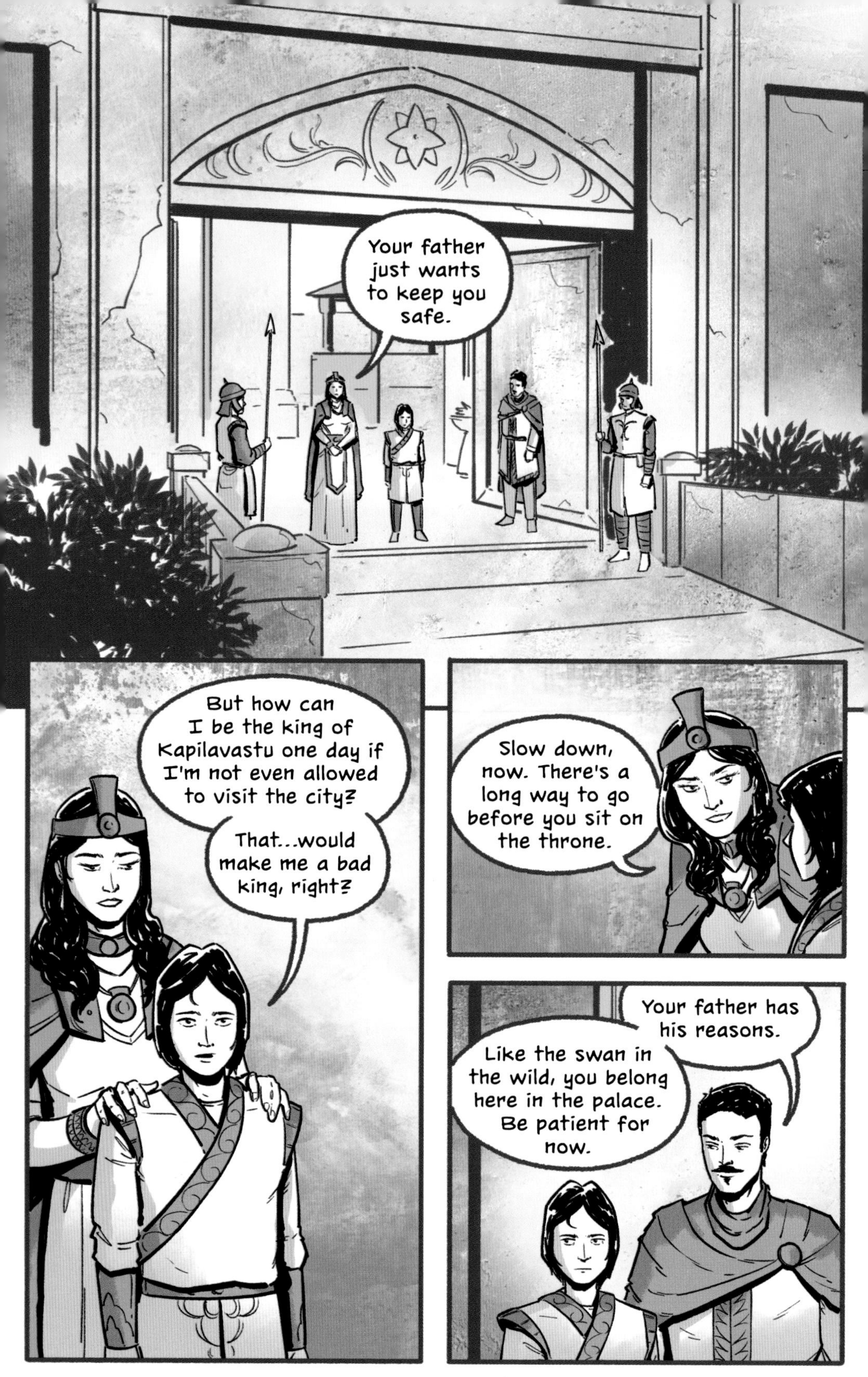
Your father just wants to keep you safe.
But how can I be the king of Kapilavastu one day if I'm not even allowed to visit the city?
That...would make me a bad king, right?
Slow down, now. There's a long way to go before you sit on the throne.
Your father has his reasons.
Like the swan in the wild, you belong here in the palace. Be patient for now.

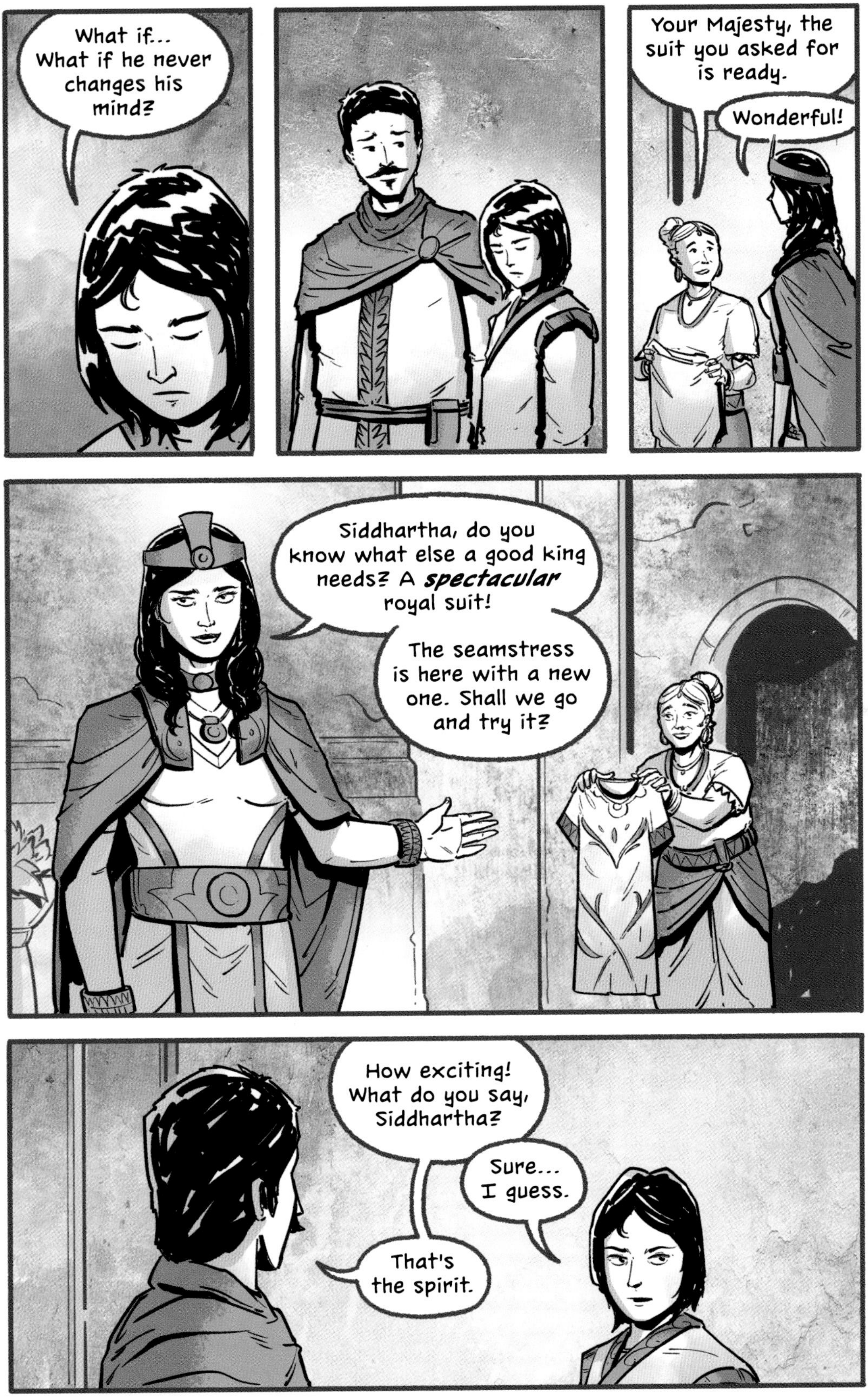
What if...
What if he never changes his mind?
Your Majesty, the suit you asked for is ready.
Wonderful!
Siddhartha, do you know what else a good king needs? A *spectacular* royal suit!
The seamstress is here with a new one. Shall we go and try it?
How exciting! What do you say, Siddhartha?
Sure... I guess.
That's the spirit.

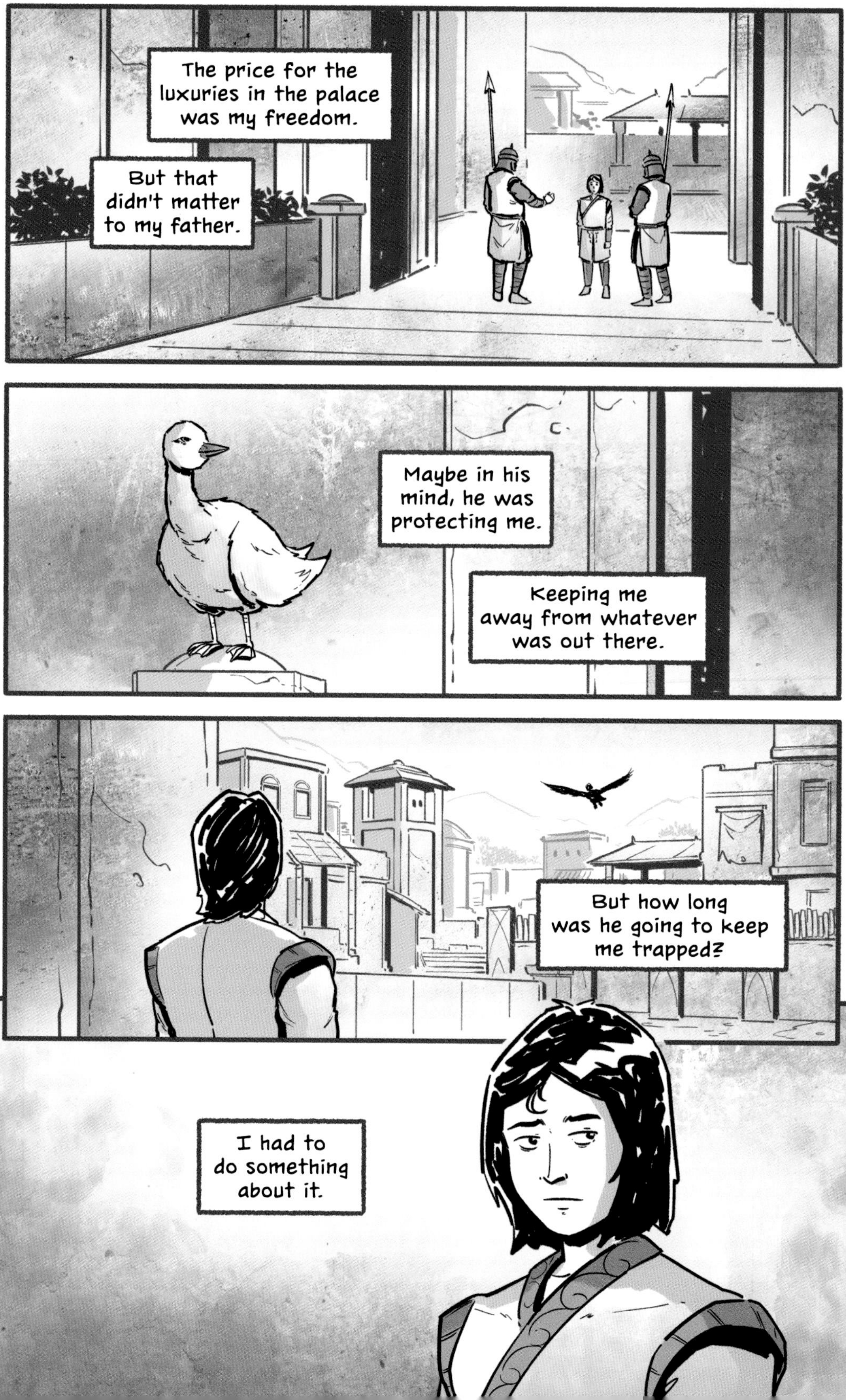
The price for the luxuries in the palace was my freedom.
But that didn't matter to my father.
Maybe in his mind, he was protecting me.
Keeping me away from whatever was out there.
But how long was he going to keep me trapped?
I had to do something about it.

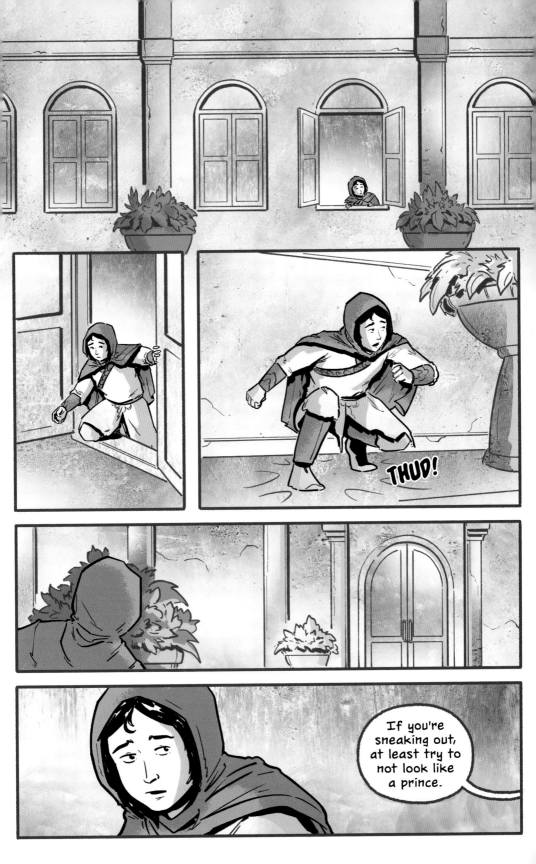

THUD!

If you're sneaking out, at least try to not look like a prince.

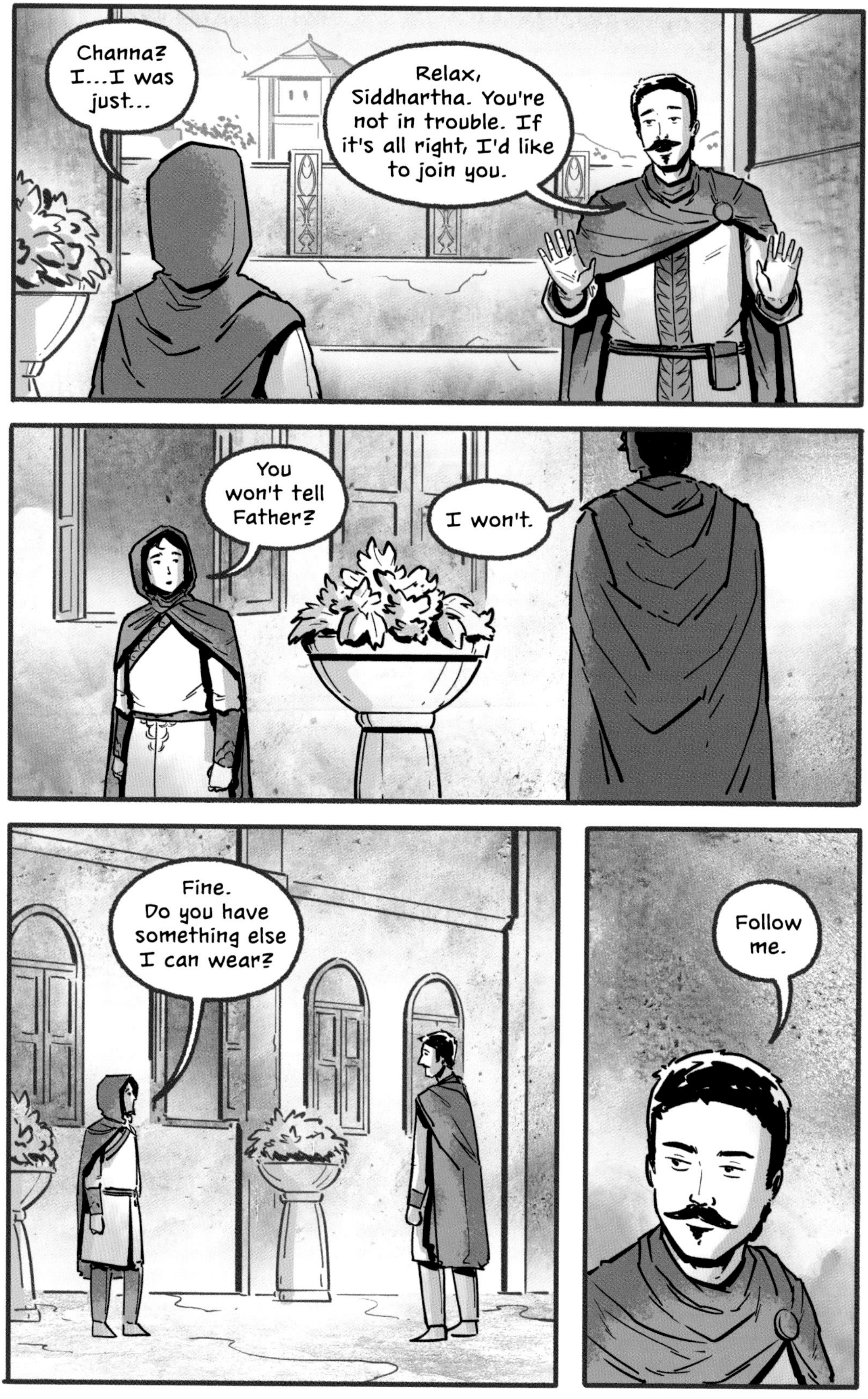
Channa? I...I was just...
Relax, Siddhartha. You're not in trouble. If it's all right, I'd like to join you.
You won't tell Father?
I won't.
Fine. Do you have something else I can wear?
Follow me.

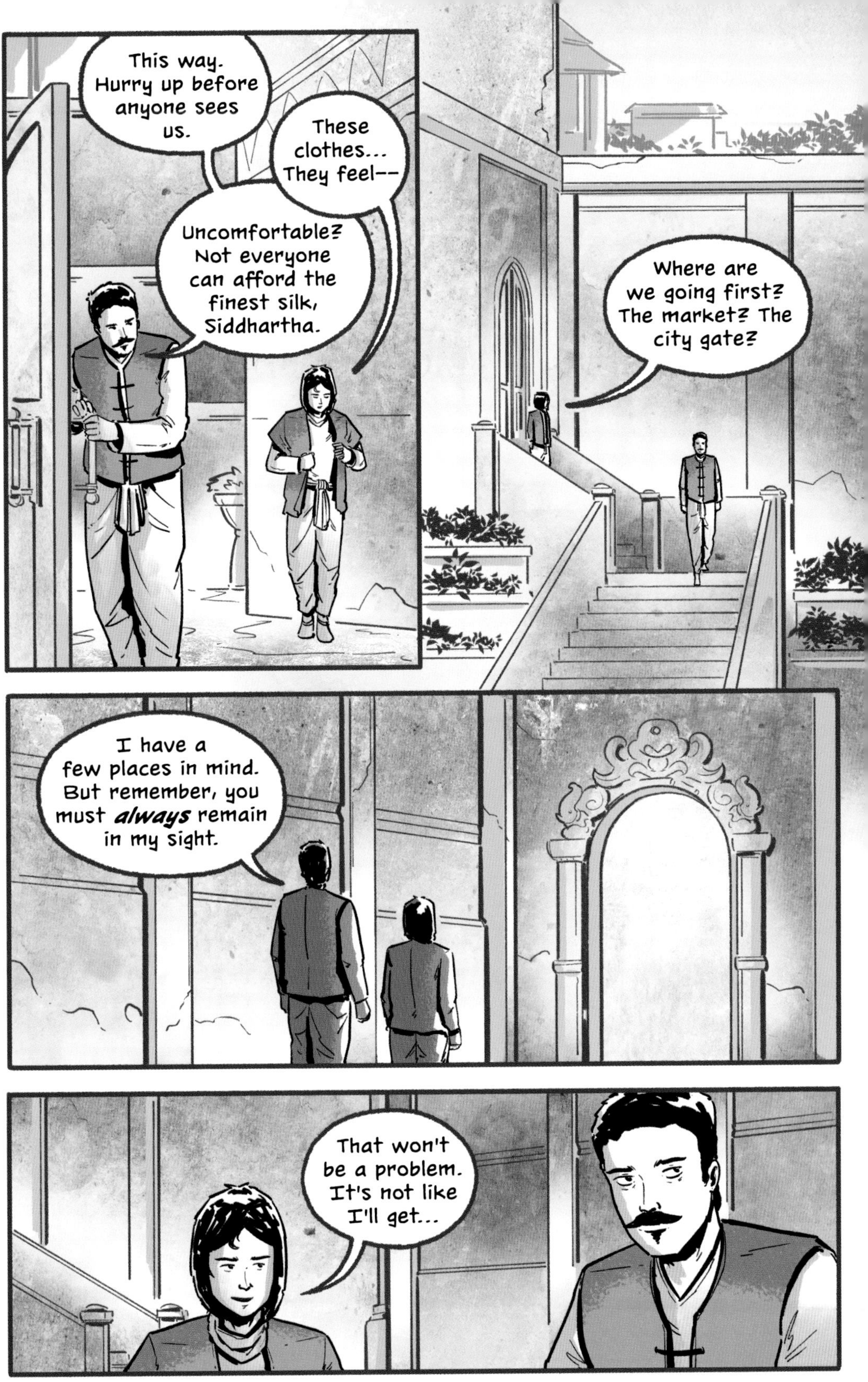
This way. Hurry up before anyone sees us.
These clothes... They feel--
Uncomfortable? Not everyone can afford the finest silk, Siddhartha.
Where are we going first? The market? The city gate?
I have a few places in mind. But remember, you must *always* remain in my sight.
That won't be a problem. It's not like I'll get...

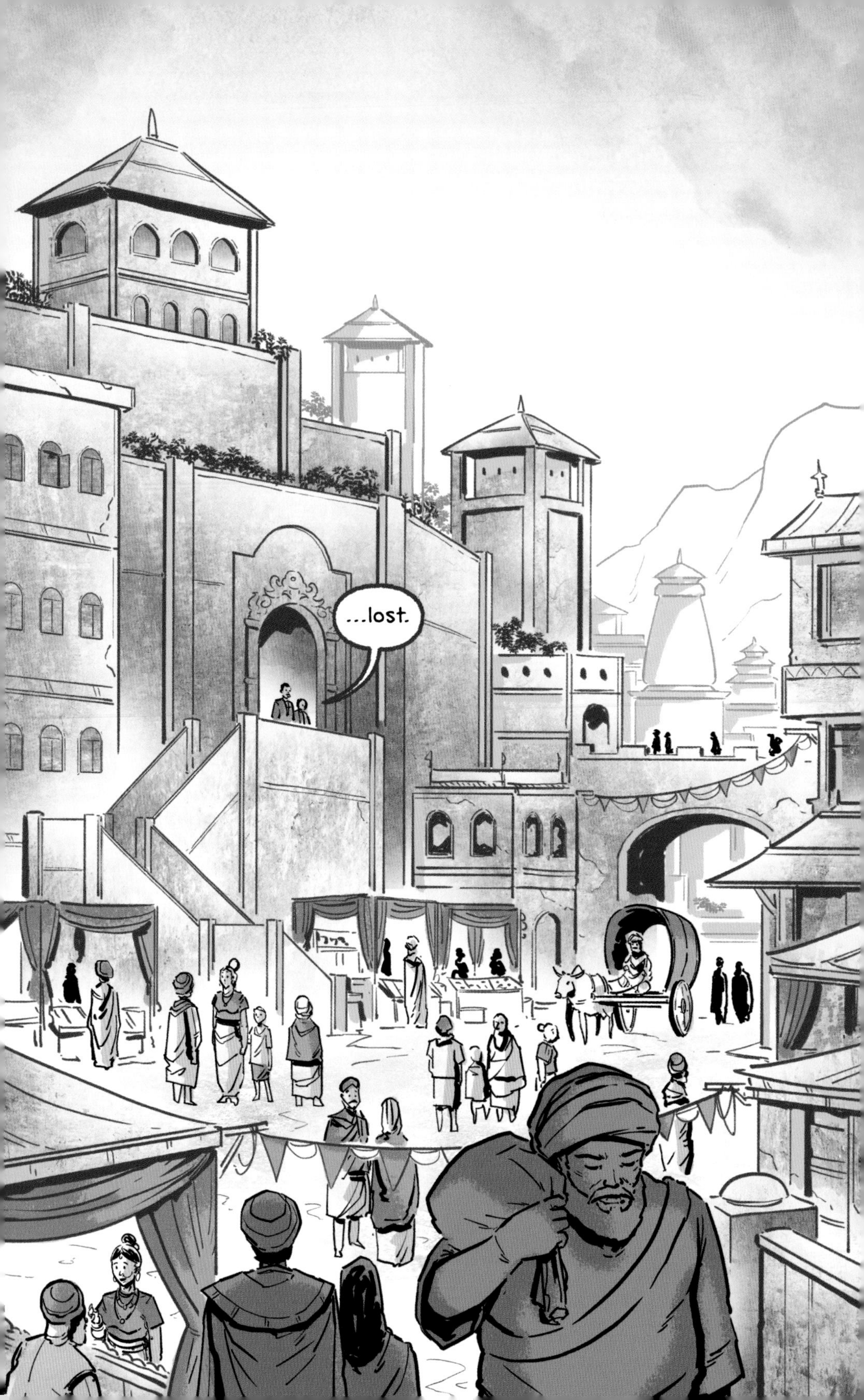
...lost.

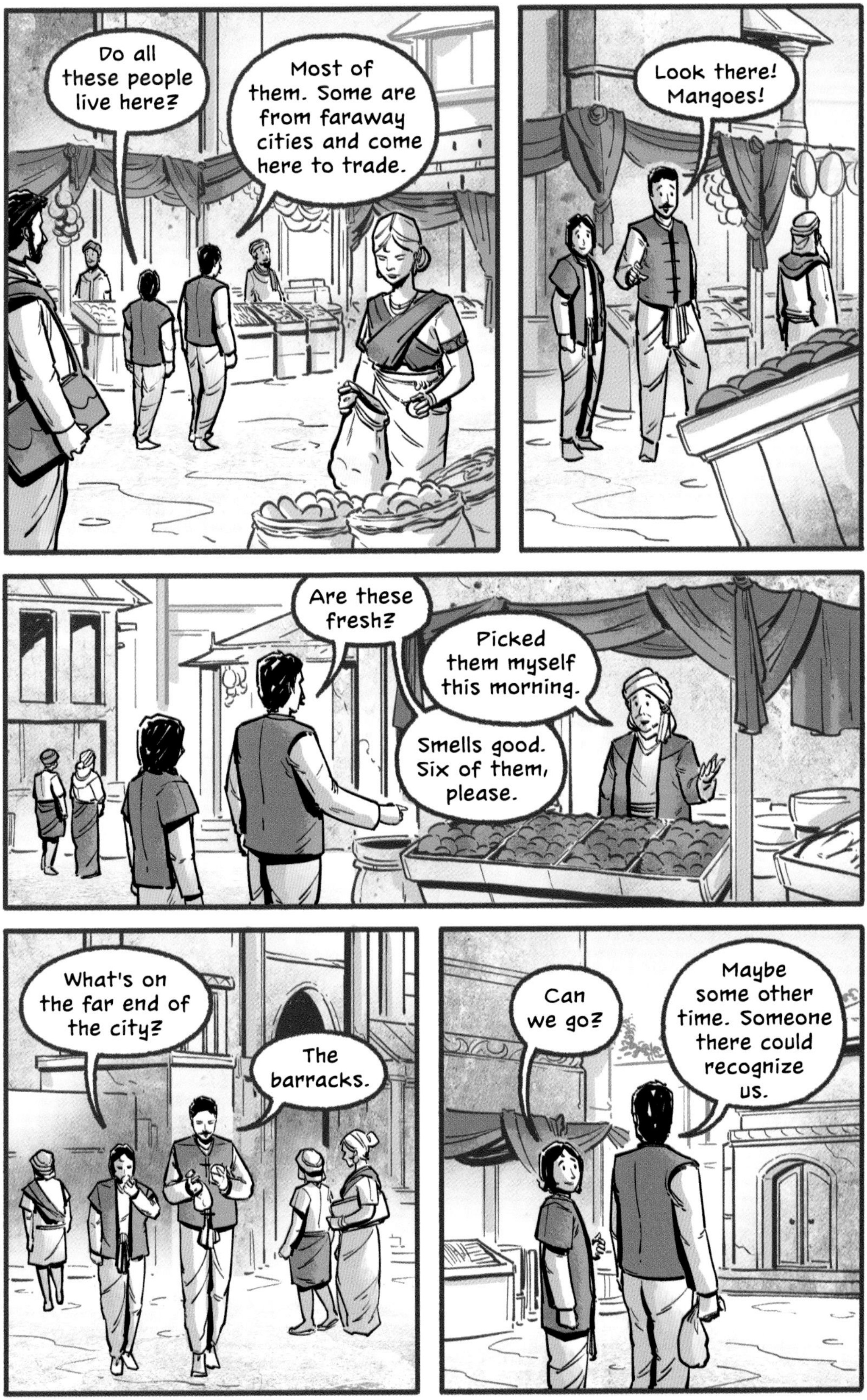
Do all these people live here?
Most of them. Some are from faraway cities and come here to trade.
Look there! Mangoes!
Are these fresh?
Picked them myself this morning.
Smells good. Six of them, please.
What's on the far end of the city?
The barracks.
Can we go?
Maybe some other time. Someone there could recognize us.

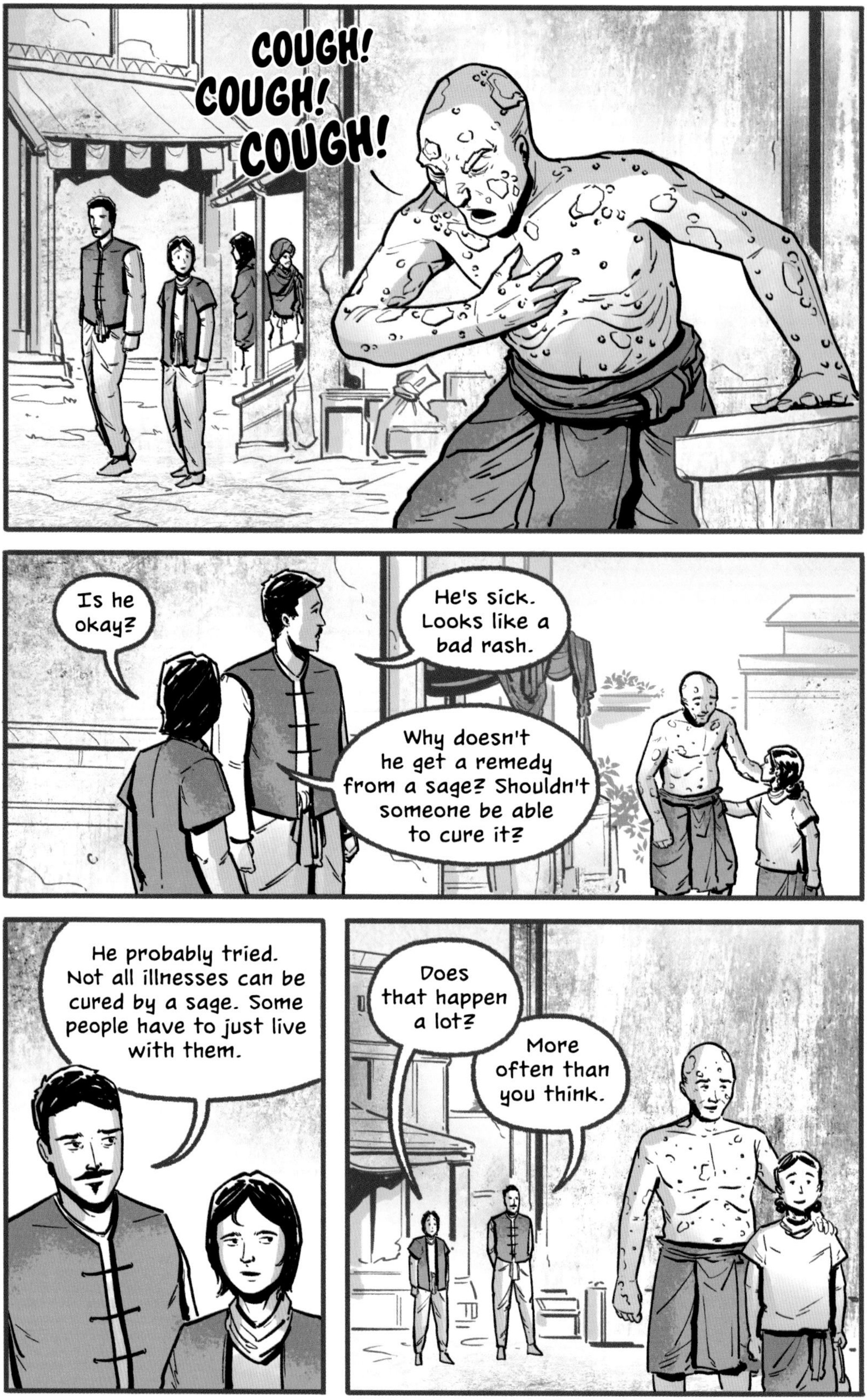
COUGH! COUGH! COUGH!
Is he okay?
He's sick. Looks like a bad rash.
Why doesn't he get a remedy from a sage? Shouldn't someone be able to cure it?
He probably tried. Not all illnesses can be cured by a sage. Some people have to just live with them.
Does that happen a lot?
More often than you think.

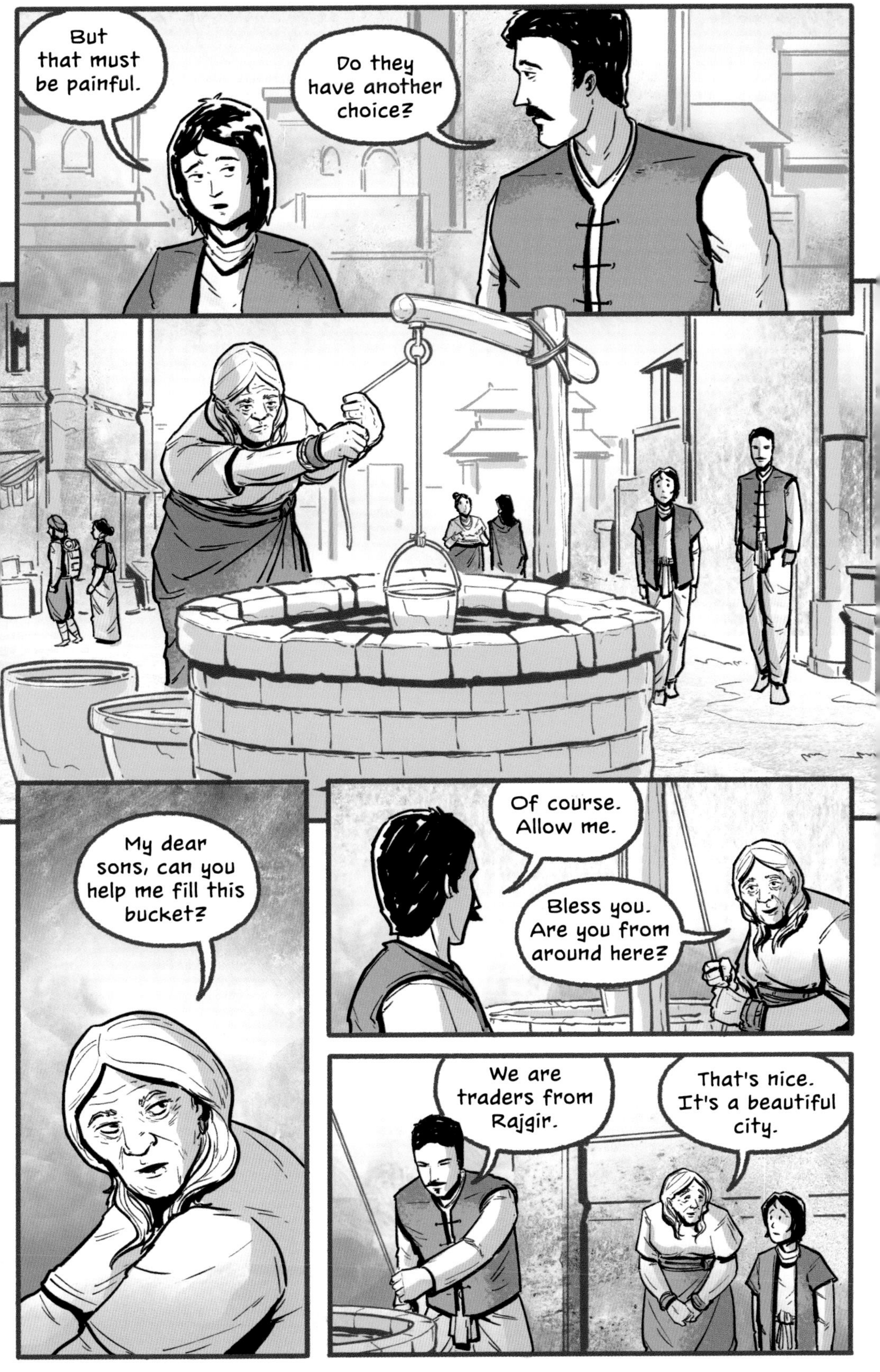

But that must be painful.
Do they have another choice?
My dear sons, can you help me fill this bucket?
Of course. Allow me.
Bless you. Are you from around here?
We are traders from Rajgir.
That's nice. It's a beautiful city.

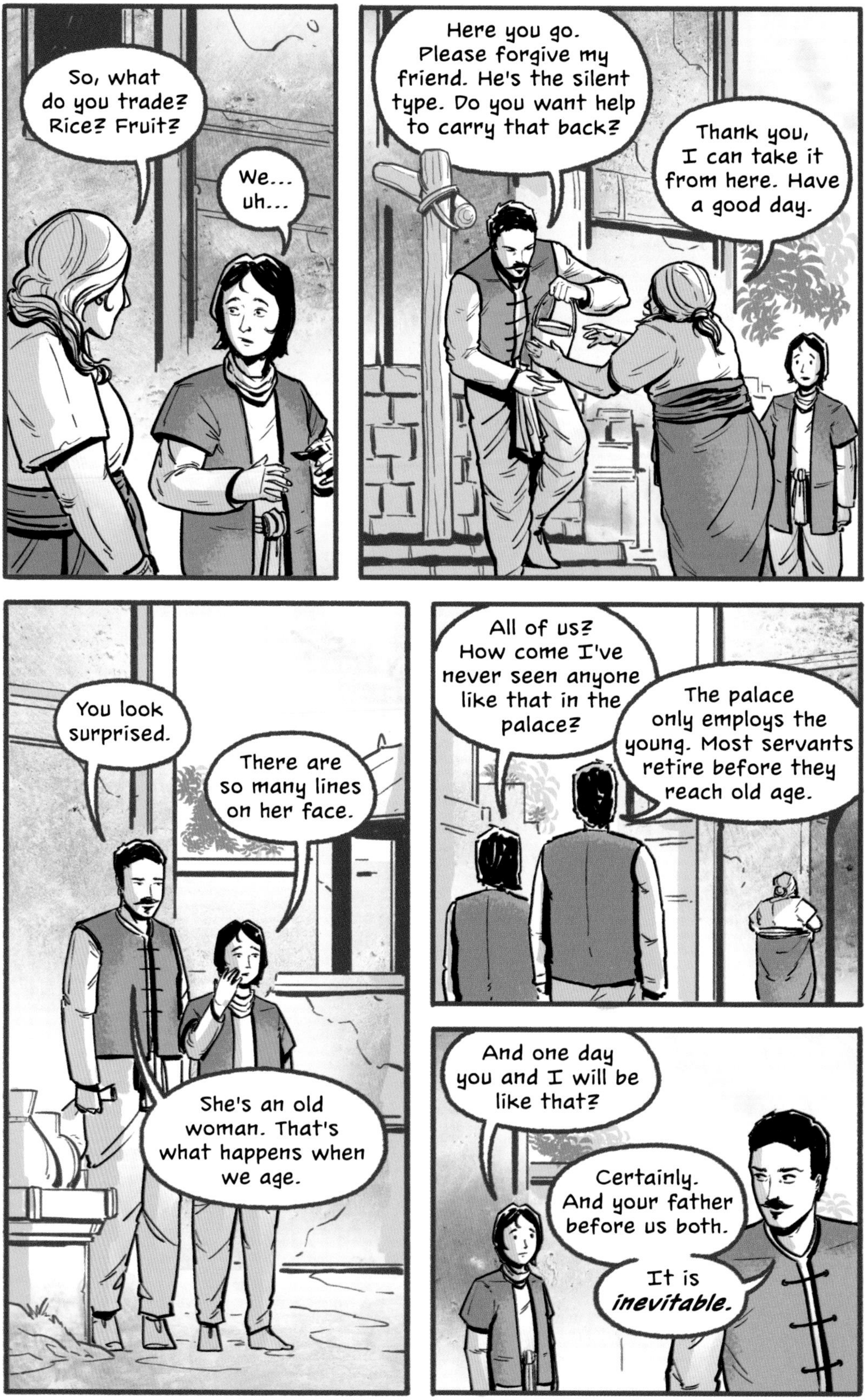
So, what do you trade? Rice? Fruit?
We... uh...
Here you go. Please forgive my friend. He's the silent type. Do you want help to carry that back?
Thank you, I can take it from here. Have a good day.
You look surprised.
There are so many lines on her face.
She's an old woman. That's what happens when we age.
All of us? How come I've never seen anyone like that in the palace?
The palace only employs the young. Most servants retire before they reach old age.
And one day you and I will be like that?
Certainly. And your father before us both.
It is *inevitable.*

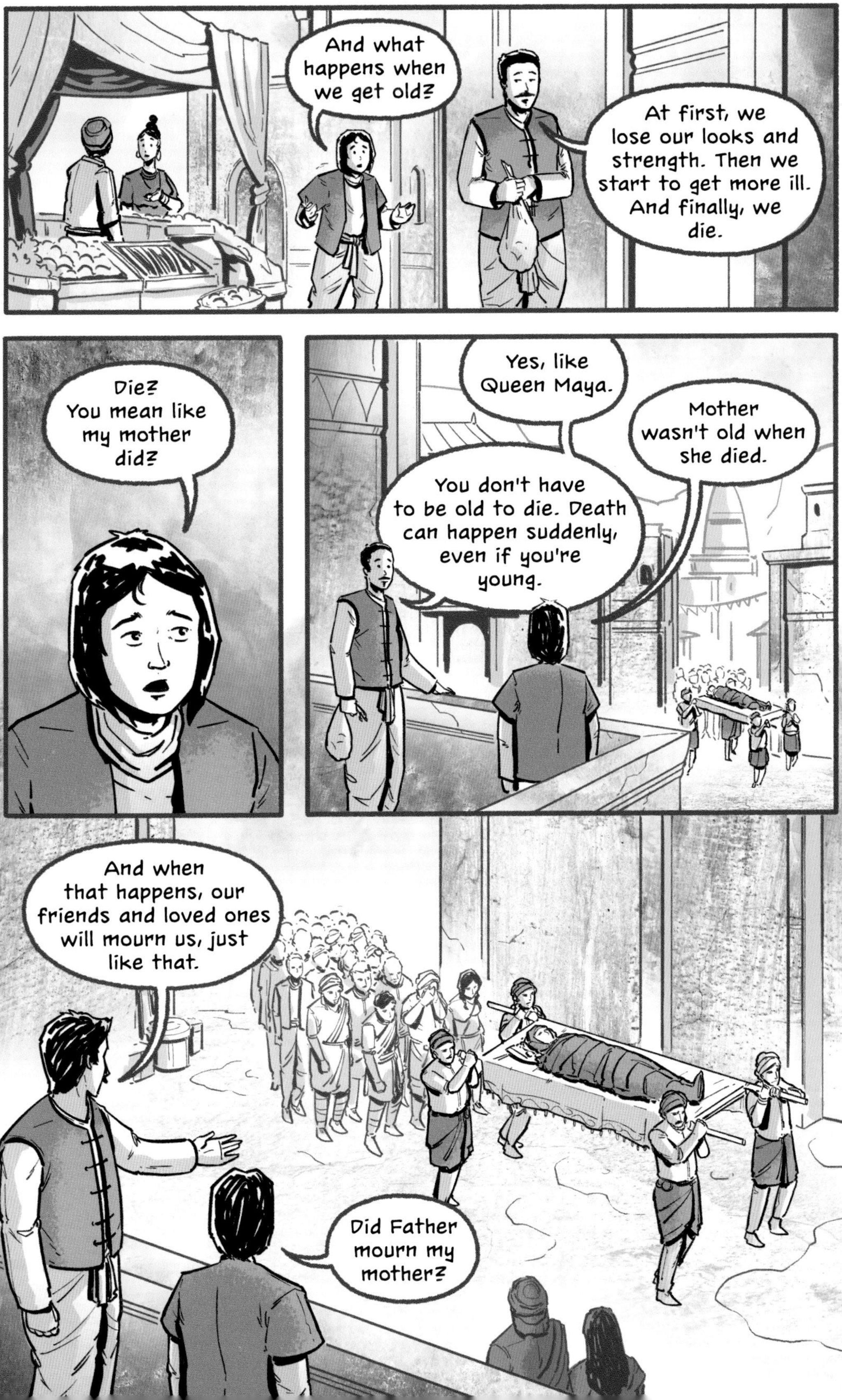
And what happens when we get old?
At first, we lose our looks and strength. Then we start to get more ill. And finally, we die.
Die? You mean like my mother did?
Yes, like Queen Maya.
Mother wasn't old when she died.
You don't have to be old to die. Death can happen suddenly, even if you're young.
And when that happens, our friends and loved ones will mourn us, just like that.
Did Father mourn my mother?

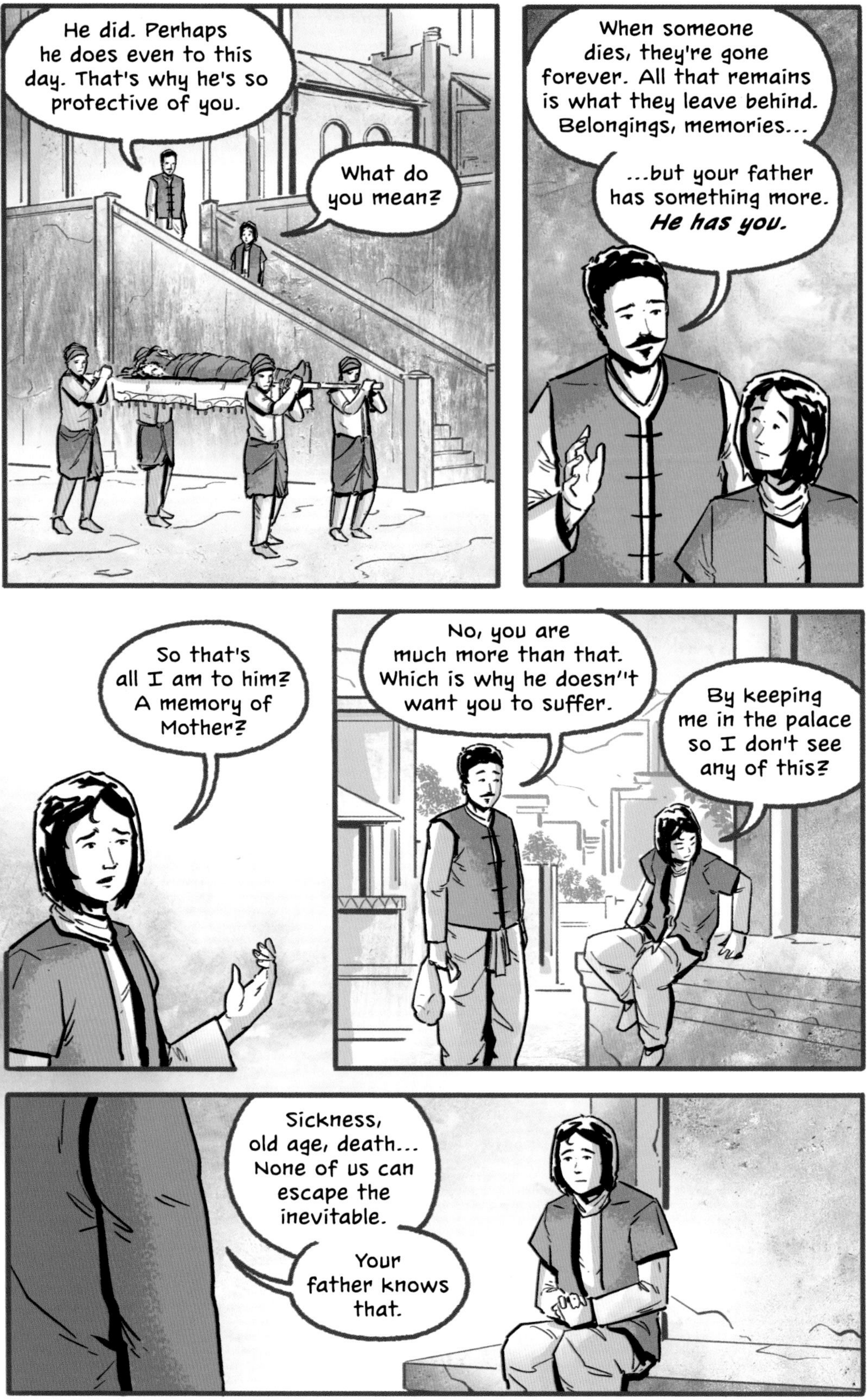
He did. Perhaps he does even to this day. That's why he's so protective of you.
What do you mean?
When someone dies, they're gone forever. All that remains is what they leave behind. Belongings, memories...
...but your father has something more. *He has you.*
So that's all I am to him? A memory of Mother?
No, you are much more than that. Which is why he doesn't want you to suffer.
By keeping me in the palace so I don't see any of this?
Sickness, old age, death... None of us can escape the inevitable.
Your father knows that.

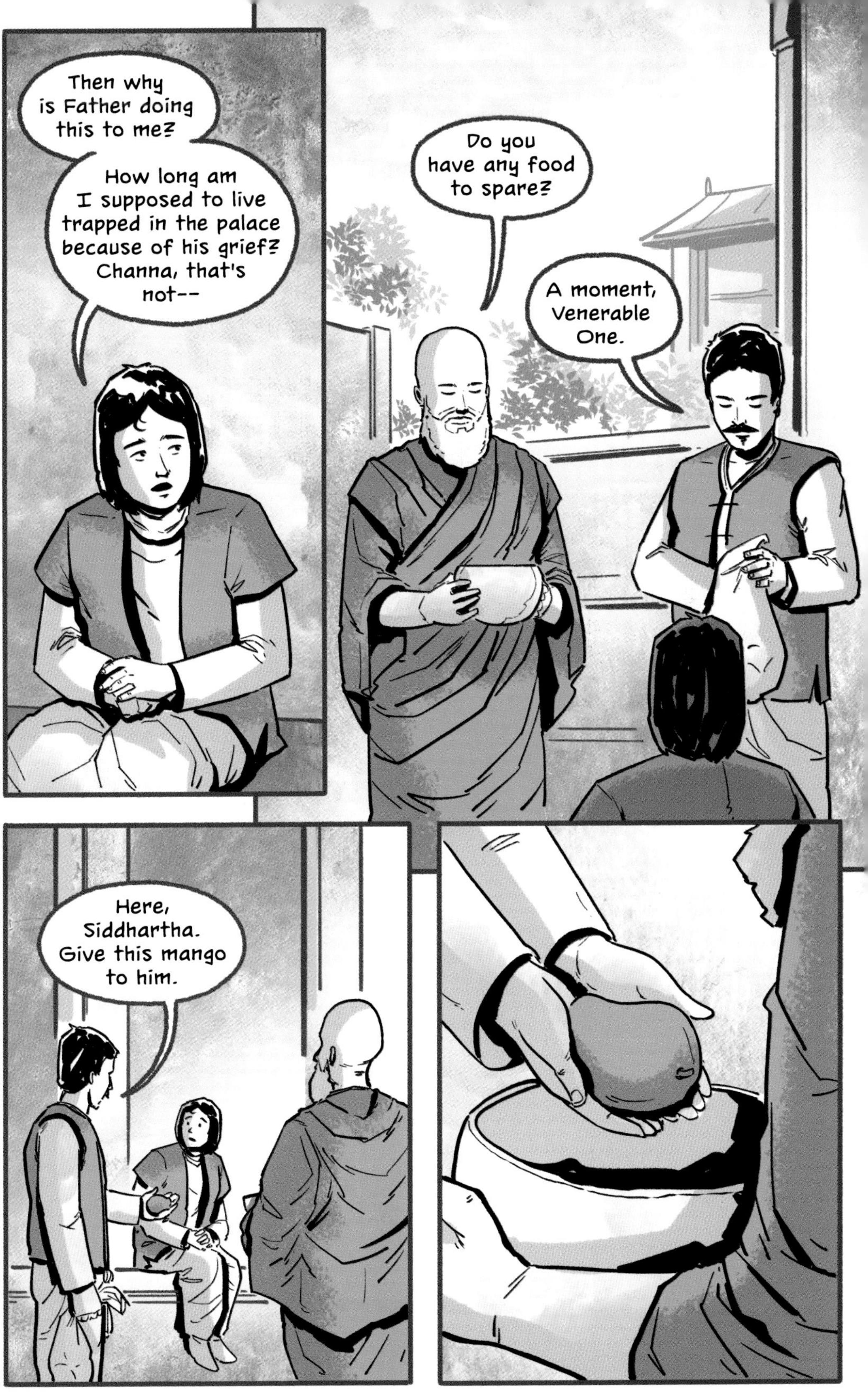
Then why is Father doing this to me?
How long am I supposed to live trapped in the palace because of his grief? Channa, that's not--
Do you have any food to spare?
A moment, Venerable One.
Here, Siddhartha. Give this mango to him.

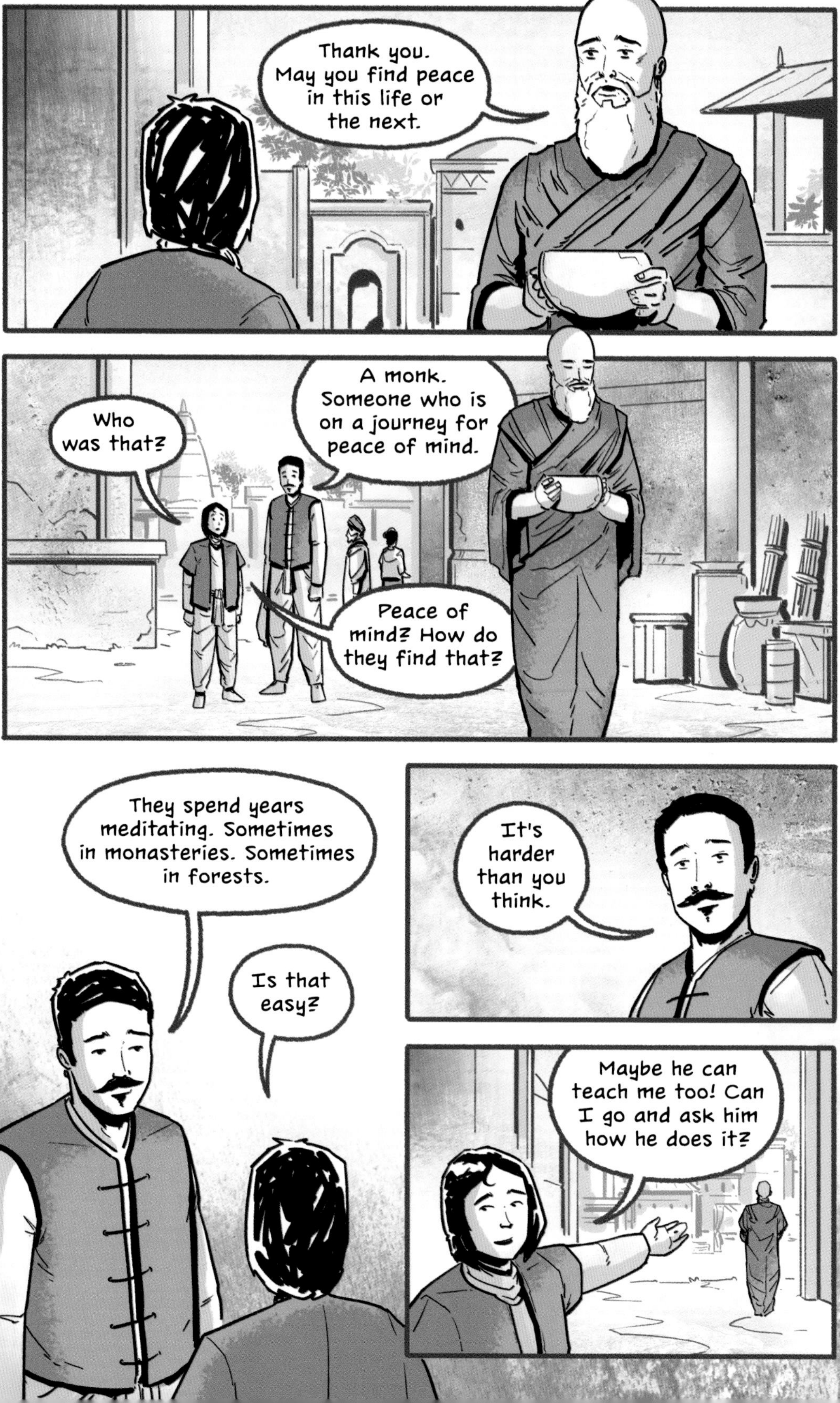
Thank you. May you find peace in this life or the next.
Who was that?
A monk. Someone who is on a journey for peace of mind.
Peace of mind? How do they find that?
They spend years meditating. Sometimes in monasteries. Sometimes in forests.
Is that easy?
It's harder than you think.
Maybe he can teach me too! Can I go and ask him how he does it?

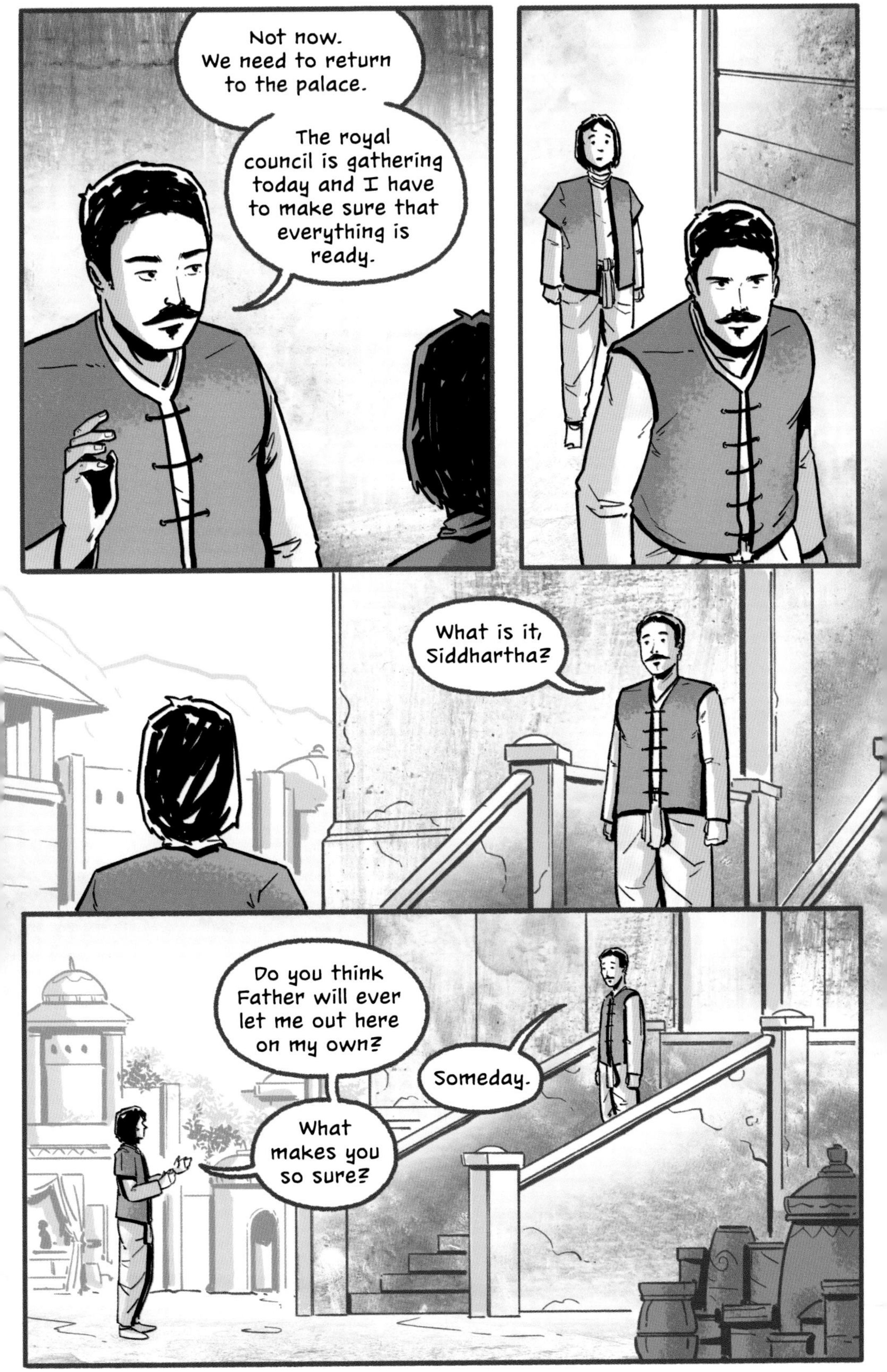
Not now. We need to return to the palace.
The royal council is gathering today and I have to make sure that everything is ready.
What is it, Siddhartha?
Do you think Father will ever let me out here on my own?
Someday.
What makes you so sure?

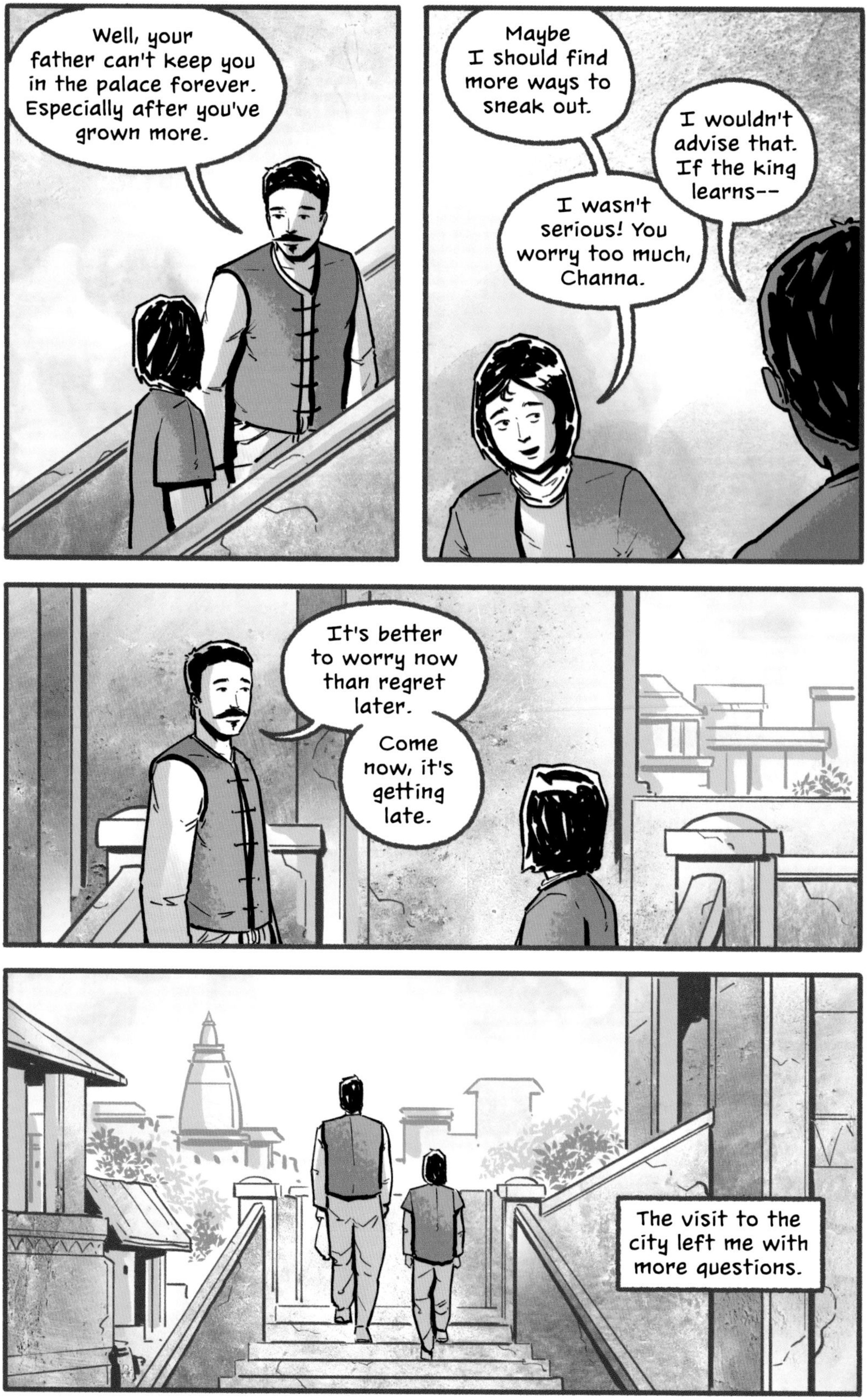
Well, your father can't keep you in the palace forever. Especially after you've grown more.
Maybe I should find more ways to sneak out.
I wouldn't advise that. If the king learns--
I wasn't serious! You worry too much, Channa.
It's better to worry now than regret later.
Come now, it's getting late.
The visit to the city left me with more questions.

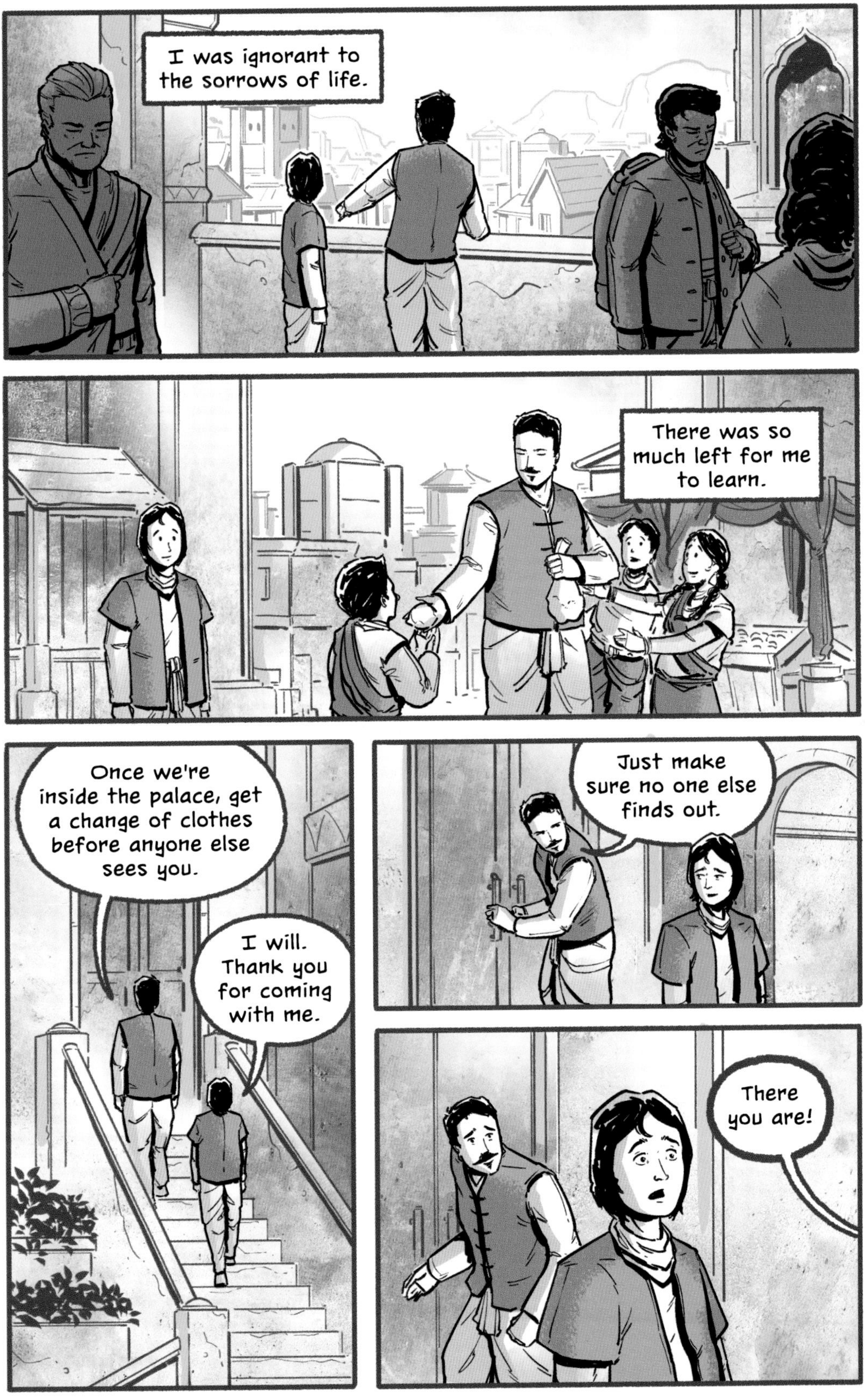
I was ignorant to the sorrows of life.
There was so much left for me to learn.
Once we're inside the palace, get a change of clothes before anyone else sees you.
I will. Thank you for coming with me.
Just make sure no one else finds out.
There you are!

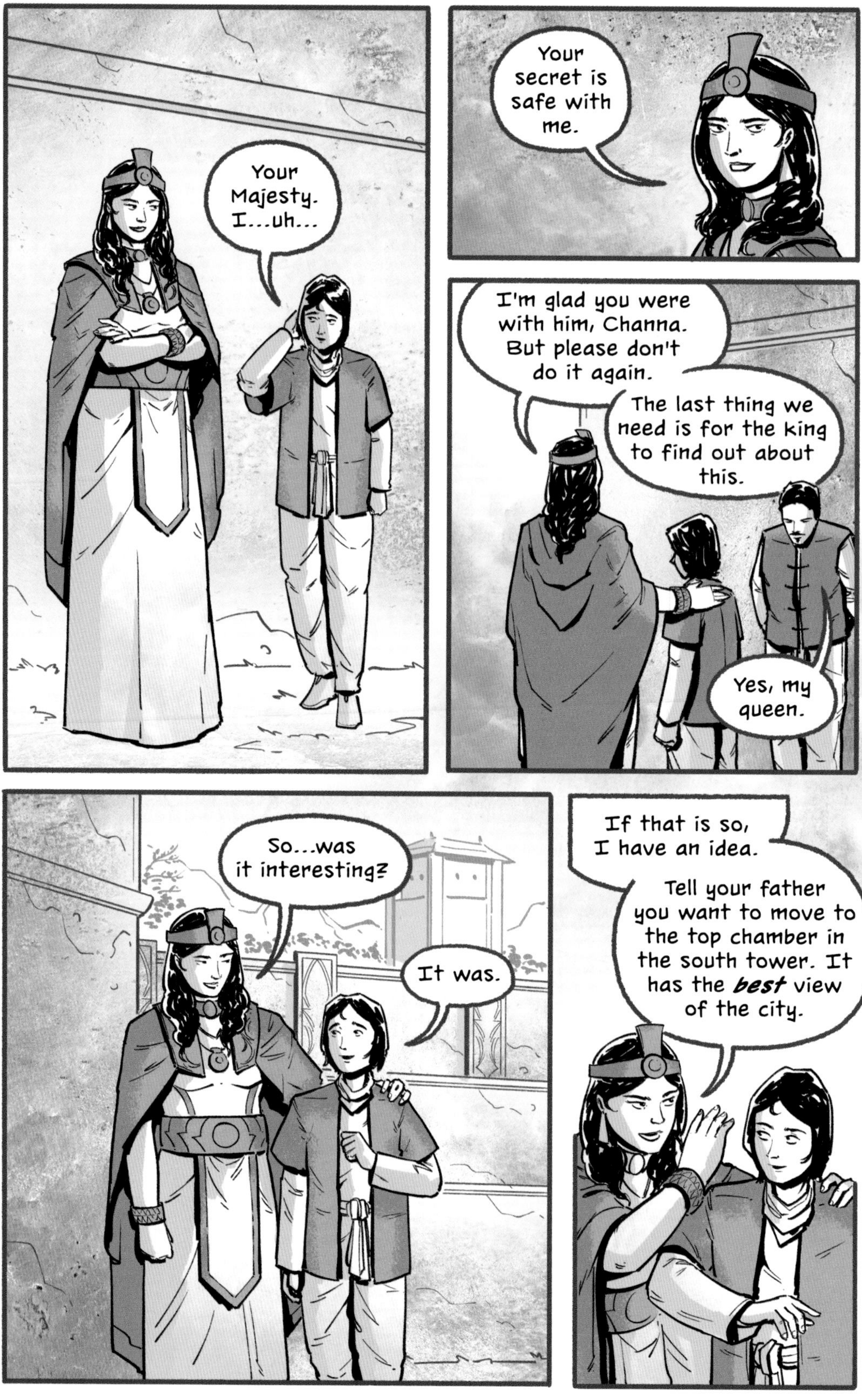
Your Majesty. I...uh...
Your secret is safe with me.
I'm glad you were with him, Channa. But please don't do it again.
The last thing we need is for the king to find out about this.
Yes, my queen.
So...was it interesting?
It was.
If that is so, I have an idea.
Tell your father you want to move to the top chamber in the south tower. It has the *best* view of the city.

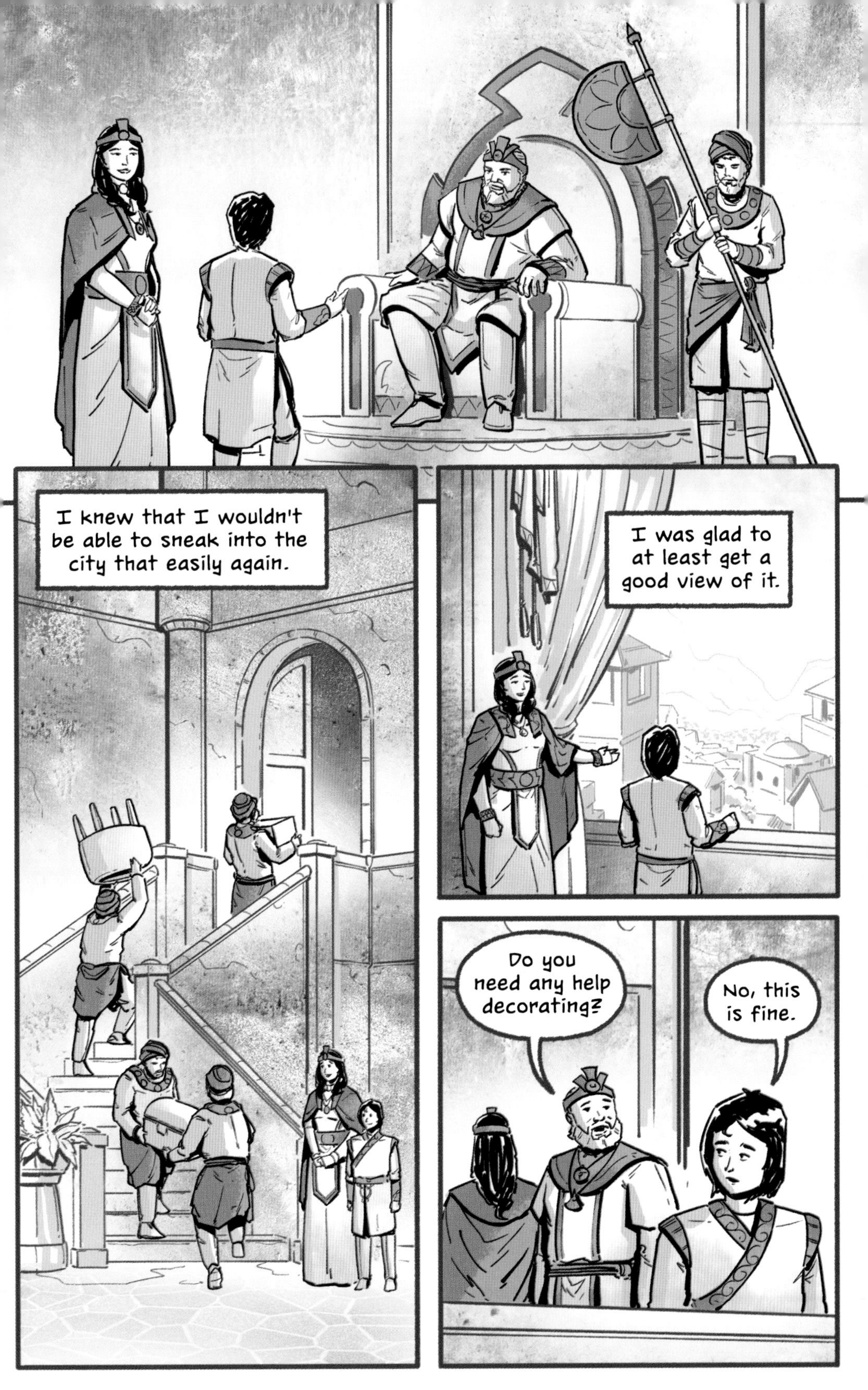
I knew that I wouldn't be able to sneak into the city that easily again.
I was glad to at least get a good view of it.
Do you need any help decorating?
No, this is fine.

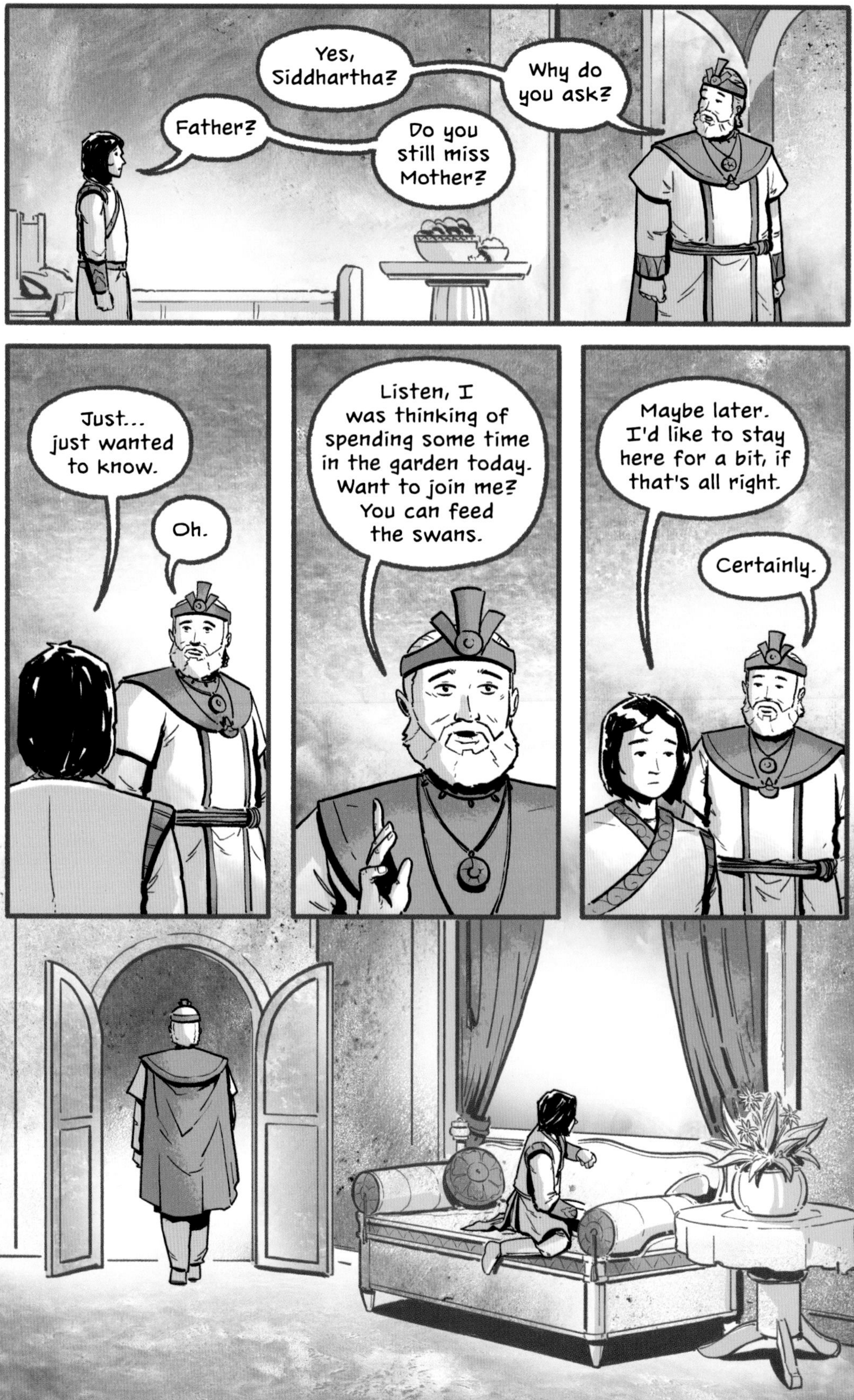
Father?
Yes, Siddhartha?
Do you still miss Mother?
Why do you ask?
Just... just wanted to know.
Oh.
Listen, I was thinking of spending some time in the garden today. Want to join me? You can feed the swans.
Maybe later. I'd like to stay here for a bit, if that's all right.
Certainly.

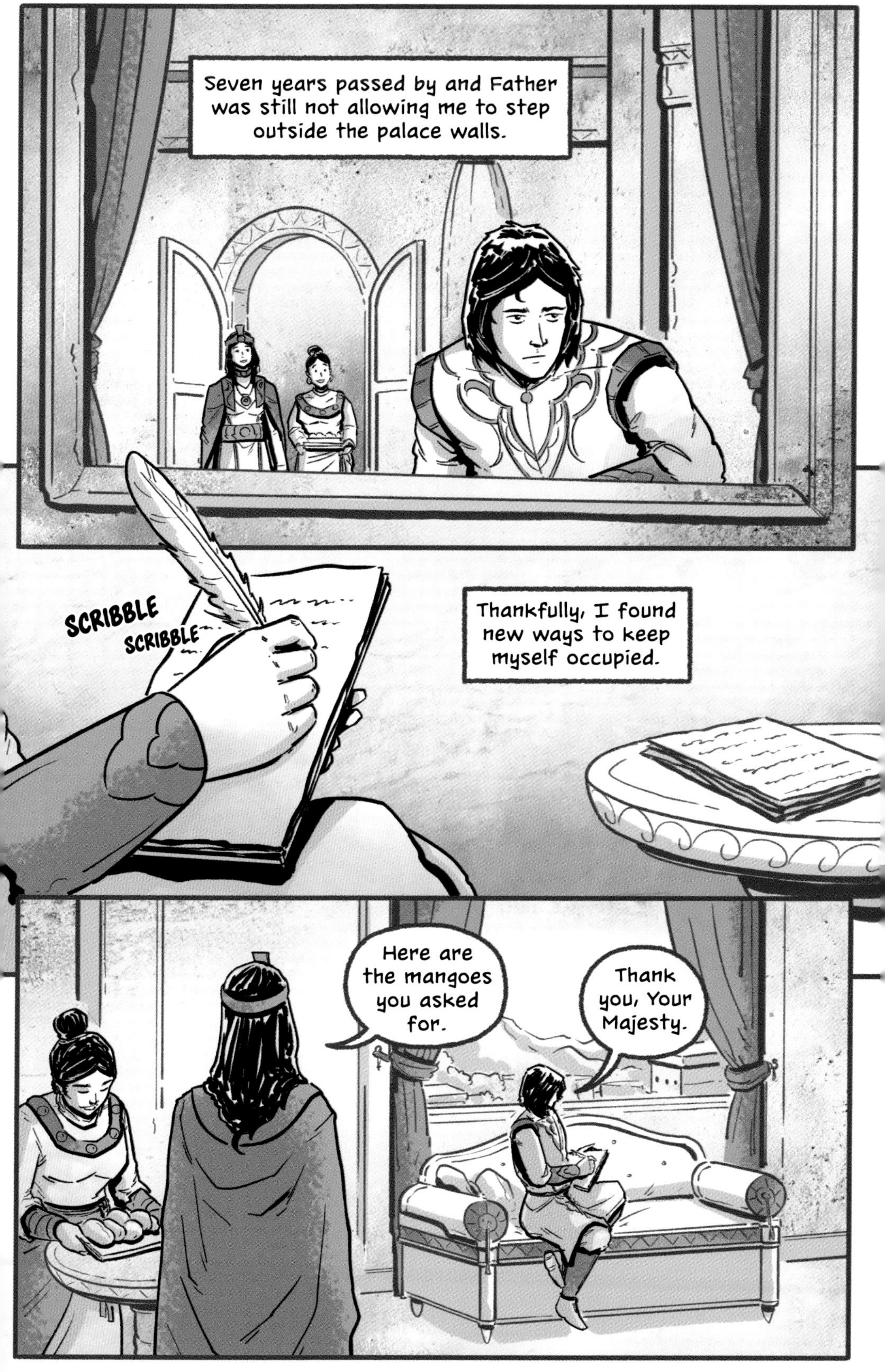
Seven years passed by and Father was still not allowing me to step outside the palace walls.
SCRIBBLE
SCRIBBLE
Thankfully, I found new ways to keep myself occupied.
Here are the mangoes you asked for.
Thank you, Your Majesty.

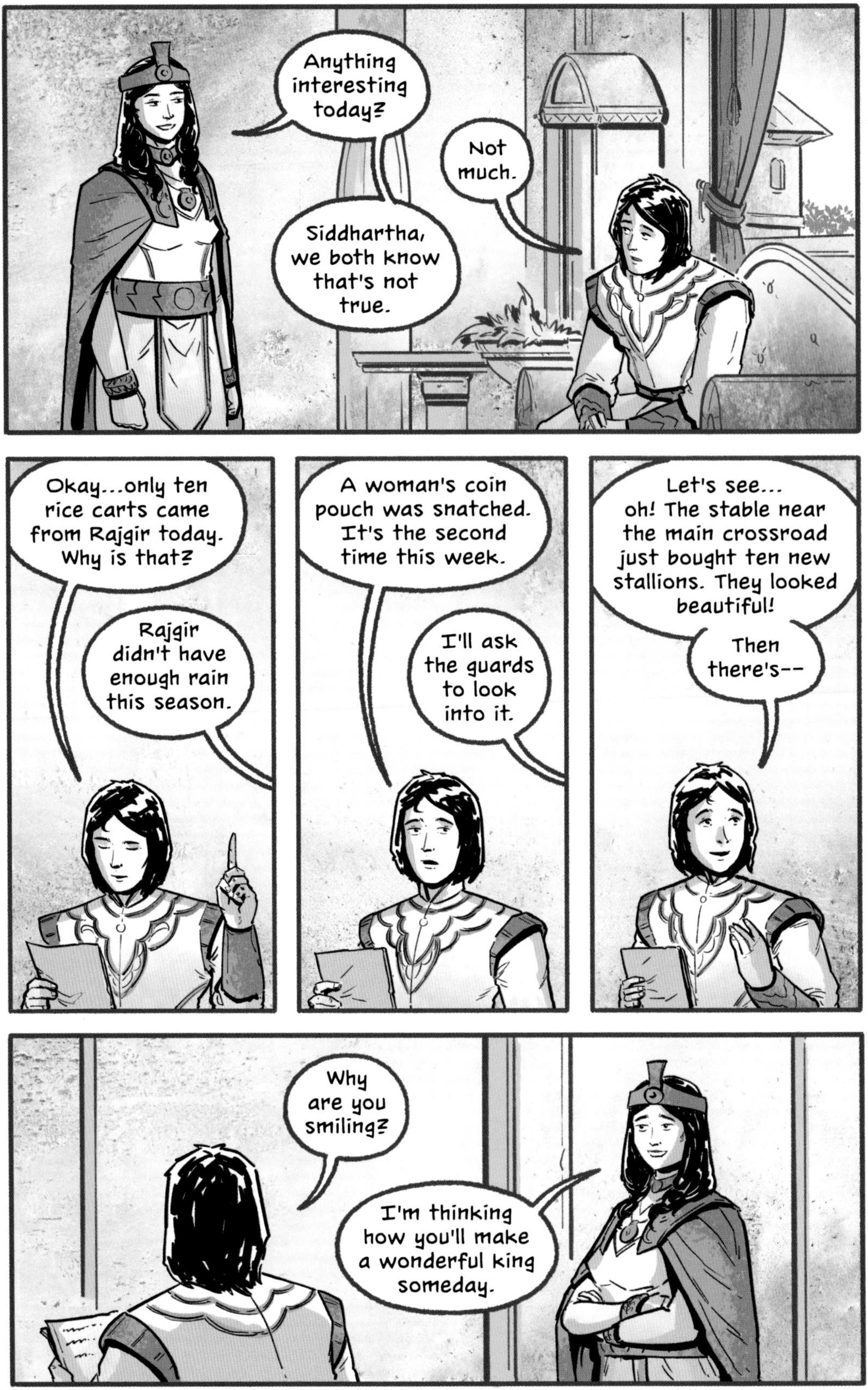
Anything interesting today?
Not much.
Siddhartha, we both know that's not true.
Okay...only ten rice carts came from Rajgir today. Why is that?
Rajgir didn't have enough rain this season.
A woman's coin pouch was snatched. It's the second time this week.
I'll ask the guards to look into it.
Let's see... oh! The stable near the main crossroad just bought ten new stallions. They looked beautiful!
Then there's--
Why are you smiling?
I'm thinking how you'll make a wonderful king someday.

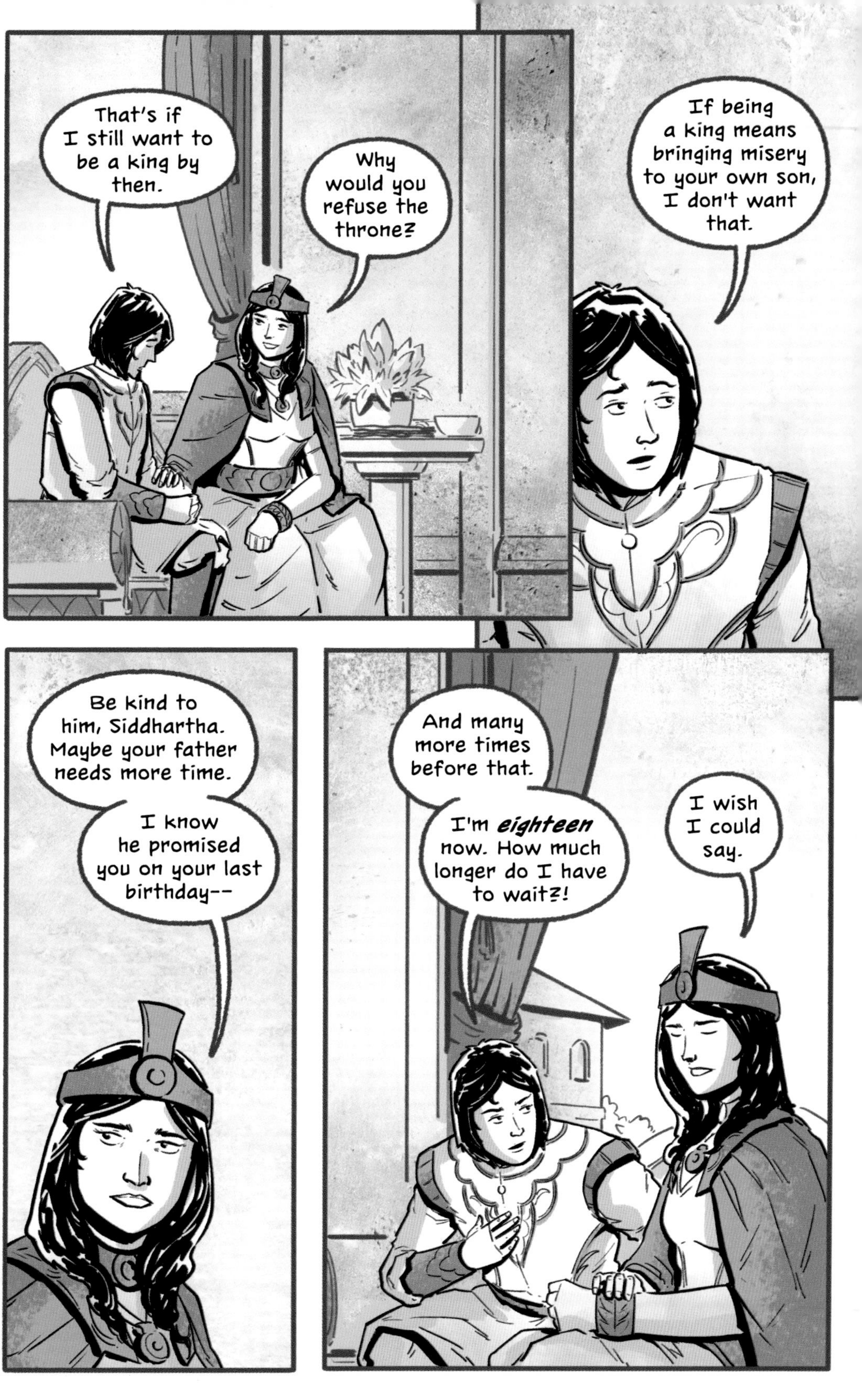
That's if I still want to be a king by then.
Why would you refuse the throne?
If being a king means bringing misery to your own son, I don't want that.
Be kind to him, Siddhartha. Maybe your father needs more time.
I know he promised you on your last birthday--
And many more times before that.
I'm *eighteen* now. How much longer do I have to wait?!
I wish I could say.

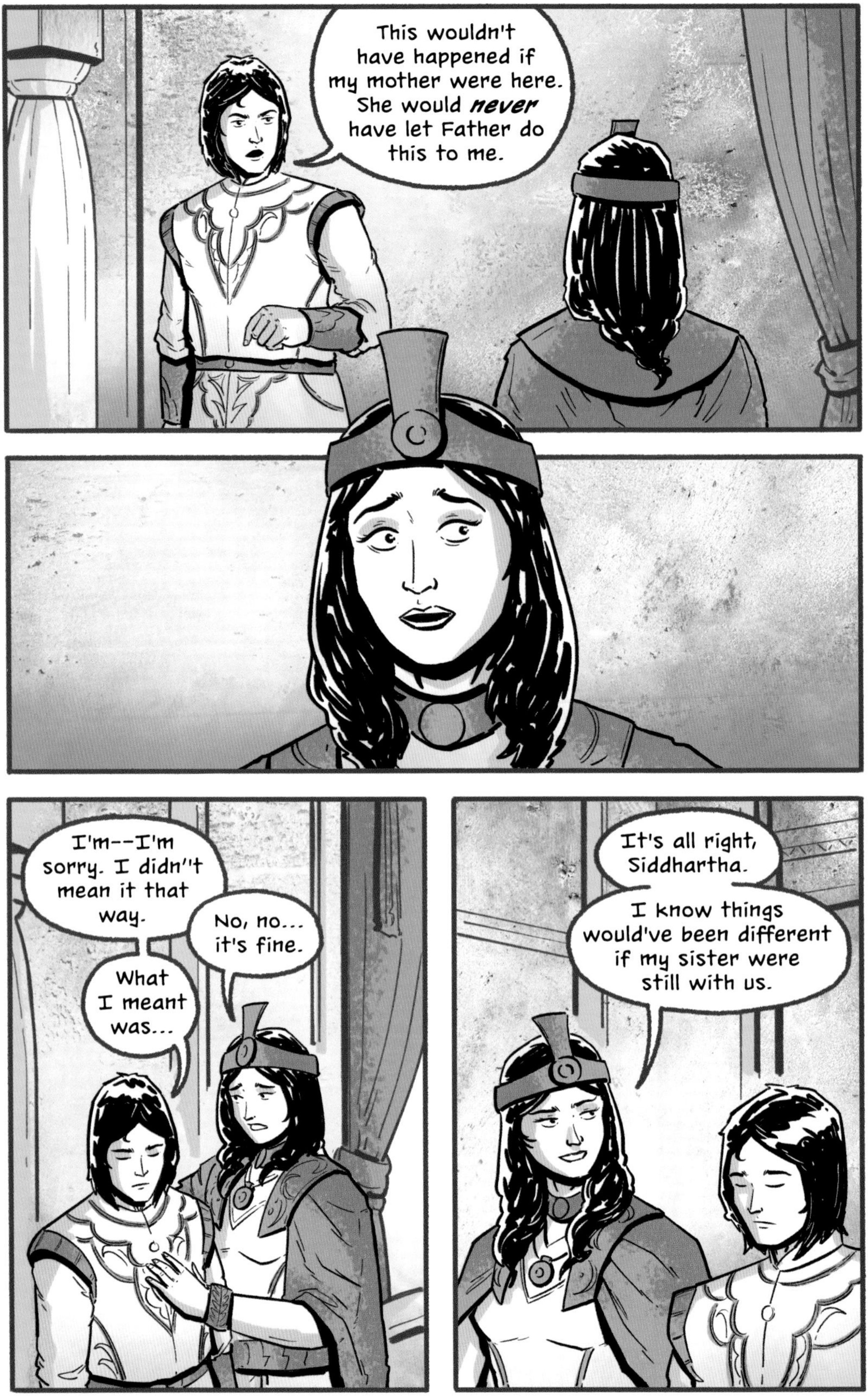
This wouldn't have happened if my mother were here. She would *never* have let Father do this to me.
I'm--I'm sorry. I didn't mean it that way.
What I meant was...
No, no... it's fine.
It's all right, Siddhartha.
I know things would've been different if my sister were still with us.

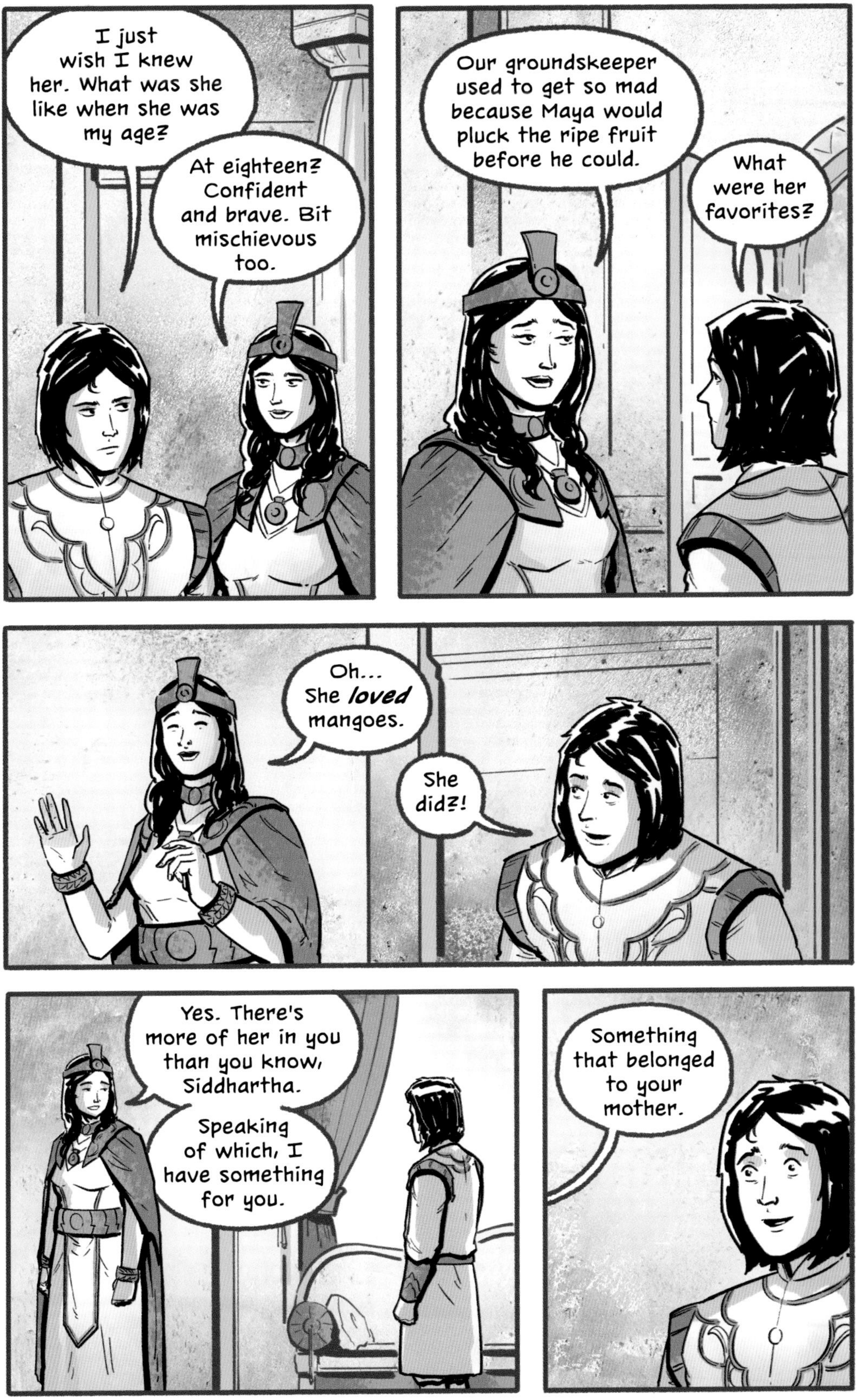
I just wish I knew her. What was she like when she was my age?
At eighteen? Confident and brave. Bit mischievous too.
Our groundskeeper used to get so mad because Maya would pluck the ripe fruit before he could.
What were her favorites?
Oh... She *loved* mangoes.
She did?!
Yes. There's more of her in you than you know, Siddhartha.
Speaking of which, I have something for you.
Something that belonged to your mother.

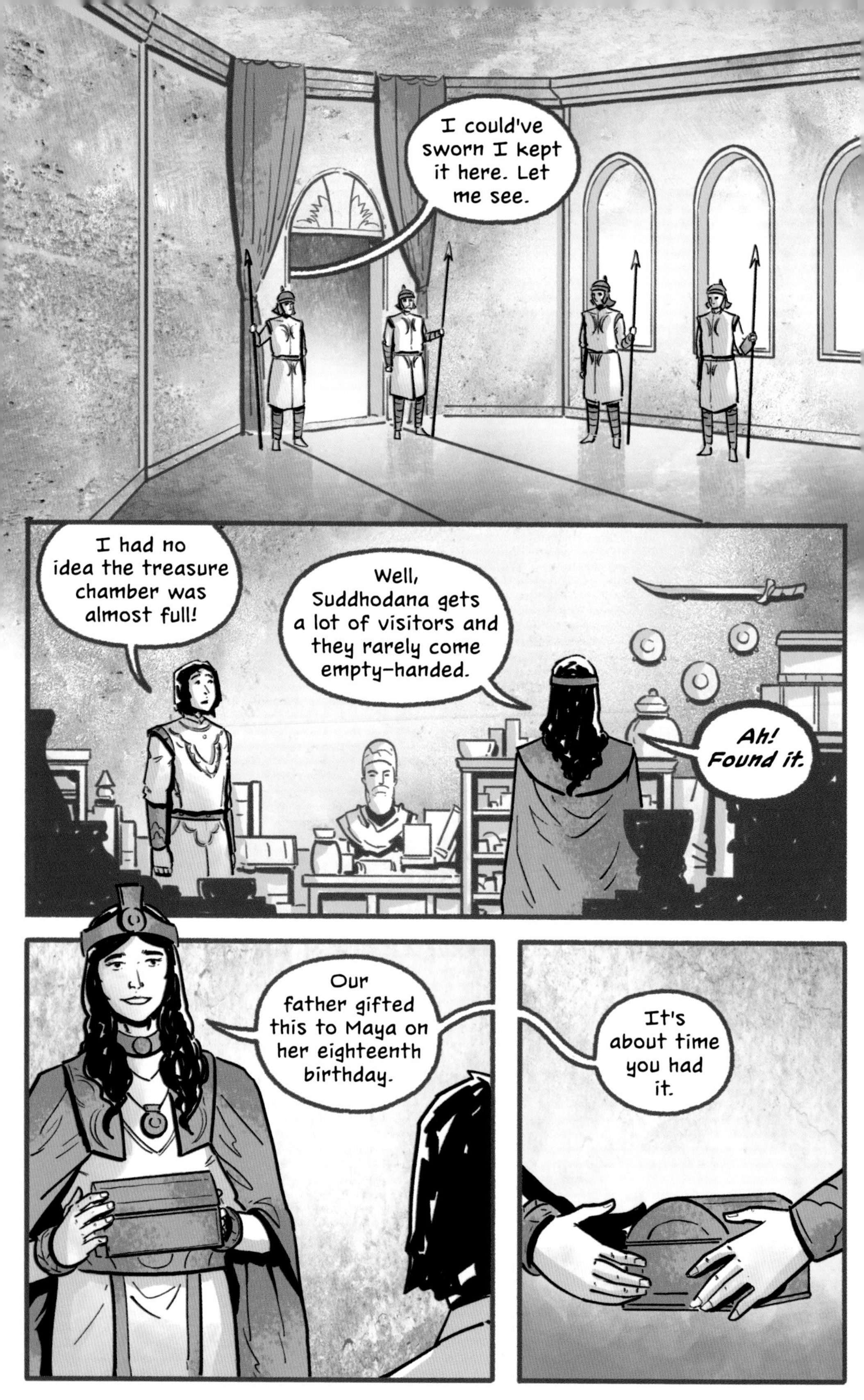
I could've sworn I kept it here. Let me see.
I had no idea the treasure chamber was almost full!
Well, Suddhodana gets a lot of visitors and they rarely come empty-handed.
Ah! Found it.
Our father gifted this to Maya on her eighteenth birthday.
It's about time you had it.

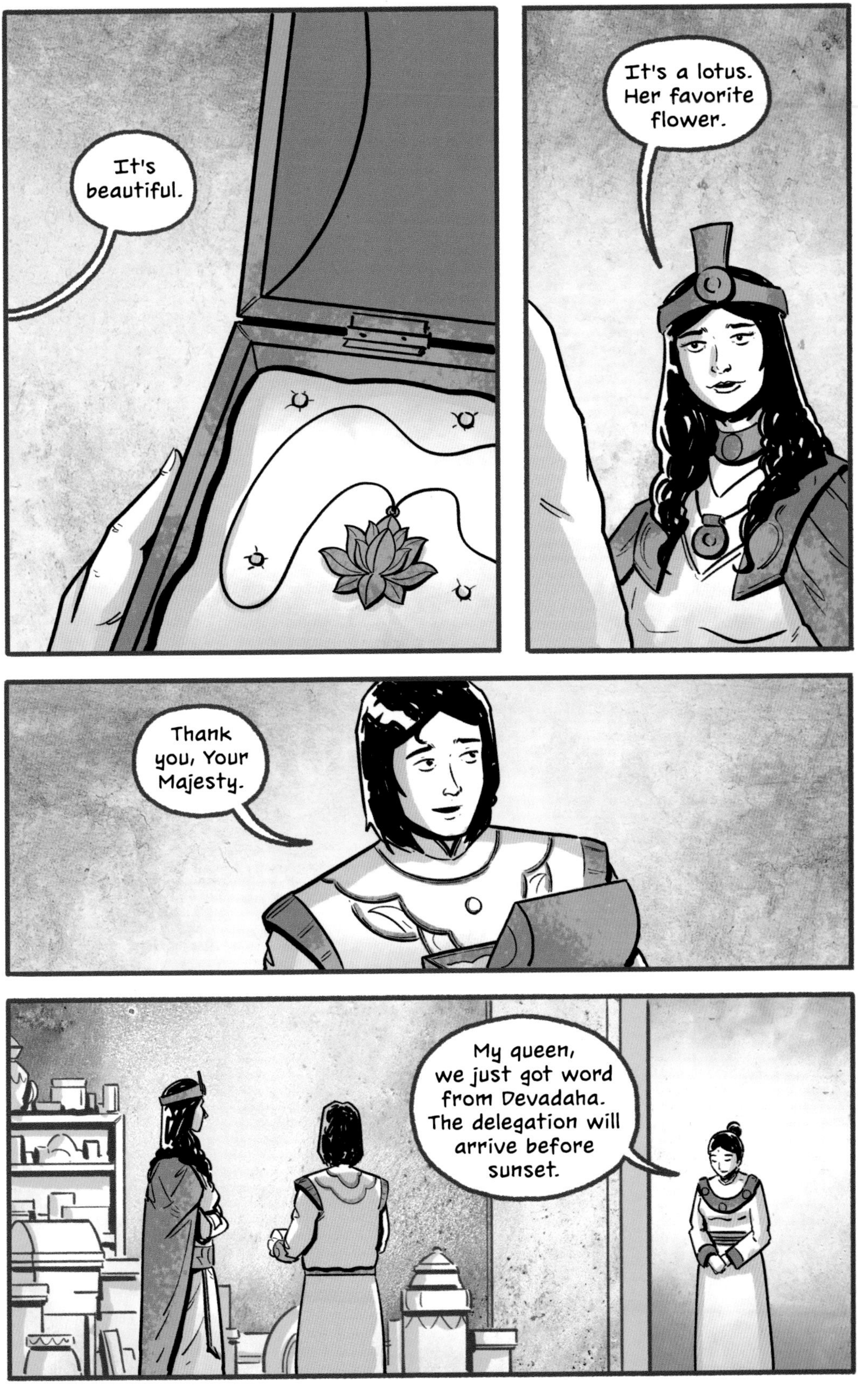
It's beautiful.
It's a lotus. Her favorite flower.
Thank you, Your Majesty.
My queen, we just got word from Devadaha. The delegation will arrive before sunset.

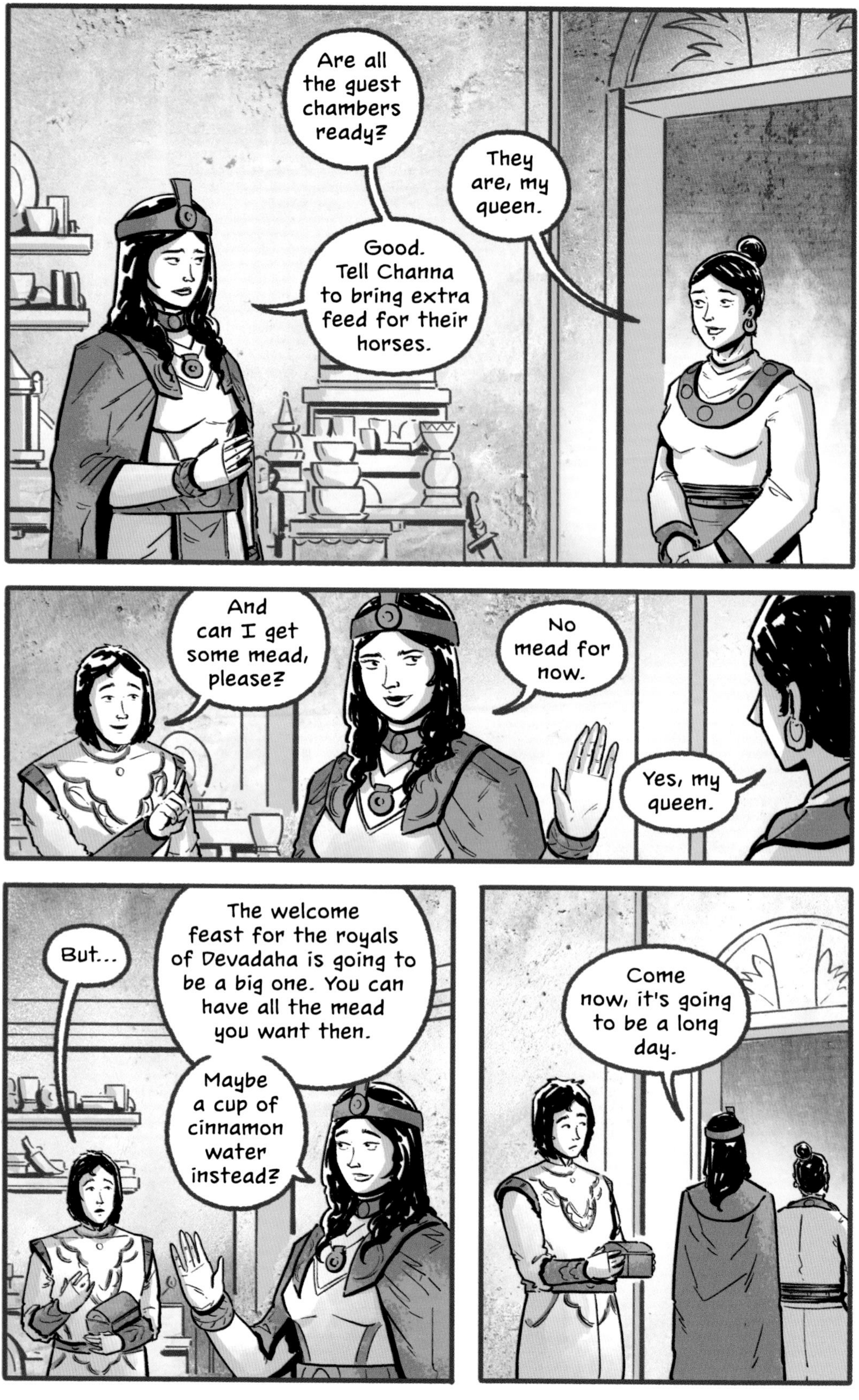
Are all the guest chambers ready?
They are, my queen.
Good. Tell Channa to bring extra feed for their horses.
And can I get some mead, please?
No mead for now.
Yes, my queen.
But...
The welcome feast for the royals of Devadaha is going to be a big one. You can have all the mead you want then.
Maybe a cup of cinnamon water instead?
Come now, it's going to be a long day.

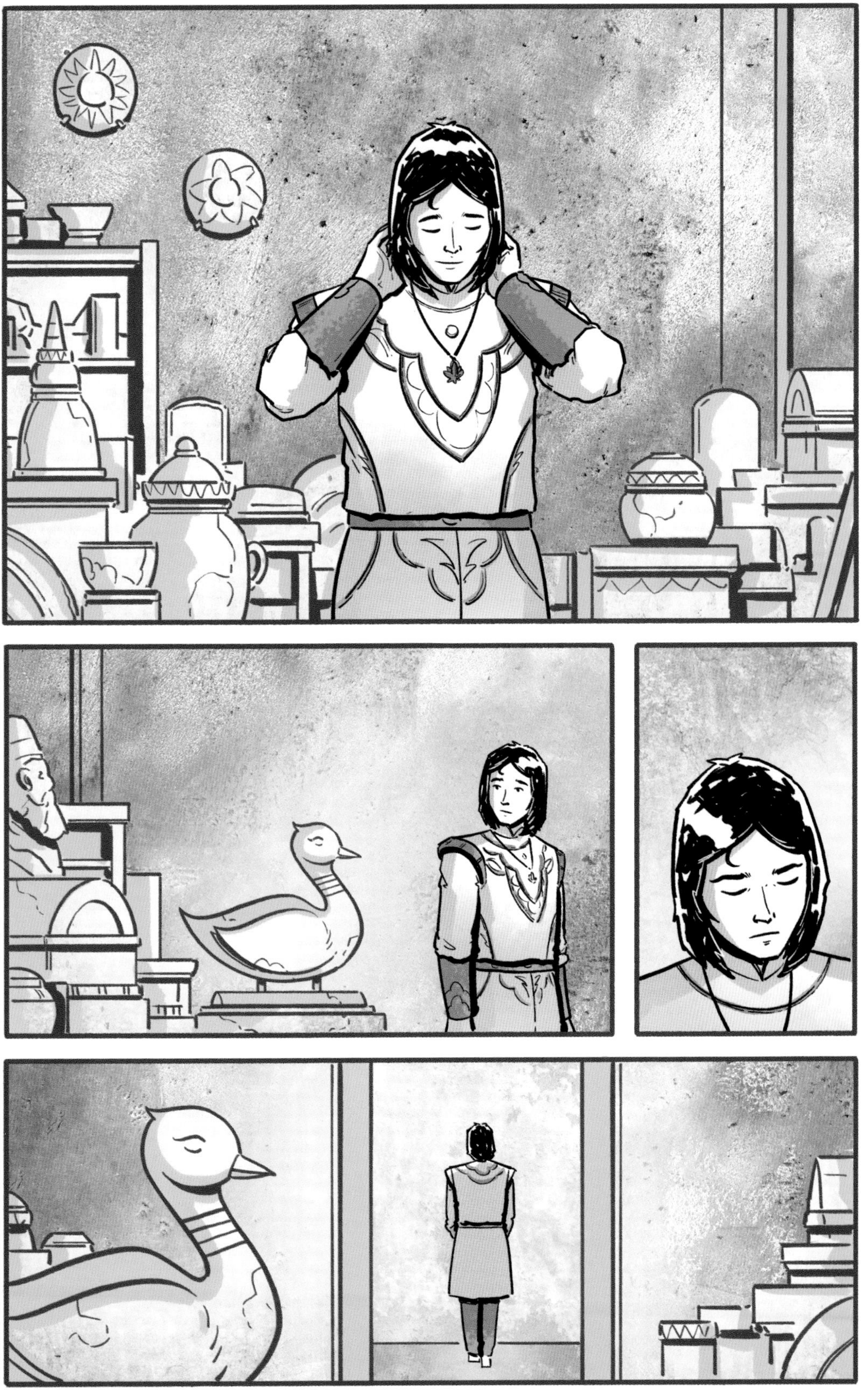

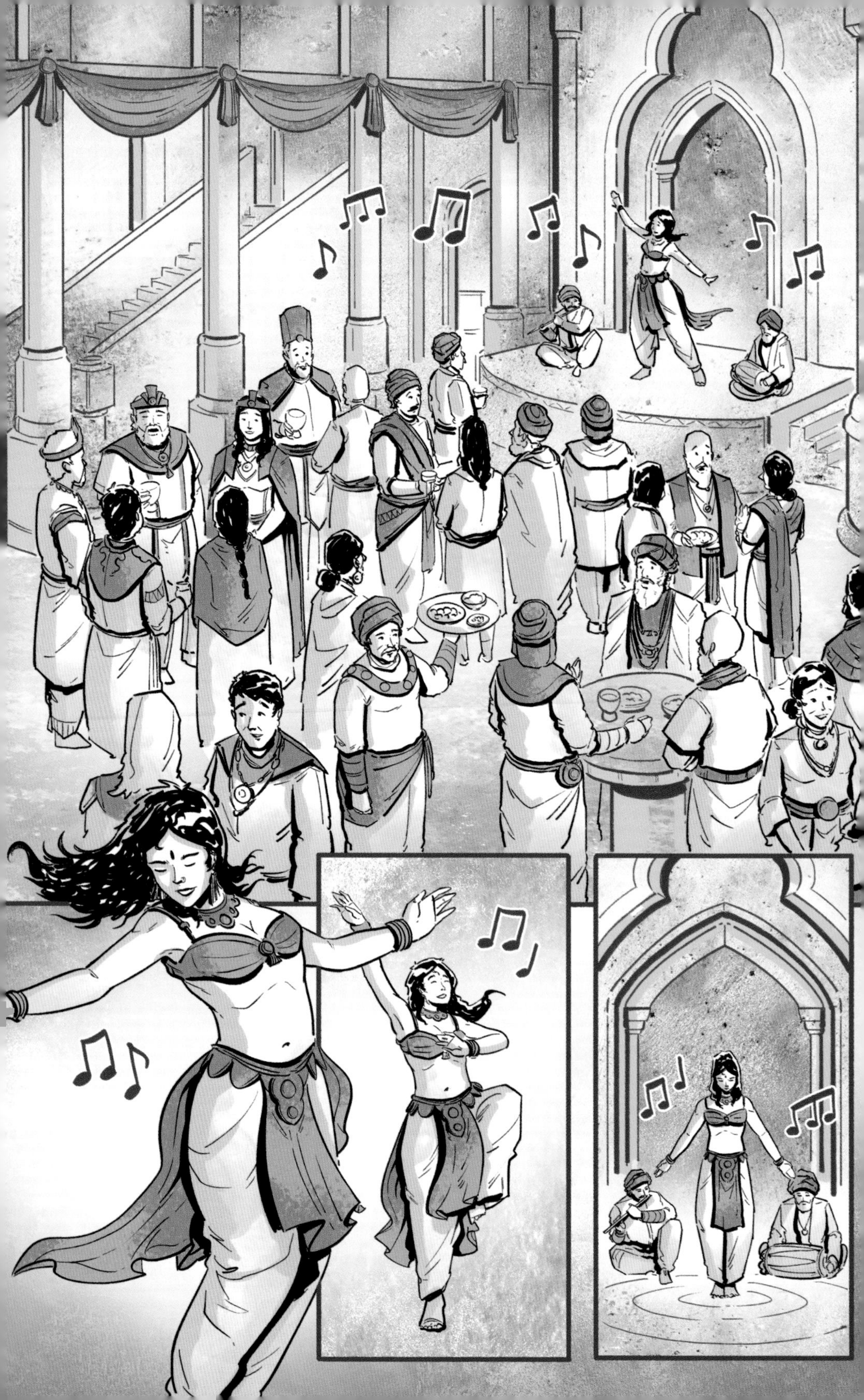

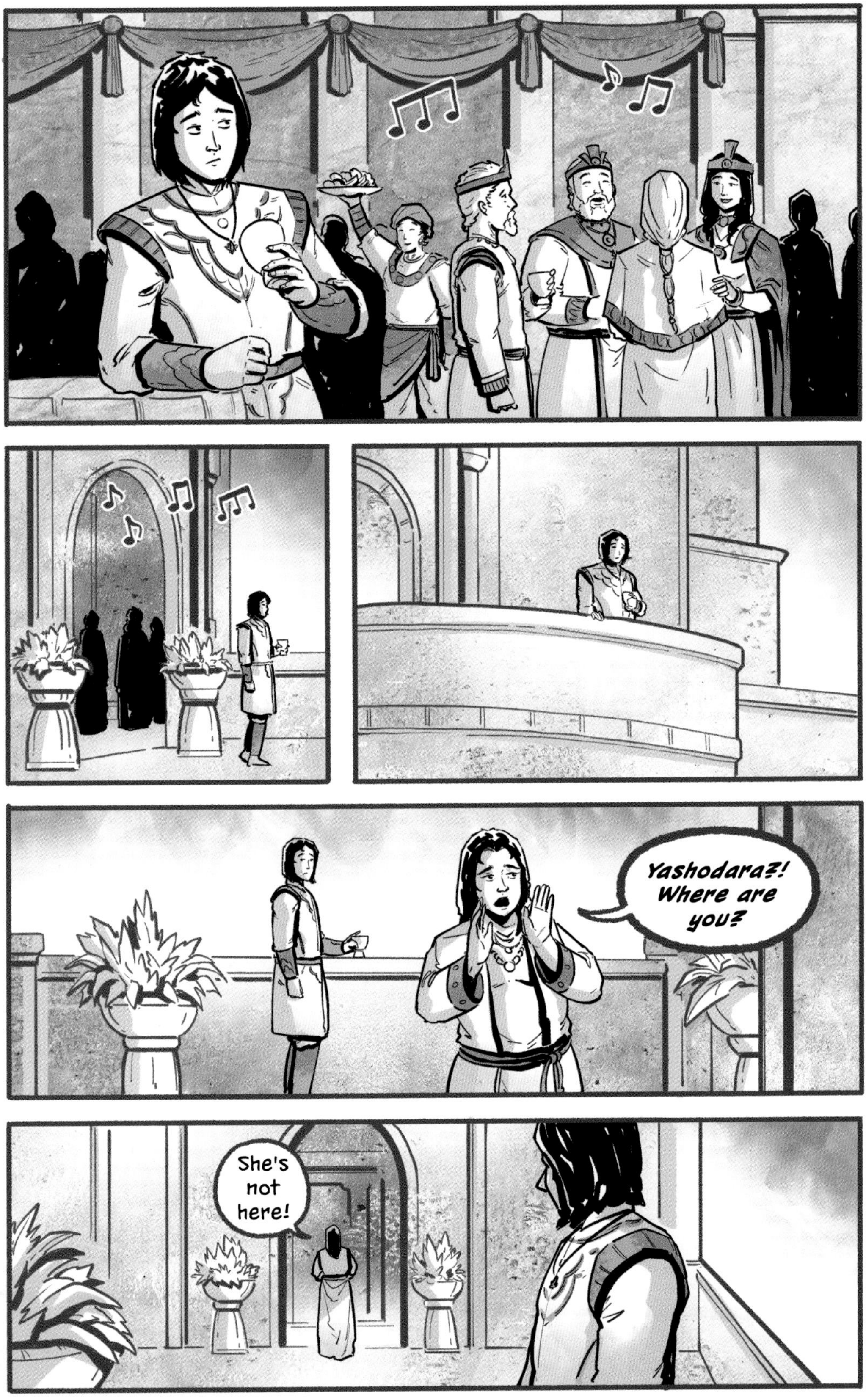
Yashodara?! Where are you?
She's not here!

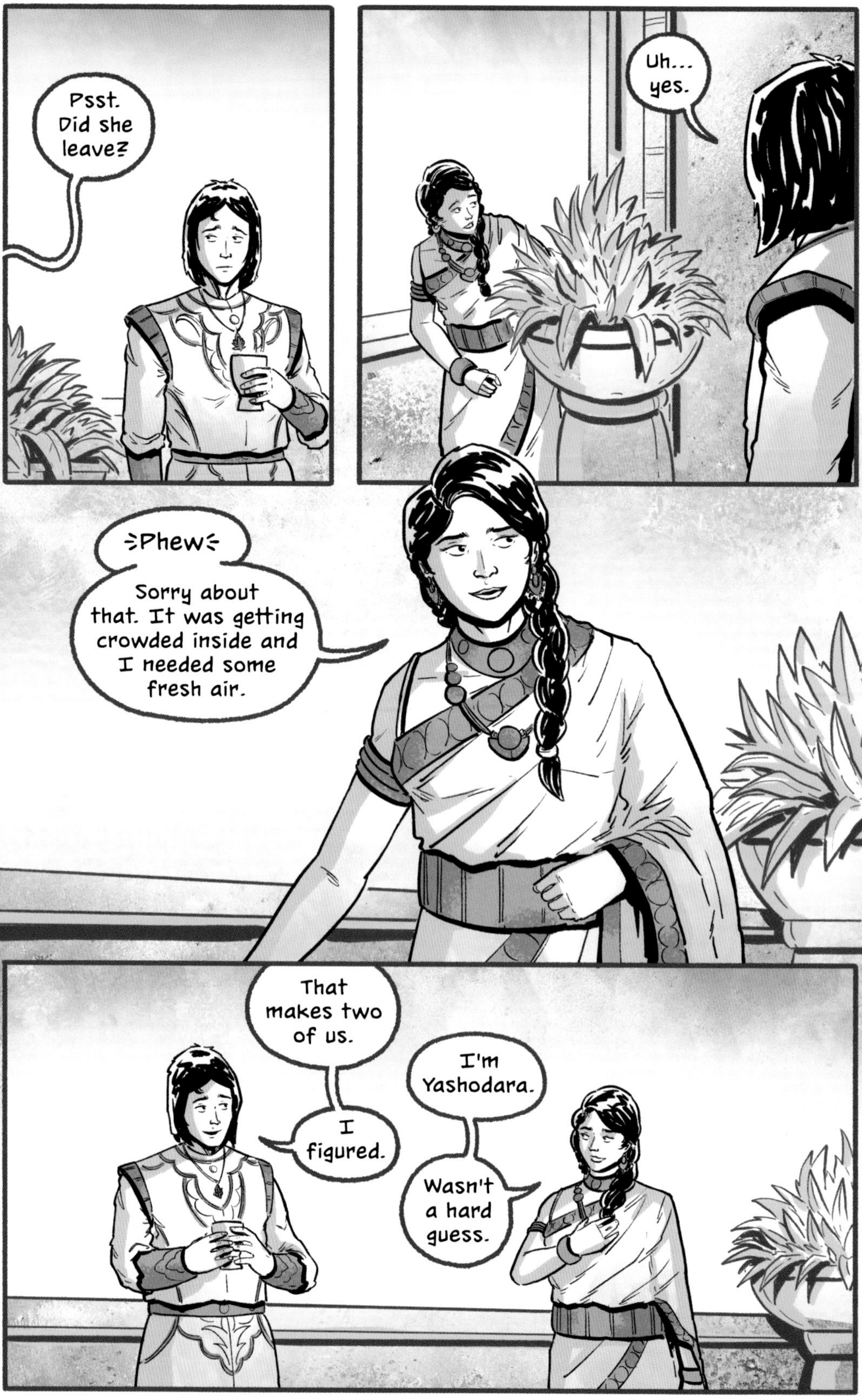
Psst. Did she leave?
Uh... yes.
Phew
Sorry about that. It was getting crowded inside and I needed some fresh air.
That makes two of us.
I figured.
I'm Yashodara.
Wasn't a hard guess.

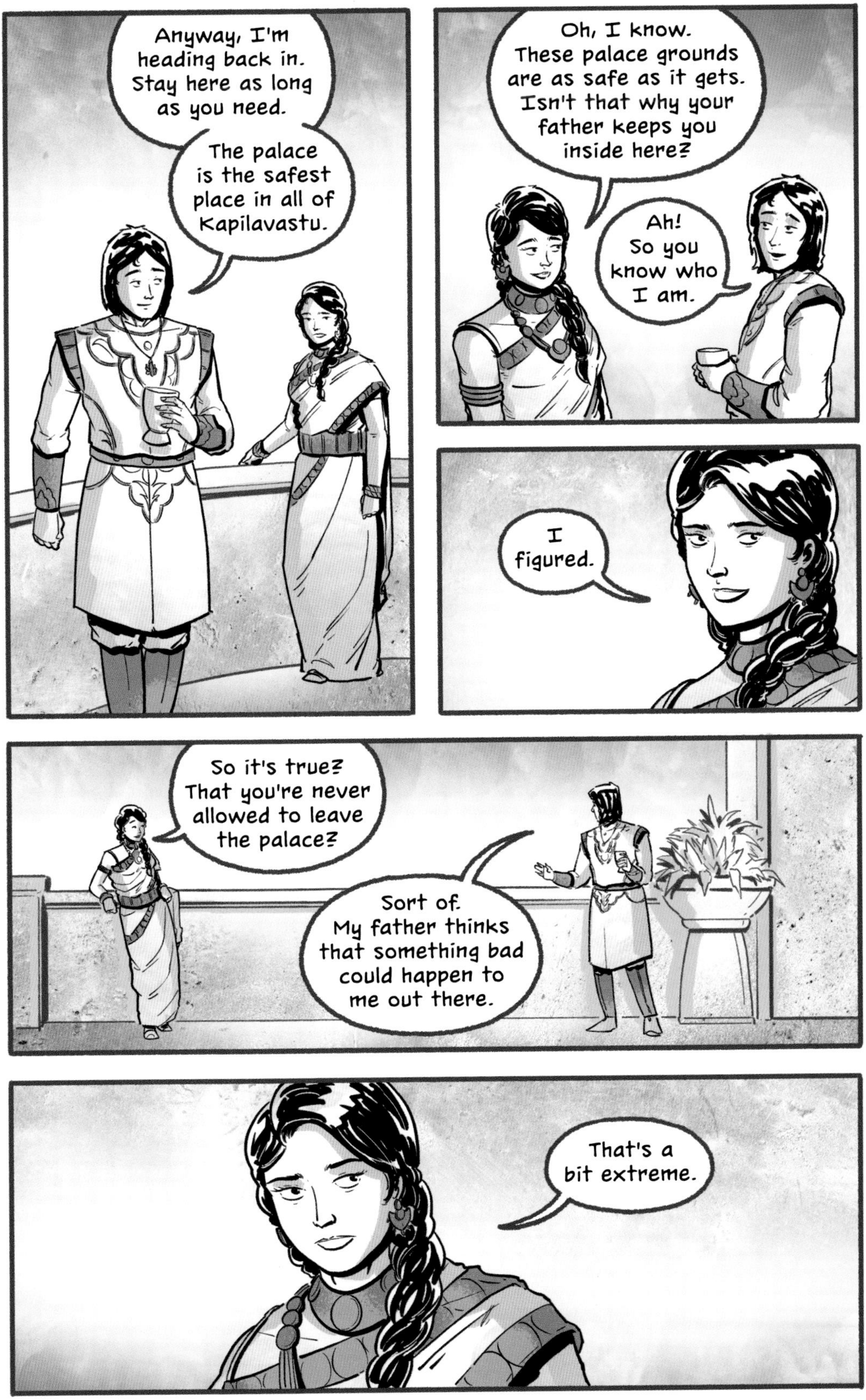
Anyway, I'm heading back in. Stay here as long as you need.
The palace is the safest place in all of Kapilavastu.
Oh, I know. These palace grounds are as safe as it gets. Isn't that why your father keeps you inside here?
Ah! So you know who I am.
I figured.
So it's true? That you're never allowed to leave the palace?
Sort of. My father thinks that something bad could happen to me out there.
That's a bit extreme.

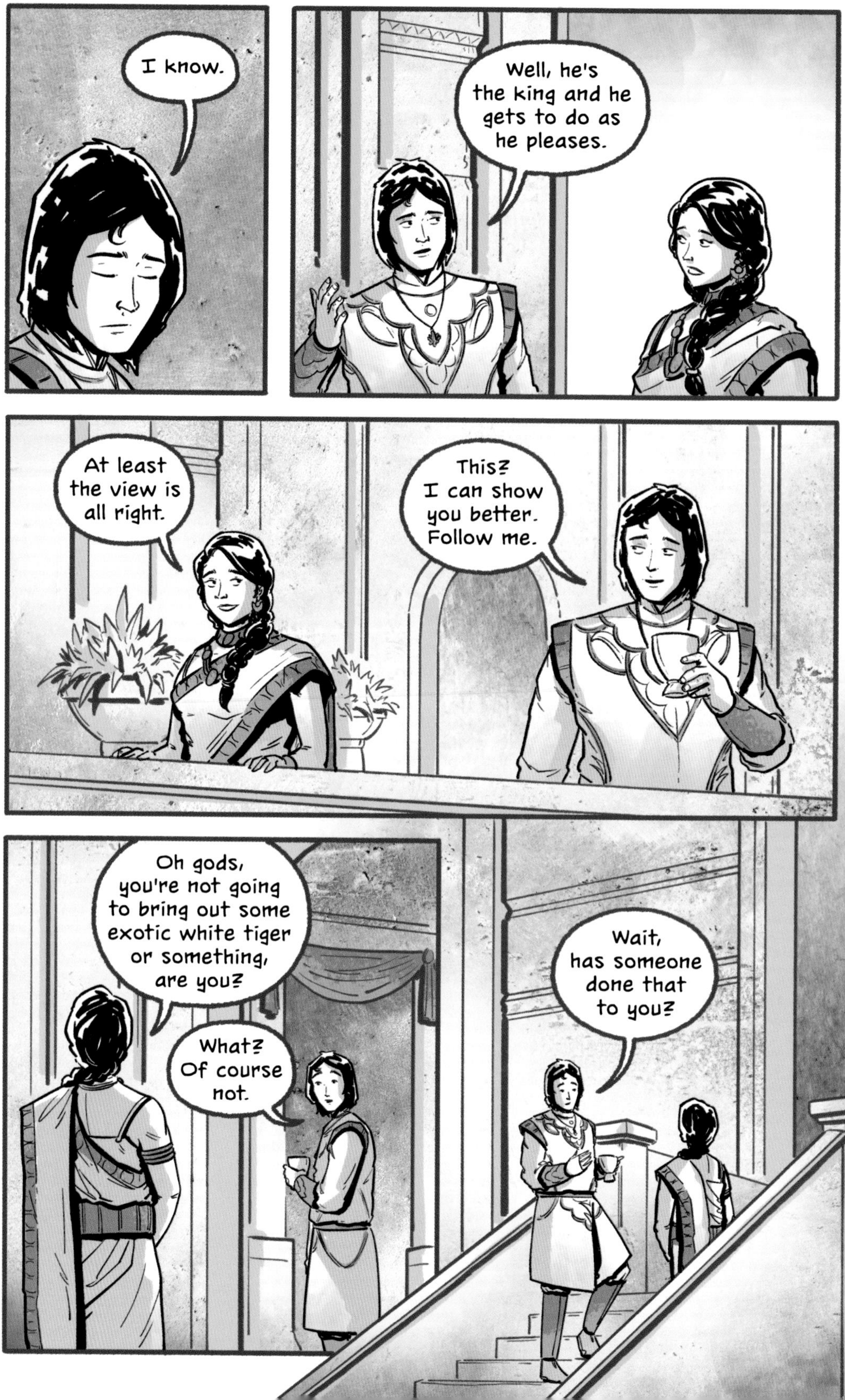
I know.
Well, he's the king and he gets to do as he pleases.
At least the view is all right.
This? I can show you better. Follow me.
Oh gods, you're not going to bring out some exotic white tiger or something, are you?
What? Of course not.
Wait, has someone done that to you?

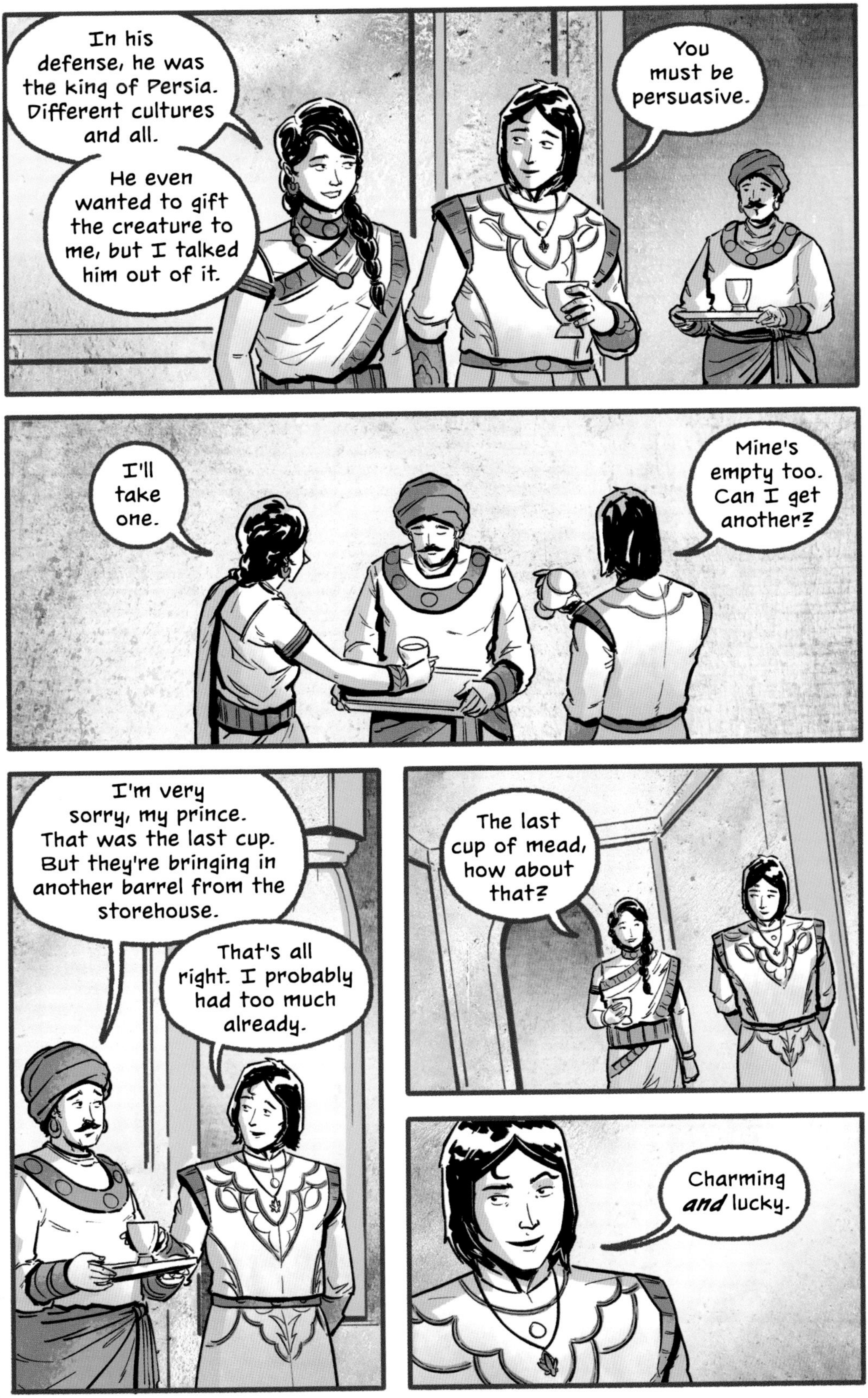
In his defense, he was the king of Persia. Different cultures and all.
He even wanted to gift the creature to me, but I talked him out of it.
You must be persuasive.
I'll take one.
Mine's empty too. Can I get another?
I'm very sorry, my prince. That was the last cup. But they're bringing in another barrel from the storehouse.
That's all right. I probably had too much already.
The last cup of mead, how about that?
Charming *and* lucky.

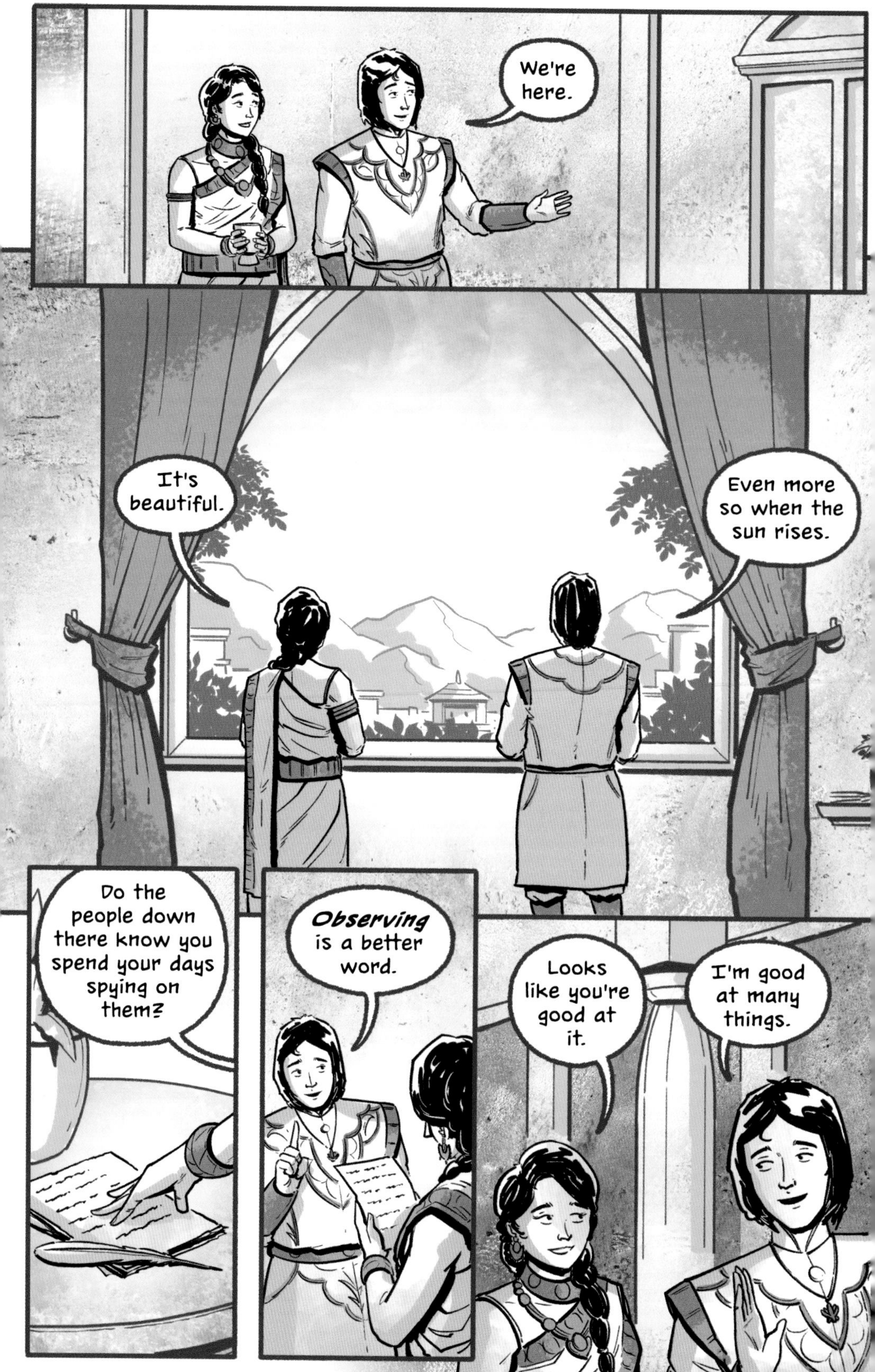
We're here.
It's beautiful.
Even more so when the sun rises.
Do the people down there know you spend your days spying on them?
Observing is a better word.
Looks like you're good at it.
I'm good at many things.

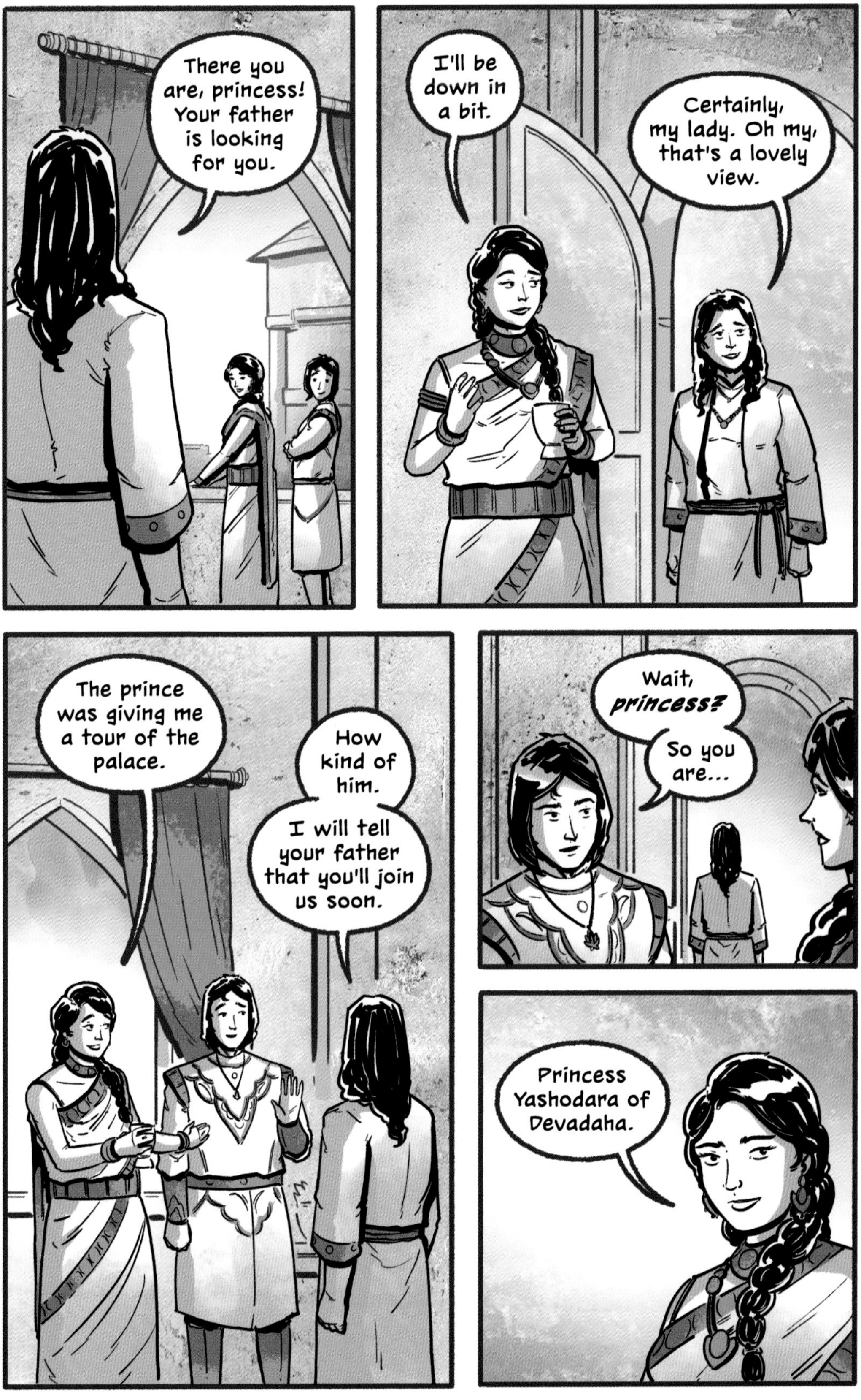
There you are, princess! Your father is looking for you.
I'll be down in a bit.
Certainly, my lady. Oh my, that's a lovely view.
The prince was giving me a tour of the palace.
How kind of him.
I will tell your father that you'll join us soon.
Wait, *princess?*
So you are...
Princess Yashodara of Devadaha.

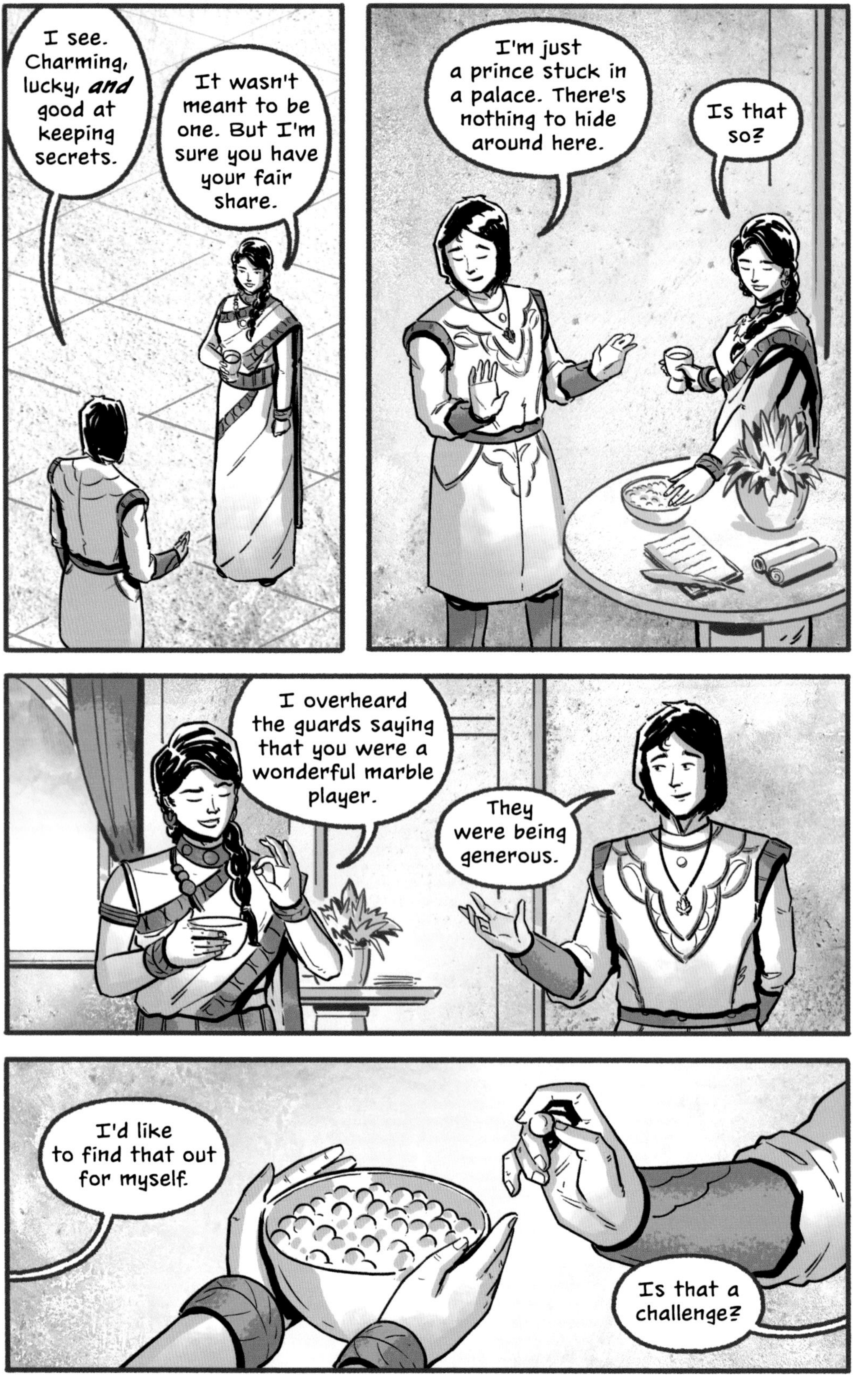
I see. Charming, lucky, *and* good at keeping secrets.
It wasn't meant to be one. But I'm sure you have your fair share.
I'm just a prince stuck in a palace. There's nothing to hide around here.
Is that so?
I overheard the guards saying that you were a wonderful marble player.
They were being generous.
I'd like to find that out for myself.
Is that a challenge?

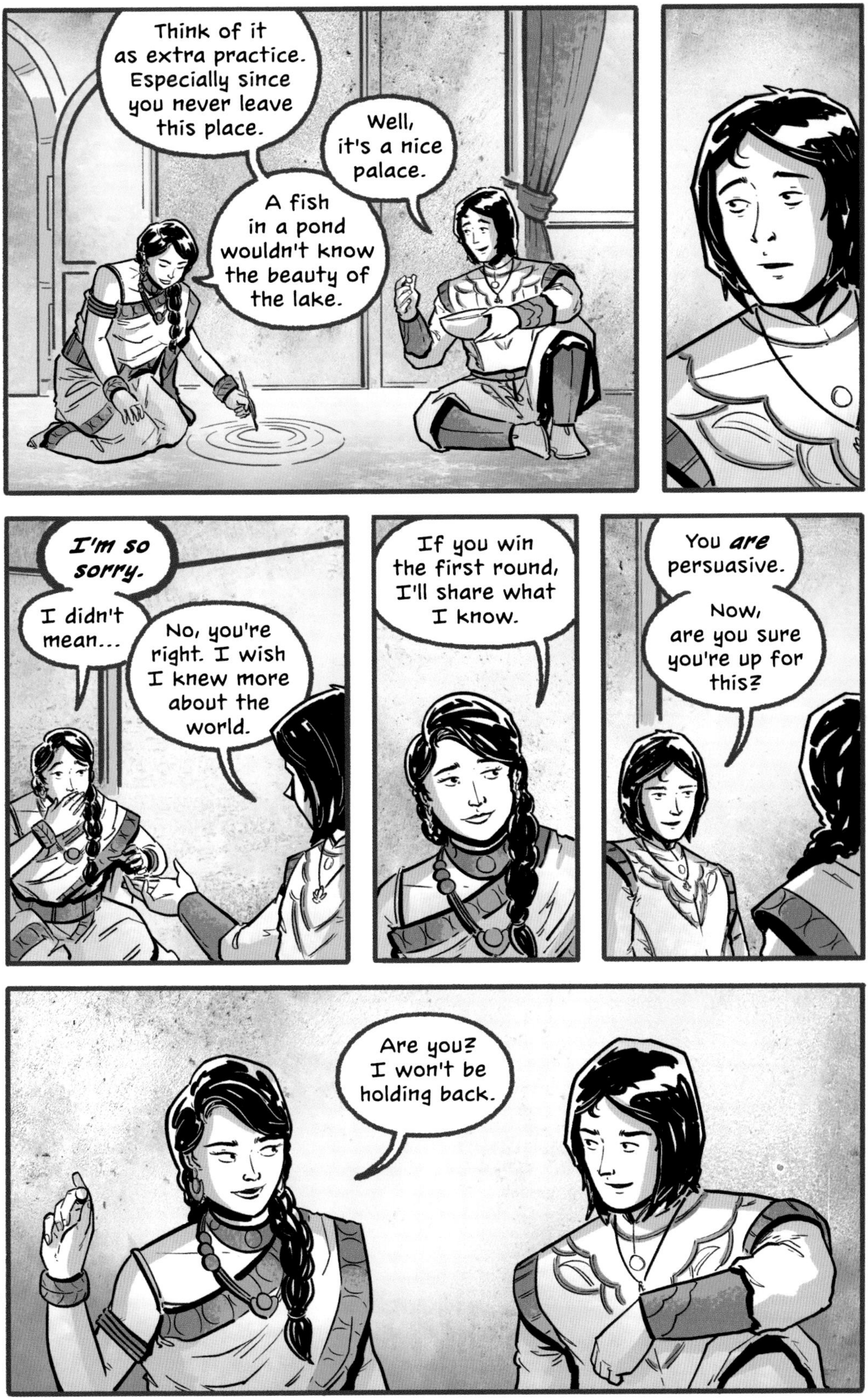
Think of it as extra practice. Especially since you never leave this place.
Well, it's a nice palace.
A fish in a pond wouldn't know the beauty of the lake.
I'm so sorry.
I didn't mean...
No, you're right. I wish I knew more about the world.
If you win the first round, I'll share what I know.
You *are* persuasive.
Now, are you sure you're up for this?
Are you? I won't be holding back.

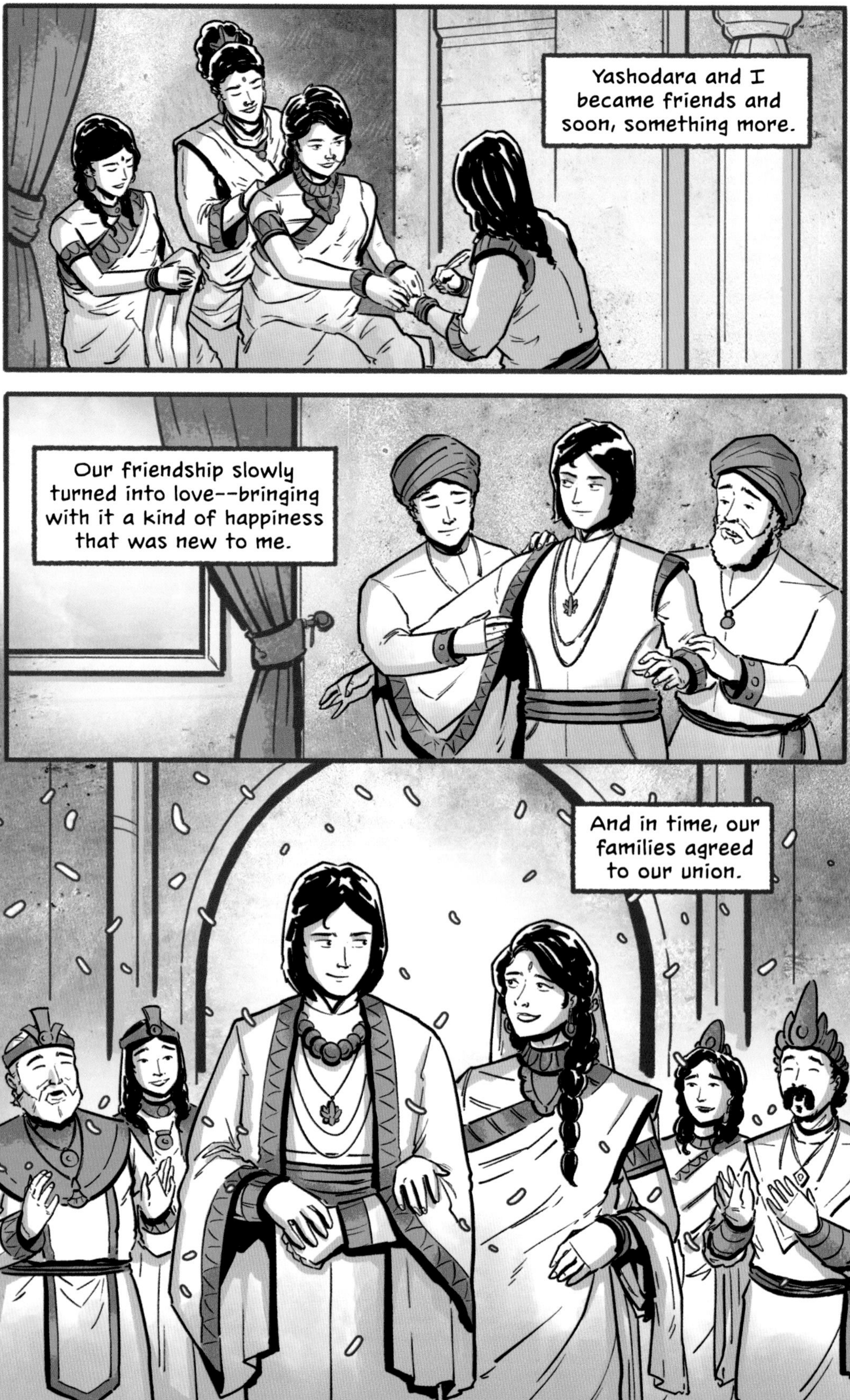
Yashodara and I became friends and soon, something more.
Our friendship slowly turned into love--bringing with it a kind of happiness that was new to me.
And in time, our families agreed to our union.

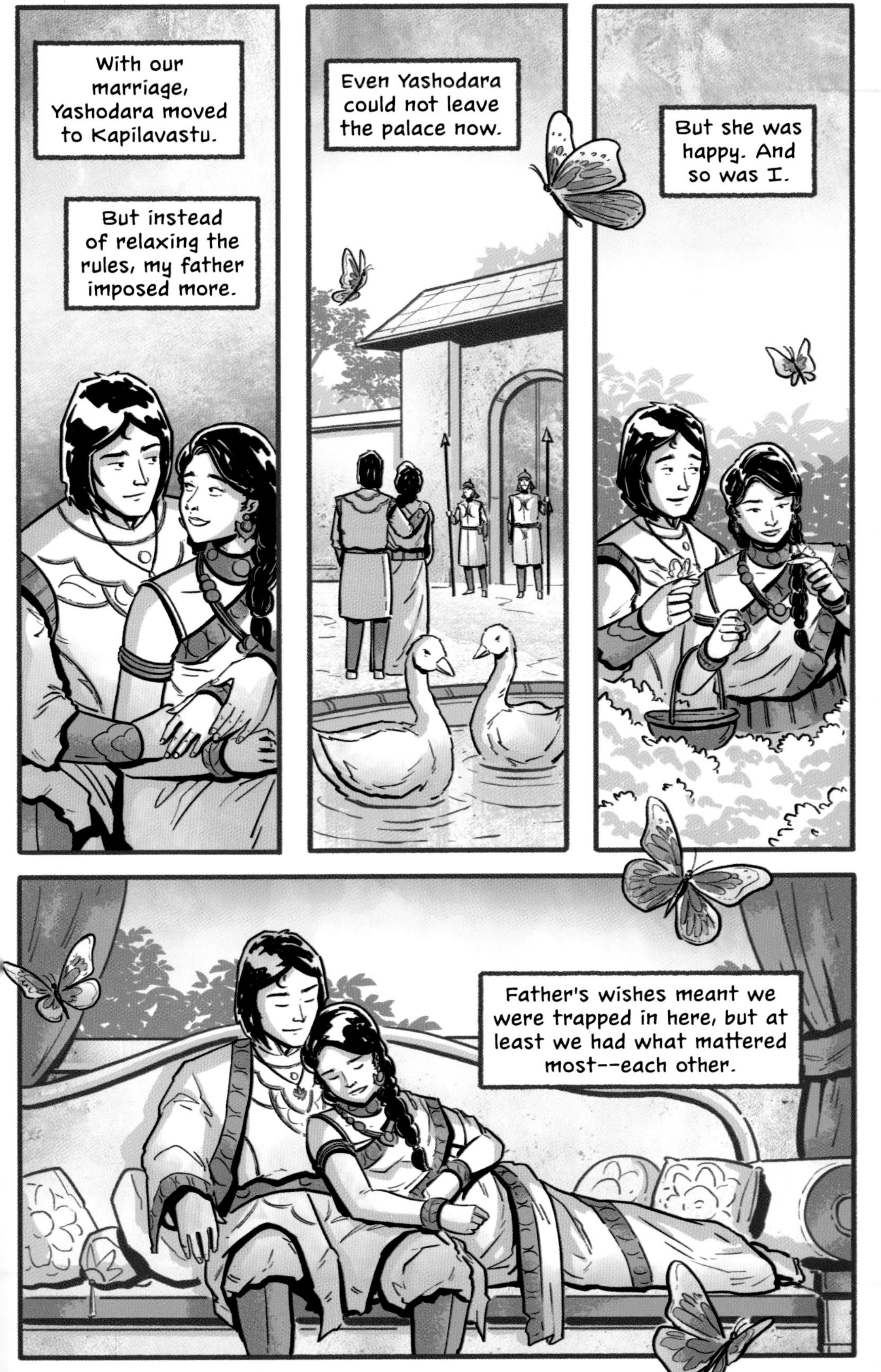

With our marriage, Yashodara moved to Kapilavastu.
But instead of relaxing the rules, my father imposed more.
Even Yashodara could not leave the palace now.
But she was happy. And so was I.
Father's wishes meant we were trapped in here, but at least we had what mattered most--each other.

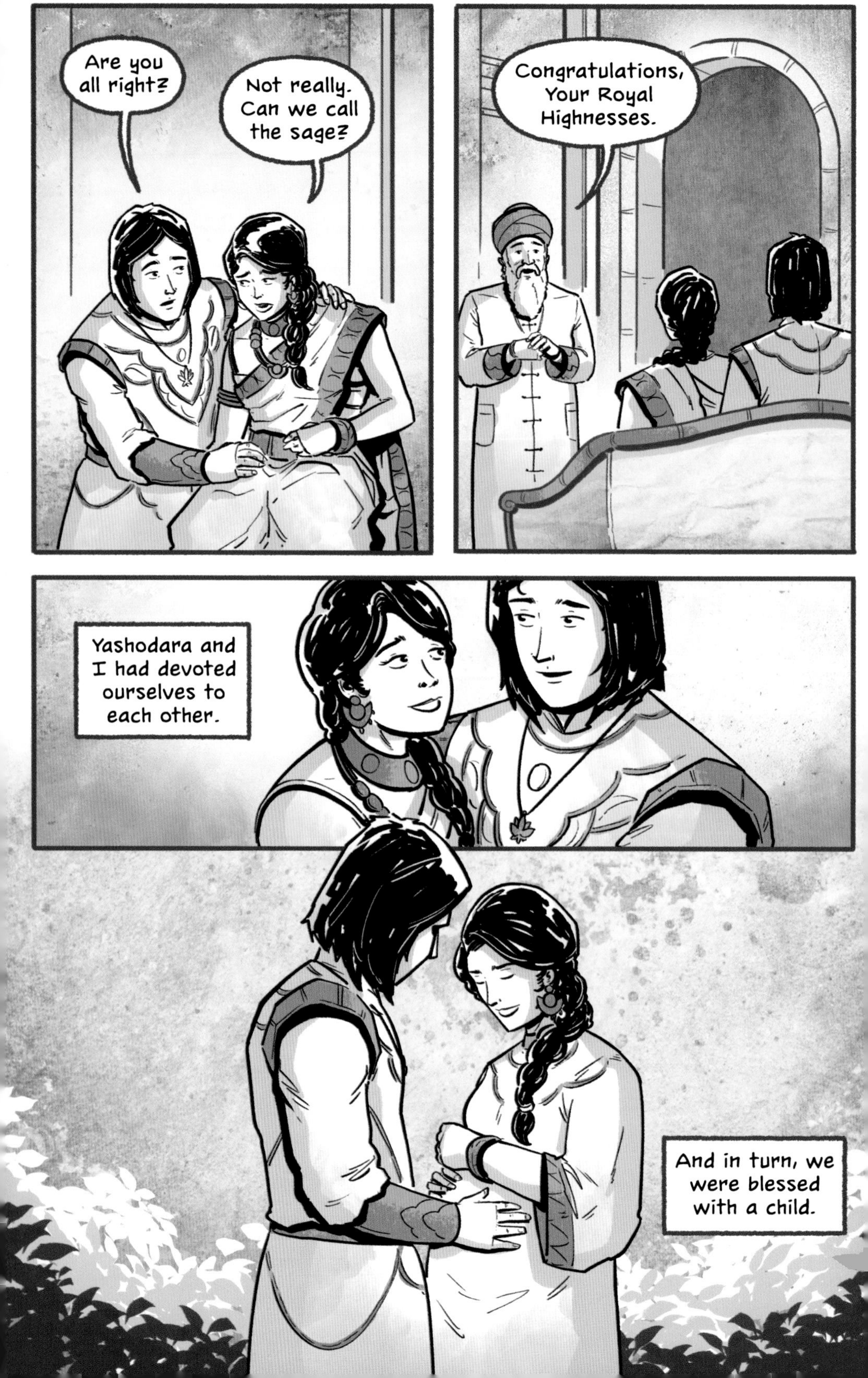
Are you all right?
Not really. Can we call the sage?
Congratulations, Your Royal Highnesses.
Yashodara and I had devoted ourselves to each other.
And in turn, we were blessed with a child.

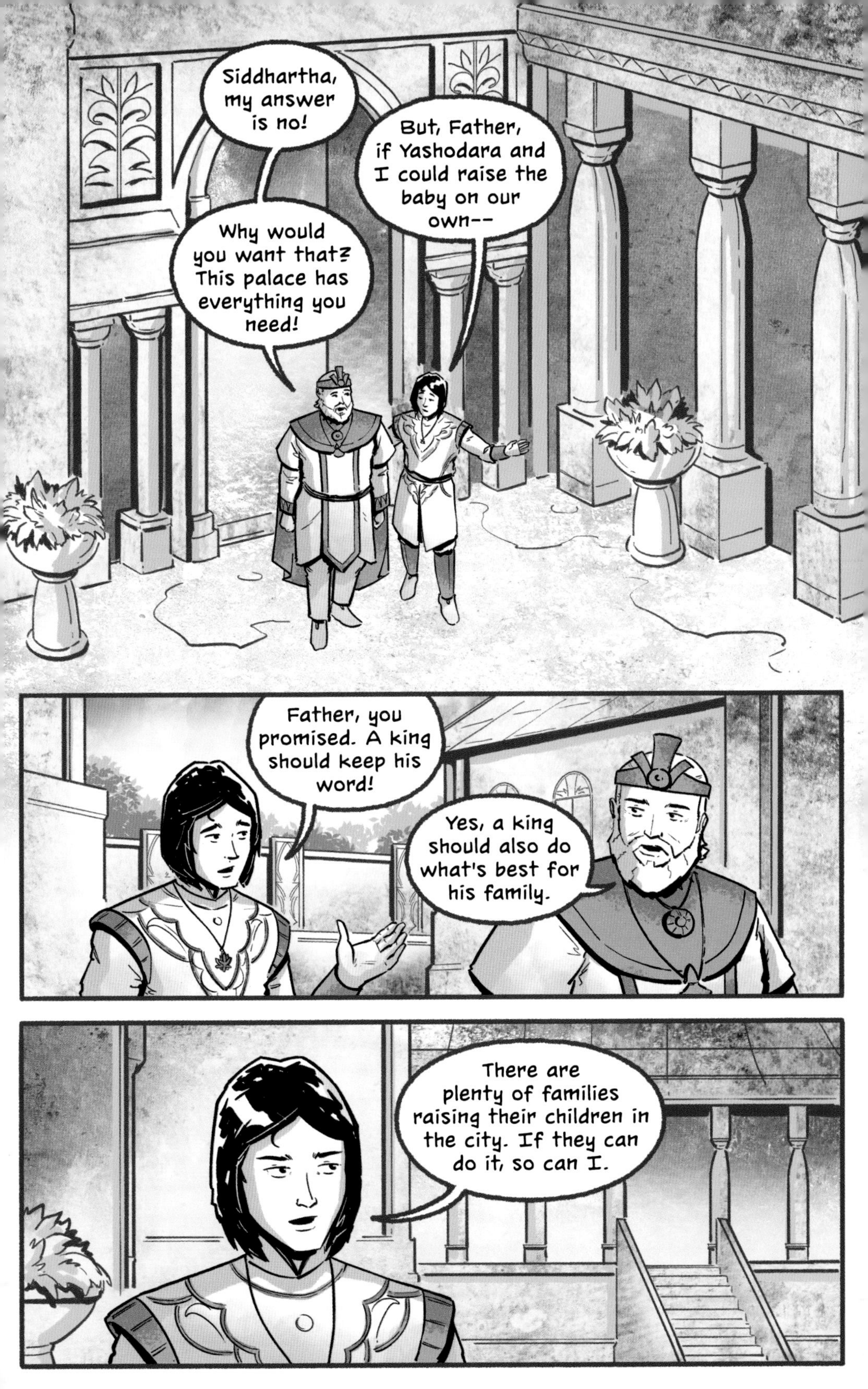
Siddhartha, my answer is no!
Why would you want that? This palace has everything you need!
But, Father, if Yashodara and I could raise the baby on our own--
Father, you promised. A king should keep his word!
Yes, a king should also do what's best for his family.
There are plenty of families raising their children in the city. If they can do it, so can I.

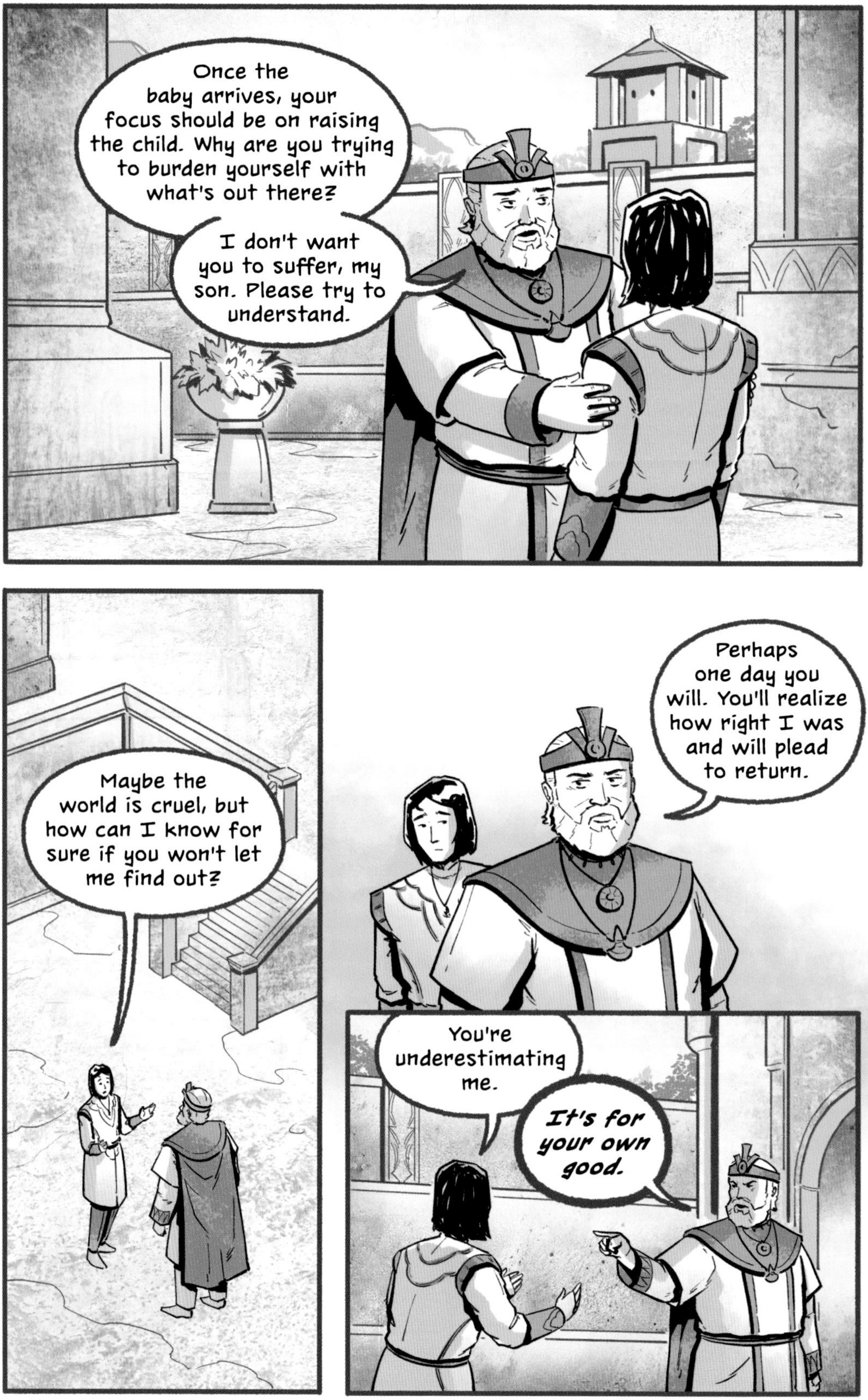
Once the baby arrives, your focus should be on raising the child. Why are you trying to burden yourself with what's out there?
I don't want you to suffer, my son. Please try to understand.
Maybe the world is cruel, but how can I know for sure if you won't let me find out?
Perhaps one day you will. You'll realize how right I was and will plead to return.
You're underestimating me.
It's for your own good.

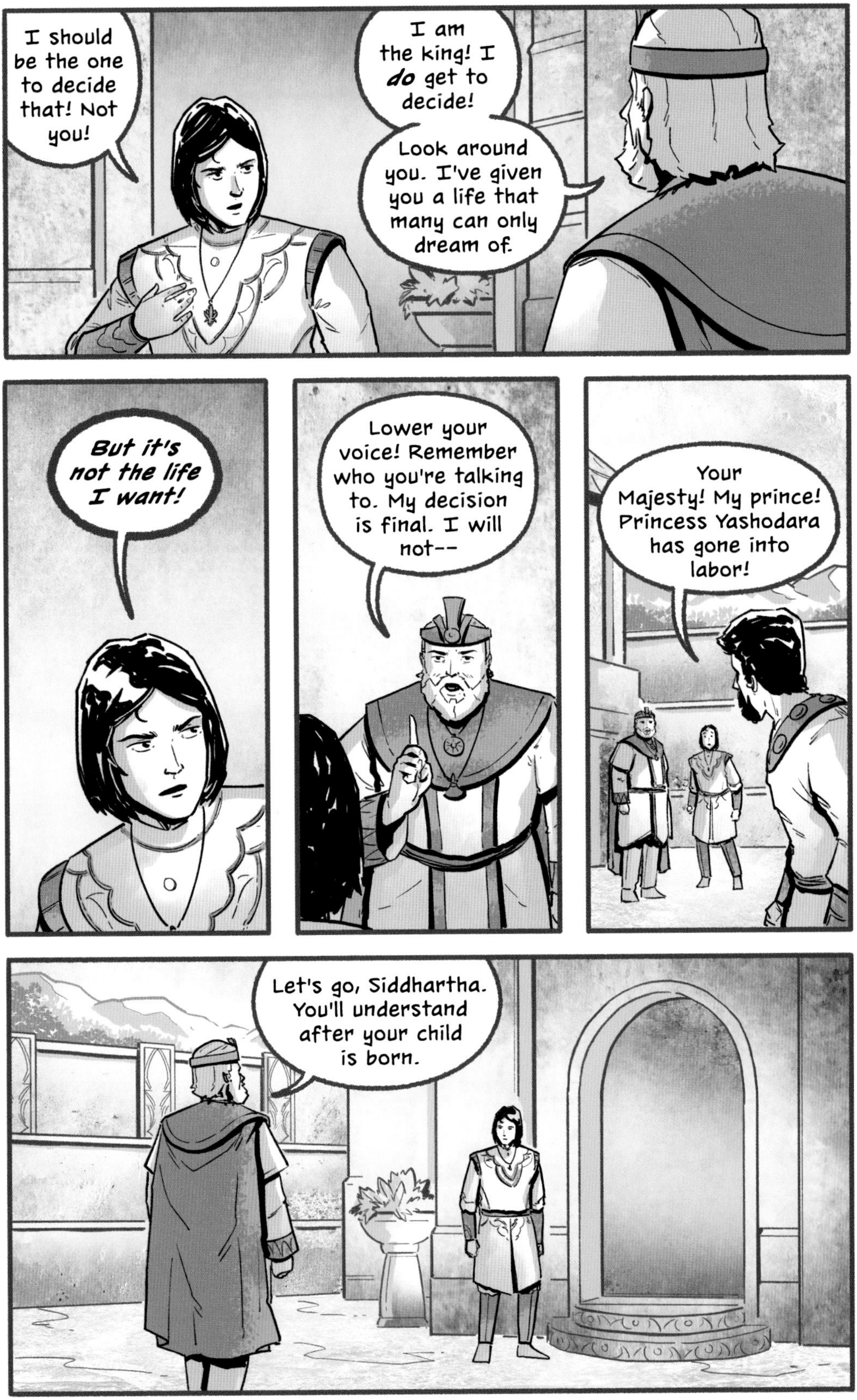
I should be the one to decide that! Not you!
I am the king! I *do* get to decide!
Look around you. I've given you a life that many can only dream of.
But it's not the life I want!
Lower your voice! Remember who you're talking to. My decision is final. I will not--
Your Majesty! My prince! Princess Yashodara has gone into labor!
Let's go, Siddhartha. You'll understand after your child is born.

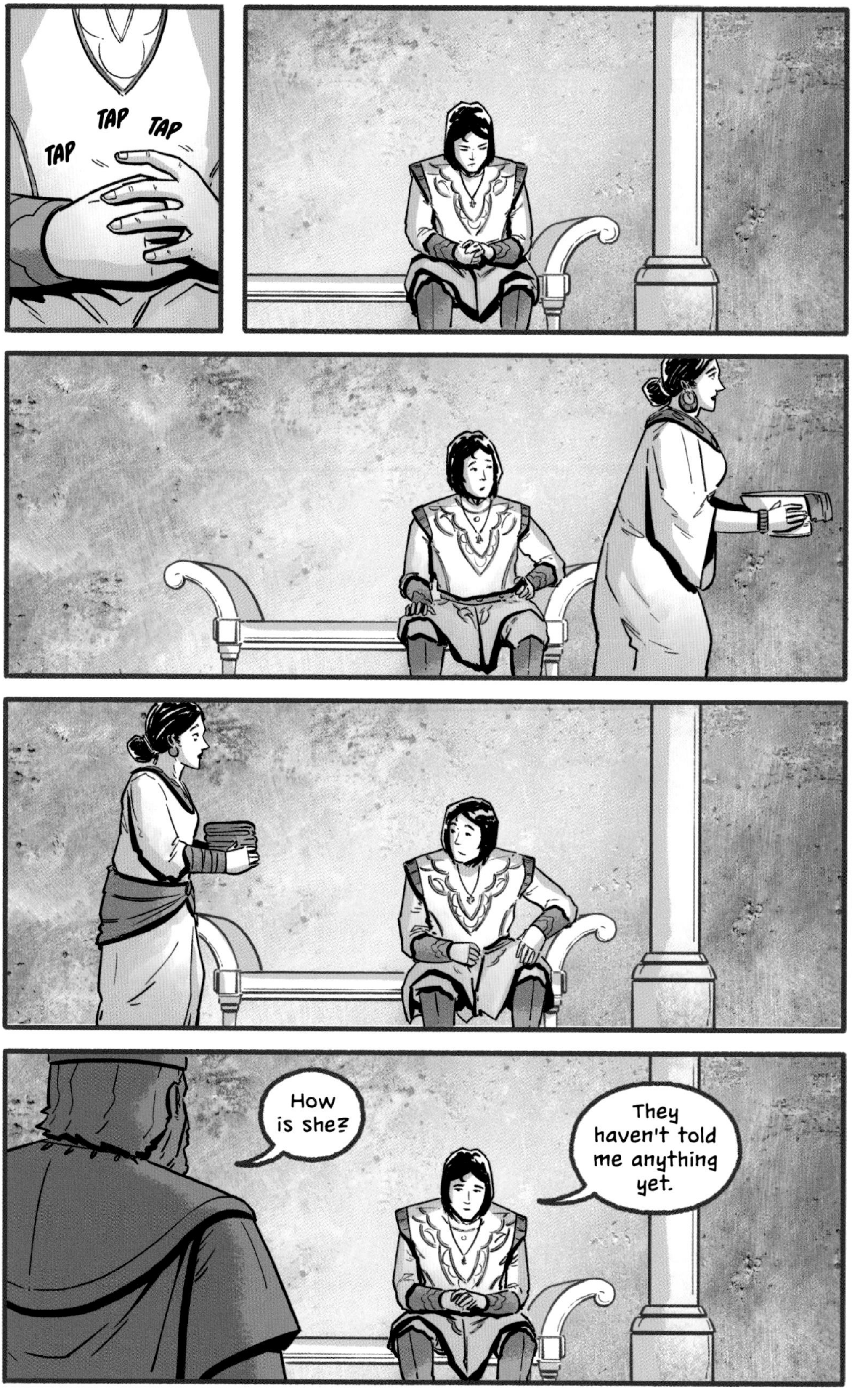
TAP
TAP
TAP
How is she?
They haven't told me anything yet.

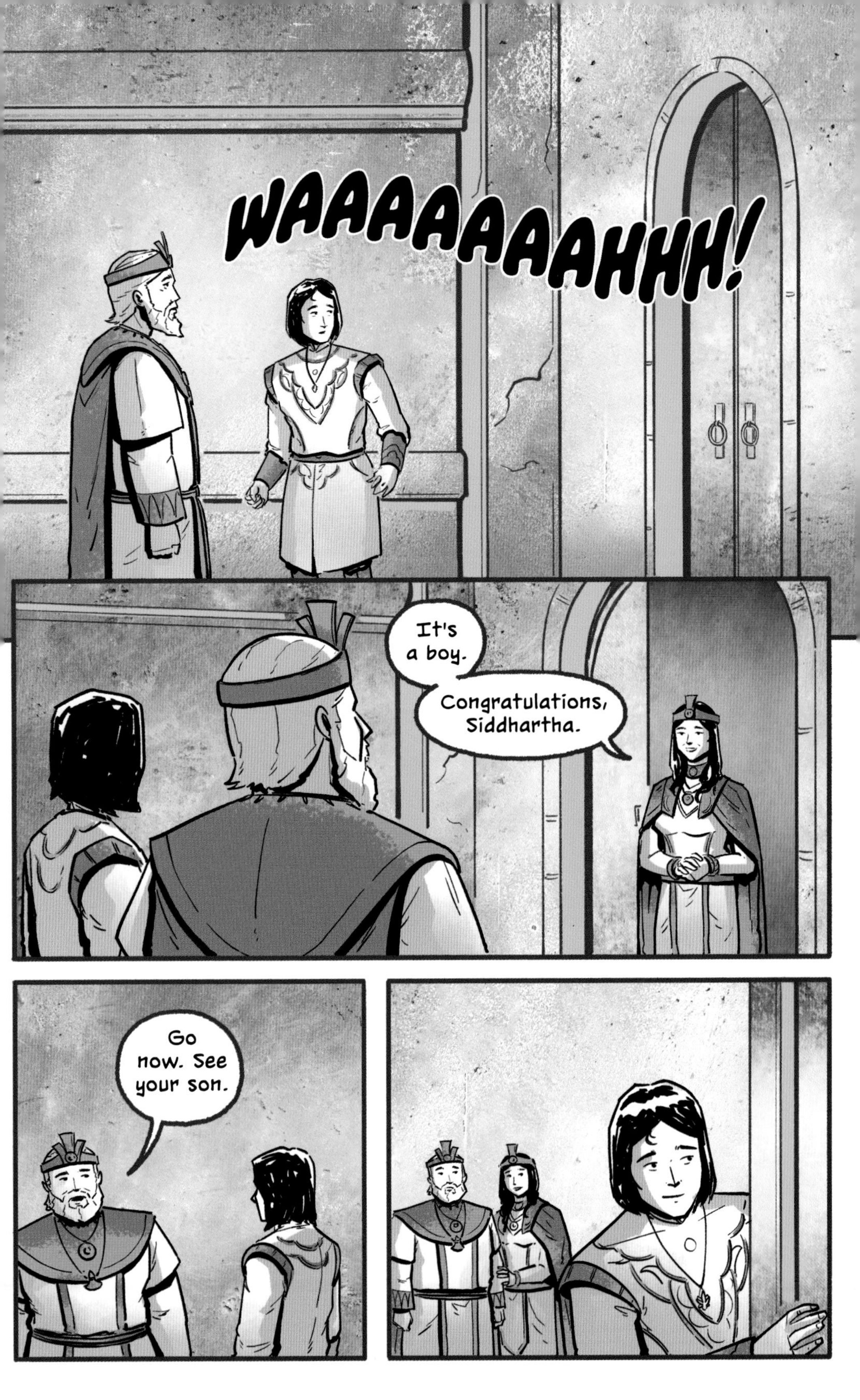

WAAAAAAAAHHH!
It's a boy.
Congratulations, Siddhartha.
Go now. See your son.

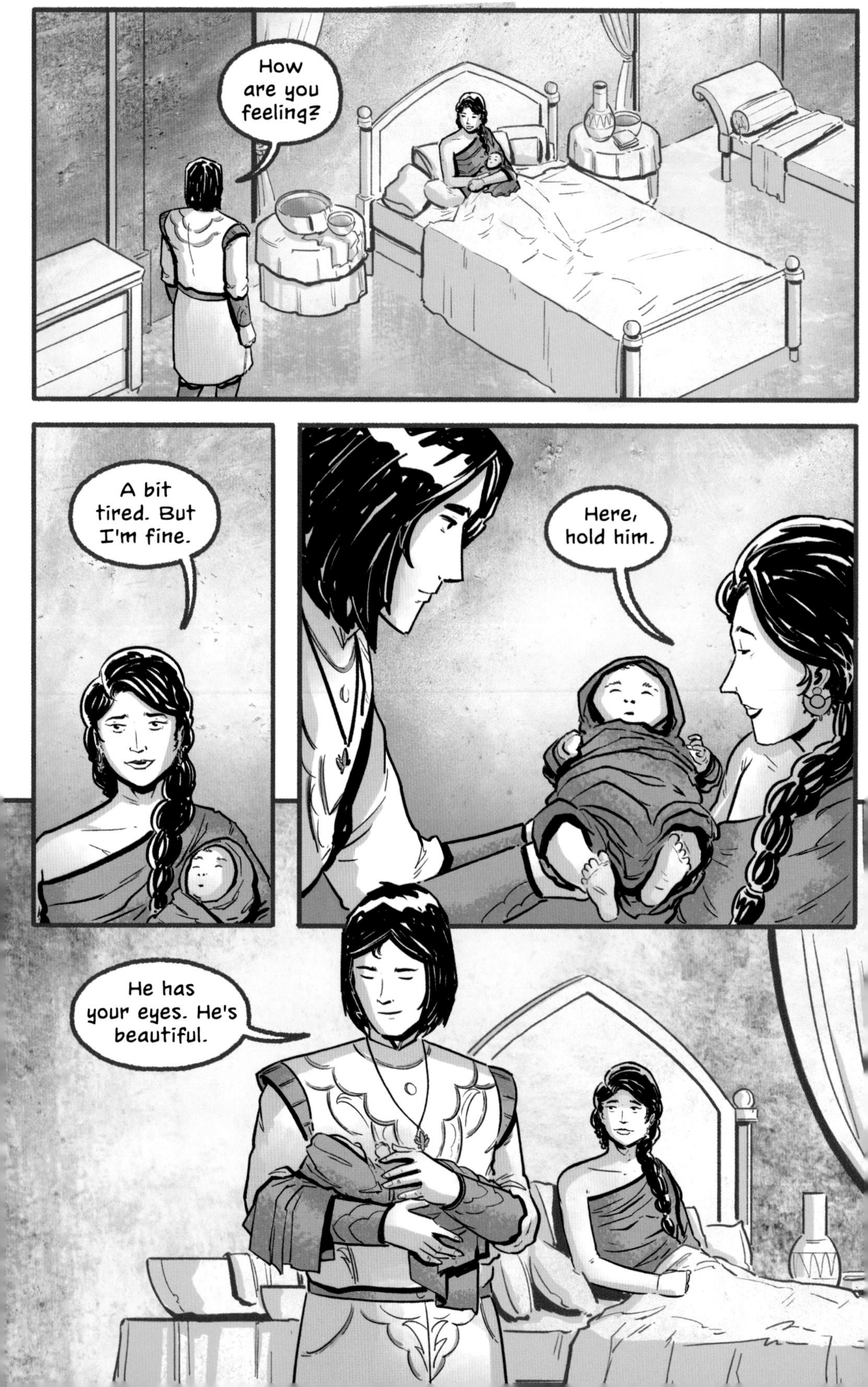
How are you feeling?
A bit tired. But I'm fine.
Here, hold him.
He has your eyes. He's beautiful.

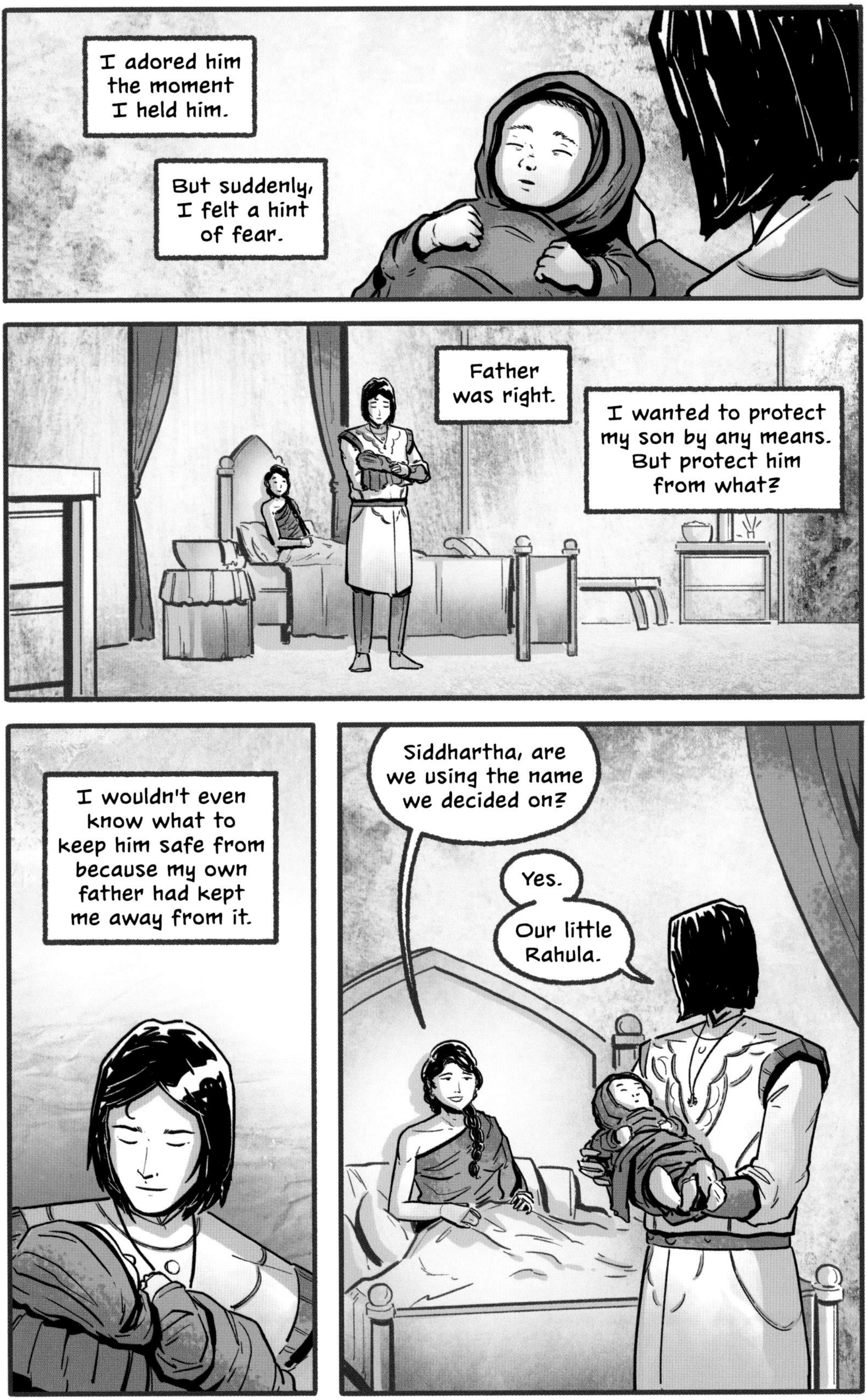
I adored him the moment I held him.
But suddenly, I felt a hint of fear.
Father was right.
I wanted to protect my son by any means. But protect him from what?
I wouldn't even know what to keep him safe from because my own father had kept me away from it.
Siddhartha, are we using the name we decided on?
Yes.
Our little Rahula.

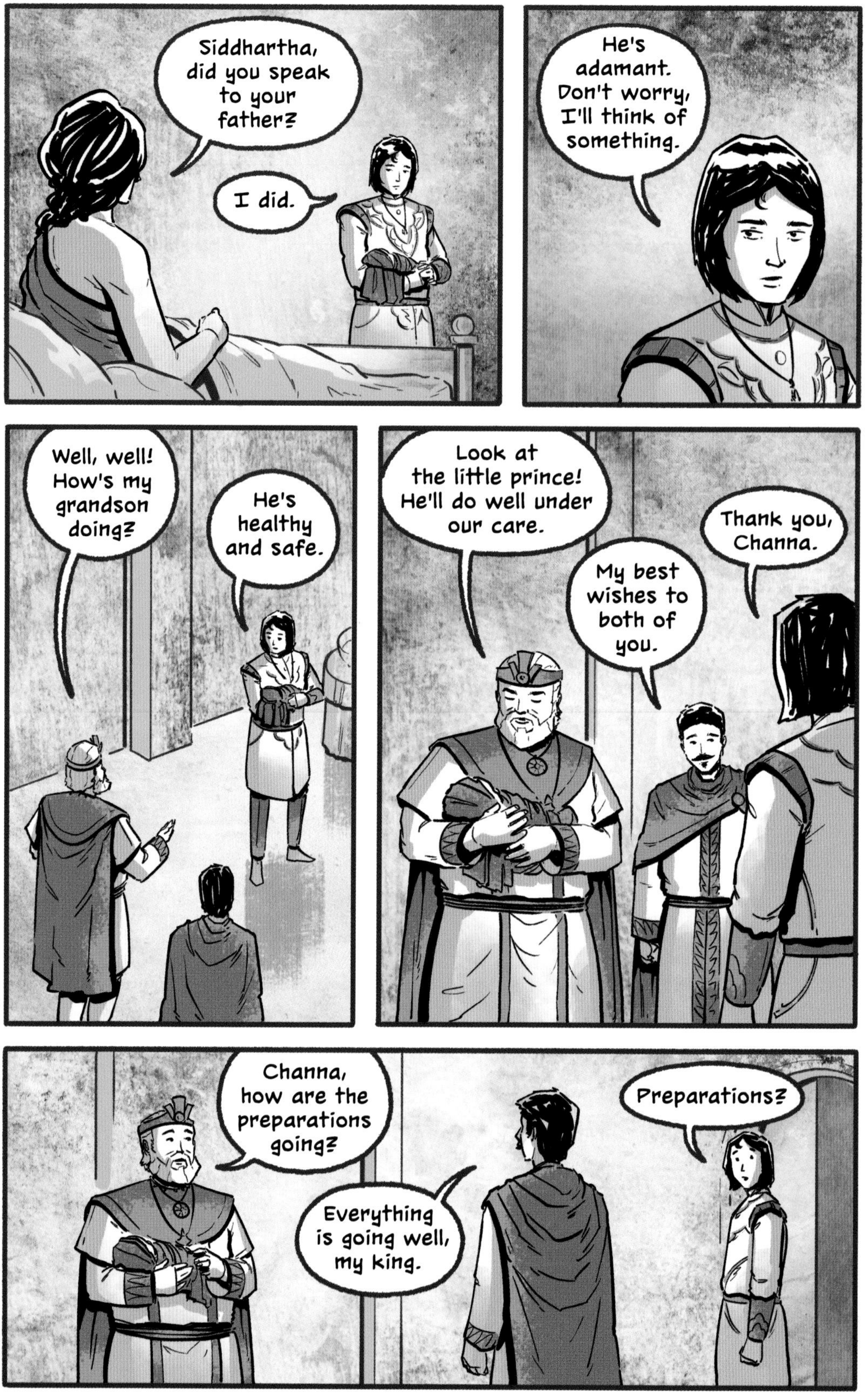
Siddhartha, did you speak to your father?
I did.
He's adamant. Don't worry, I'll think of something.
Well, well! How's my grandson doing?
He's healthy and safe.
Look at the little prince! He'll do well under our care.
Thank you, Channa.
My best wishes to both of you.
Channa, how are the preparations going?
Everything is going well, my king.
Preparations?

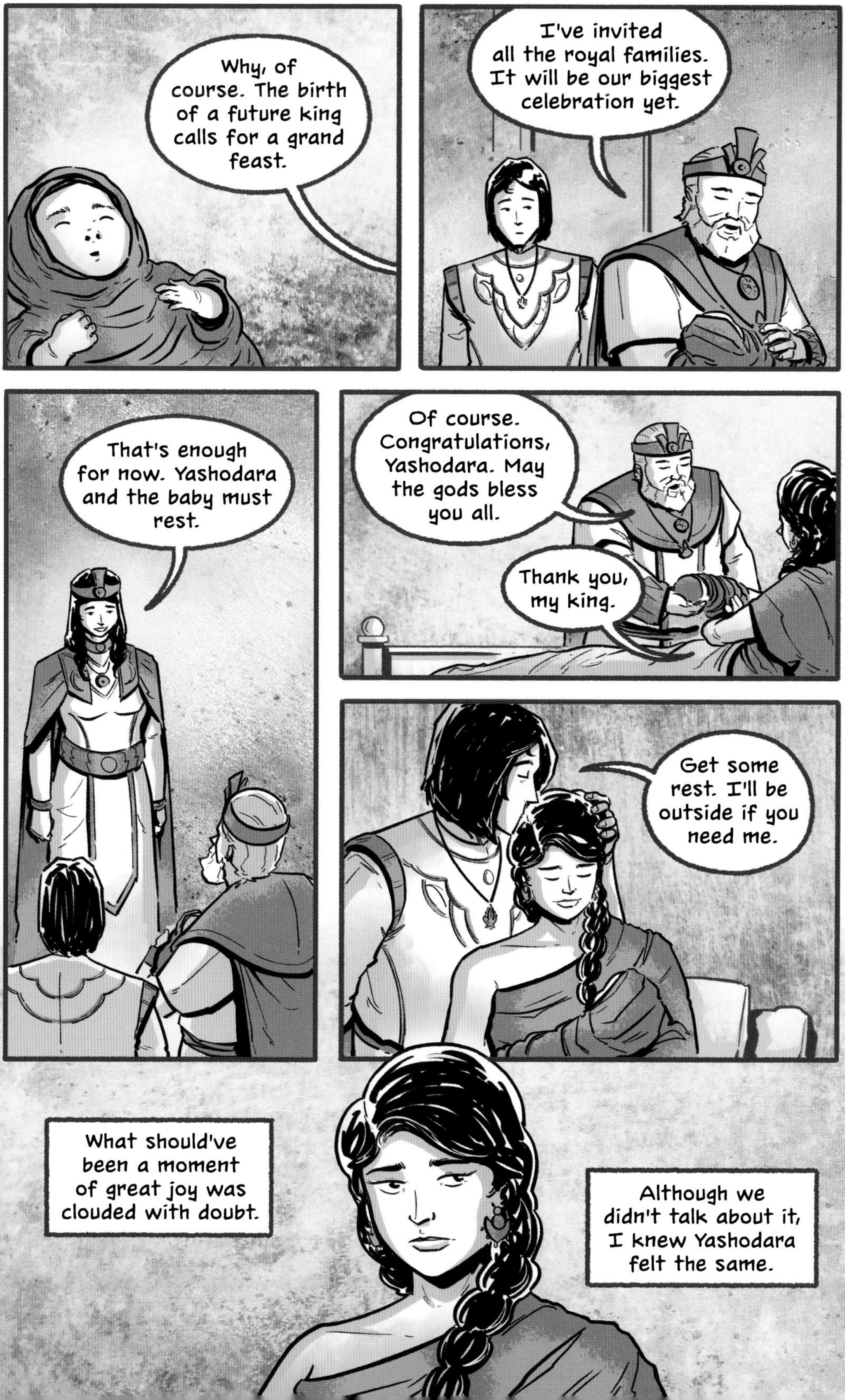
Why, of course. The birth of a future king calls for a grand feast.
I've invited all the royal families. It will be our biggest celebration yet.
That's enough for now. Yashodara and the baby must rest.
Of course. Congratulations, Yashodara. May the gods bless you all.
Thank you, my king.
Get some rest. I'll be outside if you need me.
What should've been a moment of great joy was clouded with doubt.
Although we didn't talk about it, I knew Yashodara felt the same.

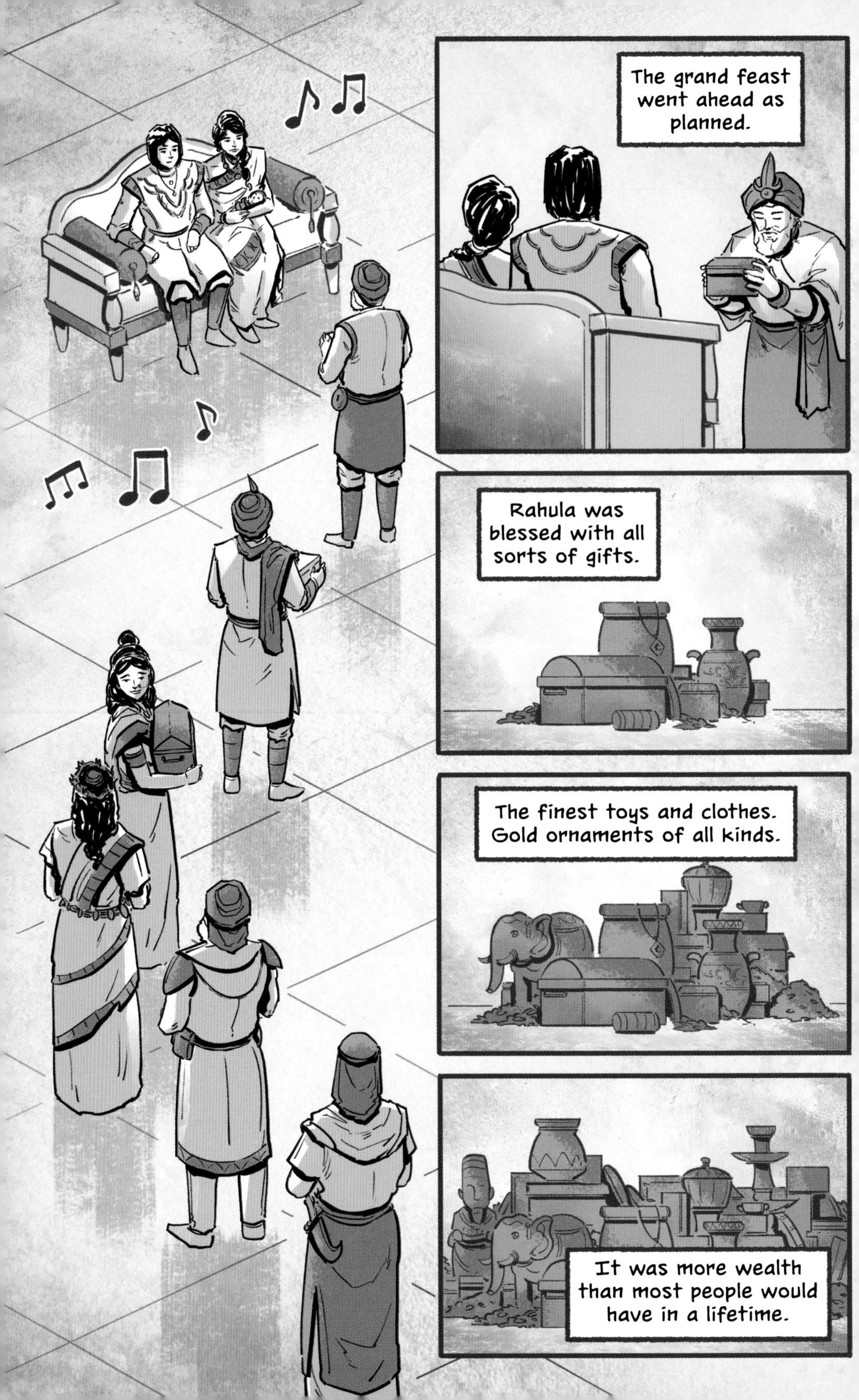
The grand feast went ahead as planned.
Rahula was blessed with all sorts of gifts.
The finest toys and clothes. Gold ornaments of all kinds.
It was more wealth than most people would have in a lifetime.

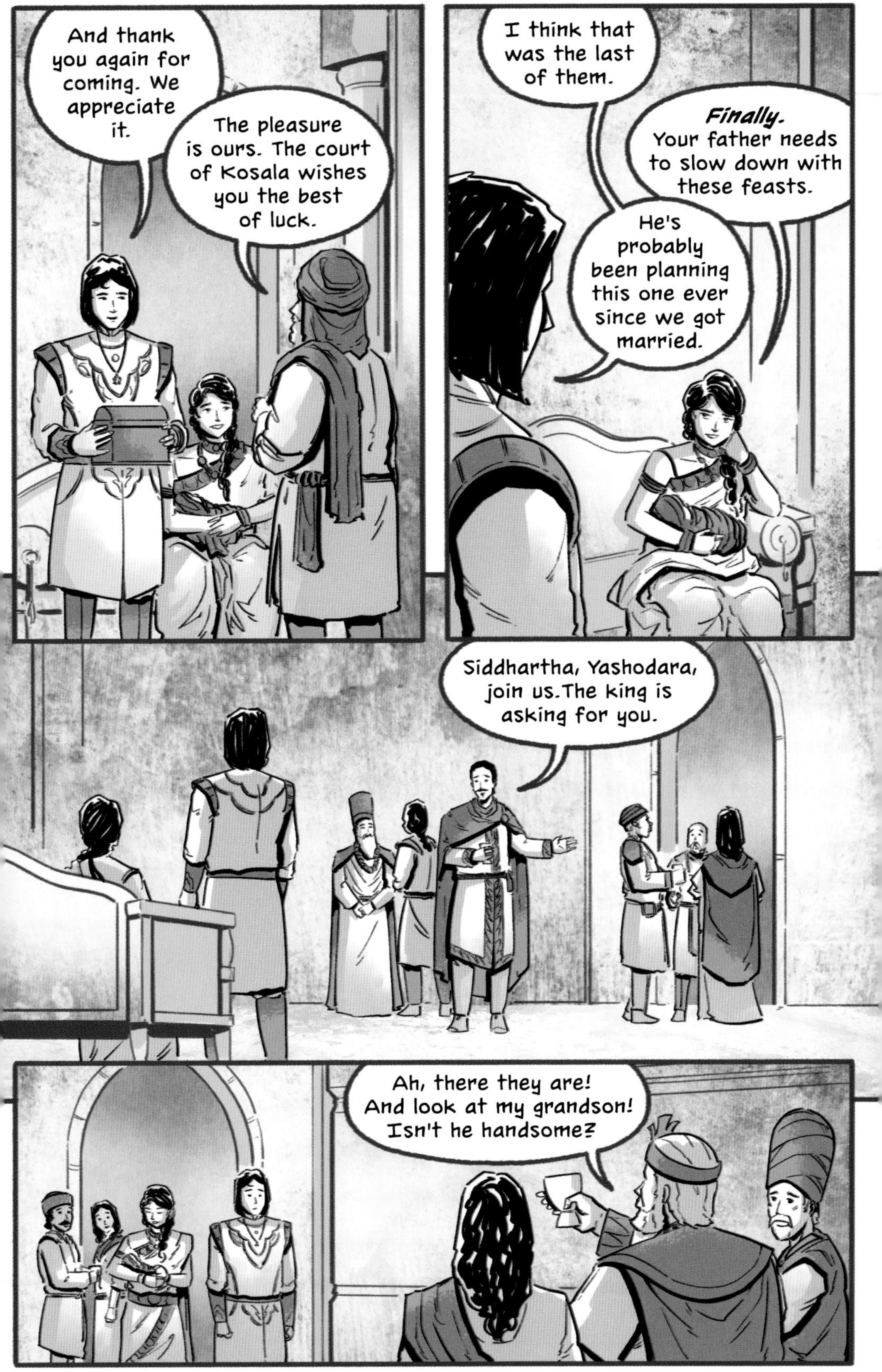
And thank you again for coming. We appreciate it.
The pleasure is ours. The court of Kosala wishes you the best of luck.
I think that was the last of them.
Finally. Your father needs to slow down with these feasts.
He's probably been planning this one ever since we got married.
Siddhartha, Yashodara, join us. The king is asking for you.
Ah, there they are! And look at my grandson! Isn't he handsome?

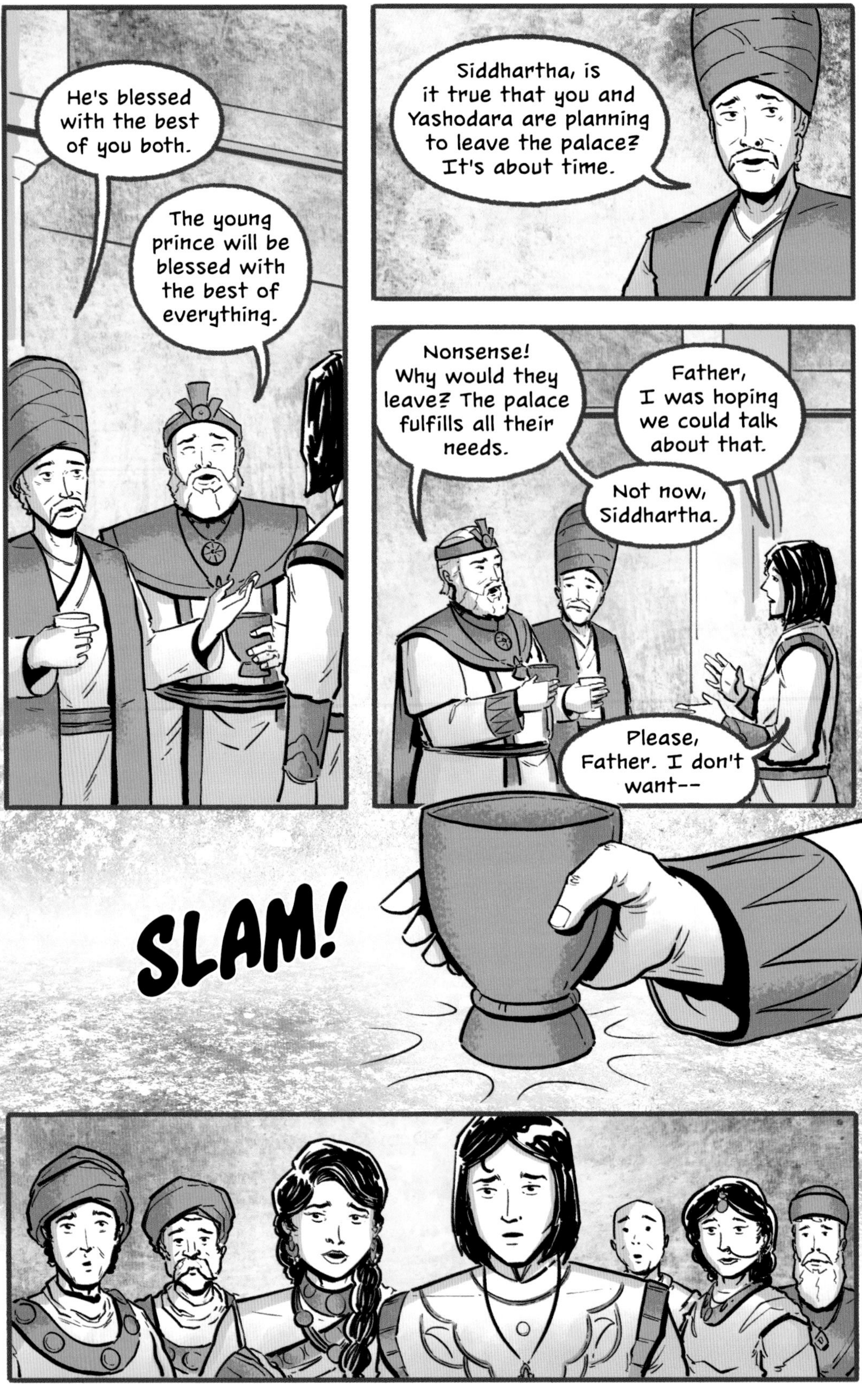
He's blessed with the best of you both.
The young prince will be blessed with the best of everything.
Siddhartha, is it true that you and Yashodara are planning to leave the palace? It's about time.
Nonsense! Why would they leave? The palace fulfills all their needs.
Father, I was hoping we could talk about that.
Not now, Siddhartha.
Please, Father. I don't want--
SLAM!

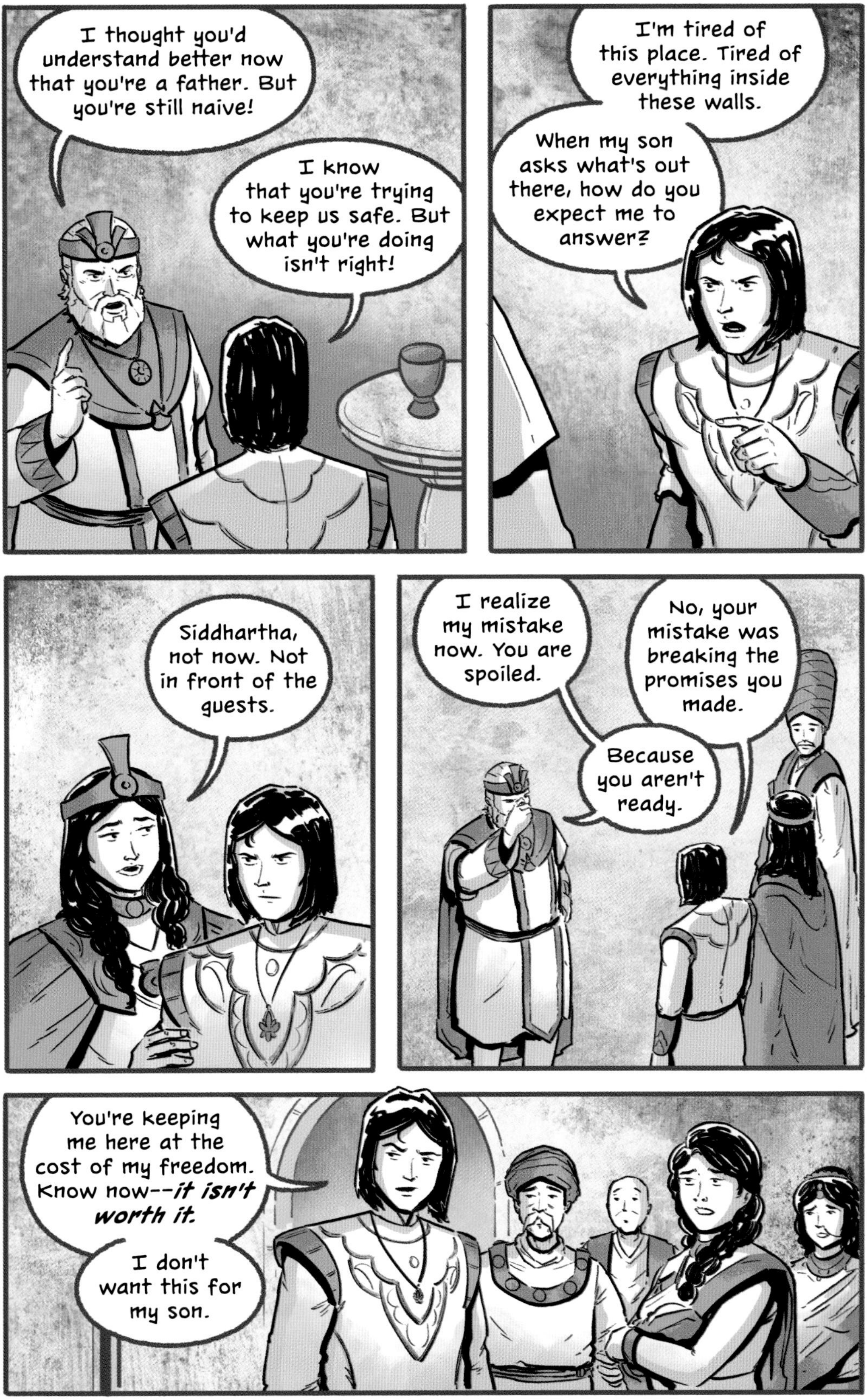
I thought you'd understand better now that you're a father. But you're still naive!
I know that you're trying to keep us safe. But what you're doing isn't right!
I'm tired of this place. Tired of everything inside these walls.
When my son asks what's out there, how do you expect me to answer?
Siddhartha, not now. Not in front of the guests.
I realize my mistake now. You are spoiled.
Because you aren't ready.
No, your mistake was breaking the promises you made.
You're keeping me here at the cost of my freedom. Know now--*it isn't worth it.*
I don't want this for my son.

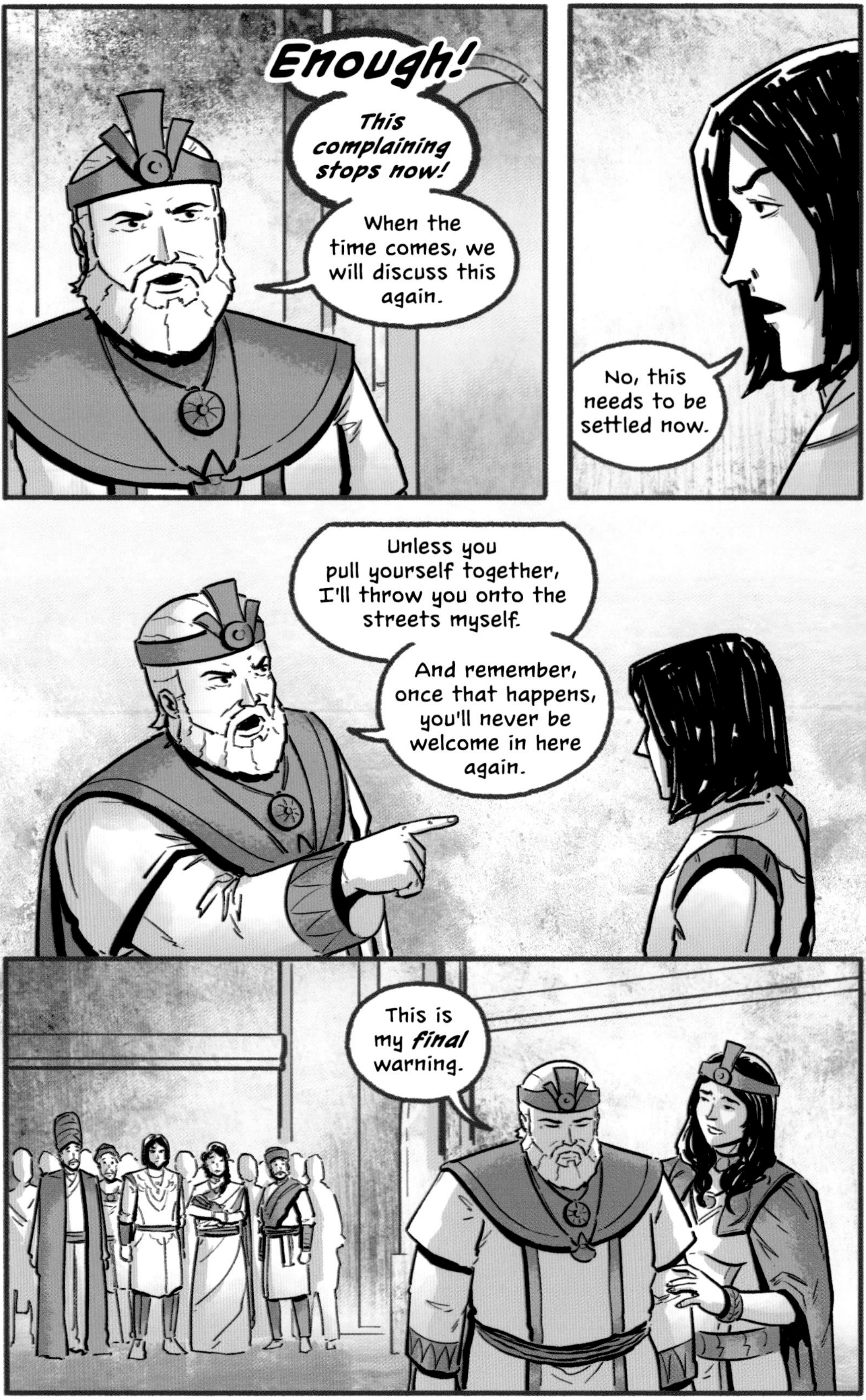
Enough!
This complaining stops now!
When the time comes, we will discuss this again.
No, this needs to be settled now.
Unless you pull yourself together, I'll throw you onto the streets myself.
And remember, once that happens, you'll never be welcome in here again.
This is my *final* warning.

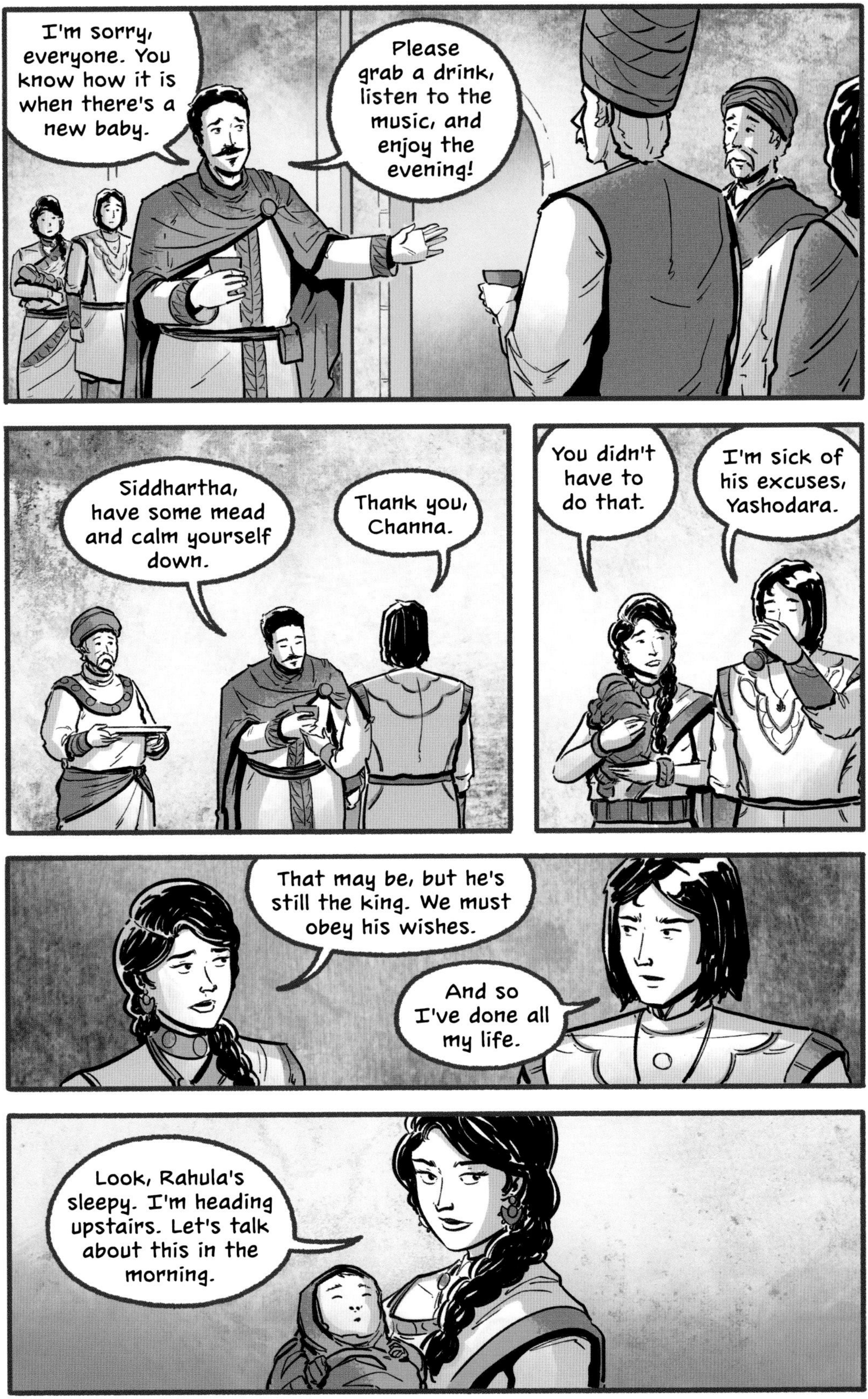
I'm sorry, everyone. You know how it is when there's a new baby.
Please grab a drink, listen to the music, and enjoy the evening!
Siddhartha, have some mead and calm yourself down.
Thank you, Channa.
You didn't have to do that.
I'm sick of his excuses, Yashodara.
That may be, but he's still the king. We must obey his wishes.
And so I've done all my life.
Look, Rahula's sleepy. I'm heading upstairs. Let's talk about this in the morning.

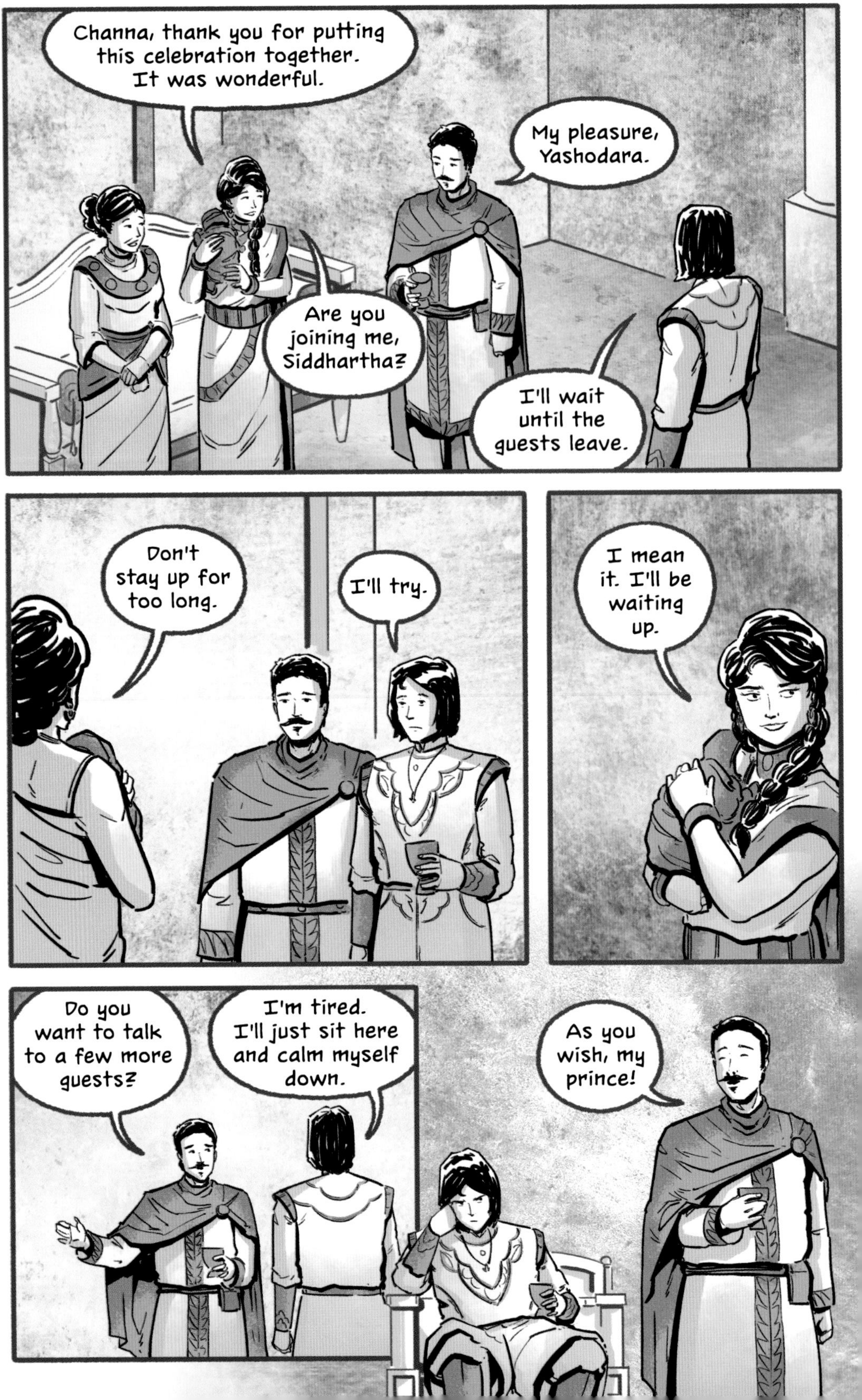
Channa, thank you for putting this celebration together. It was wonderful.
My pleasure, Yashodara.
Are you joining me, Siddhartha?
I'll wait until the guests leave.
Don't stay up for too long.
I'll try.
I mean it. I'll be waiting up.
Do you want to talk to a few more guests?
I'm tired. I'll just sit here and calm myself down.
As you wish, my prince!

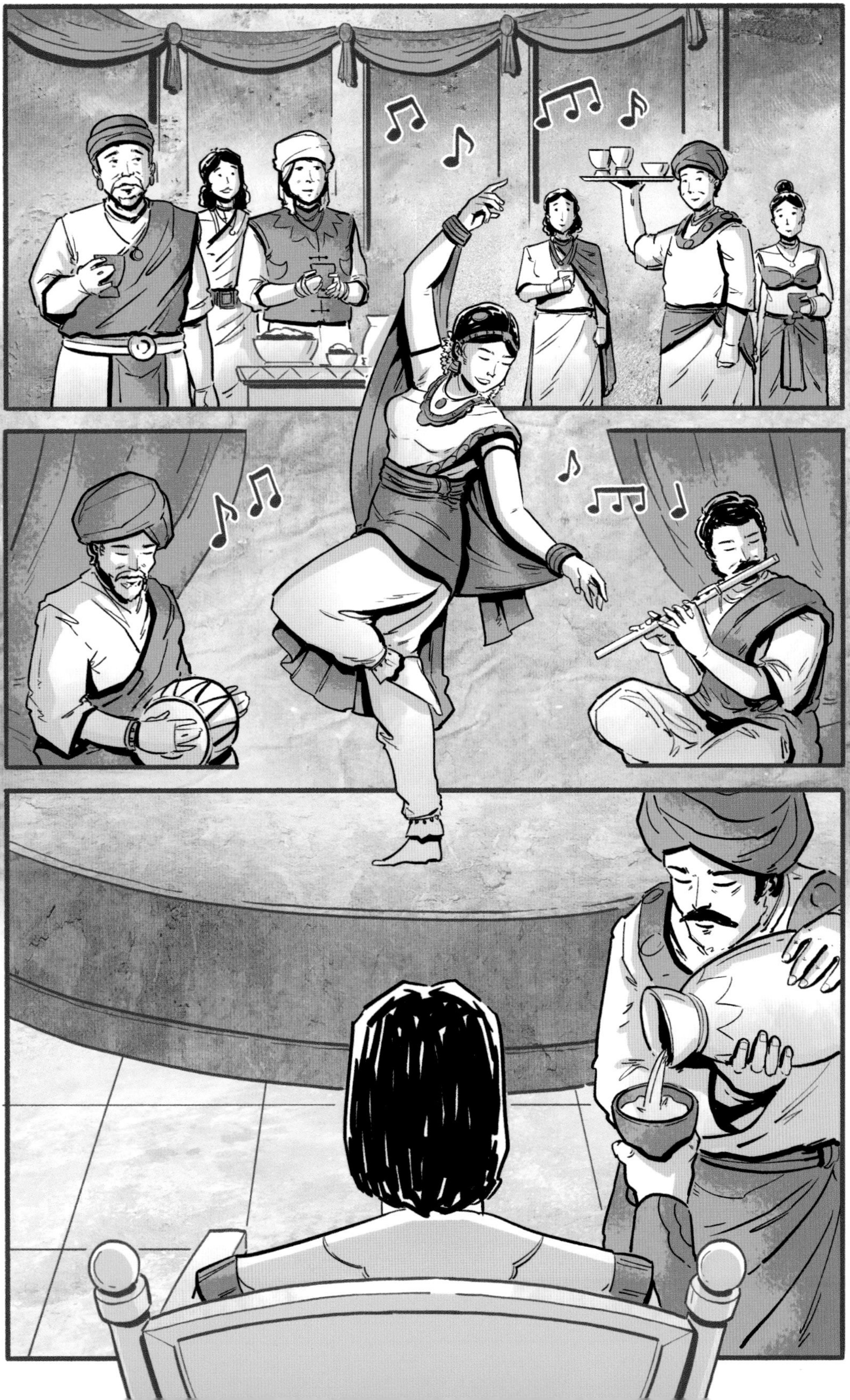

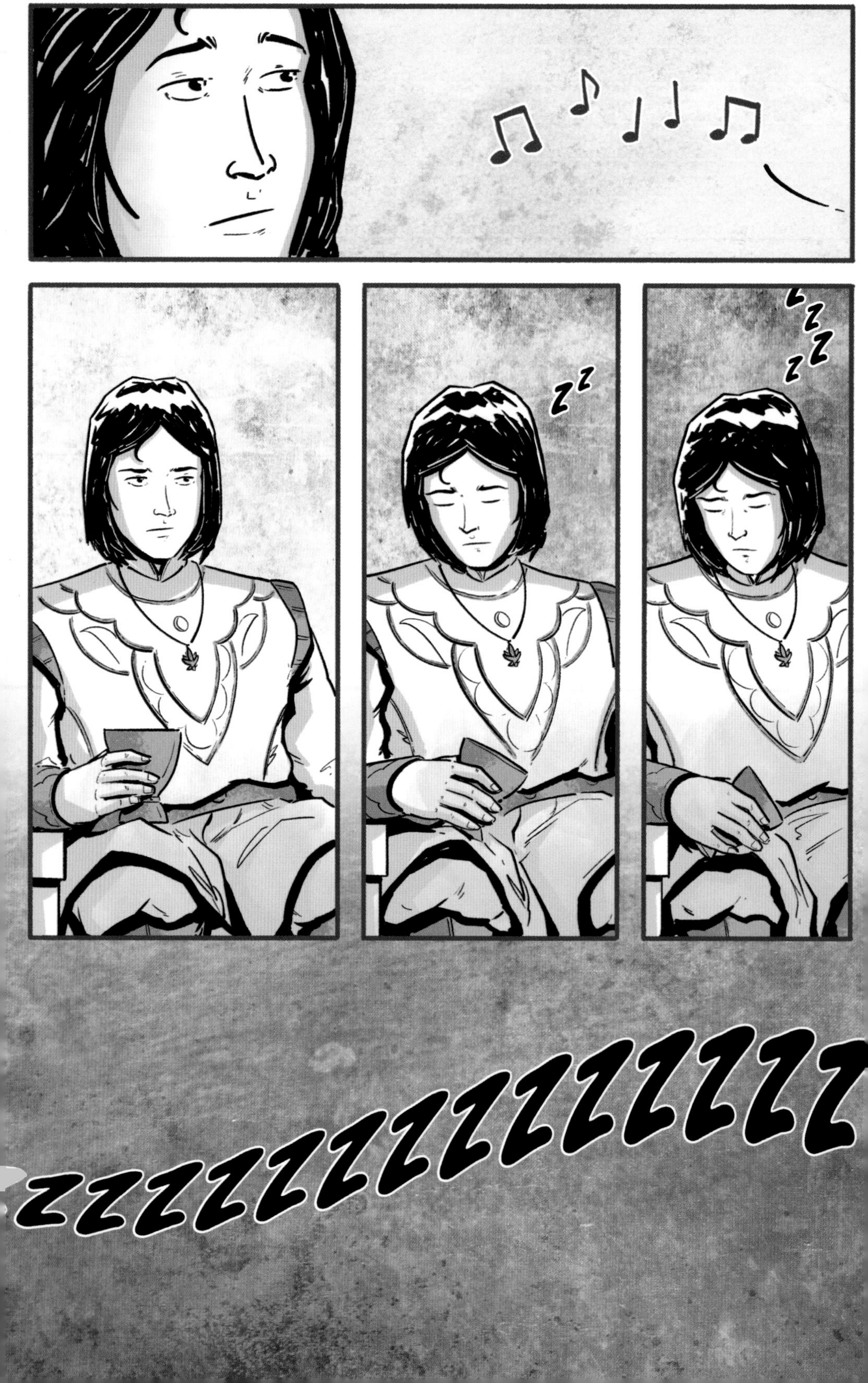

zz
zzzz
ZZZZZZZZZZZZZZ

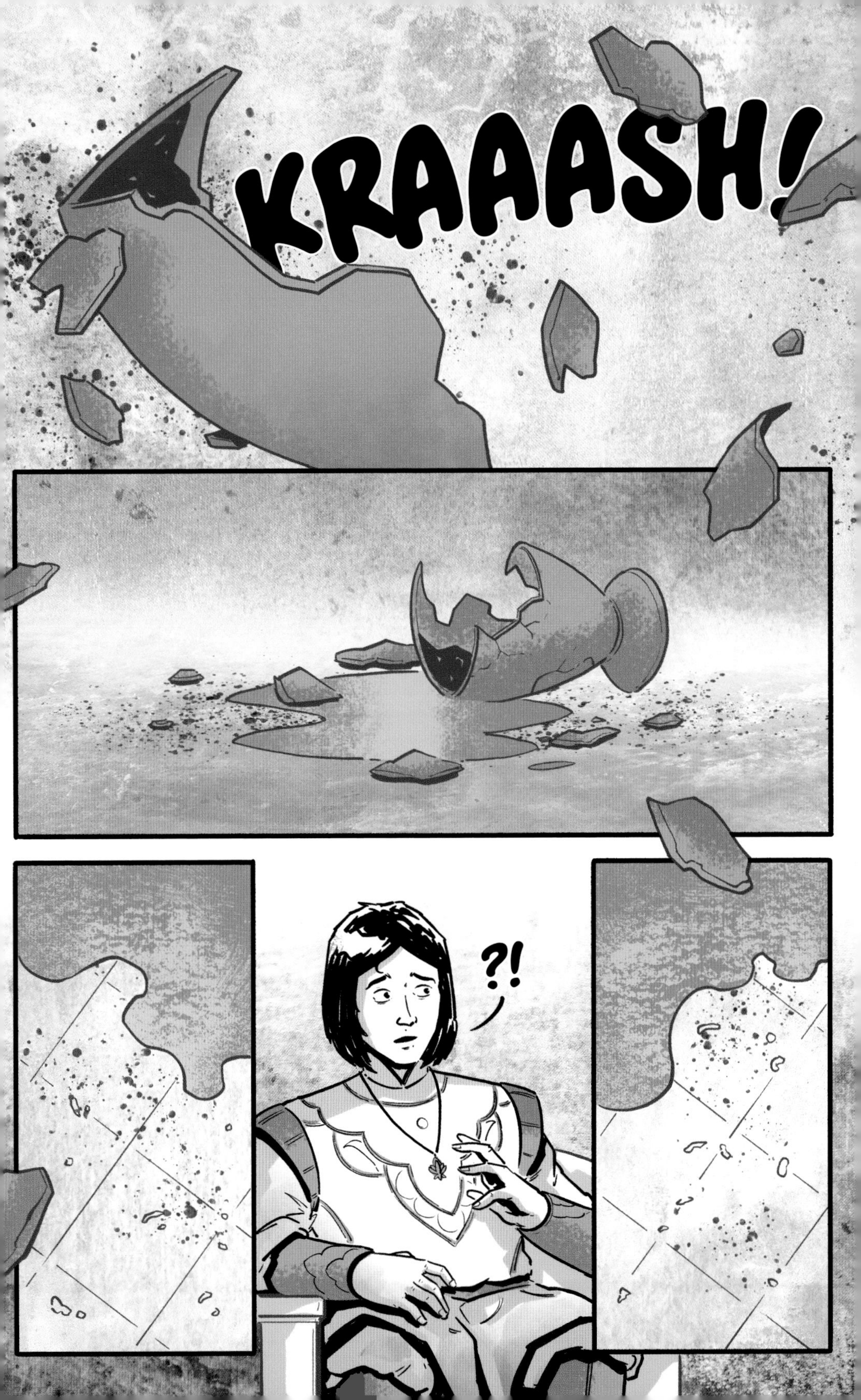
KRAAASH!
?!

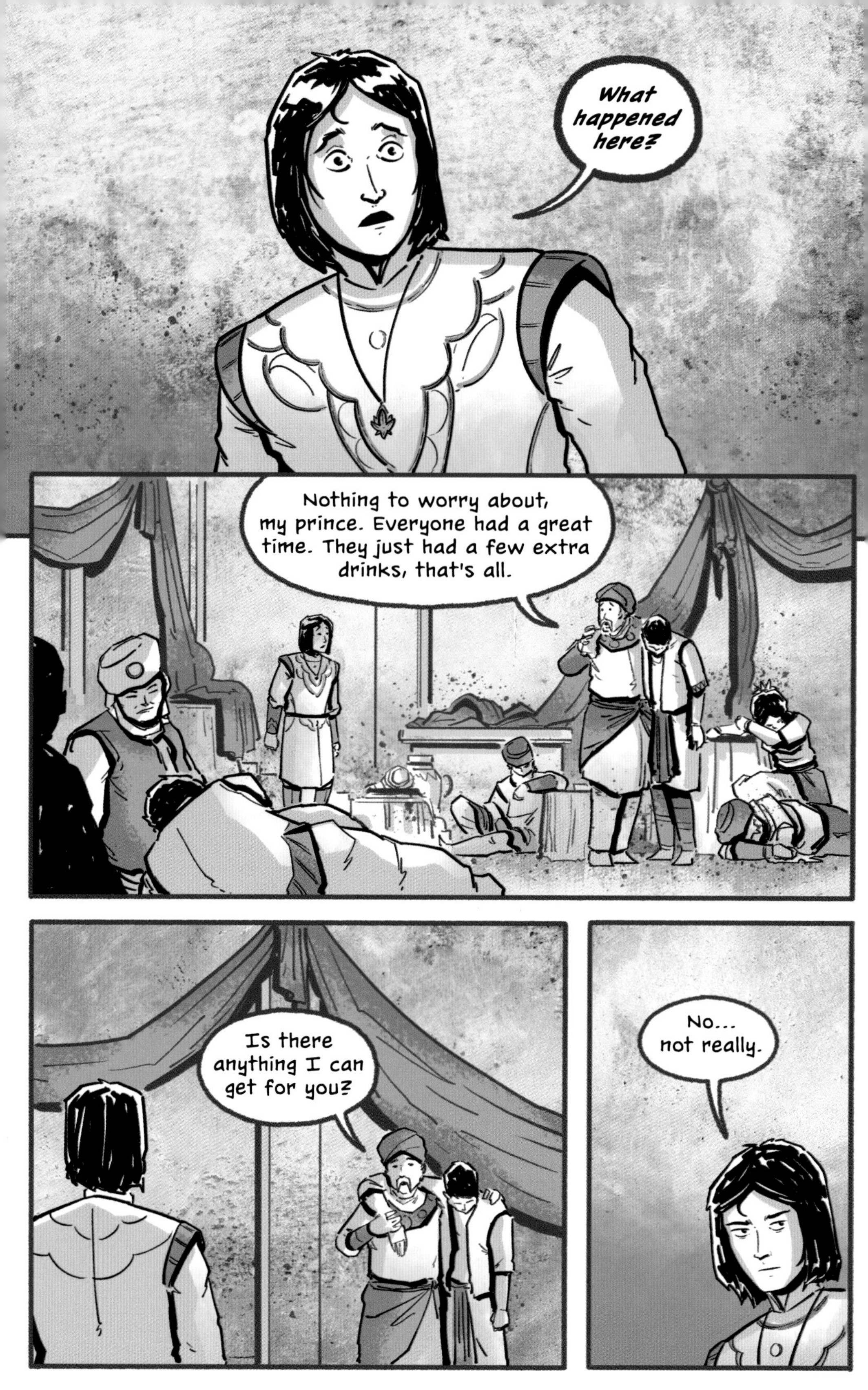
What happened here?
Nothing to worry about, my prince. Everyone had a great time. They just had a few extra drinks, that's all.
Is there anything I can get for you?
No... not really.

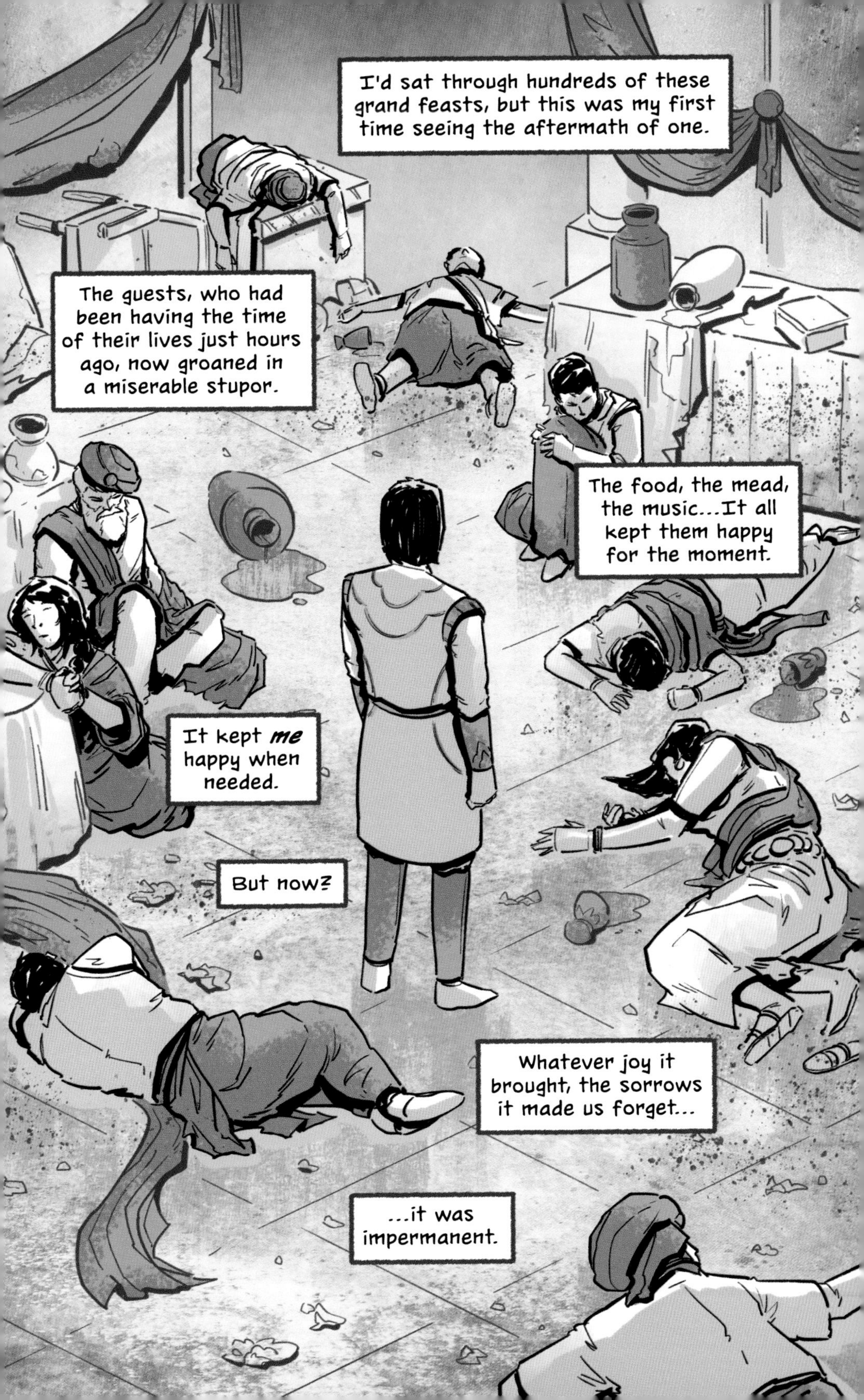
I'd sat through hundreds of these grand feasts, but this was my first time seeing the aftermath of one.
The guests, who had been having the time of their lives just hours ago, now groaned in a miserable stupor.
The food, the mead, the music...It all kept them happy for the moment.
It kept *me* happy when needed.
But now?
Whatever joy it brought, the sorrows it made us forget...
...it was impermanent.

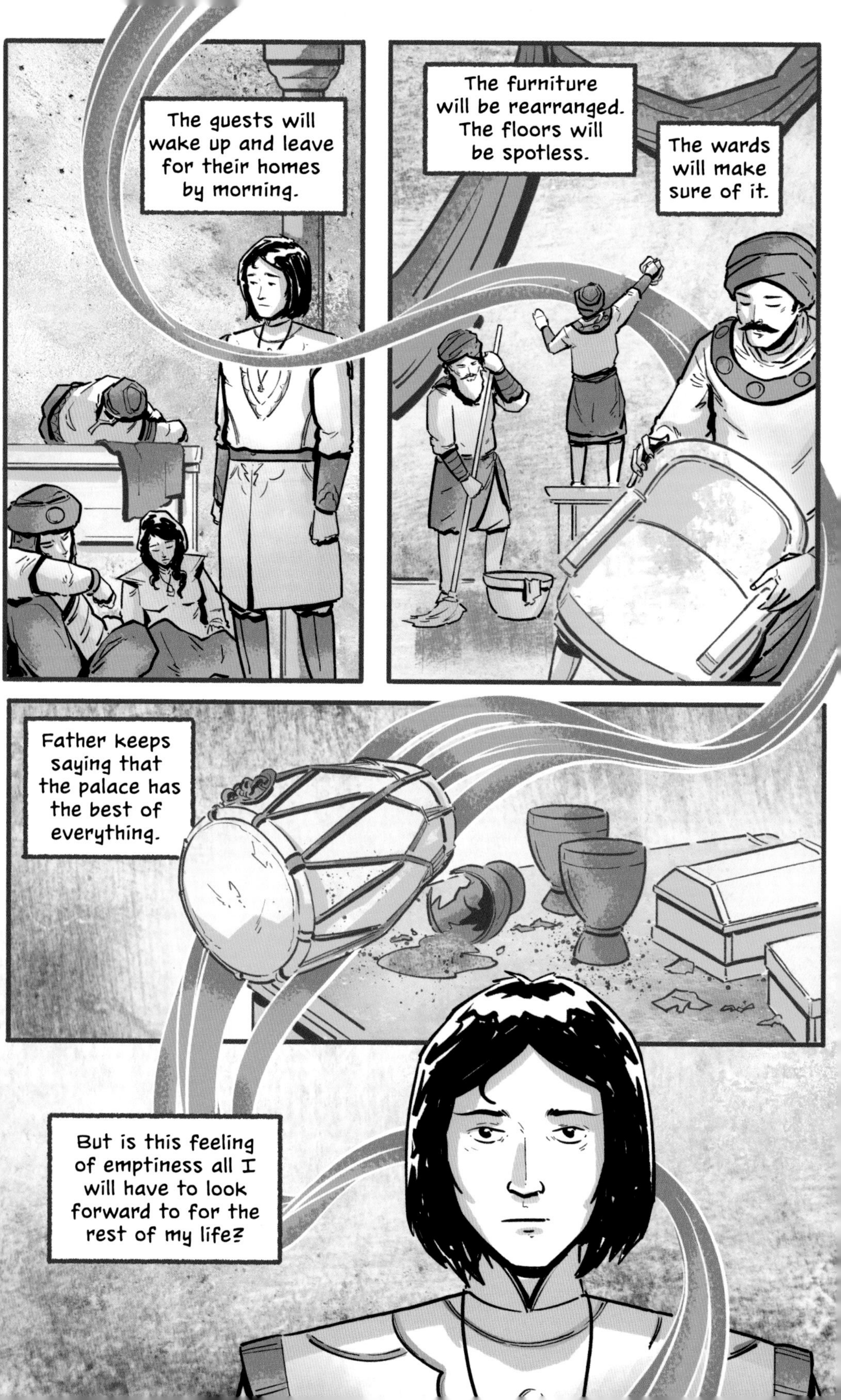
The guests will wake up and leave for their homes by morning.
The furniture will be rearranged. The floors will be spotless.
The wards will make sure of it.
Father keeps saying that the palace has the best of everything.
But is this feeling of emptiness all I will have to look forward to for the rest of my life?

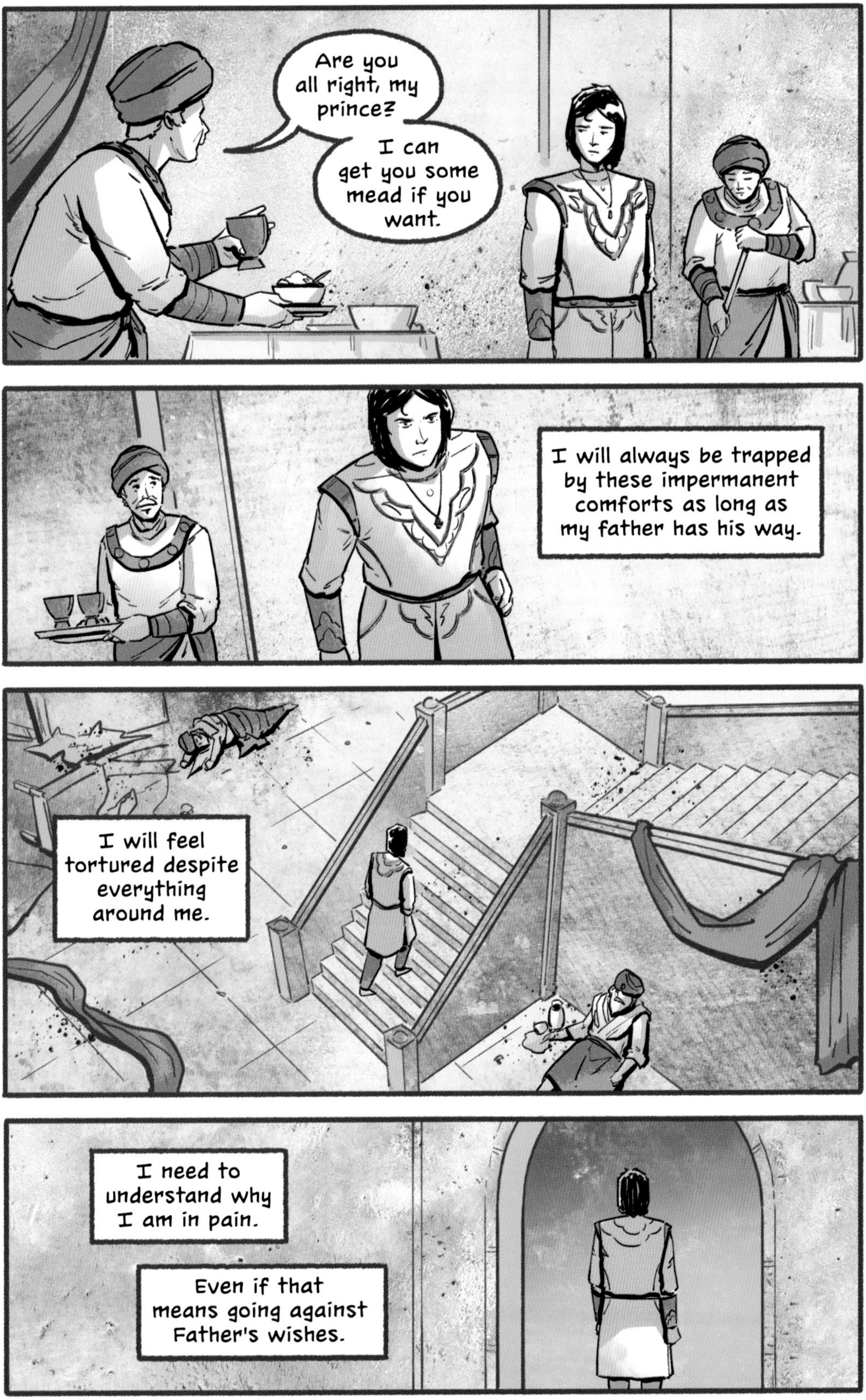
Are you all right, my prince?
I can get you some mead if you want.
I will always be trapped by these impermanent comforts as long as my father has his way.
I will feel tortured despite everything around me.
I need to understand why I am in pain.
Even if that means going against Father's wishes.

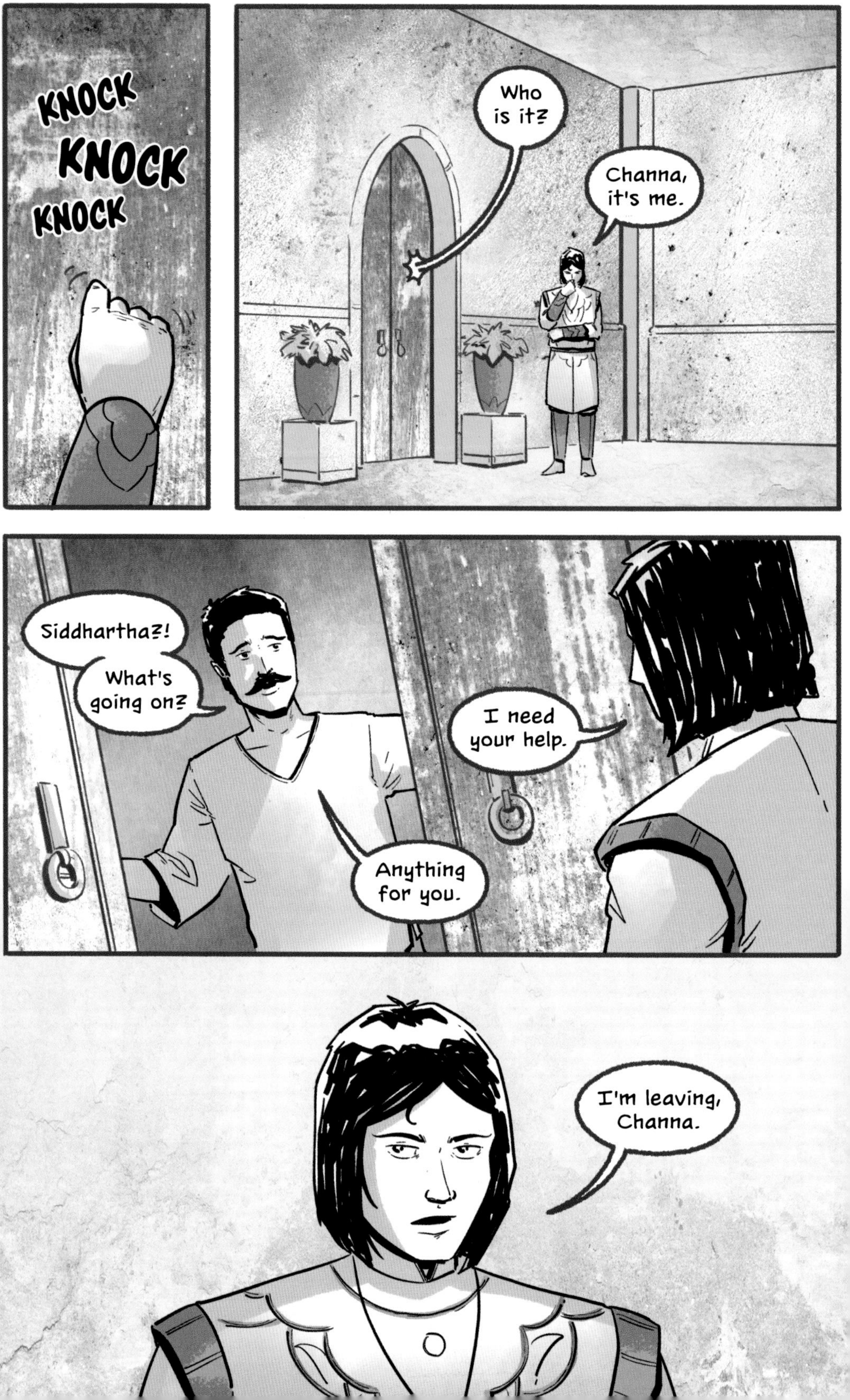
KNOCK
KNOCK
KNOCK
Who is it?
Channa, it's me.
Siddhartha?!
What's going on?
I need your help.
Anything for you.
I'm leaving, Channa.

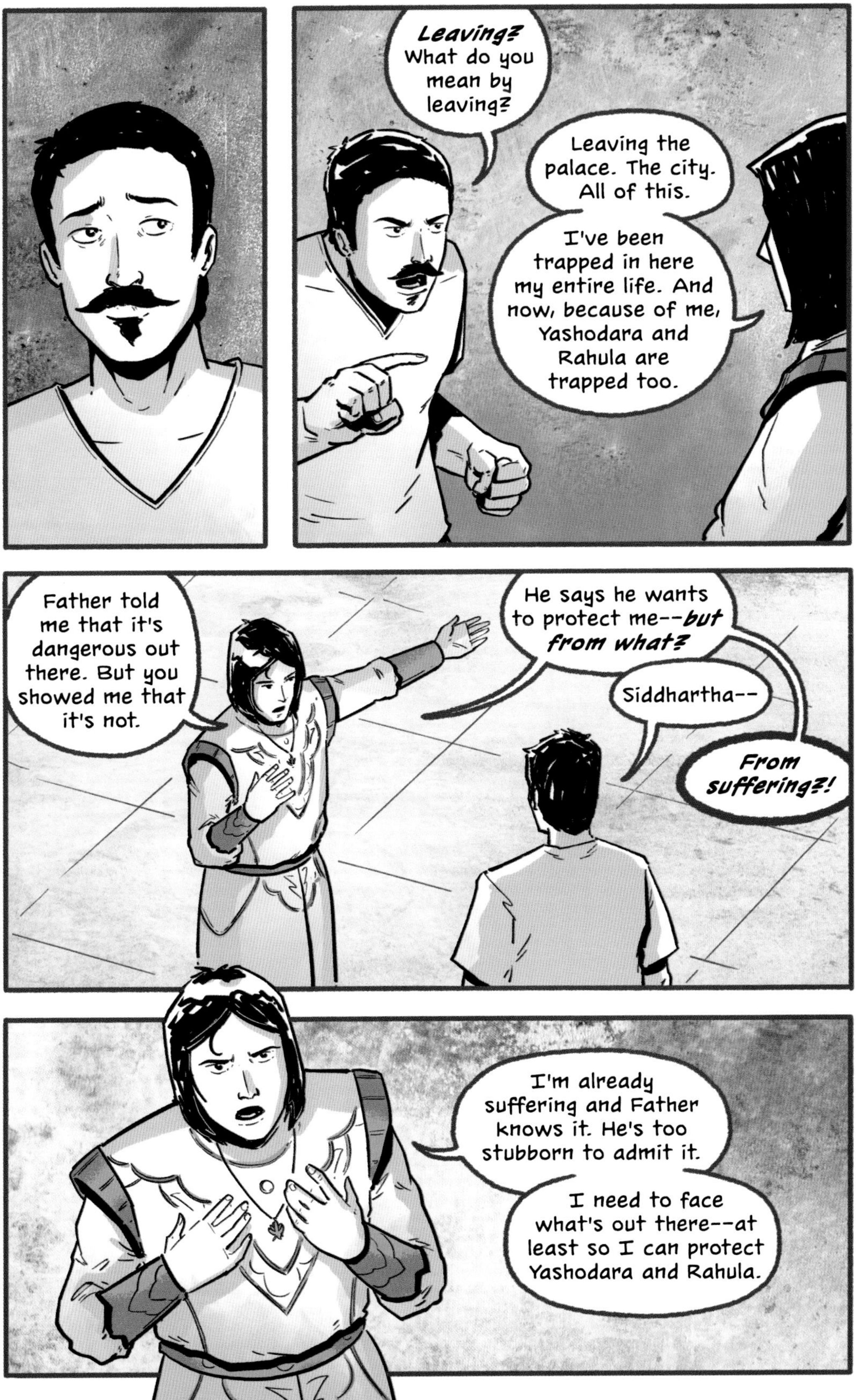
Leaving? What do you mean by leaving?
Leaving the palace. The city. All of this.
I've been trapped in here my entire life. And now, because of me, Yashodara and Rahula are trapped too.
Father told me that it's dangerous out there. But you showed me that it's not.
He says he wants to protect me--*but from what?*
Siddhartha--
From suffering?!
I'm already suffering and Father knows it. He's too stubborn to admit it.
I need to face what's out there--at least so I can protect Yashodara and Rahula.

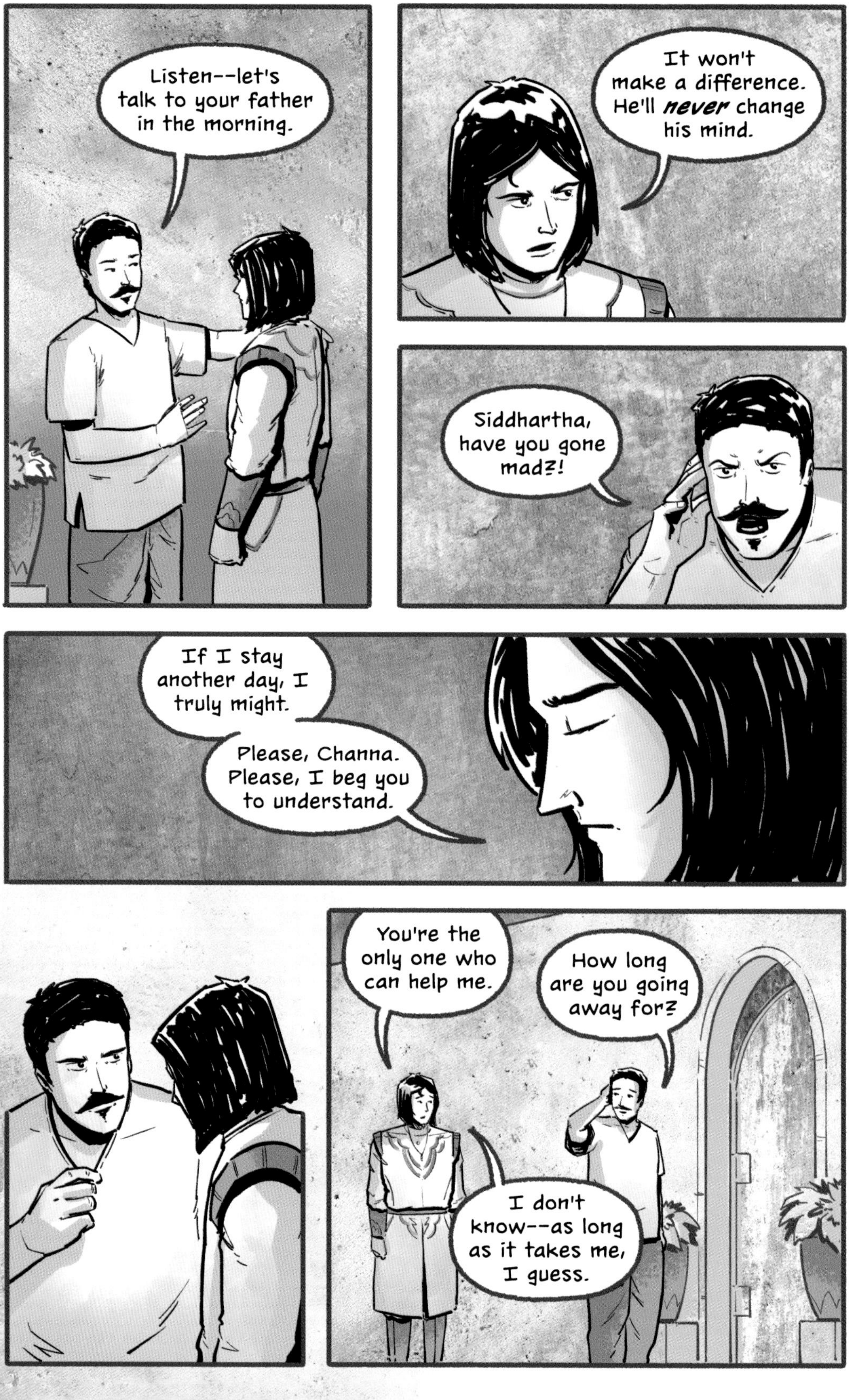
Listen--let's talk to your father in the morning.
It won't make a difference. He'll *never* change his mind.
Siddhartha, have you gone mad?!
If I stay another day, I truly might.
Please, Channa. Please, I beg you to understand.
You're the only one who can help me.
How long are you going away for?
I don't know--as long as it takes me, I guess.

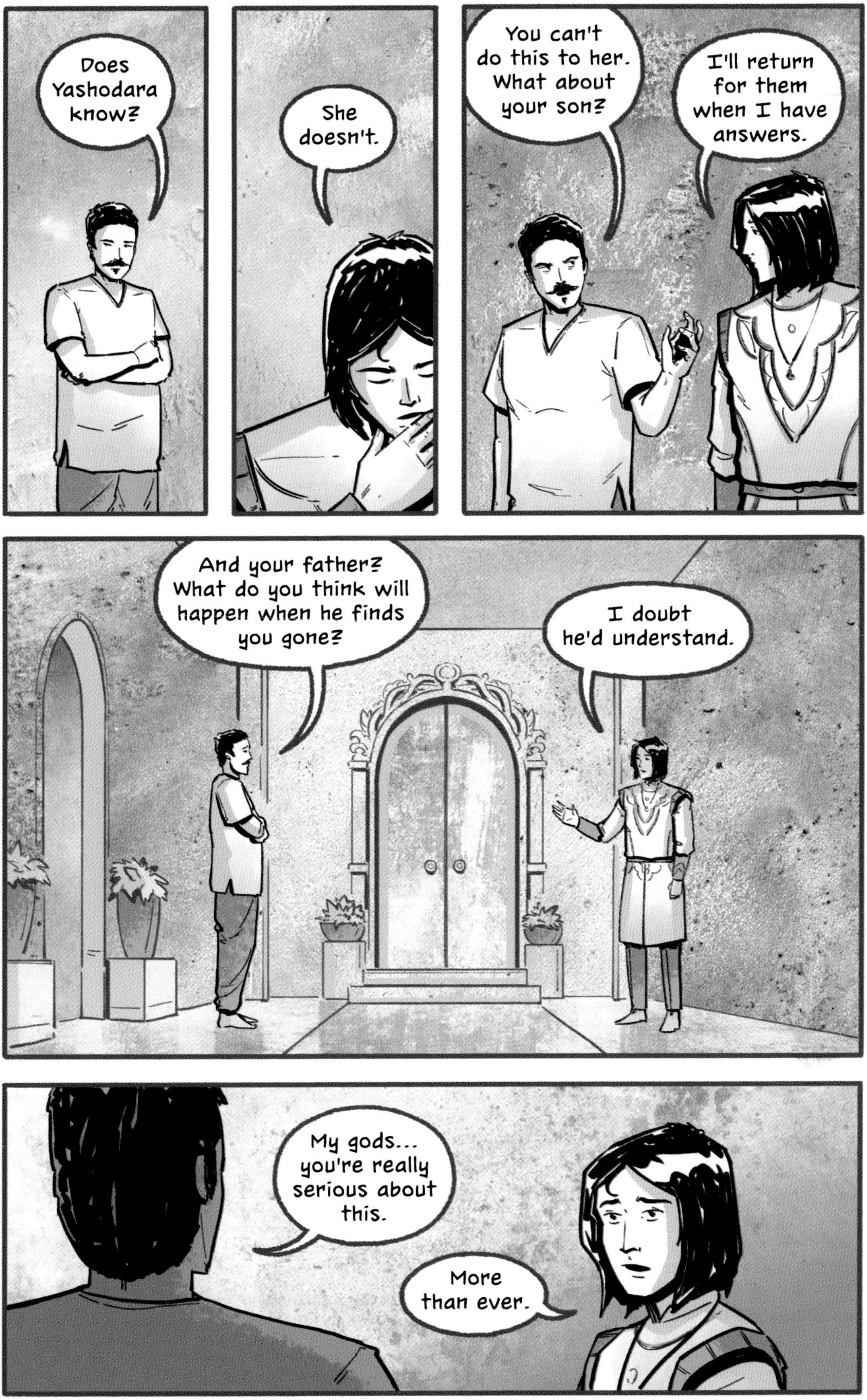
Does Yashodara know?
She doesn't.
You can't do this to her. What about your son?
I'll return for them when I have answers.
And your father? What do you think will happen when he finds you gone?
I doubt he'd understand.
My gods... you're really serious about this.
More than ever.

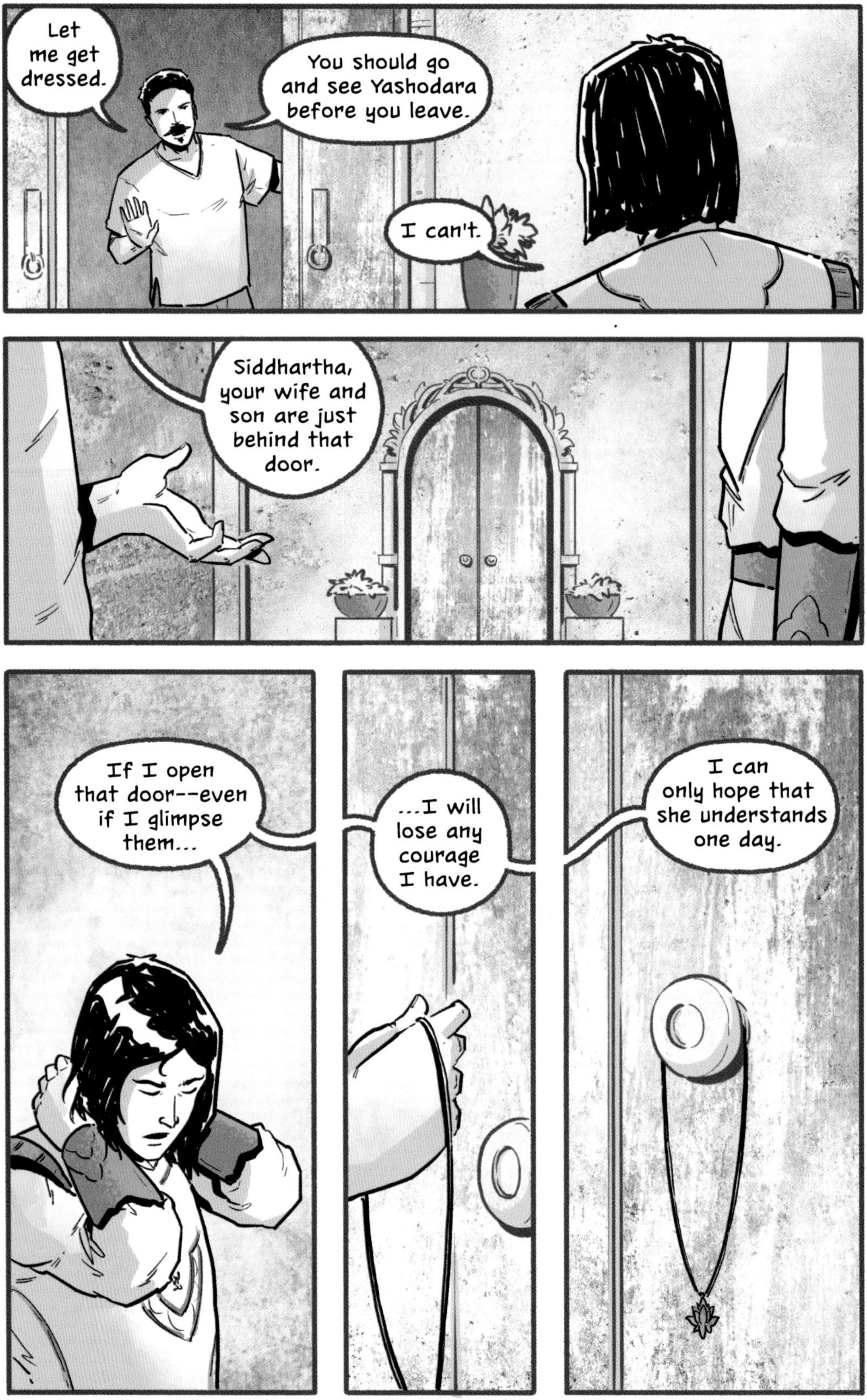
Let me get dressed.
You should go and see Yashodara before you leave.
I can't.
Siddhartha, your wife and son are just behind that door.
If I open that door--even if I glimpse them...
...I will lose any courage I have.
I can only hope that she understands one day.

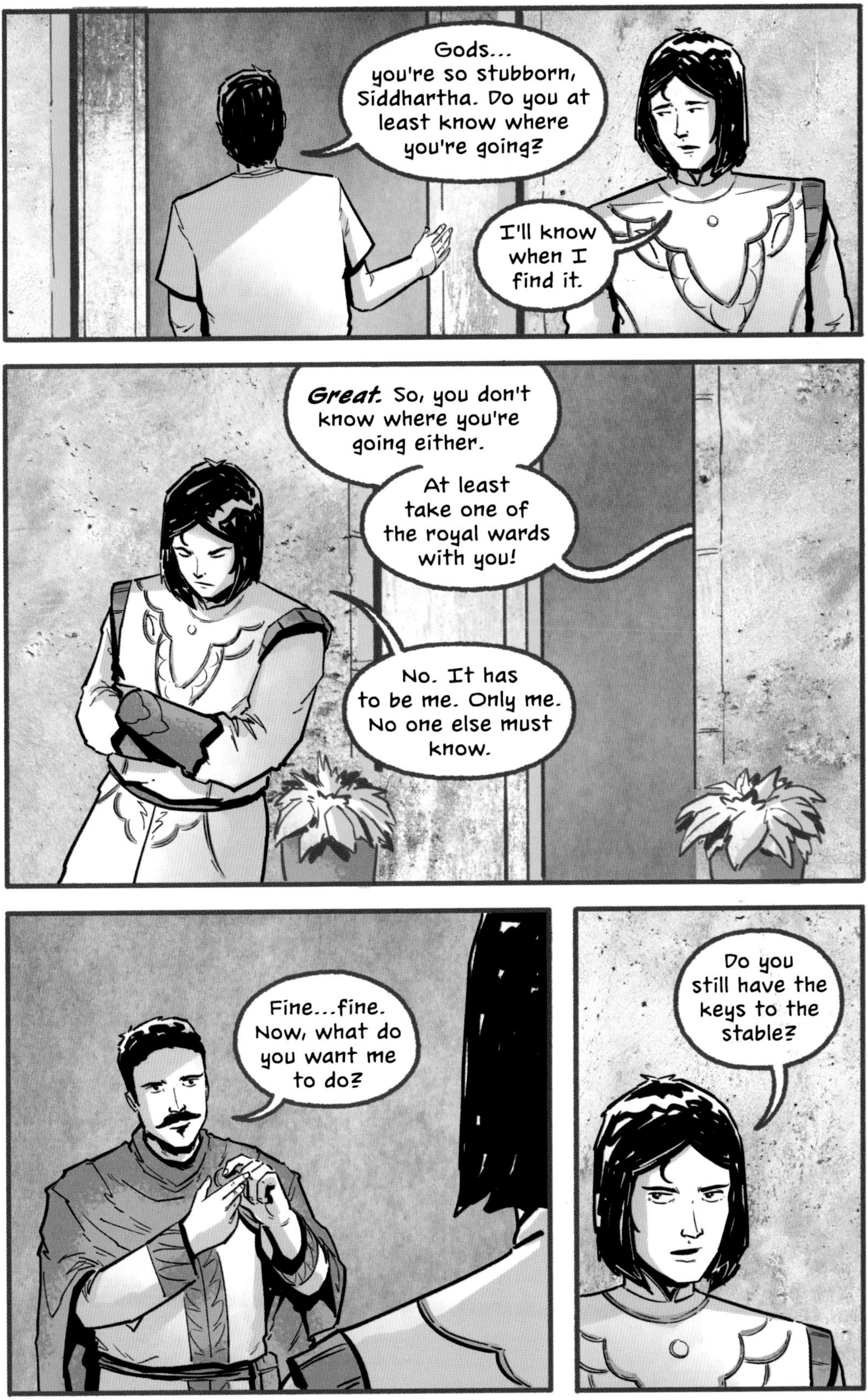
Gods... you're so stubborn, Siddhartha. Do you at least know where you're going?
I'll know when I find it.
Great. So, you don't know where you're going either.
At least take one of the royal wards with you!
No. It has to be me. Only me. No one else must know.
Fine...fine. Now, what do you want me to do?
Do you still have the keys to the stable?

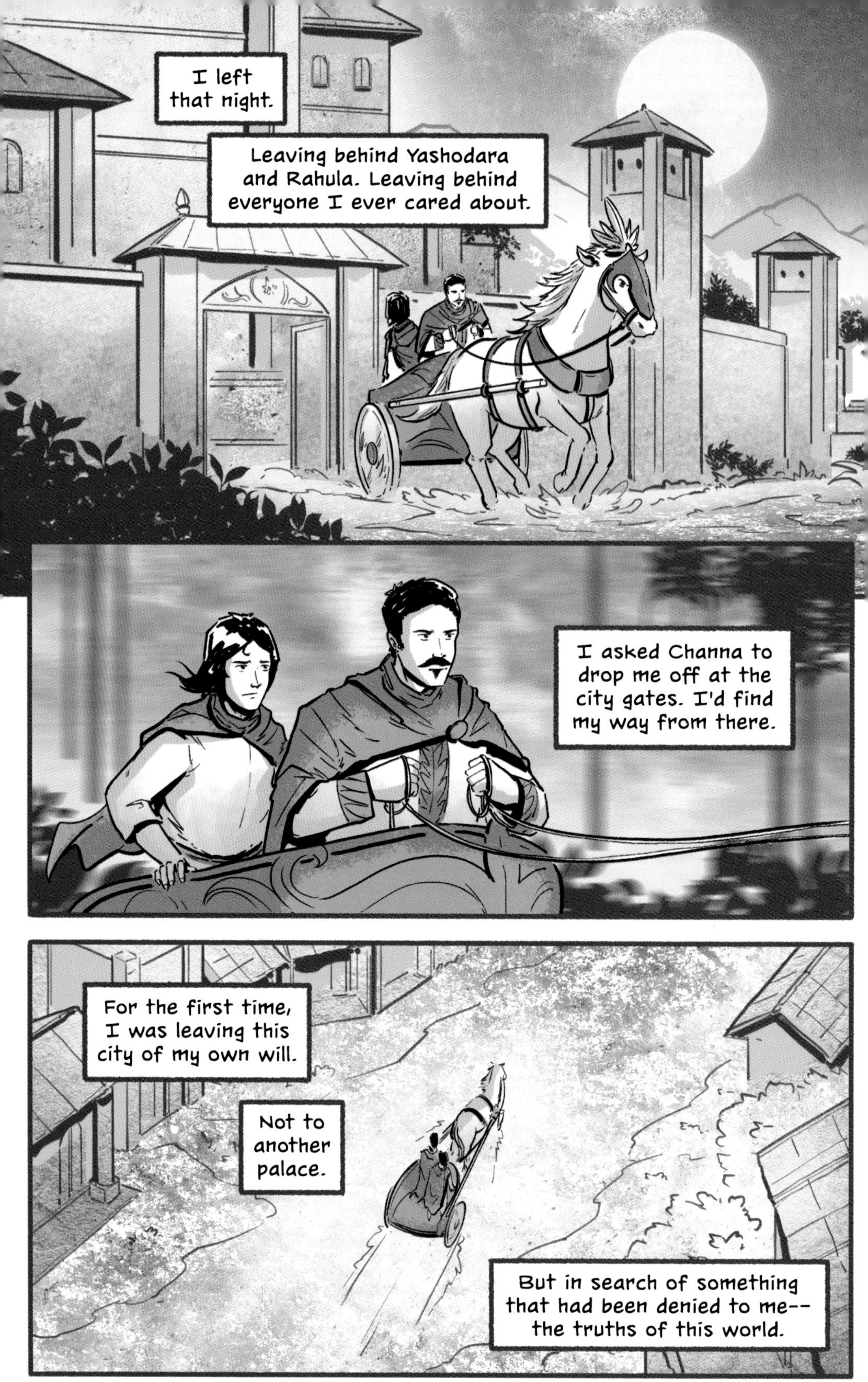
I left that night.
Leaving behind Yashodara and Rahula. Leaving behind everyone I ever cared about.
I asked Channa to drop me off at the city gates. I'd find my way from there.
For the first time, I was leaving this city of my own will.
Not to another palace.
But in search of something that had been denied to me-- the truths of this world.

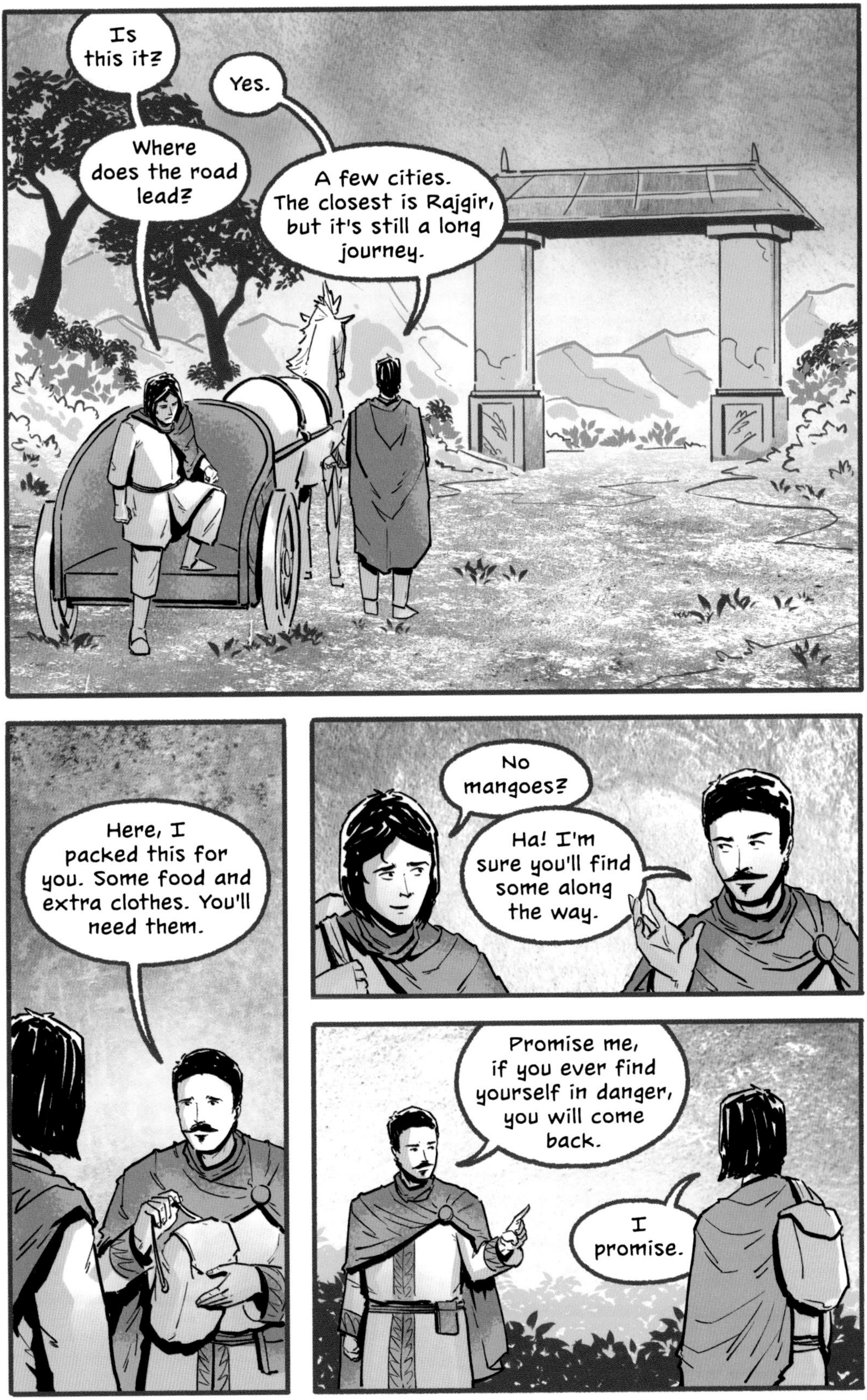
Is this it?
Yes.
Where does the road lead?
A few cities. The closest is Rajgir, but it's still a long journey.
Here, I packed this for you. Some food and extra clothes. You'll need them.
No mangoes?
Ha! I'm sure you'll find some along the way.
Promise me, if you ever find yourself in danger, you will come back.
I promise.

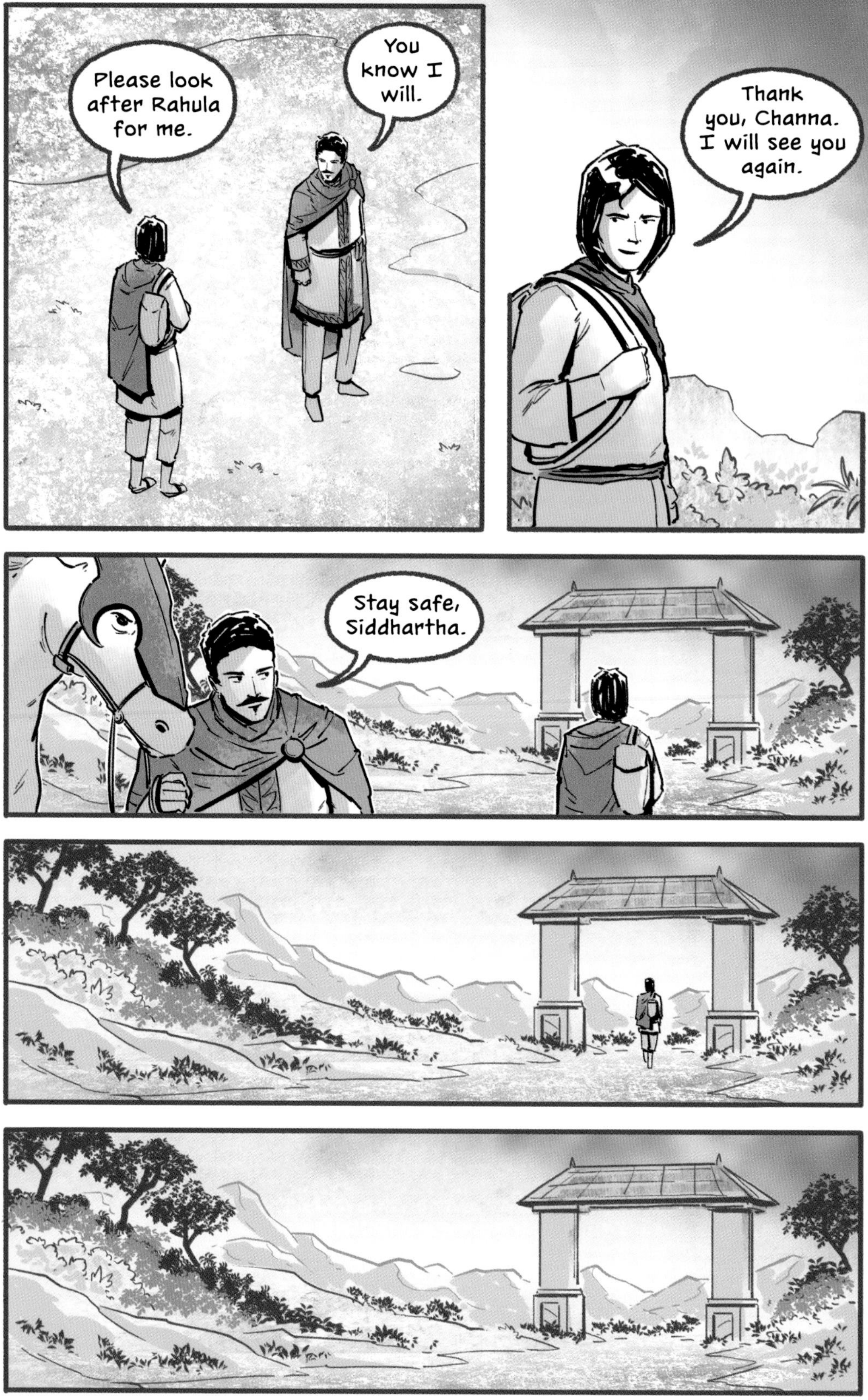
Please look after Rahula for me.
You know I will.
Thank you, Channa. I will see you again.
Stay safe, Siddhartha.

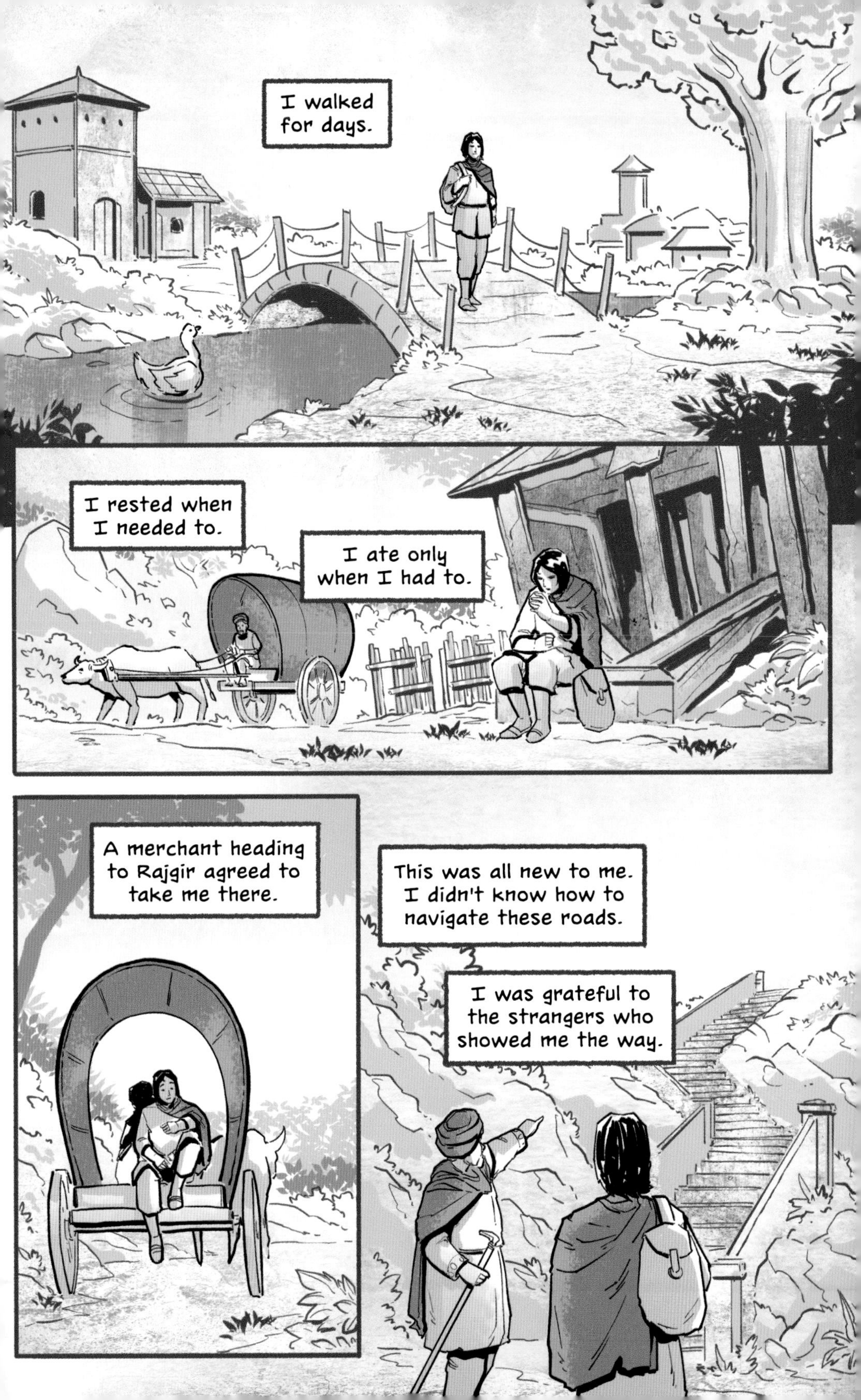
I walked for days.
I rested when I needed to.
I ate only when I had to.
A merchant heading to Rajgir agreed to take me there.
This was all new to me. I didn't know how to navigate these roads.
I was grateful to the strangers who showed me the way.

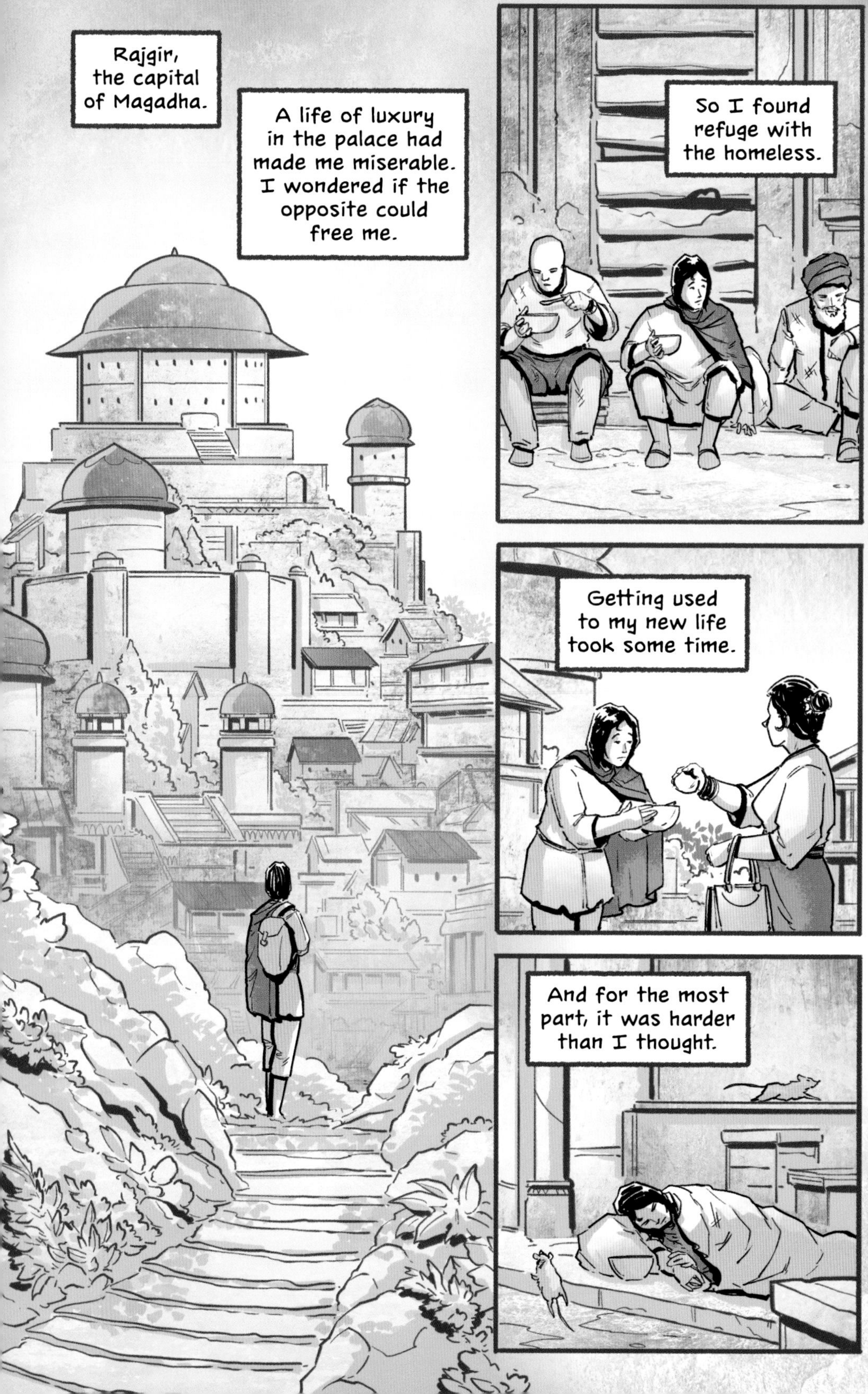
Rajgir, the capital of Magadha.
A life of luxury in the palace had made me miserable. I wondered if the opposite could free me.
So I found refuge with the homeless.
Getting used to my new life took some time.
And for the most part, it was harder than I thought.

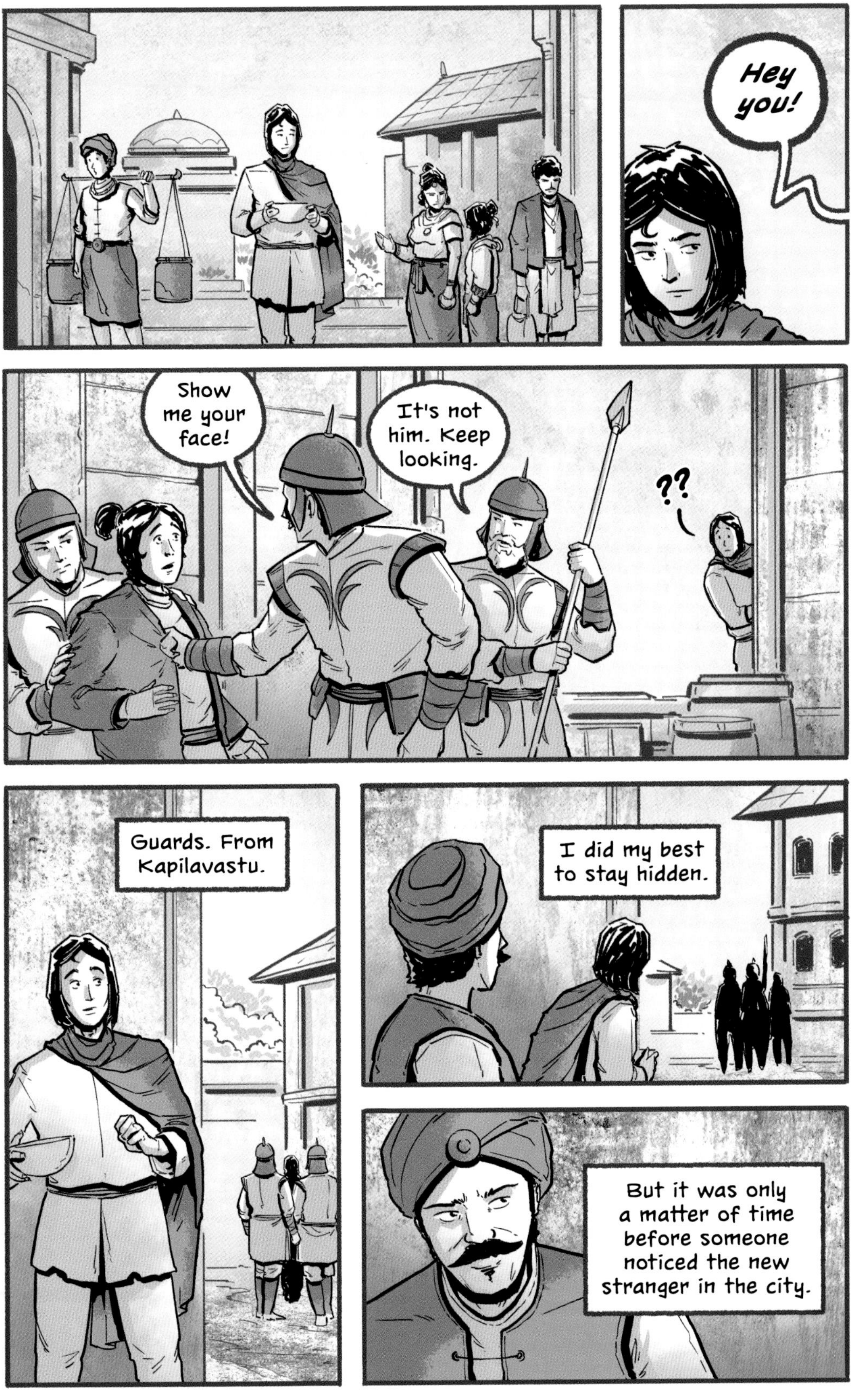
Hey you!
Show me your face!
It's not him. Keep looking.
??
Guards. From Kapilavastu.
I did my best to stay hidden.
But it was only a matter of time before someone noticed the new stranger in the city.

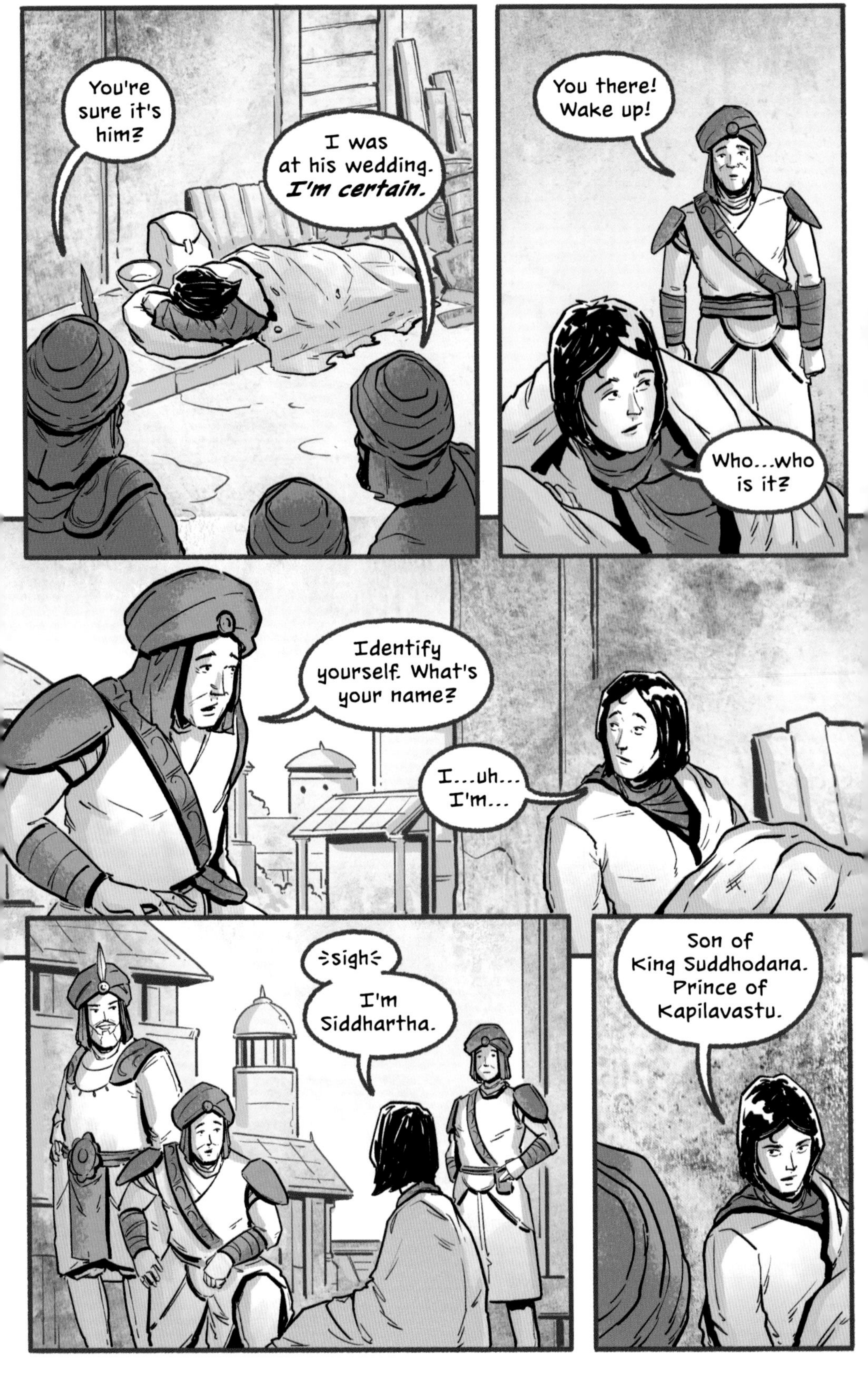
You're sure it's him?
I was at his wedding. *I'm certain.*
You there! Wake up!
Who...who is it?
Identify yourself. What's your name?
I...uh... I'm...
sigh
I'm Siddhartha.
Son of King Suddhodana. Prince of Kapilavastu.

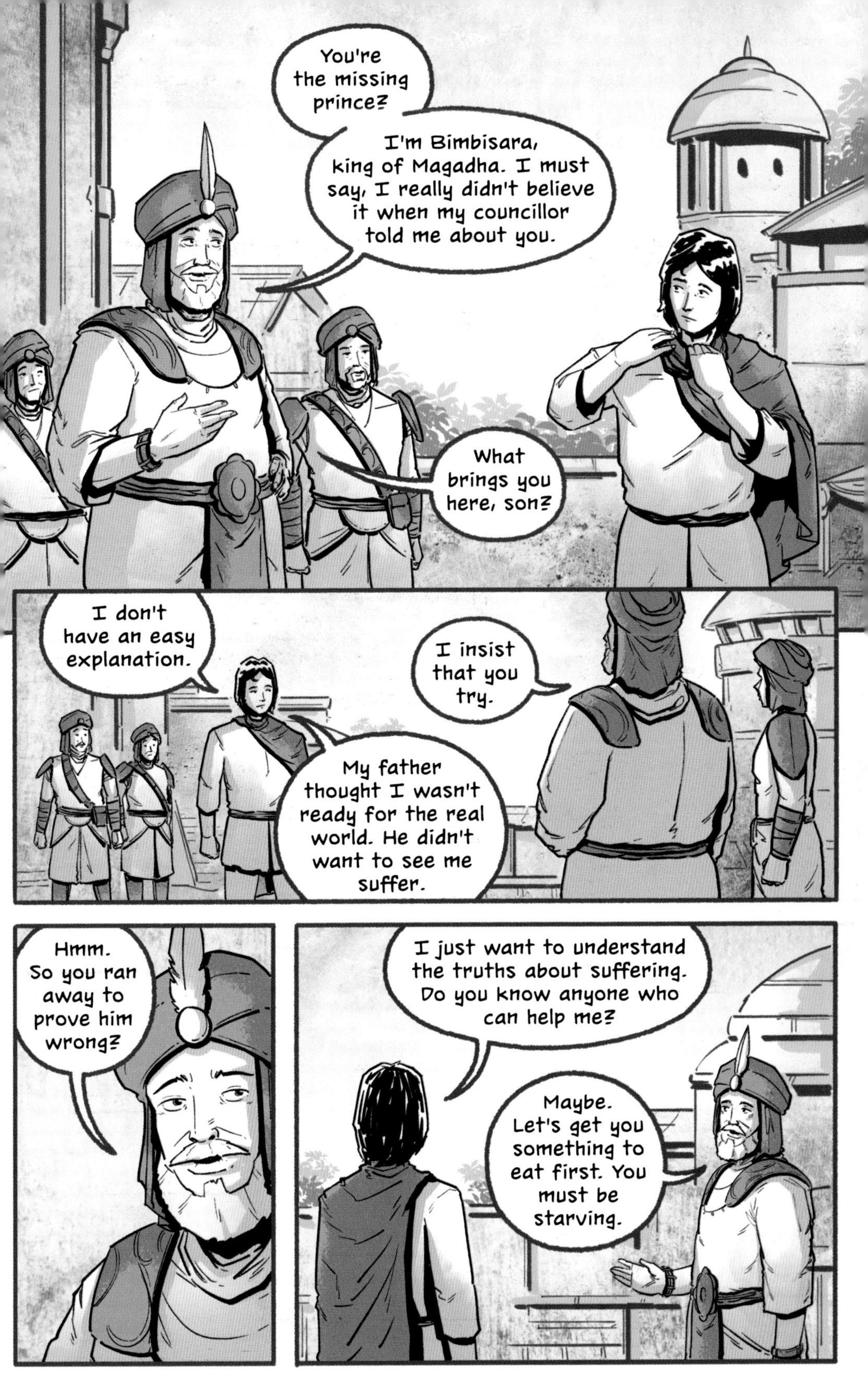

You're the missing prince?
I'm Bimbisara, king of Magadha. I must say, I really didn't believe it when my councillor told me about you.
What brings you here, son?
I don't have an easy explanation.
I insist that you try.
My father thought I wasn't ready for the real world. He didn't want to see me suffer.
Hmm. So you ran away to prove him wrong?
I just want to understand the truths about suffering. Do you know anyone who can help me?
Maybe. Let's get you something to eat first. You must be starving.

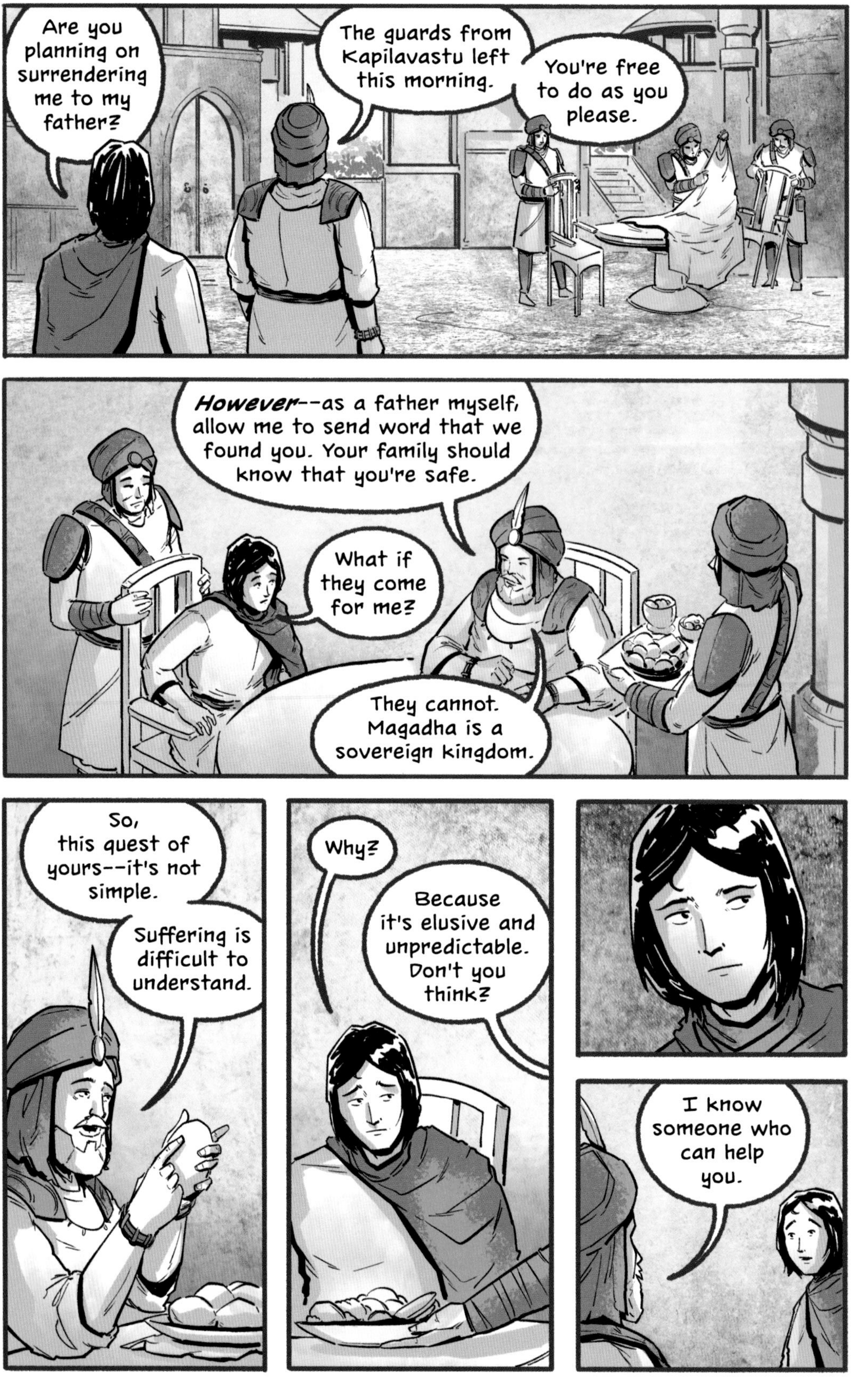
Are you planning on surrendering me to my father?
The guards from Kapilavastu left this morning.
You're free to do as you please.
However--as a father myself, allow me to send word that we found you. Your family should know that you're safe.
What if they come for me?
They cannot. Magadha is a sovereign kingdom.
So, this quest of yours--it's not simple.
Suffering is difficult to understand.
Why?
Because it's elusive and unpredictable. Don't you think?
I know someone who can help you.

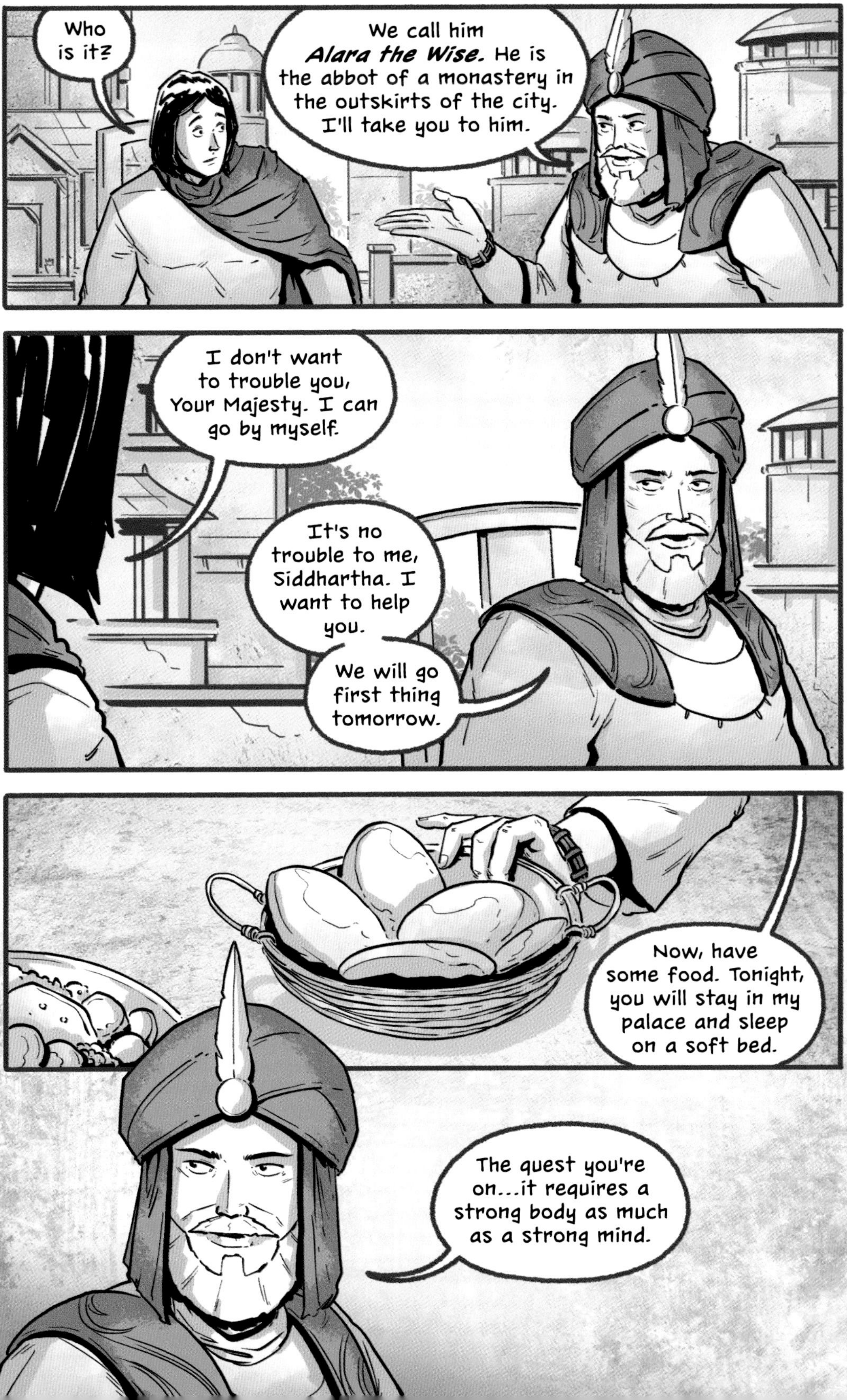
Who is it?
We call him *Alara the Wise.* He is the abbot of a monastery in the outskirts of the city. I'll take you to him.
I don't want to trouble you, Your Majesty. I can go by myself.
It's no trouble to me, Siddhartha. I want to help you.
We will go first thing tomorrow.
Now, have some food. Tonight, you will stay in my palace and sleep on a soft bed.
The quest you're on...it requires a strong body as much as a strong mind.

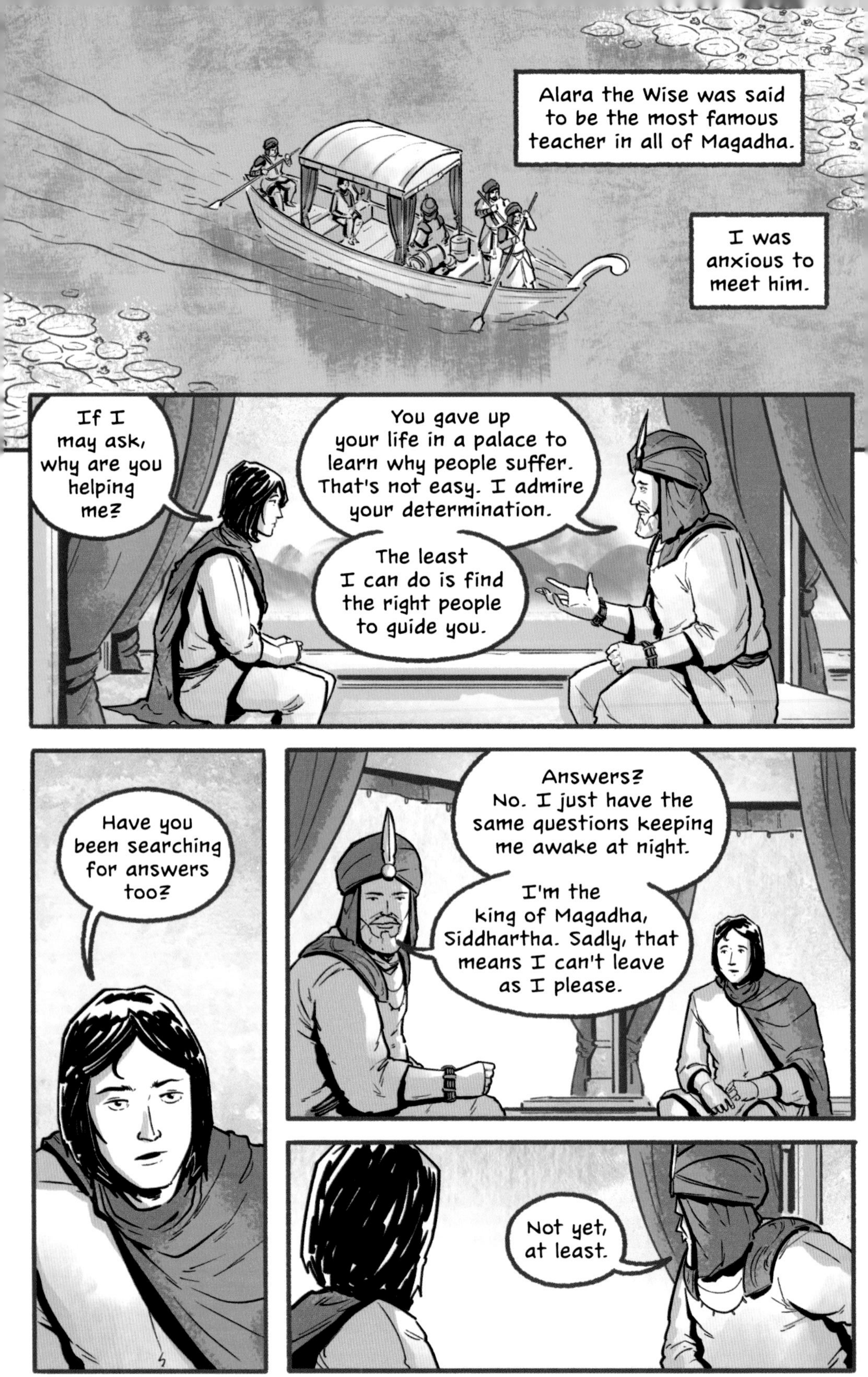
Alara the Wise was said to be the most famous teacher in all of Magadha.
I was anxious to meet him.
If I may ask, why are you helping me?
You gave up your life in a palace to learn why people suffer. That's not easy. I admire your determination.
The least I can do is find the right people to guide you.
Have you been searching for answers too?
Answers? No. I just have the same questions keeping me awake at night.
I'm the king of Magadha, Siddhartha. Sadly, that means I can't leave as I please.
Not yet, at least.

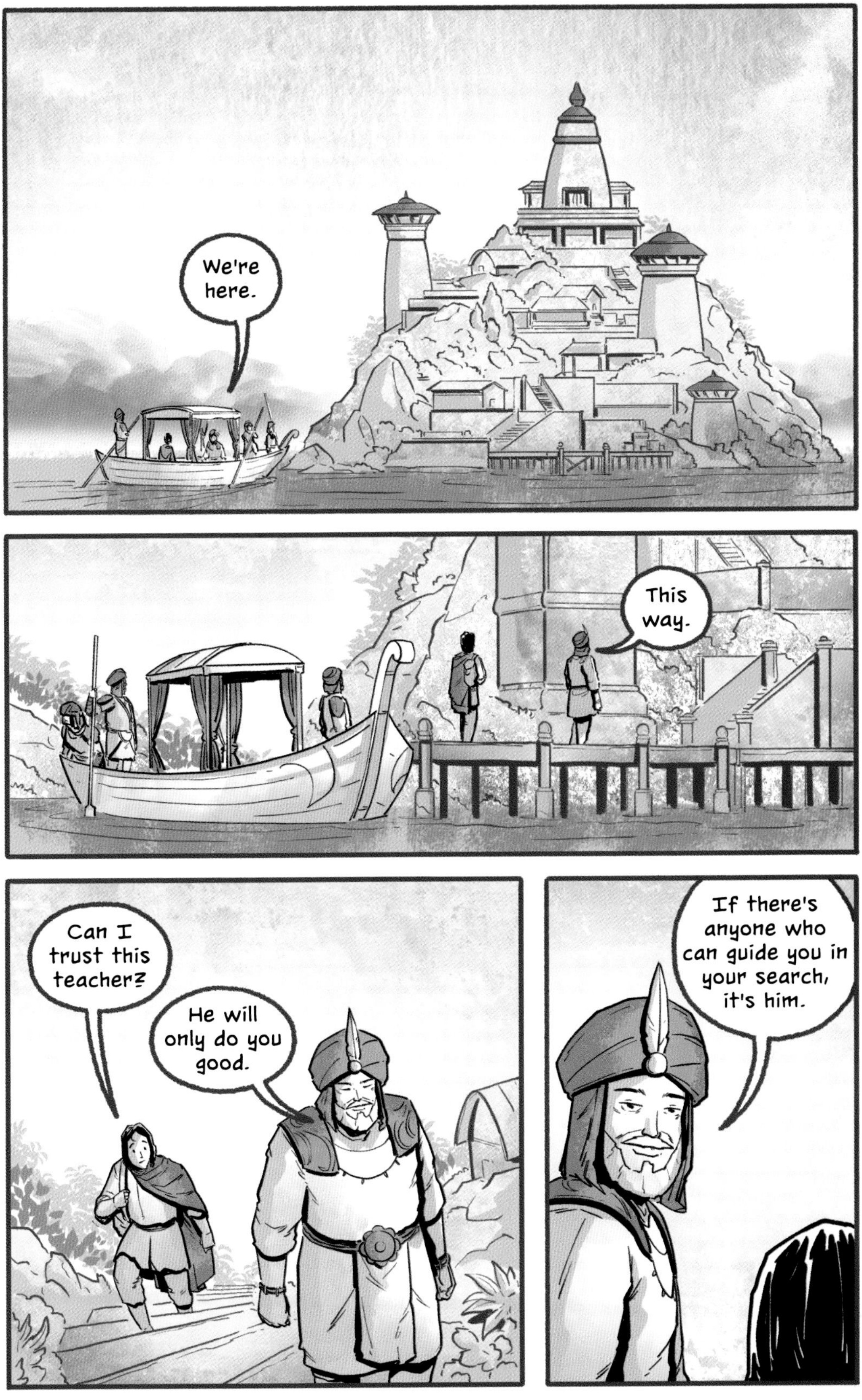
We're here.
This way.
Can I trust this teacher?
He will only do you good.
If there's anyone who can guide you in your search, it's him.

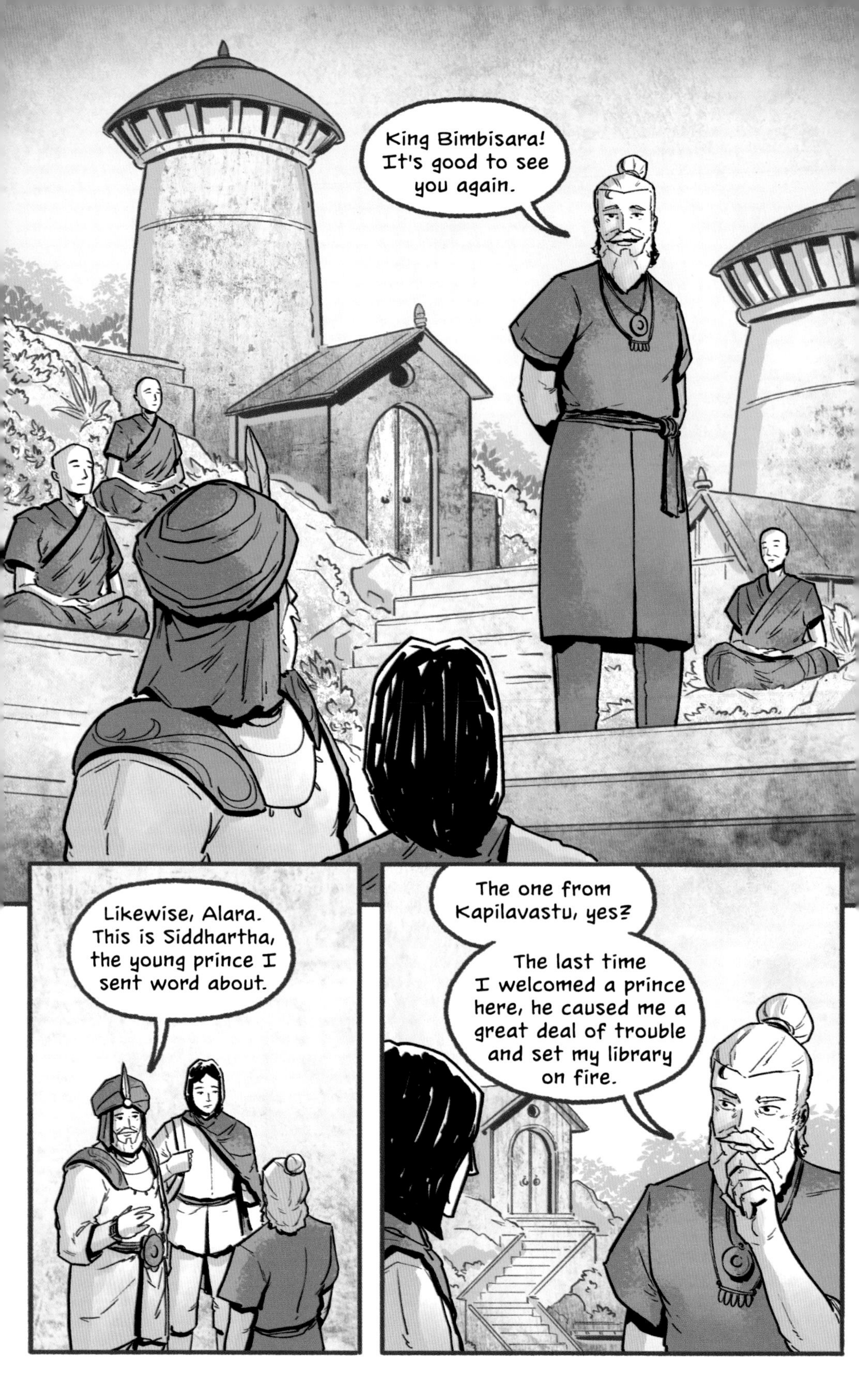
King Bimbisara! It's good to see you again.
Likewise, Alara. This is Siddhartha, the young prince I sent word about.
The one from Kapilavastu, yes?
The last time I welcomed a prince here, he caused me a great deal of trouble and set my library on fire.

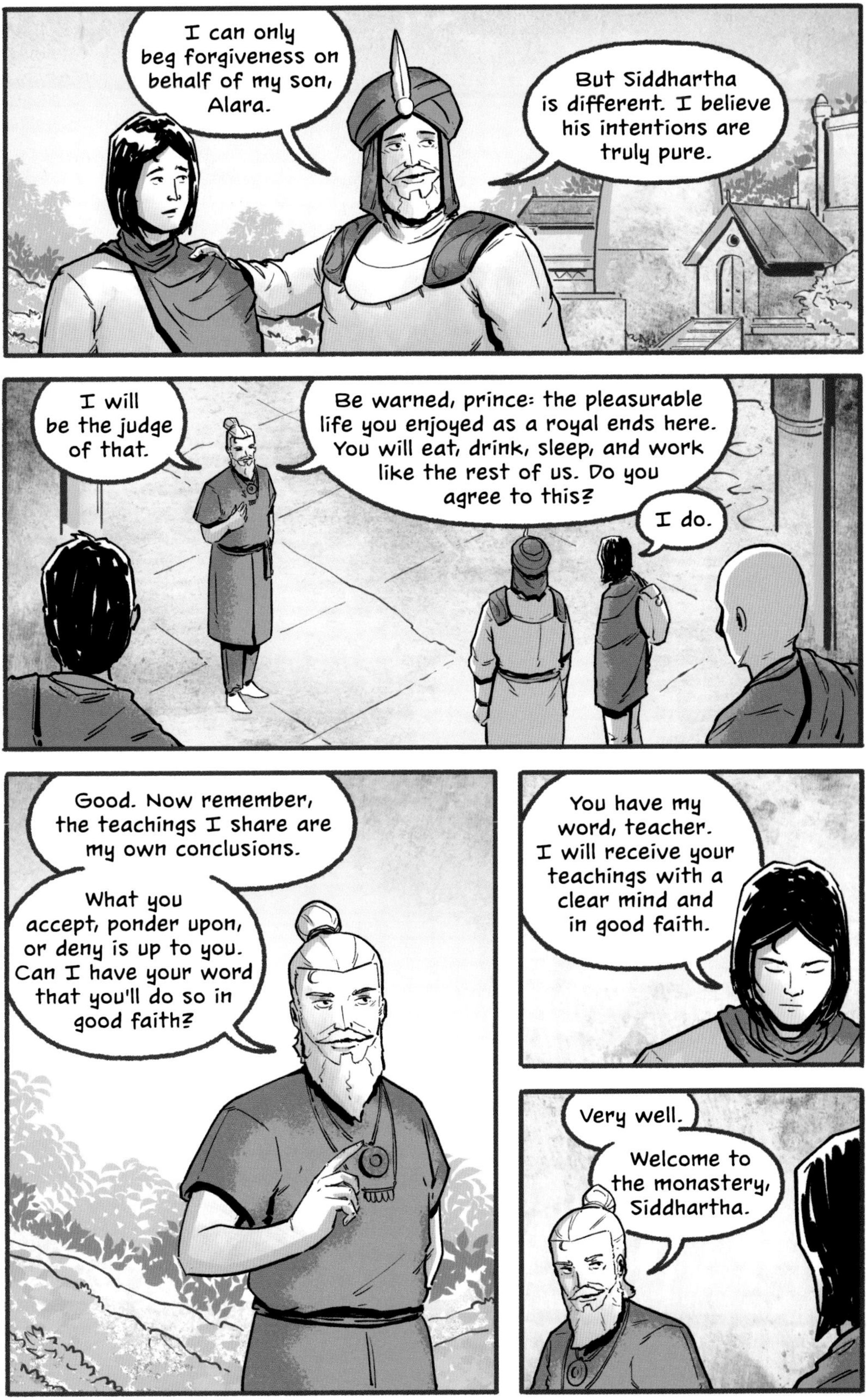
I can only beg forgiveness on behalf of my son, Alara.
But Siddhartha is different. I believe his intentions are truly pure.
I will be the judge of that.
Be warned, prince: the pleasurable life you enjoyed as a royal ends here. You will eat, drink, sleep, and work like the rest of us. Do you agree to this?
I do.
Good. Now remember, the teachings I share are my own conclusions.
What you accept, ponder upon, or deny is up to you. Can I have your word that you'll do so in good faith?
You have my word, teacher. I will receive your teachings with a clear mind and in good faith.
Very well.
Welcome to the monastery, Siddhartha.

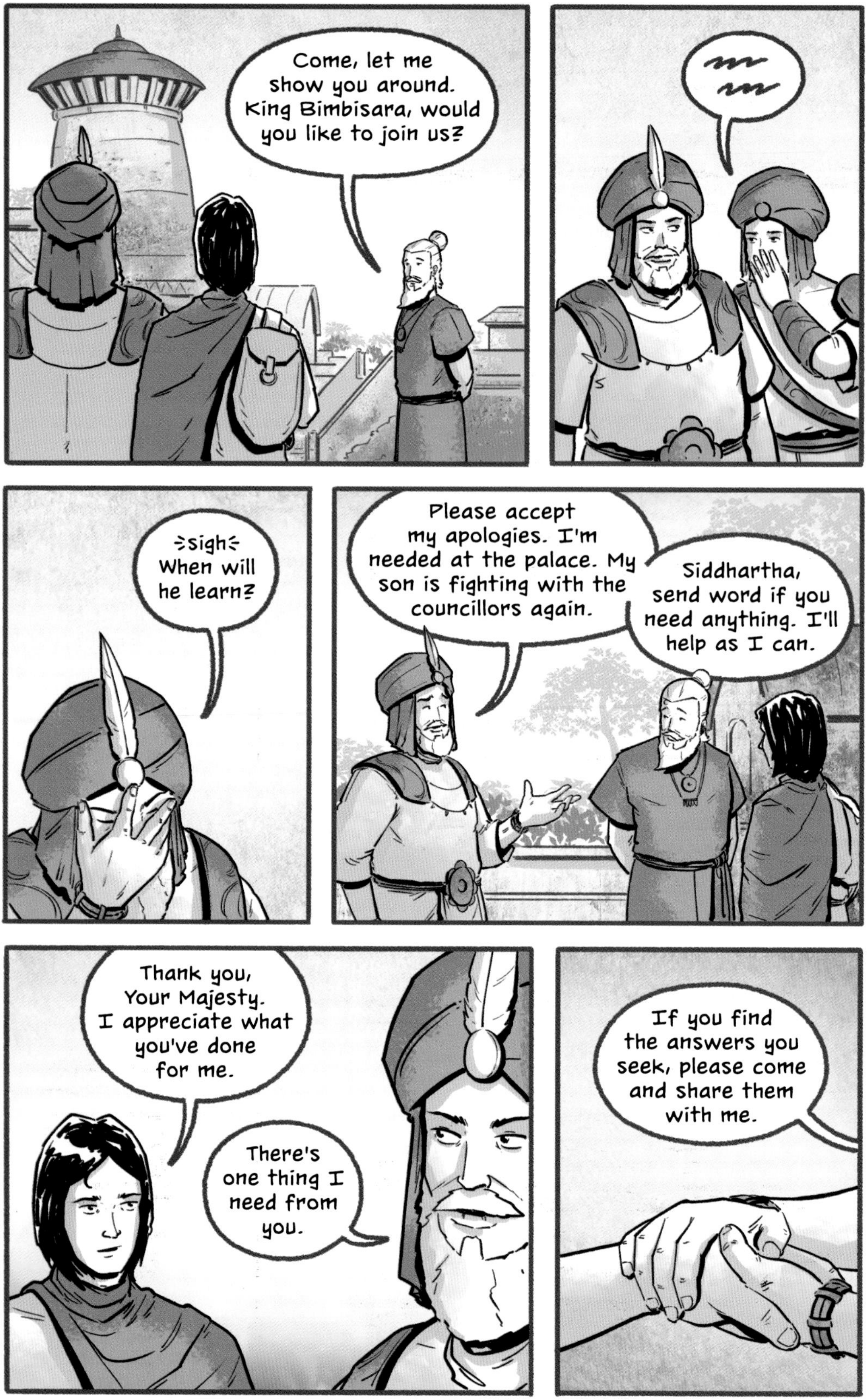
Come, let me show you around. King Bimbisara, would you like to join us?
~sigh~ When will he learn?
Please accept my apologies. I'm needed at the palace. My son is fighting with the councillors again.
Siddhartha, send word if you need anything. I'll help as I can.
Thank you, Your Majesty. I appreciate what you've done for me.
There's one thing I need from you.
If you find the answers you seek, please come and share them with me.

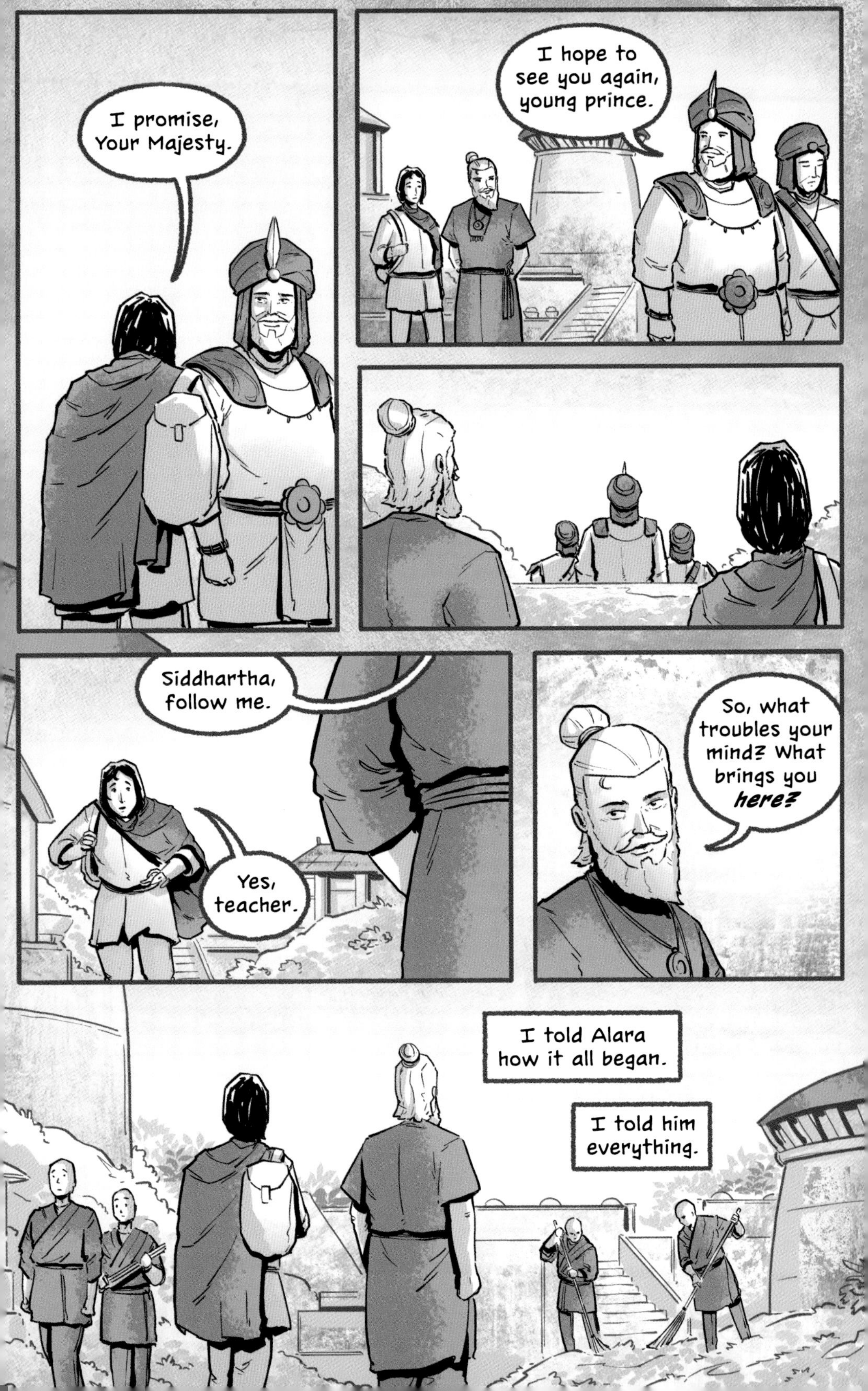
I promise, Your Majesty.
I hope to see you again, young prince.
Siddhartha, follow me.
Yes, teacher.
So, what troubles your mind? What brings you *here?*
I told Alara how it all began.
I told him everything.

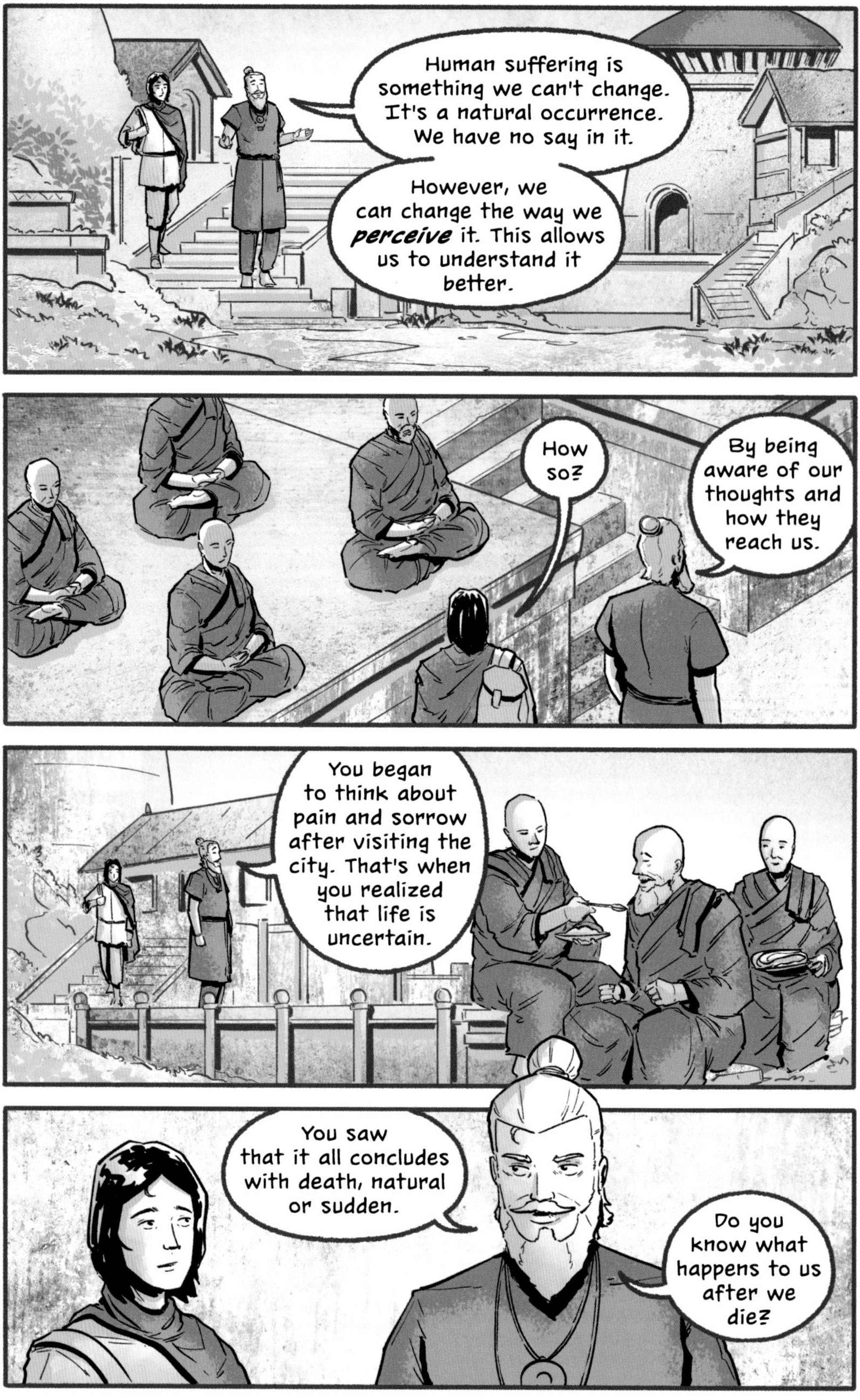
Human suffering is something we can't change. It's a natural occurrence. We have no say in it.
However, we can change the way we *perceive* it. This allows us to understand it better.
How so?
By being aware of our thoughts and how they reach us.
You began to think about pain and sorrow after visiting the city. That's when you realized that life is uncertain.
You saw that it all concludes with death, natural or sudden.
Do you know what happens to us after we die?

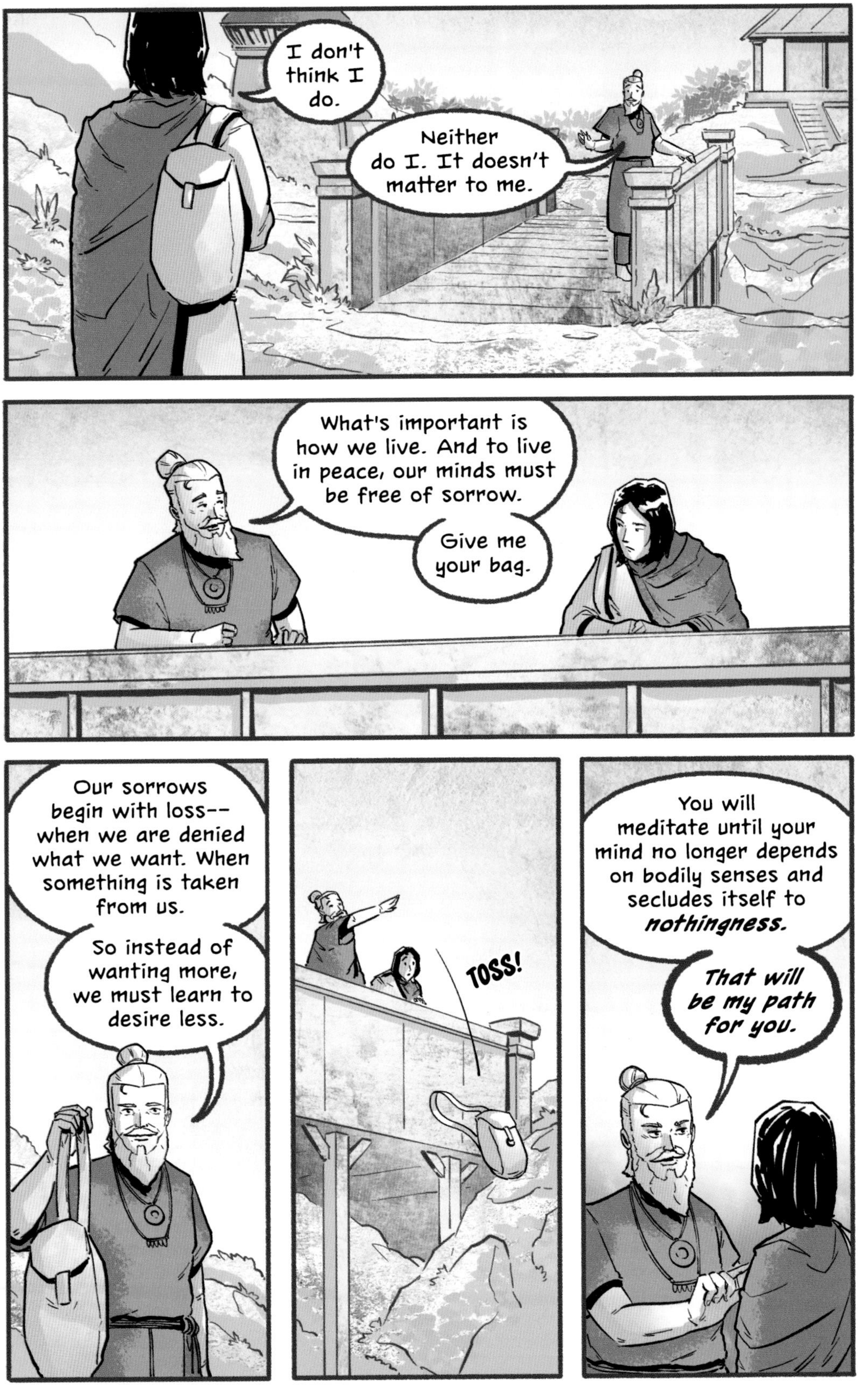
I don't think I do.
Neither do I. It doesn't matter to me.
What's important is how we live. And to live in peace, our minds must be free of sorrow.
Give me your bag.
Our sorrows begin with loss-- when we are denied what we want. When something is taken from us.
So instead of wanting more, we must learn to desire less.
TOSS!
You will meditate until your mind no longer depends on bodily senses and secludes itself to *nothingness.*
That will be my path for you.

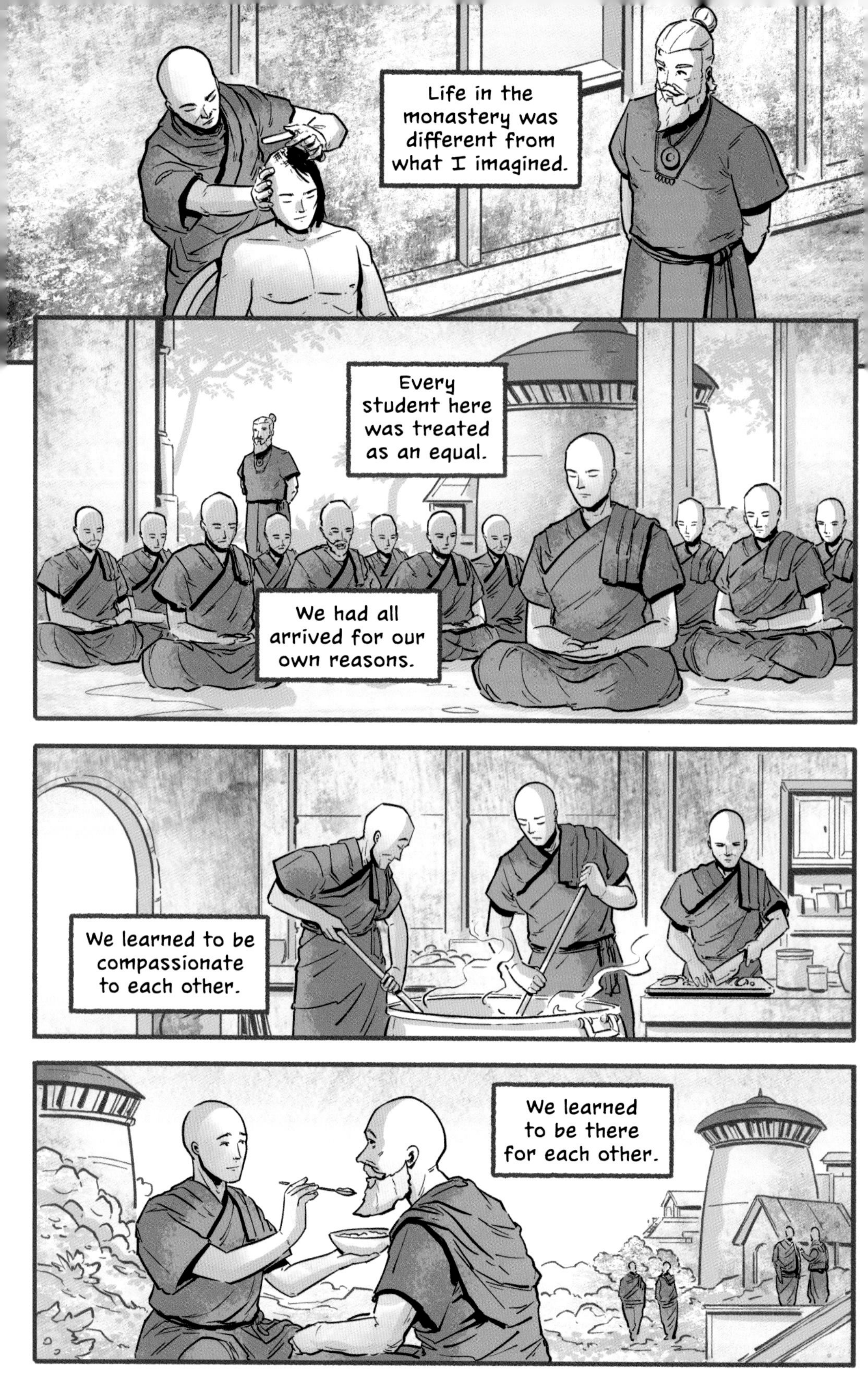
Life in the monastery was different from what I imagined.
Every student here was treated as an equal.
We had all arrived for our own reasons.
We learned to be compassionate to each other.
We learned to be there for each other.

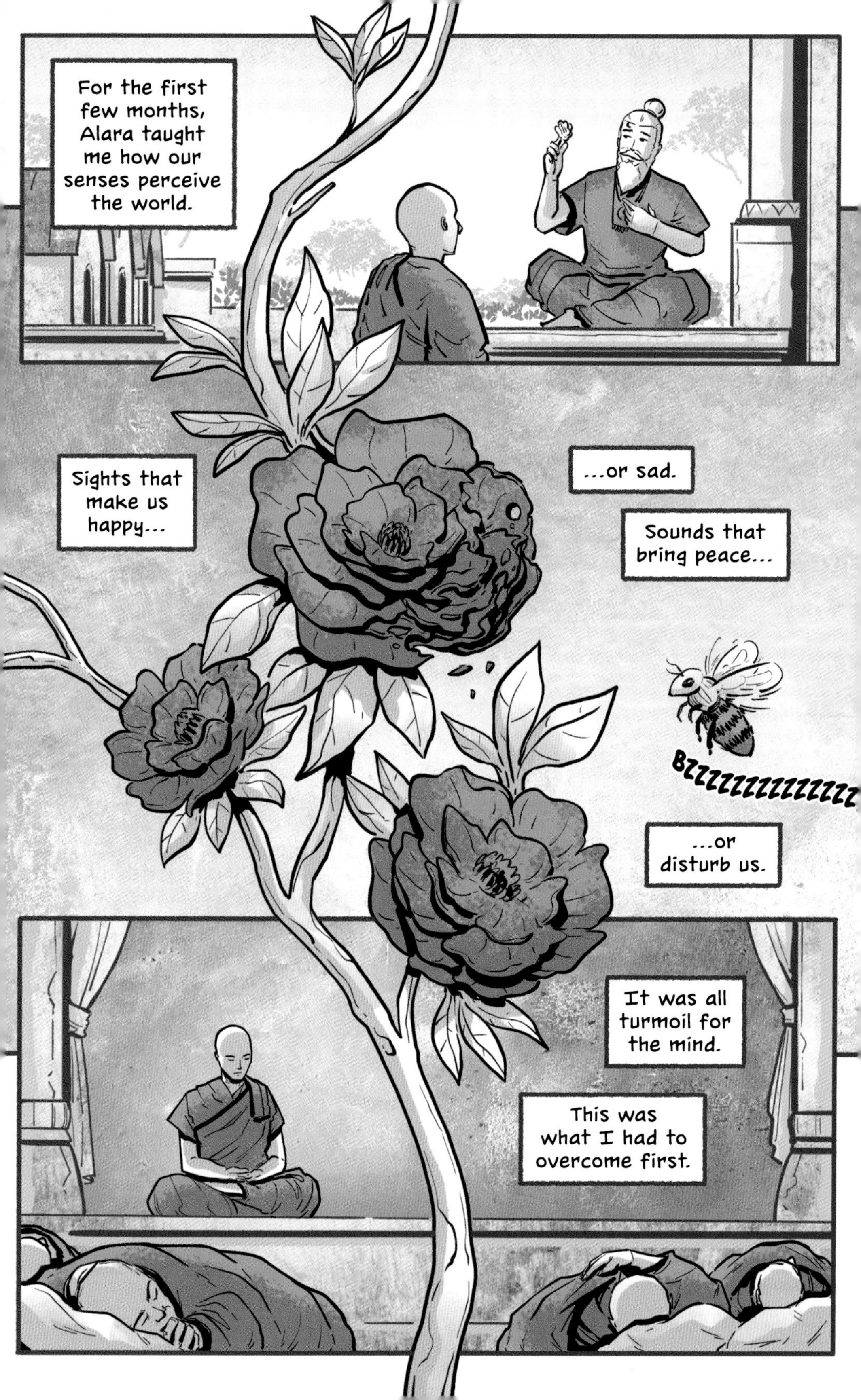
For the first few months, Alara taught me how our senses perceive the world.
Sights that make us happy...
...or sad.
Sounds that bring peace...
BZZZZZZZZZZZZZZZ
...or disturb us.
It was all turmoil for the mind.
This was what I had to overcome first.

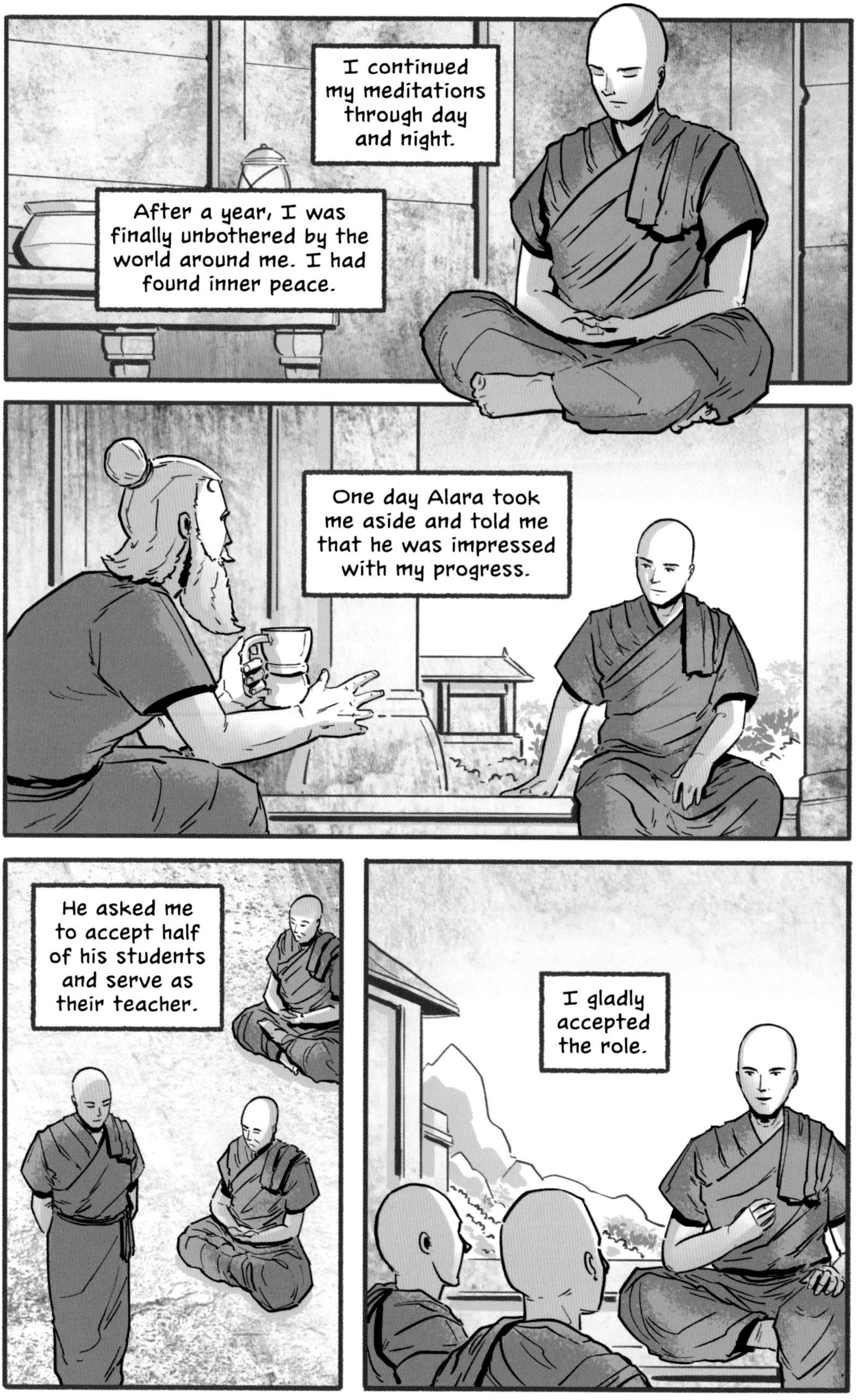
I continued my meditations through day and night.
After a year, I was finally unbothered by the world around me. I had found inner peace.
One day Alara took me aside and told me that he was impressed with my progress.
He asked me to accept half of his students and serve as their teacher.
I gladly accepted the role.

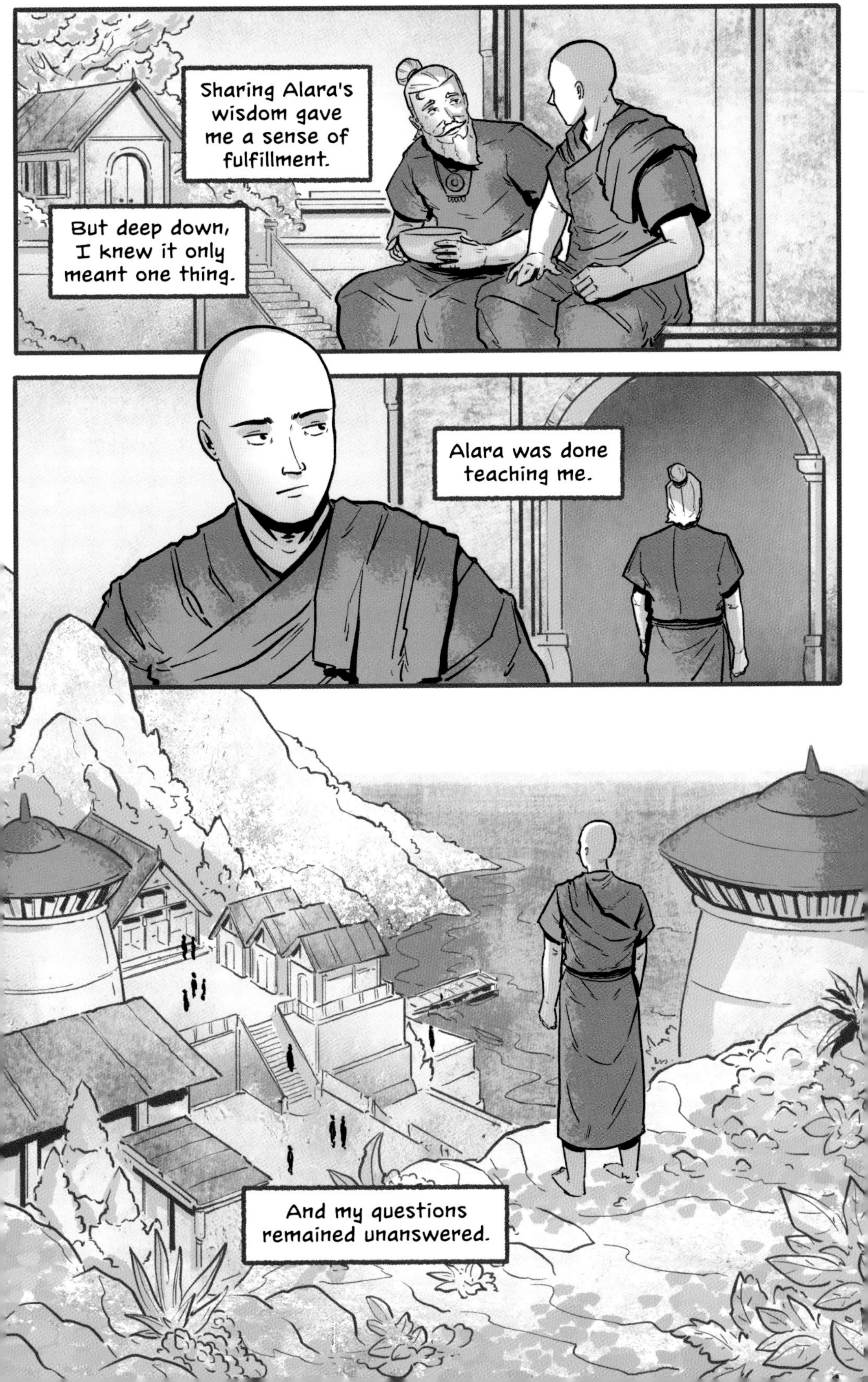
Sharing Alara's wisdom gave me a sense of fulfillment.
But deep down, I knew it only meant one thing.
Alara was done teaching me.
And my questions remained unanswered.

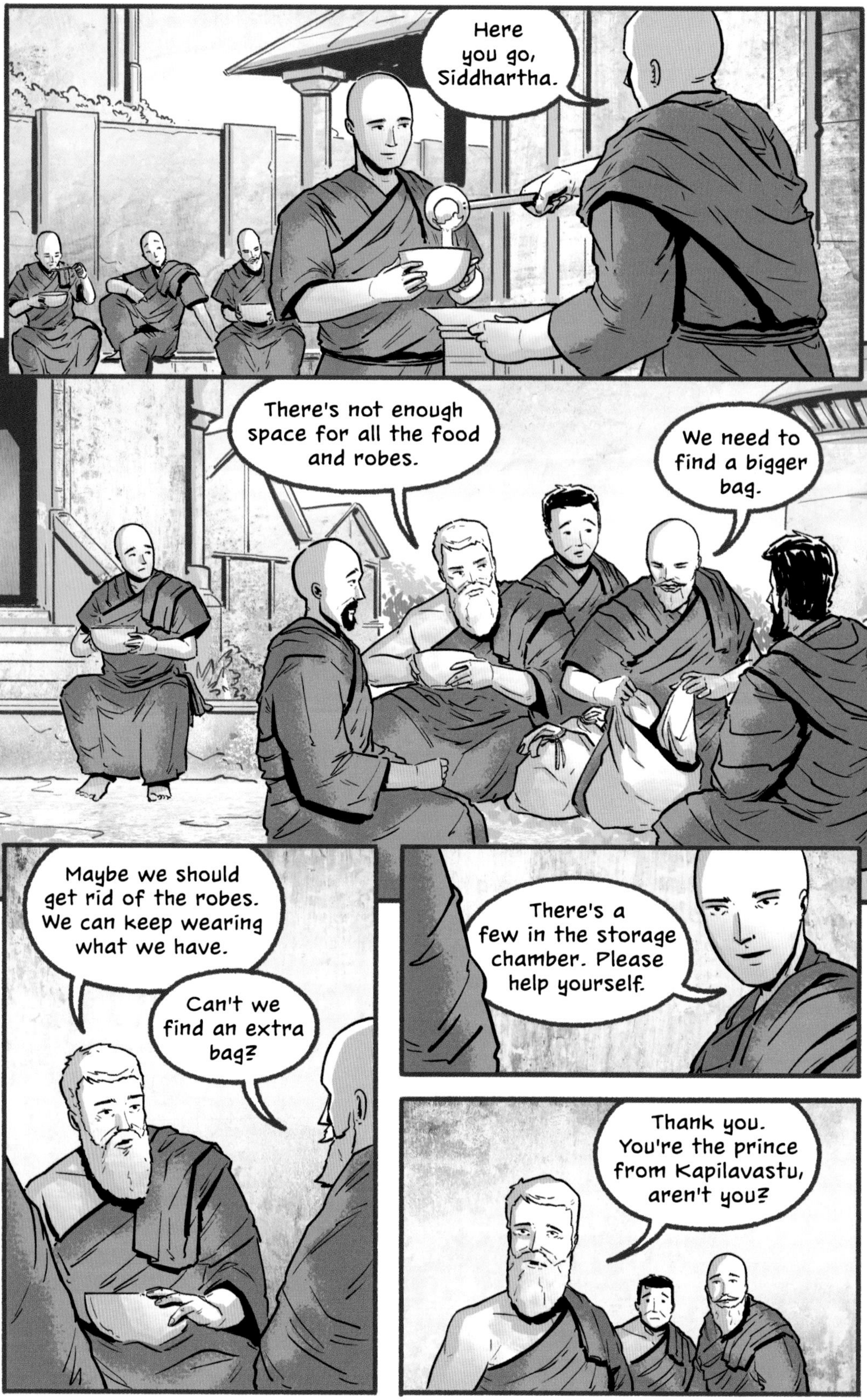
Here you go, Siddhartha.
There's not enough space for all the food and robes.
We need to find a bigger bag.
Maybe we should get rid of the robes. We can keep wearing what we have.
Can't we find an extra bag?
There's a few in the storage chamber. Please help yourself.
Thank you. You're the prince from Kapilavastu, aren't you?

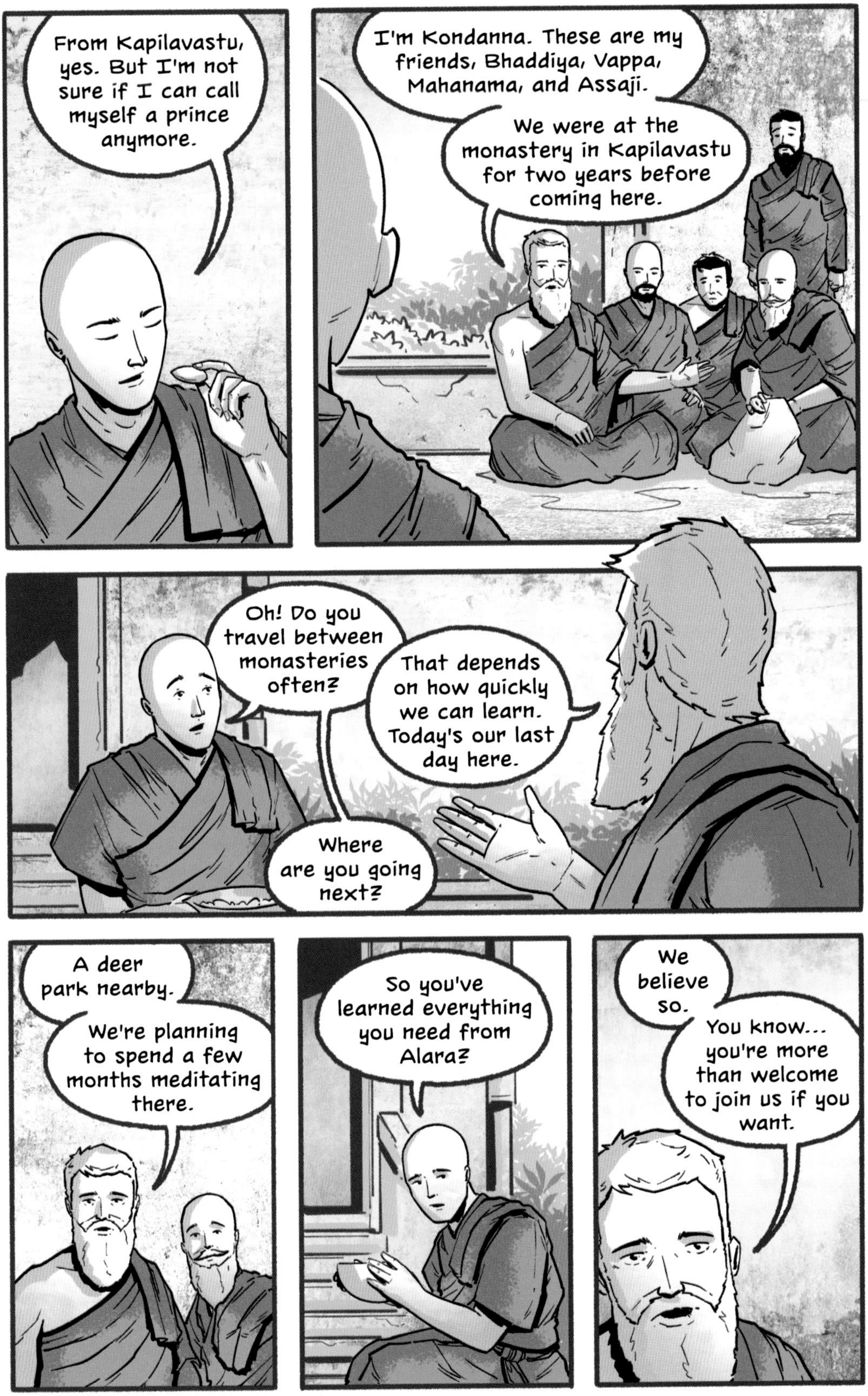
From Kapilavastu, yes. But I'm not sure if I can call myself a prince anymore.
I'm Kondanna. These are my friends, Bhaddiya, Vappa, Mahanama, and Assaji.
We were at the monastery in Kapilavastu for two years before coming here.
Oh! Do you travel between monasteries often?
That depends on how quickly we can learn. Today's our last day here.
Where are you going next?
A deer park nearby.
We're planning to spend a few months meditating there.
So you've learned everything you need from Alara?
We believe so.
You know... you're more than welcome to join us if you want.

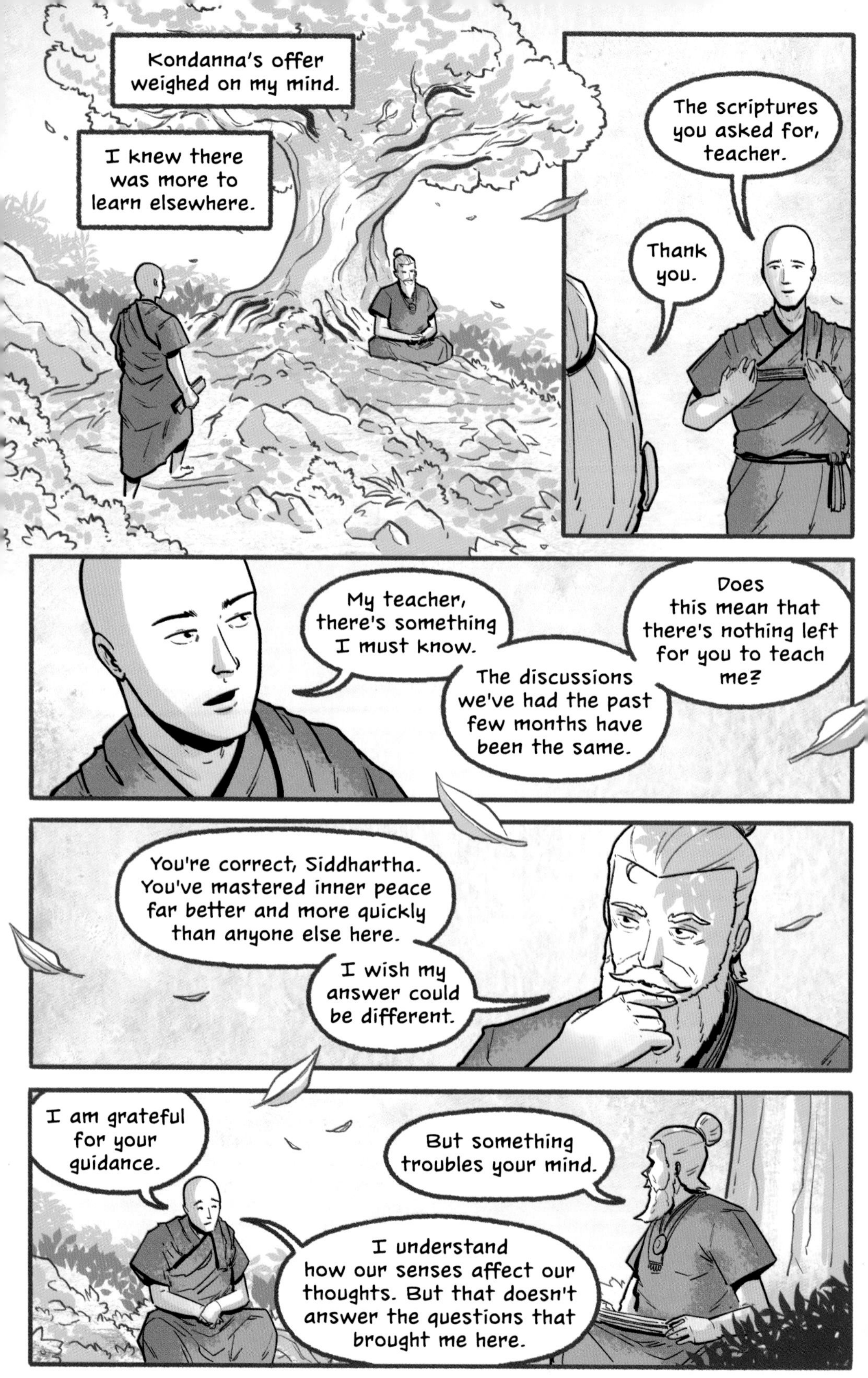
Kondanna's offer weighed on my mind.
I knew there was more to learn elsewhere.
The scriptures you asked for, teacher.
Thank you.
My teacher, there's something I must know.
The discussions we've had the past few months have been the same.
Does this mean that there's nothing left for you to teach me?
You're correct, Siddhartha. You've mastered inner peace far better and more quickly than anyone else here.
I wish my answer could be different.
I am grateful for your guidance.
But something troubles your mind.
I understand how our senses affect our thoughts. But that doesn't answer the questions that brought me here.

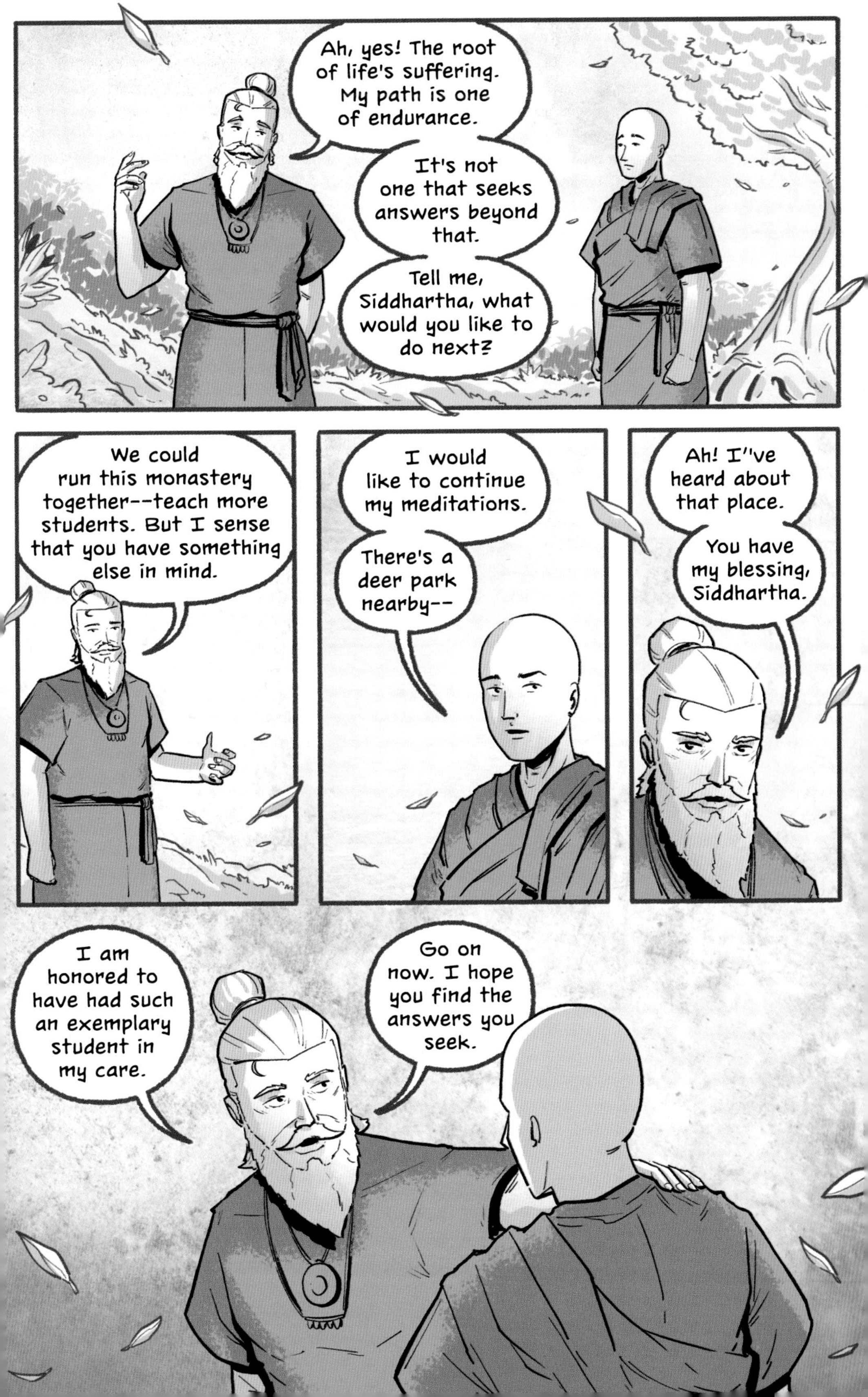
Ah, yes! The root of life's suffering. My path is one of endurance.
It's not one that seeks answers beyond that.
Tell me, Siddhartha, what would you like to do next?
We could run this monastery together--teach more students. But I sense that you have something else in mind.
I would like to continue my meditations.
There's a deer park nearby--
Ah! I've heard about that place.
You have my blessing, Siddhartha.
I am honored to have had such an exemplary student in my care.
Go on now. I hope you find the answers you seek.

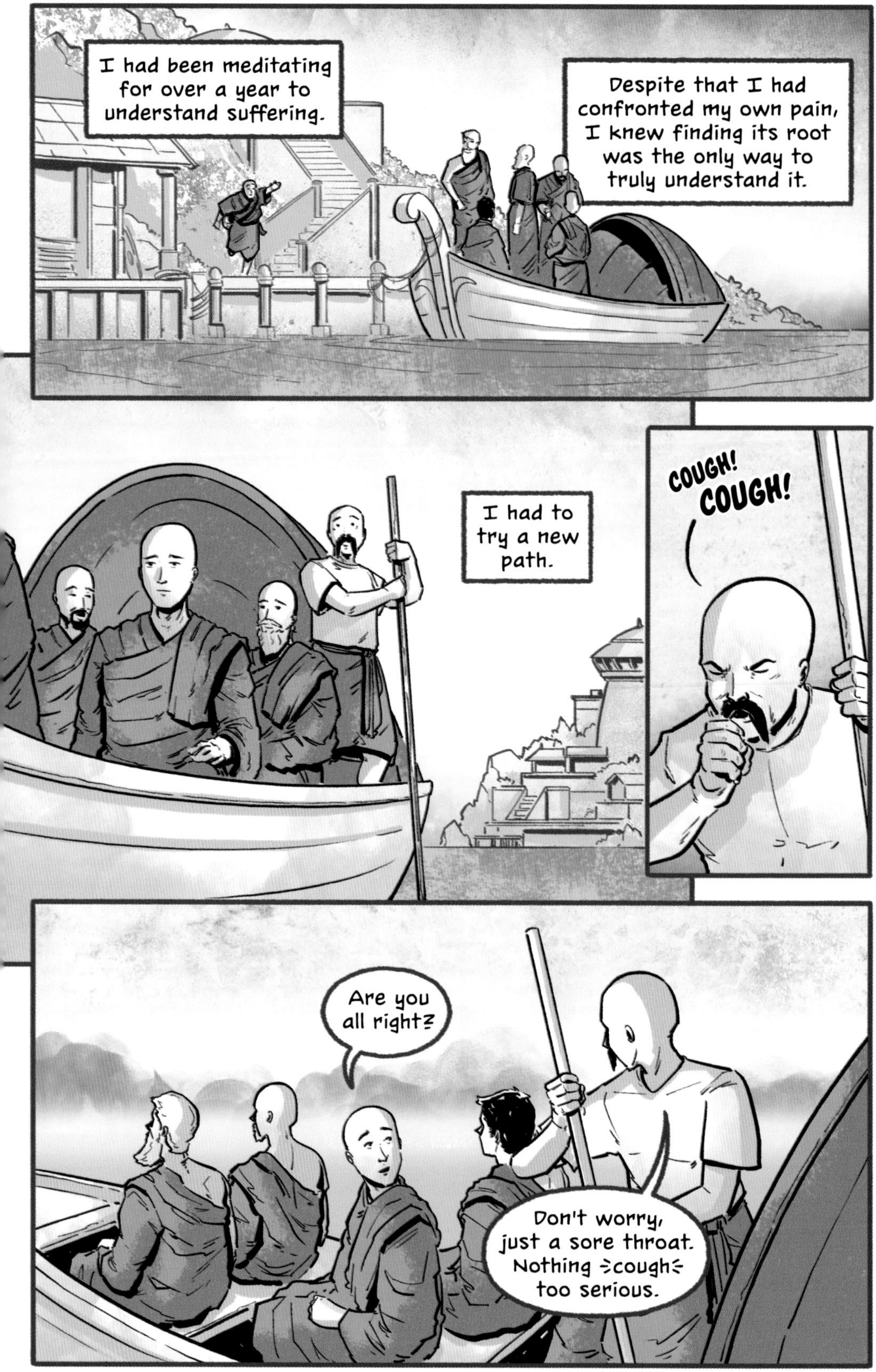
I had been meditating for over a year to understand suffering.
Despite that I had confronted my own pain, I knew finding its root was the only way to truly understand it.
I had to try a new path.
COUGH!
COUGH!
Are you all right?
Don't worry, just a sore throat. Nothing =cough= too serious.

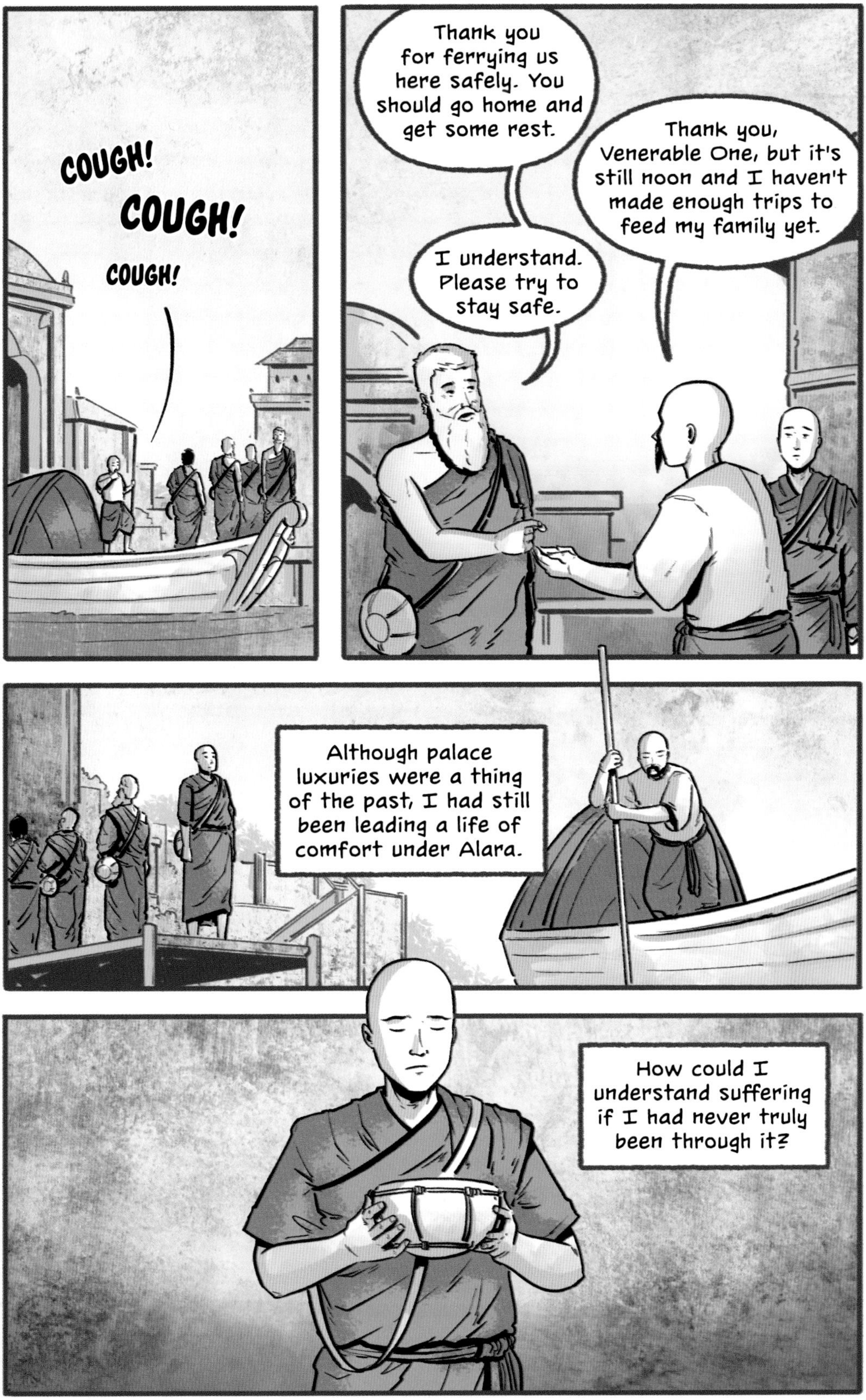

COUGH!
COUGH!
COUGH!
Thank you for ferrying us here safely. You should go home and get some rest.
Thank you, Venerable One, but it's still noon and I haven't made enough trips to feed my family yet.
I understand. Please try to stay safe.
Although palace luxuries were a thing of the past, I had still been leading a life of comfort under Alara.
How could I understand suffering if I had never truly been through it?

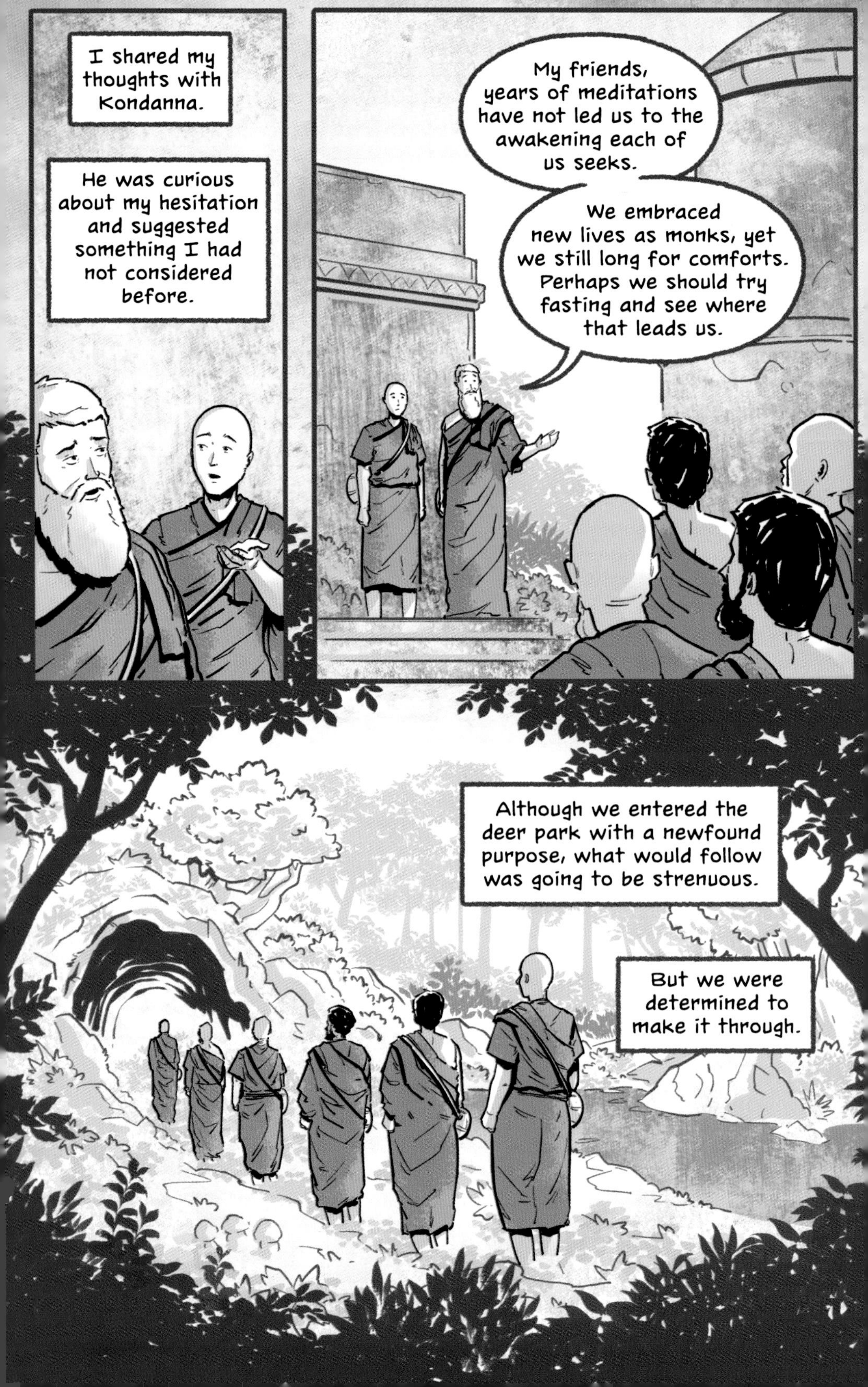

I shared my thoughts with Kondanna.
He was curious about my hesitation and suggested something I had not considered before.
My friends, years of meditations have not led us to the awakening each of us seeks.
We embraced new lives as monks, yet we still long for comforts. Perhaps we should try fasting and see where that leads us.
Although we entered the deer park with a newfound purpose, what would follow was going to be strenuous.
But we were determined to make it through.

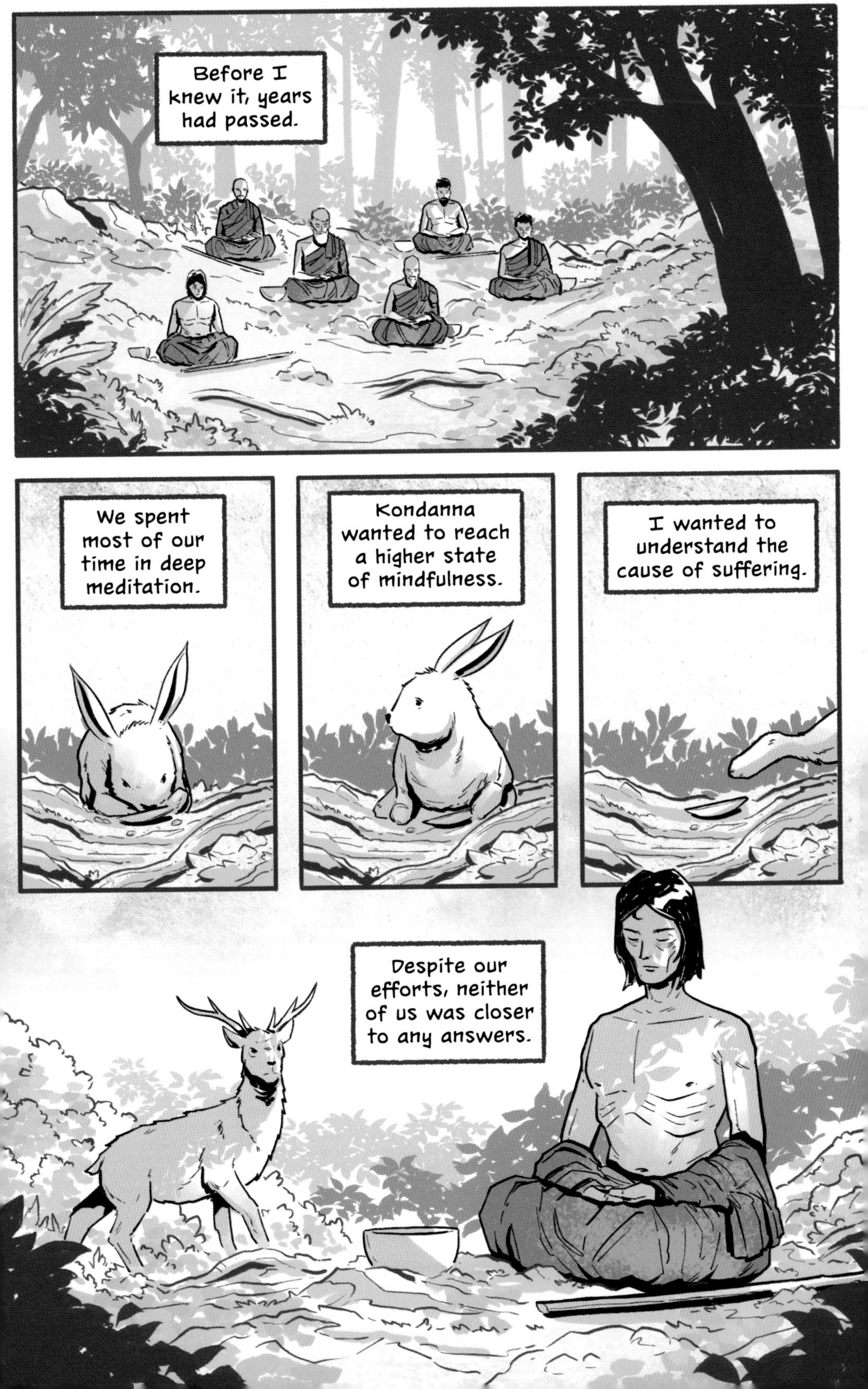
Before I knew it, years had passed.
We spent most of our time in deep meditation.
Kondanna wanted to reach a higher state of mindfulness.
I wanted to understand the cause of suffering.
Despite our efforts, neither of us was closer to any answers.

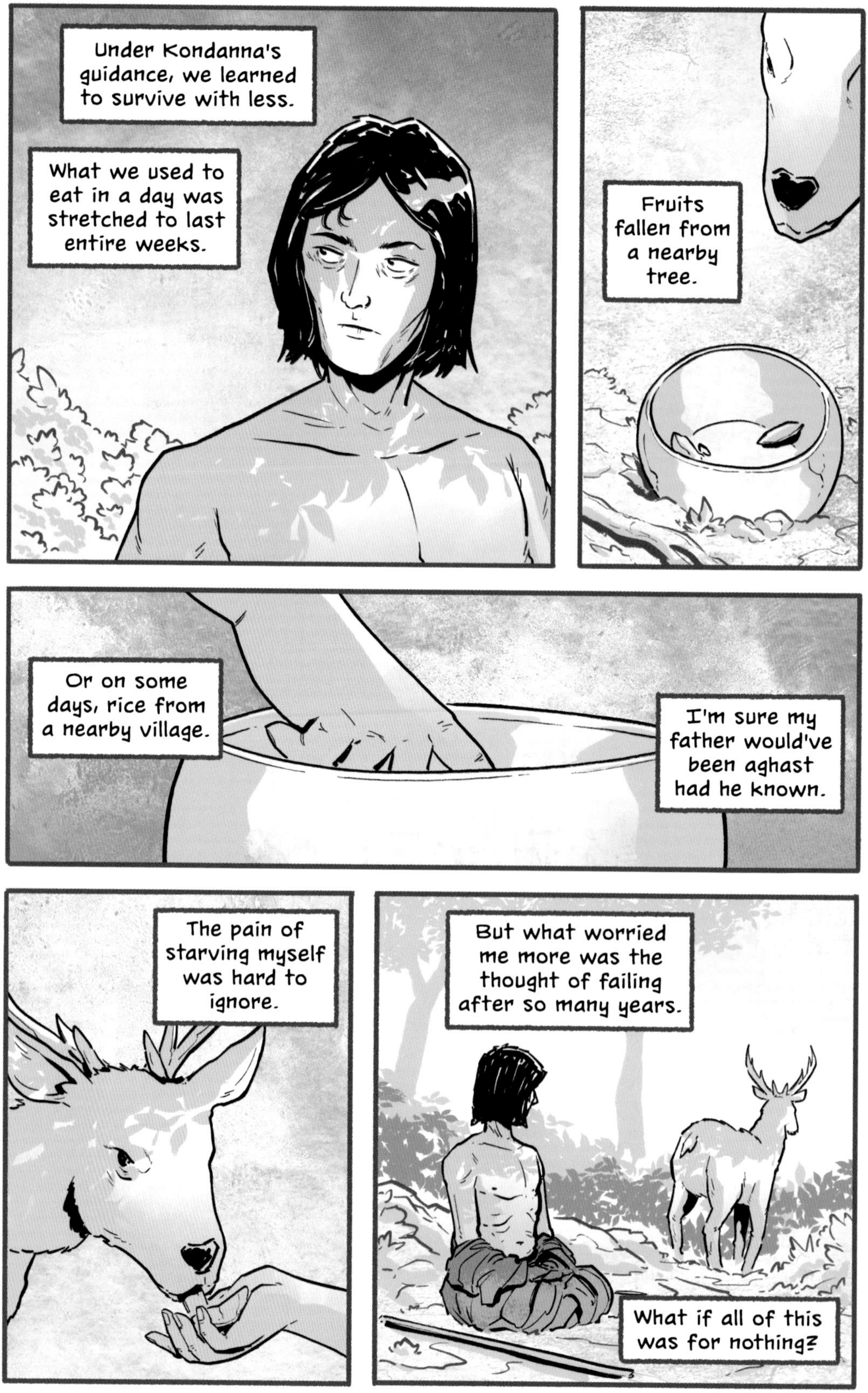
Under Kondanna's guidance, we learned to survive with less.
What we used to eat in a day was stretched to last entire weeks.
Fruits fallen from a nearby tree.
Or on some days, rice from a nearby village.
I'm sure my father would've been aghast had he known.
The pain of starving myself was hard to ignore.
But what worried me more was the thought of failing after so many years.
What if all of this was for nothing?

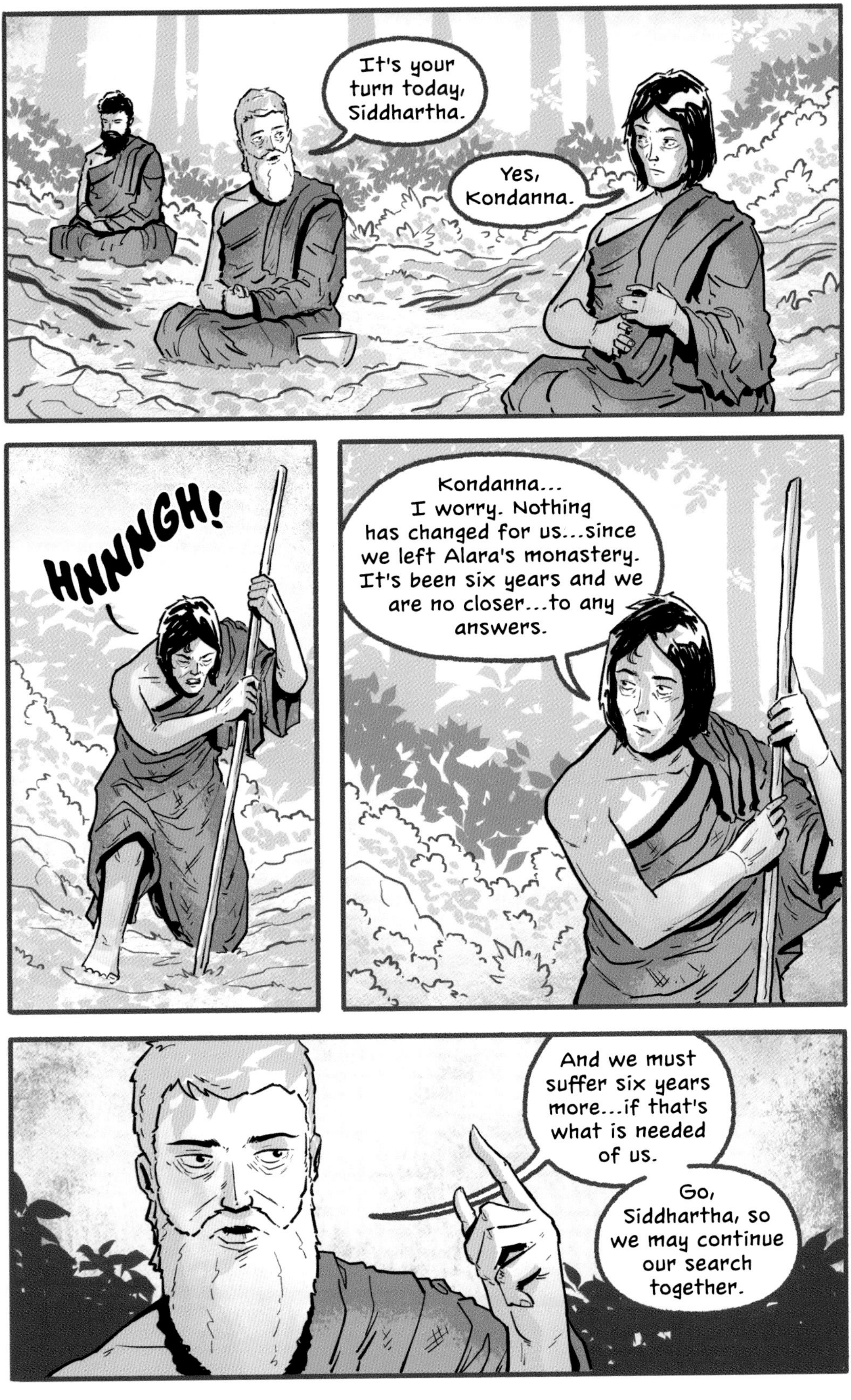
It's your turn today, Siddhartha.
Yes, Kondanna.
HNNNGH!
Kondanna... I worry. Nothing has changed for us...since we left Alara's monastery. It's been six years and we are no closer...to any answers.
And we must suffer six years more...if that's what is needed of us.
Go, Siddhartha, so we may continue our search together.

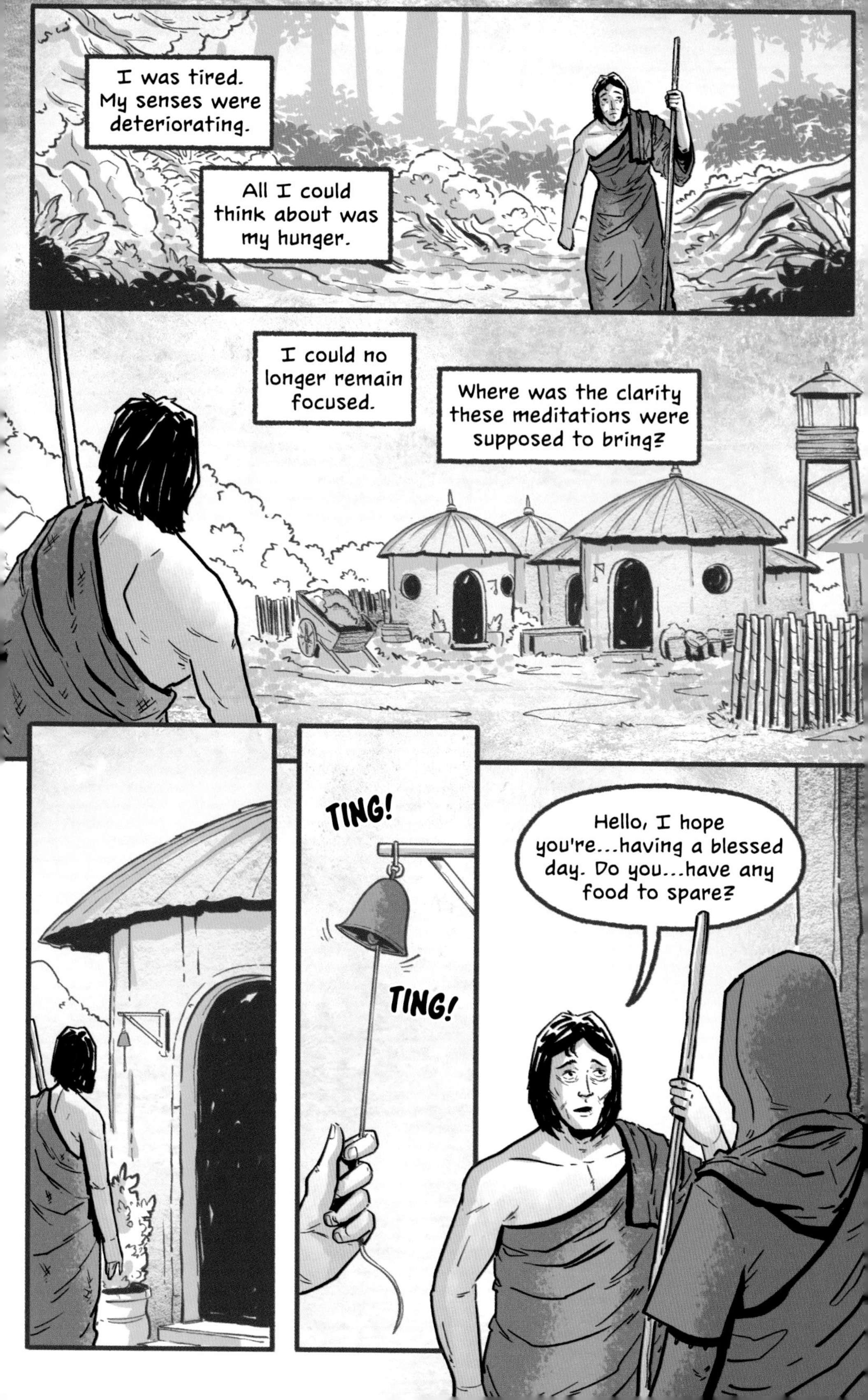
I was tired. My senses were deteriorating.
All I could think about was my hunger.
I could no longer remain focused.
Where was the clarity these meditations were supposed to bring?
TING!
TING!
Hello, I hope you're...having a blessed day. Do you...have any food to spare?

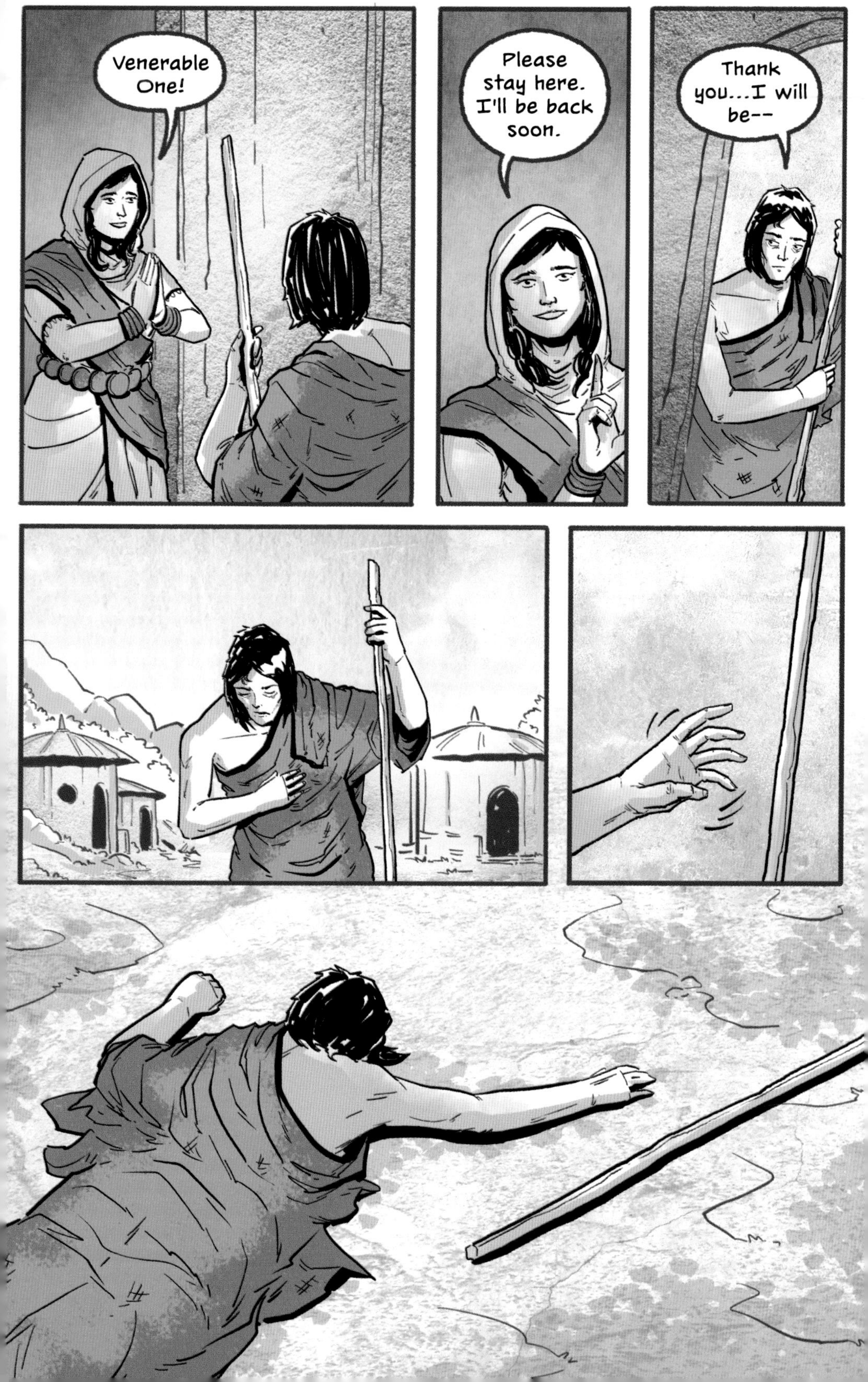
Venerable One!
Please stay here. I'll be back soon.
Thank you...I will be--

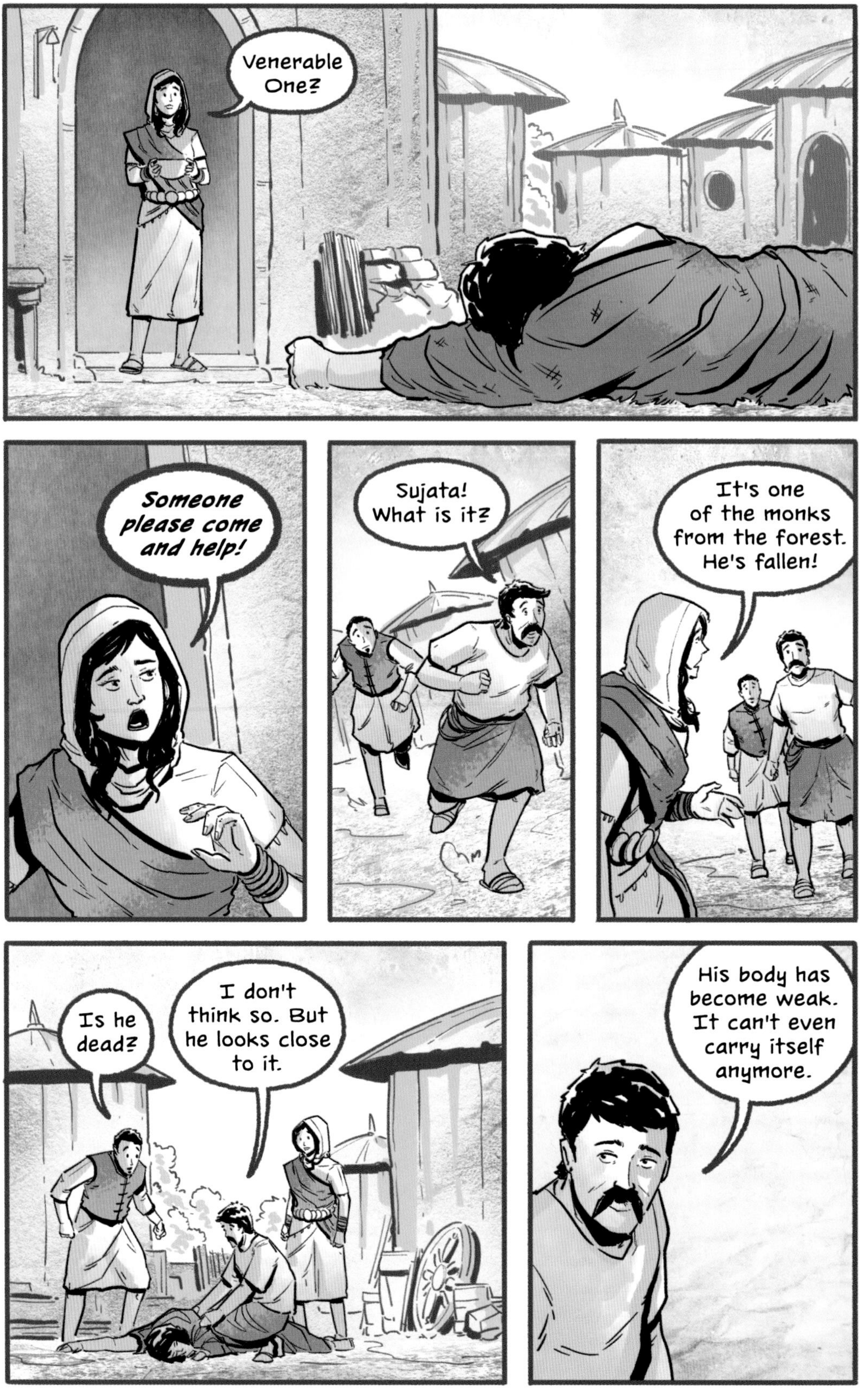
Venerable One?
Someone please come and help!
Sujata! What is it?
It's one of the monks from the forest. He's fallen!
Is he dead?
I don't think so. But he looks close to it.
His body has become weak. It can't even carry itself anymore.

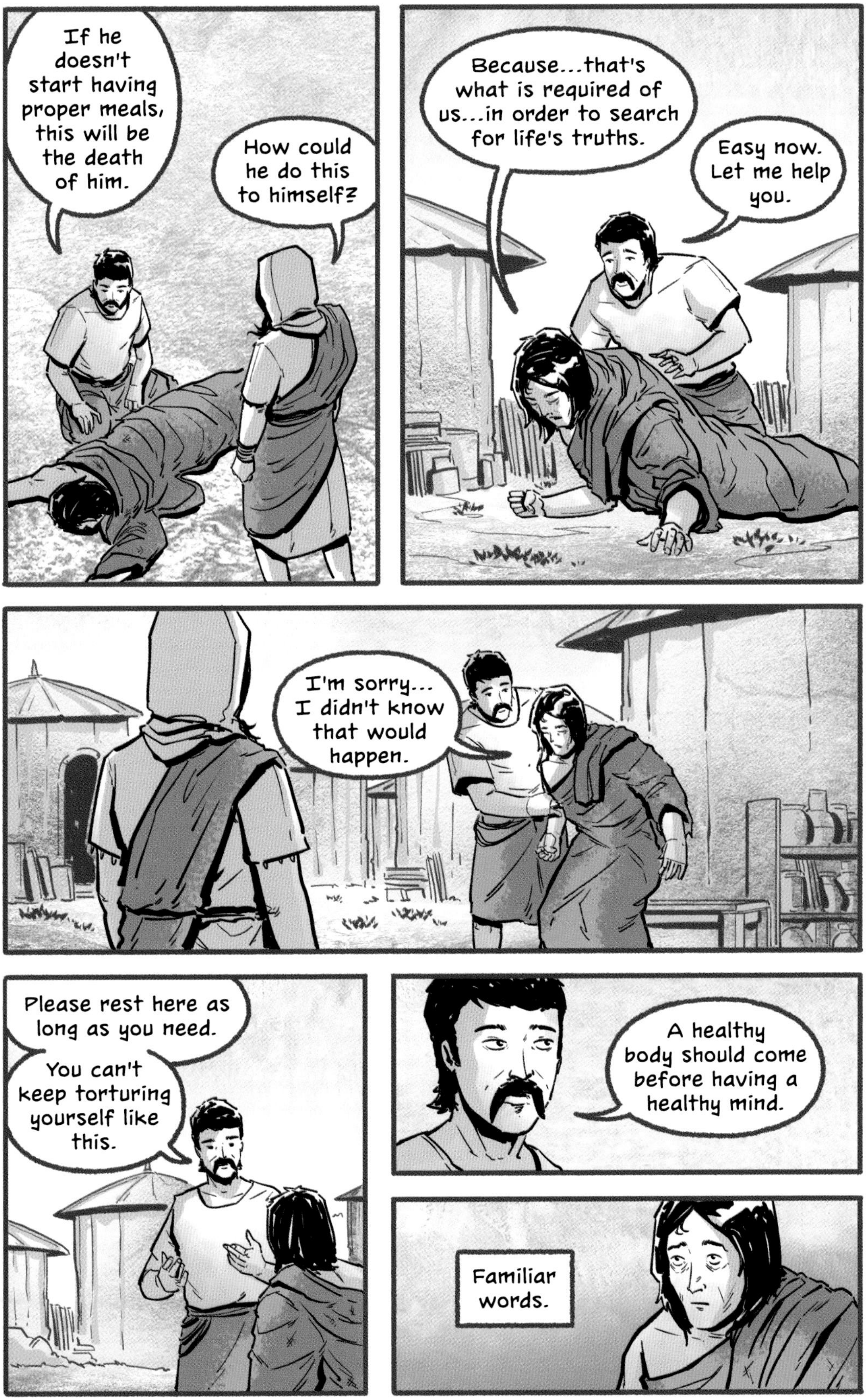

If he doesn't start having proper meals, this will be the death of him.
How could he do this to himself?
Because...that's what is required of us...in order to search for life's truths.
Easy now. Let me help you.
I'm sorry... I didn't know that would happen.
Please rest here as long as you need.
You can't keep torturing yourself like this.
A healthy body should come before having a healthy mind.
Familiar words.

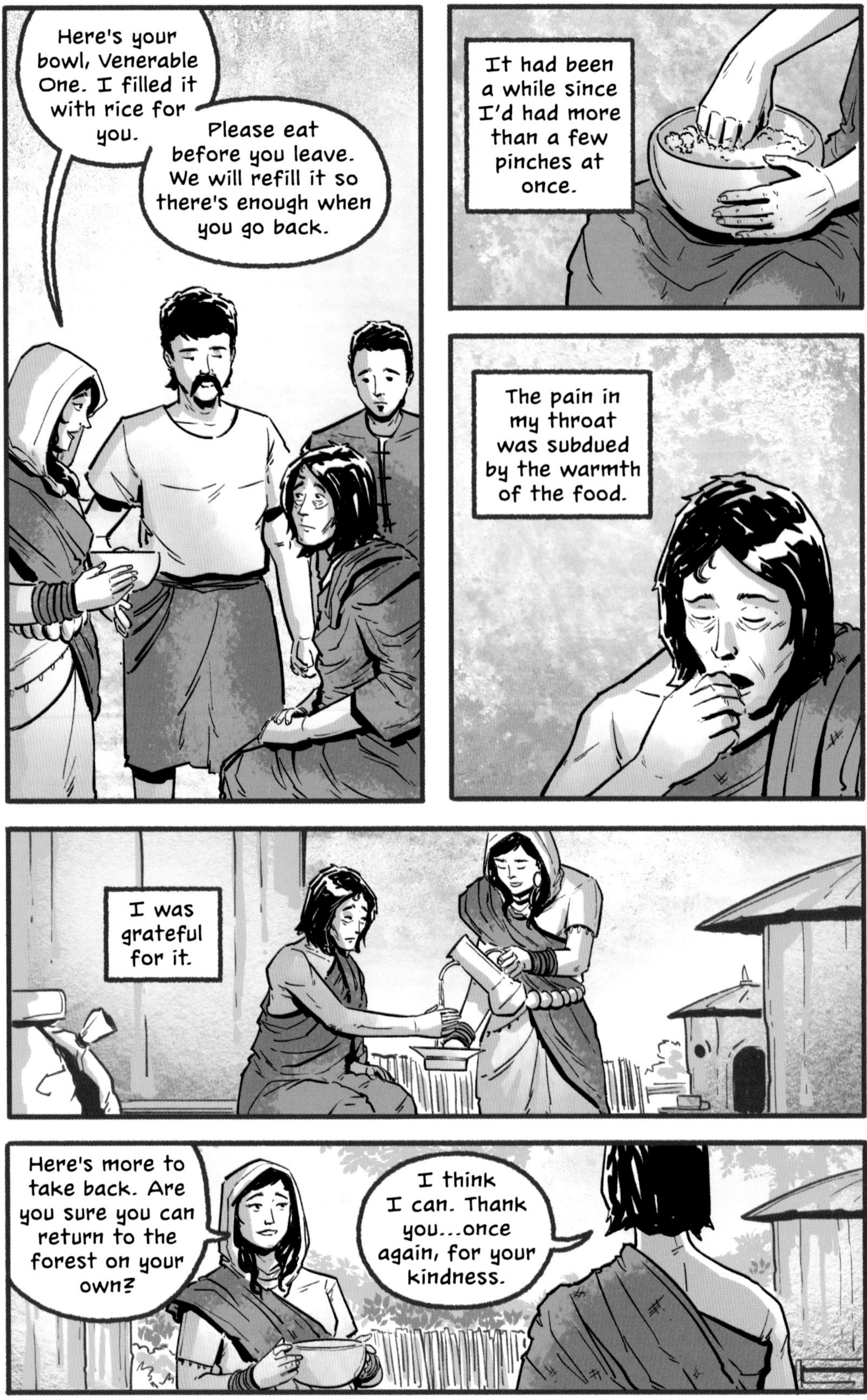
Here's your bowl, Venerable One. I filled it with rice for you.
Please eat before you leave. We will refill it so there's enough when you go back.
It had been a while since I'd had more than a few pinches at once.
The pain in my throat was subdued by the warmth of the food.
I was grateful for it.
Here's more to take back. Are you sure you can return to the forest on your own?
I think I can. Thank you...once again, for your kindness.

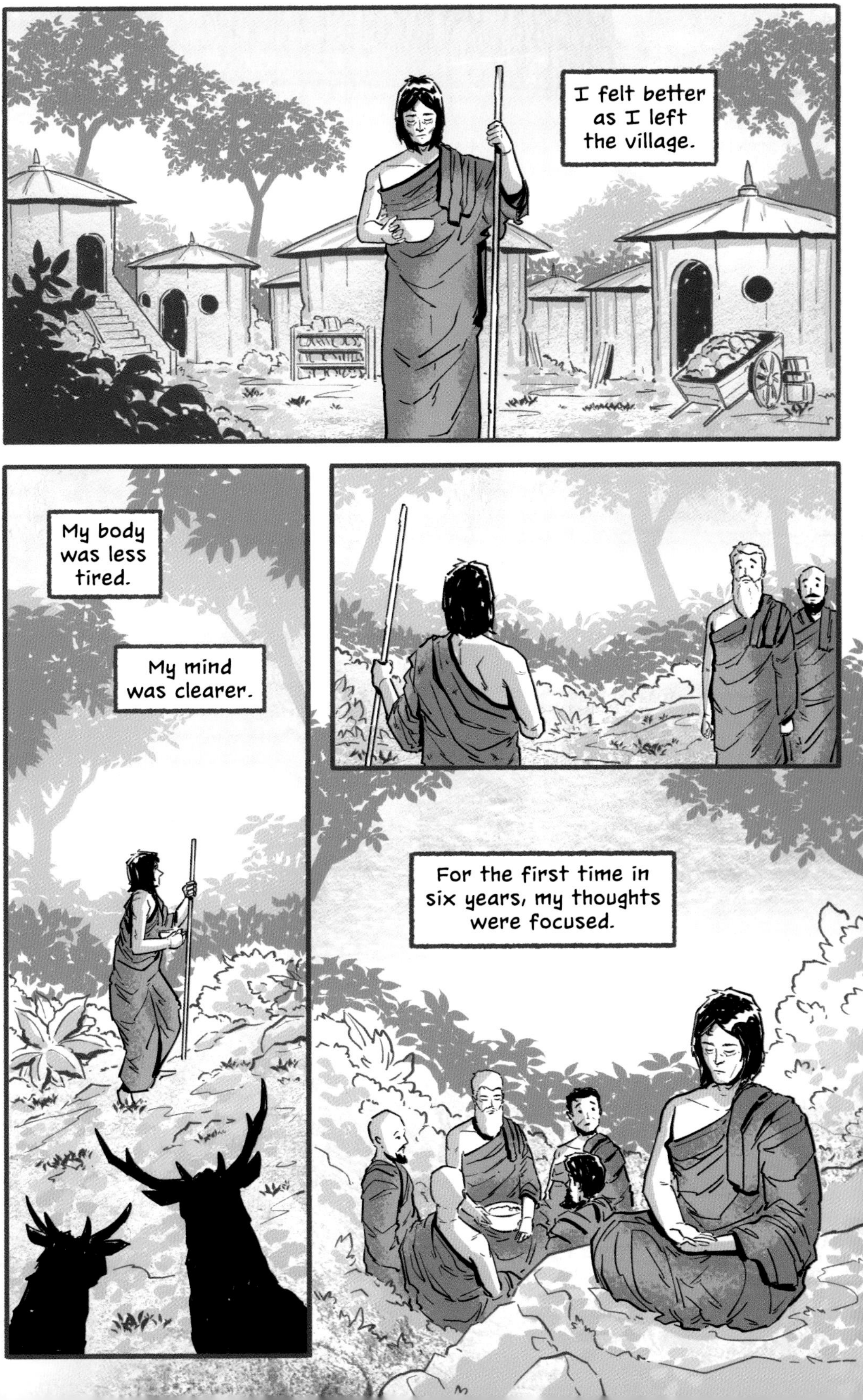
I felt better as I left the village.
My body was less tired.
My mind was clearer.
For the first time in six years, my thoughts were focused.

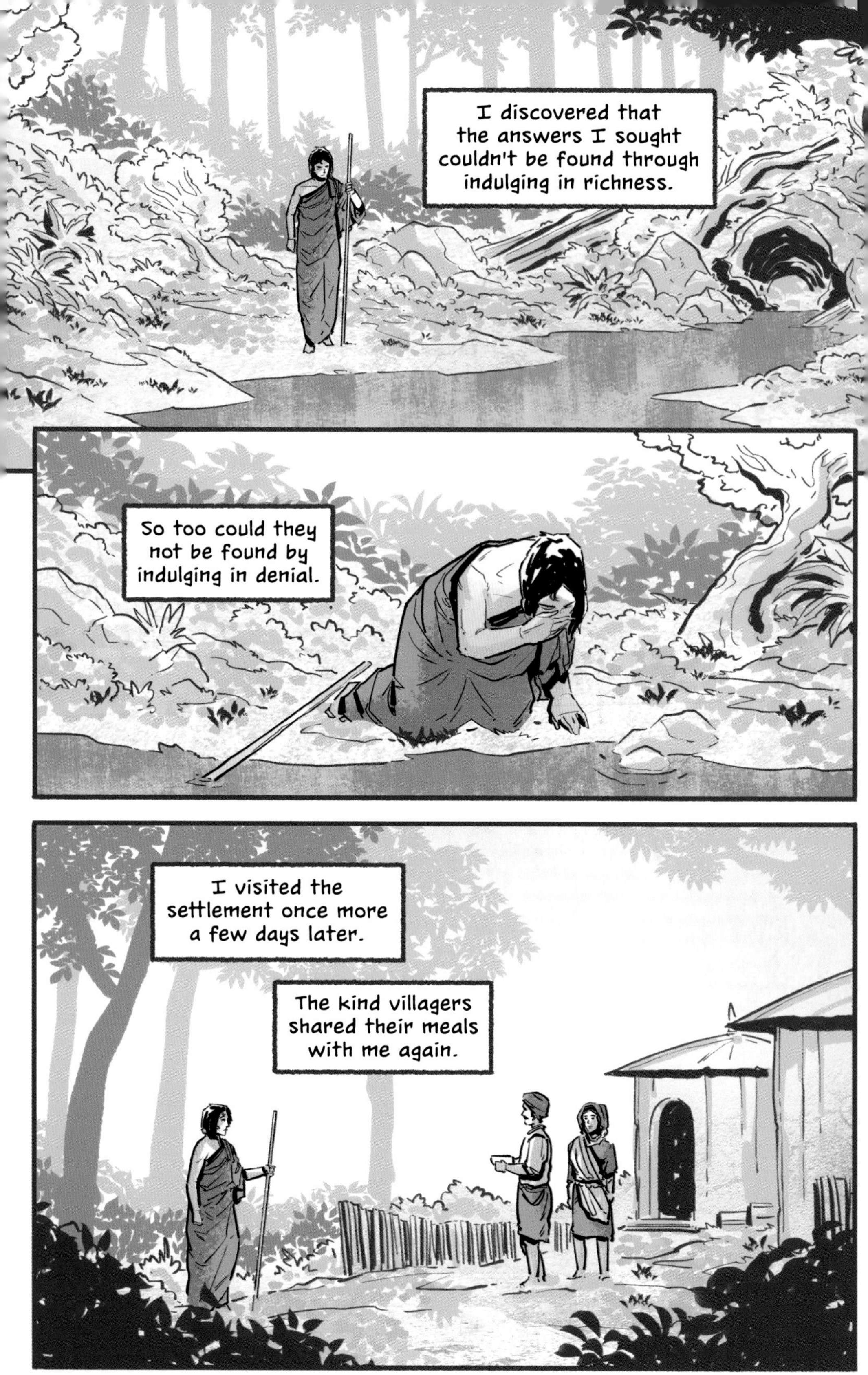
I discovered that the answers I sought couldn't be found through indulging in richness.
So too could they not be found by indulging in denial.
I visited the settlement once more a few days later.
The kind villagers shared their meals with me again.

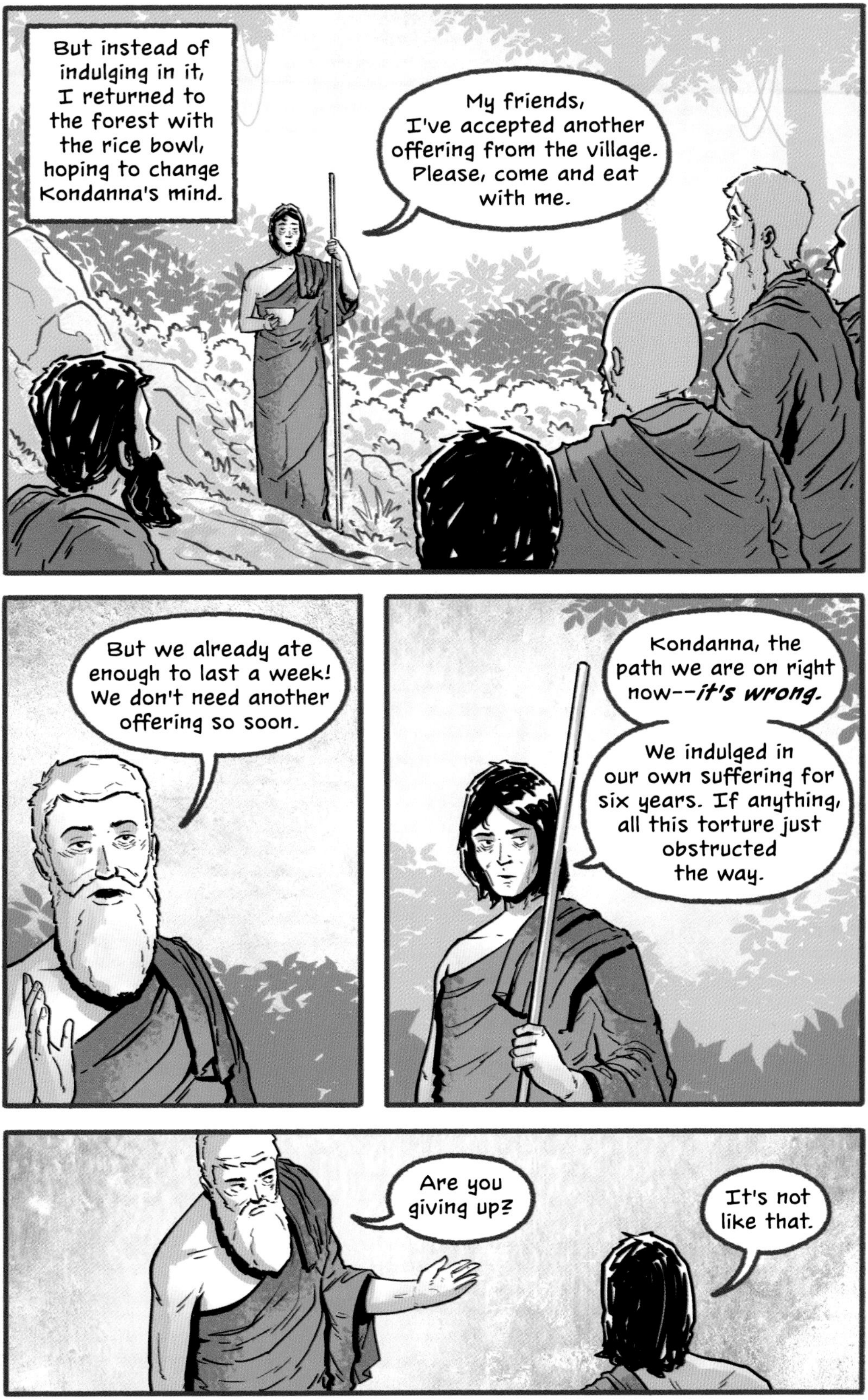

But instead of indulging in it, I returned to the forest with the rice bowl, hoping to change Kondanna's mind.
My friends, I've accepted another offering from the village. Please, come and eat with me.
But we already ate enough to last a week! We don't need another offering so soon.
Kondanna, the path we are on right now--*it's wrong.*
We indulged in our own suffering for six years. If anything, all this torture just obstructed the way.
Are you giving up?
It's not like that.

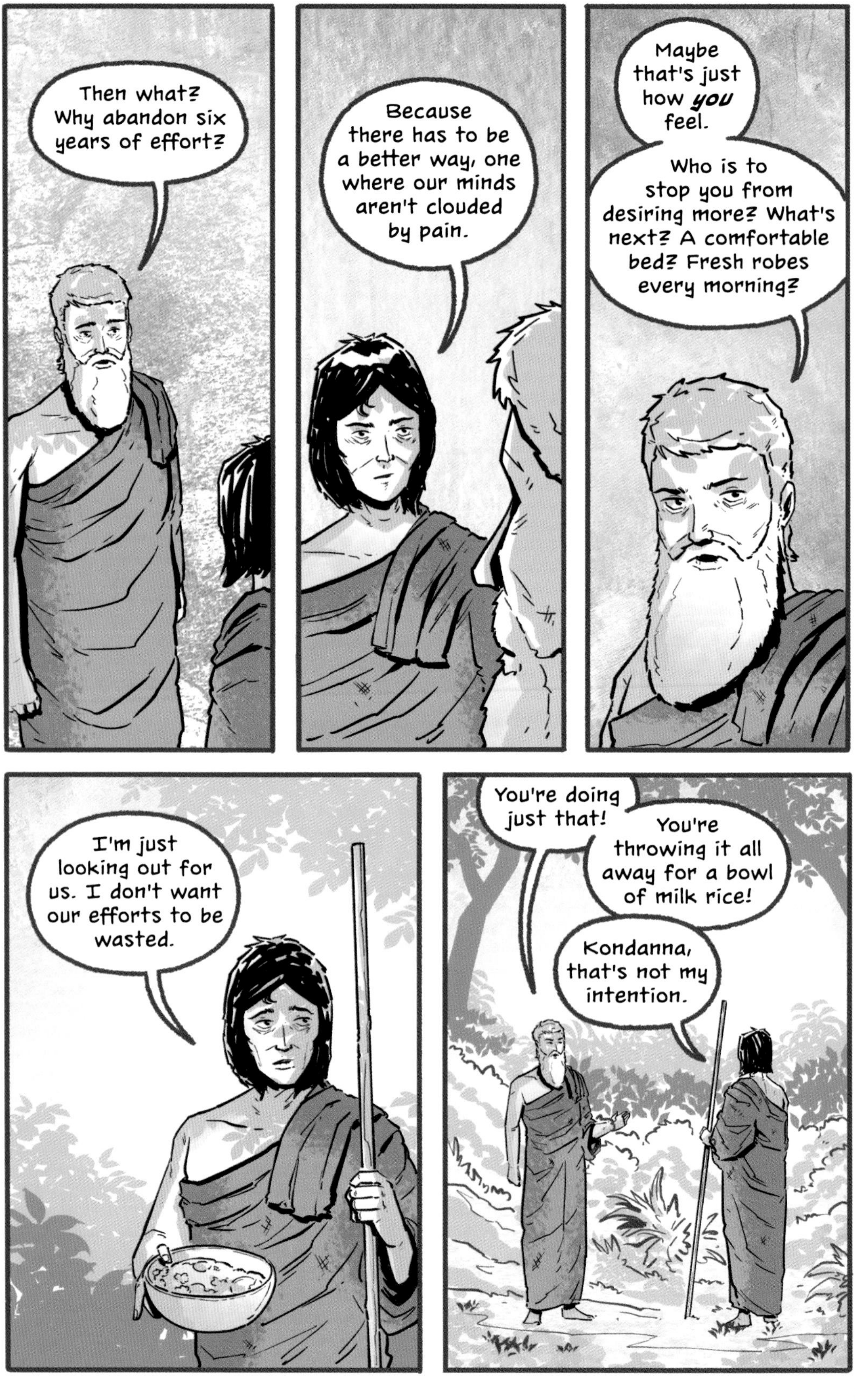
Then what? Why abandon six years of effort?
Because there has to be a better way, one where our minds aren't clouded by pain.
Maybe that's just how *you* feel.
Who is to stop you from desiring more? What's next? A comfortable bed? Fresh robes every morning?
I'm just looking out for us. I don't want our efforts to be wasted.
You're doing just that!
You're throwing it all away for a bowl of milk rice!
Kondanna, that's not my intention.

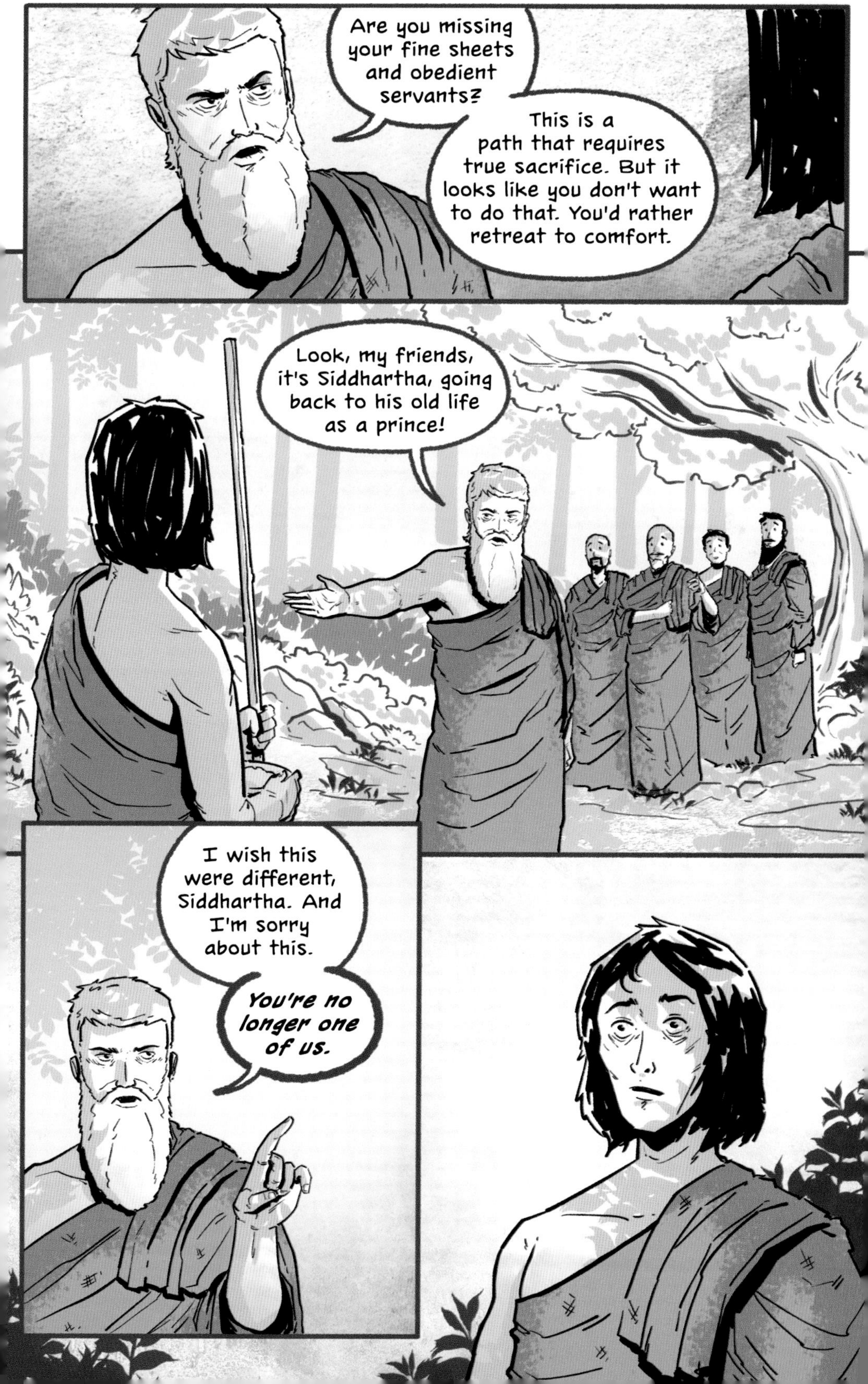
Are you missing your fine sheets and obedient servants?
This is a path that requires true sacrifice. But it looks like you don't want to do that. You'd rather retreat to comfort.
Look, my friends, it's Siddhartha, going back to his old life as a prince!
I wish this were different, Siddhartha. And I'm sorry about this.
You're no longer one of us.

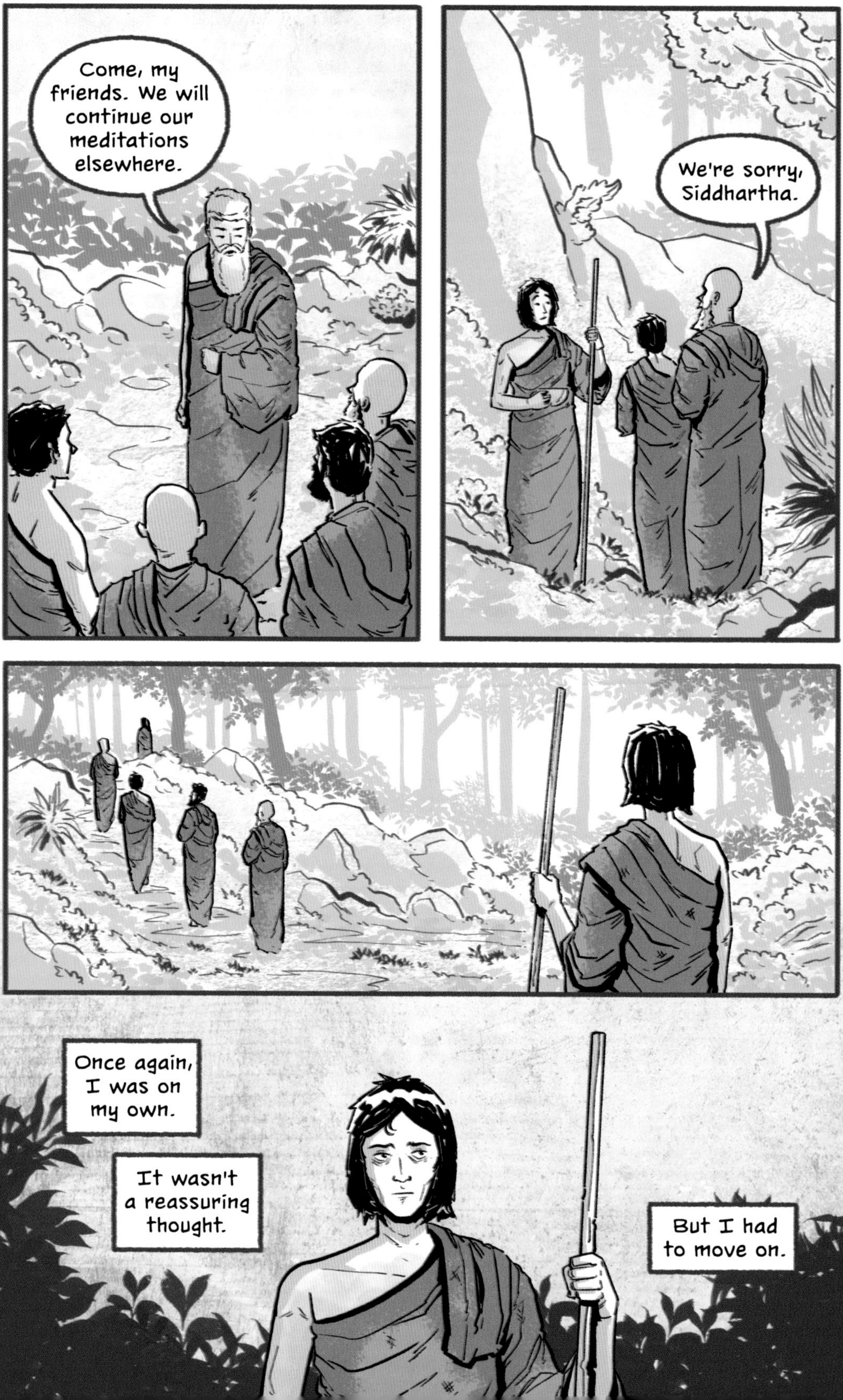
Come, my friends. We will continue our meditations elsewhere.
We're sorry, Siddhartha.
Once again, I was on my own.
It wasn't a reassuring thought.
But I had to move on.

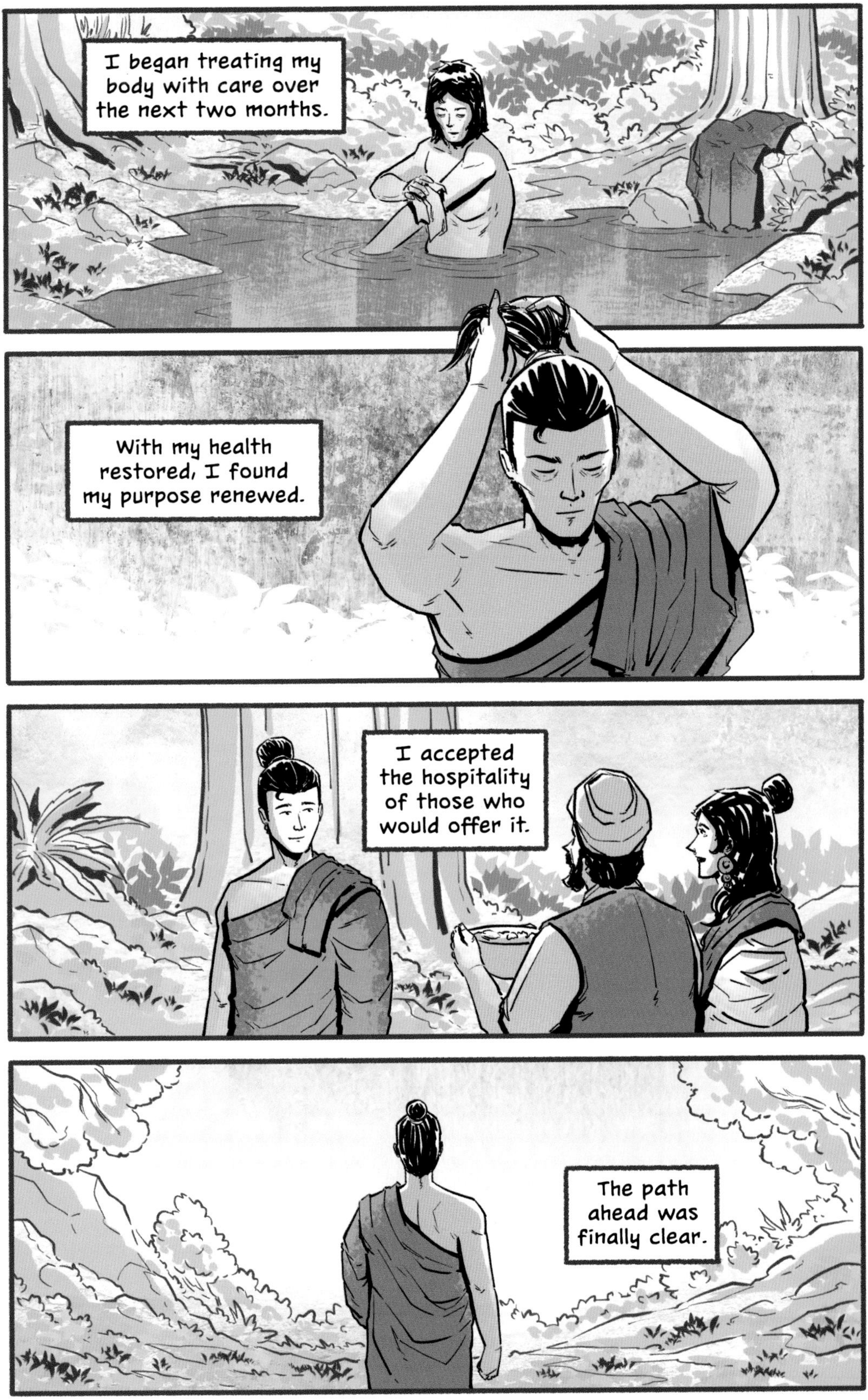
I began treating my body with care over the next two months.
With my health restored, I found my purpose renewed.
I accepted the hospitality of those who would offer it.
The path ahead was finally clear.

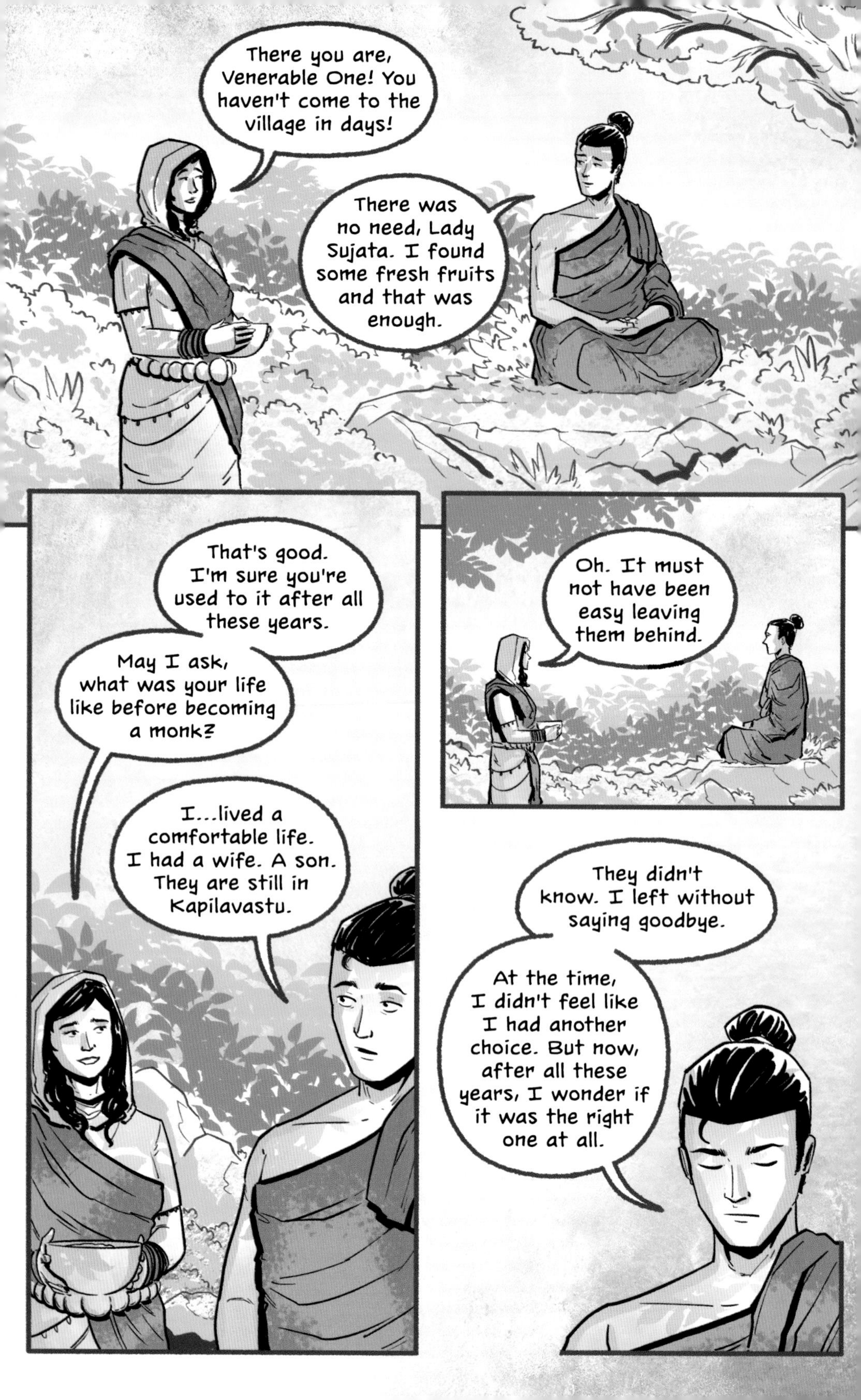
There you are, Venerable One! You haven't come to the village in days!
There was no need, Lady Sujata. I found some fresh fruits and that was enough.
That's good. I'm sure you're used to it after all these years.
May I ask, what was your life like before becoming a monk?
I...lived a comfortable life. I had a wife. A son. They are still in Kapilavastu.
Oh. It must not have been easy leaving them behind.
They didn't know. I left without saying goodbye.
At the time, I didn't feel like I had another choice. But now, after all these years, I wonder if it was the right one at all.

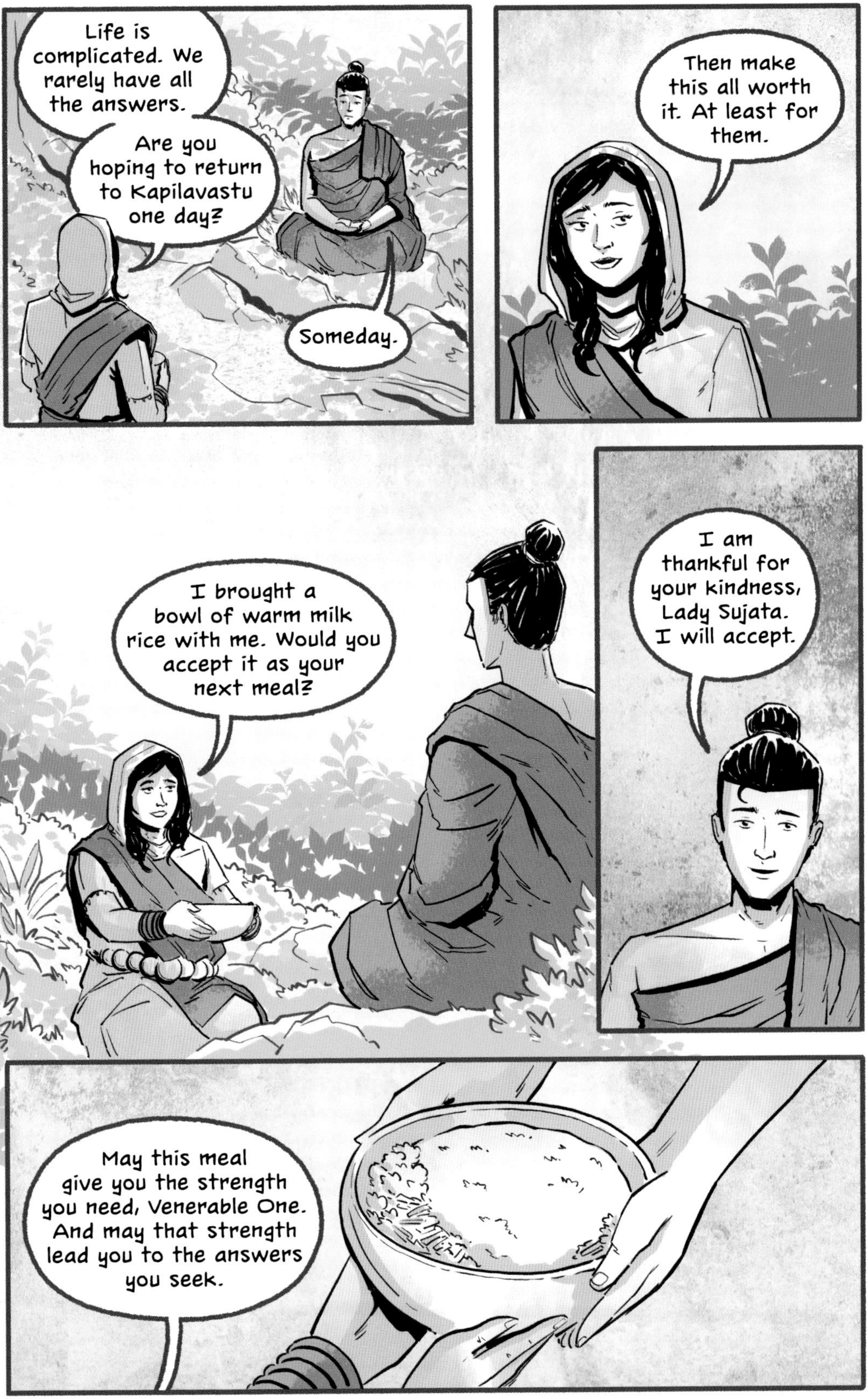
Life is complicated. We rarely have all the answers.
Are you hoping to return to Kapilavastu one day?
Someday.
Then make this all worth it. At least for them.
I brought a bowl of warm milk rice with me. Would you accept it as your next meal?
I am thankful for your kindness, Lady Sujata. I will accept.
May this meal give you the strength you need, Venerable One. And may that strength lead you to the answers you seek.

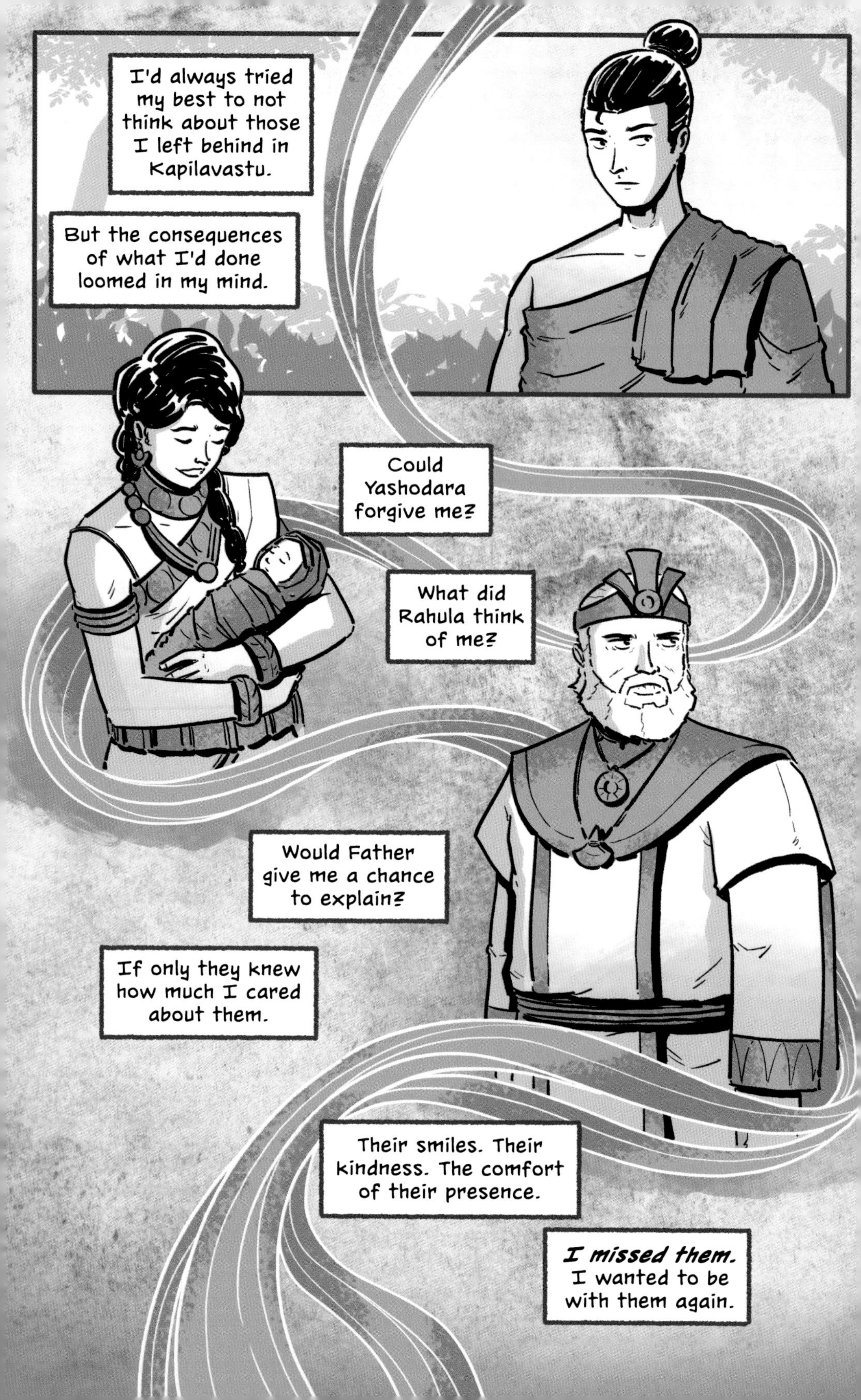
I'd always tried my best to not think about those I left behind in Kapilavastu.
But the consequences of what I'd done loomed in my mind.
Could Yashodara forgive me?
What did Rahula think of me?
Would Father give me a chance to explain?
If only they knew how much I cared about them.
Their smiles. Their kindness. The comfort of their presence.
I missed them. I wanted to be with them again.

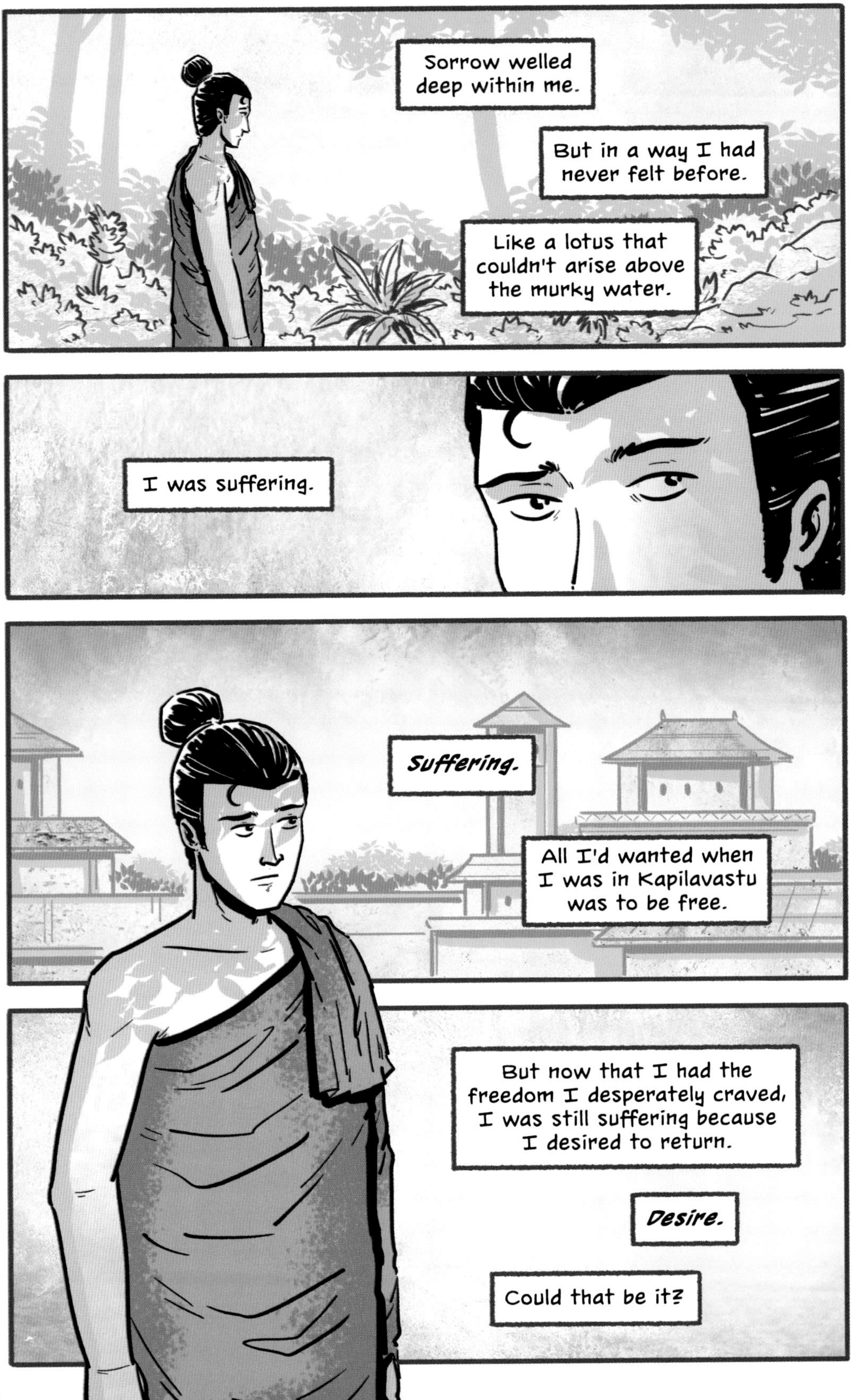
Sorrow welled deep within me.
But in a way I had never felt before.
Like a lotus that couldn't arise above the murky water.
I was suffering.
Suffering.
All I'd wanted when I was in Kapilavastu was to be free.
But now that I had the freedom I desperately craved, I was still suffering because I desired to return.
Desire.
Could that be it?

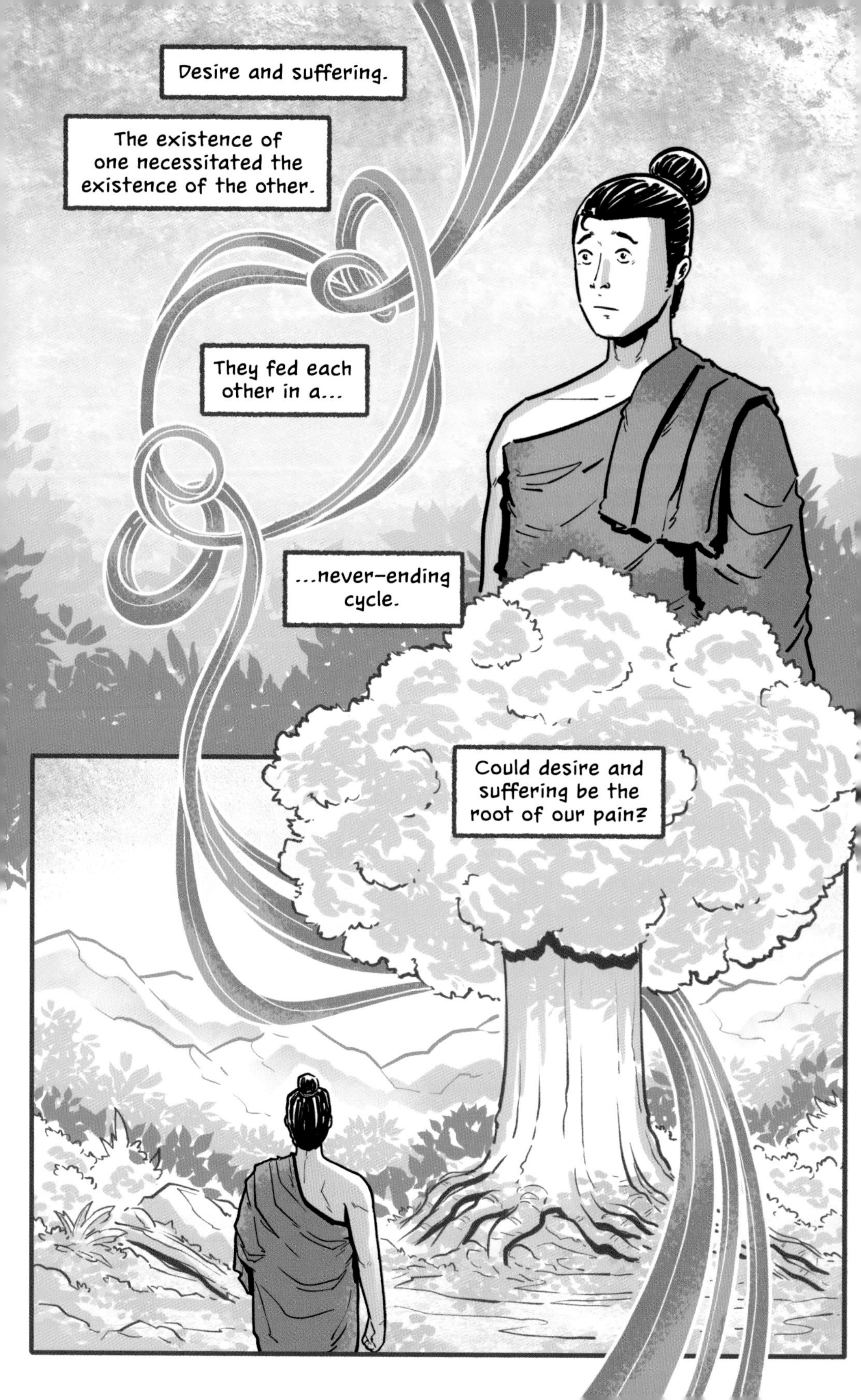
Desire and suffering.
The existence of one necessitated the existence of the other.
They fed each other in a...
...never-ending cycle.
Could desire and suffering be the root of our pain?

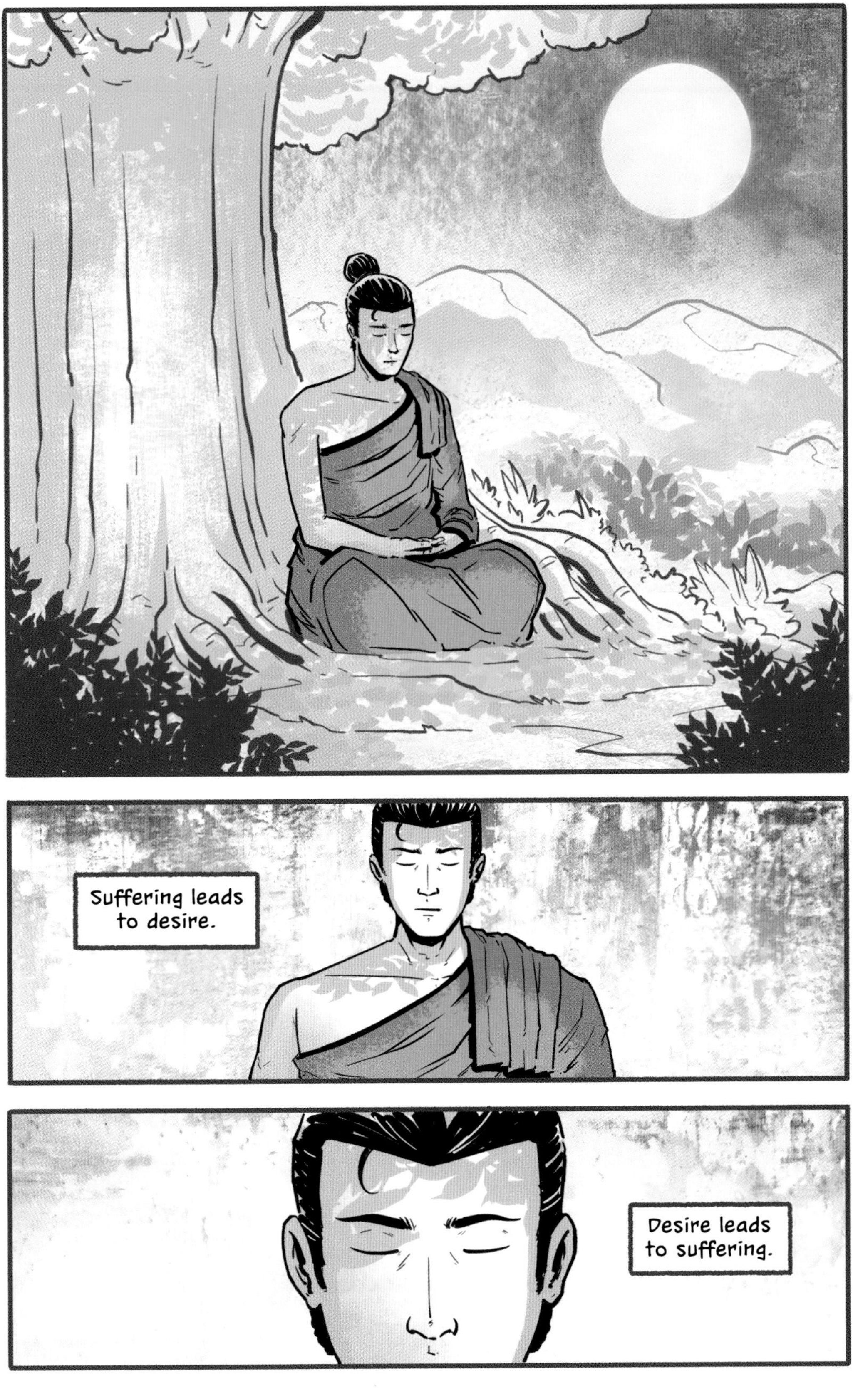
Suffering leads to desire.
Desire leads to suffering.

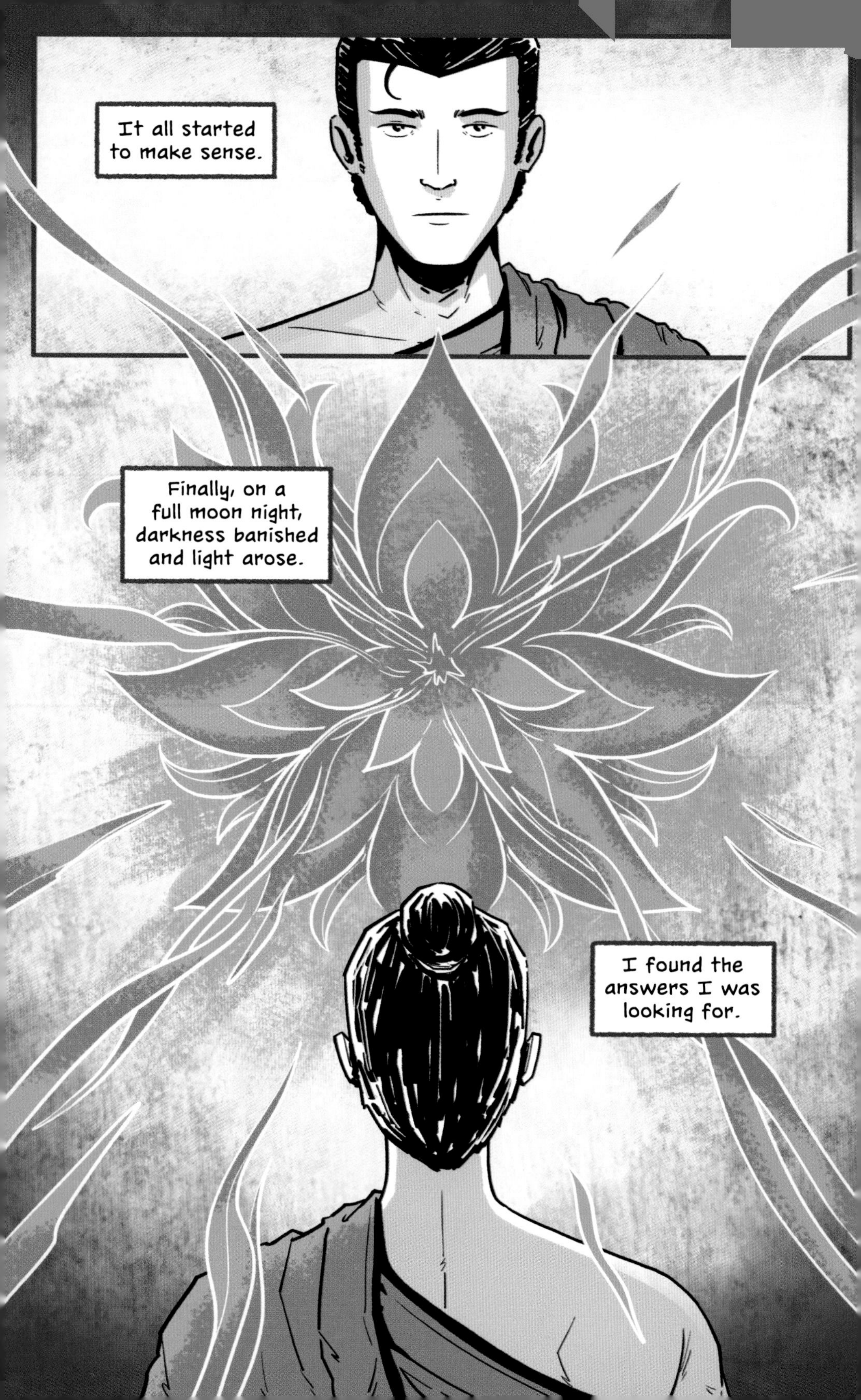
It all started to make sense.
Finally, on a full moon night, darkness banished and light arose.
I found the answers I was looking for.

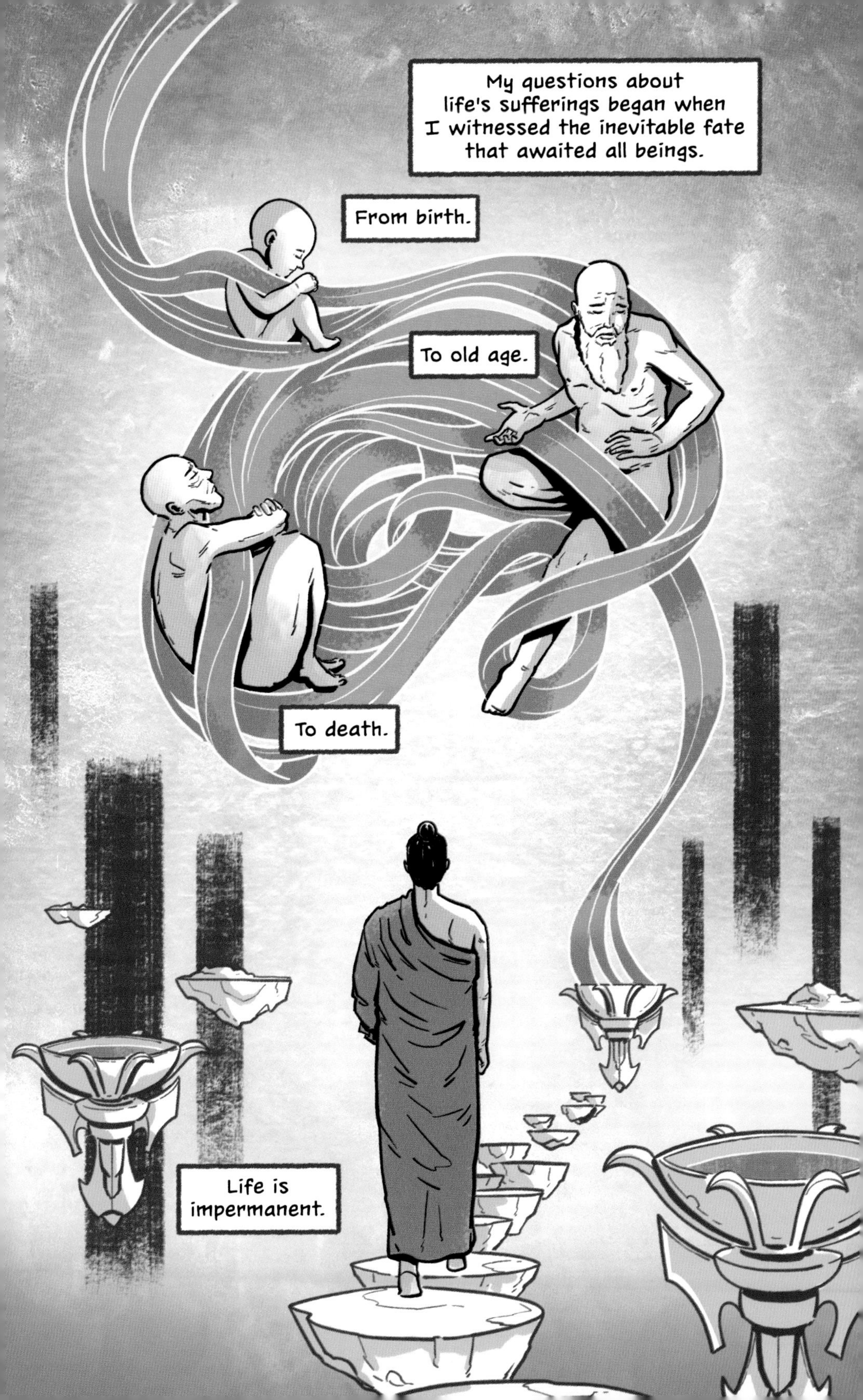
My questions about life's sufferings began when I witnessed the inevitable fate that awaited all beings.
From birth.
To old age.
To death.
Life is impermanent.

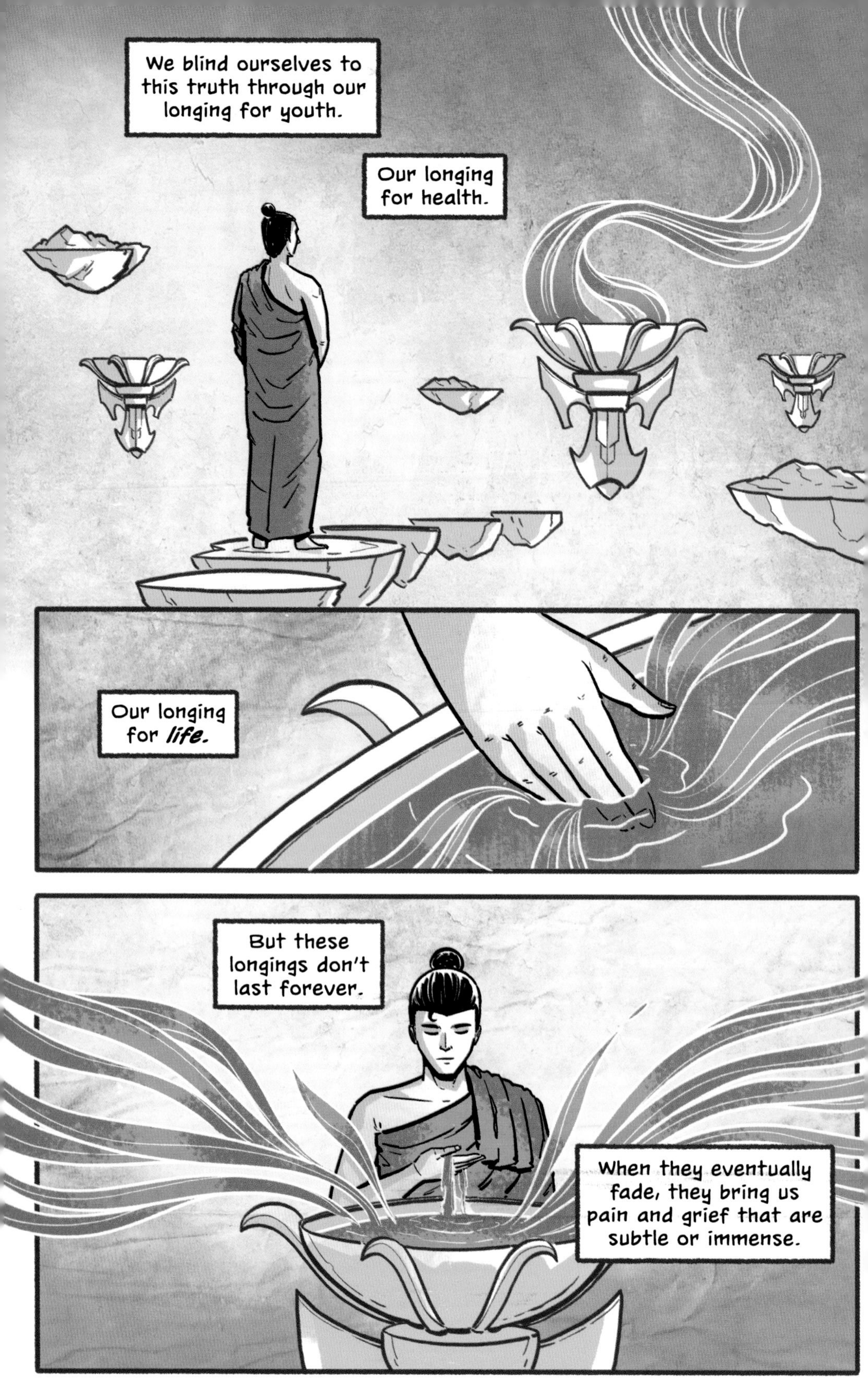
We blind ourselves to this truth through our longing for youth.
Our longing for health.
Our longing for *life.*
But these longings don't last forever.
When they eventually fade, they bring us pain and grief that are subtle or immense.

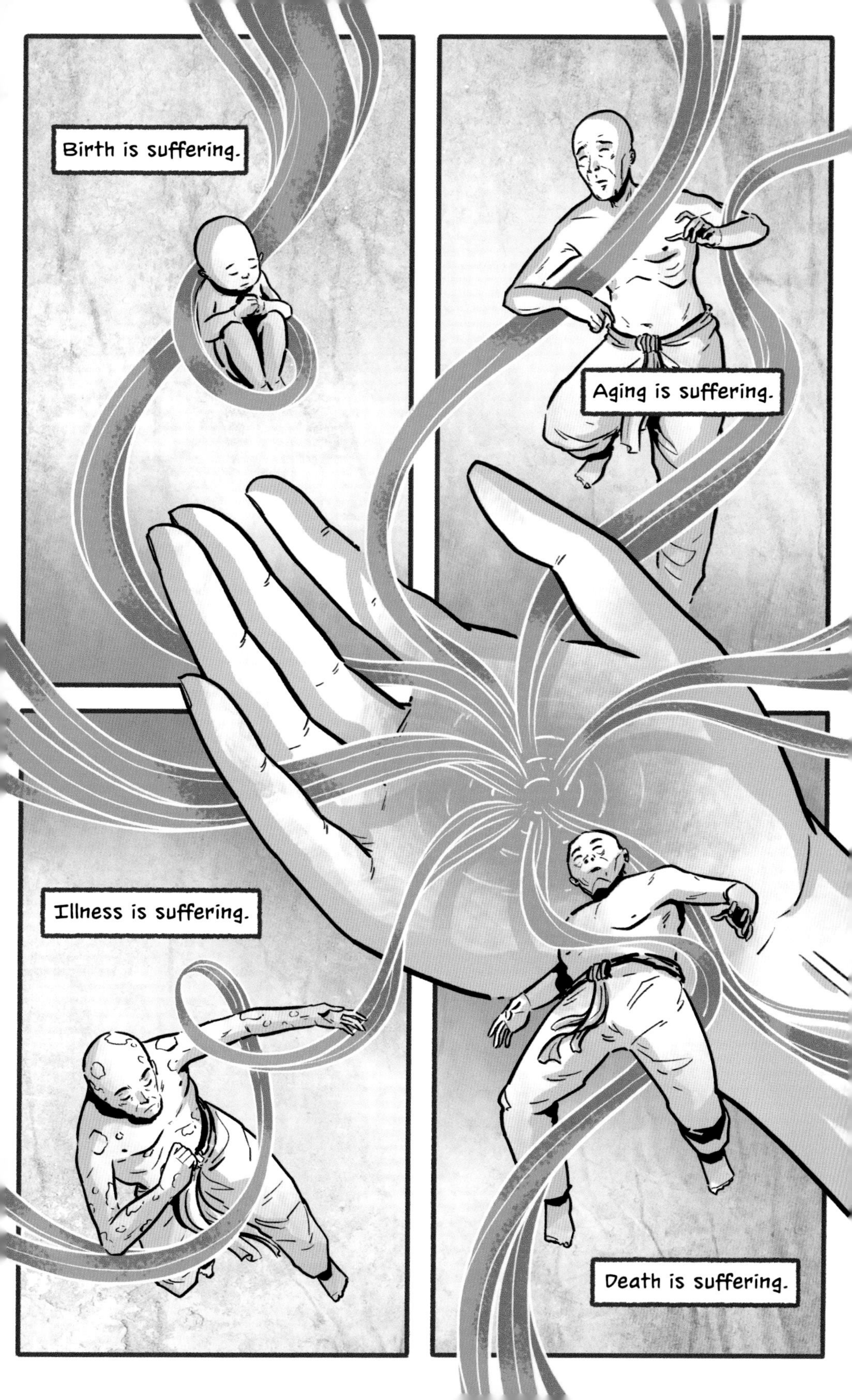
Birth is suffering.
Aging is suffering.
Illness is suffering.
Death is suffering.

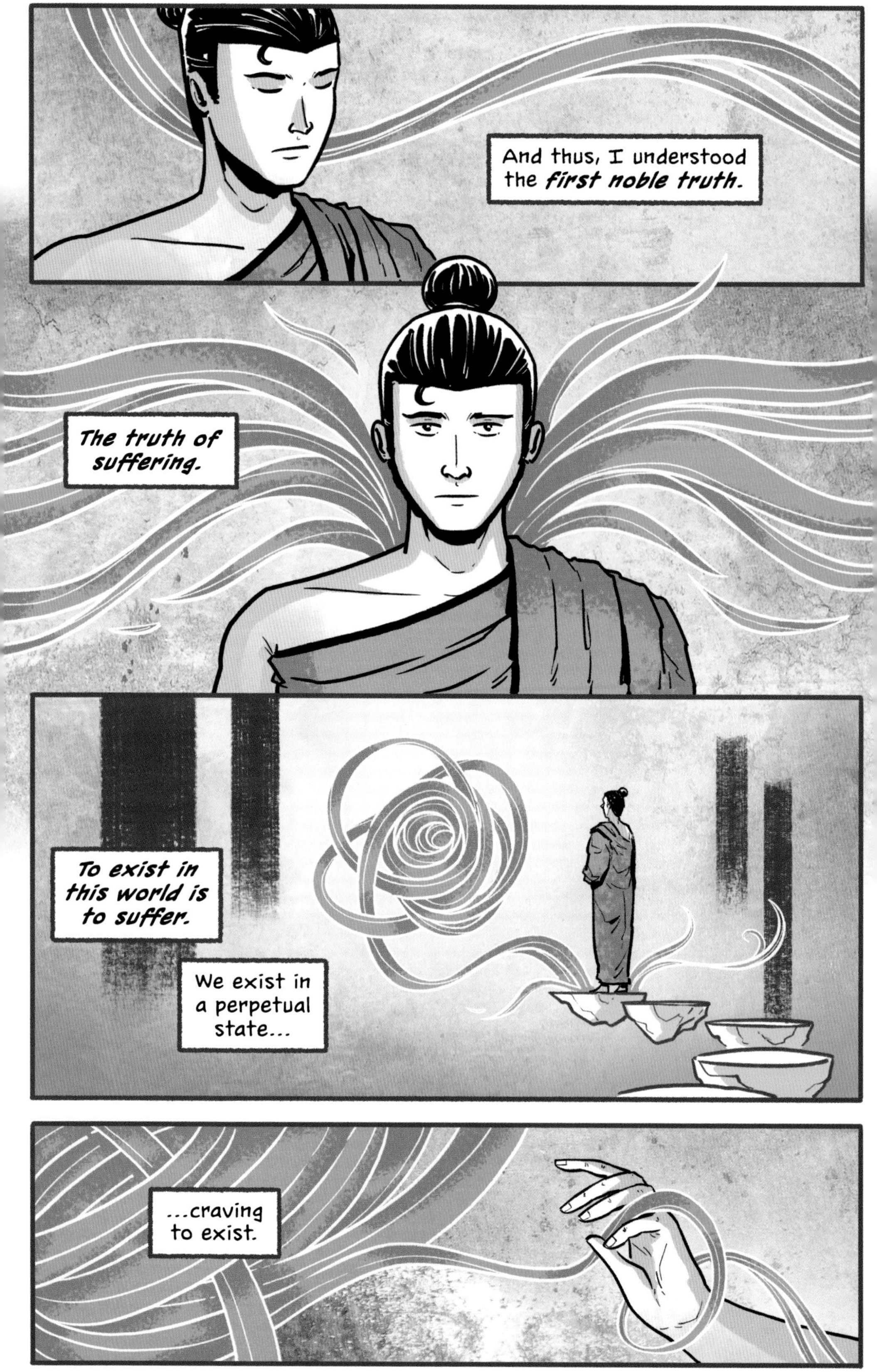
And thus, I understood the *first noble truth.*
The truth of suffering.
To exist in this world is to suffer.
We exist in a perpetual state...
...craving to exist.

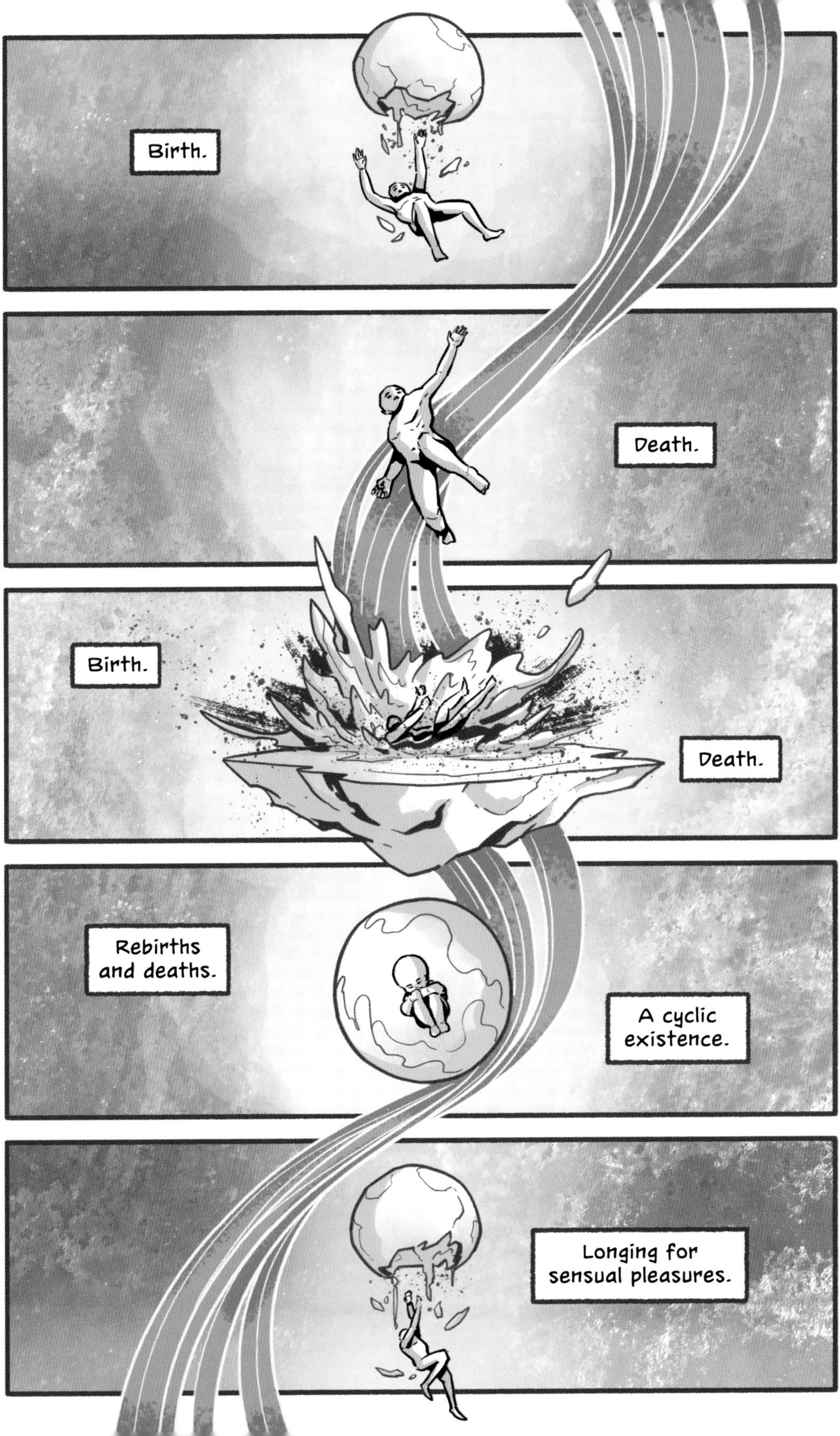
Birth.
Death.
Birth.
Death.
Rebirths and deaths.
A cyclic existence.
Longing for sensual pleasures.

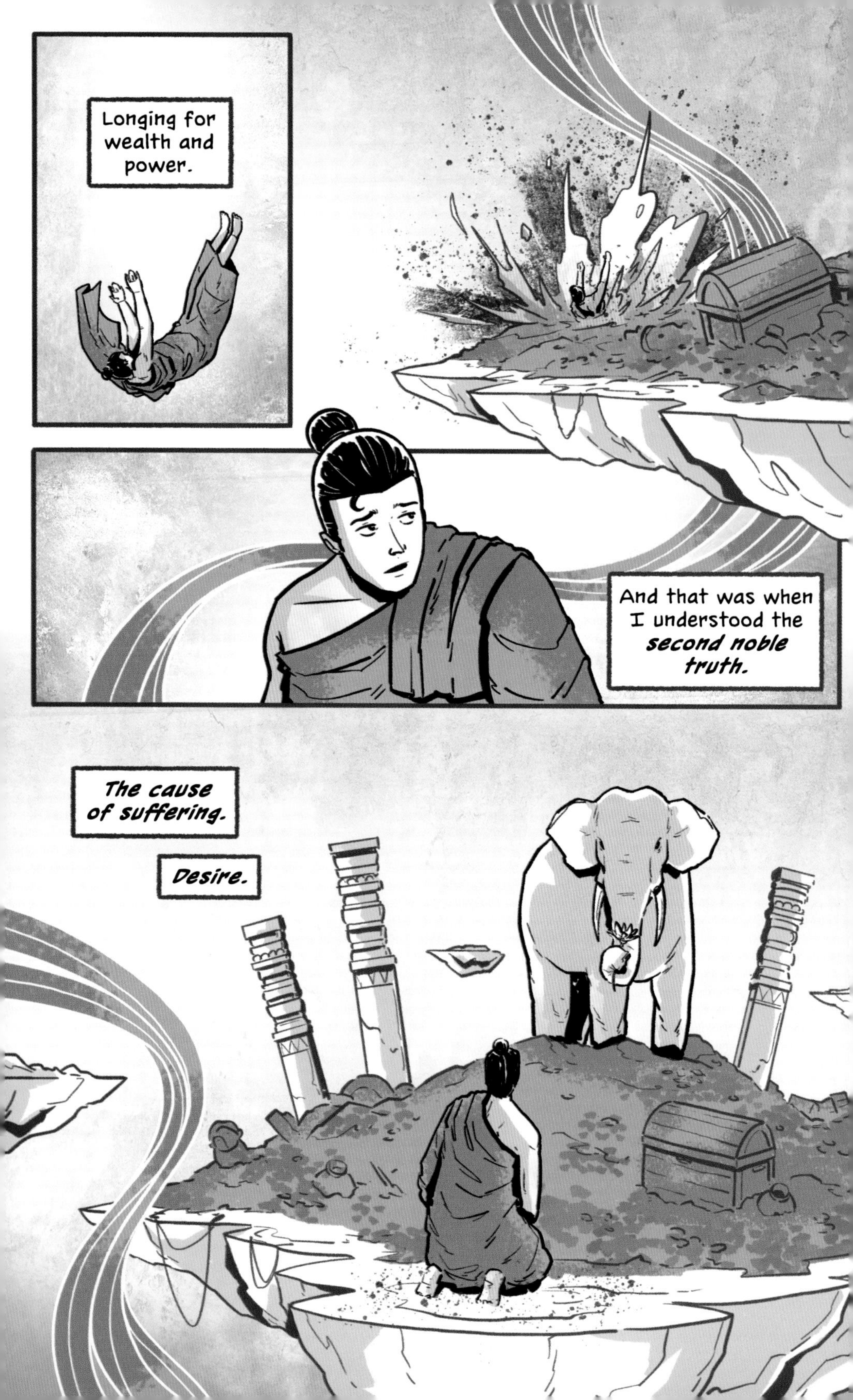

Longing for wealth and power.
And that was when I understood the *second noble truth.*
The cause of suffering.
Desire.

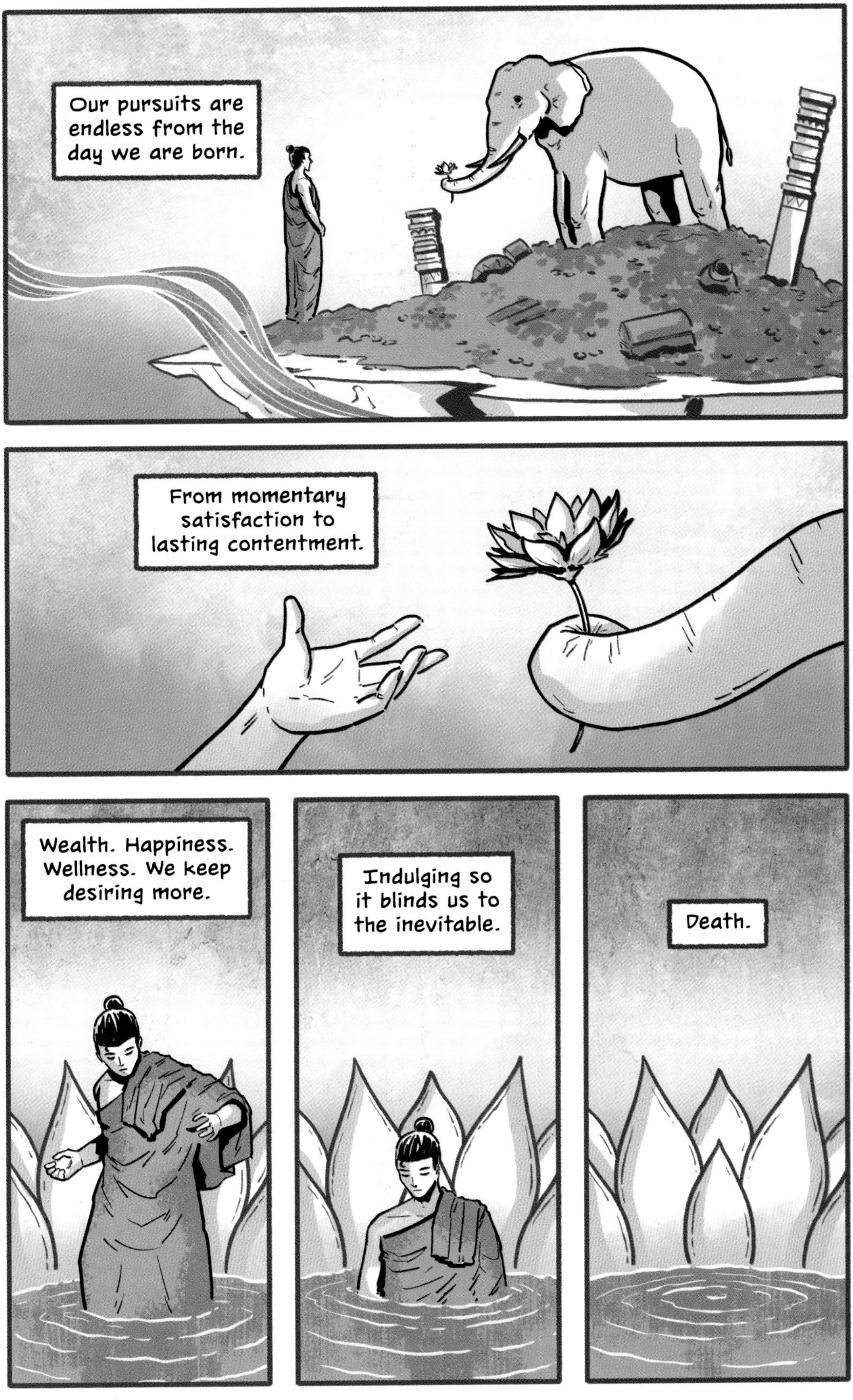
Our pursuits are endless from the day we are born.
From momentary satisfaction to lasting contentment.
Wealth. Happiness. Wellness. We keep desiring more.
Indulging so it blinds us to the inevitable.
Death.

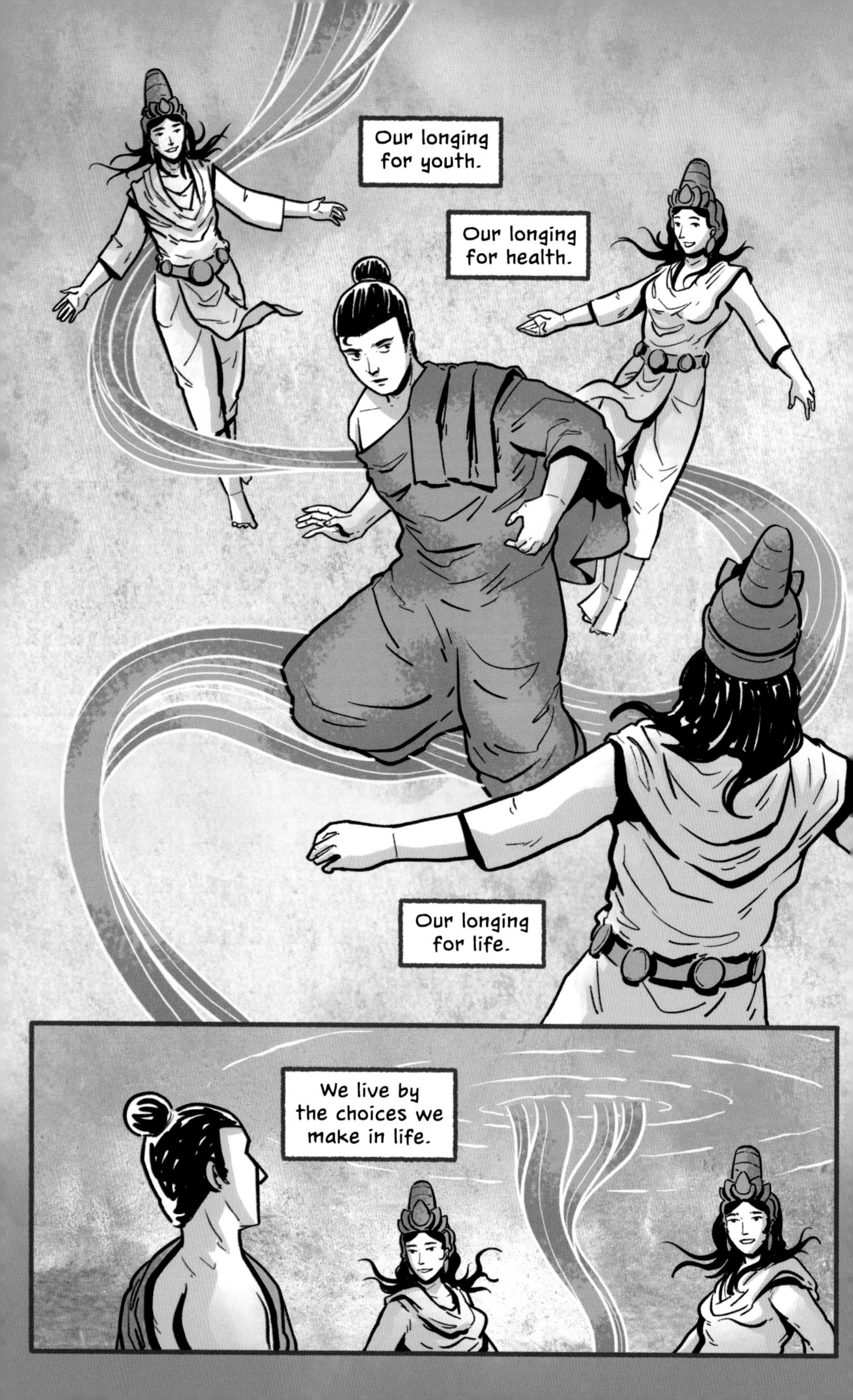
Our longing for youth.
Our longing for health.
Our longing for life.
We live by the choices we make in life.

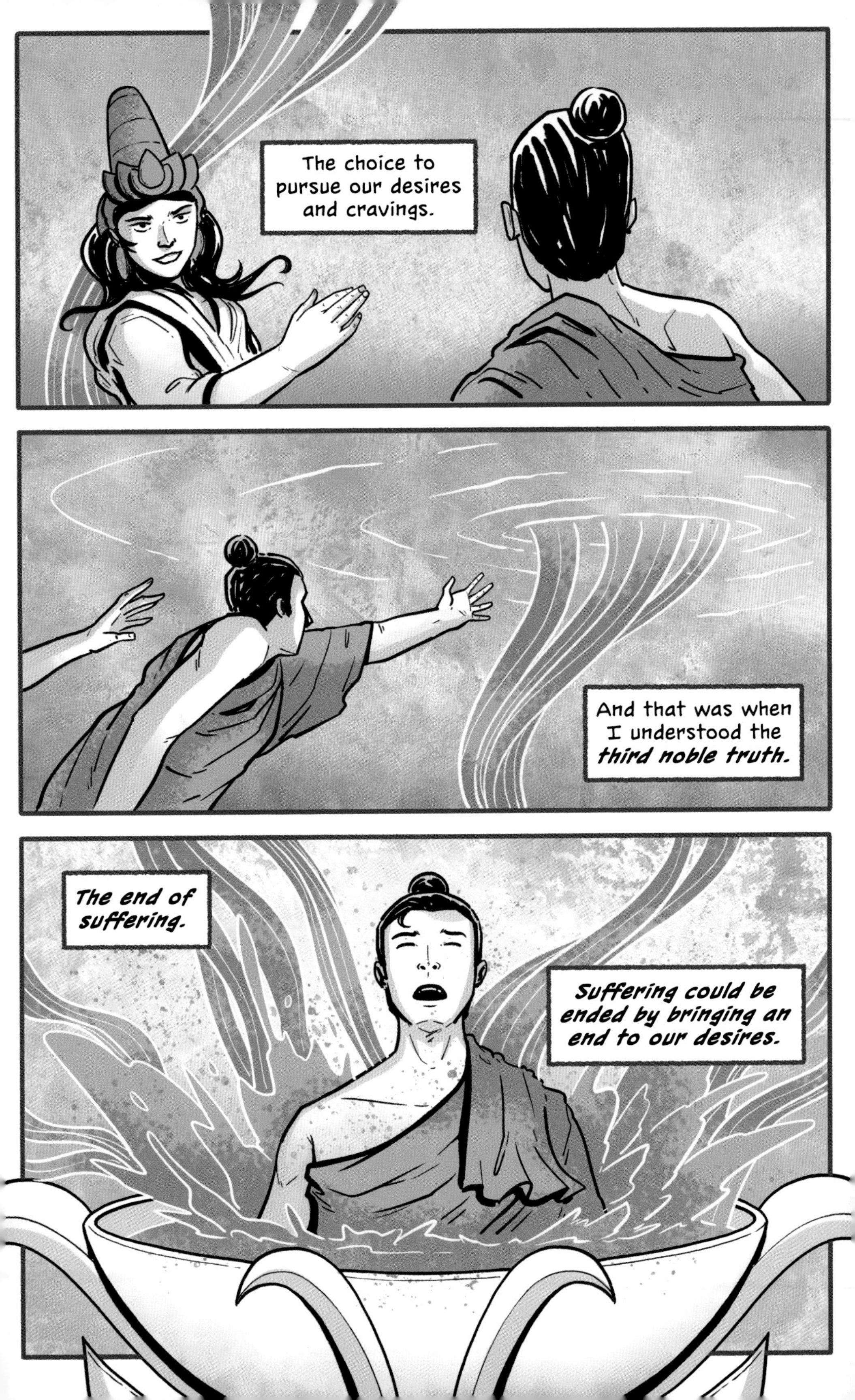
The choice to pursue our desires and cravings.
And that was when I understood the *third noble truth.*
The end of suffering.
Suffering could be ended by bringing an end to our desires.

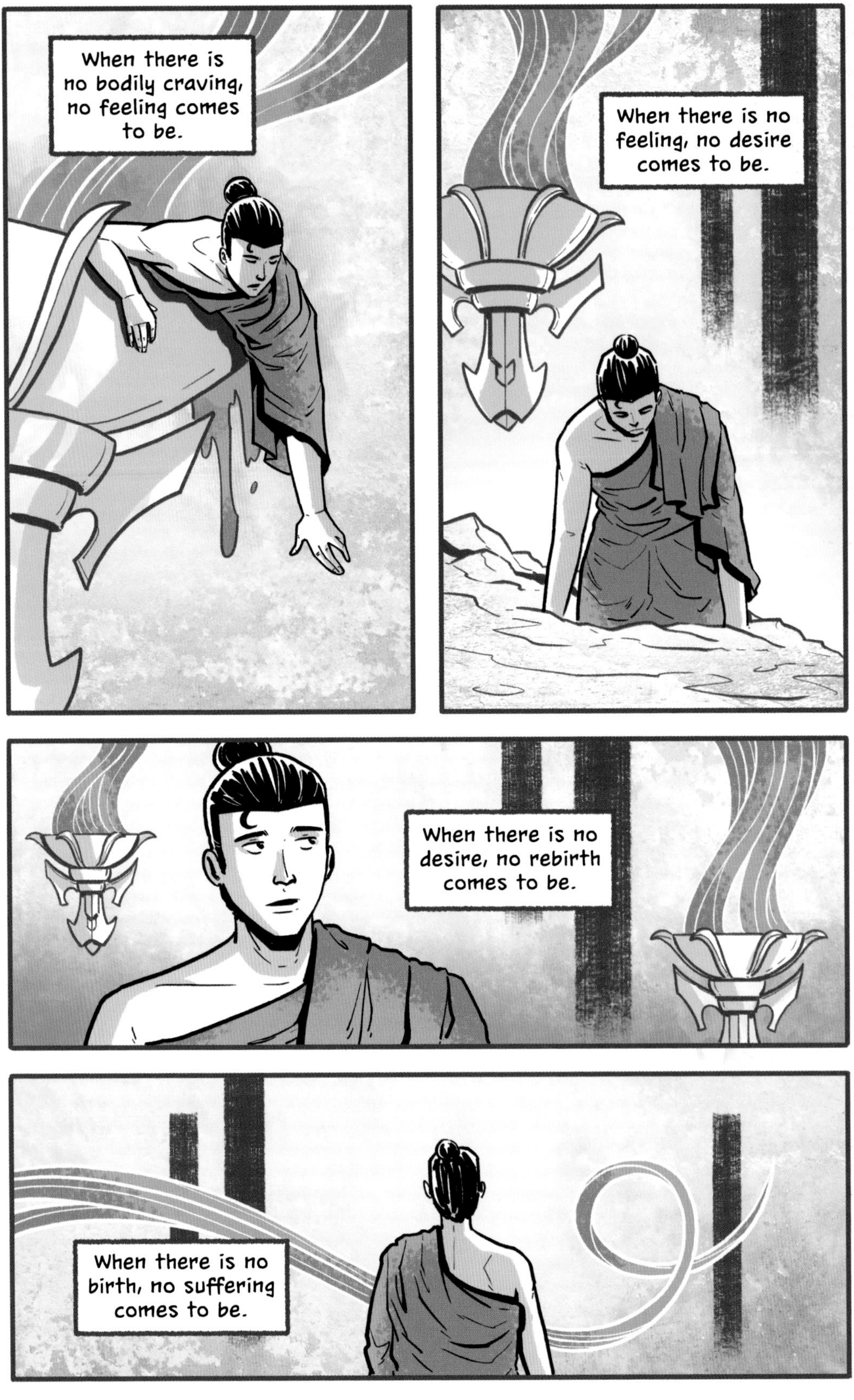
When there is no bodily craving, no feeling comes to be.
When there is no feeling, no desire comes to be.
When there is no desire, no rebirth comes to be.
When there is no birth, no suffering comes to be.

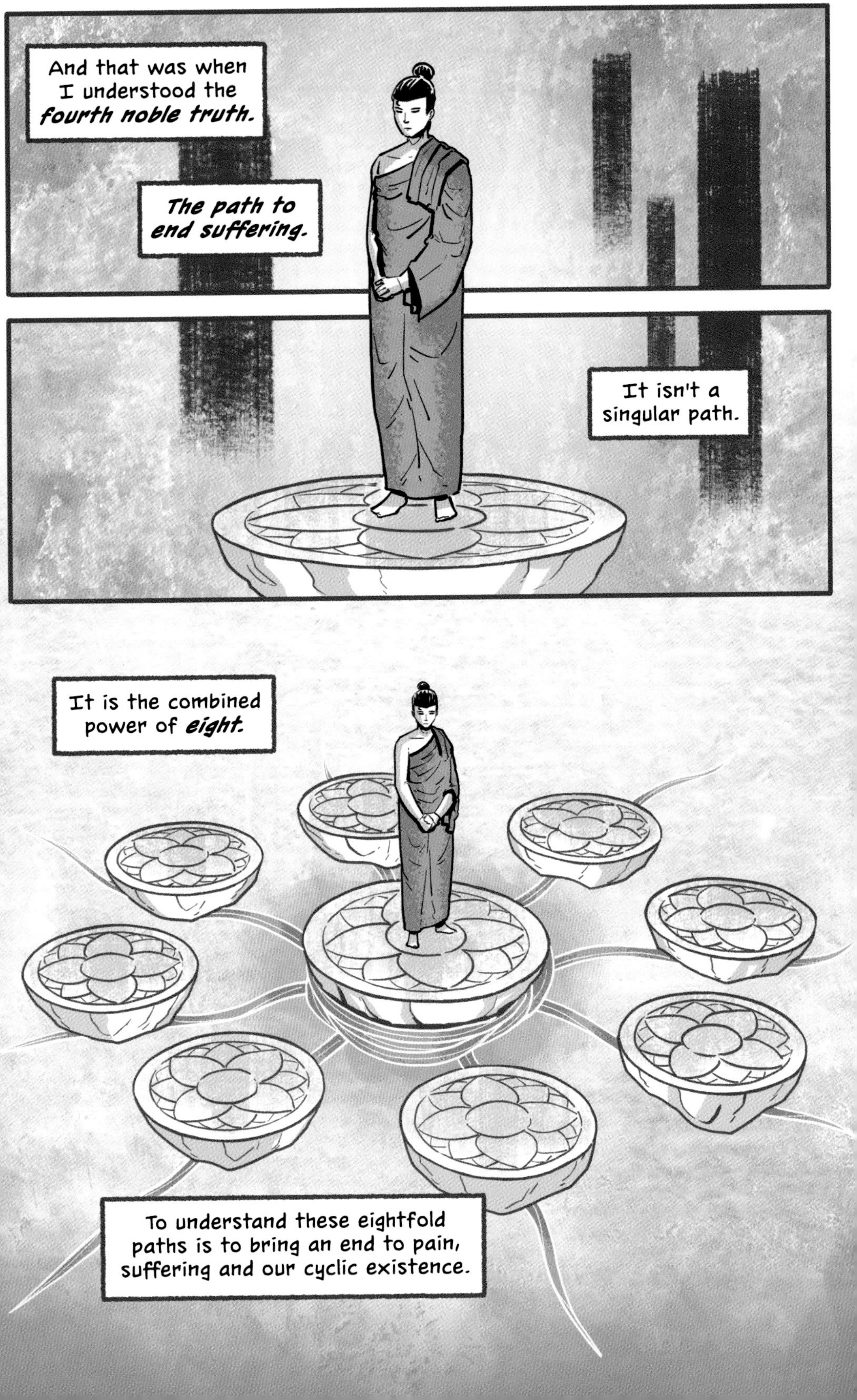
And that was when I understood the *fourth noble truth.*
The path to end suffering.
It isn't a singular path.
It is the combined power of *eight.*
To understand these eightfold paths is to bring an end to pain, suffering and our cyclic existence.

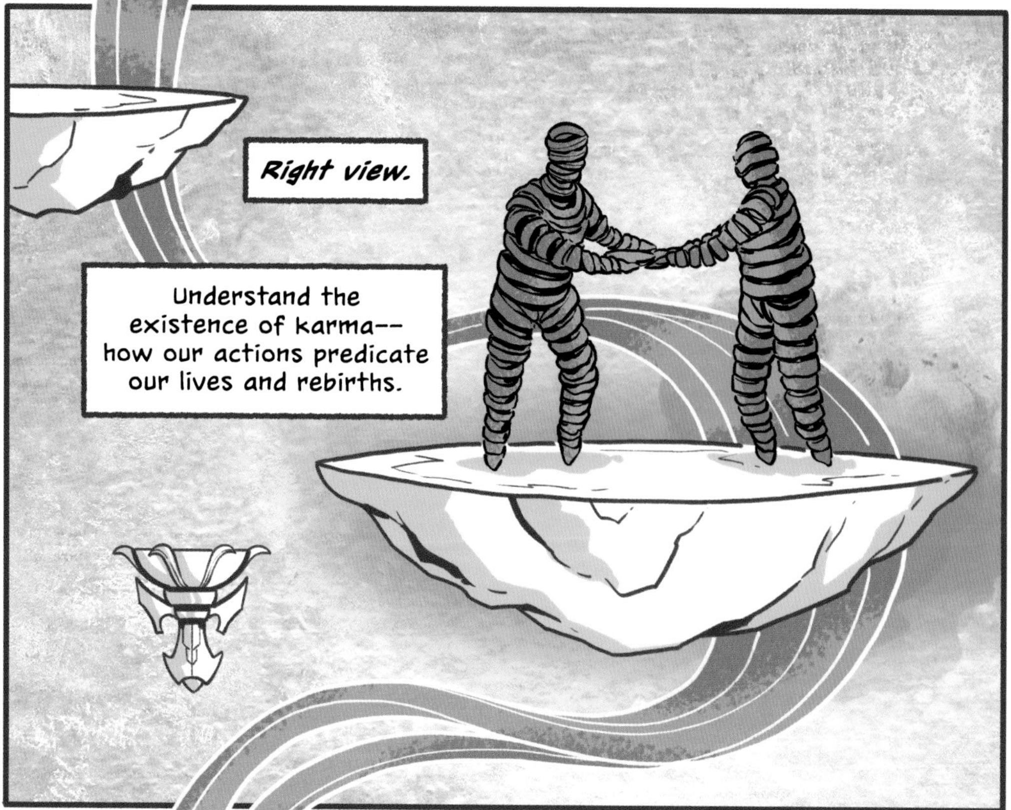
Right view.
Understand the existence of karma-- how our actions predicate our lives and rebirths.

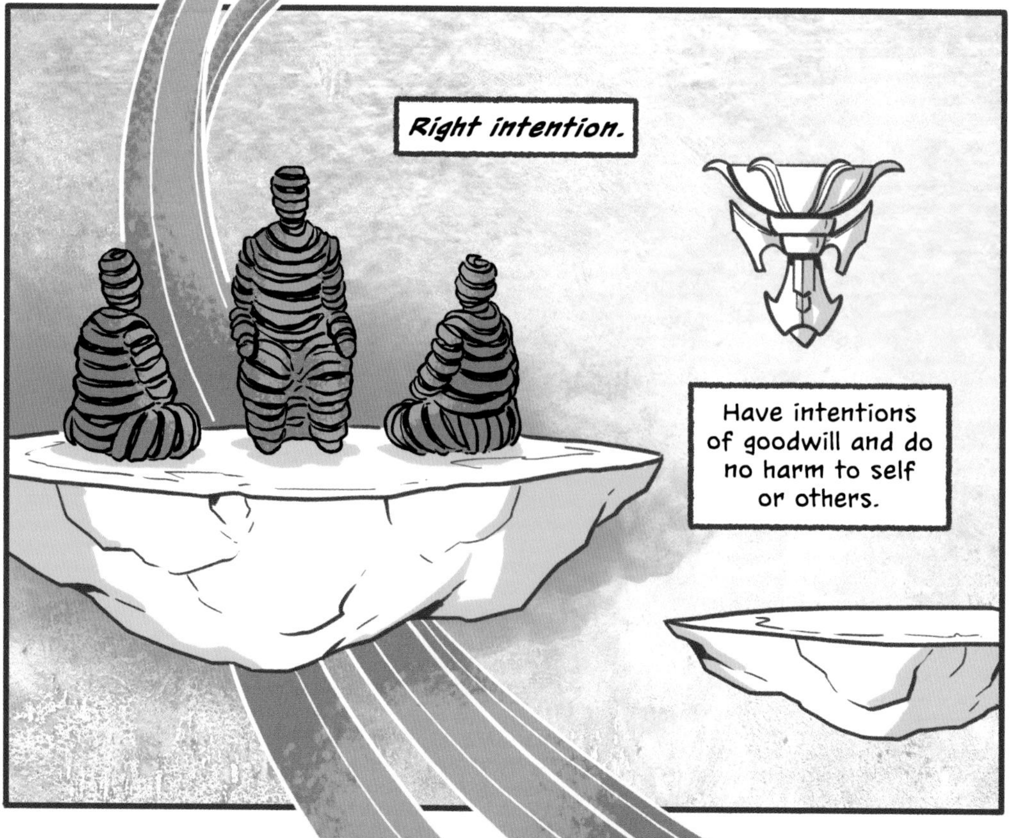
Right intention.
Have intentions of goodwill and do no harm to self or others.

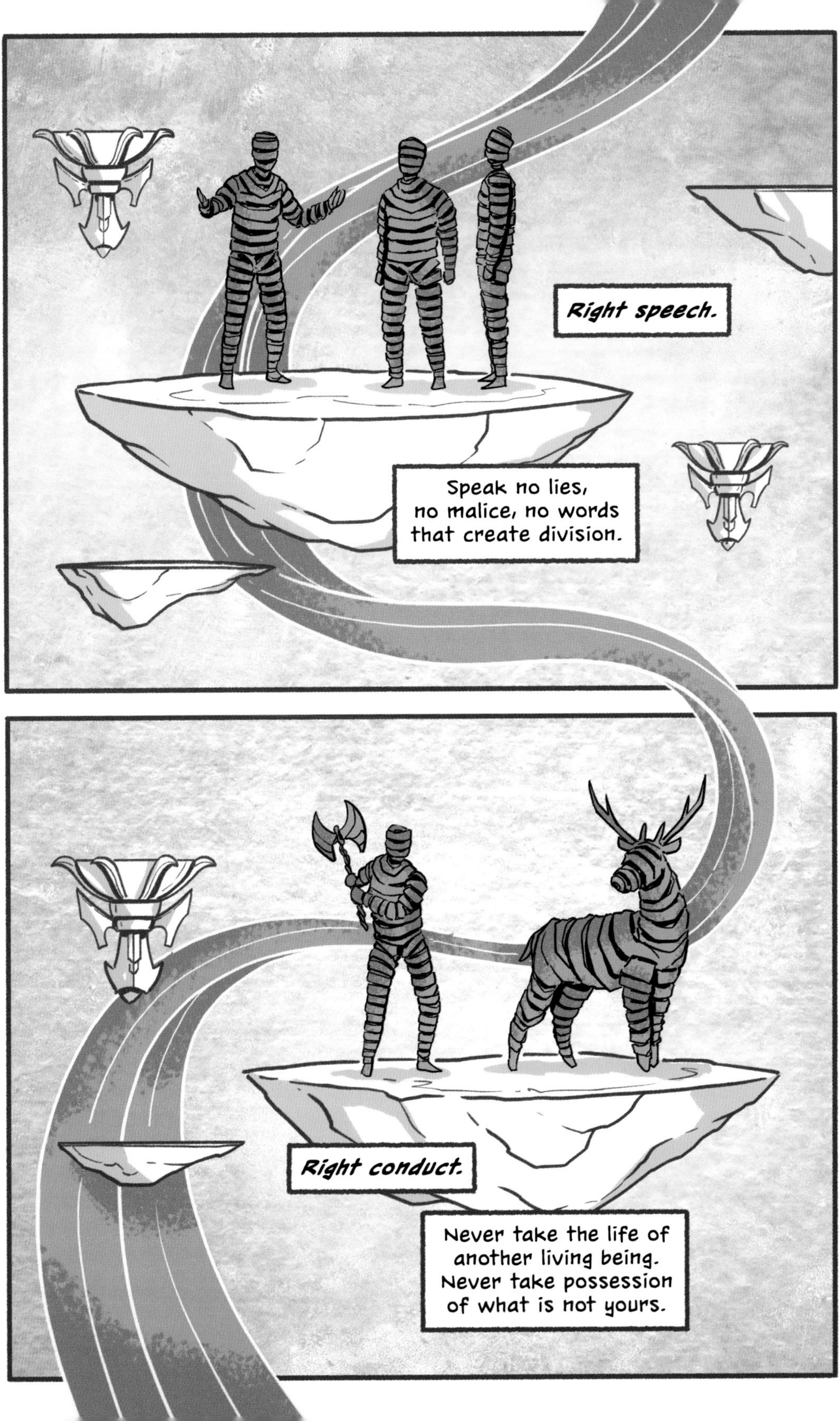
Right speech.
Speak no lies, no malice, no words that create division.
Right conduct.
Never take the life of another living being. Never take possession of what is not yours.

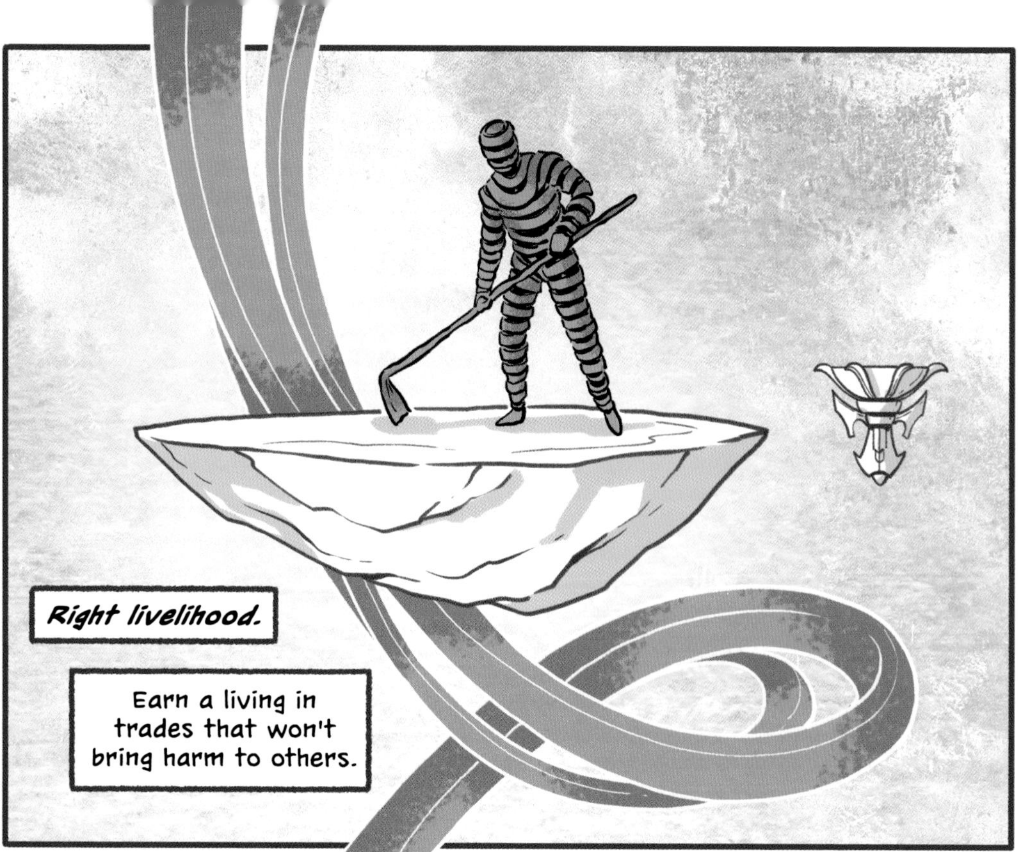
Right livelihood.
Earn a living in trades that won't bring harm to others.

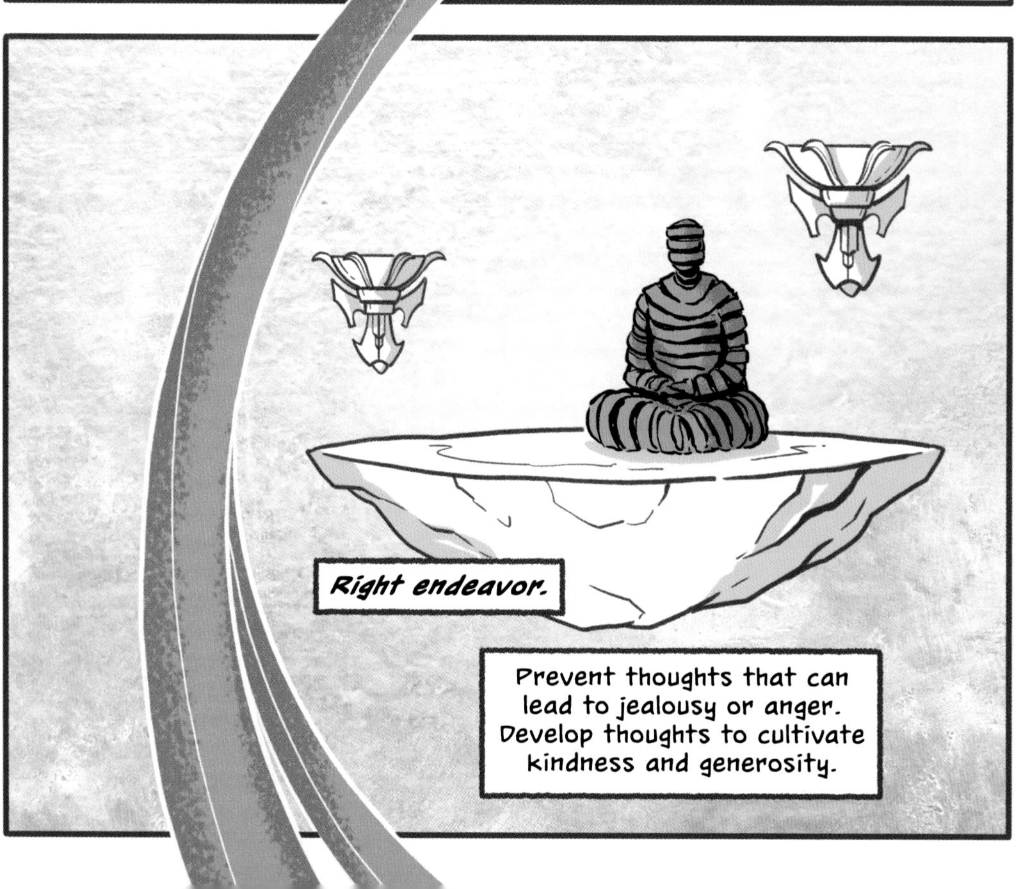
Right endeavor.
Prevent thoughts that can lead to jealousy or anger. Develop thoughts to cultivate kindness and generosity.

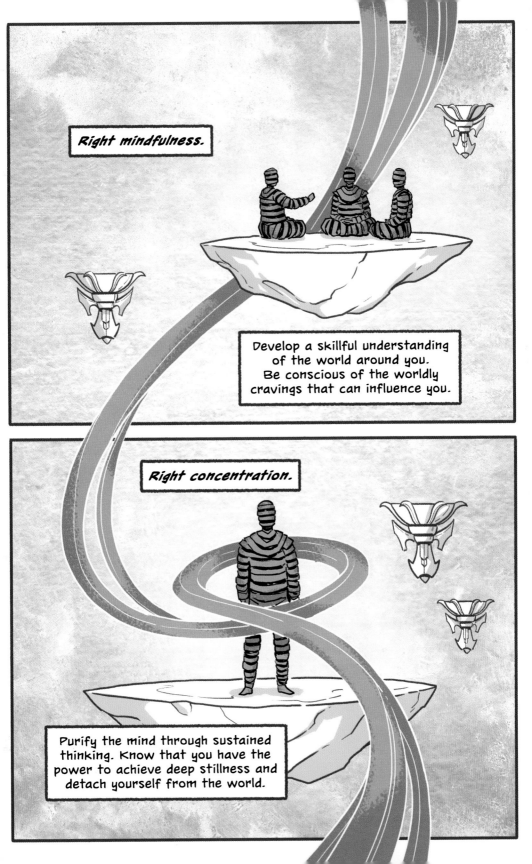

Right mindfulness.

Develop a skillful understanding
of the world around you.
Be conscious of the worldly
cravings that can influence you.

Right concentration.

Purify the mind through sustained
thinking. Know that you have the
power to achieve deep stillness and
detach yourself from the world.

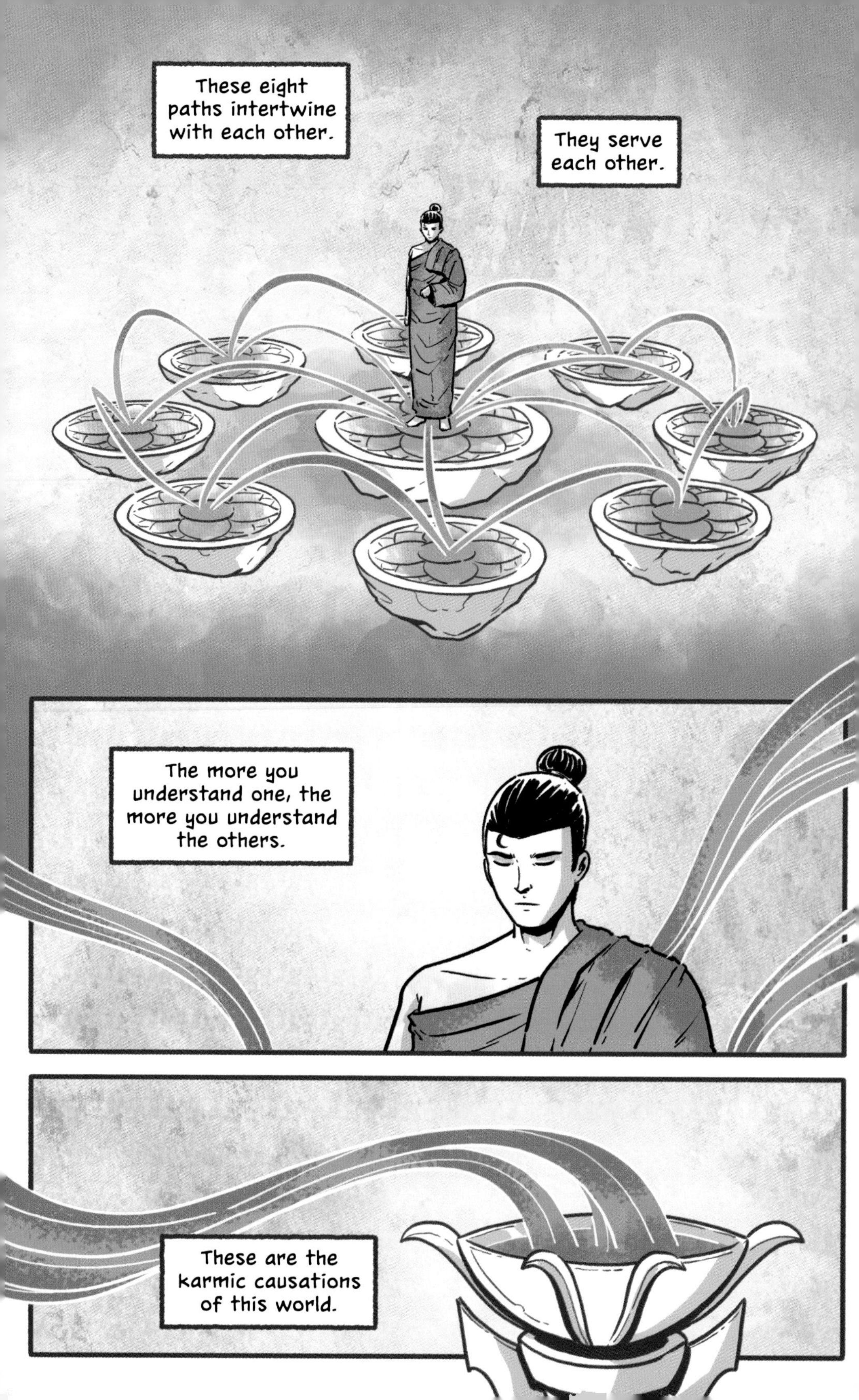
These eight paths intertwine with each other.
They serve each other.
The more you understand one, the more you understand the others.
These are the karmic causations of this world.

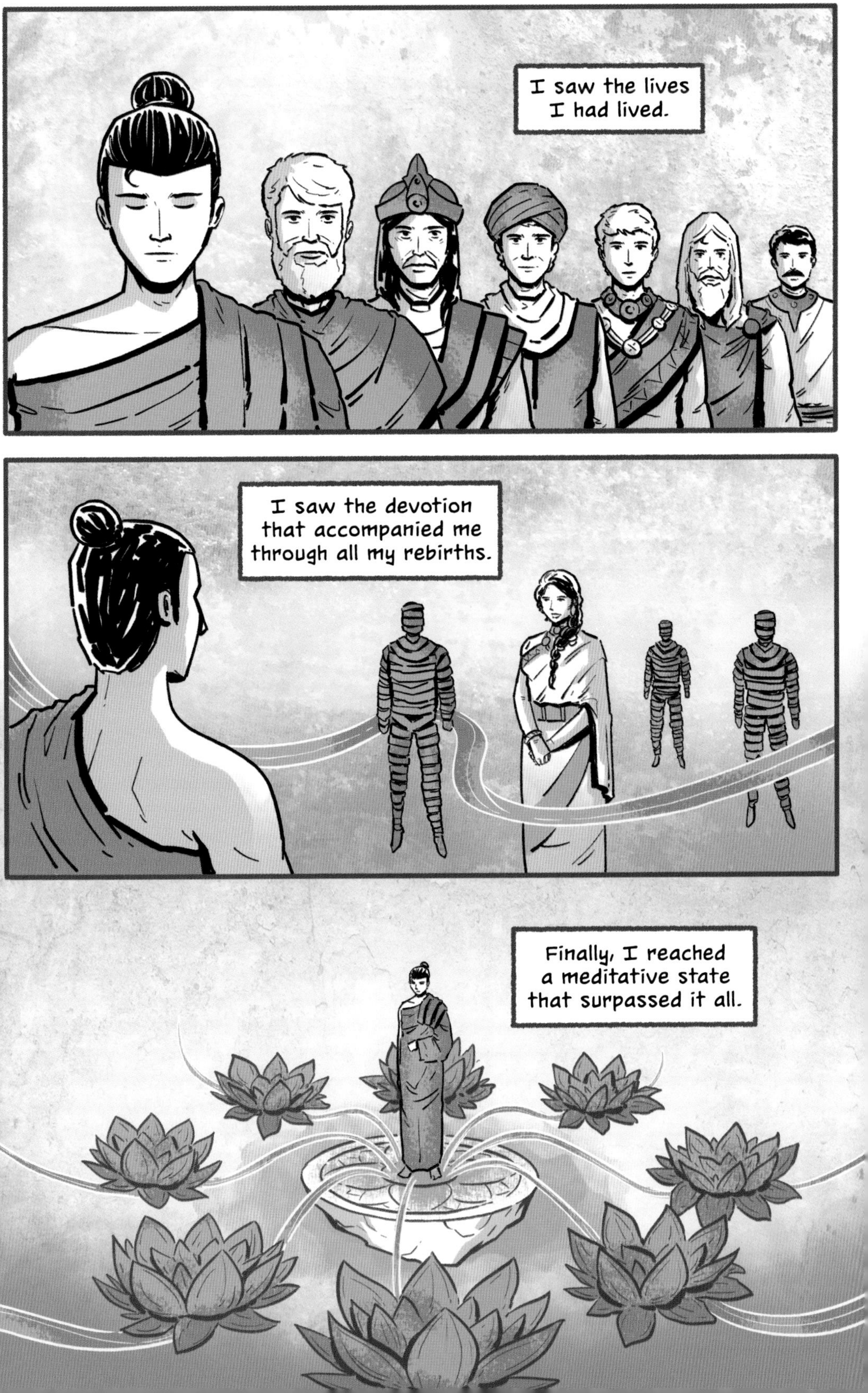
I saw the lives I had lived.
I saw the devotion that accompanied me through all my rebirths.
Finally, I reached a meditative state that surpassed it all.

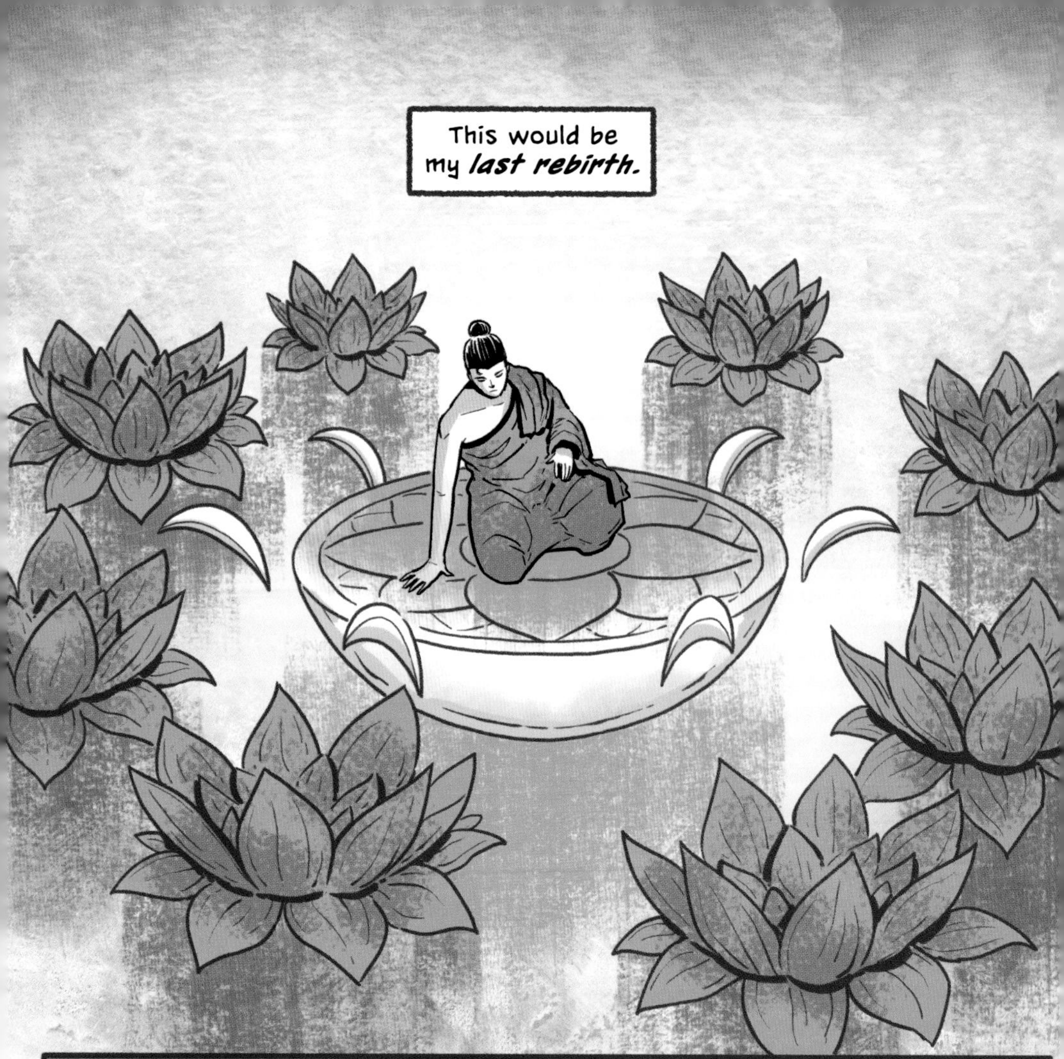
This would be my *last rebirth.*

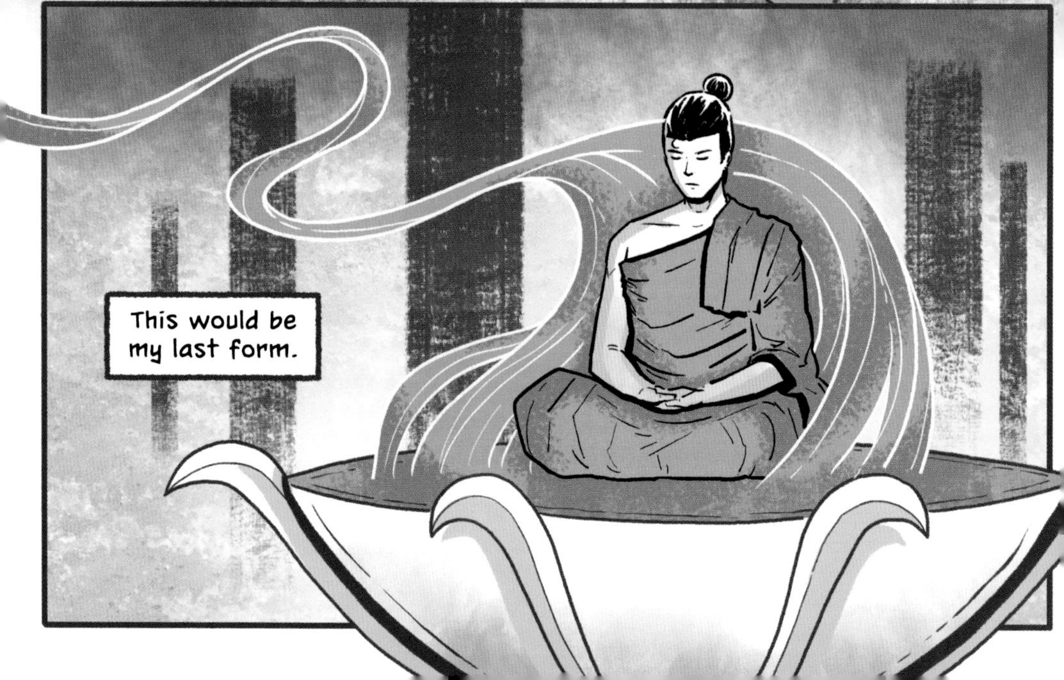
This would be my last form.

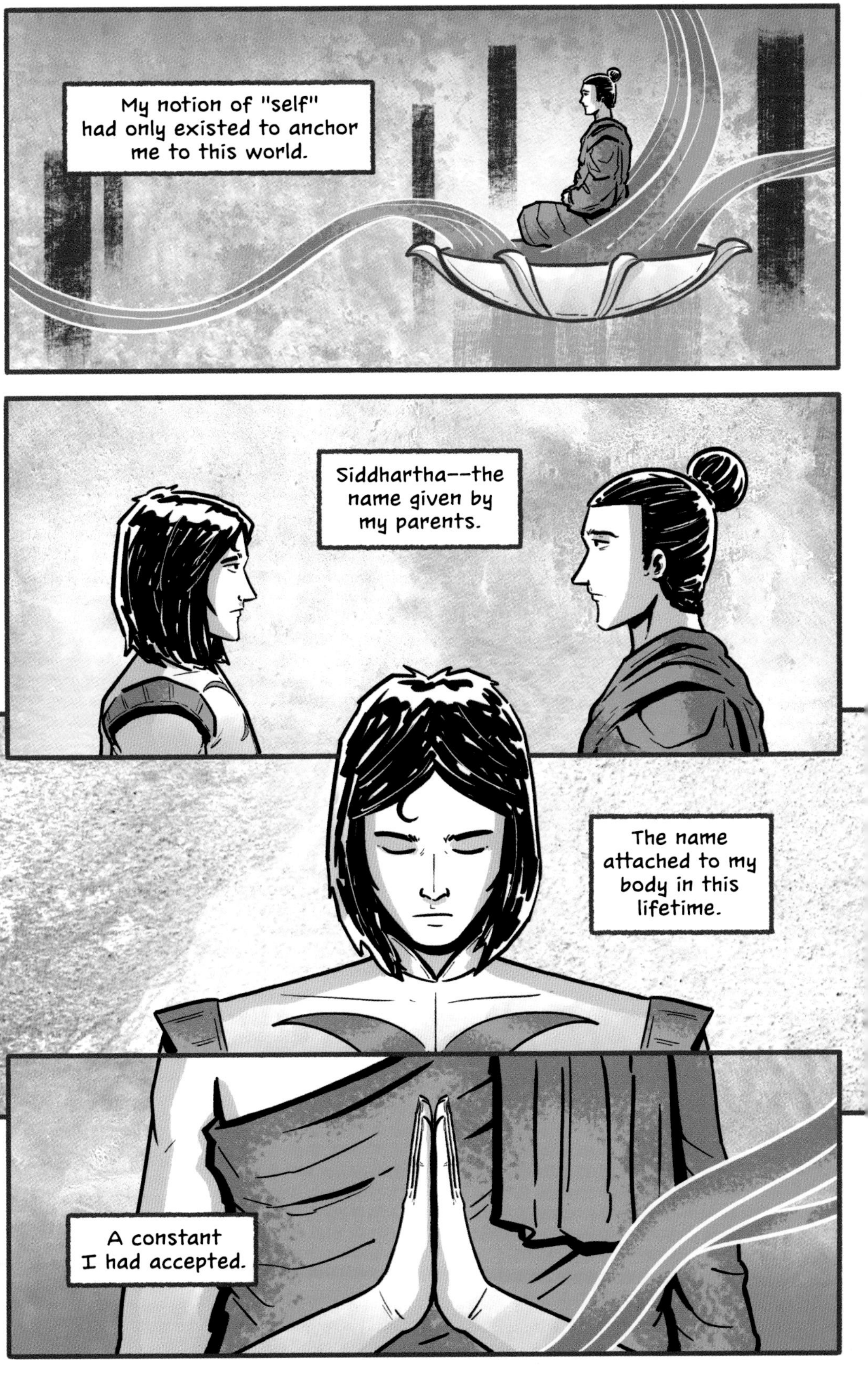
My notion of "self" had only existed to anchor me to this world.
Siddhartha--the name given by my parents.
The name attached to my body in this lifetime.
A constant I had accepted.

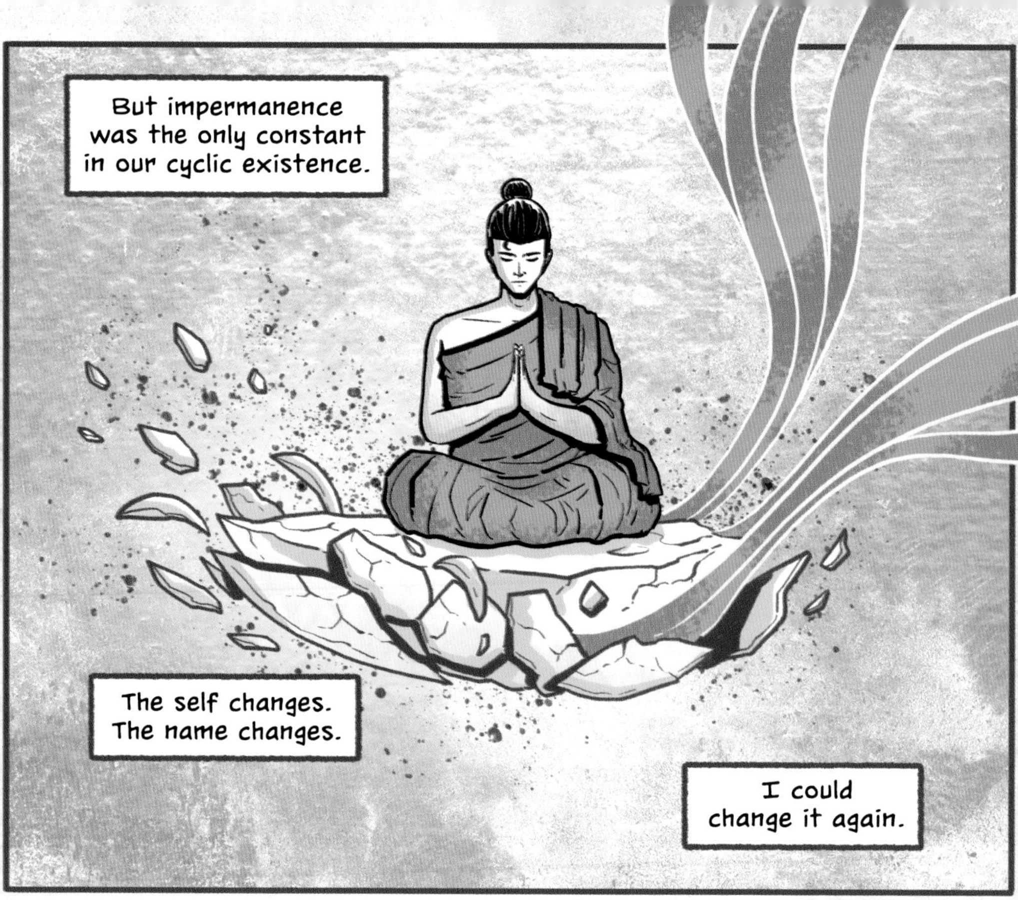
But impermanence was the only constant in our cyclic existence.
The self changes. The name changes.
I could change it again.

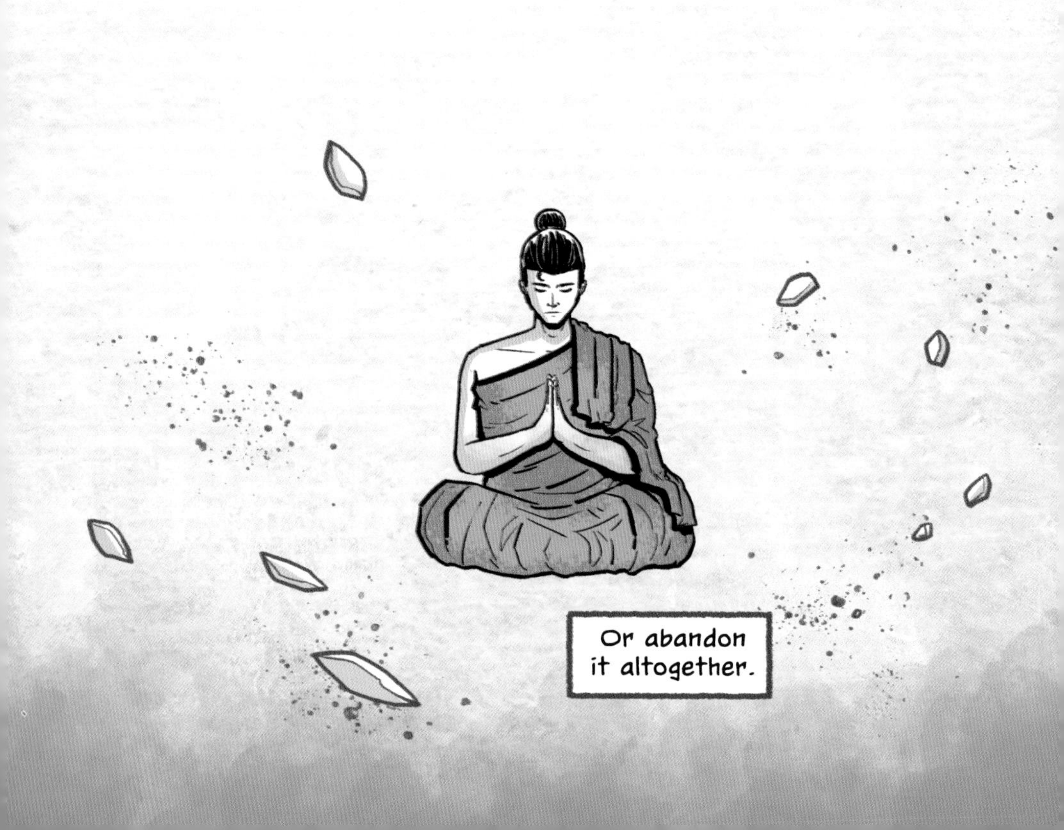
Or abandon it altogether.

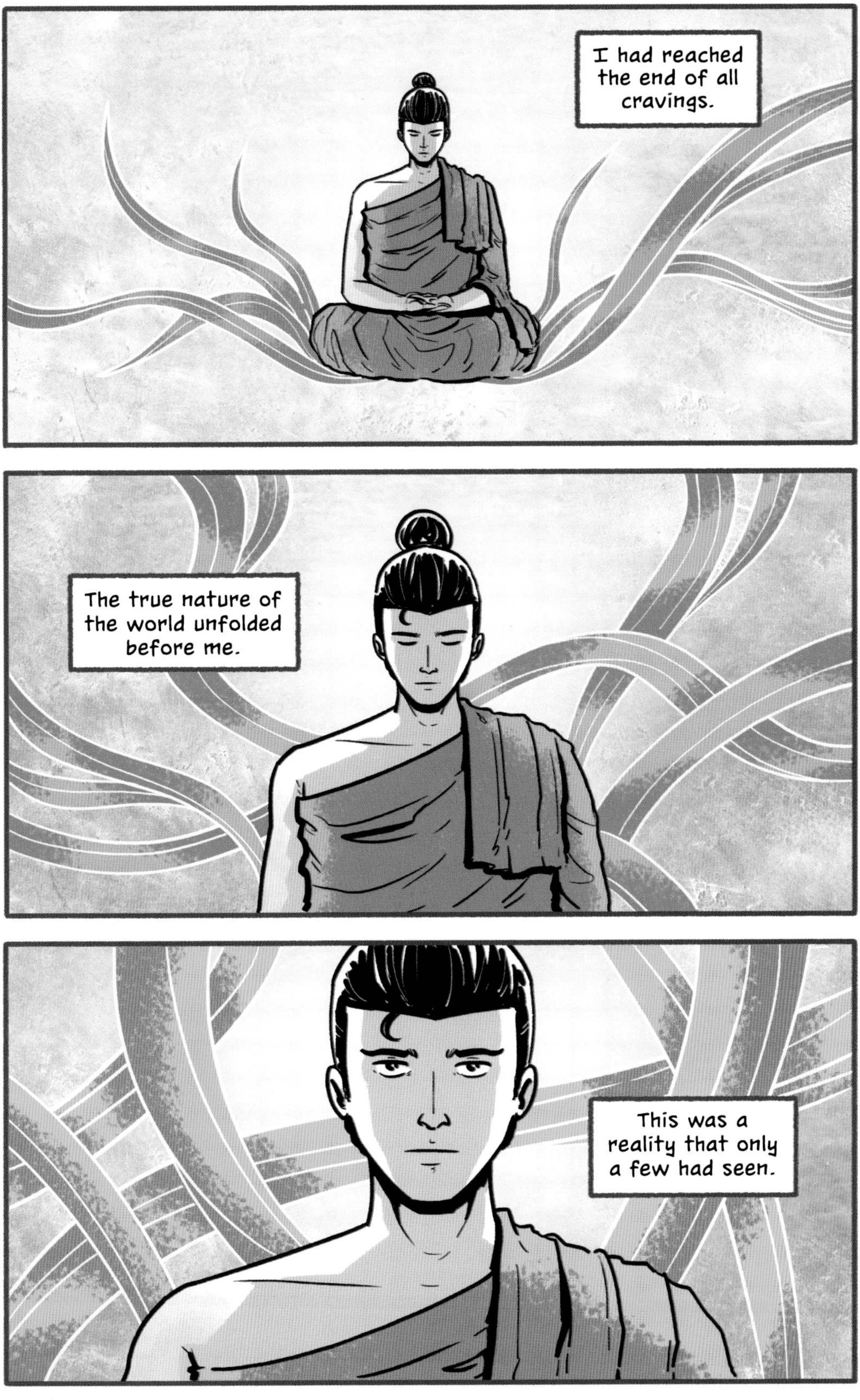
I had reached the end of all cravings.
The true nature of the world unfolded before me.
This was a reality that only a few had seen.

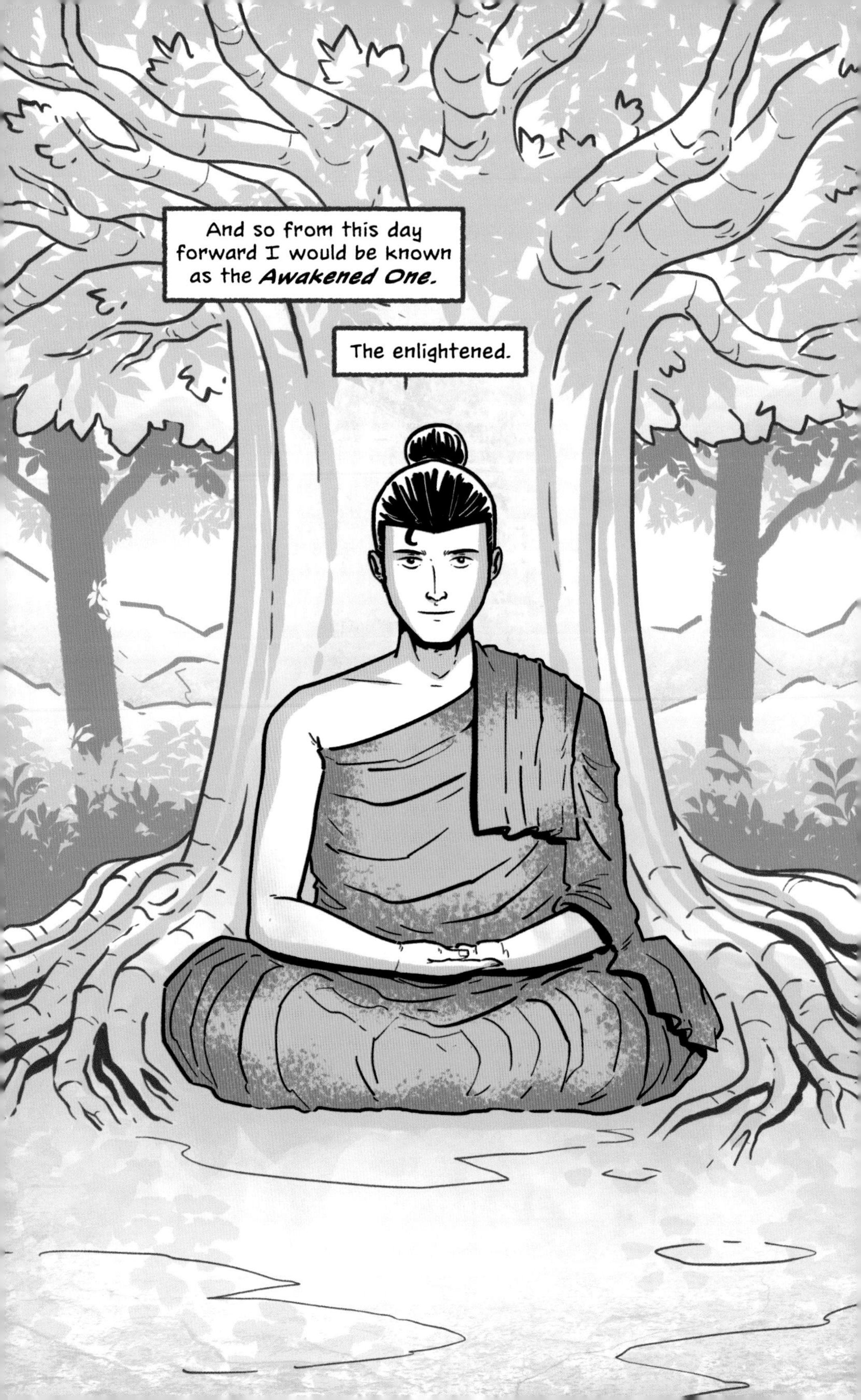
And so from this day forward I would be known as the *Awakened One.*
The enlightened.

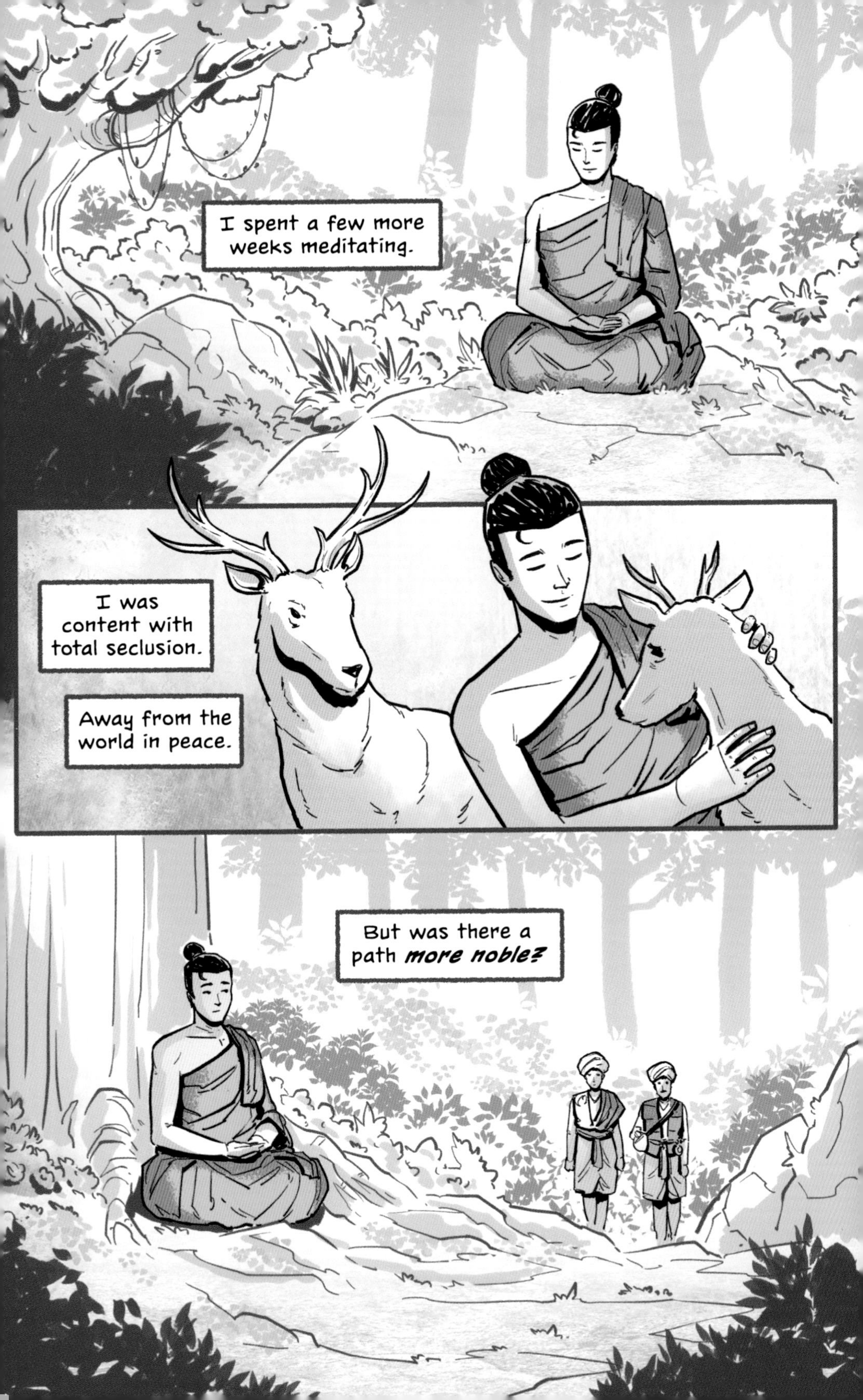
I spent a few more weeks meditating.
I was content with total seclusion.
Away from the world in peace.
But was there a path *more noble?*

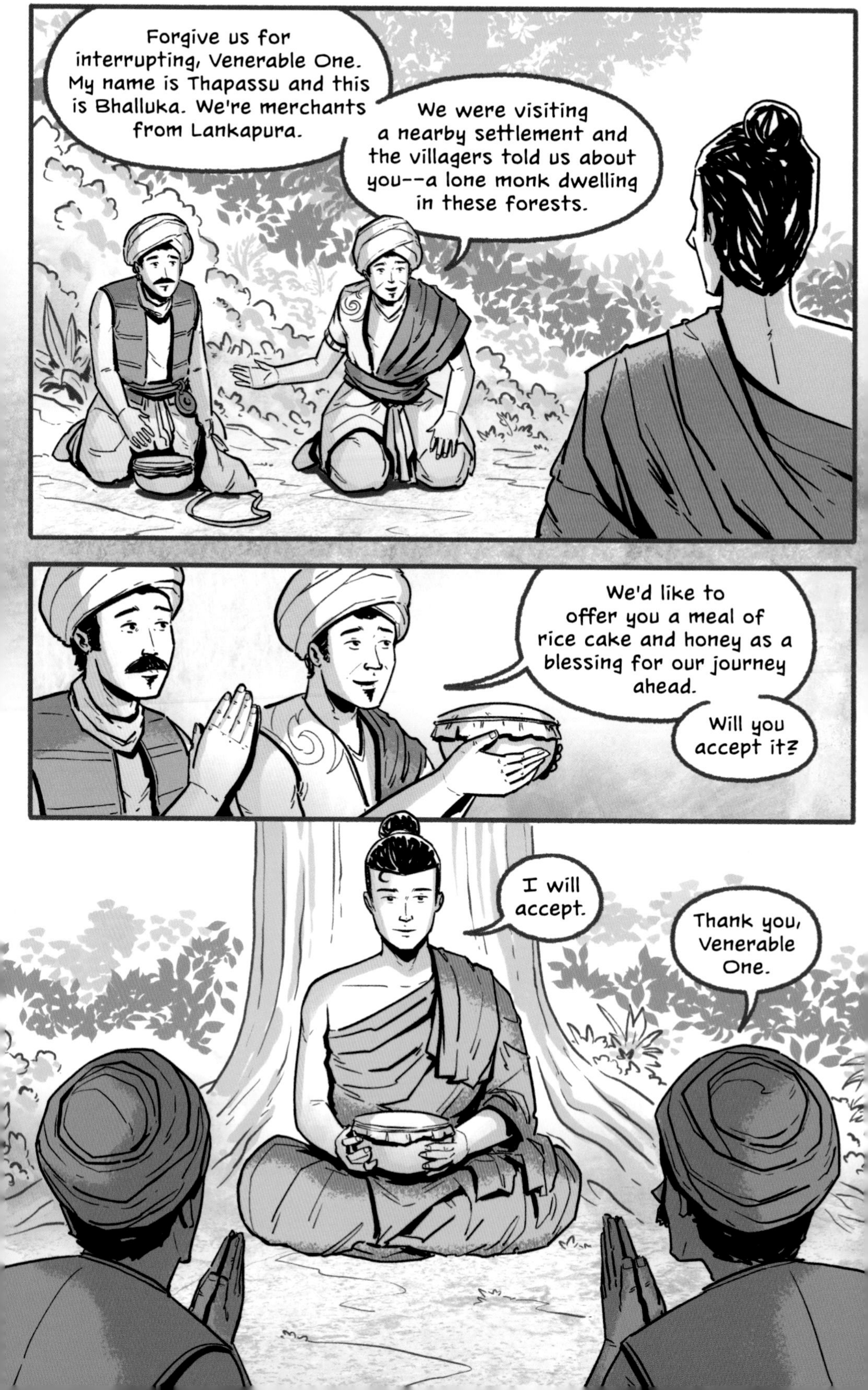
Forgive us for interrupting, Venerable One. My name is Thapassu and this is Bhalluka. We're merchants from Lankapura.
We were visiting a nearby settlement and the villagers told us about you--a lone monk dwelling in these forests.
We'd like to offer you a meal of rice cake and honey as a blessing for our journey ahead.
Will you accept it?
I will accept.
Thank you, Venerable One.

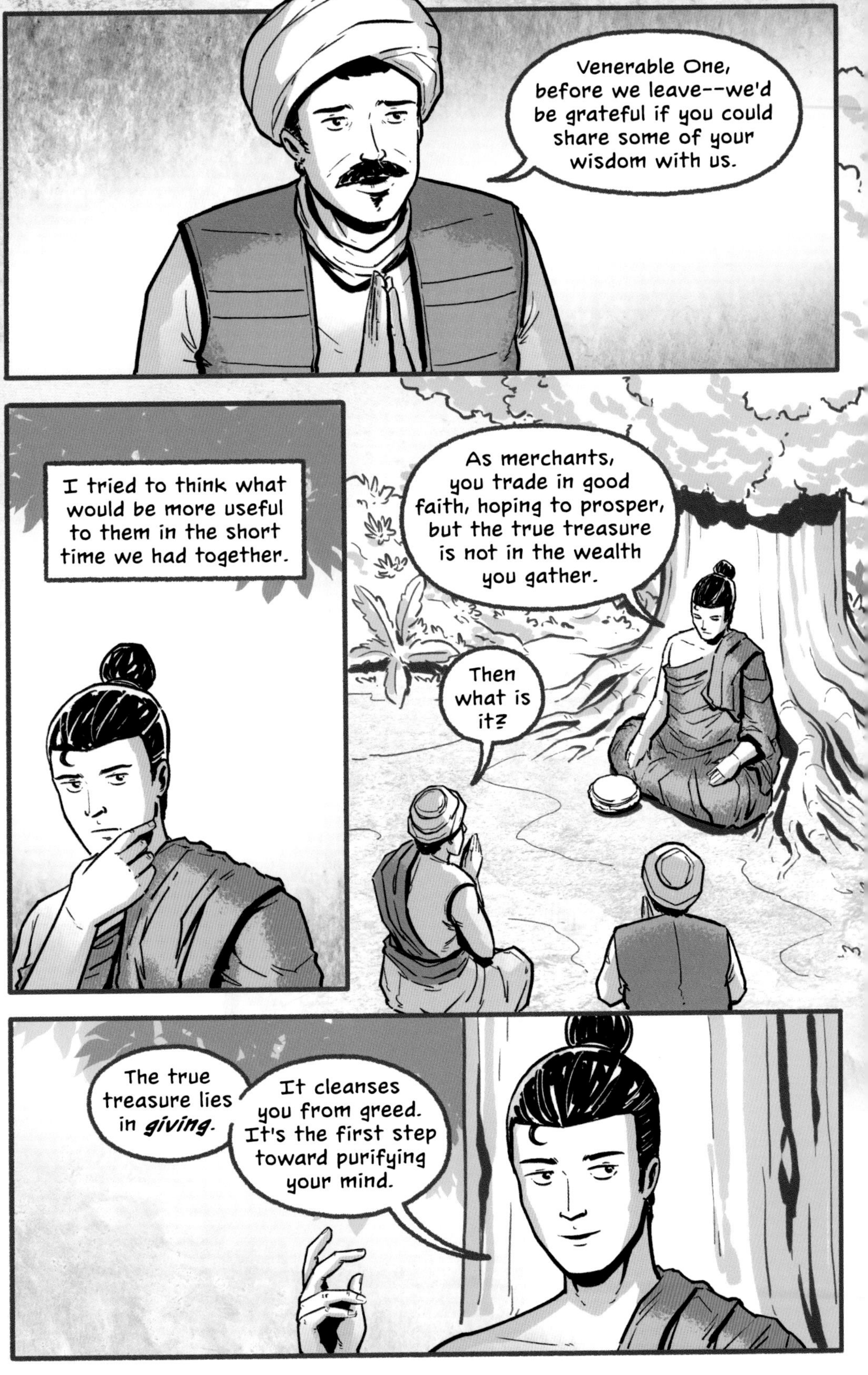
Venerable One, before we leave--we'd be grateful if you could share some of your wisdom with us.
I tried to think what would be more useful to them in the short time we had together.
As merchants, you trade in good faith, hoping to prosper, but the true treasure is not in the wealth you gather.
Then what is it?
The true treasure lies in *giving*.
It cleanses you from greed. It's the first step toward purifying your mind.

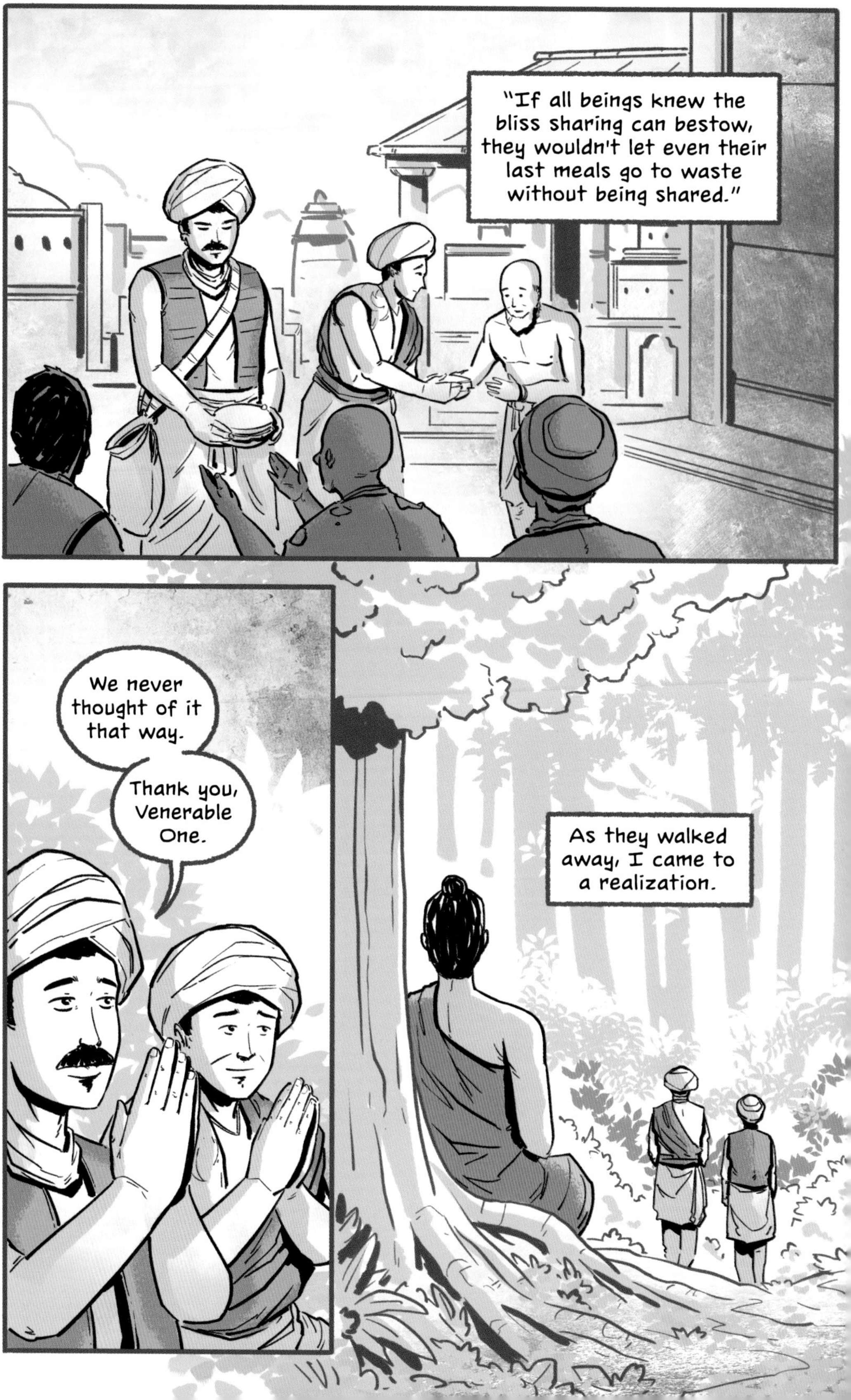
"If all beings knew the bliss sharing can bestow, they wouldn't let even their last meals go to waste without being shared."
We never thought of it that way.
Thank you, Venerable One.
As they walked away, I came to a realization.

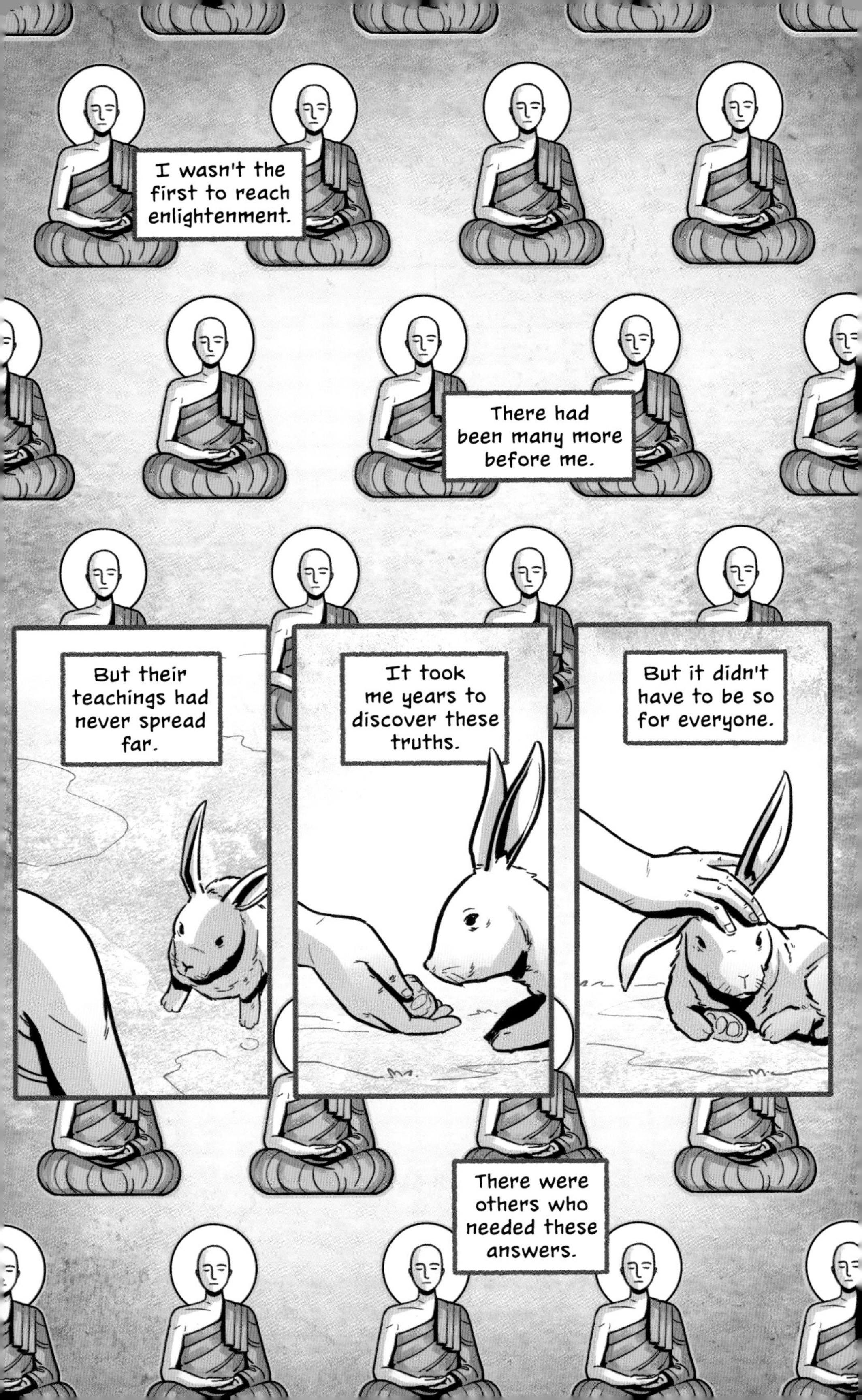
I wasn't the first to reach enlightenment.
There had been many more before me.
But their teachings had never spread far.
It took me years to discover these truths.
But it didn't have to be so for everyone.
There were others who needed these answers.

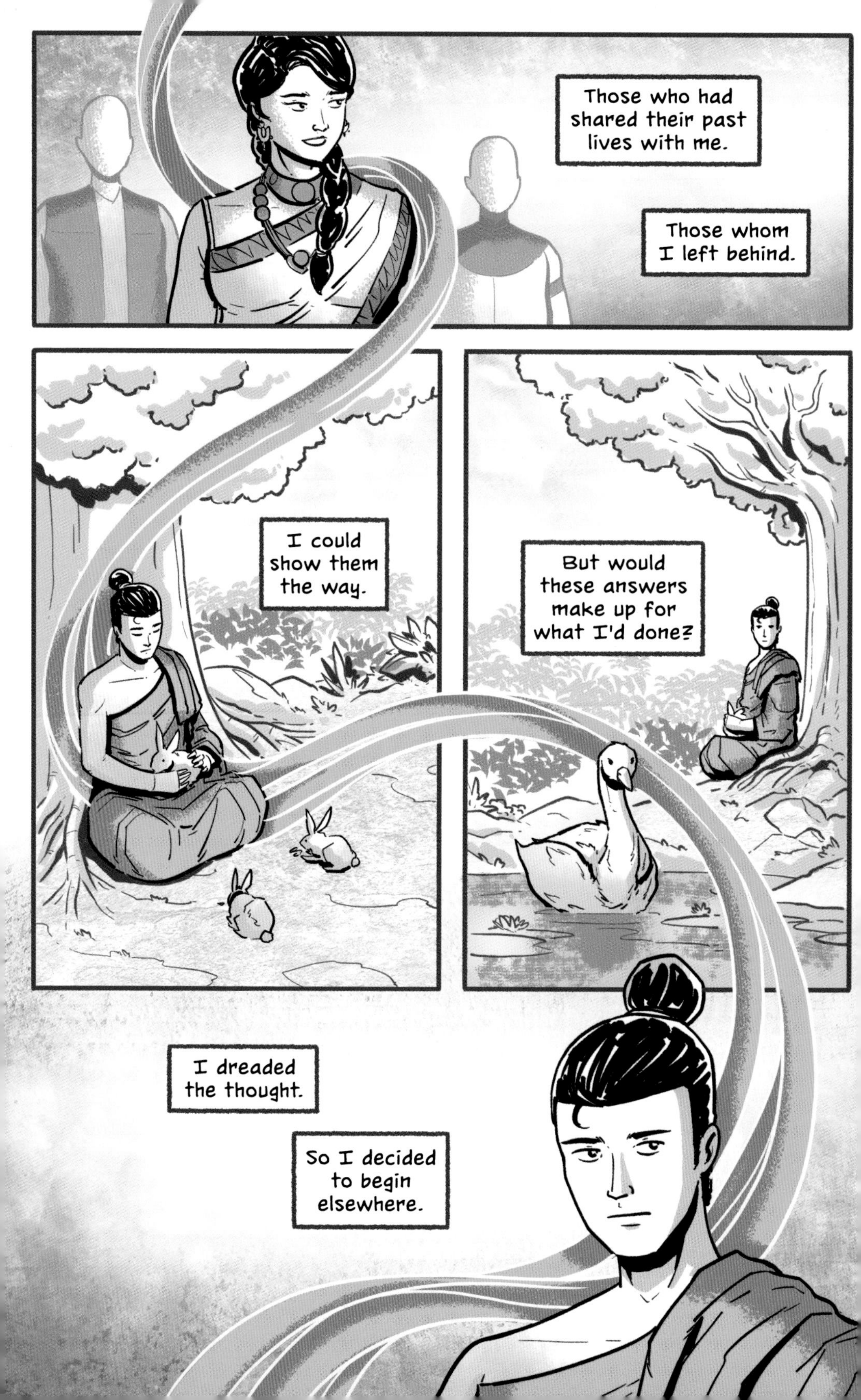
Those who had shared their past lives with me.
Those whom I left behind.
I could show them the way.
But would these answers make up for what I'd done?
I dreaded the thought.
So I decided to begin elsewhere.

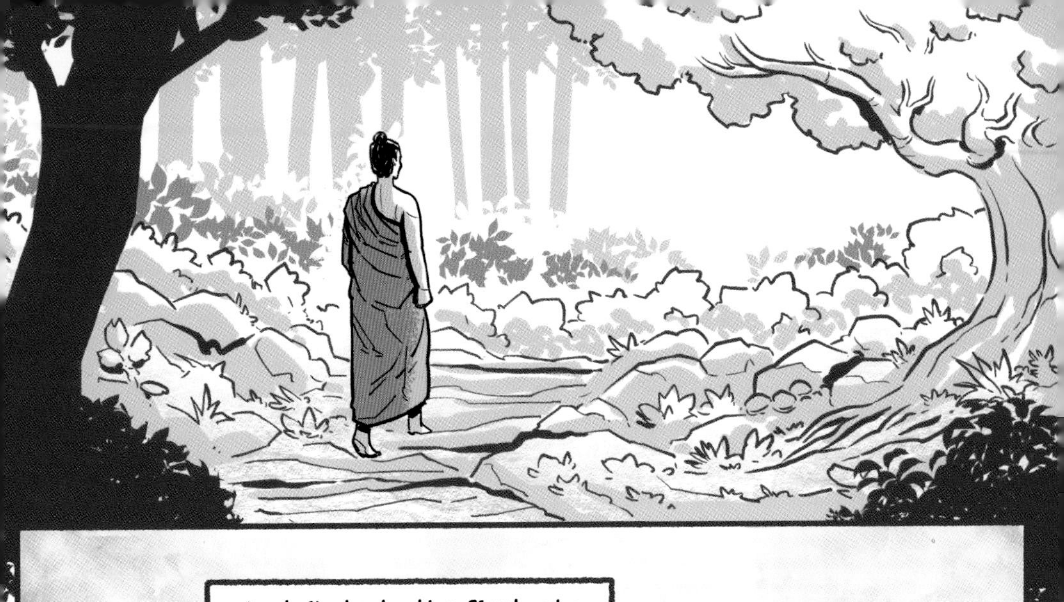

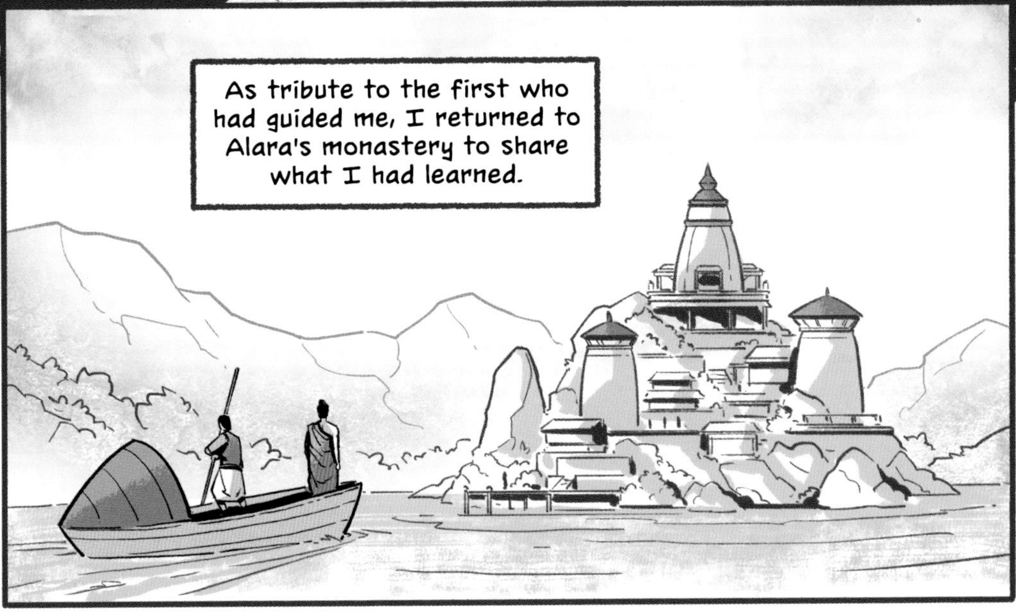
As tribute to the first who had guided me, I returned to Alara's monastery to share what I had learned.

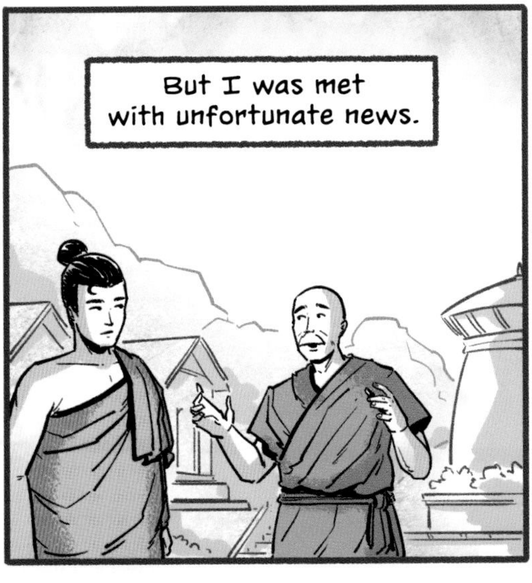
But I was met with unfortunate news.

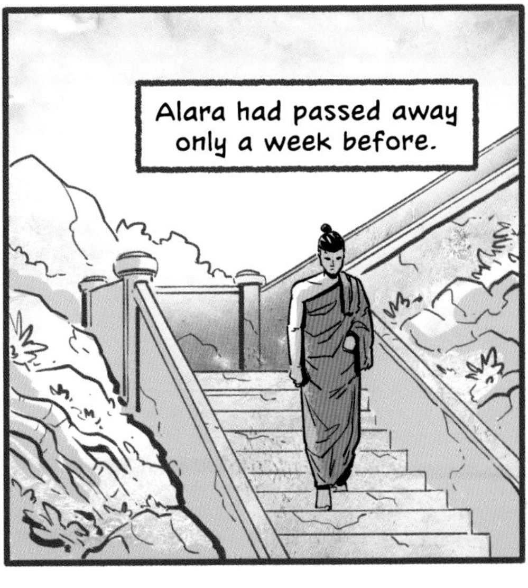
Alara had passed away only a week before.

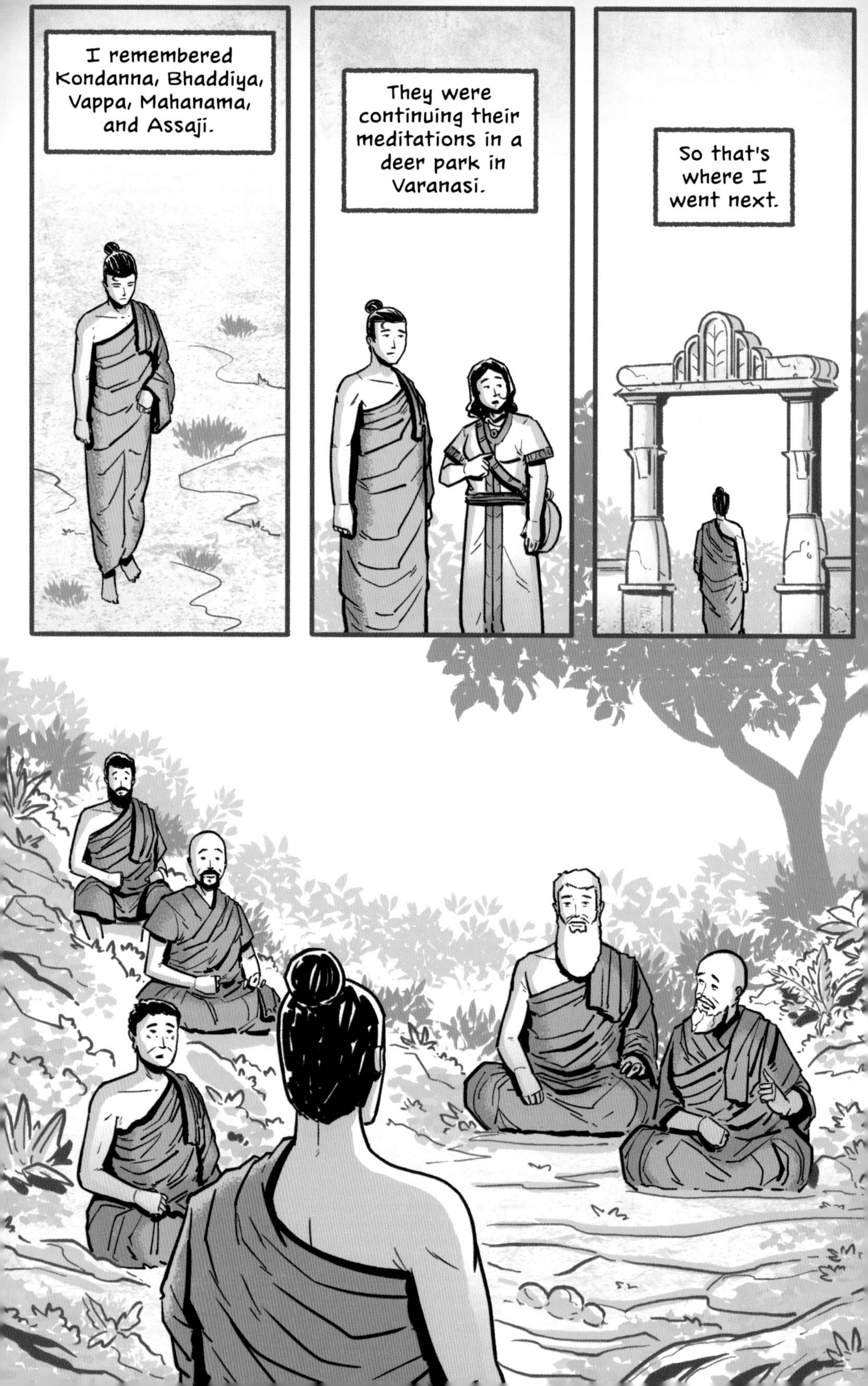
I remembered Kondanna, Bhaddiya, Vappa, Mahanama, and Assaji.
They were continuing their meditations in a deer park in Varanasi.
So that's where I went next.

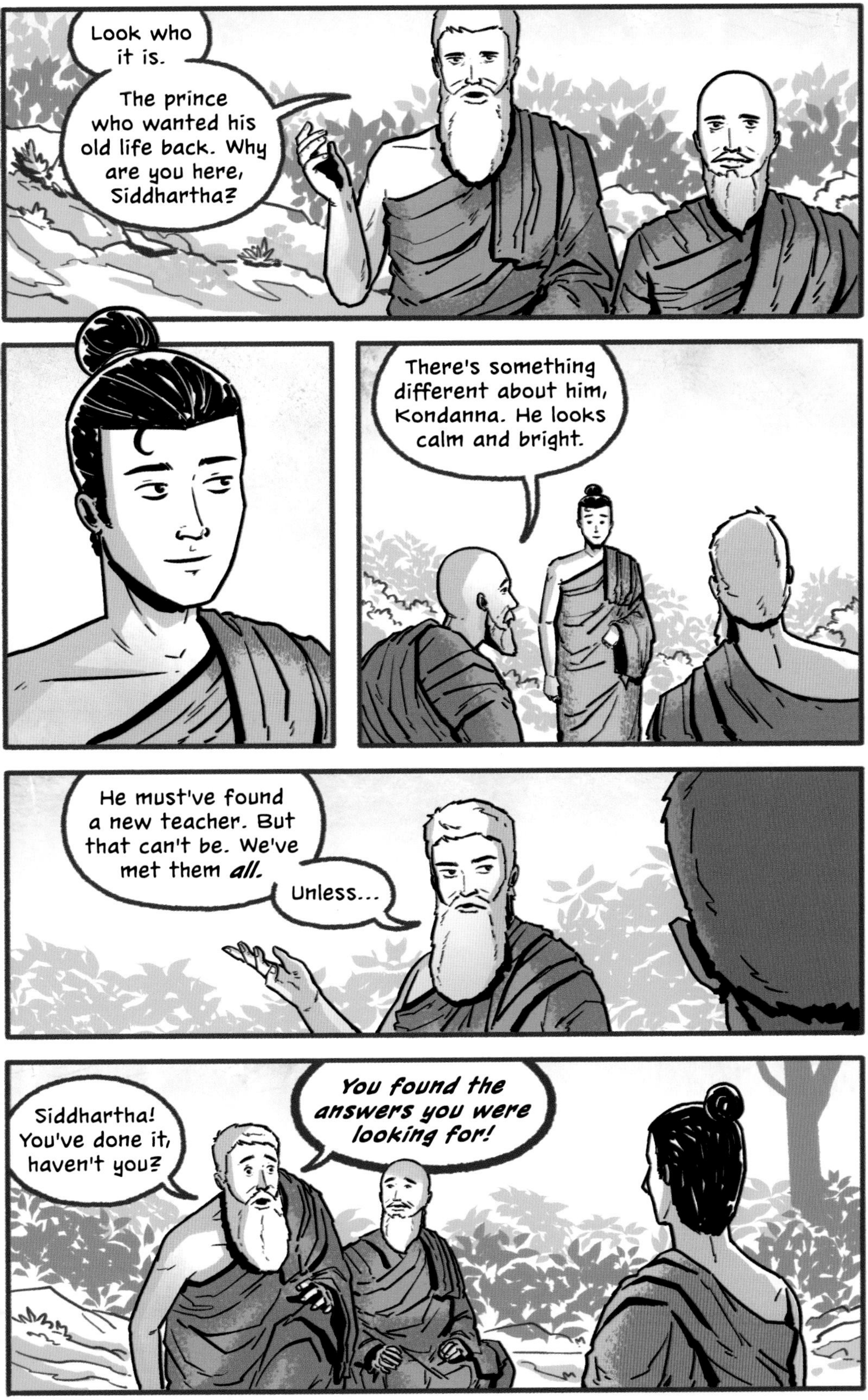

Look who it is.
The prince who wanted his old life back. Why are you here, Siddhartha?
There's something different about him, Kondanna. He looks calm and bright.
He must've found a new teacher. But that can't be. We've met them *all.*
Unless...
Siddhartha! You've done it, haven't you?
You found the answers you were looking for!

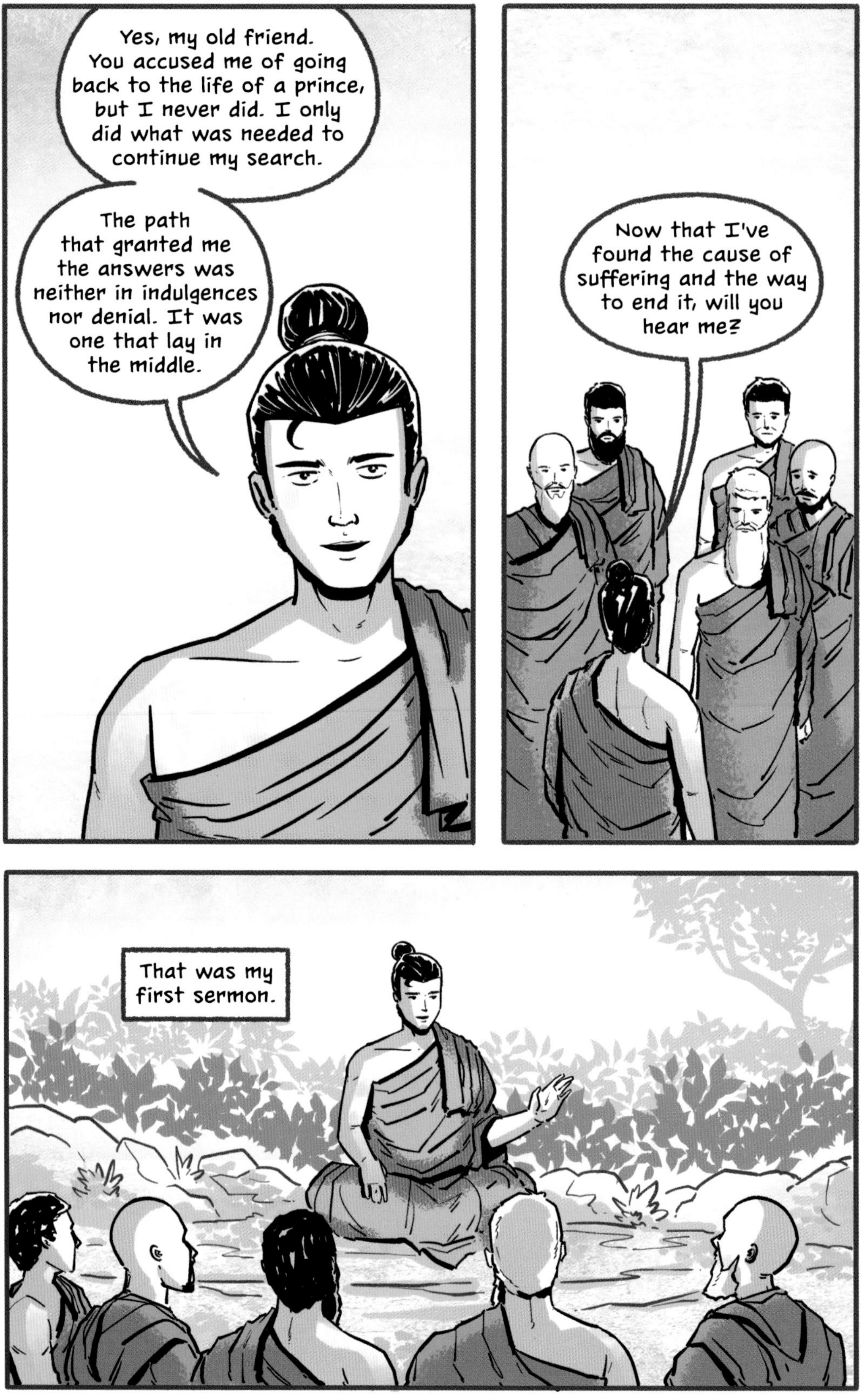
Yes, my old friend. You accused me of going back to the life of a prince, but I never did. I only did what was needed to continue my search.
The path that granted me the answers was neither in indulgences nor denial. It was one that lay in the middle.
Now that I've found the cause of suffering and the way to end it, will you hear me?
That was my first sermon.

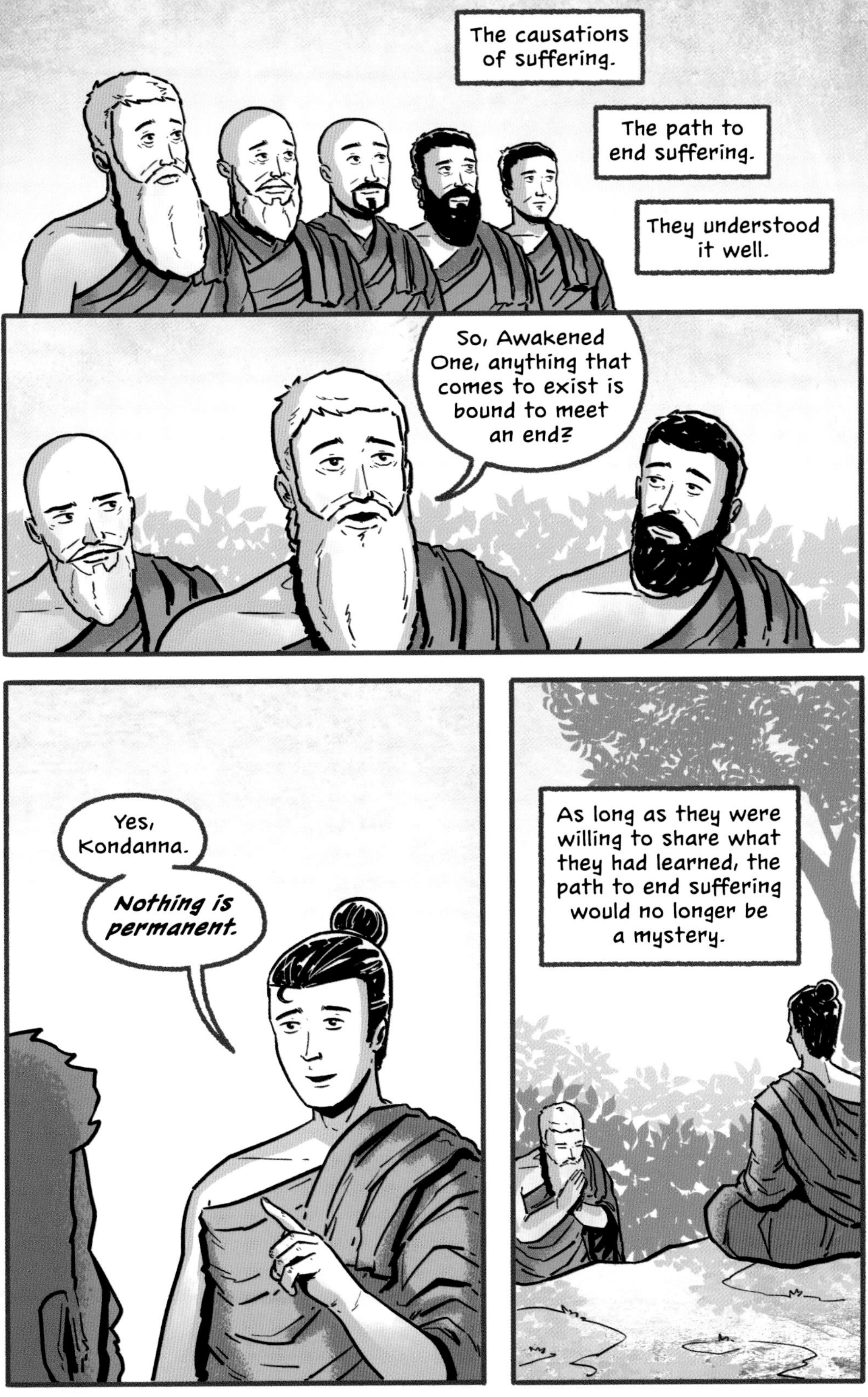
The causations of suffering.
The path to end suffering.
They understood it well.
So, Awakened One, anything that comes to exist is bound to meet an end?
Yes, Kondanna.
Nothing is permanent.
As long as they were willing to share what they had learned, the path to end suffering would no longer be a mystery.

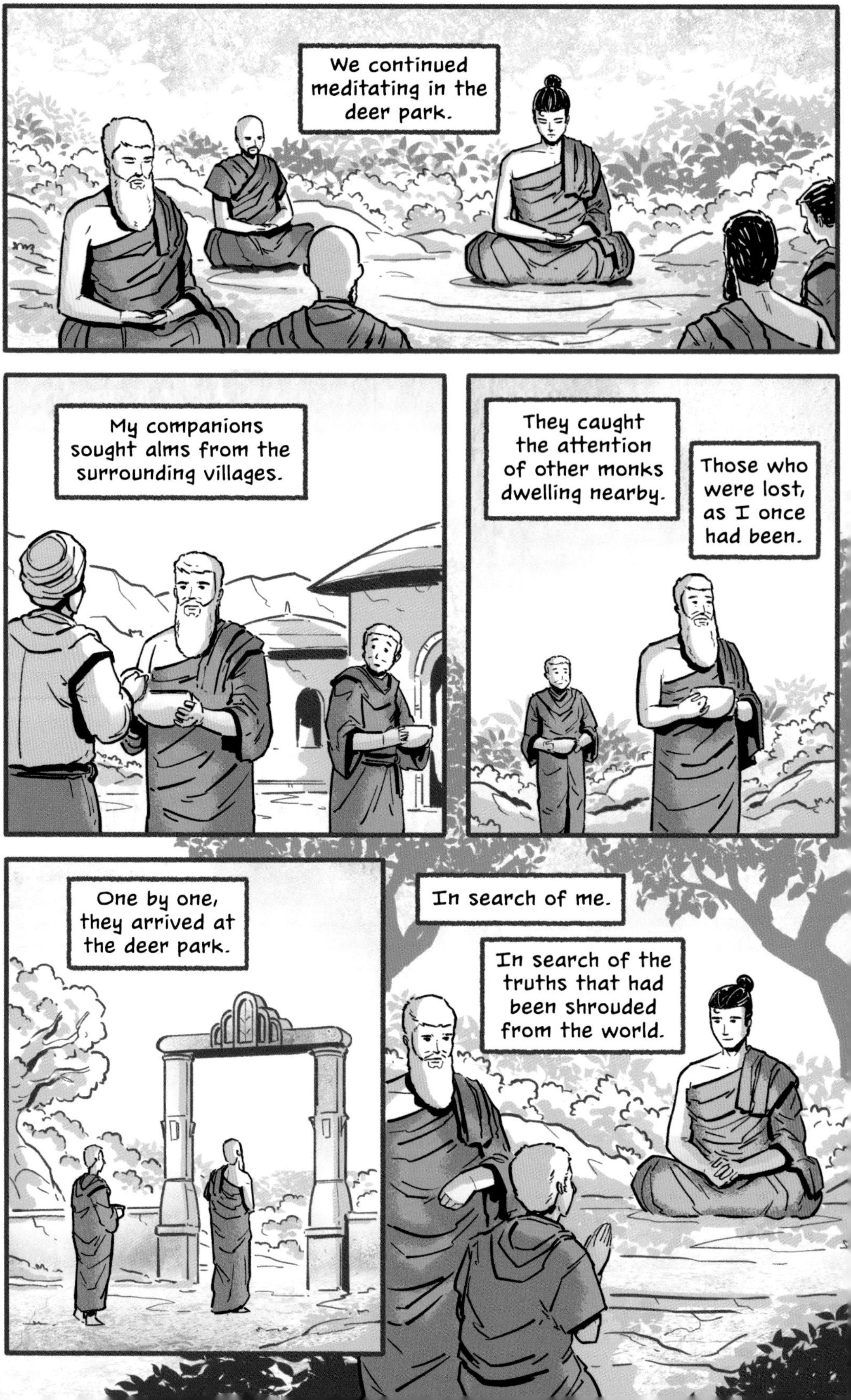
We continued meditating in the deer park.
My companions sought alms from the surrounding villages.
They caught the attention of other monks dwelling nearby.
Those who were lost, as I once had been.
One by one, they arrived at the deer park.
In search of me.
In search of the truths that had been shrouded from the world.

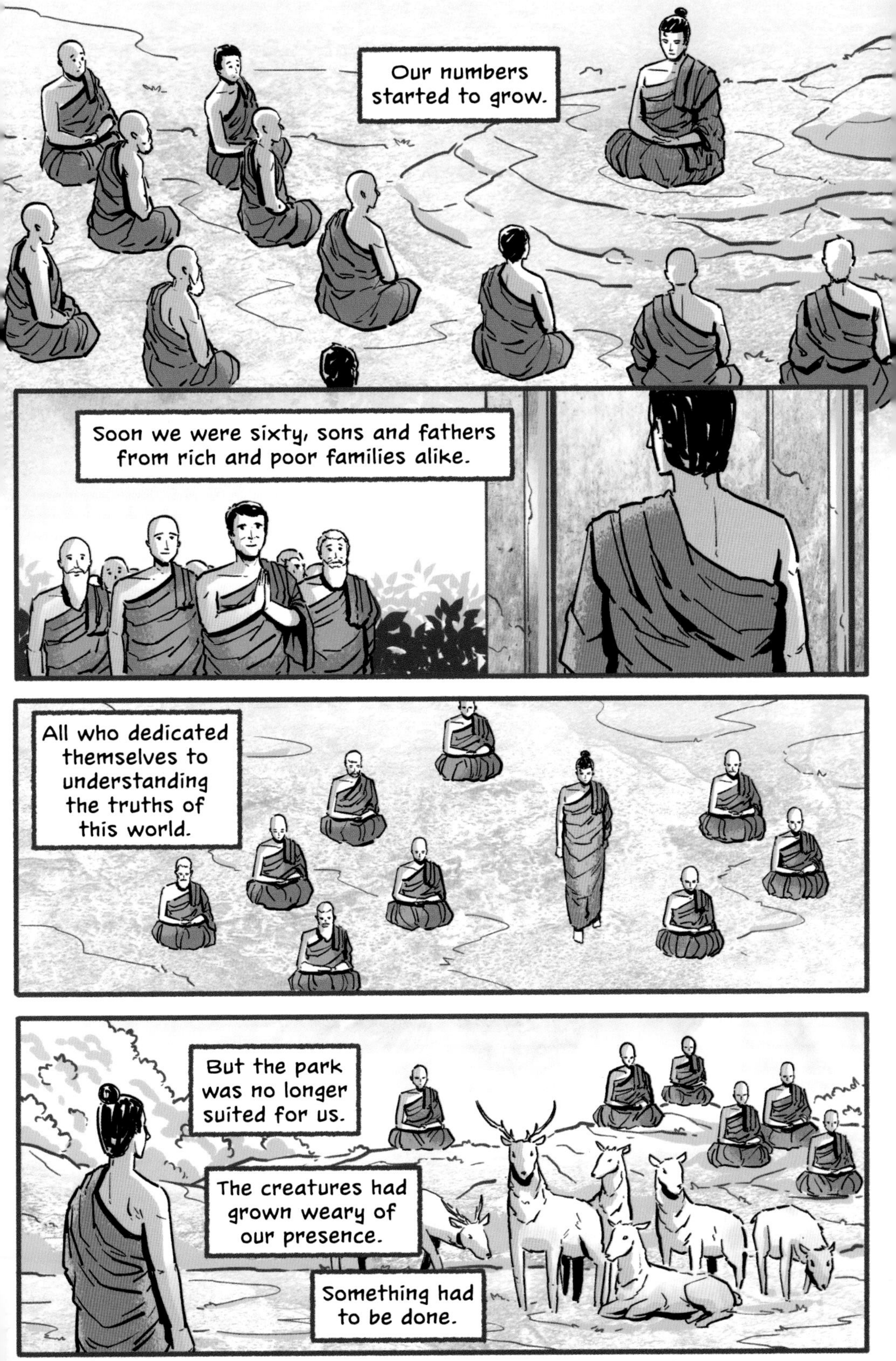
Our numbers started to grow.
Soon we were sixty, sons and fathers from rich and poor families alike.
All who dedicated themselves to understanding the truths of this world.
But the park was no longer suited for us.
The creatures had grown weary of our presence.
Something had to be done.

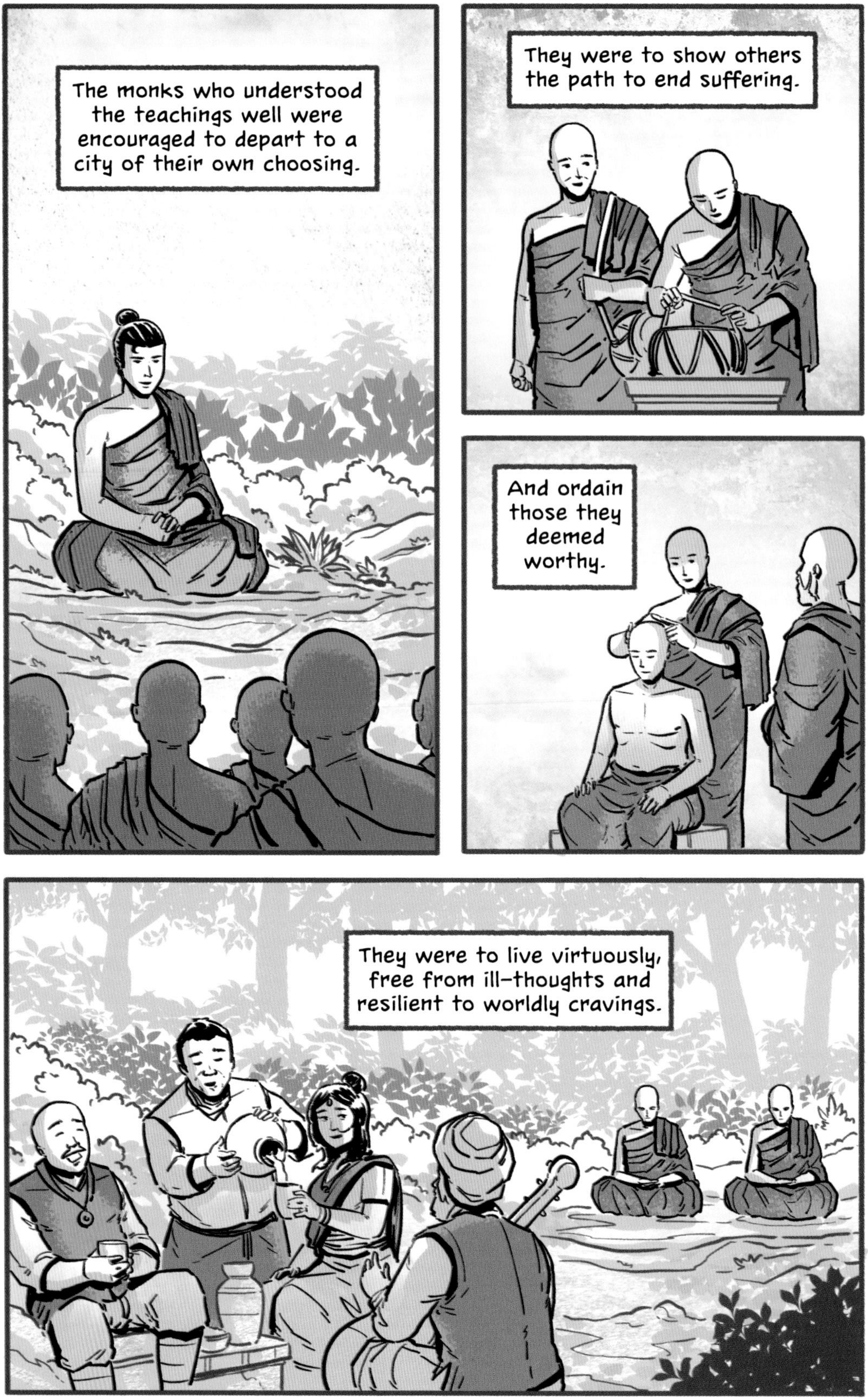
The monks who understood the teachings well were encouraged to depart to a city of their own choosing.
They were to show others the path to end suffering.
And ordain those they deemed worthy.
They were to live virtuously, free from ill-thoughts and resilient to worldly cravings.

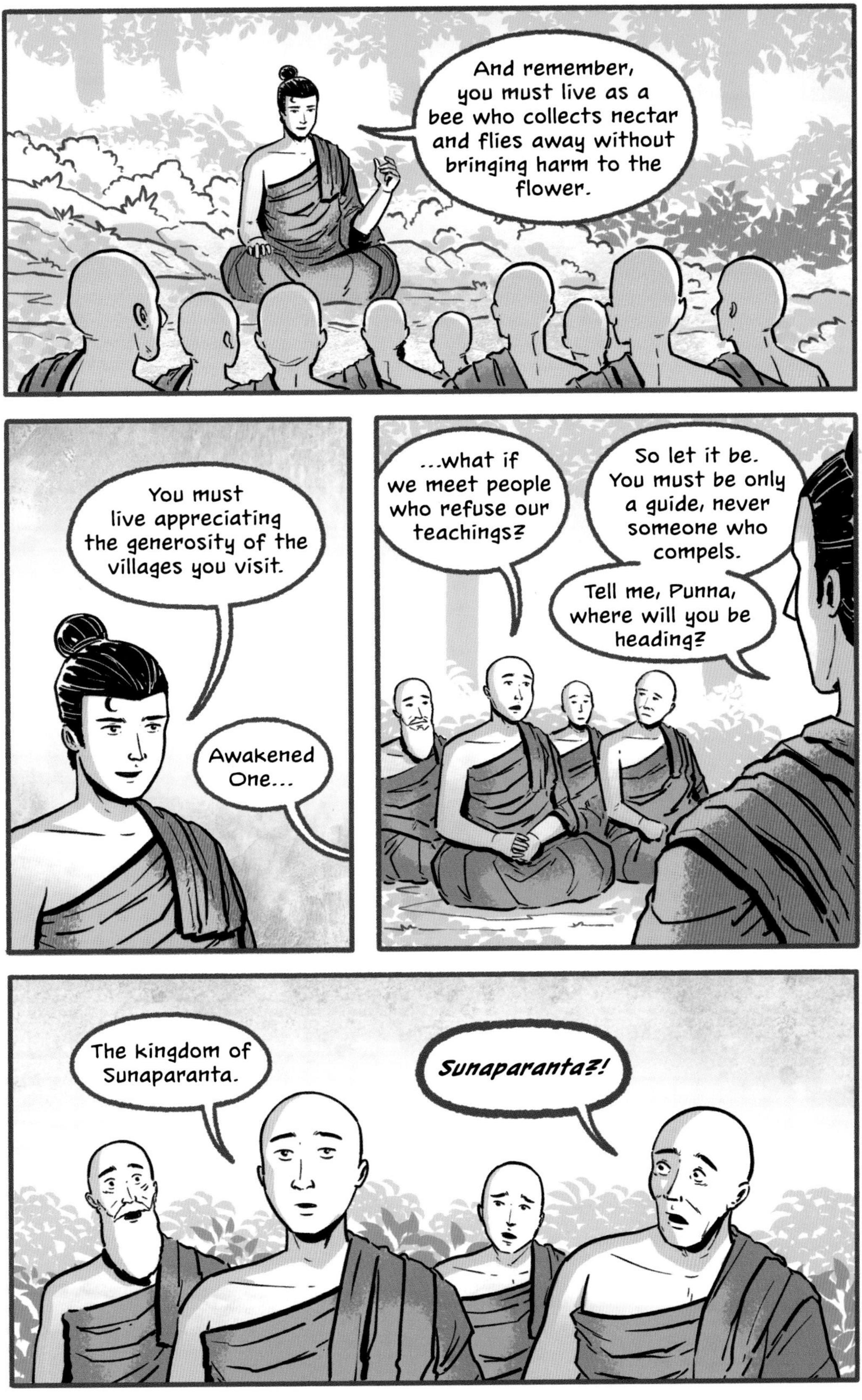
And remember, you must live as a bee who collects nectar and flies away without bringing harm to the flower.
You must live appreciating the generosity of the villages you visit.
Awakened One...
...what if we meet people who refuse our teachings?
So let it be. You must be only a guide, never someone who compels.
Tell me, Punna, where will you be heading?
The kingdom of Sunaparanta.
Sunaparanta?!

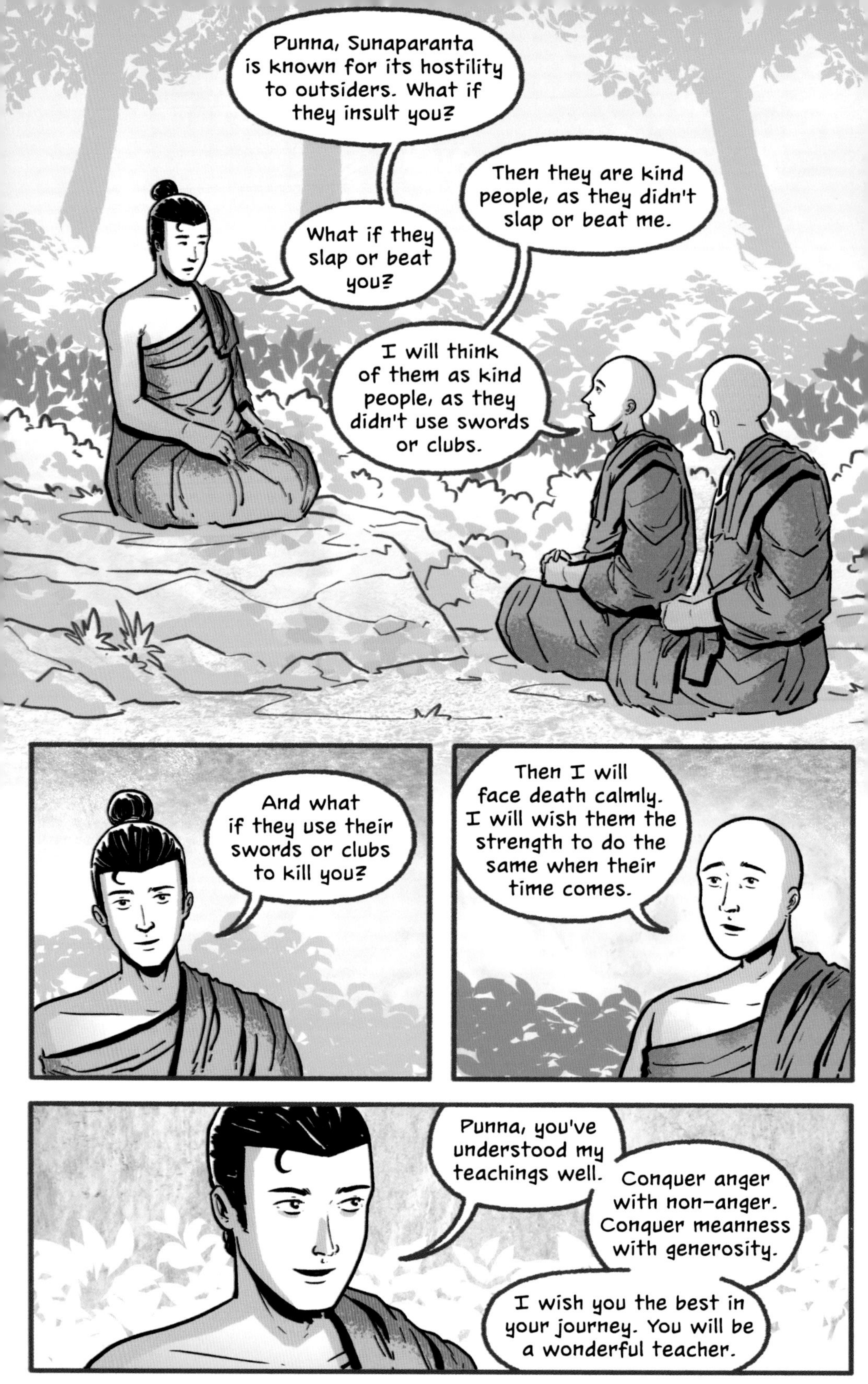
Punna, Sunaparanta is known for its hostility to outsiders. What if they insult you?
What if they slap or beat you?
Then they are kind people, as they didn't slap or beat me.
I will think of them as kind people, as they didn't use swords or clubs.
And what if they use their swords or clubs to kill you?
Then I will face death calmly. I will wish them the strength to do the same when their time comes.
Punna, you've understood my teachings well.
Conquer anger with non-anger. Conquer meanness with generosity.
I wish you the best in your journey. You will be a wonderful teacher.

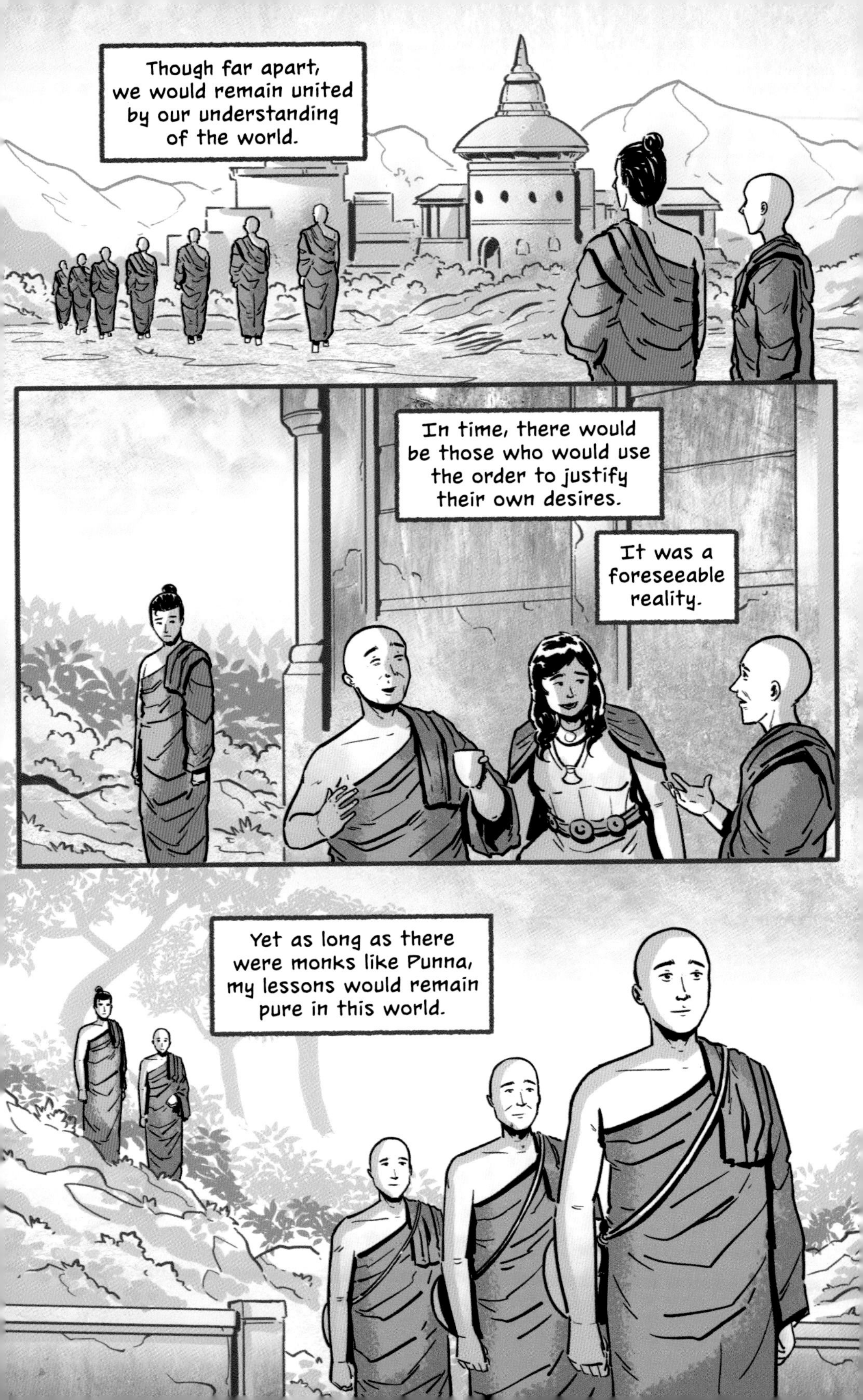
Though far apart, we would remain united by our understanding of the world.
In time, there would be those who would use the order to justify their own desires.
It was a foreseeable reality.
Yet as long as there were monks like Punna, my lessons would remain pure in this world.

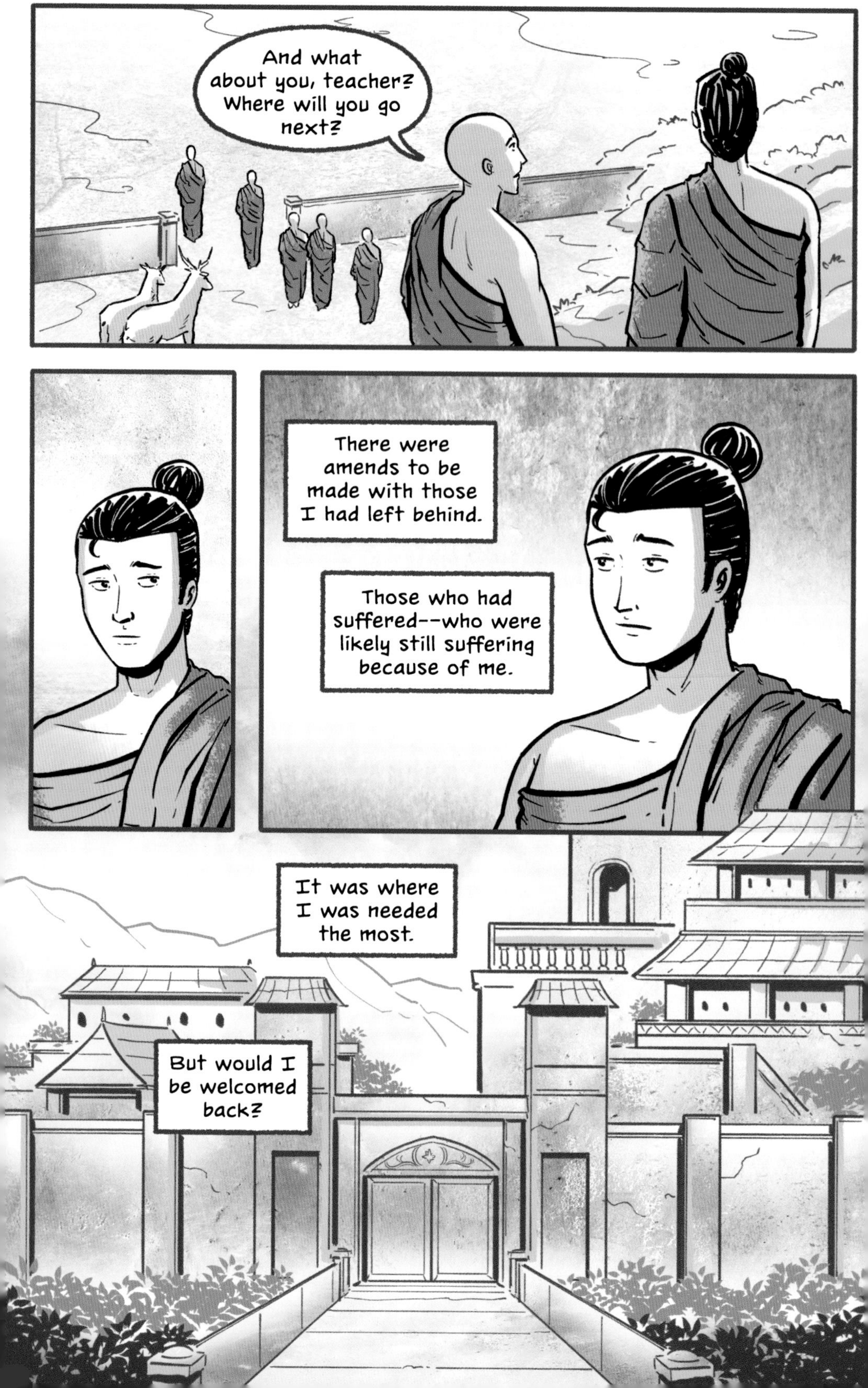
And what about you, teacher? Where will you go next?
There were amends to be made with those I had left behind.
Those who had suffered--who were likely still suffering because of me.
It was where I was needed the most.
But would I be welcomed back?

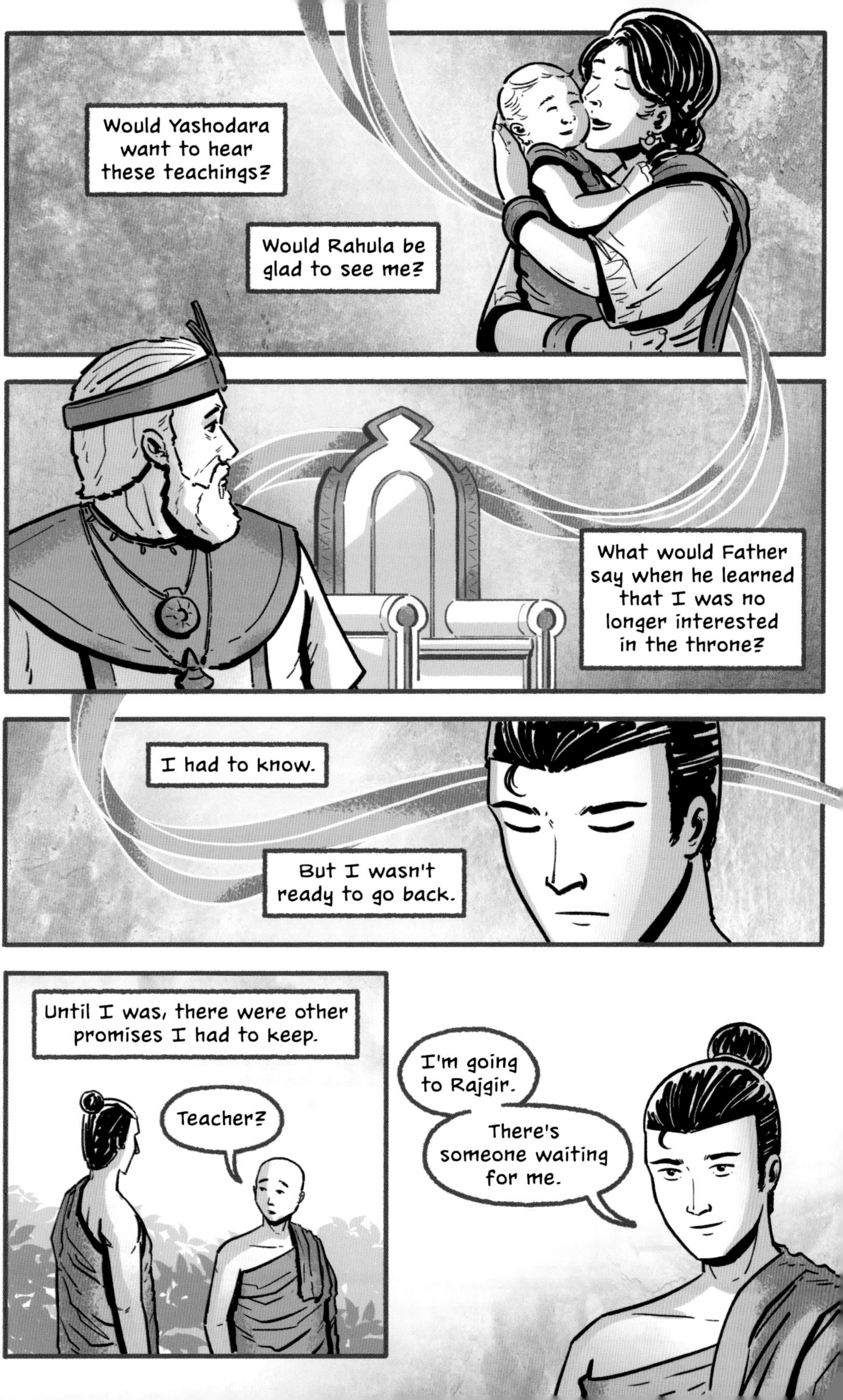
Would Yashodara want to hear these teachings?
Would Rahula be glad to see me?
What would Father say when he learned that I was no longer interested in the throne?
I had to know.
But I wasn't ready to go back.
Until I was, there were other promises I had to keep.
Teacher?
I'm going to Rajgir.
There's someone waiting for me.

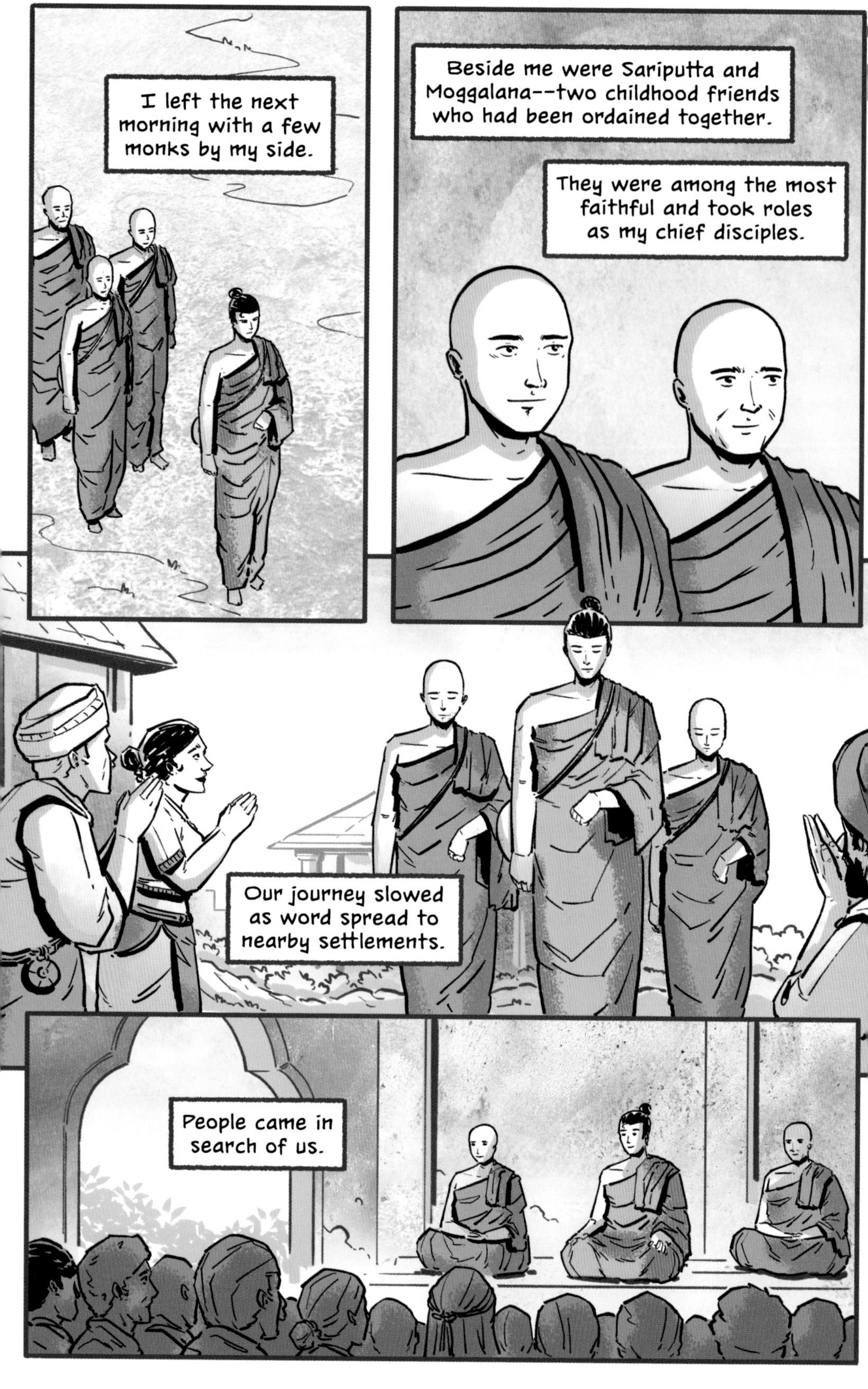
I left the next morning with a few monks by my side.
Beside me were Sariputta and Moggalana--two childhood friends who had been ordained together.
They were among the most faithful and took roles as my chief disciples.
Our journey slowed as word spread to nearby settlements.
People came in search of us.

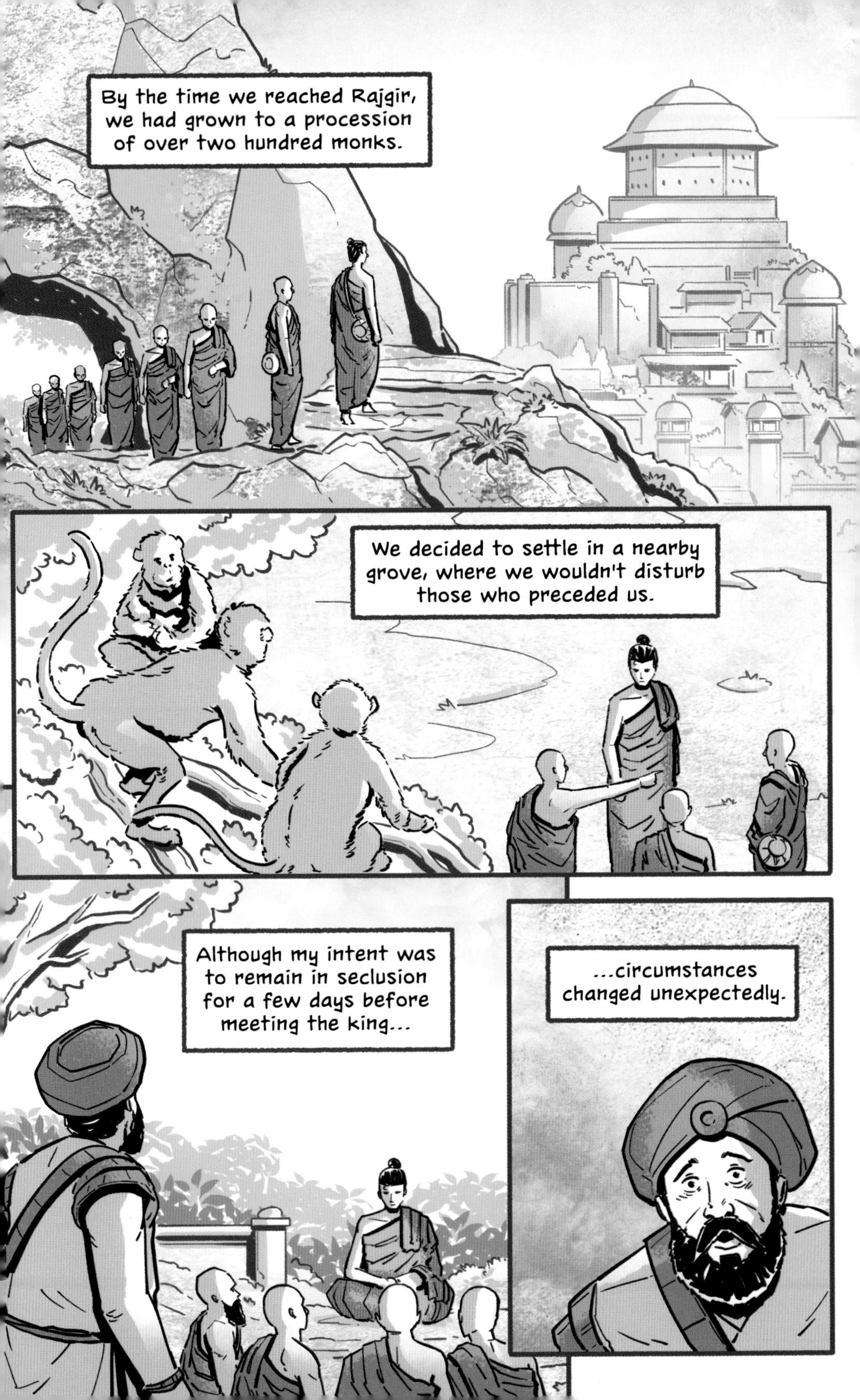
By the time we reached Rajgir, we had grown to a procession of over two hundred monks.
We decided to settle in a nearby grove, where we wouldn't disturb those who preceded us.
Although my intent was to remain in seclusion for a few days before meeting the king...
...circumstances changed unexpectedly.

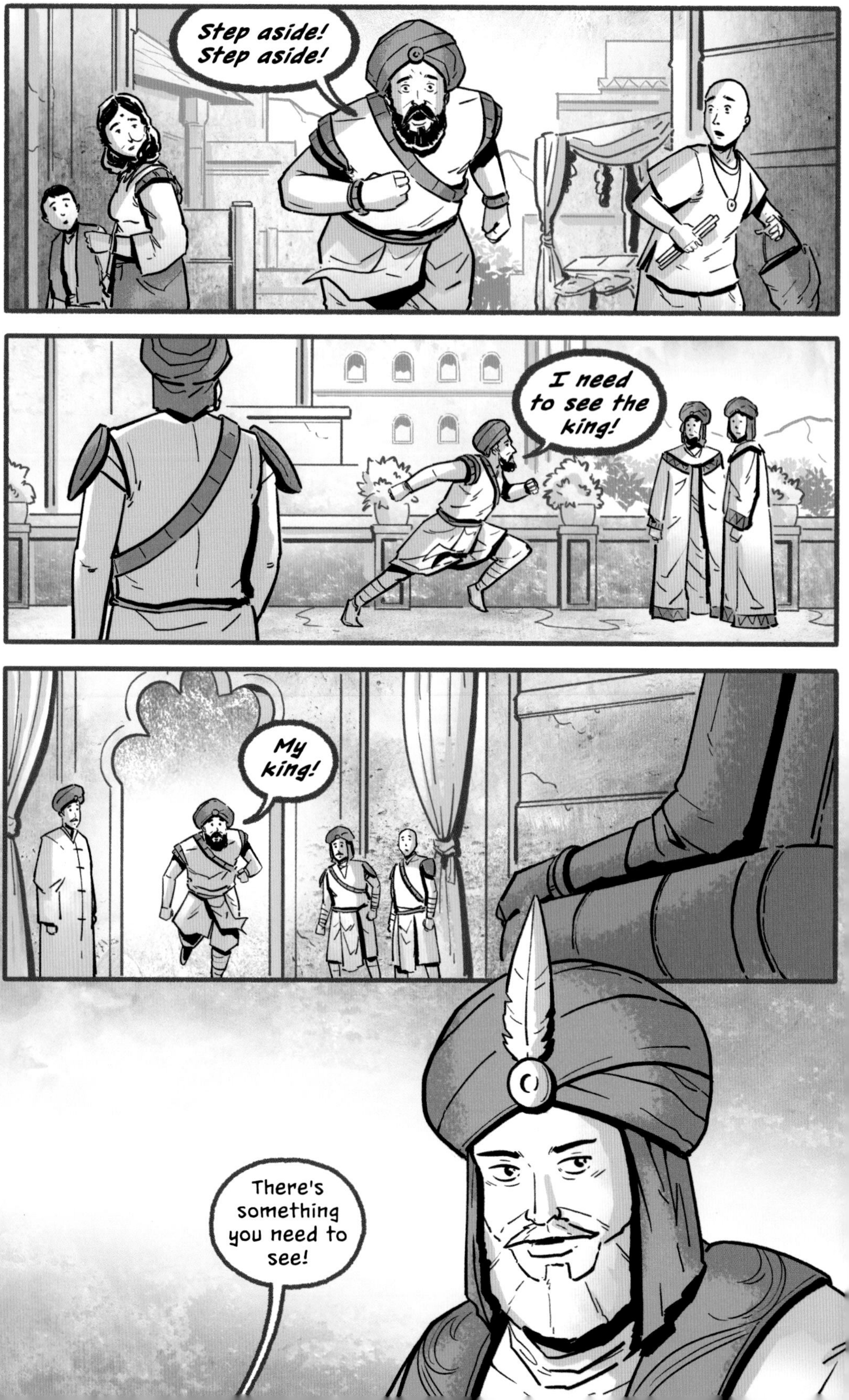
Step aside! Step aside!
I need to see the king!
My king!
There's something you need to see!

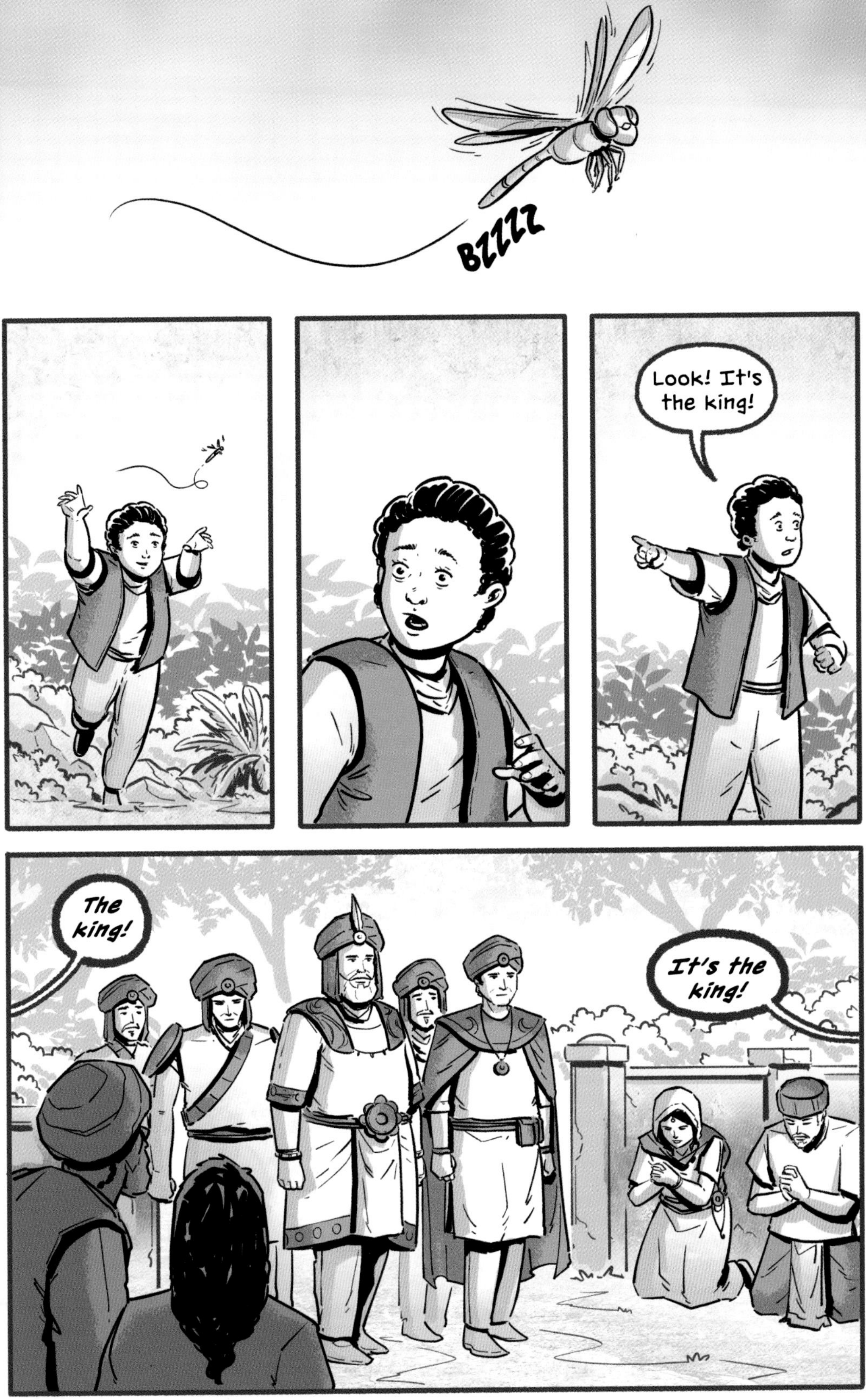
BZZZZ
Look! It's the king!
The king!
It's the king!

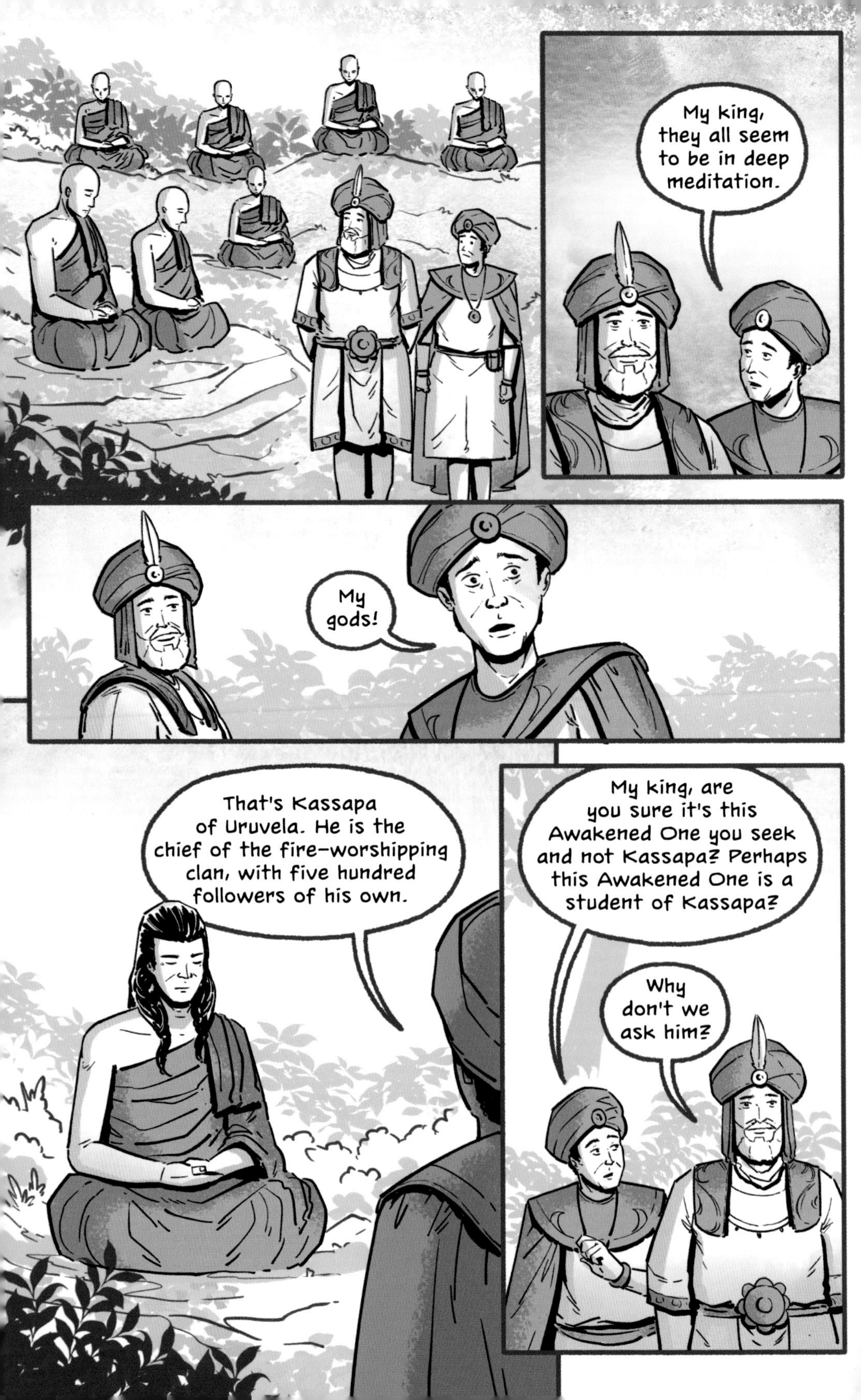
My king, they all seem to be in deep meditation.
My gods!
That's Kassapa of Uruvela. He is the chief of the fire-worshipping clan, with five hundred followers of his own.
My king, are you sure it's this Awakened One you seek and not Kassapa? Perhaps this Awakened One is a student of Kassapa?
Why don't we ask him?

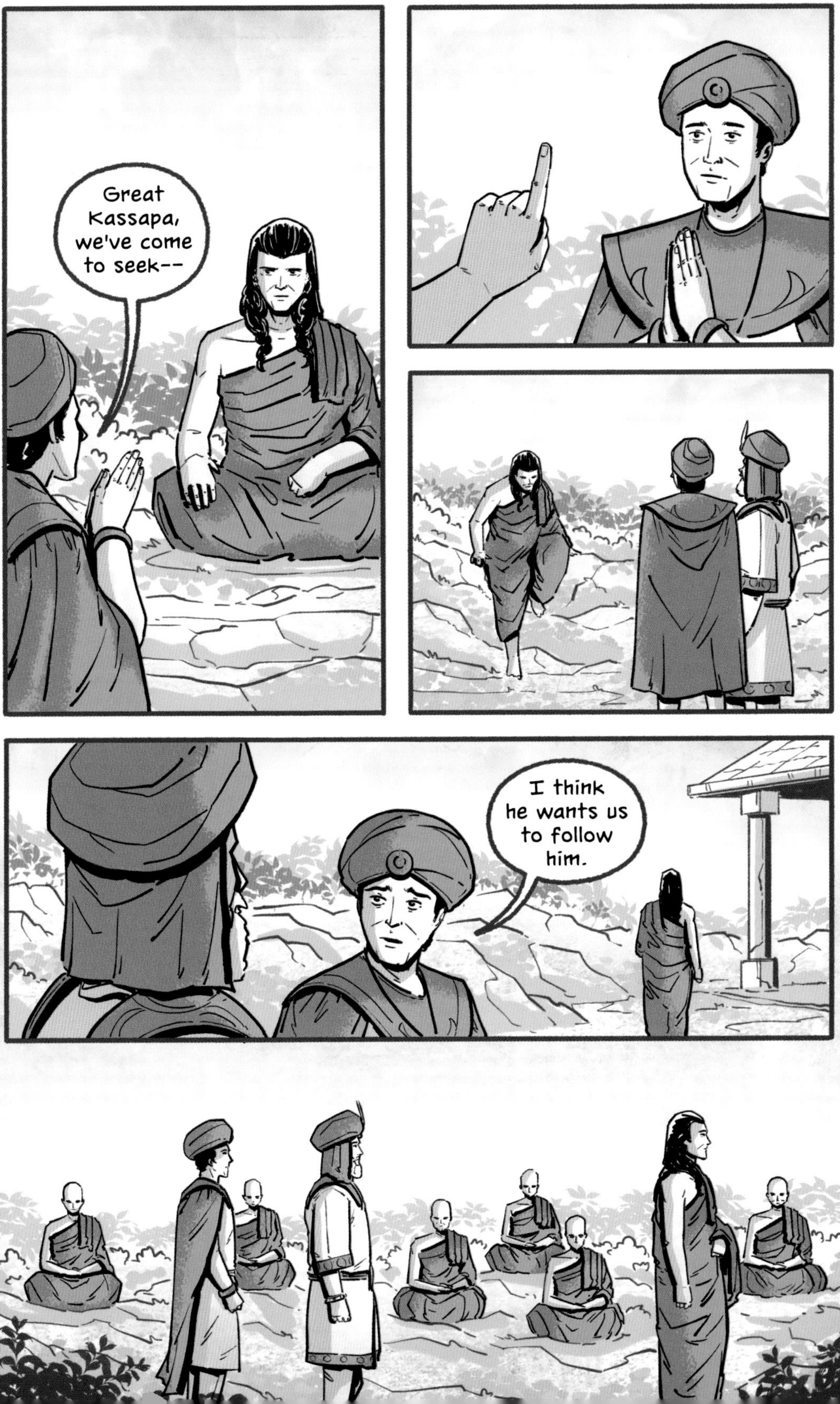
Great Kassapa, we've come to seek--
I think he wants us to follow him.

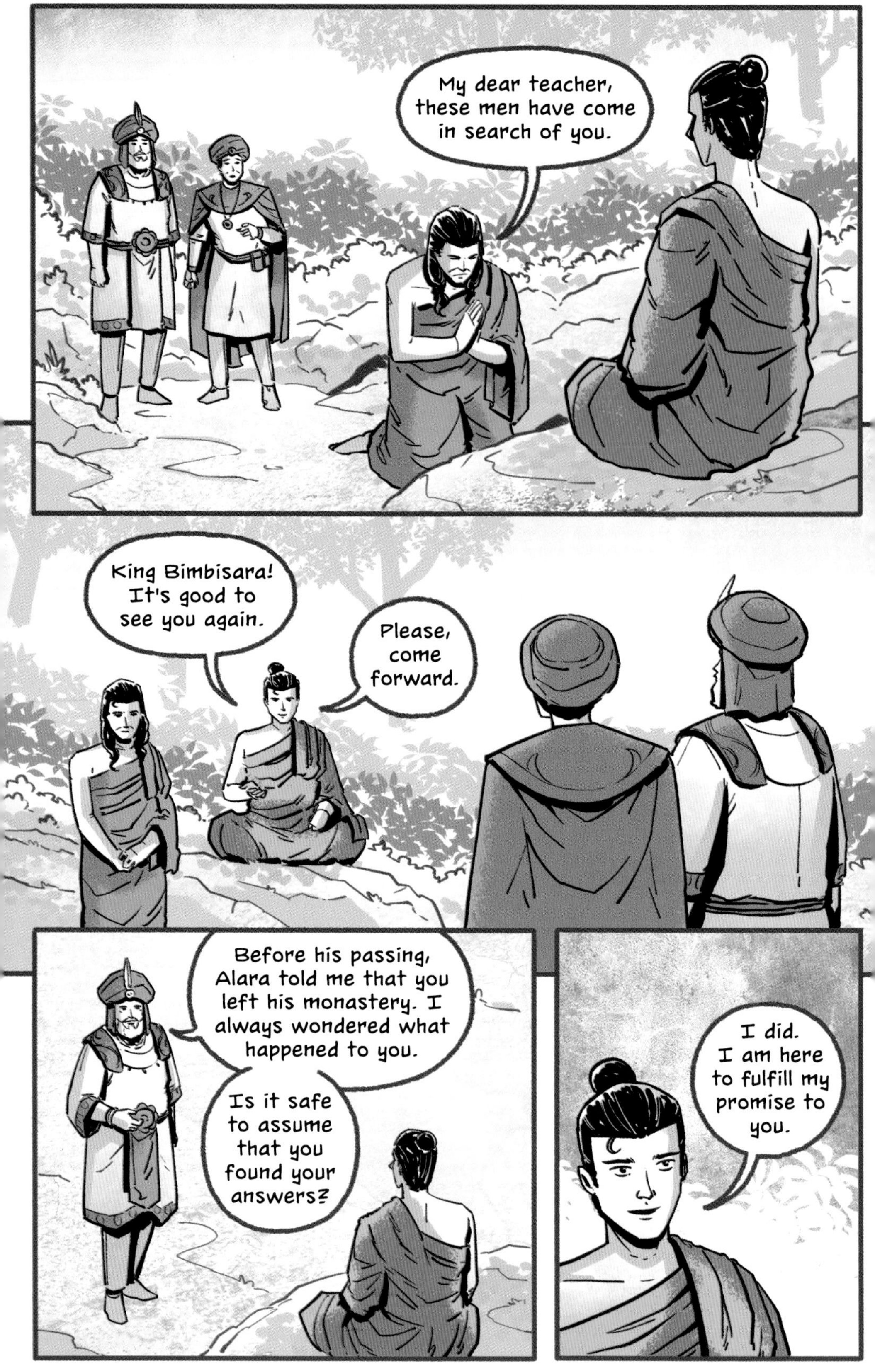
My dear teacher, these men have come in search of you.
King Bimbisara! It's good to see you again.
Please, come forward.
Before his passing, Alara told me that you left his monastery. I always wondered what happened to you.
Is it safe to assume that you found your answers?
I did. I am here to fulfill my promise to you.

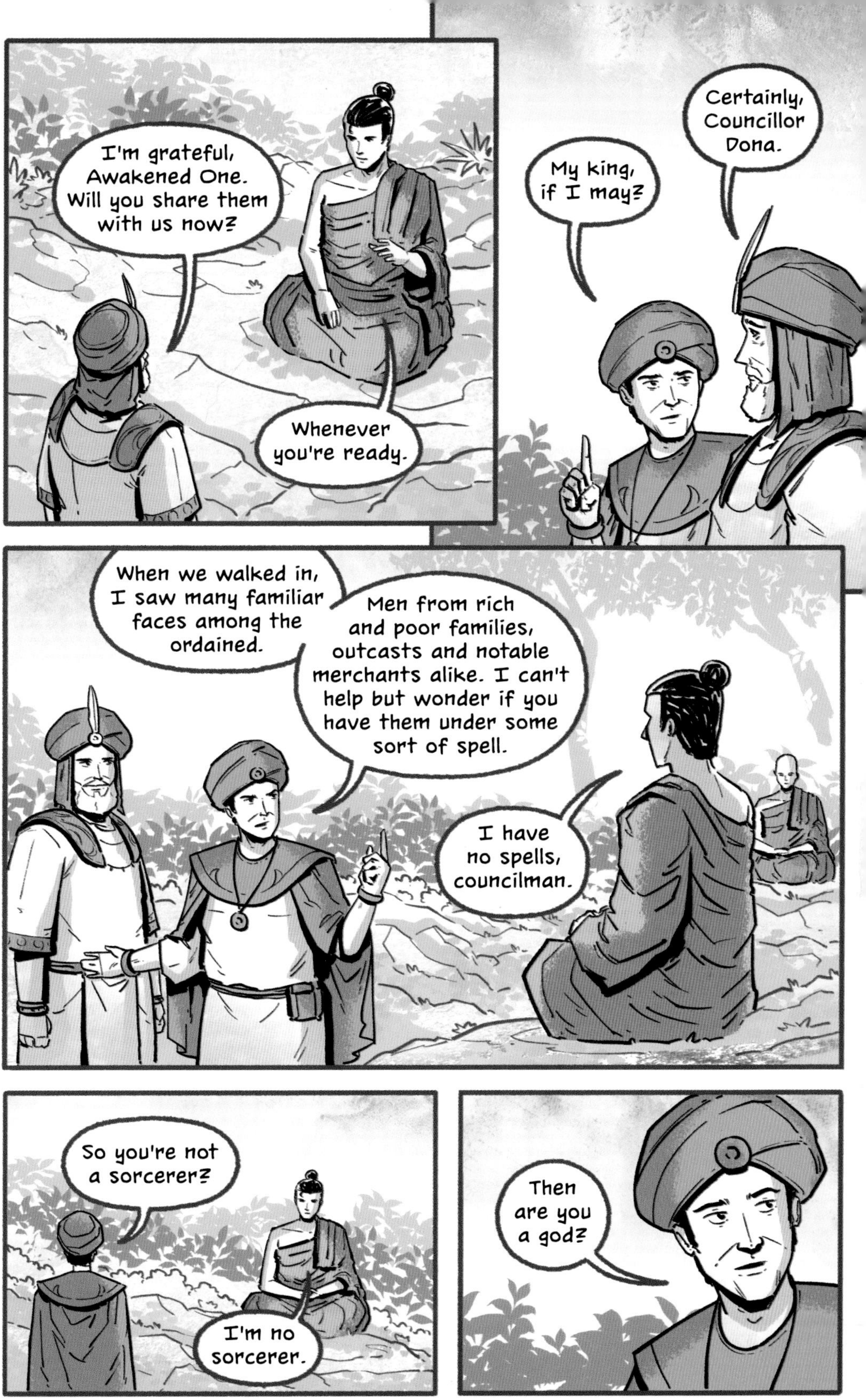
I'm grateful, Awakened One. Will you share them with us now?
Whenever you're ready.
My king, if I may?
Certainly, Councillor Dona.
When we walked in, I saw many familiar faces among the ordained.
Men from rich and poor families, outcasts and notable merchants alike. I can't help but wonder if you have them under some sort of spell.
I have no spells, councilman.
So you're not a sorcerer?
I'm no sorcerer.
Then are you a god?

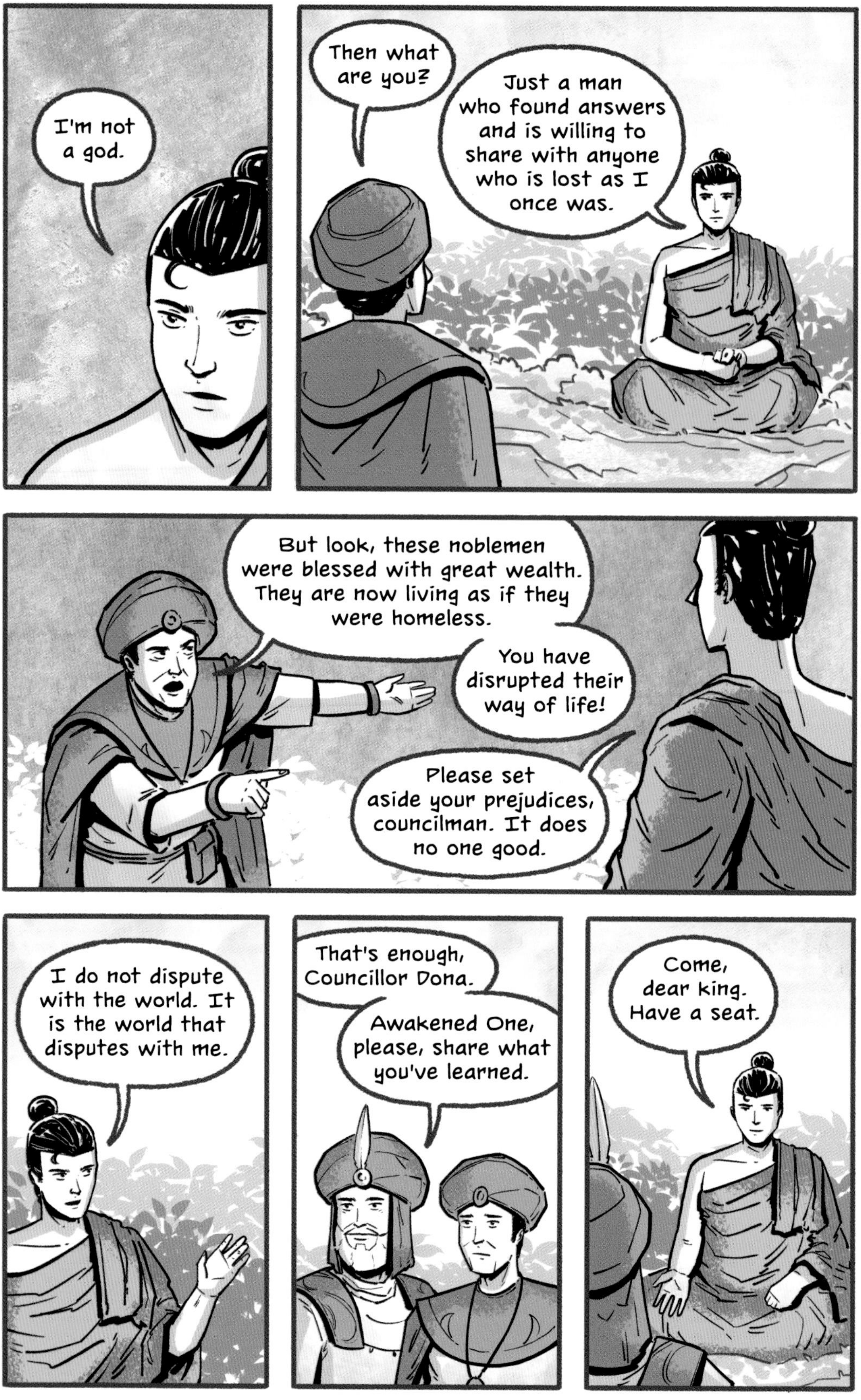
I'm not a god.
Then what are you?
Just a man who found answers and is willing to share with anyone who is lost as I once was.
But look, these noblemen were blessed with great wealth. They are now living as if they were homeless.
You have disrupted their way of life!
Please set aside your prejudices, councilman. It does no one good.
I do not dispute with the world. It is the world that disputes with me.
That's enough, Councillor Dona.
Awakened One, please, share what you've learned.
Come, dear king. Have a seat.

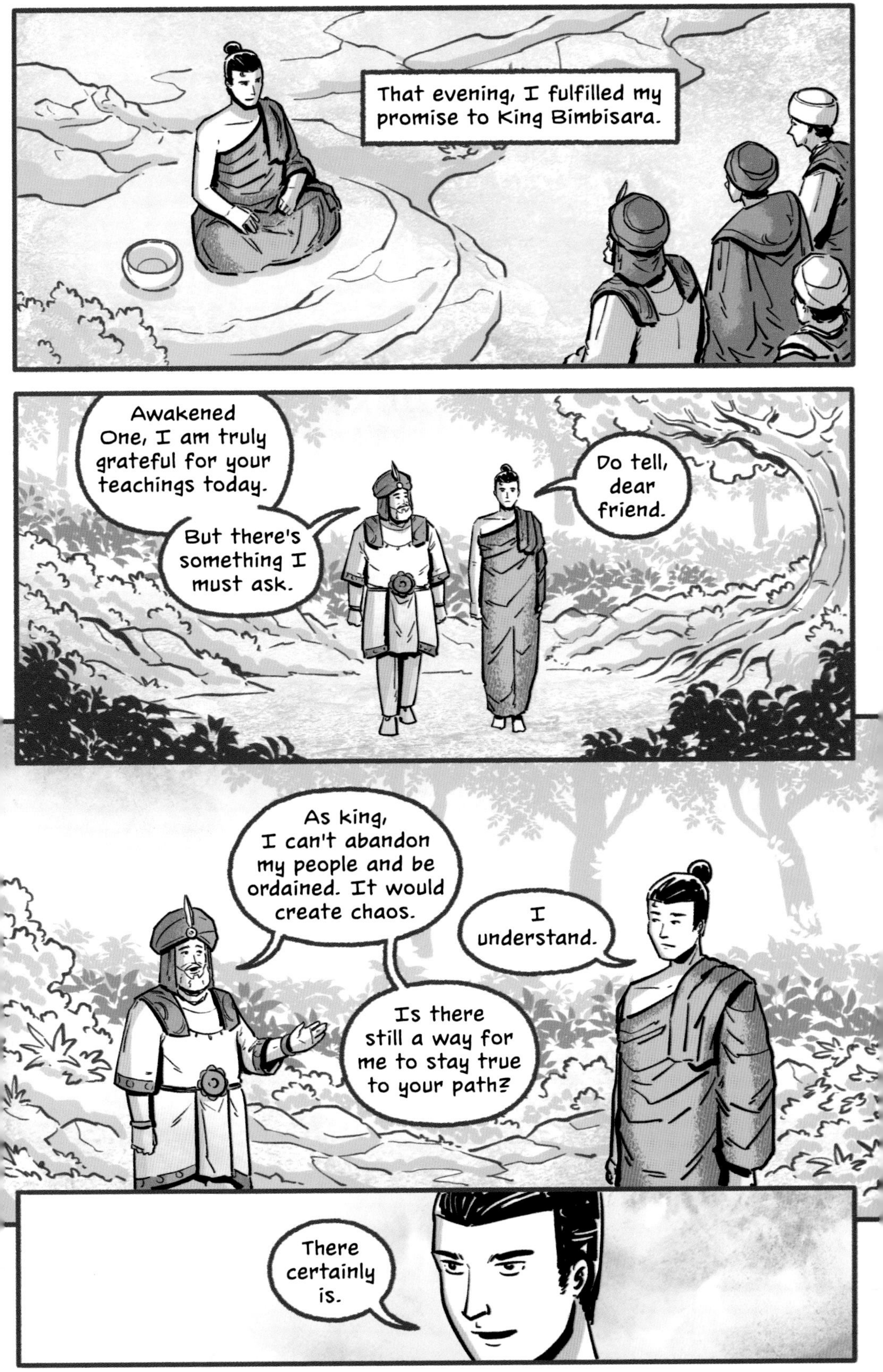
That evening, I fulfilled my promise to King Bimbisara.
Awakened One, I am truly grateful for your teachings today.
But there's something I must ask.
Do tell, dear friend.
As king, I can't abandon my people and be ordained. It would create chaos.
I understand.
Is there still a way for me to stay true to your path?
There certainly is.

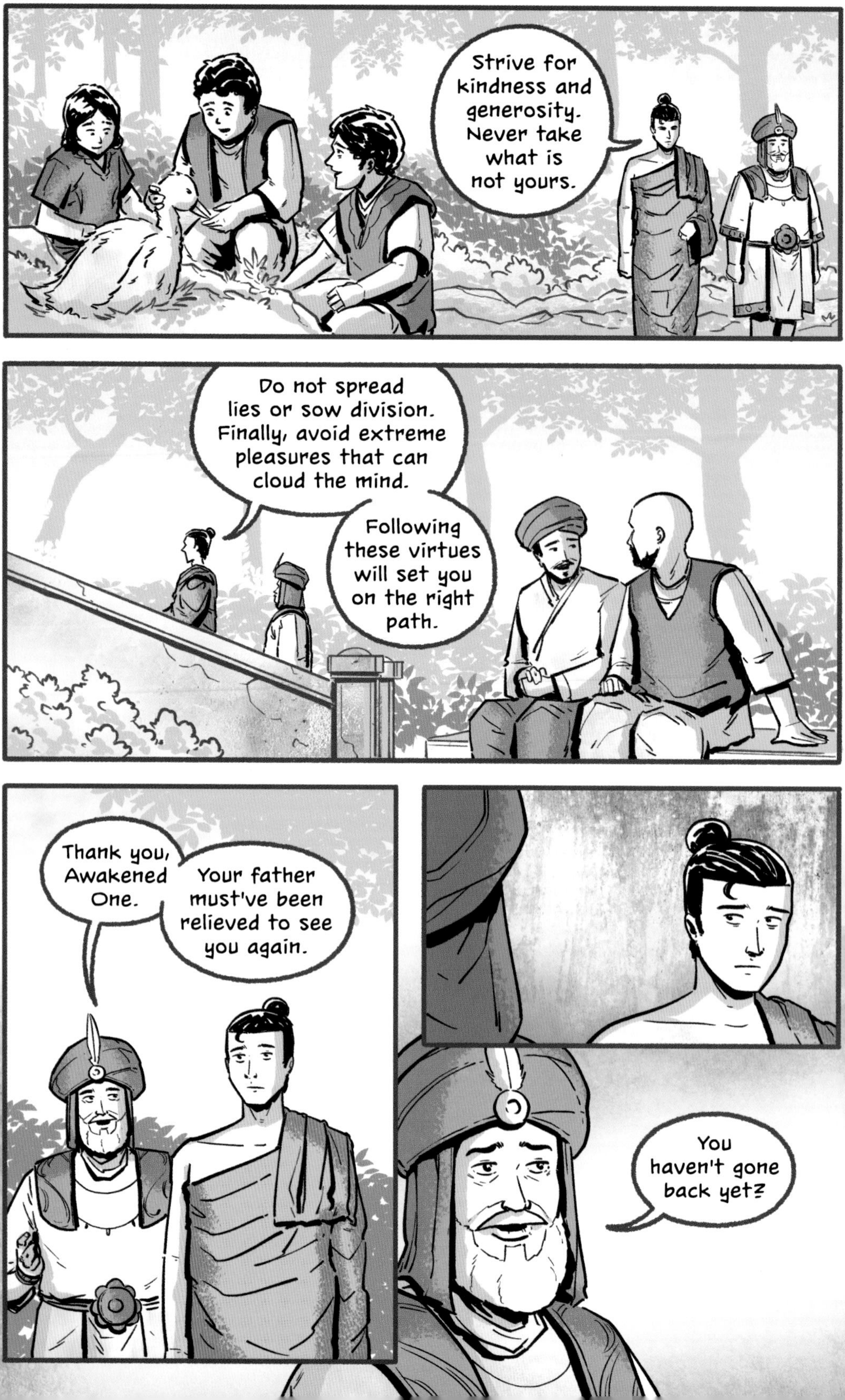
Strive for kindness and generosity. Never take what is not yours.
Do not spread lies or sow division. Finally, avoid extreme pleasures that can cloud the mind.
Following these virtues will set you on the right path.
Thank you, Awakened One.
Your father must've been relieved to see you again.
You haven't gone back yet?

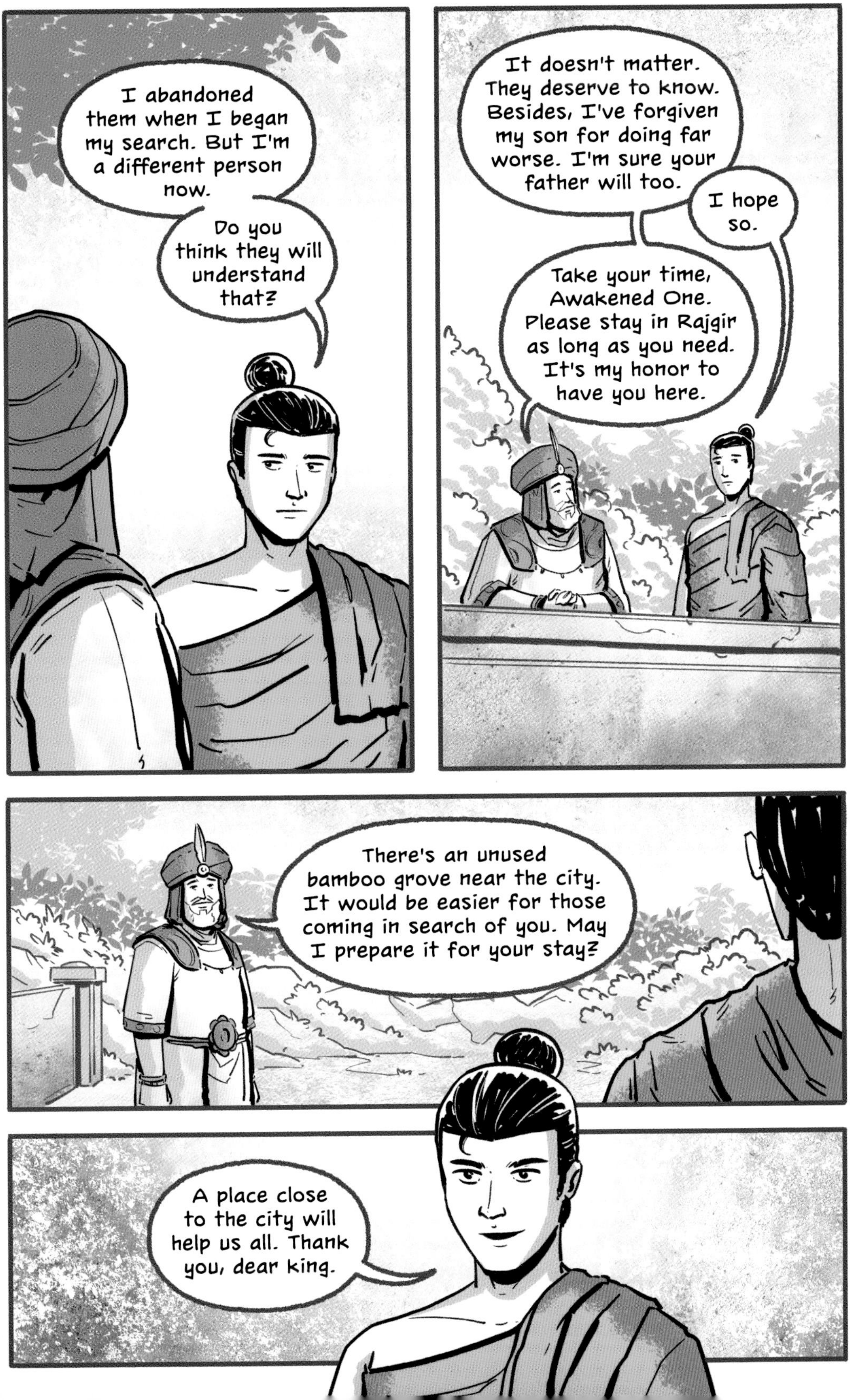
I abandoned them when I began my search. But I'm a different person now.
Do you think they will understand that?
It doesn't matter. They deserve to know. Besides, I've forgiven my son for doing far worse. I'm sure your father will too.
I hope so.
Take your time, Awakened One. Please stay in Rajgir as long as you need. It's my honor to have you here.
There's an unused bamboo grove near the city. It would be easier for those coming in search of you. May I prepare it for your stay?
A place close to the city will help us all. Thank you, dear king.

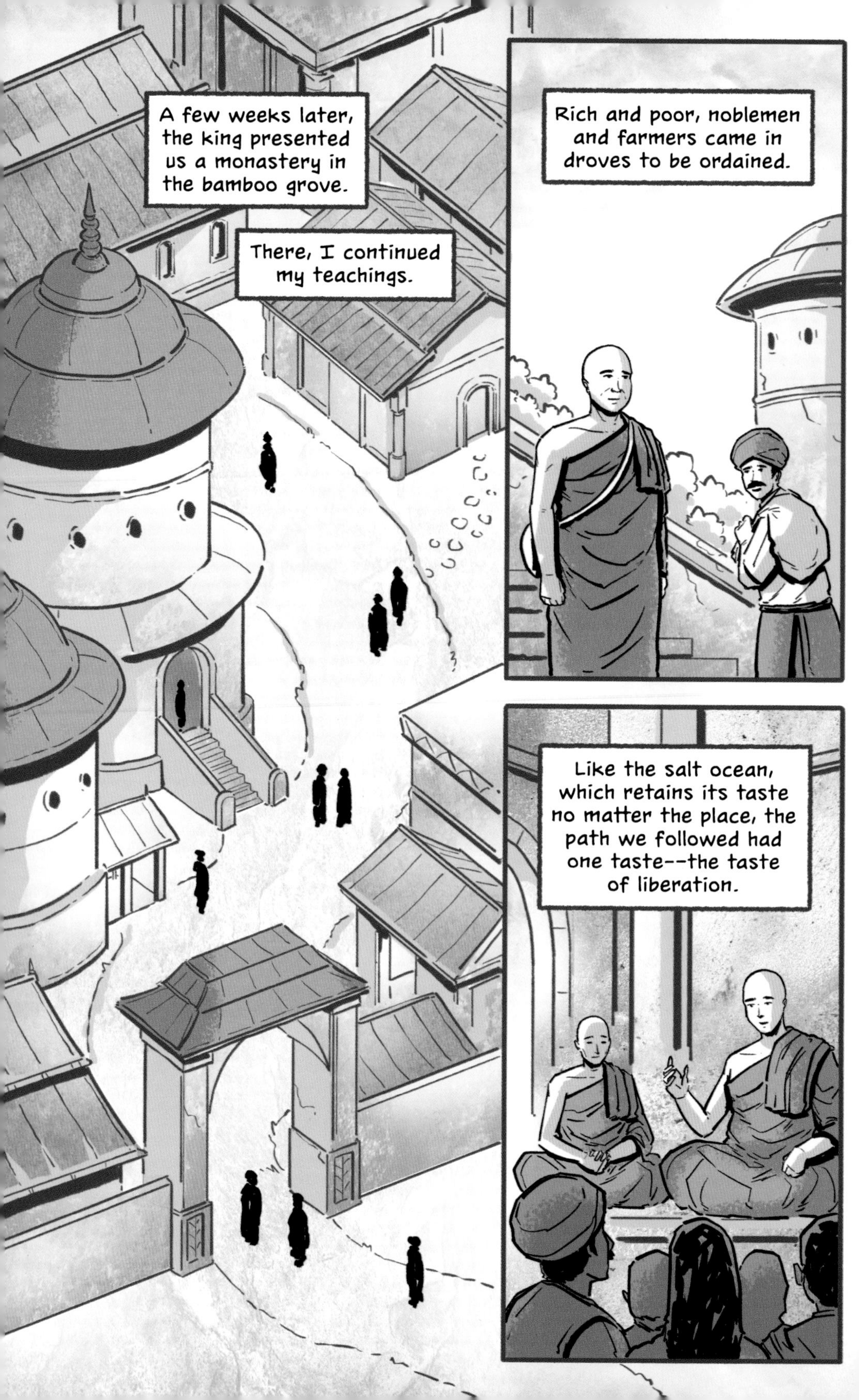
A few weeks later, the king presented us a monastery in the bamboo grove.
There, I continued my teachings.
Rich and poor, noblemen and farmers came in droves to be ordained.
Like the salt ocean, which retains its taste no matter the place, the path we followed had one taste--the taste of liberation.

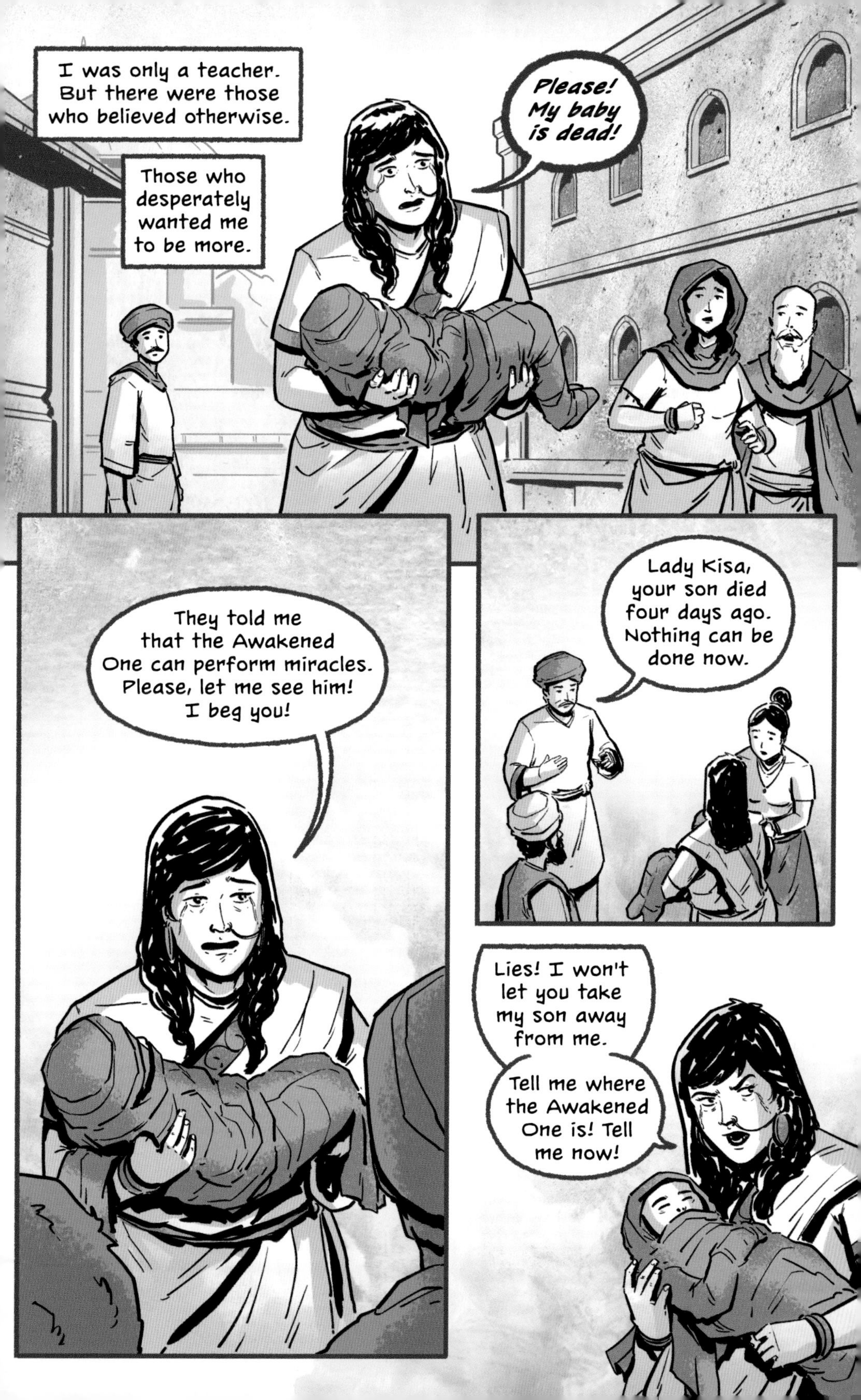
I was only a teacher. But there were those who believed otherwise.
Those who desperately wanted me to be more.
Please! My baby is dead!
They told me that the Awakened One can perform miracles. Please, let me see him! I beg you!
Lady Kisa, your son died four days ago. Nothing can be done now.
Lies! I won't let you take my son away from me.
Tell me where the Awakened One is! Tell me now!

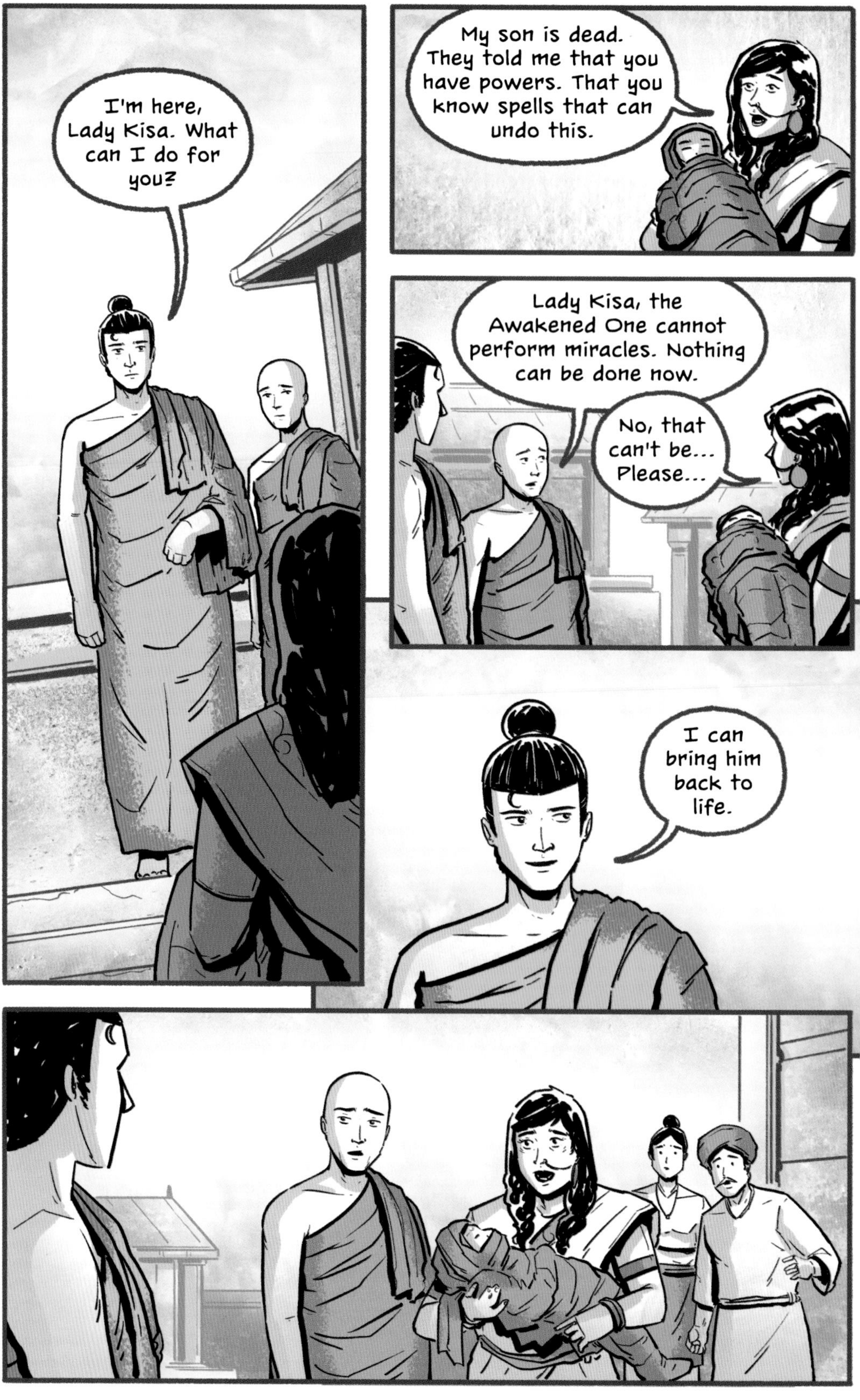
I'm here, Lady Kisa. What can I do for you?
My son is dead. They told me that you have powers. That you know spells that can undo this.
Lady Kisa, the Awakened One cannot perform miracles. Nothing can be done now.
No, that can't be... Please...
I can bring him back to life.

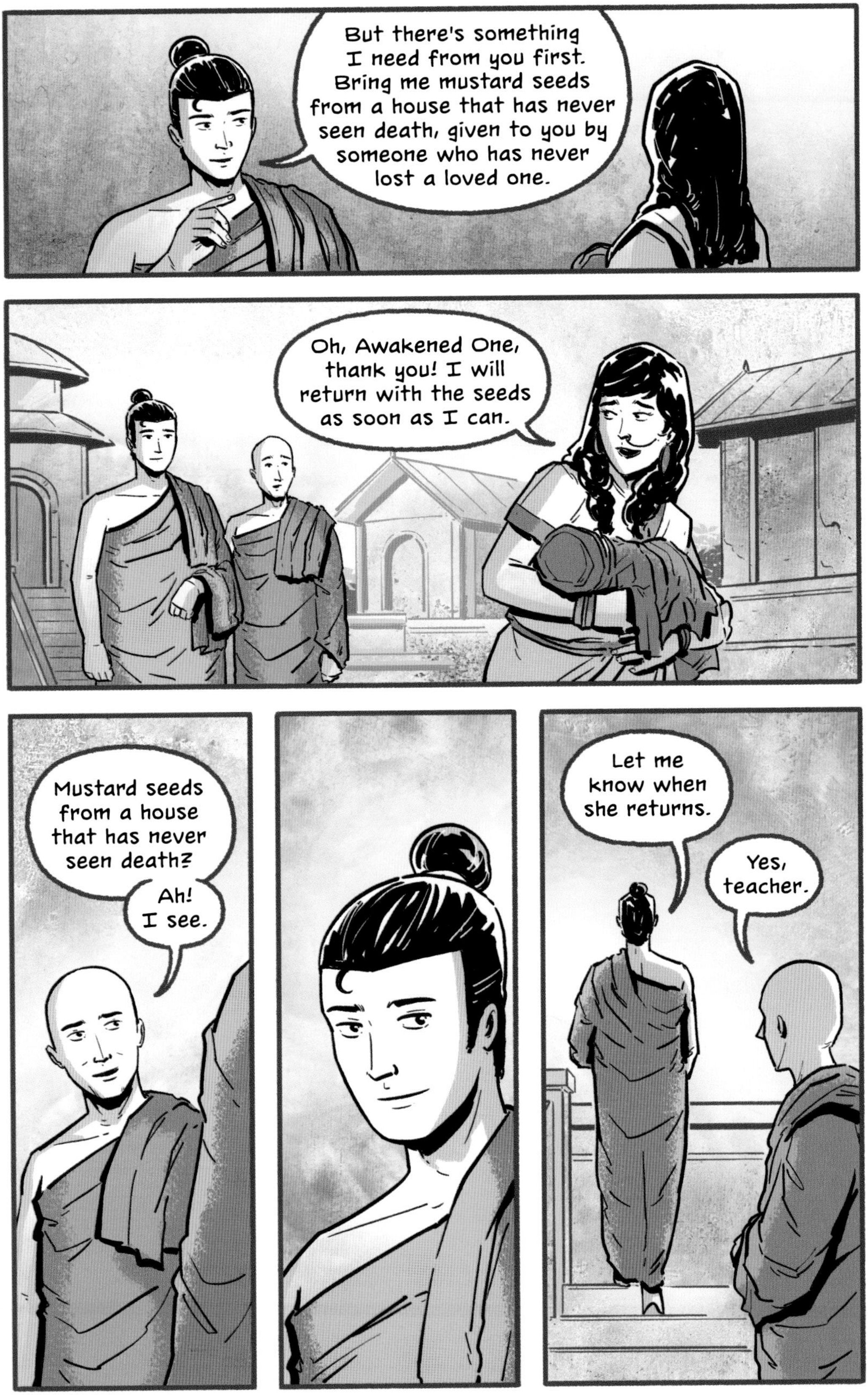
But there's something I need from you first. Bring me mustard seeds from a house that has never seen death, given to you by someone who has never lost a loved one.
Oh, Awakened One, thank you! I will return with the seeds as soon as I can.
Mustard seeds from a house that has never seen death?
Ah! I see.
Let me know when she returns.
Yes, teacher.

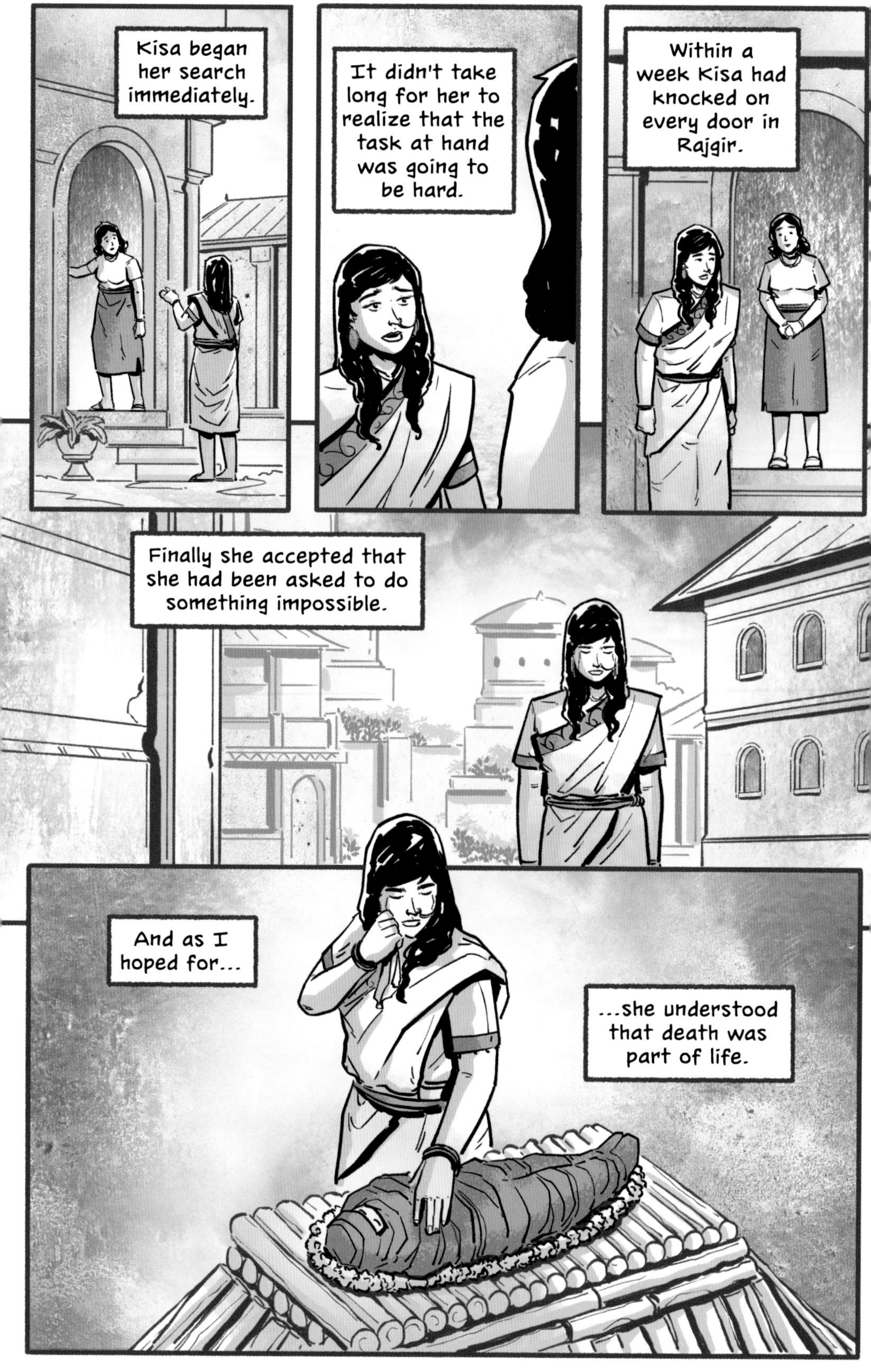
Kisa began her search immediately.
It didn't take long for her to realize that the task at hand was going to be hard.
Within a week Kisa had knocked on every door in Rajgir.
Finally she accepted that she had been asked to do something impossible.
And as I hoped for...
...she understood that death was part of life.

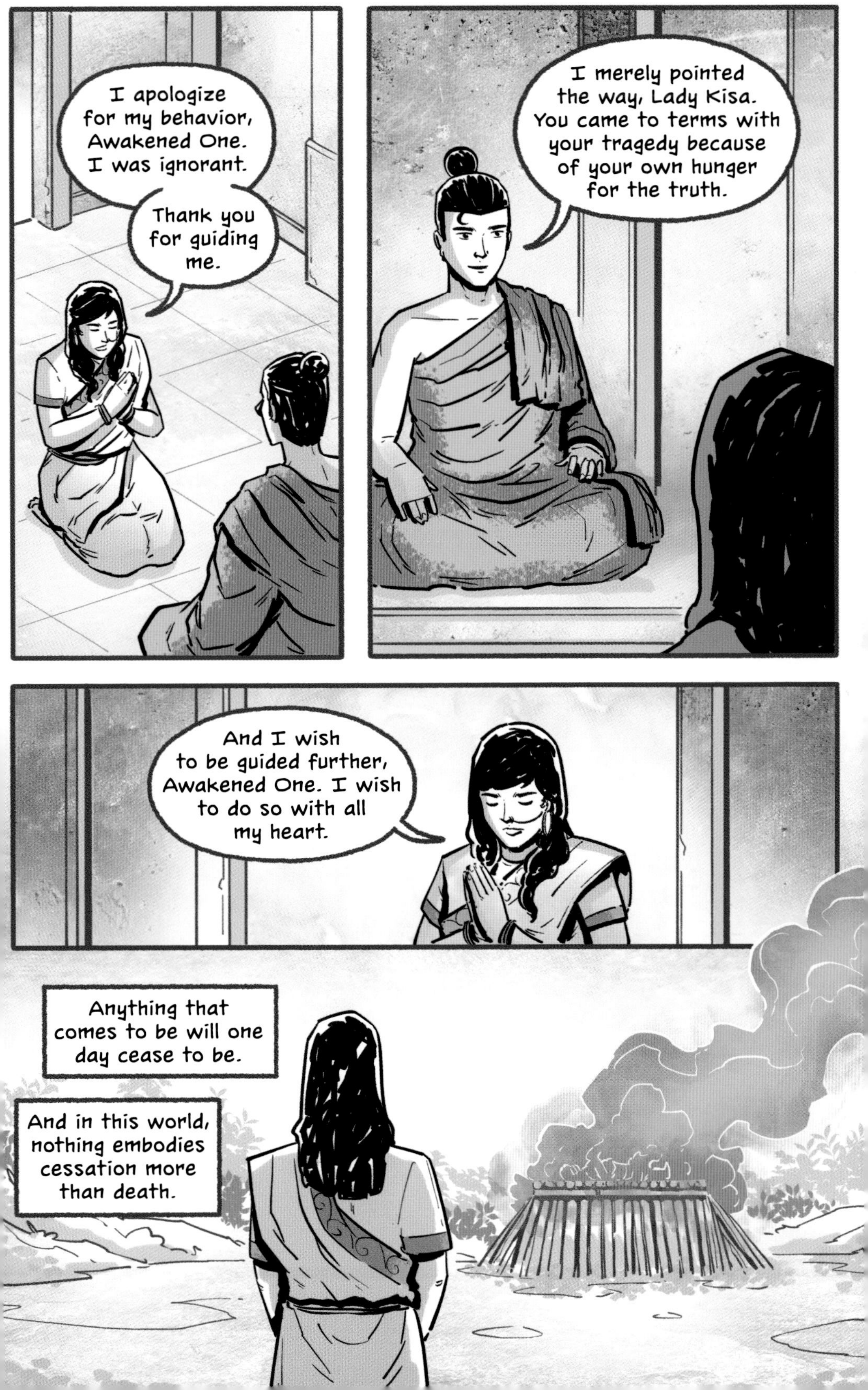
I apologize for my behavior, Awakened One. I was ignorant.
Thank you for guiding me.
I merely pointed the way, Lady Kisa. You came to terms with your tragedy because of your own hunger for the truth.
And I wish to be guided further, Awakened One. I wish to do so with all my heart.
Anything that comes to be will one day cease to be.
And in this world, nothing embodies cessation more than death.

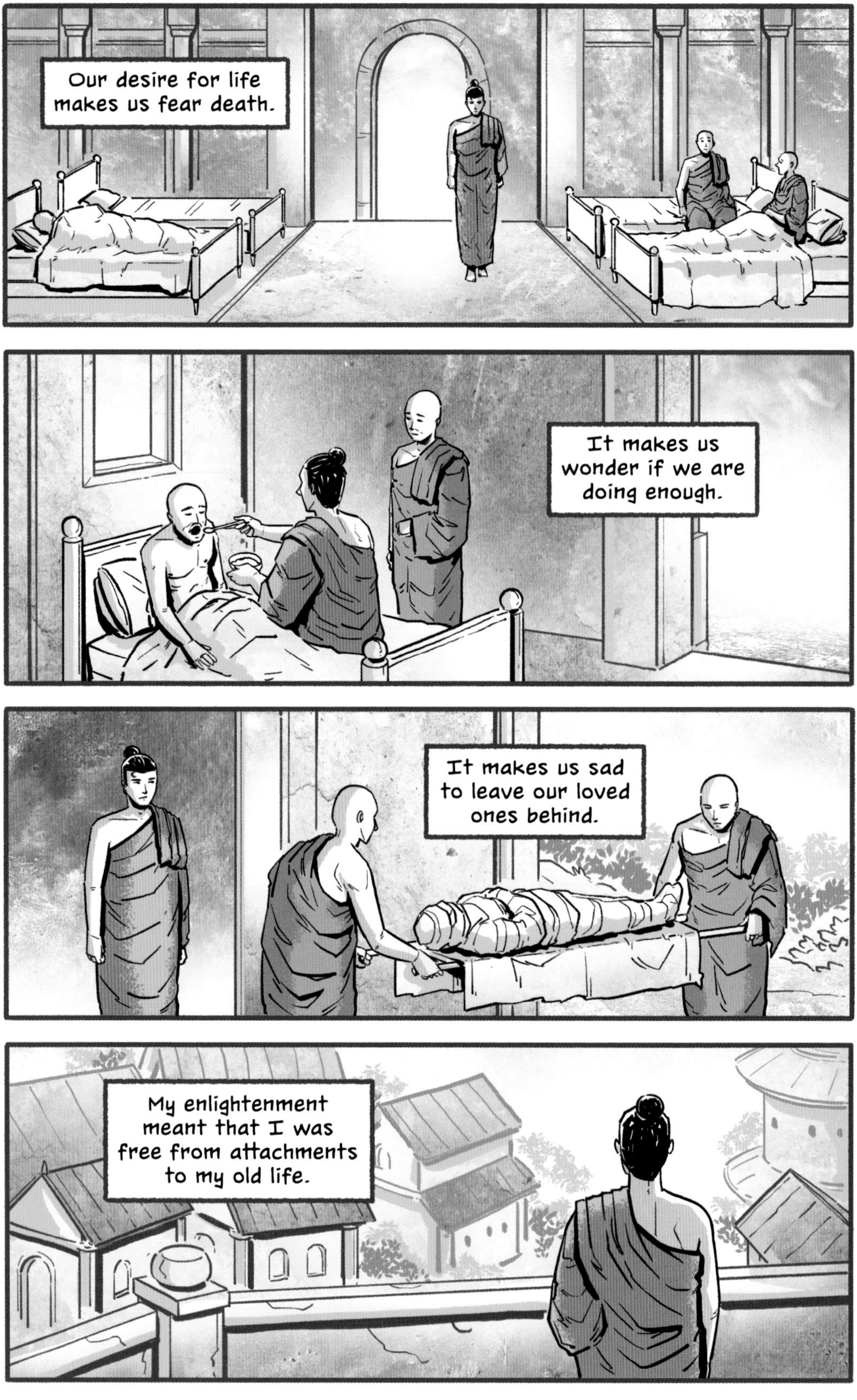
Our desire for life makes us fear death.
It makes us wonder if we are doing enough.
It makes us sad to leave our loved ones behind.
My enlightenment meant that I was free from attachments to my old life.

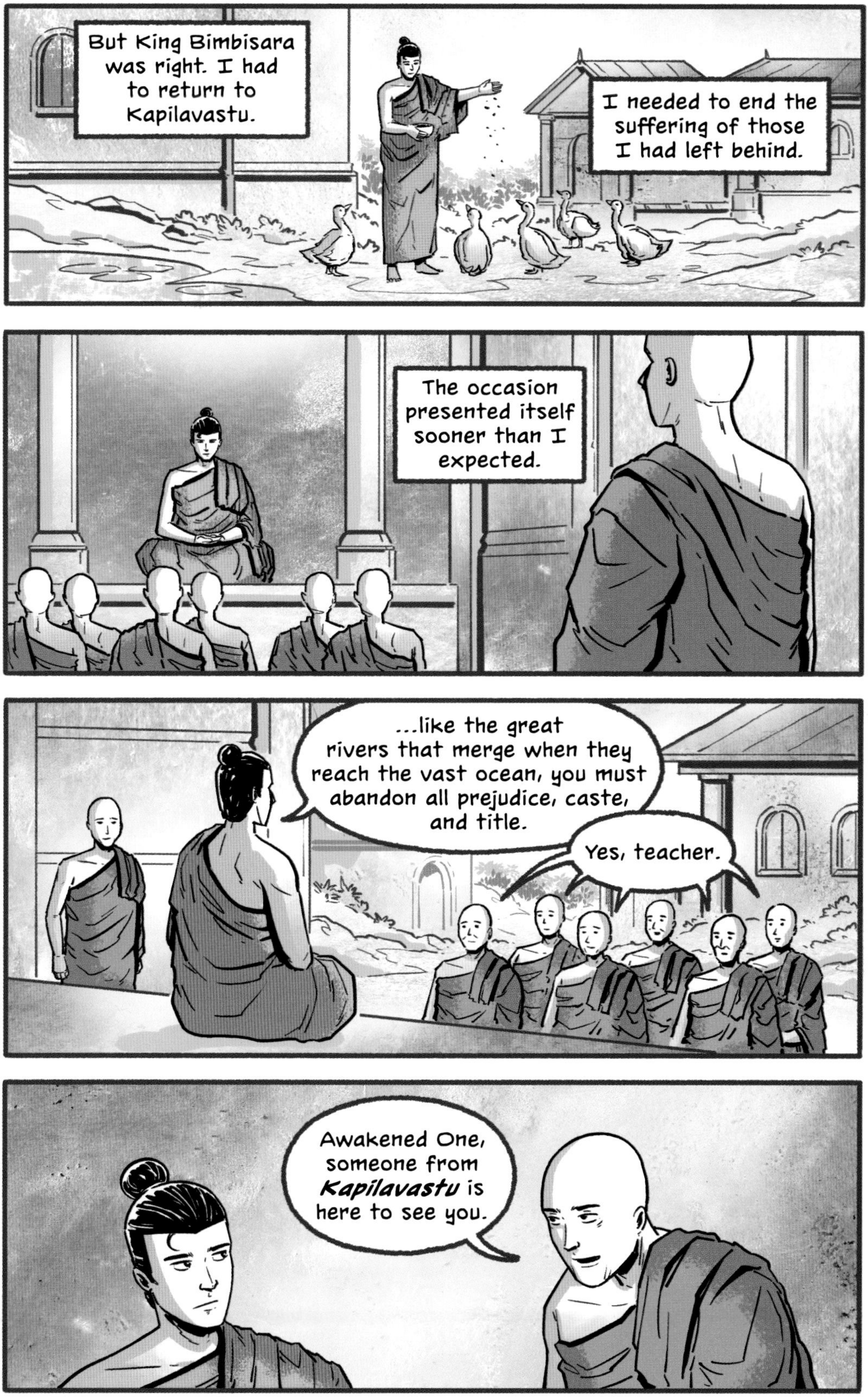

But King Bimbisara was right. I had to return to Kapilavastu.
I needed to end the suffering of those I had left behind.
The occasion presented itself sooner than I expected.
...like the great rivers that merge when they reach the vast ocean, you must abandon all prejudice, caste, and title.
Yes, teacher.
Awakened One, someone from *Kapilavastu* is here to see you.

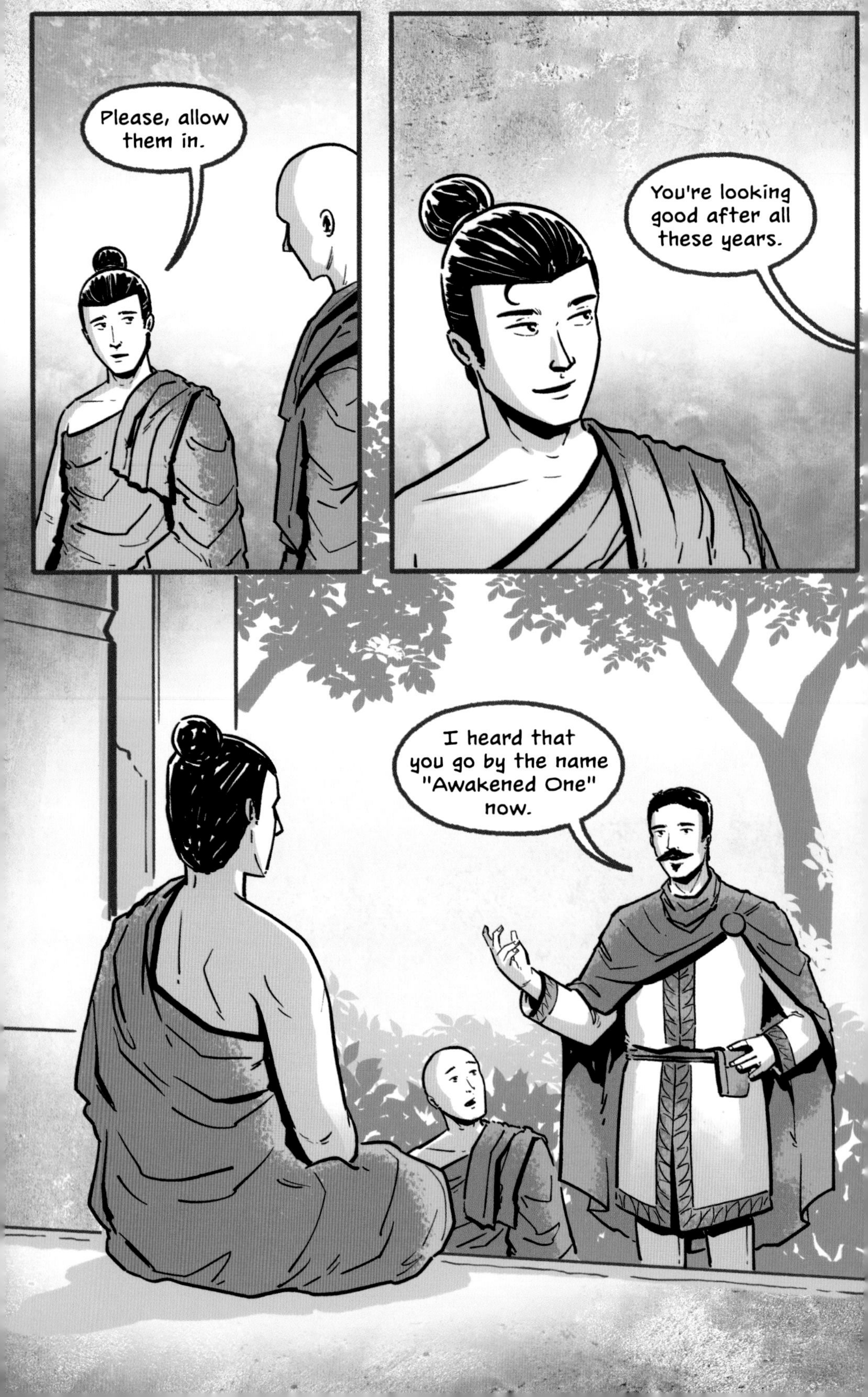
Please, allow them in.
You're looking good after all these years.
I heard that you go by the name "Awakened One" now.

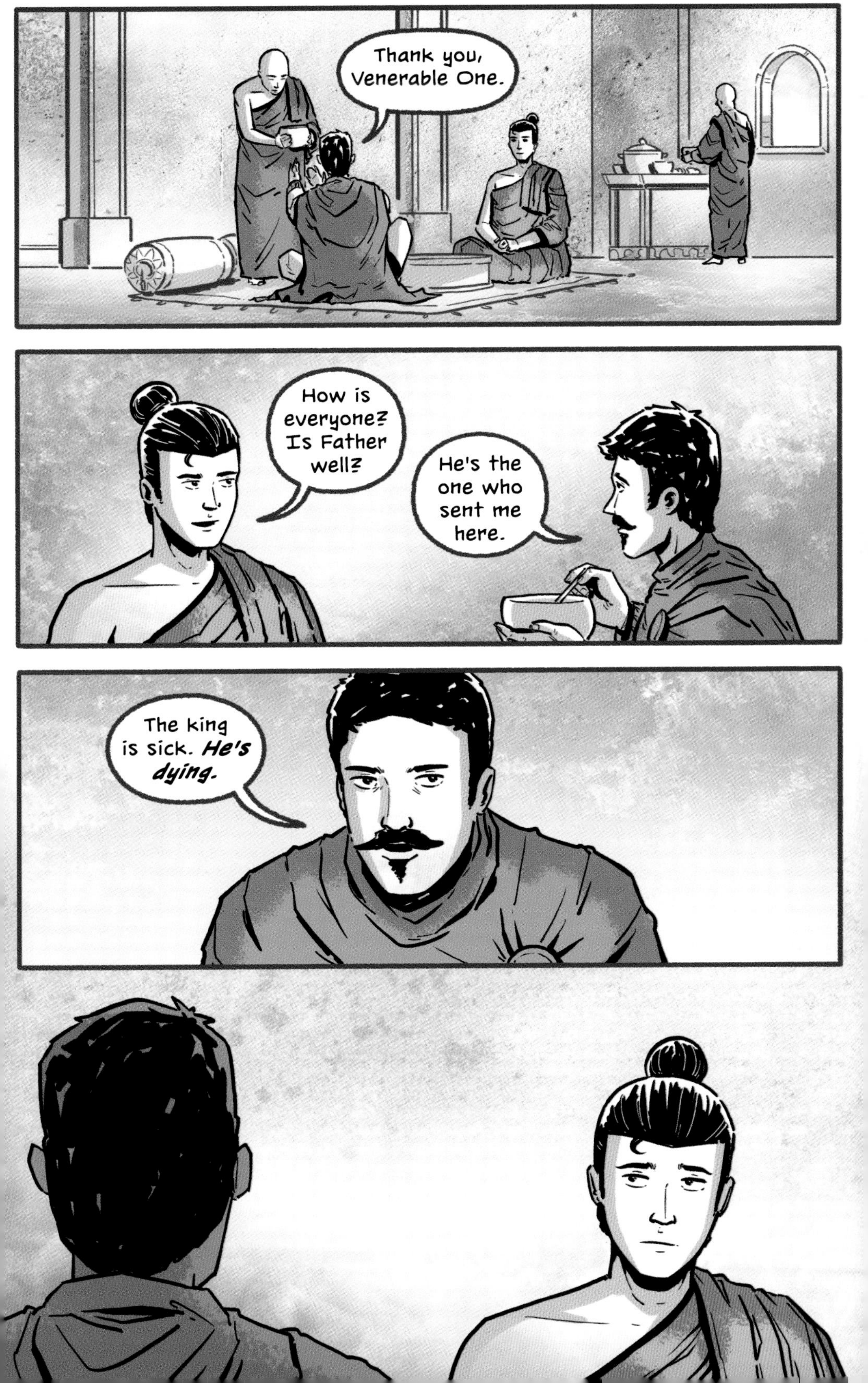
Thank you, Venerable One.
How is everyone? Is Father well?
He's the one who sent me here.
The king is sick. *He's dying.*

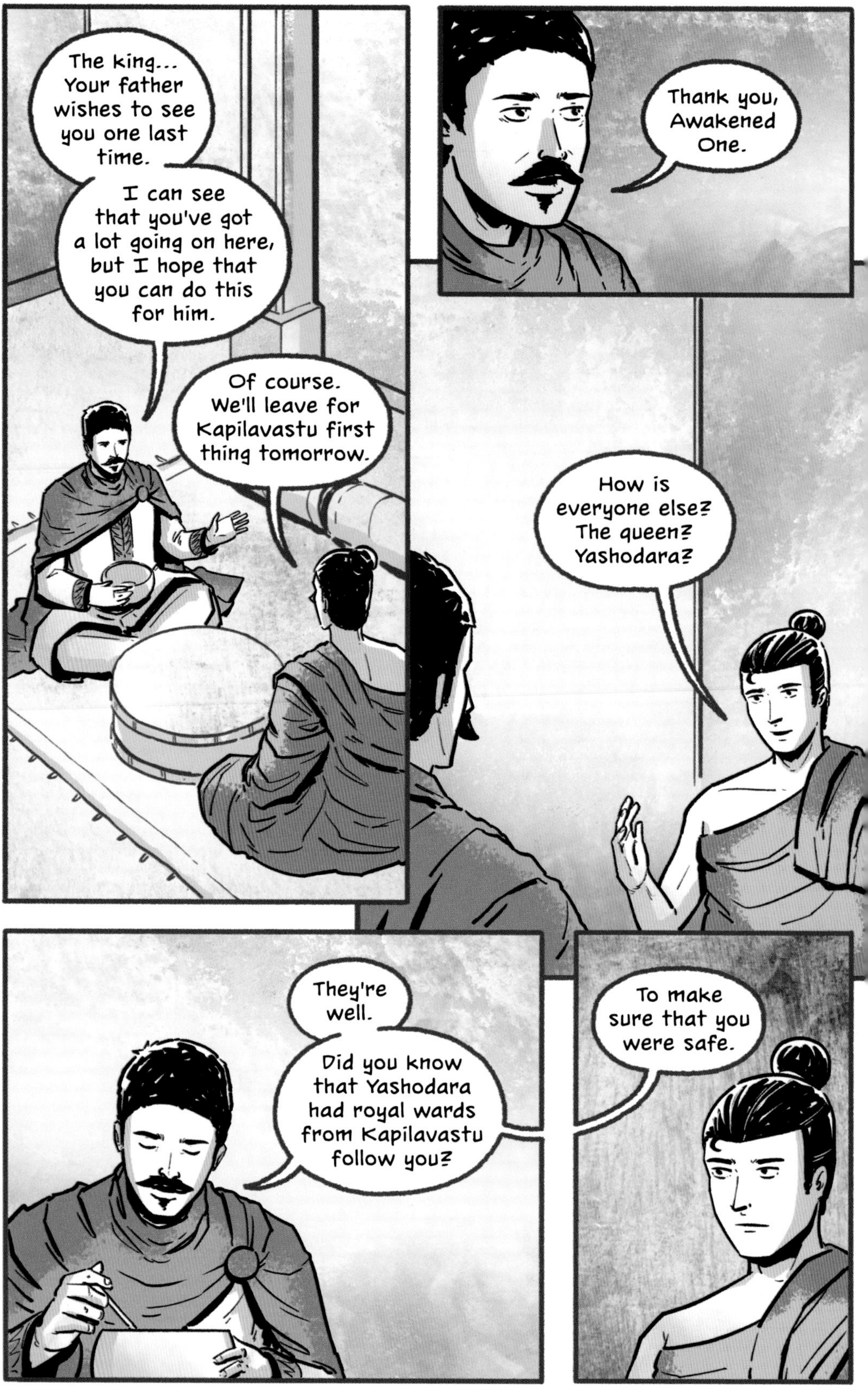

The king... Your father wishes to see you one last time.
I can see that you've got a lot going on here, but I hope that you can do this for him.
Of course. We'll leave for Kapilavastu first thing tomorrow.
Thank you, Awakened One.
How is everyone else? The queen? Yashodara?
They're well.
Did you know that Yashodara had royal wards from Kapilavastu follow you?
To make sure that you were safe.

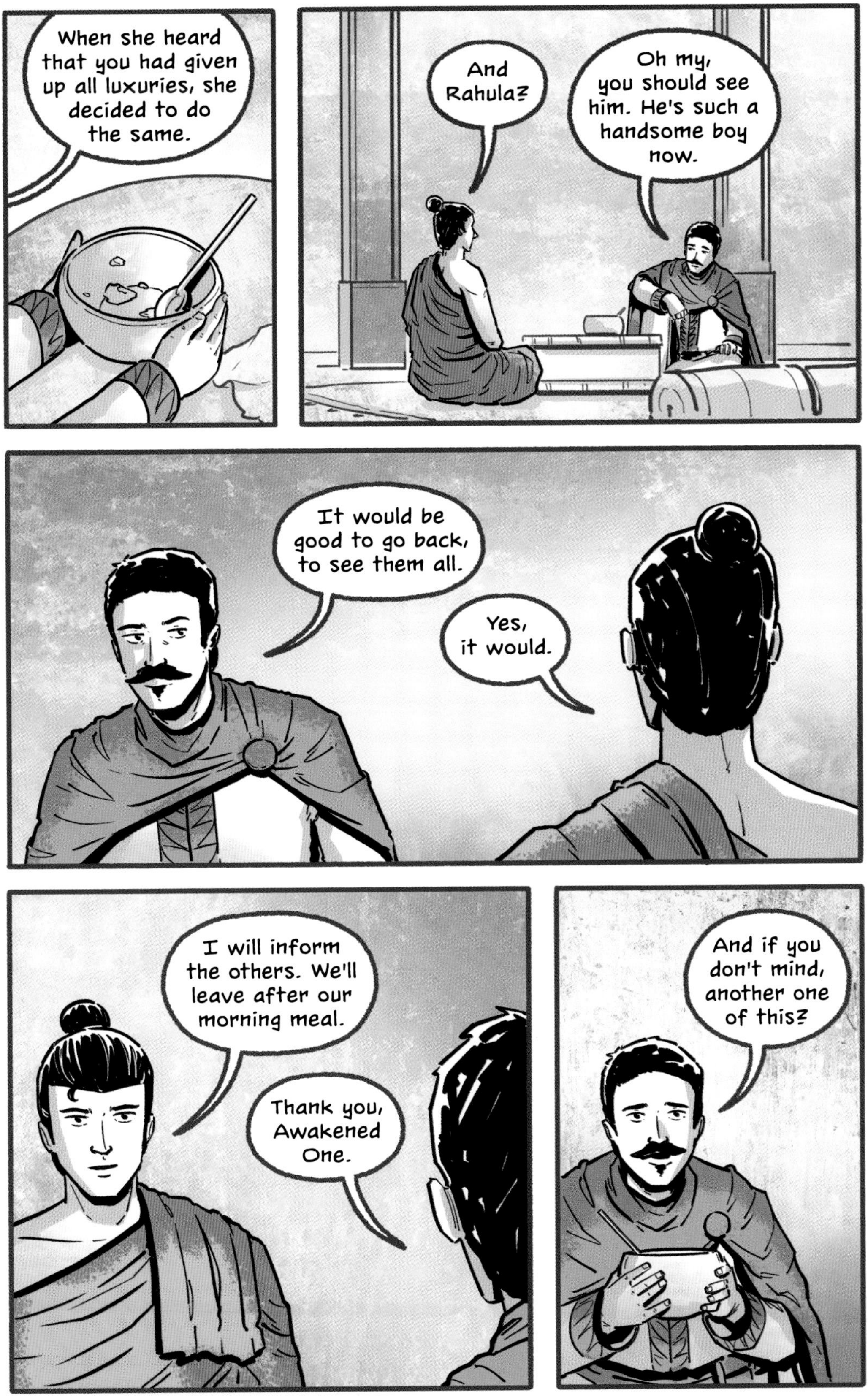
When she heard that you had given up all luxuries, she decided to do the same.
And Rahula?
Oh my, you should see him. He's such a handsome boy now.
It would be good to go back, to see them all.
Yes, it would.
I will inform the others. We'll leave after our morning meal.
Thank you, Awakened One.
And if you don't mind, another one of this?

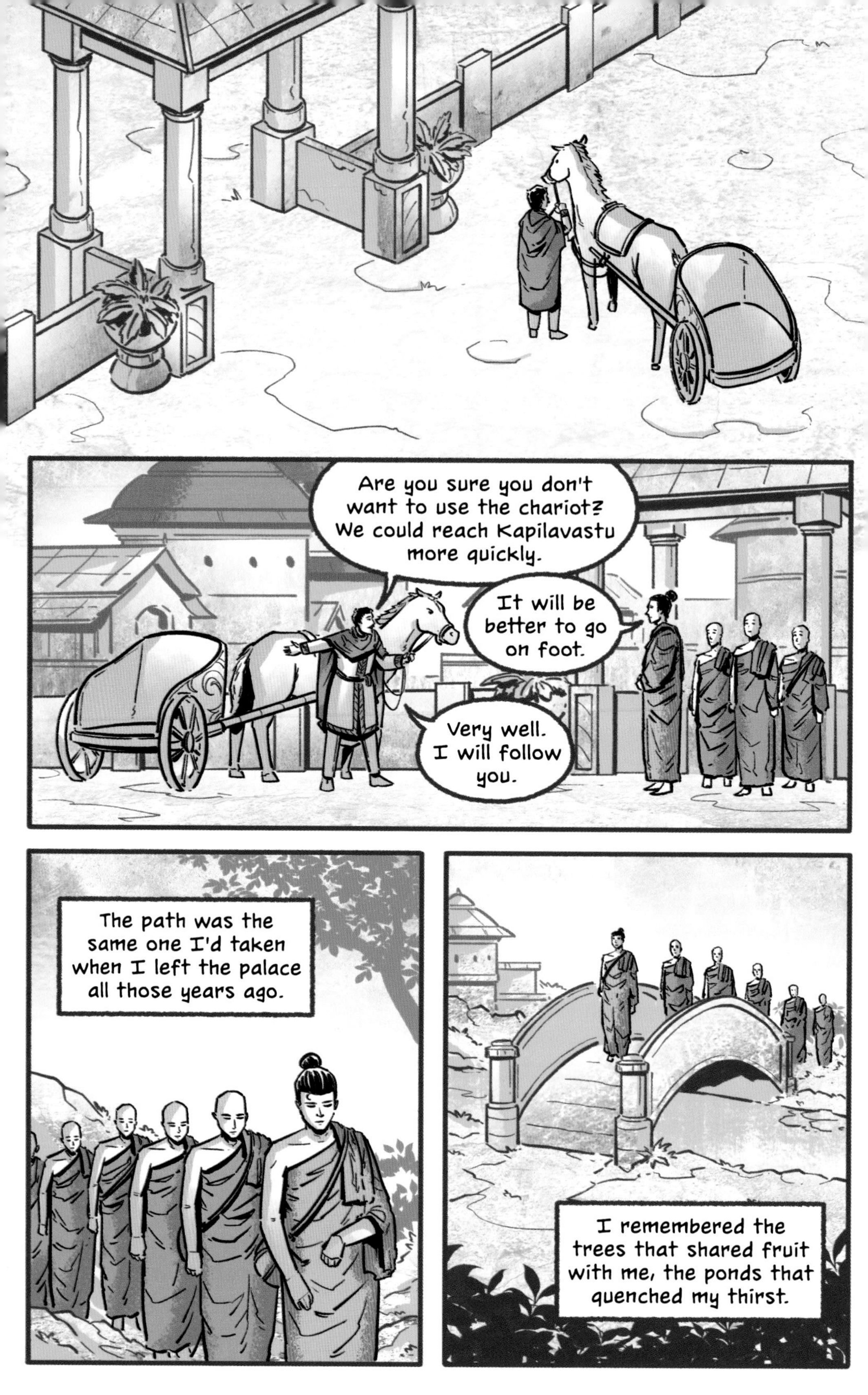
Are you sure you don't want to use the chariot? We could reach Kapilavastu more quickly.
It will be better to go on foot.
Very well. I will follow you.
The path was the same one I'd taken when I left the palace all those years ago.
I remembered the trees that shared fruit with me, the ponds that quenched my thirst.

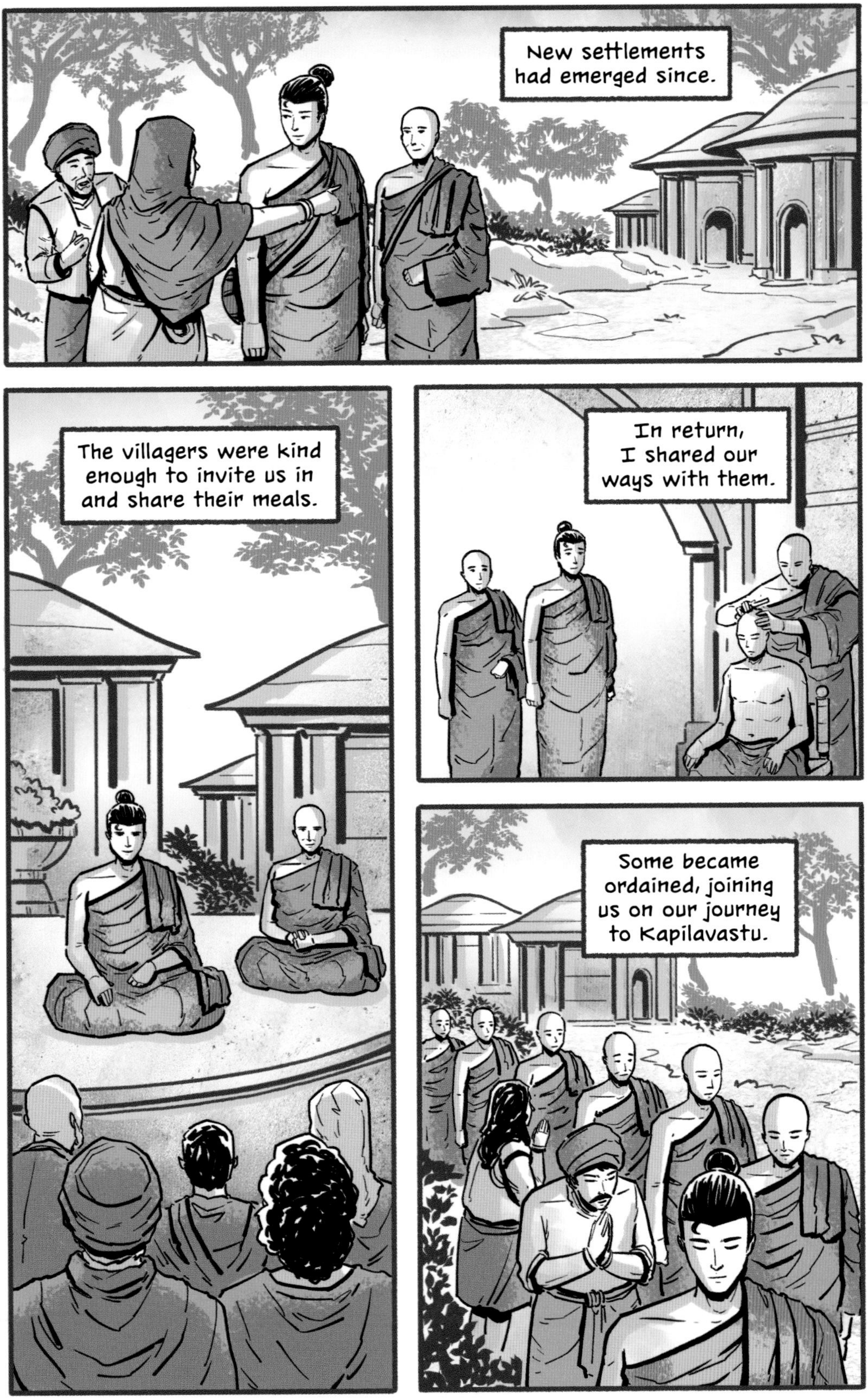
New settlements had emerged since.
The villagers were kind enough to invite us in and share their meals.
In return, I shared our ways with them.
Some became ordained, joining us on our journey to Kapilavastu.

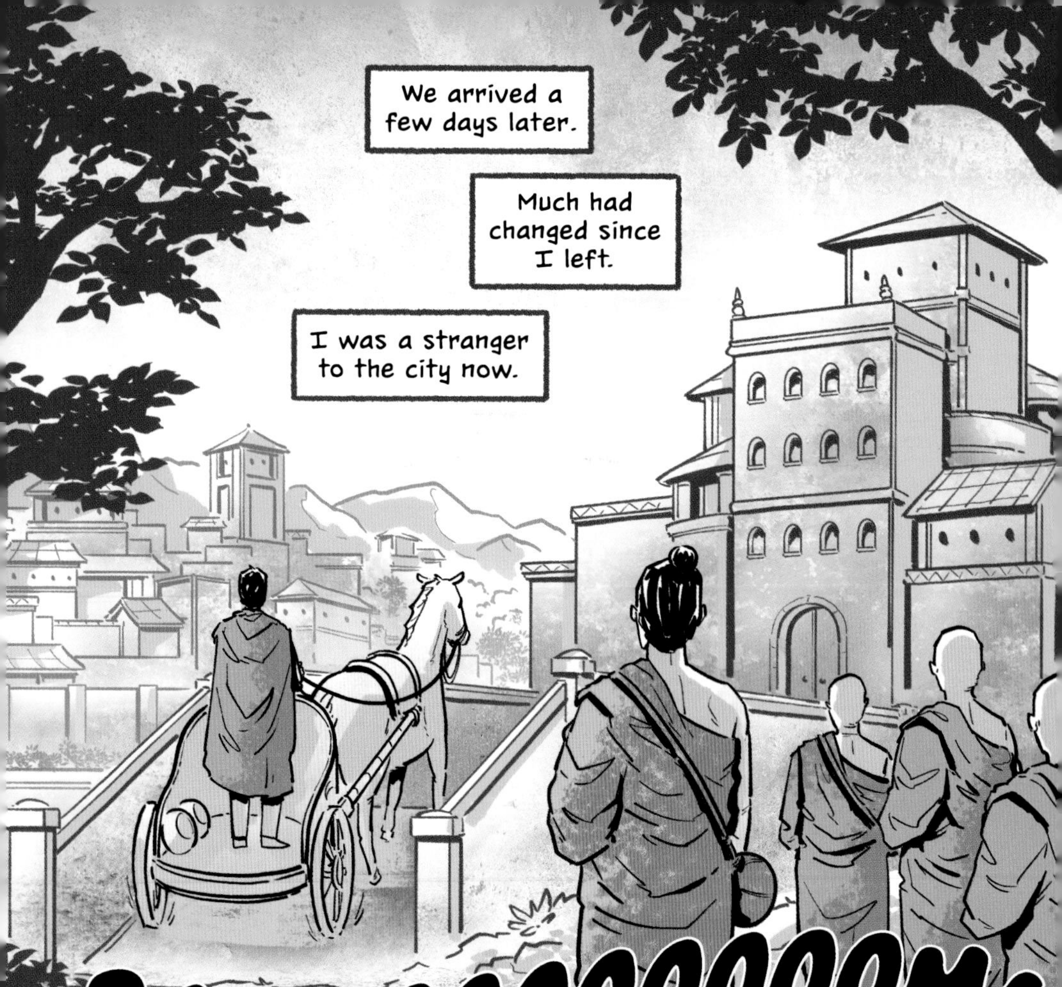
We arrived a few days later.
Much had changed since I left.
I was a stranger to the city now.

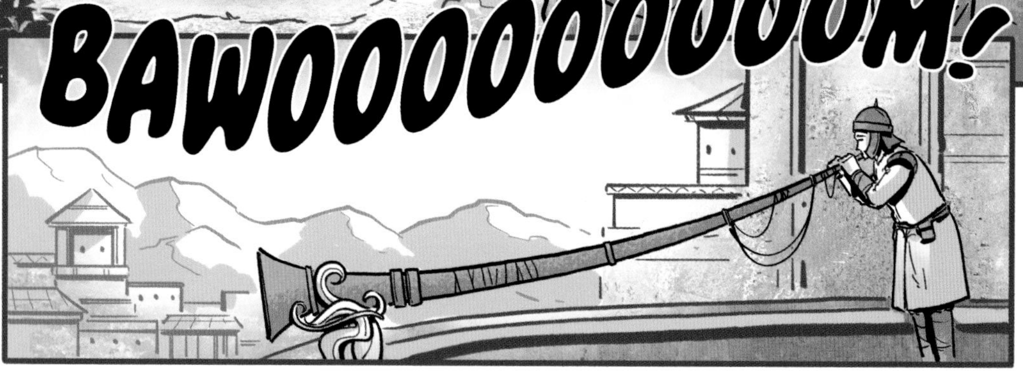
BAWOOOOOOOOOOM!

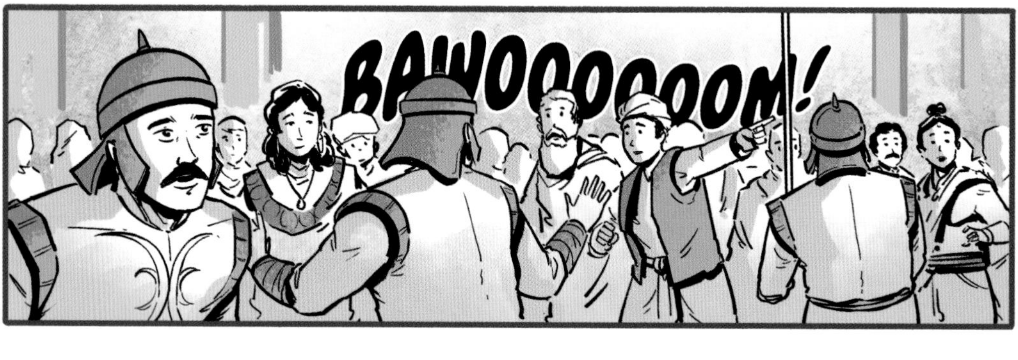
BAWOOOOOOOM!

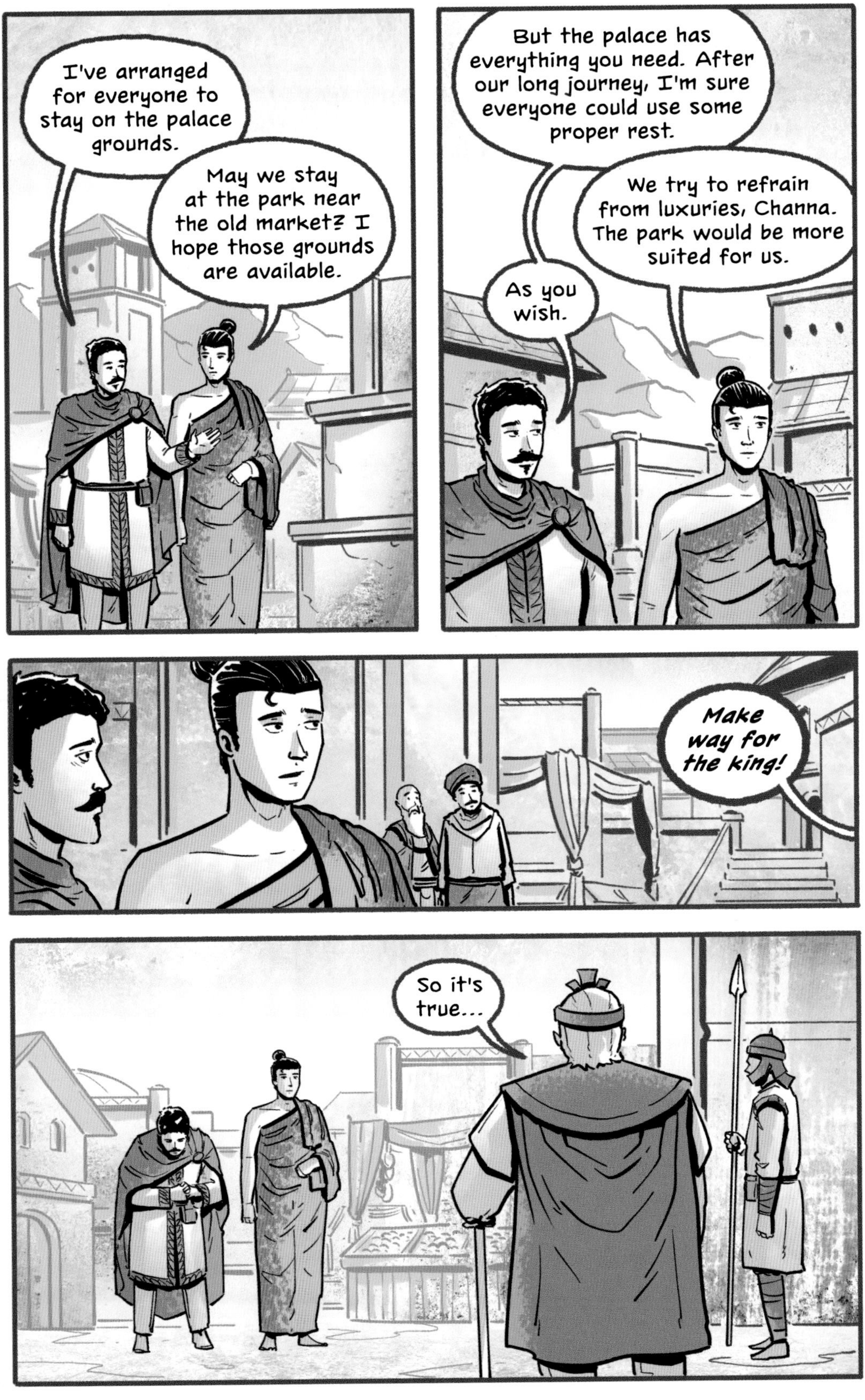
I've arranged for everyone to stay on the palace grounds.
May we stay at the park near the old market? I hope those grounds are available.
But the palace has everything you need. After our long journey, I'm sure everyone could use some proper rest.
We try to refrain from luxuries, Channa. The park would be more suited for us.
As you wish.
Make way for the king!
So it's true...

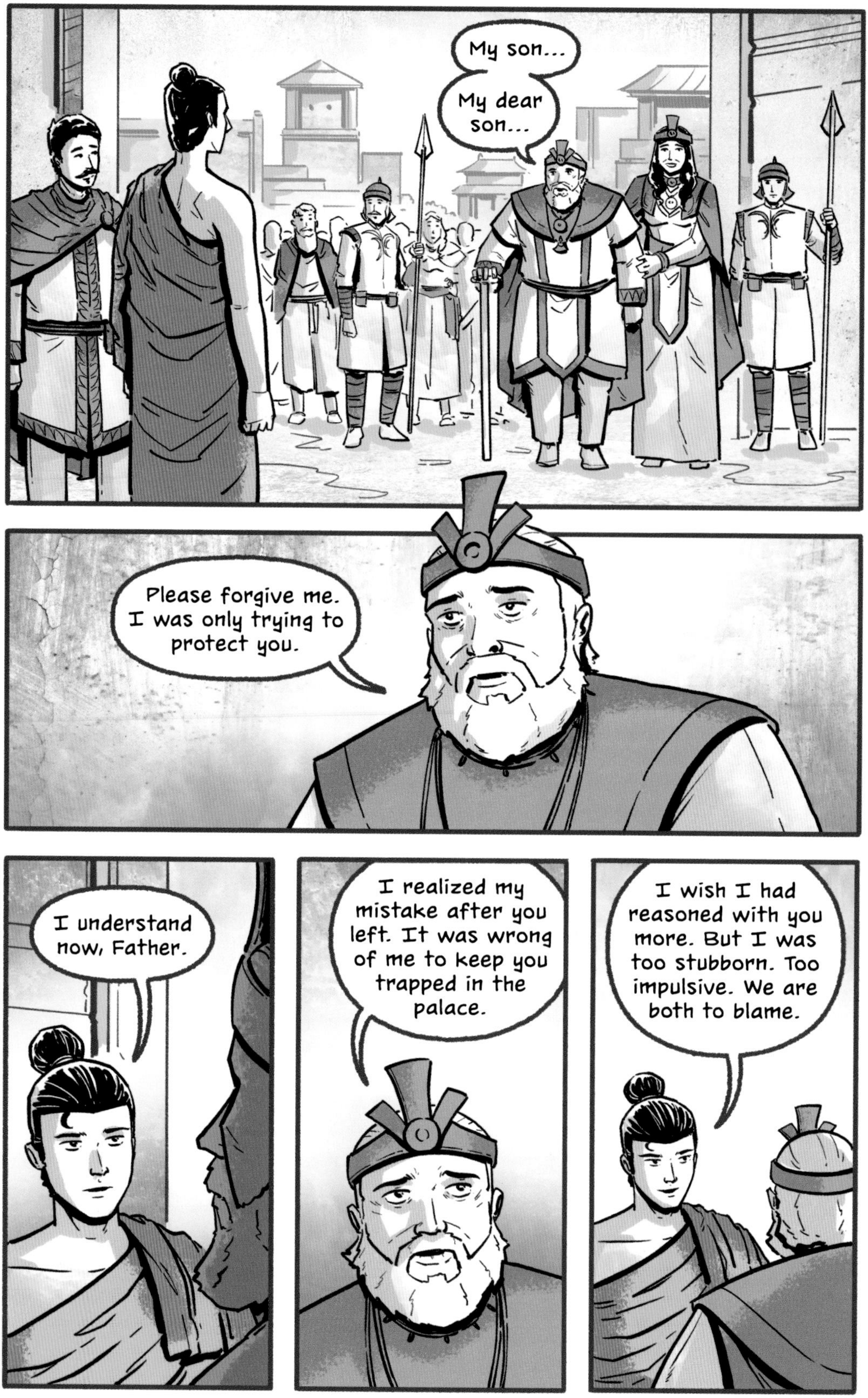
My son...
My dear son...
Please forgive me. I was only trying to protect you.
I understand now, Father.
I realized my mistake after you left. It was wrong of me to keep you trapped in the palace.
I wish I had reasoned with you more. But I was too stubborn. Too impulsive. We are both to blame.

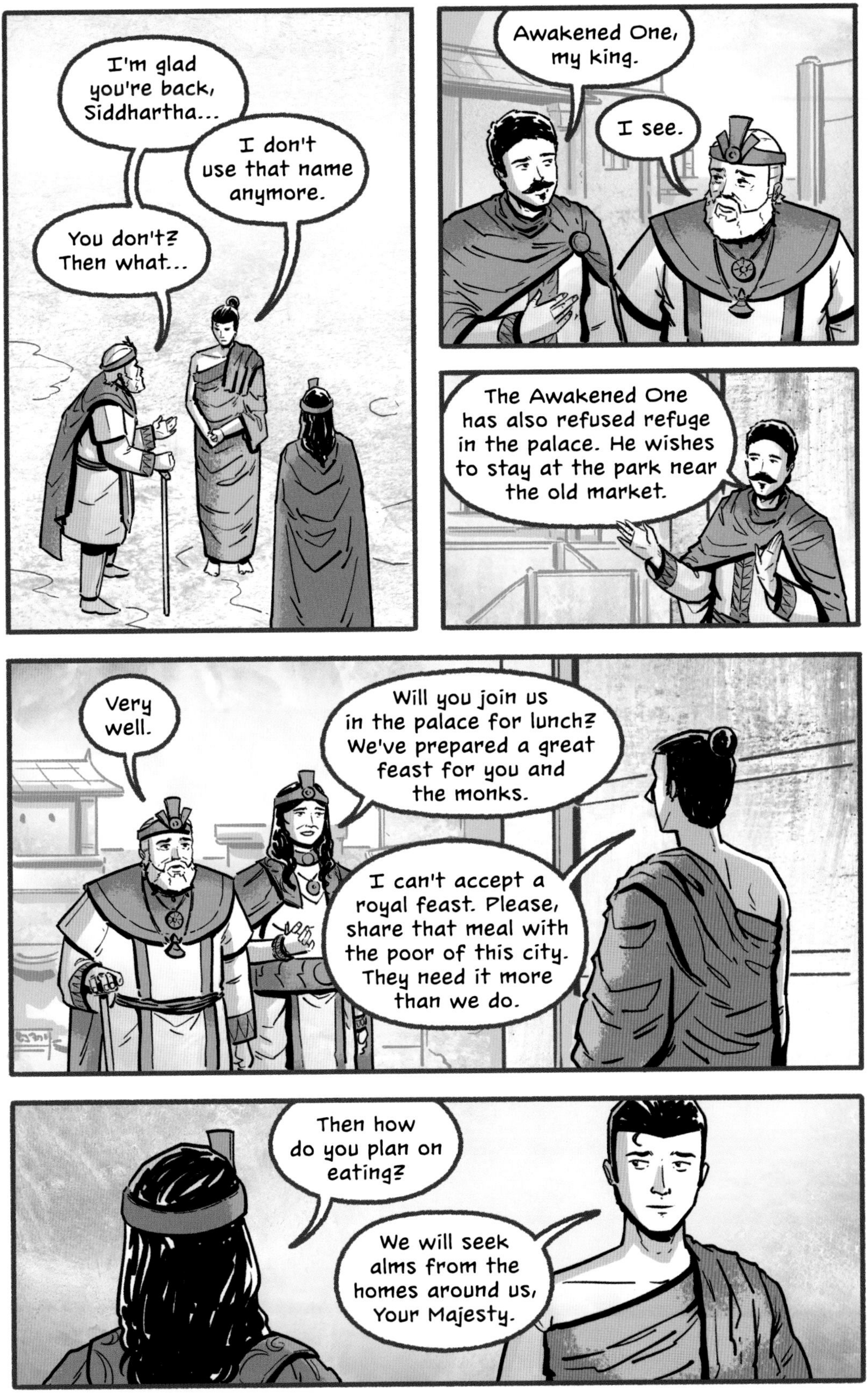
I'm glad you're back, Siddhartha...
I don't use that name anymore.
You don't? Then what...
Awakened One, my king.
I see.
The Awakened One has also refused refuge in the palace. He wishes to stay at the park near the old market.
Very well.
Will you join us in the palace for lunch? We've prepared a great feast for you and the monks.
I can't accept a royal feast. Please, share that meal with the poor of this city. They need it more than we do.
Then how do you plan on eating?
We will seek alms from the homes around us, Your Majesty.

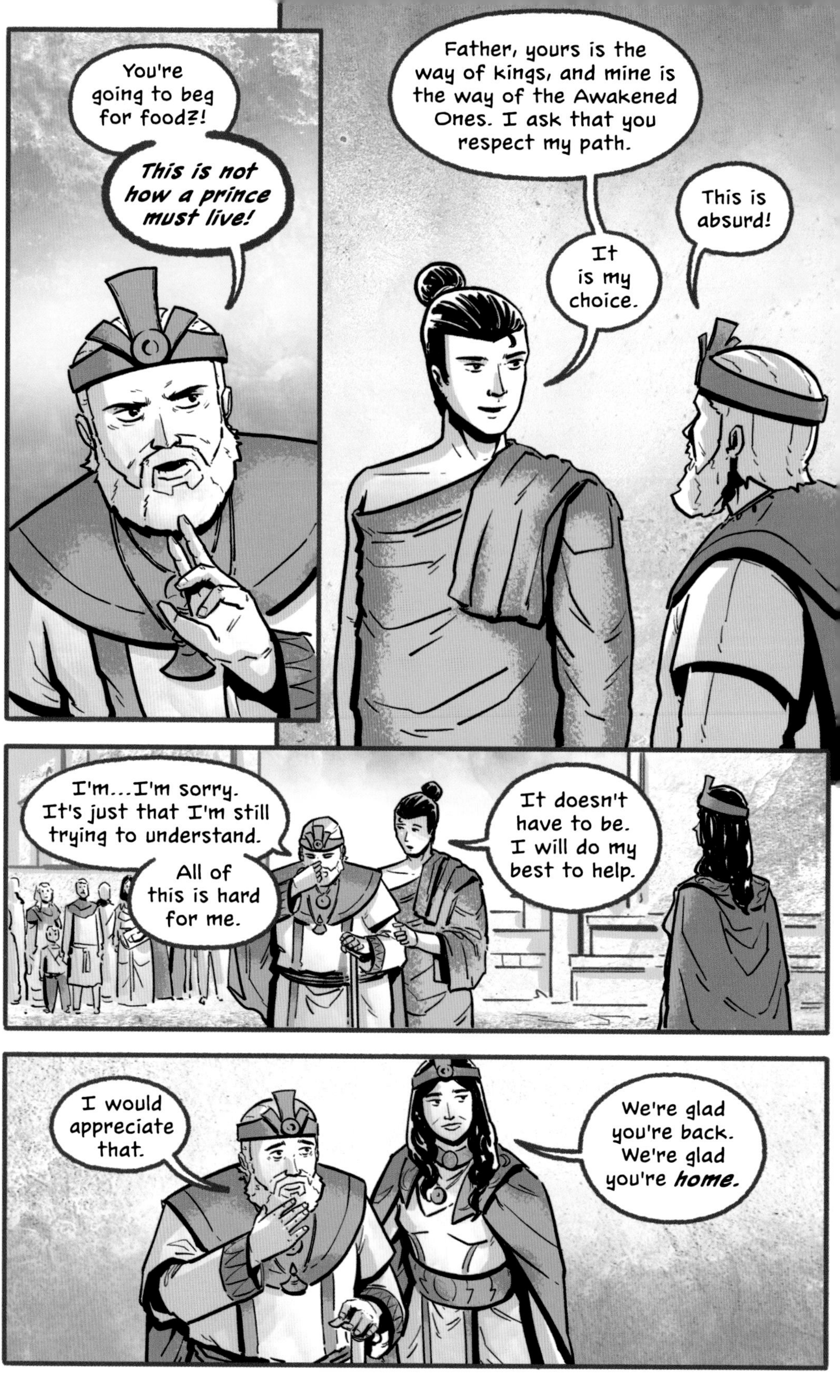
You're going to beg for food?!
This is not how a prince must live!
Father, yours is the way of kings, and mine is the way of the Awakened Ones. I ask that you respect my path.
It is my choice.
This is absurd!
I'm...I'm sorry. It's just that I'm still trying to understand.
All of this is hard for me.
It doesn't have to be. I will do my best to help.
I would appreciate that.
We're glad you're back. We're glad you're *home.*

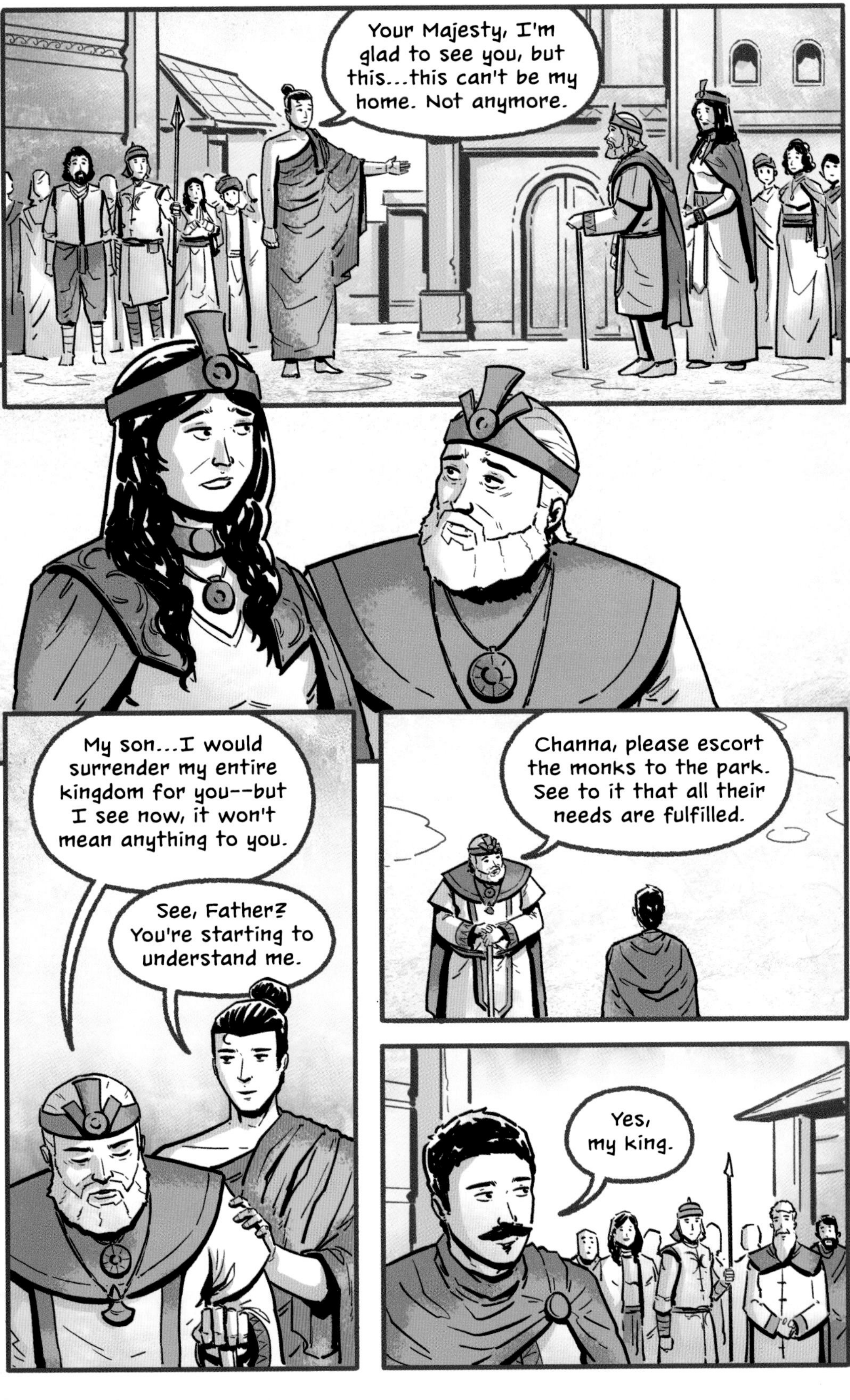
Your Majesty, I'm glad to see you, but this...this can't be my home. Not anymore.
My son...I would surrender my entire kingdom for you--but I see now, it won't mean anything to you.
See, Father? You're starting to understand me.
Channa, please escort the monks to the park. See to it that all their needs are fulfilled.
Yes, my king.

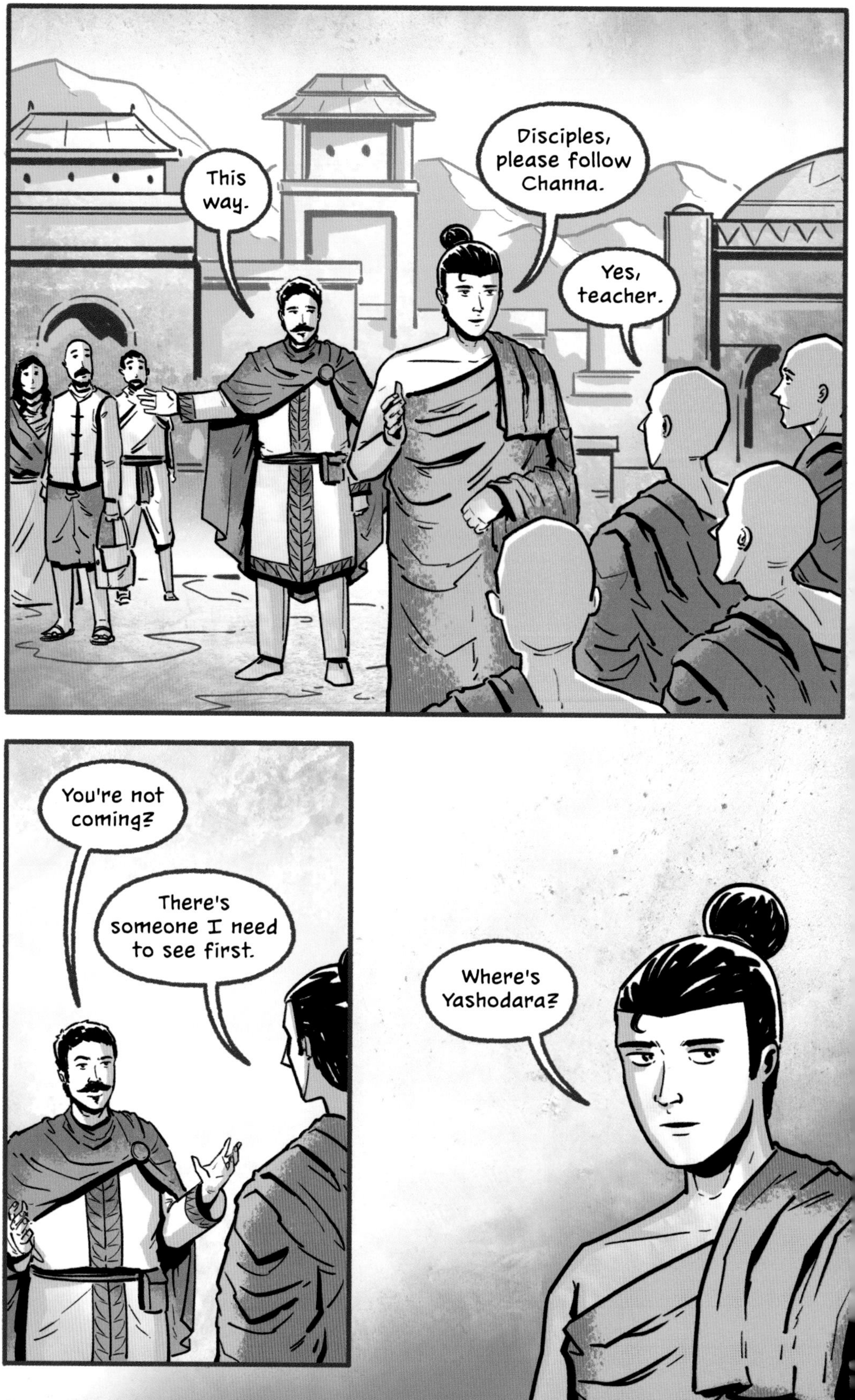
This way.
Disciples, please follow Channa.
Yes, teacher.
You're not coming?
There's someone I need to see first.
Where's Yashodara?

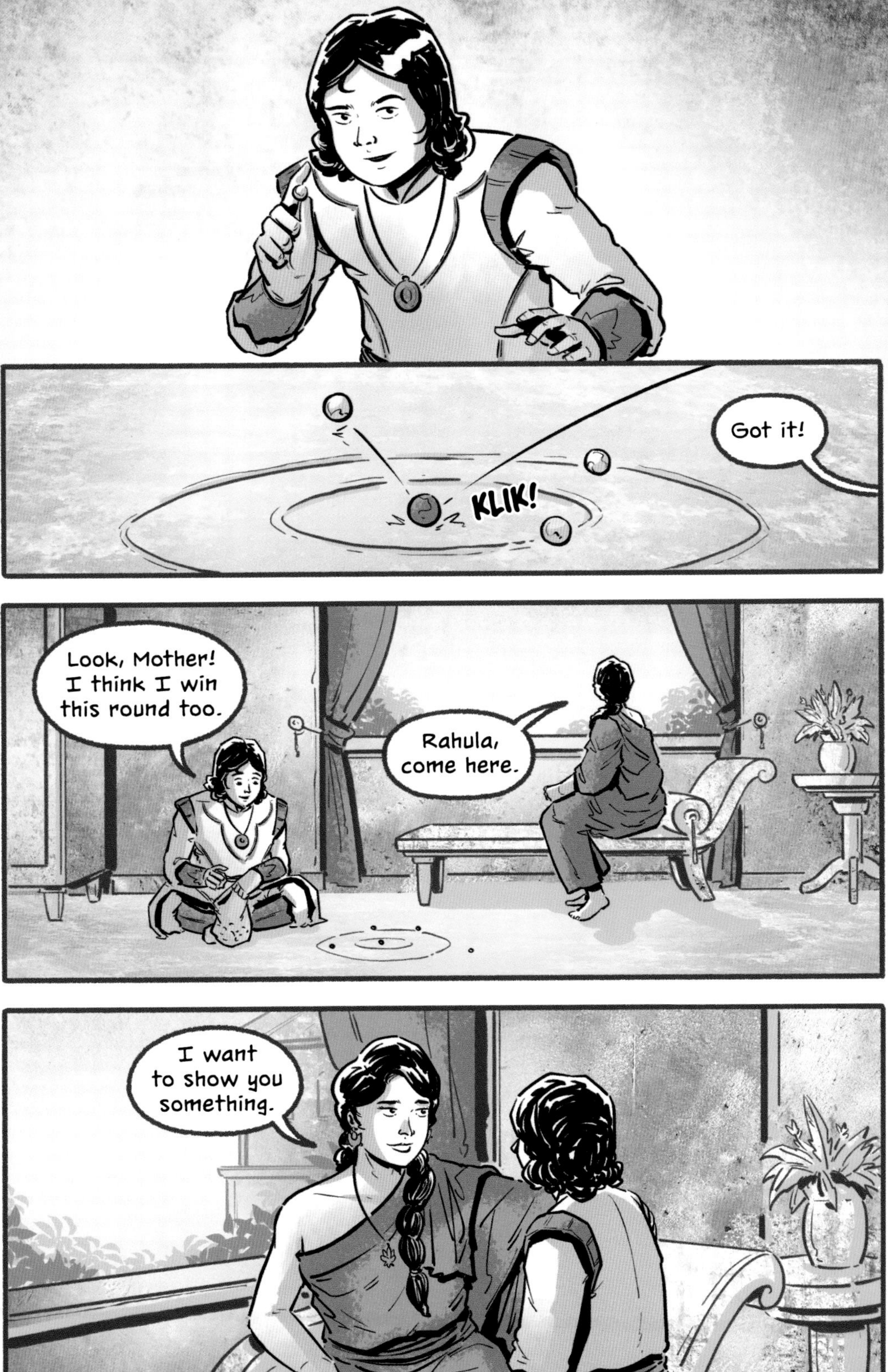
Got it!
KLIK!
Look, Mother! I think I win this round too.
Rahula, come here.
I want to show you something.

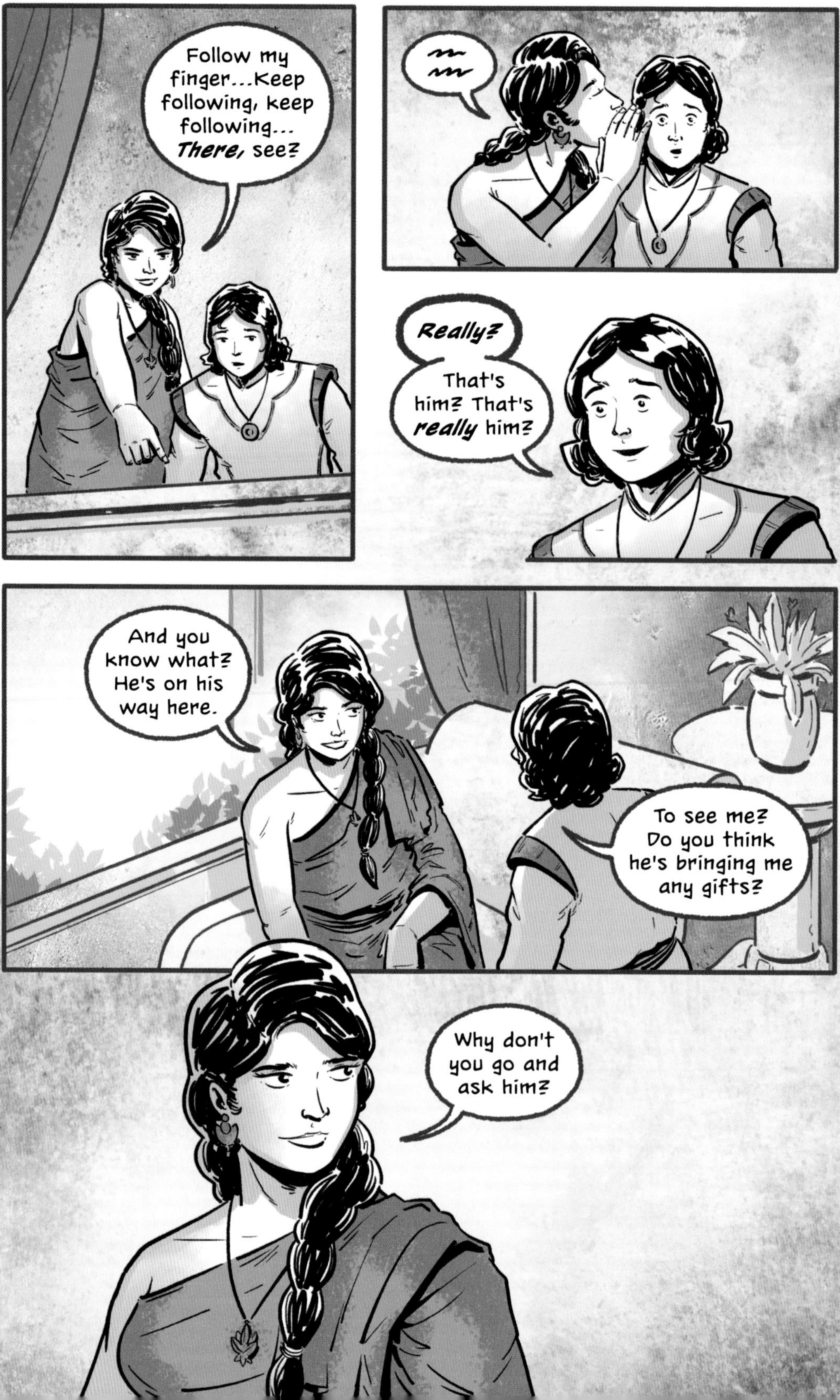
Follow my finger...Keep following, keep following... *There,* see?
Really?
That's him? That's *really* him?
And you know what? He's on his way here.
To see me? Do you think he's bringing me any gifts?
Why don't you go and ask him?

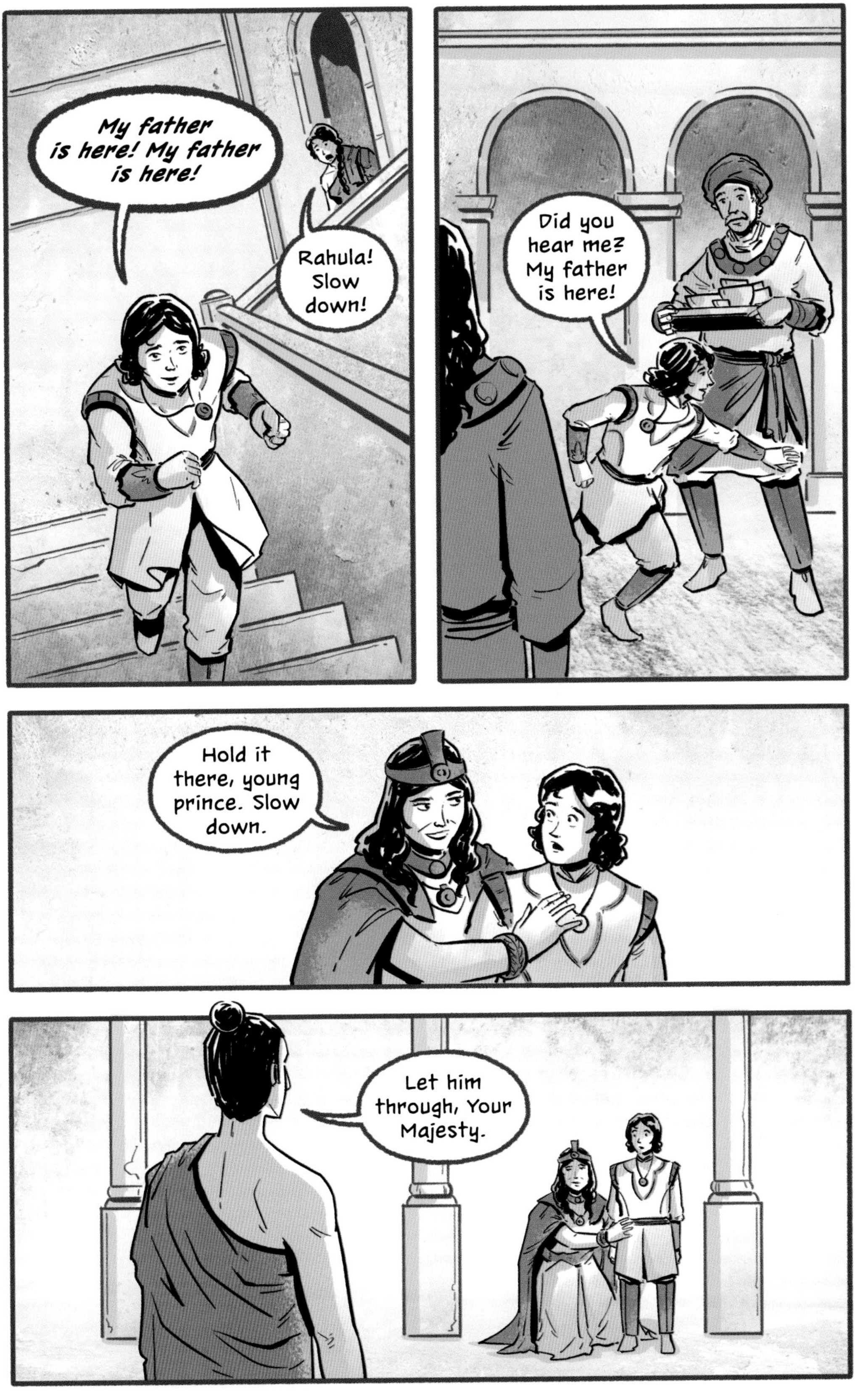
My father is here! My father is here!
Rahula! Slow down!
Did you hear me? My father is here!
Hold it there, young prince. Slow down.
Let him through, Your Majesty.

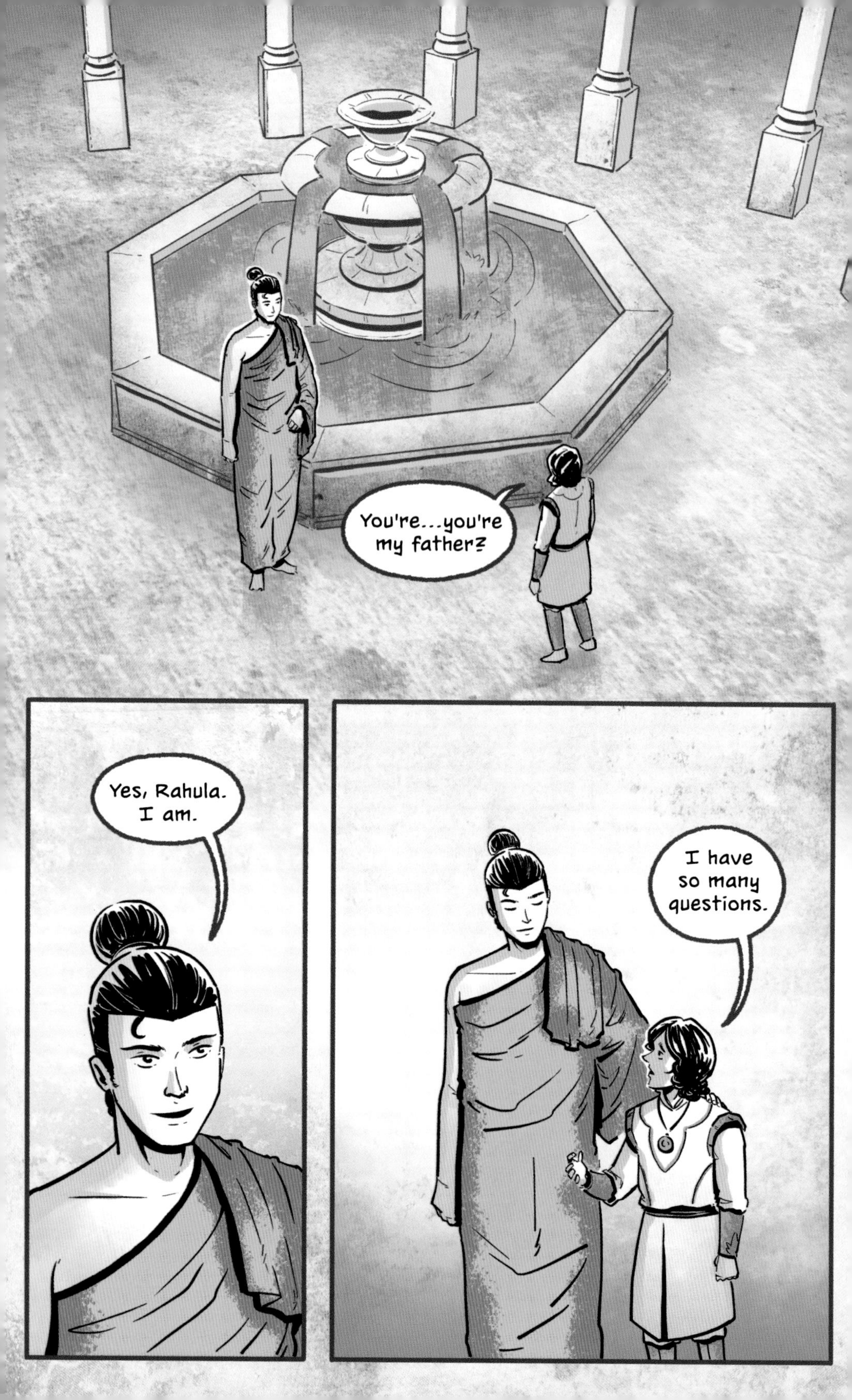
You're...you're my father?
Yes, Rahula. I am.
I have so many questions.

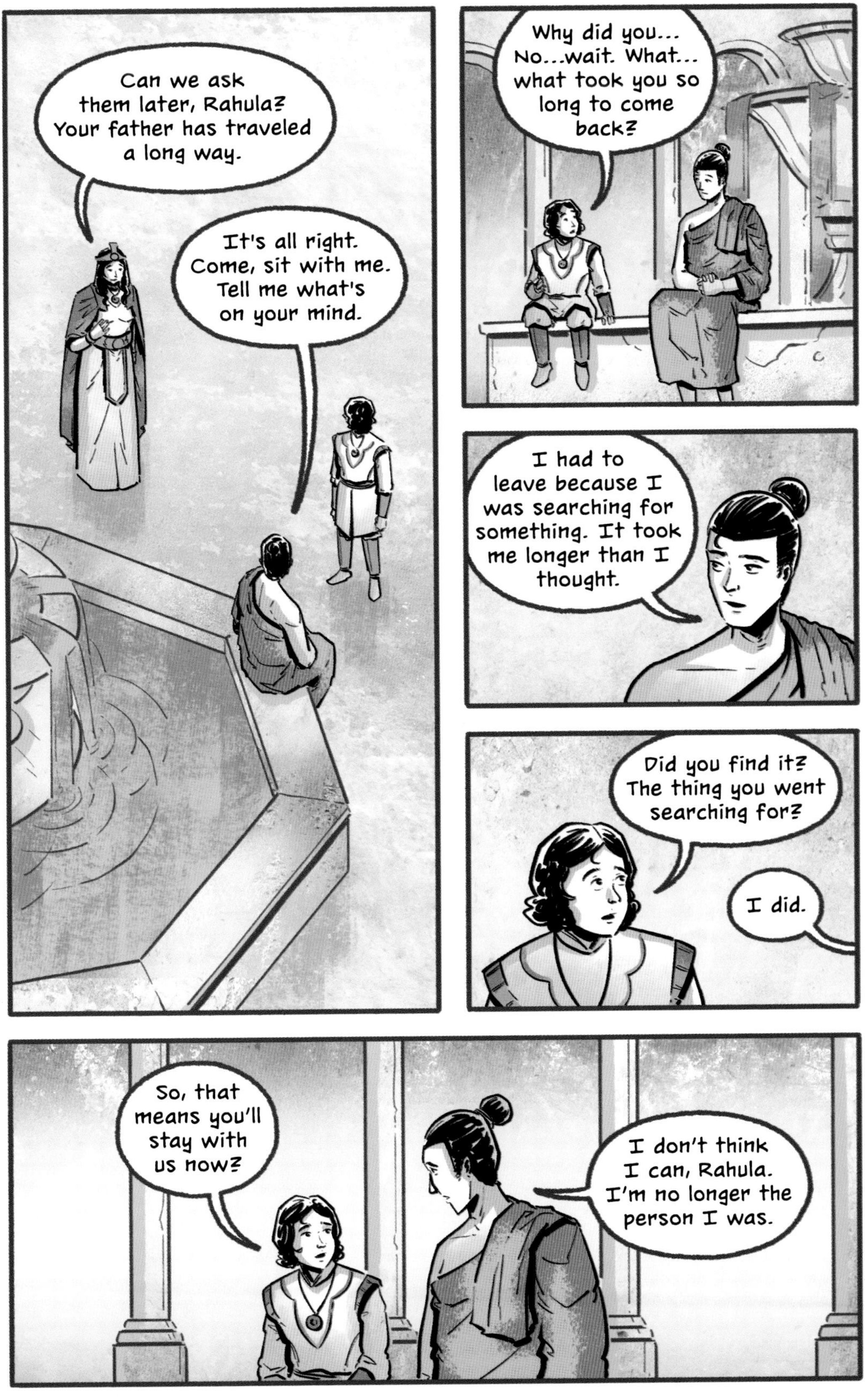
Can we ask them later, Rahula? Your father has traveled a long way.
It's all right. Come, sit with me. Tell me what's on your mind.
Why did you... No...wait. What... what took you so long to come back?
I had to leave because I was searching for something. It took me longer than I thought.
Did you find it? The thing you went searching for?
I did.
So, that means you'll stay with us now?
I don't think I can, Rahula. I'm no longer the person I was.

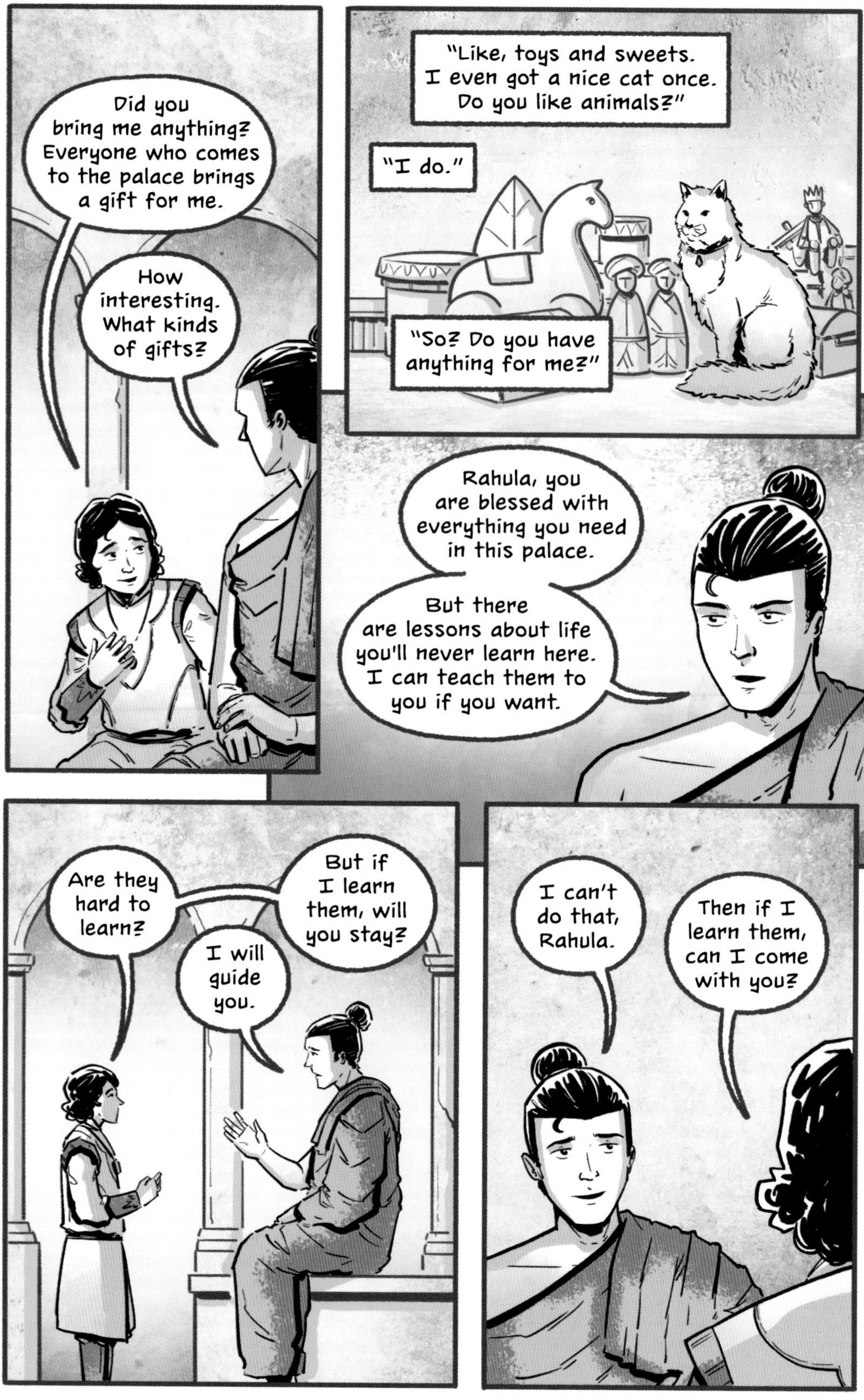
Did you bring me anything? Everyone who comes to the palace brings a gift for me.
How interesting. What kinds of gifts?
"Like, toys and sweets. I even got a nice cat once. Do you like animals?"
"I do."
"So? Do you have anything for me?"
Rahula, you are blessed with everything you need in this palace.
But there are lessons about life you'll never learn here. I can teach them to you if you want.
Are they hard to learn?
I will guide you.
But if I learn them, will you stay?
I can't do that, Rahula.
Then if I learn them, can I come with you?

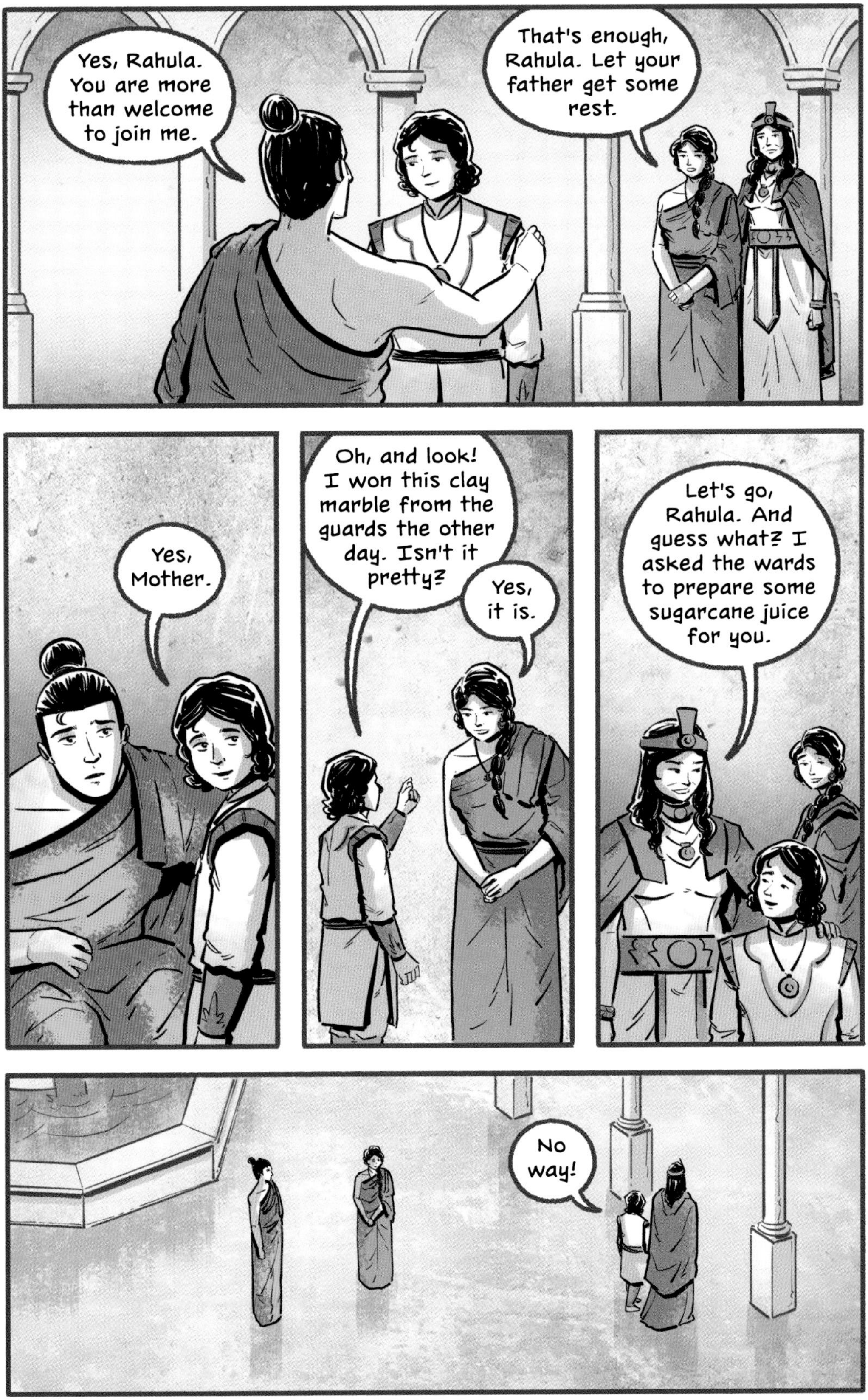
Yes, Rahula. You are more than welcome to join me.
That's enough, Rahula. Let your father get some rest.
Yes, Mother.
Oh, and look! I won this clay marble from the guards the other day. Isn't it pretty?
Yes, it is.
Let's go, Rahula. And guess what? I asked the wards to prepare some sugarcane juice for you.
No way!

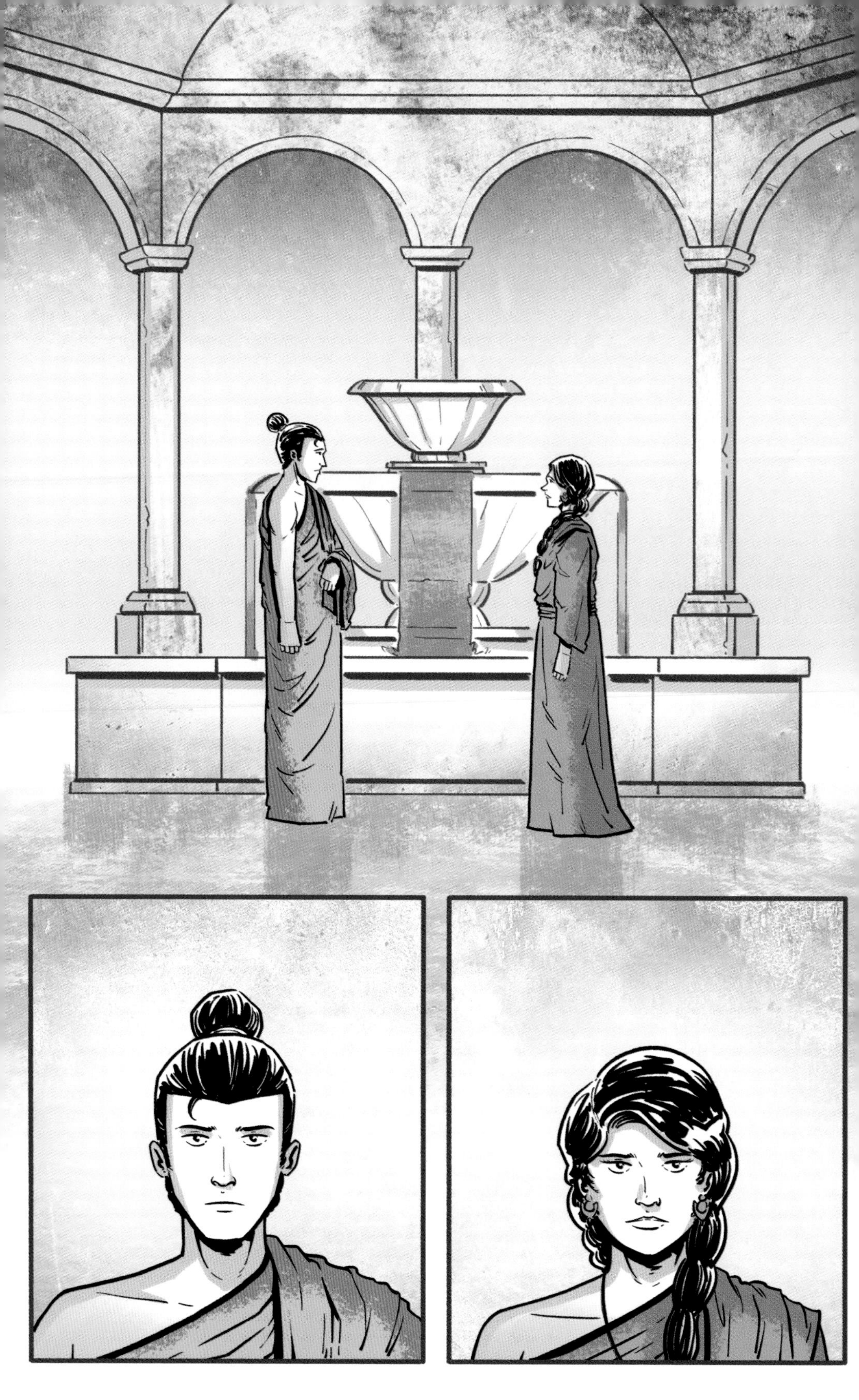

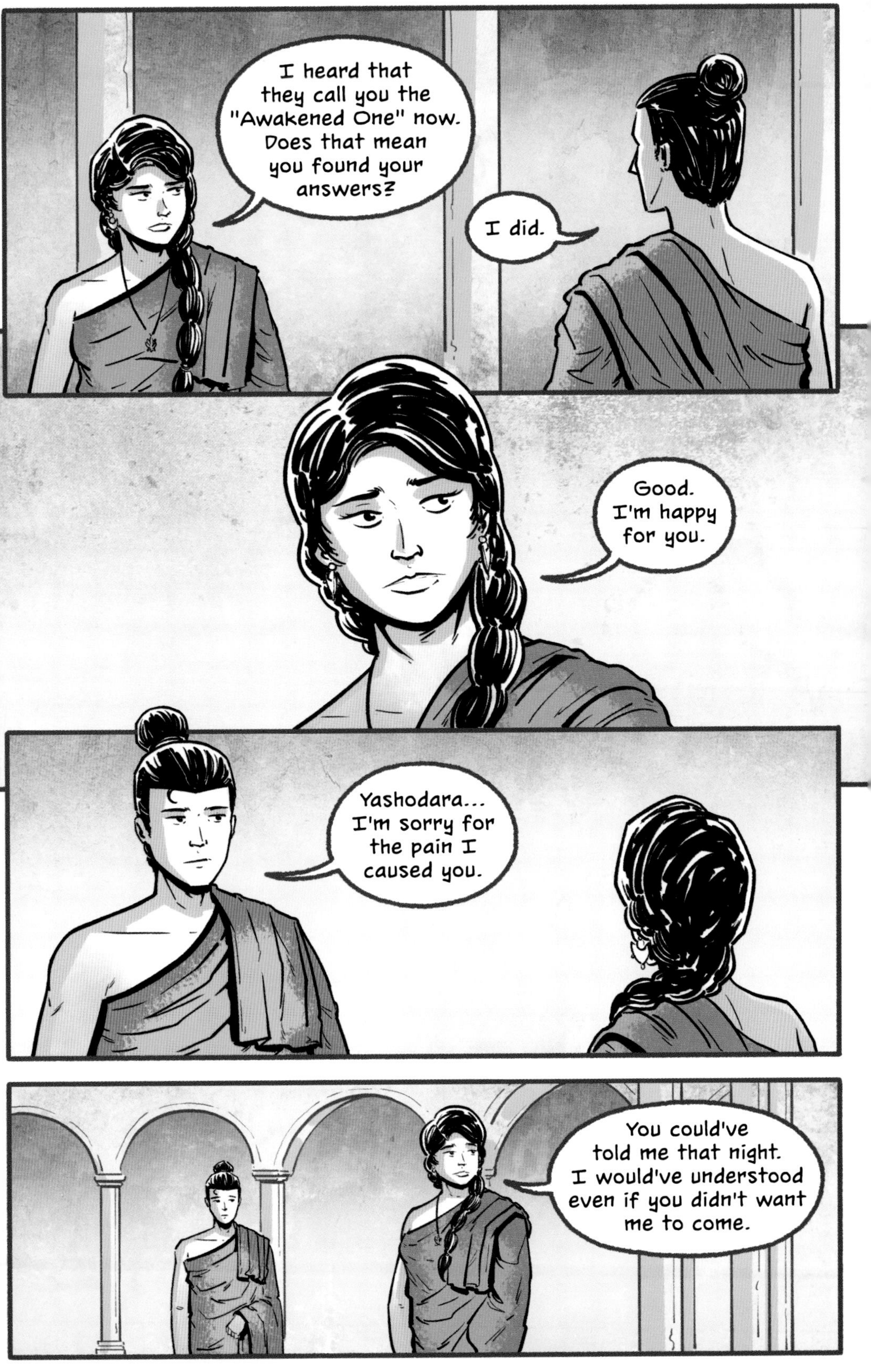
I heard that they call you the "Awakened One" now. Does that mean you found your answers?
I did.
Good. I'm happy for you.
Yashodara... I'm sorry for the pain I caused you.
You could've told me that night. I would've understood even if you didn't want me to come.

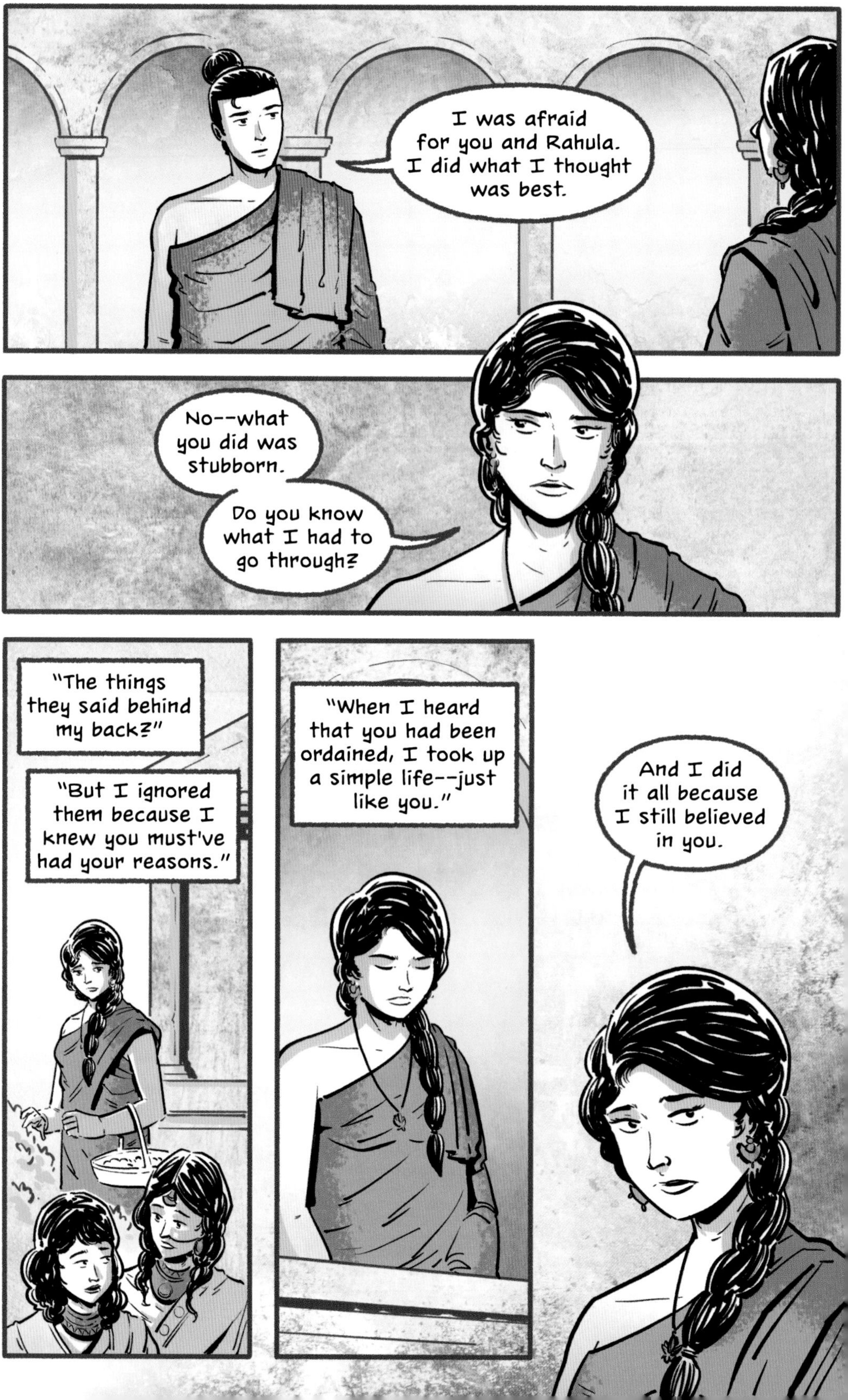
I was afraid for you and Rahula. I did what I thought was best.
No--what you did was stubborn.
Do you know what I had to go through?
"The things they said behind my back?"
"But I ignored them because I knew you must've had your reasons."
"When I heard that you had been ordained, I took up a simple life--just like you."
And I did it all because I still believed in you.

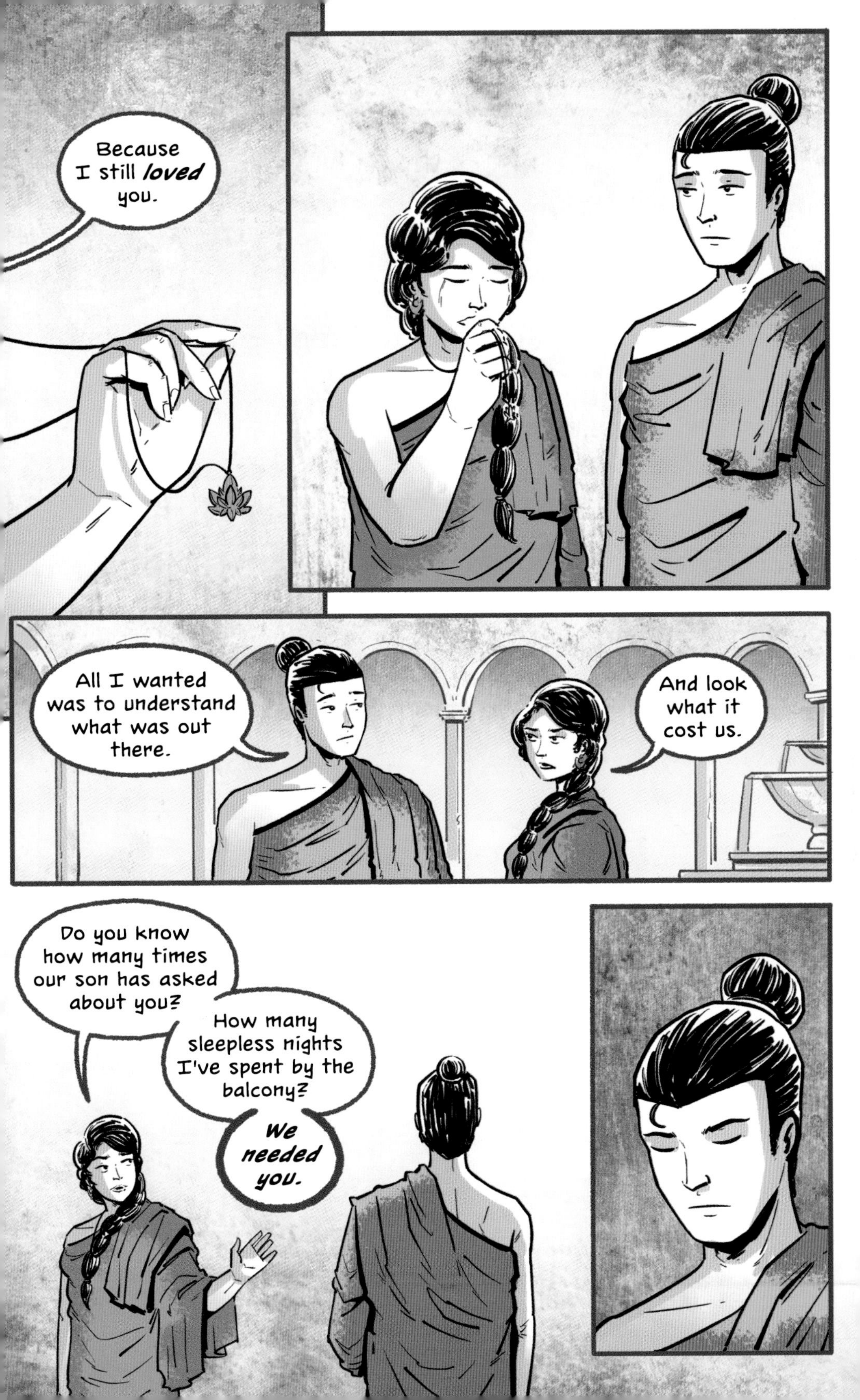
Because I still *loved* you.
All I wanted was to understand what was out there.
And look what it cost us.
Do you know how many times our son has asked about you?
How many sleepless nights I've spent by the balcony?
We needed you.

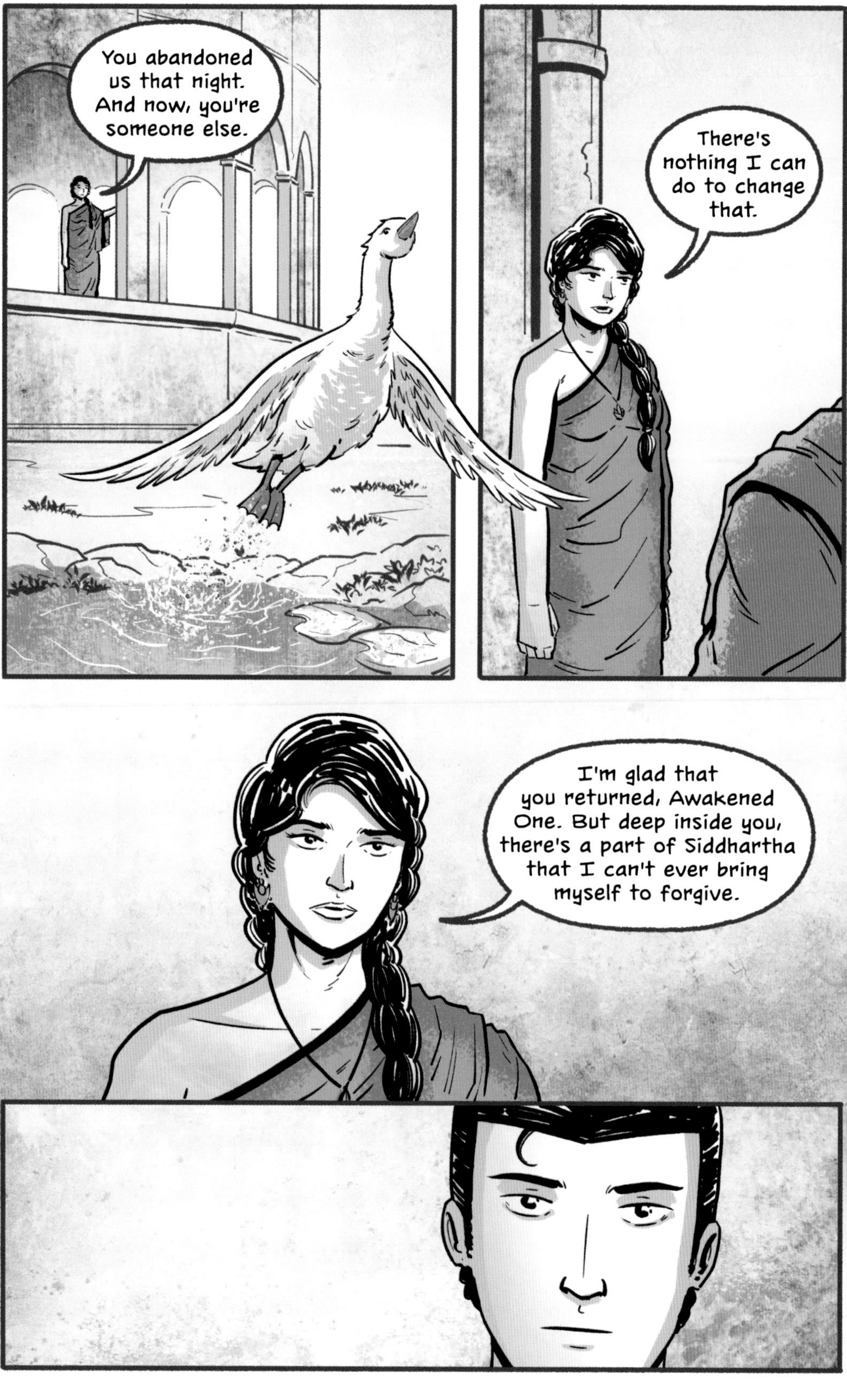
You abandoned us that night. And now, you're someone else.
There's nothing I can do to change that.
I'm glad that you returned, Awakened One. But deep inside you, there's a part of Siddhartha that I can't ever bring myself to forgive.

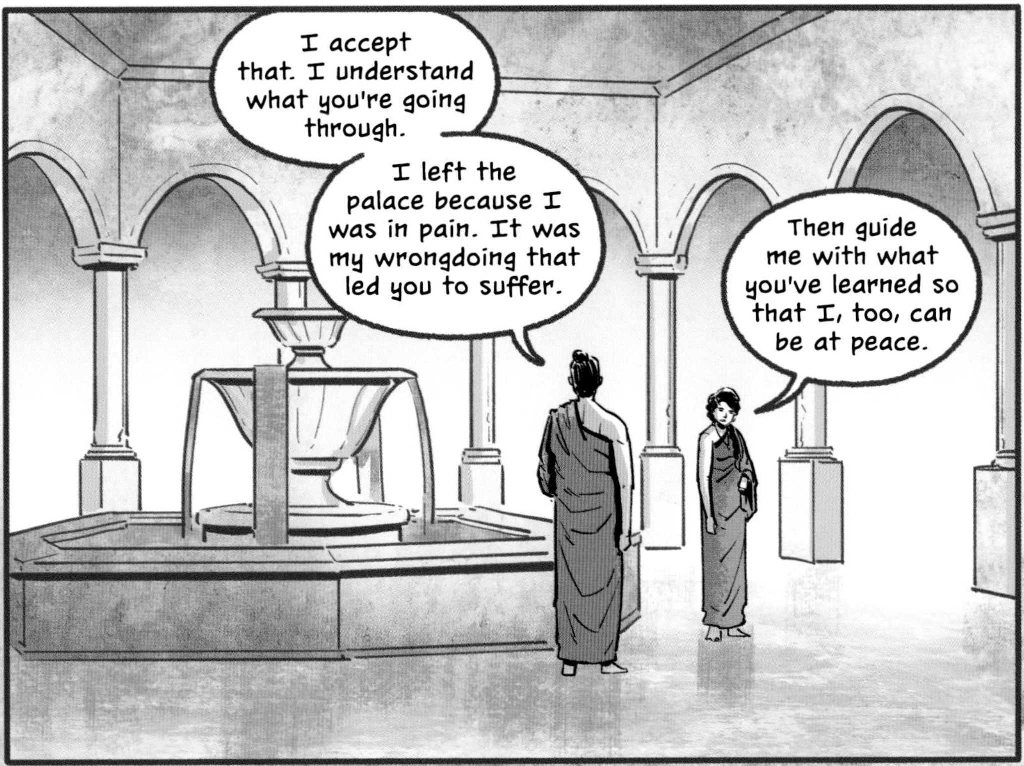
I accept that. I understand what you're going through.
I left the palace because I was in pain. It was my wrongdoing that led you to suffer.
Then guide me with what you've learned so that I, too, can be at peace.

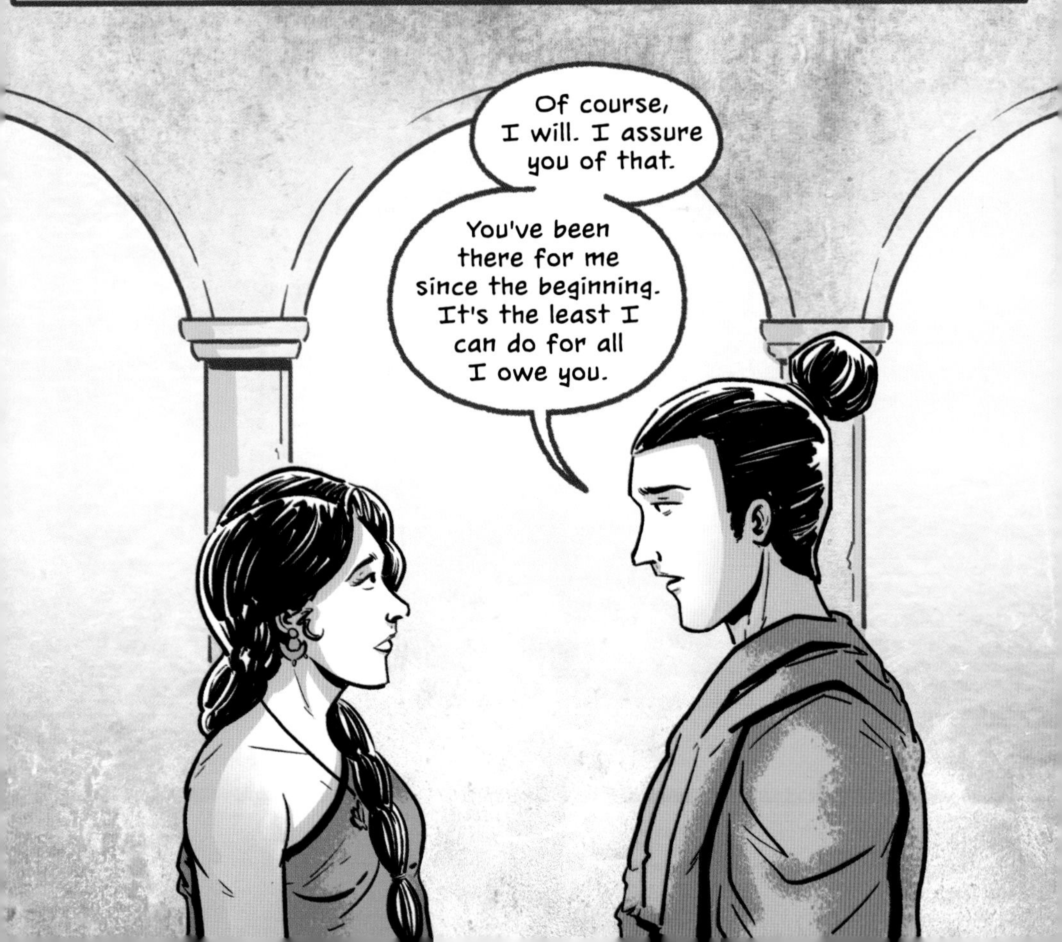
Of course, I will. I assure you of that.
You've been there for me since the beginning. It's the least I can do for all I owe you.

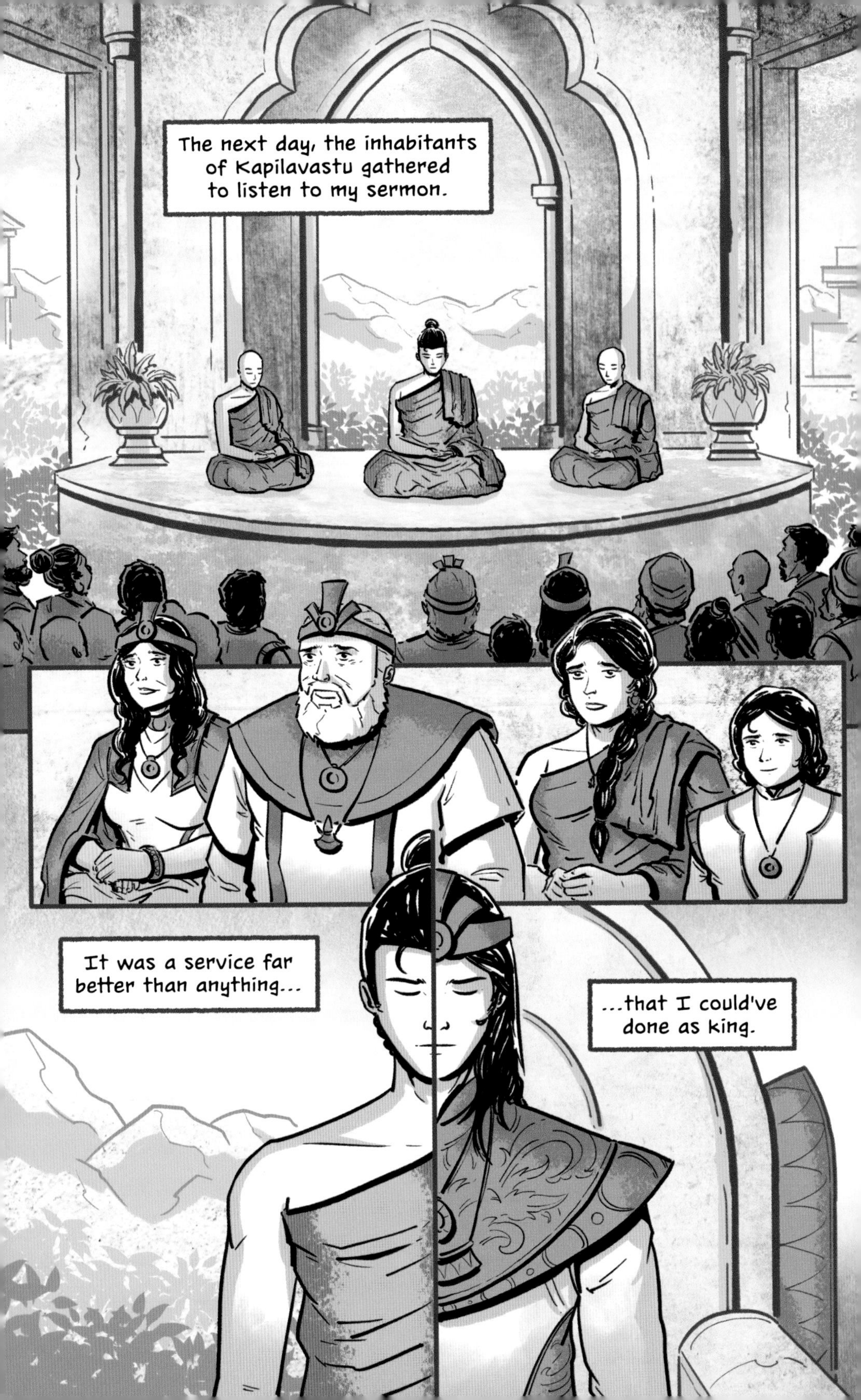
The next day, the inhabitants of Kapilavastu gathered to listen to my sermon.
It was a service far better than anything...
...that I could've done as king.

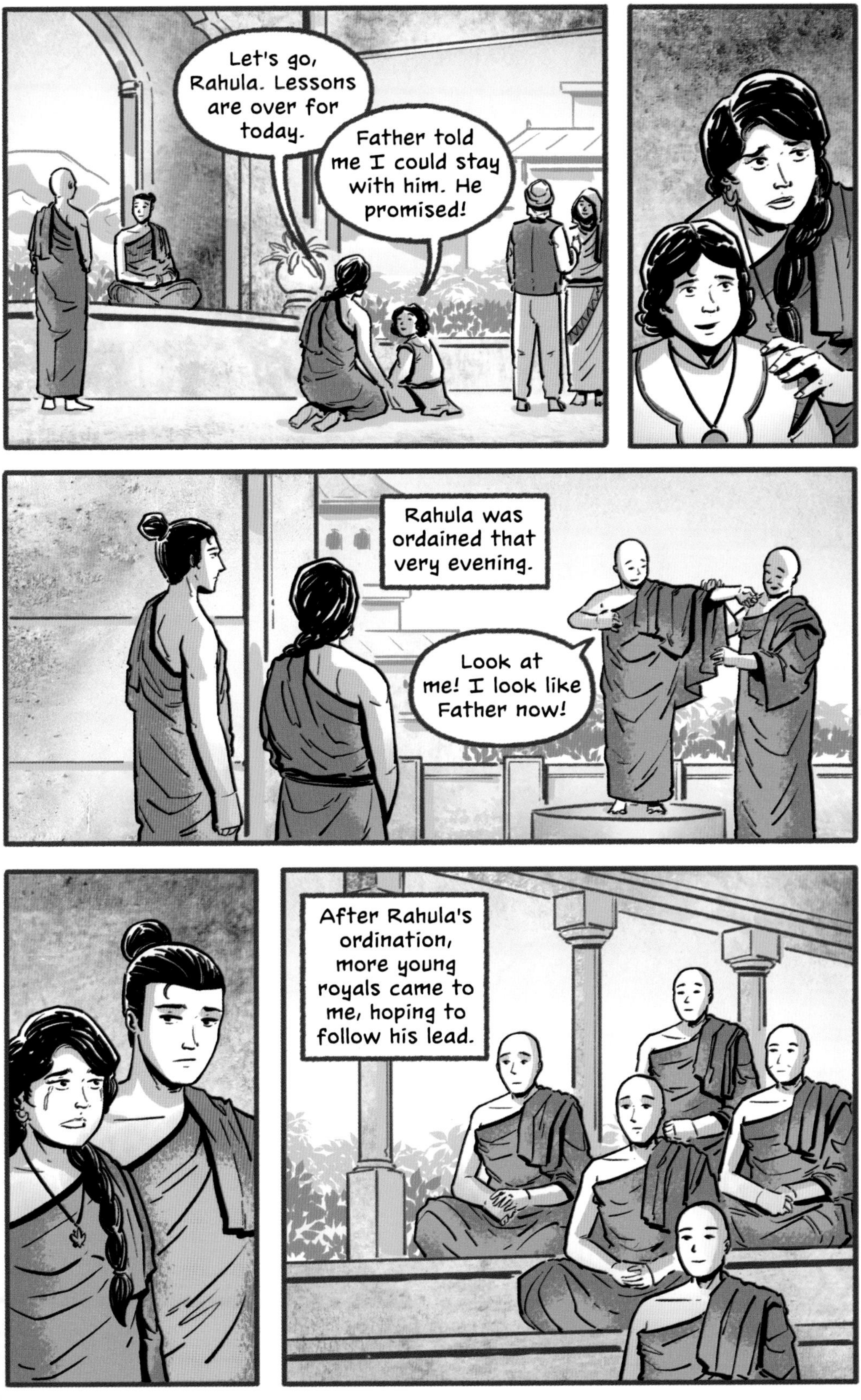
Let's go, Rahula. Lessons are over for today.
Father told me I could stay with him. He promised!
Rahula was ordained that very evening.
Look at me! I look like Father now!
After Rahula's ordination, more young royals came to me, hoping to follow his lead.

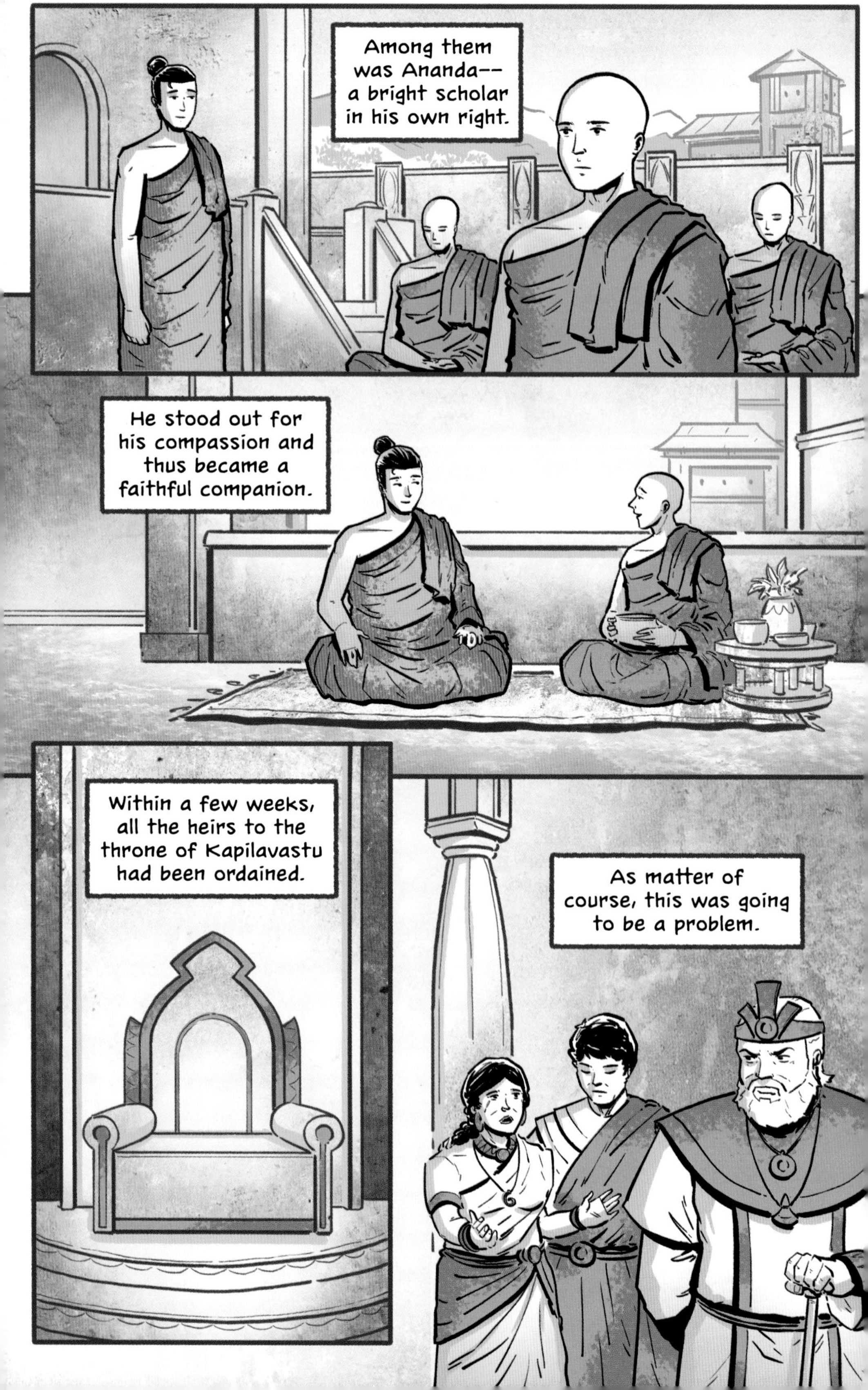
Among them was Ananda-- a bright scholar in his own right.
He stood out for his compassion and thus became a faithful companion.
Within a few weeks, all the heirs to the throne of Kapilavastu had been ordained.
As matter of course, this was going to be a problem.

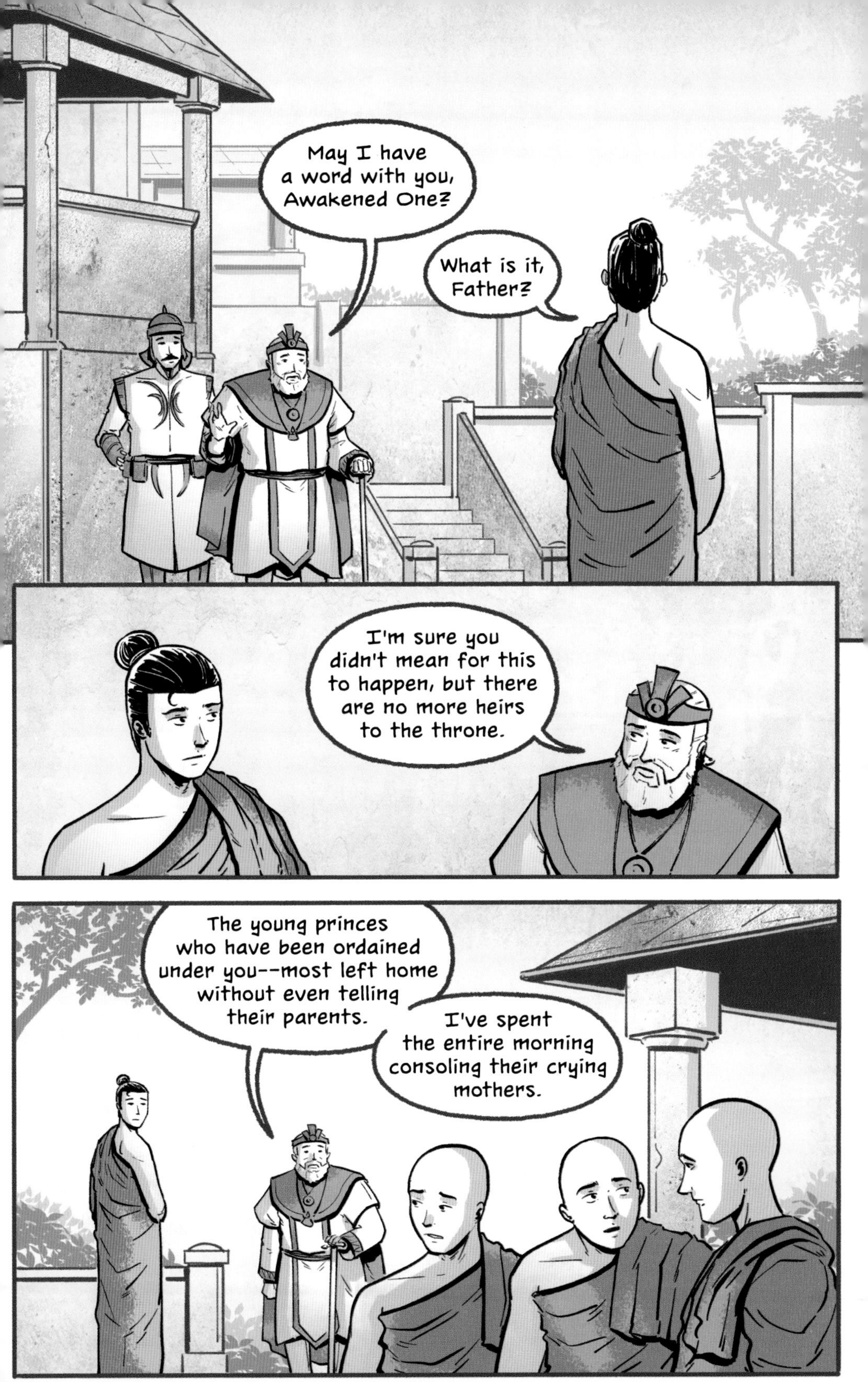
May I have a word with you, Awakened One?
What is it, Father?
I'm sure you didn't mean for this to happen, but there are no more heirs to the throne.
The young princes who have been ordained under you--most left home without even telling their parents.
I've spent the entire morning consoling their crying mothers.

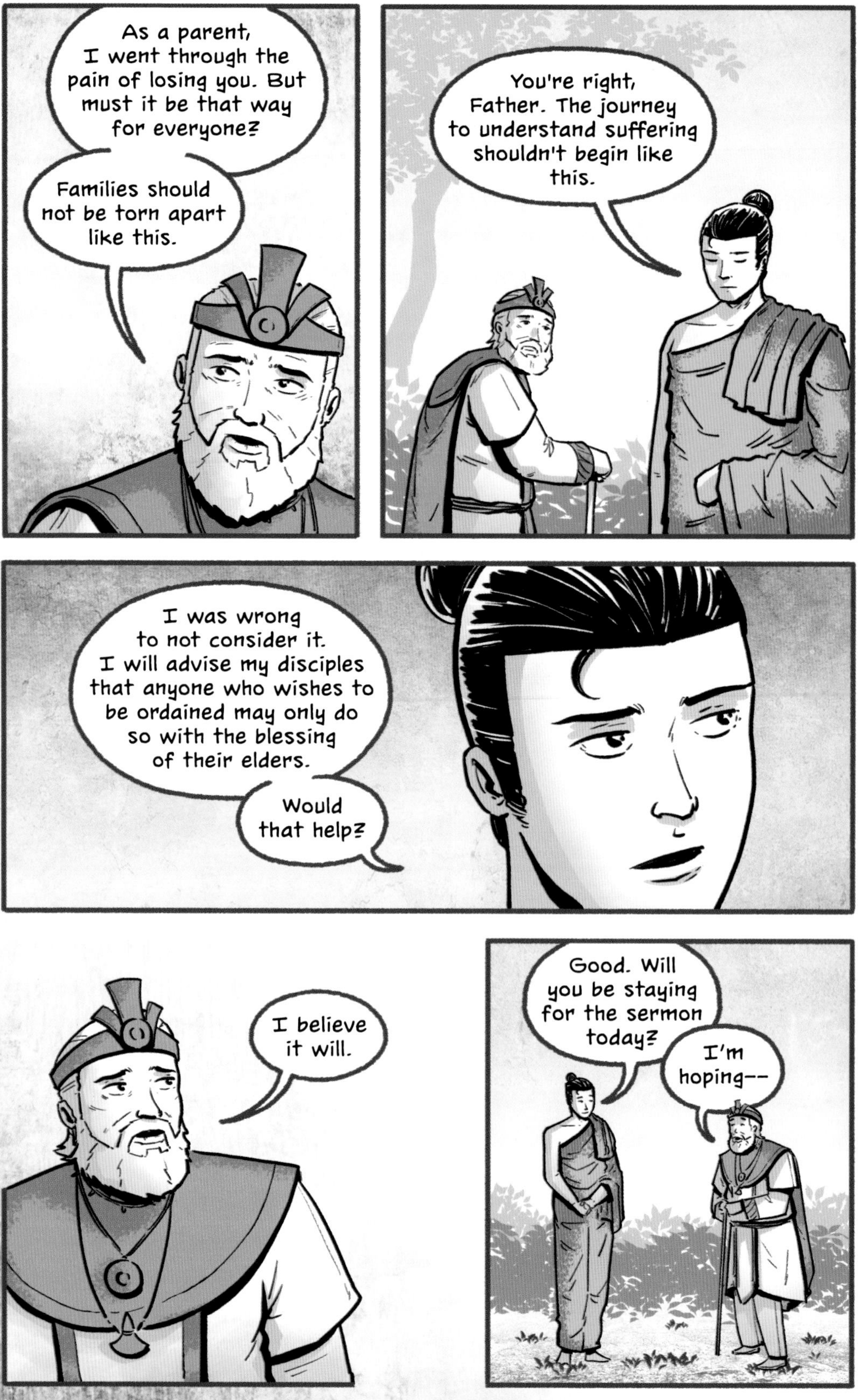
As a parent, I went through the pain of losing you. But must it be that way for everyone?
Families should not be torn apart like this.
You're right, Father. The journey to understand suffering shouldn't begin like this.
I was wrong to not consider it. I will advise my disciples that anyone who wishes to be ordained may only do so with the blessing of their elders.
Would that help?
I believe it will.
Good. Will you be staying for the sermon today?
I'm hoping--

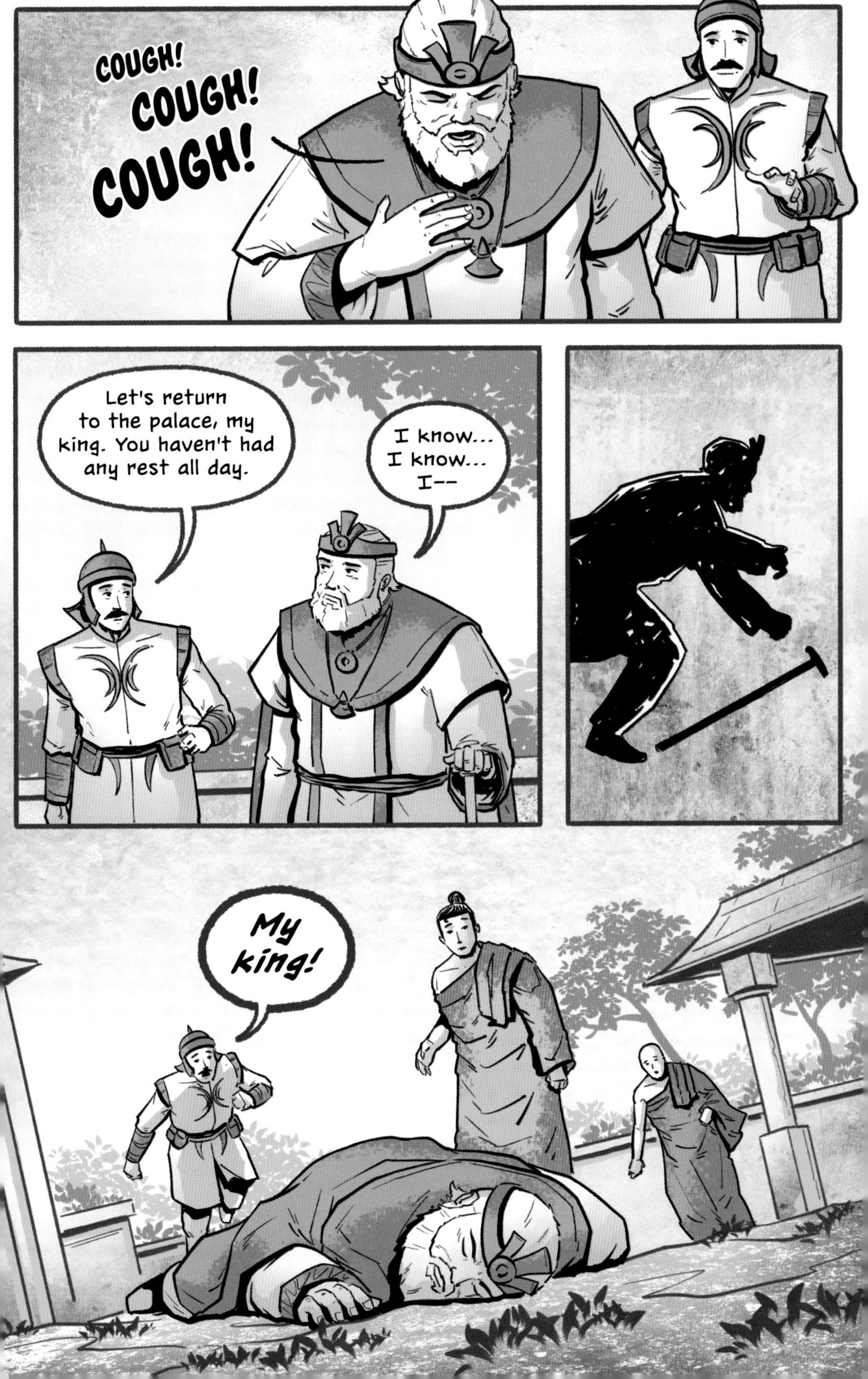
COUGH! COUGH! COUGH!
Let's return to the palace, my king. You haven't had any rest all day.
I know... I know... I--
My king!

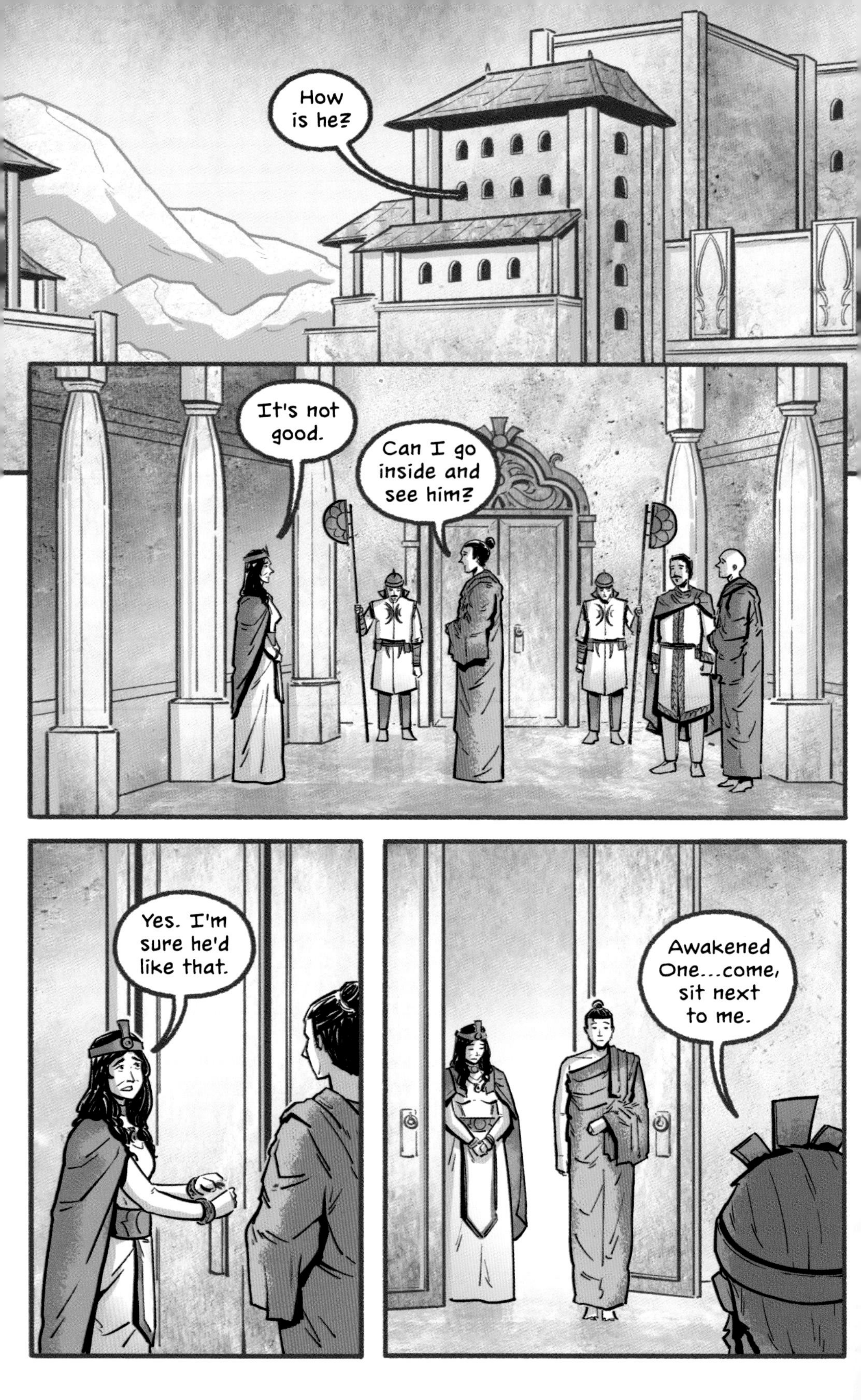
How is he?
It's not good.
Can I go inside and see him?
Yes. I'm sure he'd like that.
Awakened One...come, sit next to me.

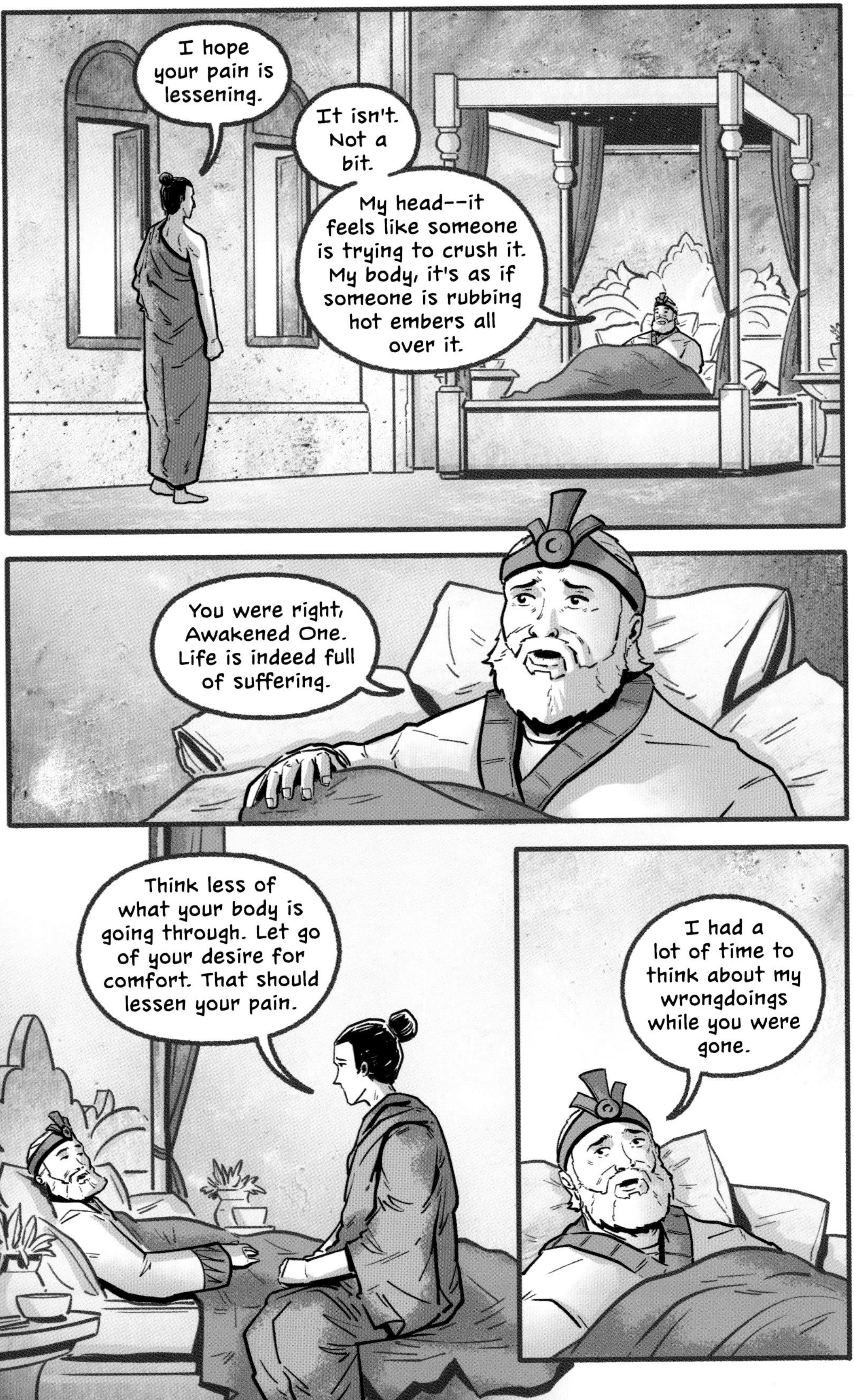
I hope your pain is lessening.
It isn't. Not a bit.
My head--it feels like someone is trying to crush it. My body, it's as if someone is rubbing hot embers all over it.
You were right, Awakened One. Life is indeed full of suffering.
Think less of what your body is going through. Let go of your desire for comfort. That should lessen your pain.
I had a lot of time to think about my wrongdoings while you were gone.

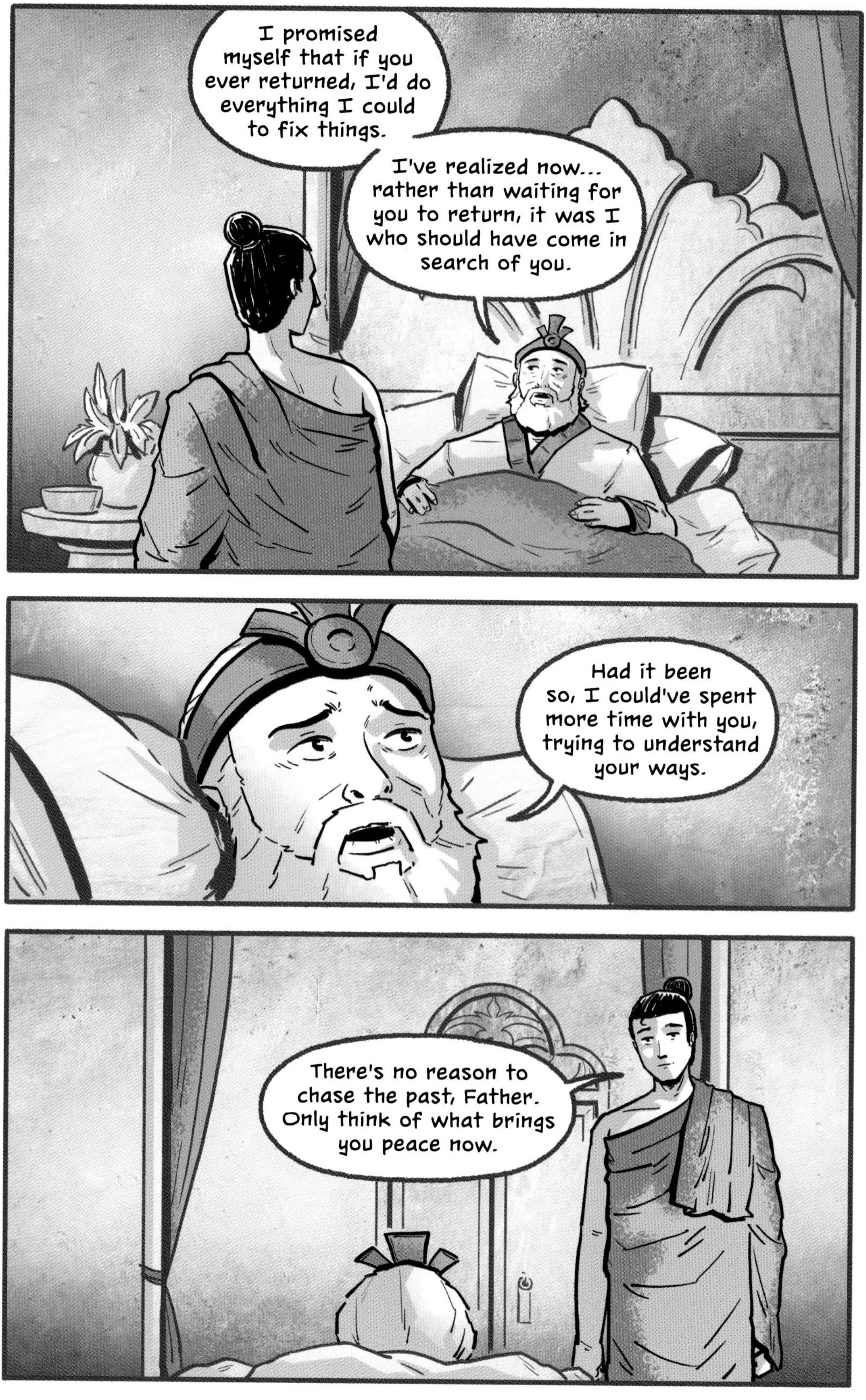
I promised myself that if you ever returned, I'd do everything I could to fix things.
I've realized now... rather than waiting for you to return, it was I who should have come in search of you.
Had it been so, I could've spent more time with you, trying to understand your ways.
There's no reason to chase the past, Father. Only think of what brings you peace now.

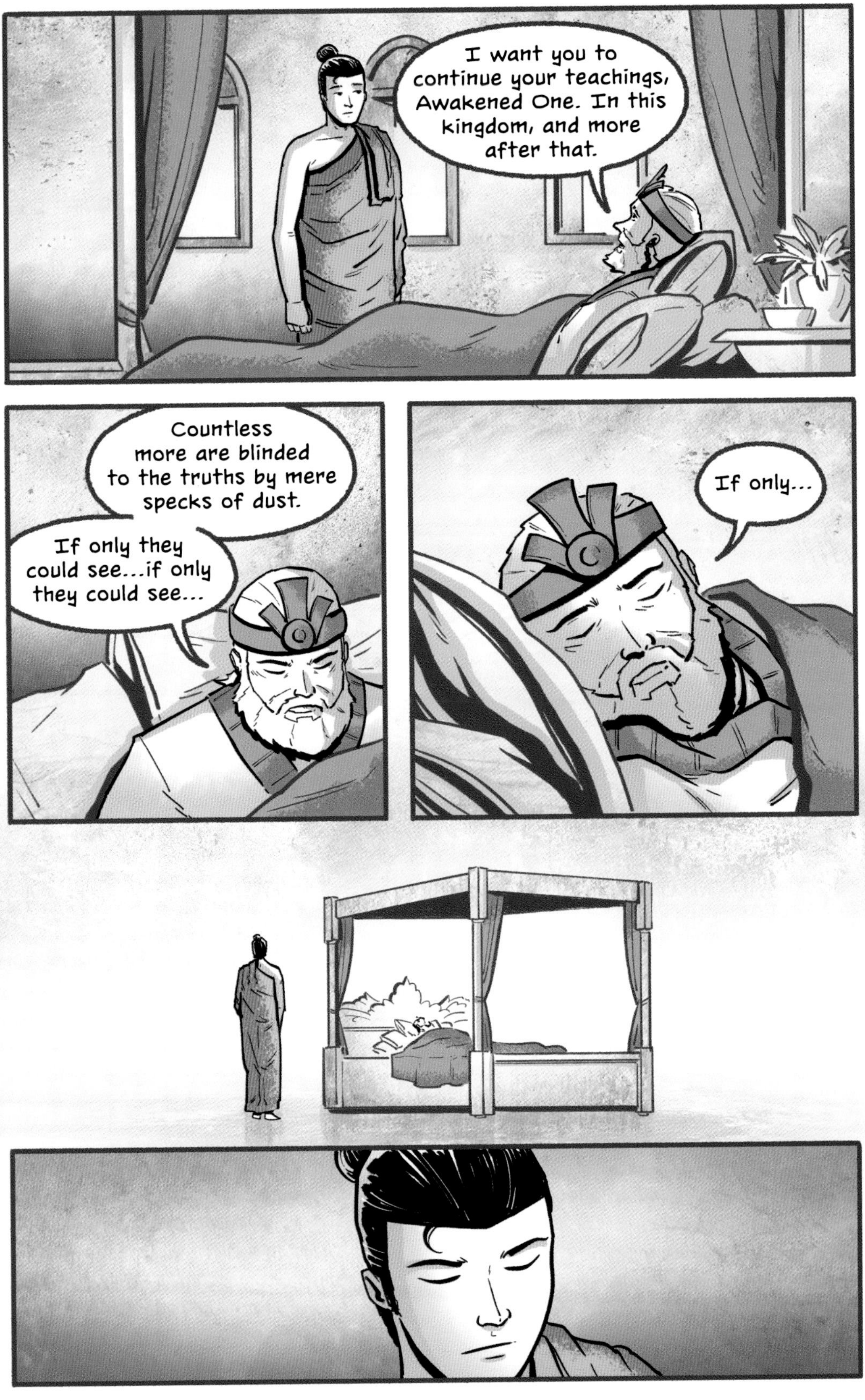
I want you to continue your teachings, Awakened One. In this kingdom, and more after that.
Countless more are blinded to the truths by mere specks of dust.
If only they could see...if only they could see...
If only...

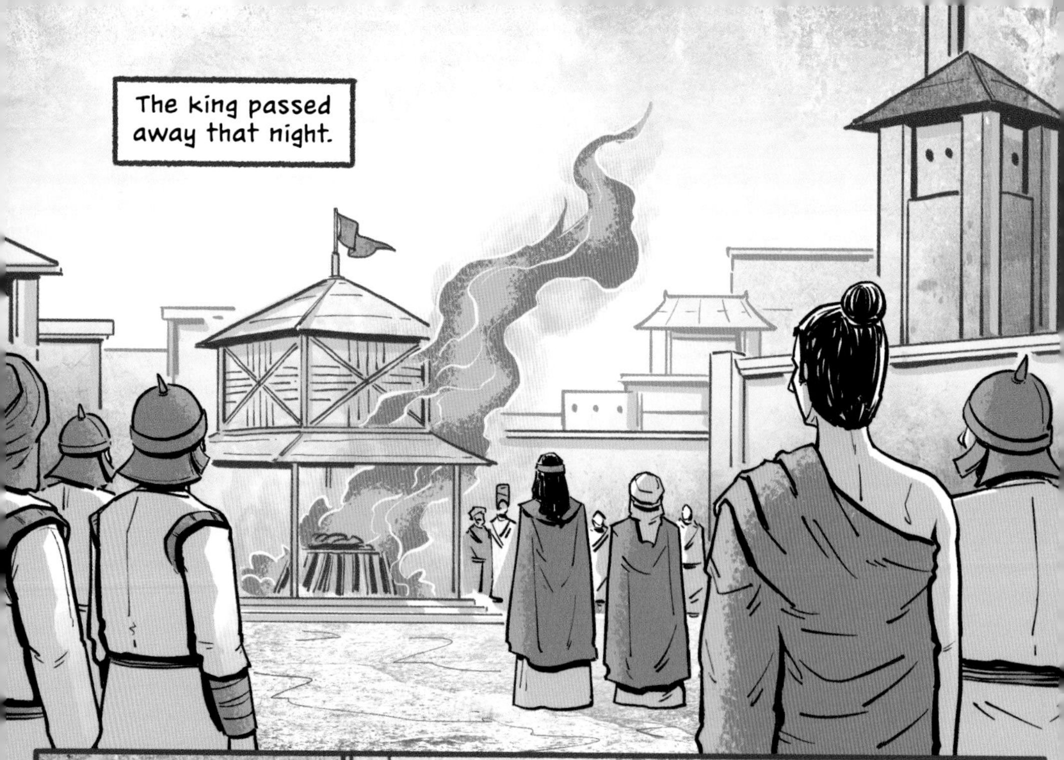
The king passed away that night.

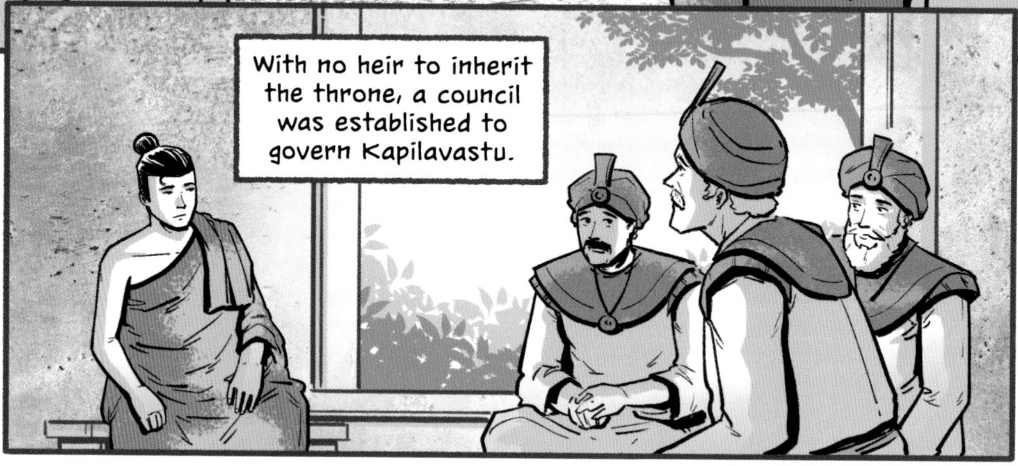
With no heir to inherit the throne, a council was established to govern Kapilavastu.

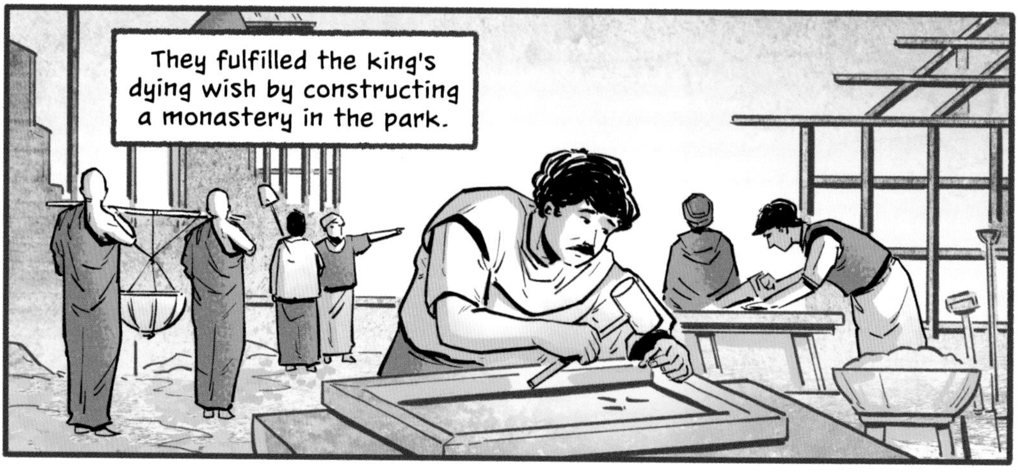
They fulfilled the king's dying wish by constructing a monastery in the park.

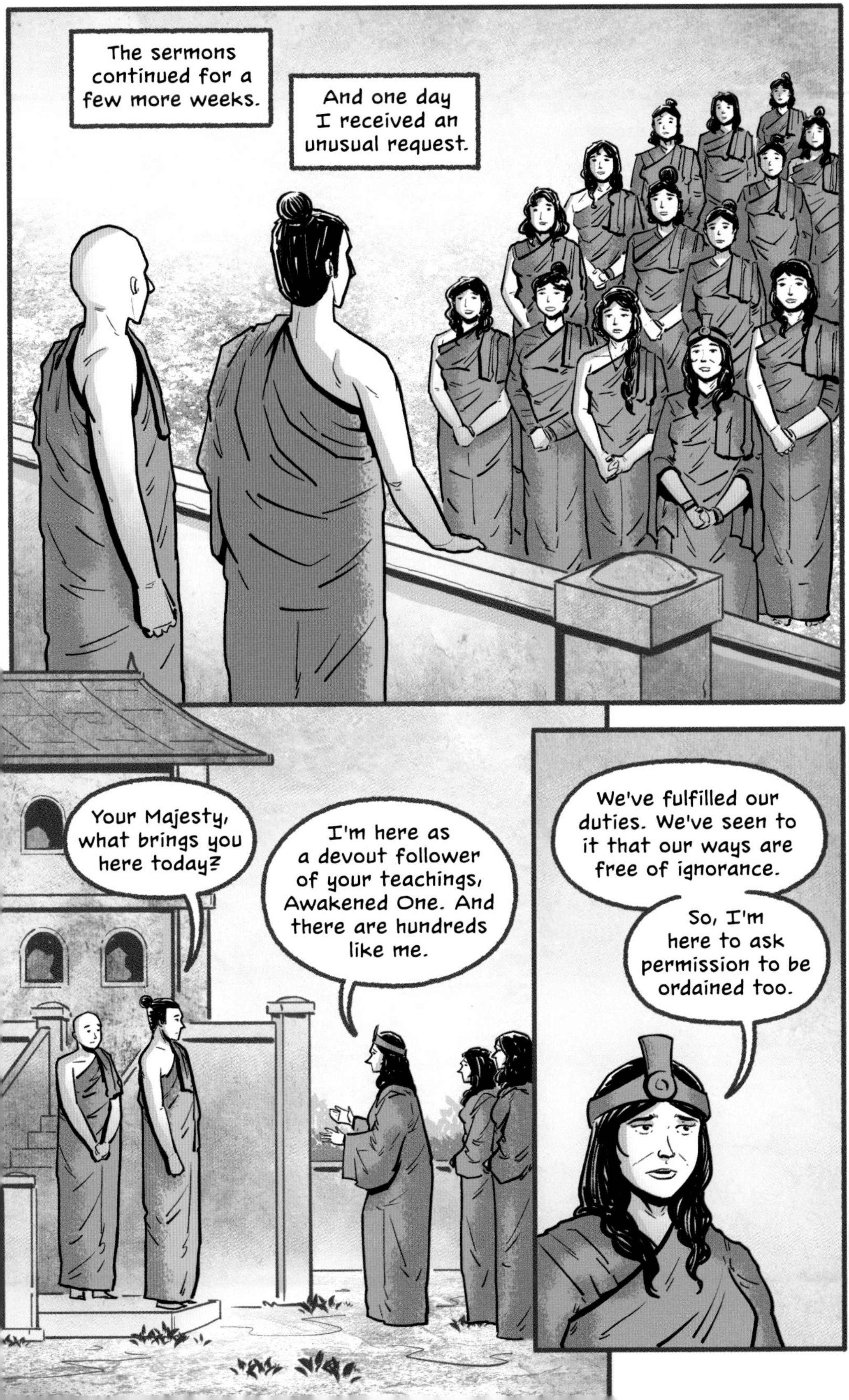
The sermons continued for a few more weeks.
And one day I received an unusual request.
Your Majesty, what brings you here today?
I'm here as a devout follower of your teachings, Awakened One. And there are hundreds like me.
We've fulfilled our duties. We've seen to it that our ways are free of ignorance.
So, I'm here to ask permission to be ordained too.

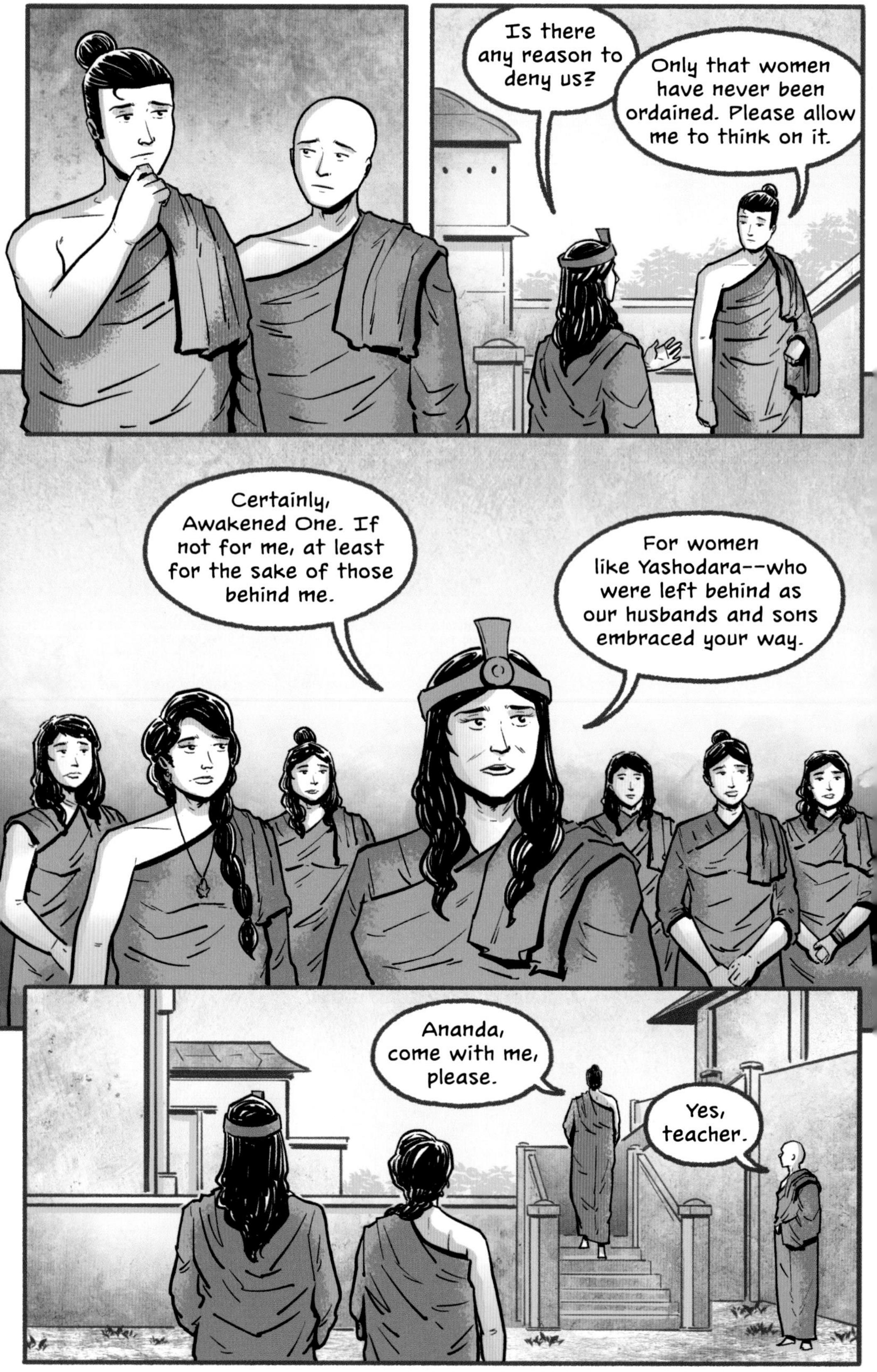
Is there any reason to deny us?
Only that women have never been ordained. Please allow me to think on it.
Certainly, Awakened One. If not for me, at least for the sake of those behind me.
For women like Yashodara--who were left behind as our husbands and sons embraced your way.
Ananda, come with me, please.
Yes, teacher.

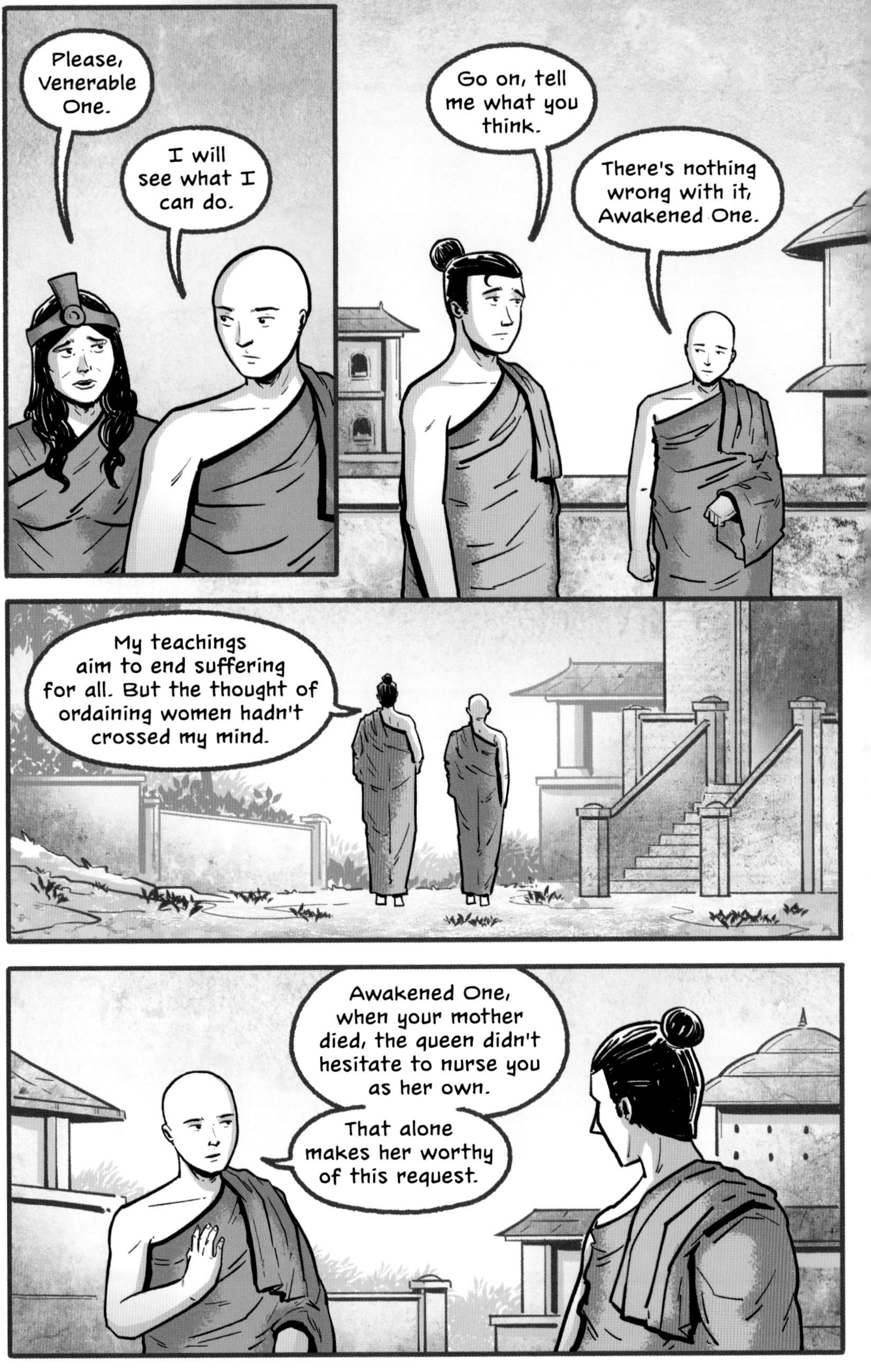
Please, Venerable One.
I will see what I can do.
Go on, tell me what you think.
There's nothing wrong with it, Awakened One.
My teachings aim to end suffering for all. But the thought of ordaining women hadn't crossed my mind.
Awakened One, when your mother died, the queen didn't hesitate to nurse you as her own.
That alone makes her worthy of this request.

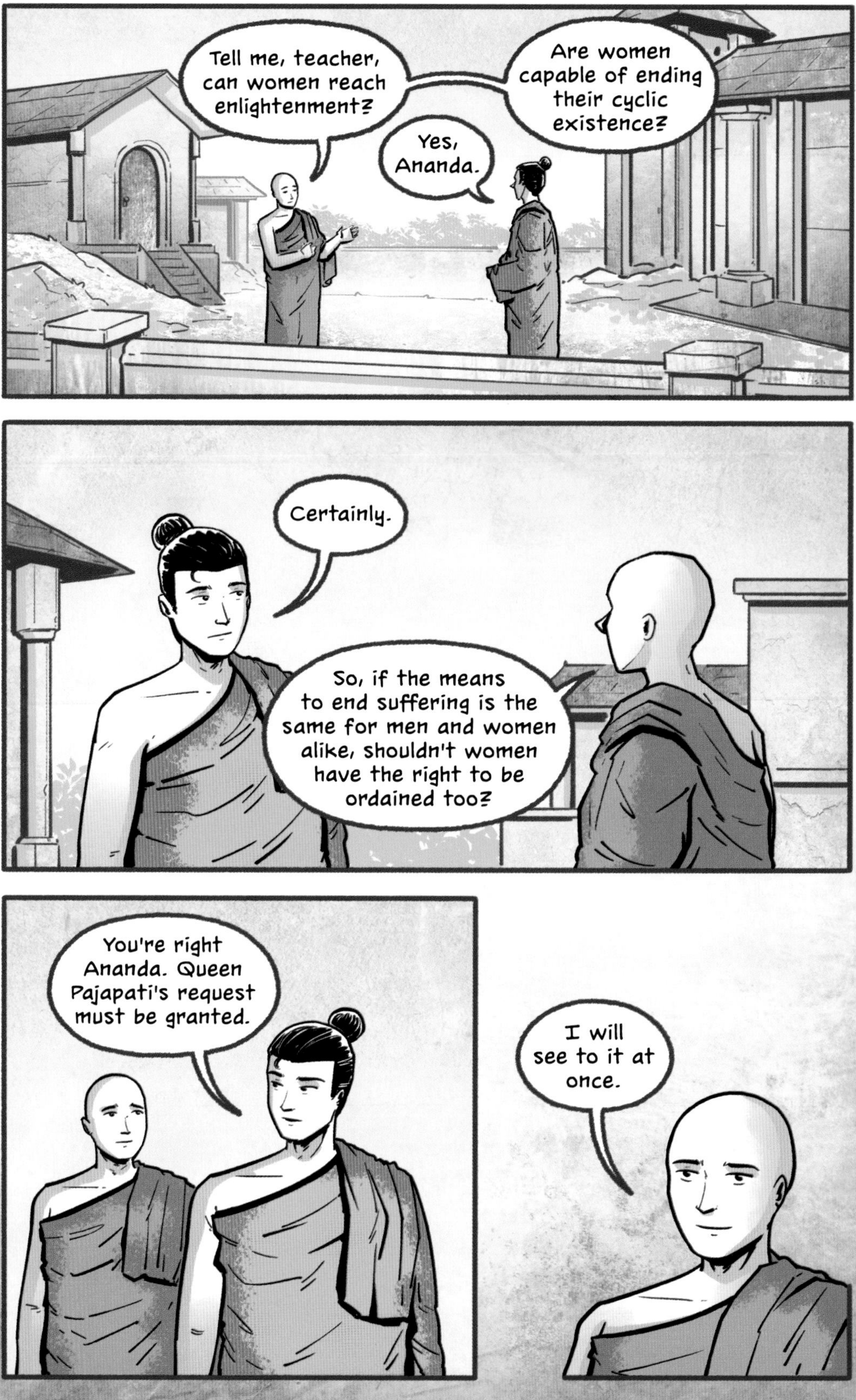
Tell me, teacher, can women reach enlightenment?
Are women capable of ending their cyclic existence?
Yes, Ananda.
Certainly.
So, if the means to end suffering is the same for men and women alike, shouldn't women have the right to be ordained too?
You're right Ananda. Queen Pajapati's request must be granted.
I will see to it at once.

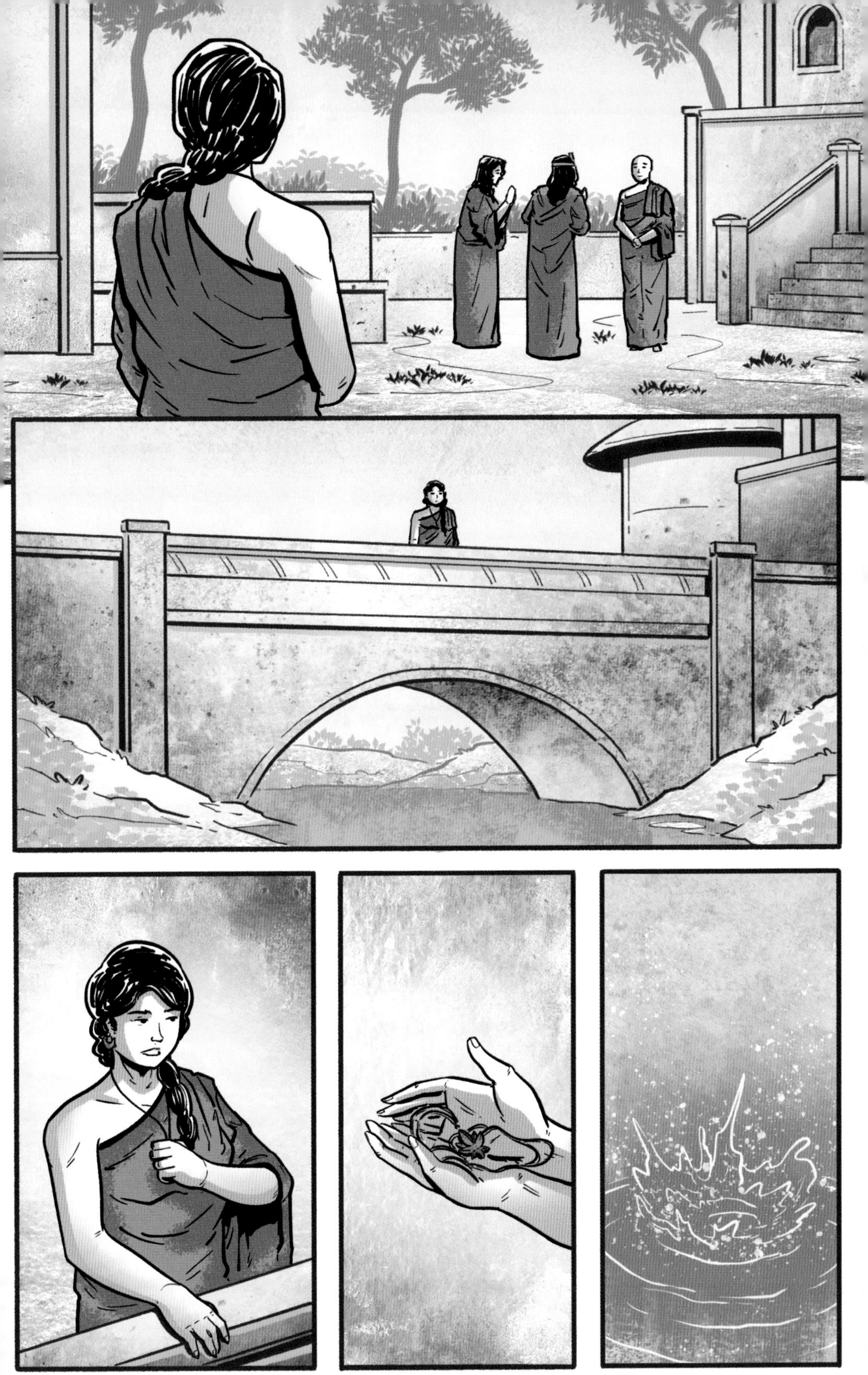

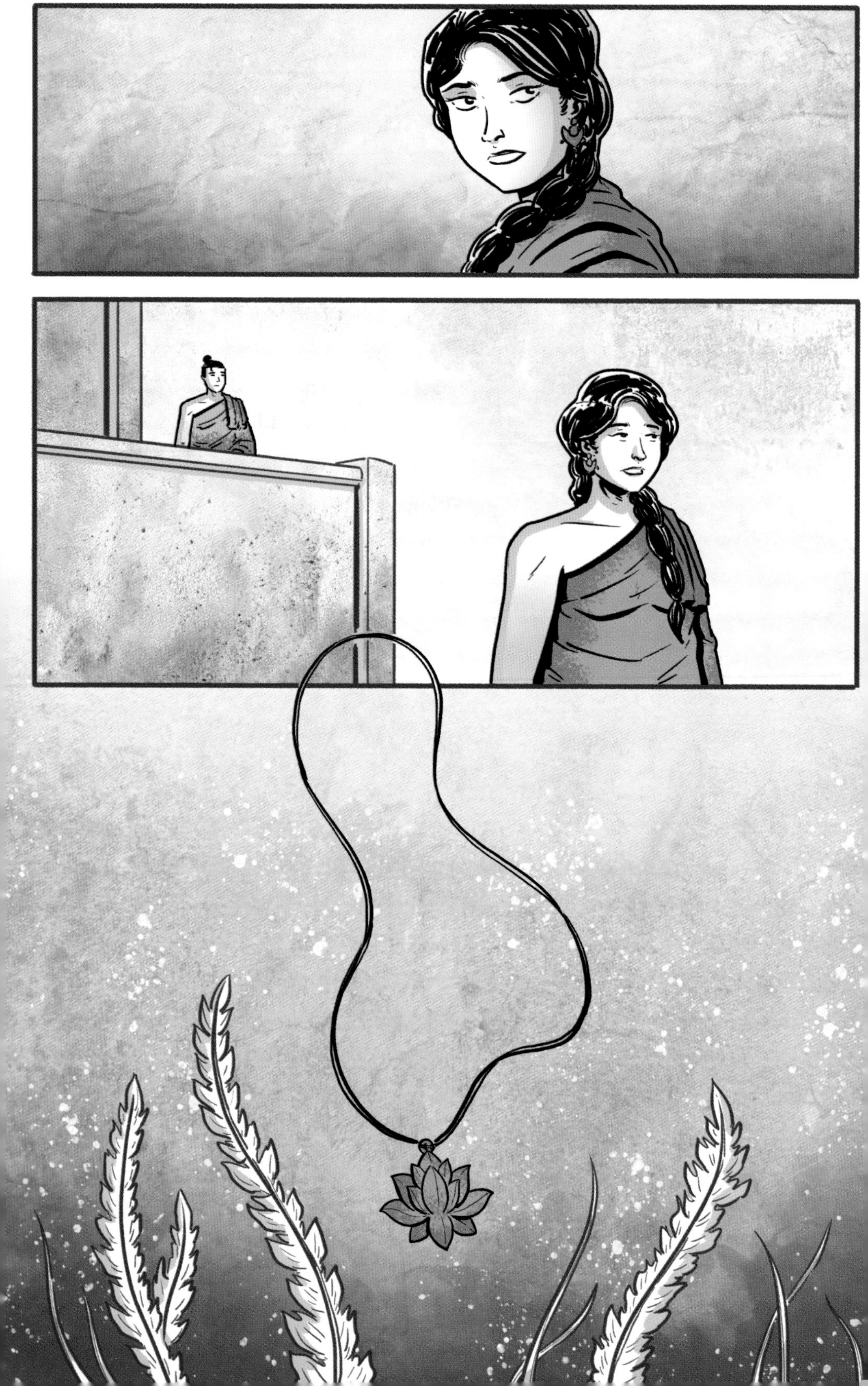

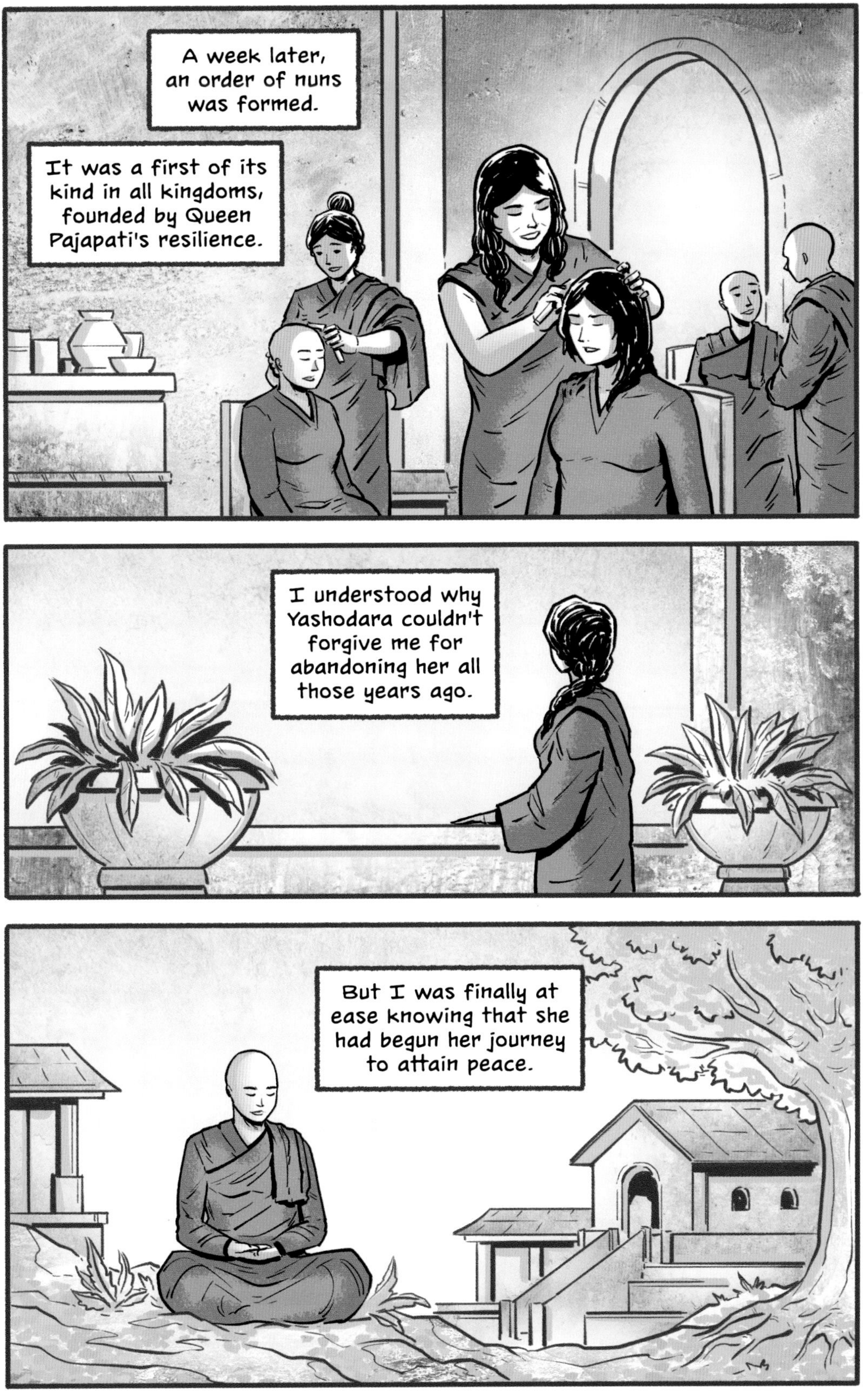
A week later, an order of nuns was formed.
It was a first of its kind in all kingdoms, founded by Queen Pajapati's resilience.
I understood why Yashodara couldn't forgive me for abandoning her all those years ago.
But I was finally at ease knowing that she had begun her journey to attain peace.

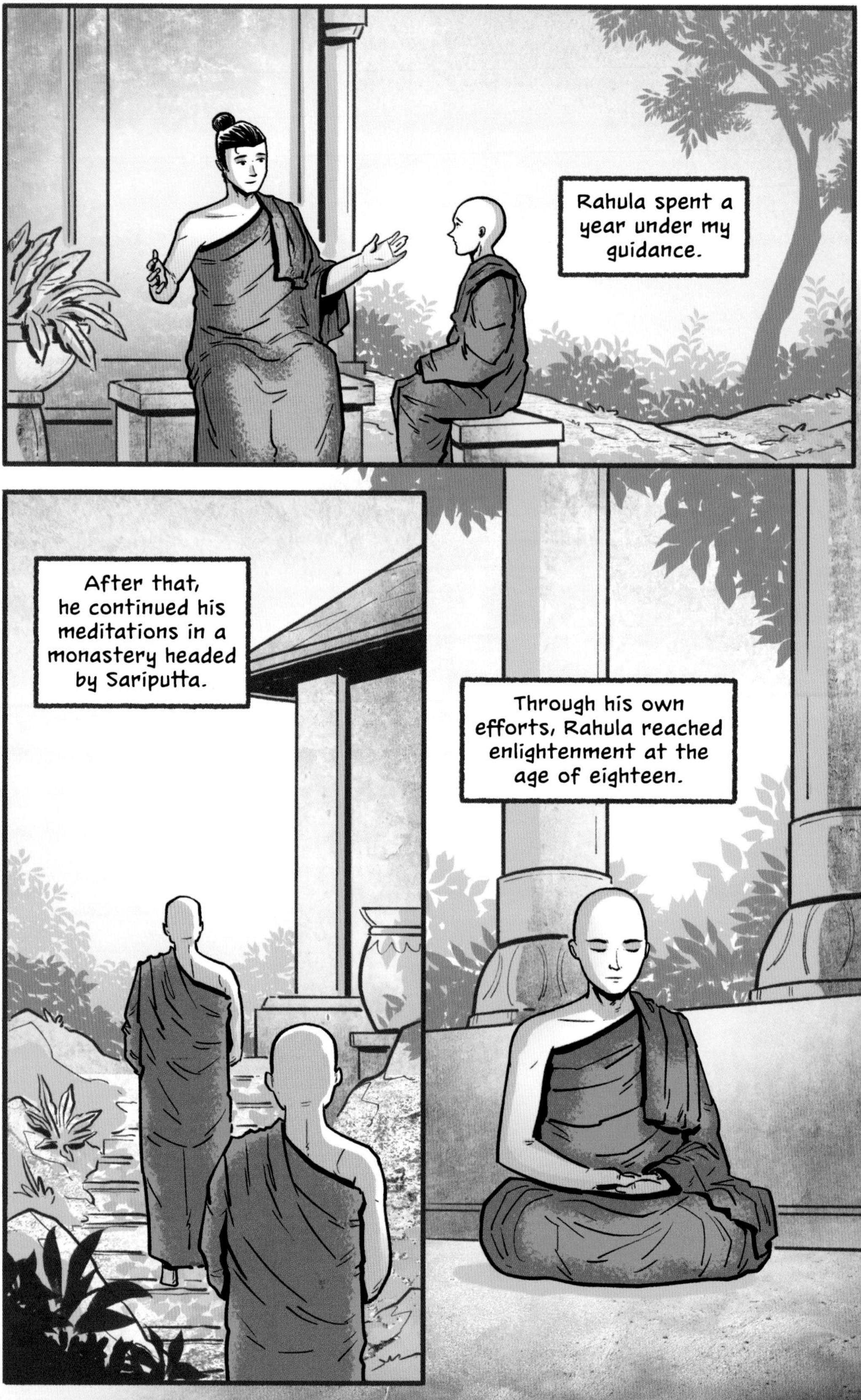
Rahula spent a year under my guidance.
After that, he continued his meditations in a monastery headed by Sariputta.
Through his own efforts, Rahula reached enlightenment at the age of eighteen.

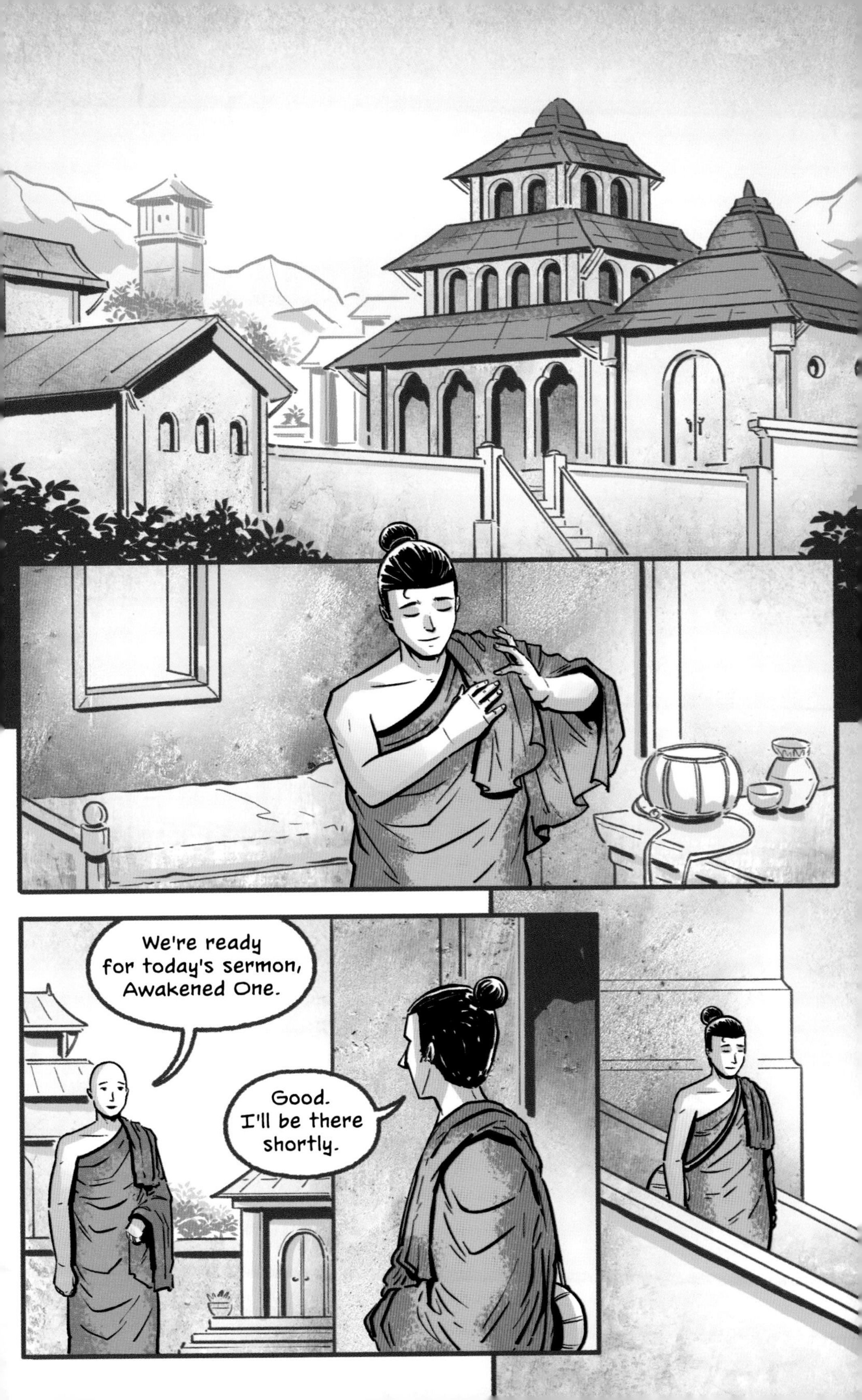
We're ready for today's sermon, Awakened One.
Good. I'll be there shortly.

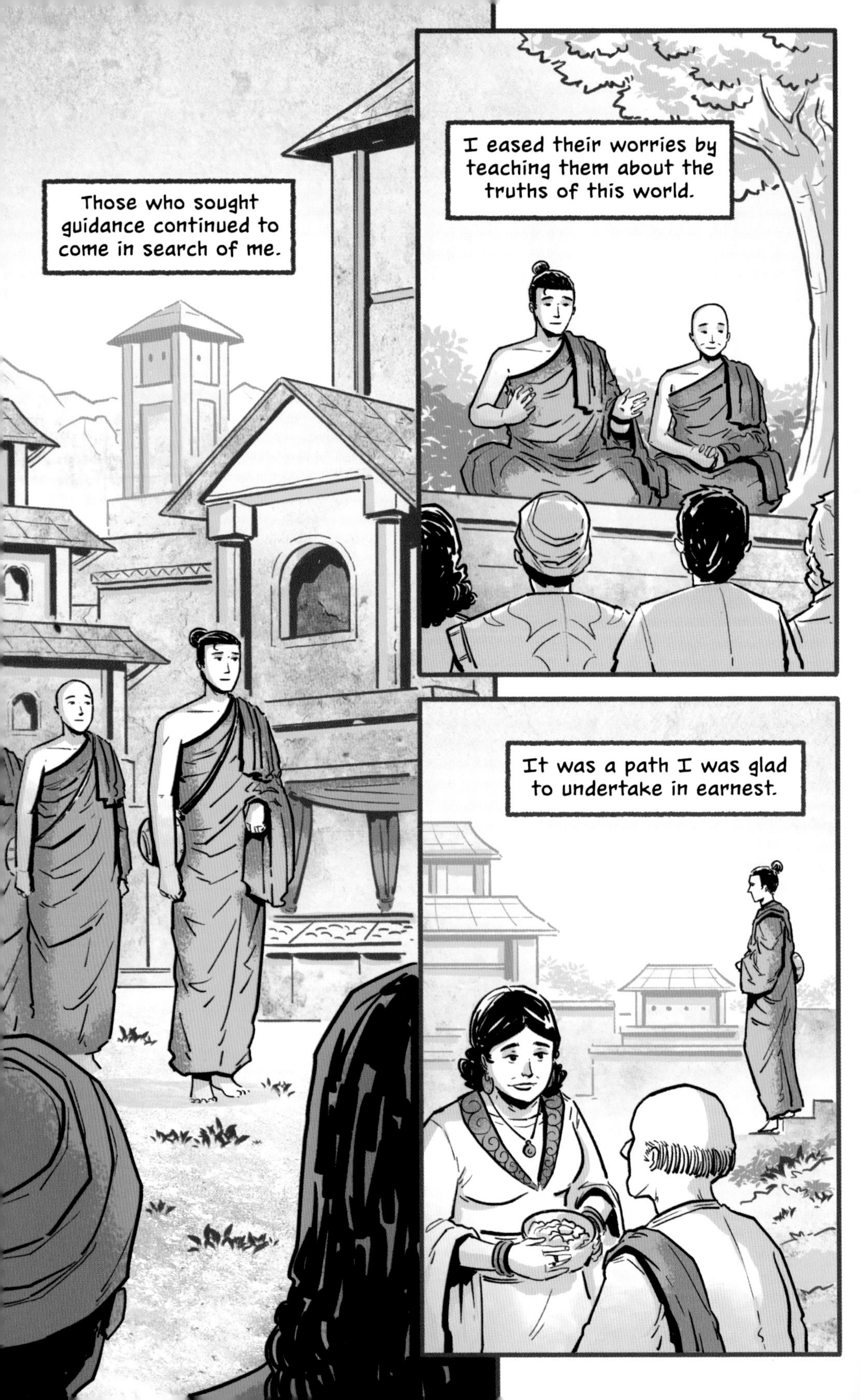
Those who sought guidance continued to come in search of me.
I eased their worries by teaching them about the truths of this world.
It was a path I was glad to undertake in earnest.

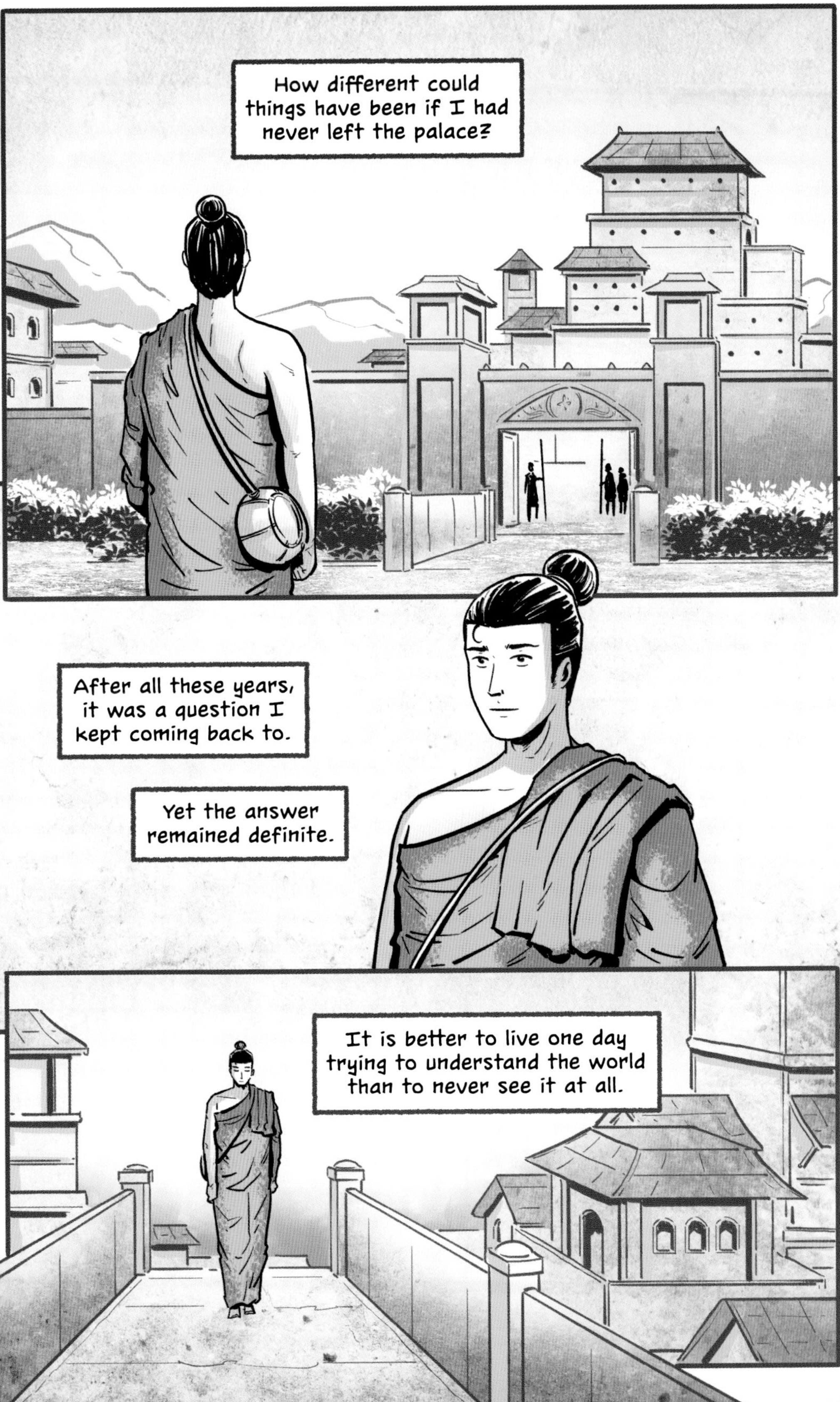
How different could things have been if I had never left the palace?
After all these years, it was a question I kept coming back to.
Yet the answer remained definite.
It is better to live one day trying to understand the world than to never see it at all.

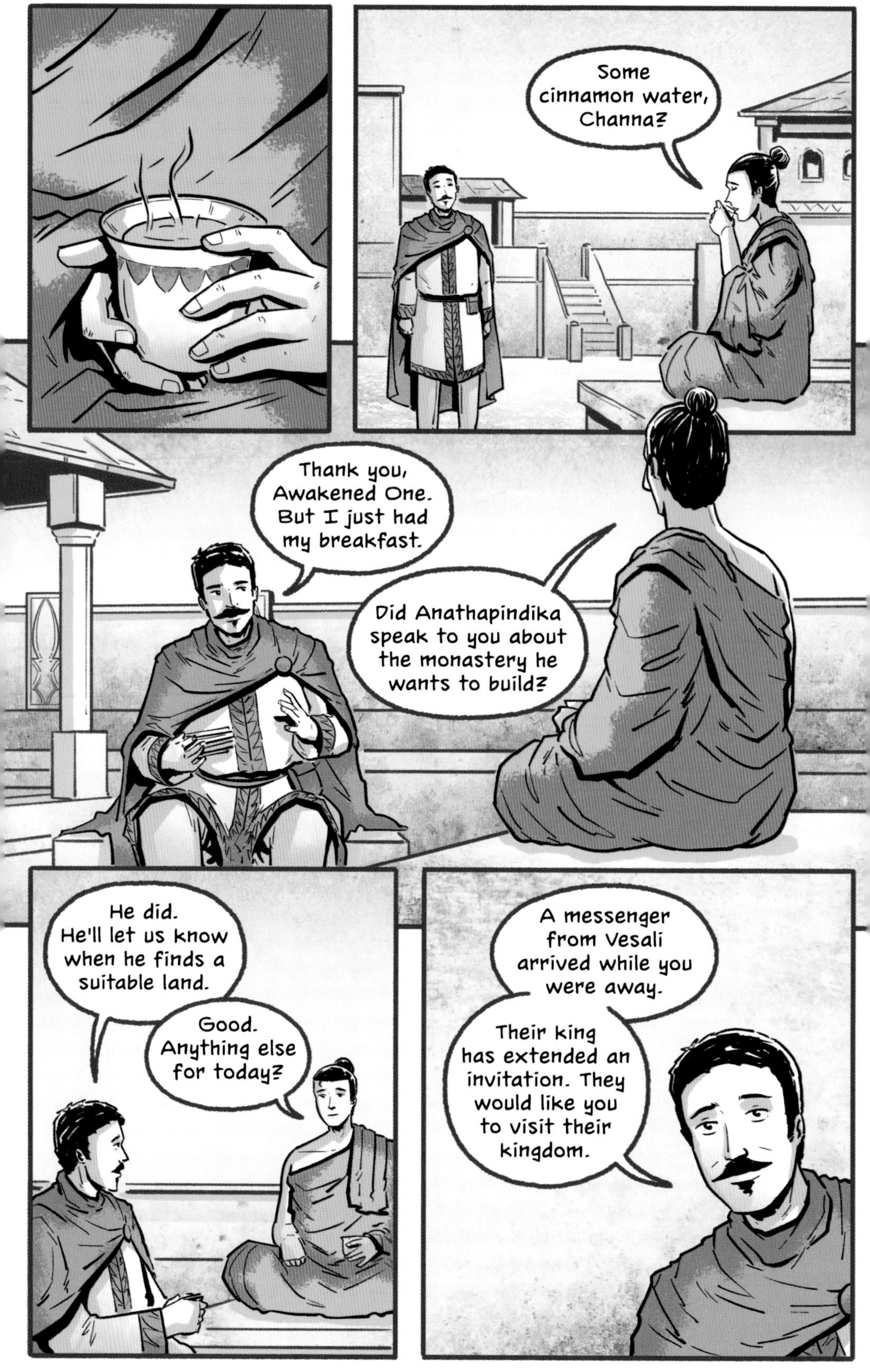
Some cinnamon water, Channa?
Thank you, Awakened One. But I just had my breakfast.
Did Anathapindika speak to you about the monastery he wants to build?
He did. He'll let us know when he finds a suitable land.
Good. Anything else for today?
A messenger from Vesali arrived while you were away.
Their king has extended an invitation. They would like you to visit their kingdom.

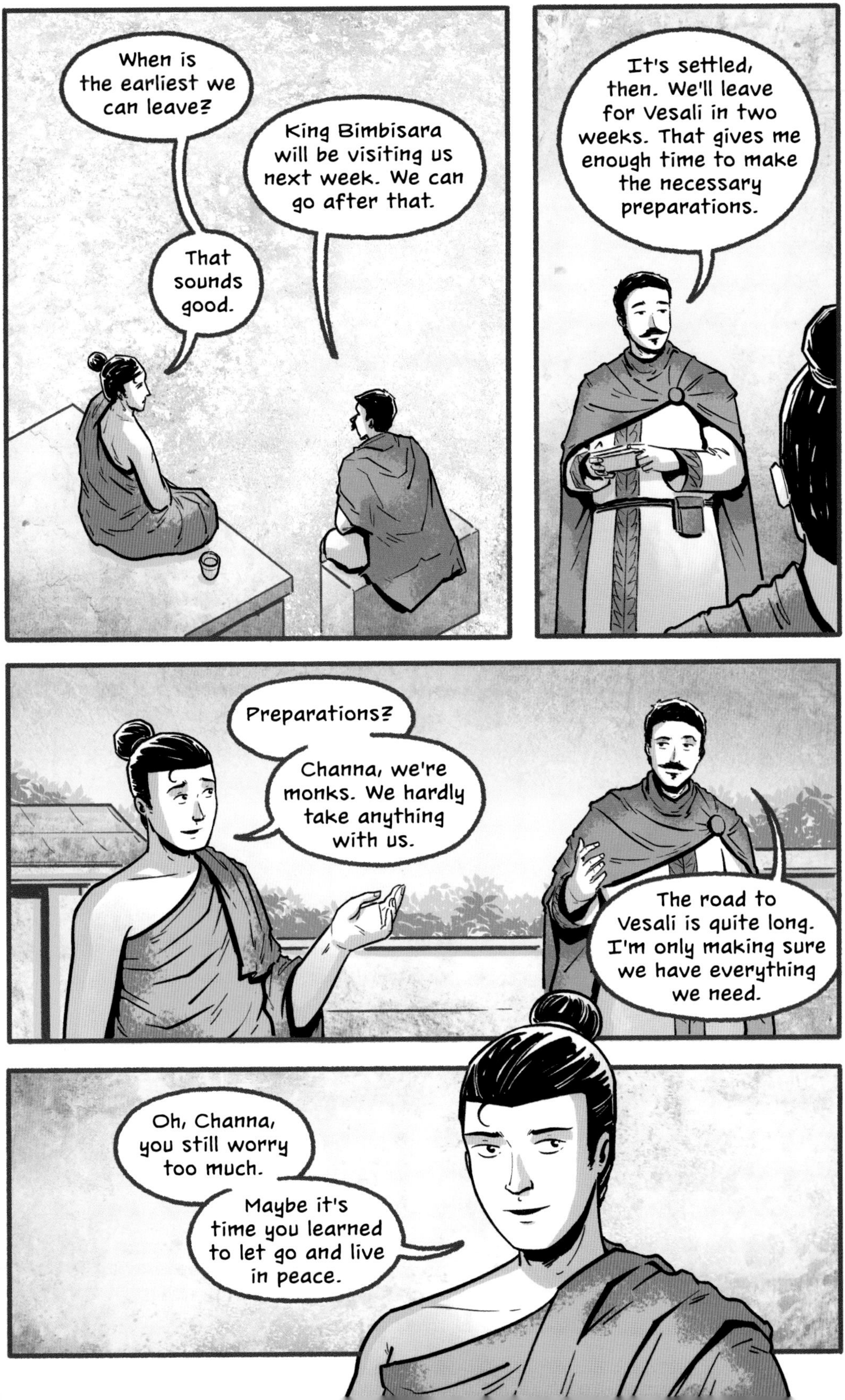
When is the earliest we can leave?
King Bimbisara will be visiting us next week. We can go after that.
That sounds good.
It's settled, then. We'll leave for Vesali in two weeks. That gives me enough time to make the necessary preparations.
Preparations?
Channa, we're monks. We hardly take anything with us.
The road to Vesali is quite long. I'm only making sure we have everything we need.
Oh, Channa, you still worry too much.
Maybe it's time you learned to let go and live in peace.

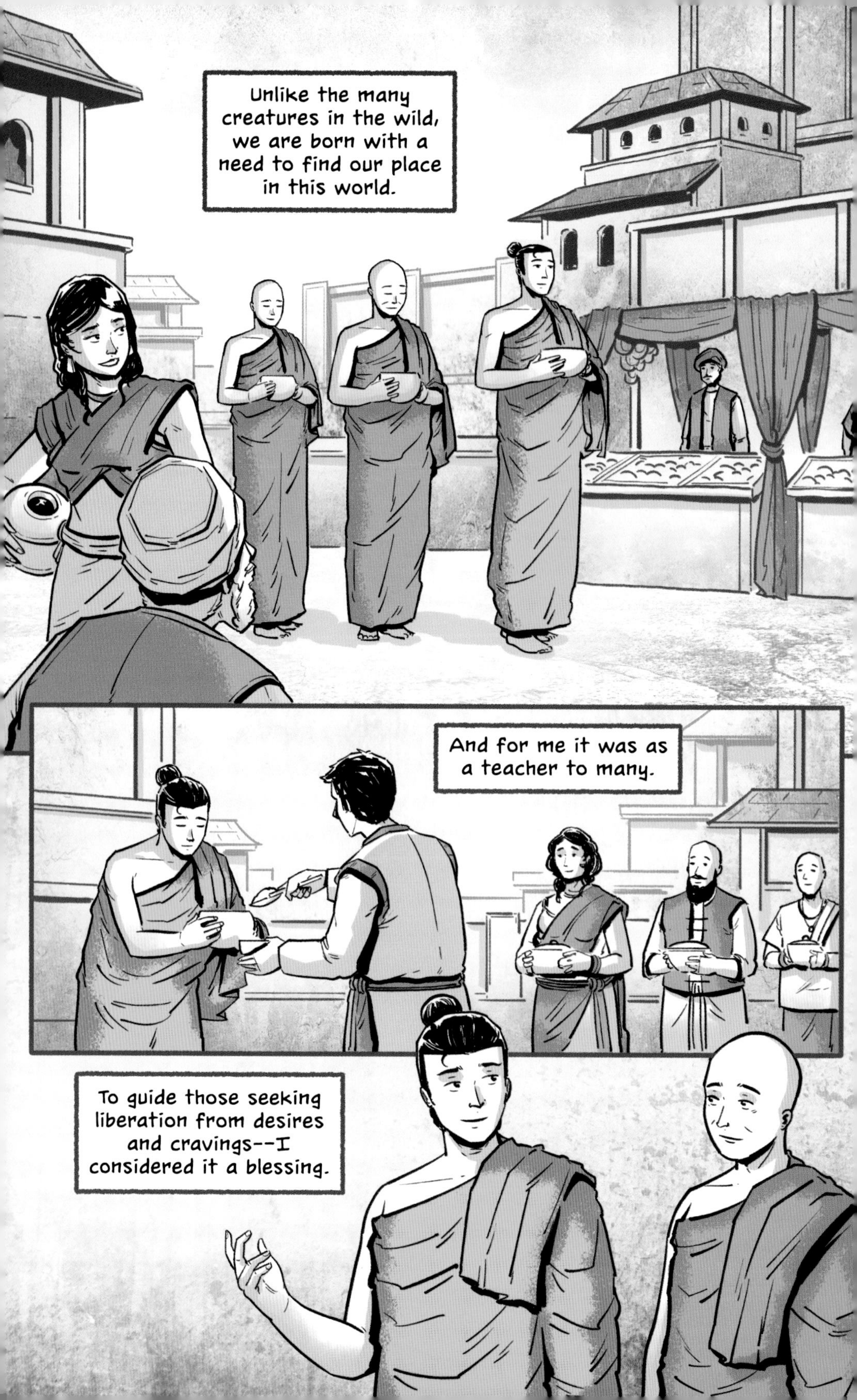
Unlike the many creatures in the wild, we are born with a need to find our place in this world.
And for me it was as a teacher to many.
To guide those seeking liberation from desires and cravings--I considered it a blessing.

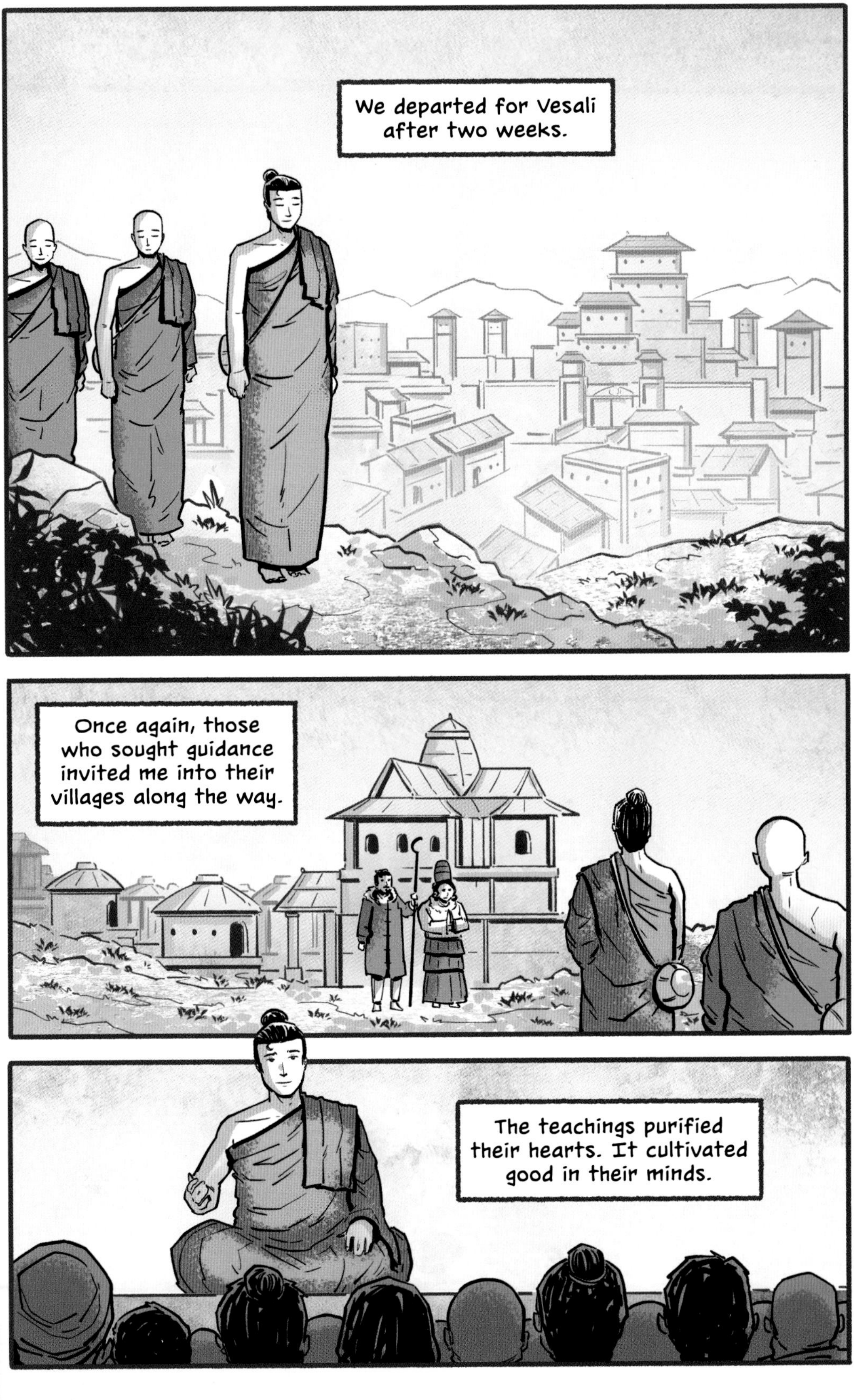
We departed for Vesali after two weeks.
Once again, those who sought guidance invited me into their villages along the way.
The teachings purified their hearts. It cultivated good in their minds.

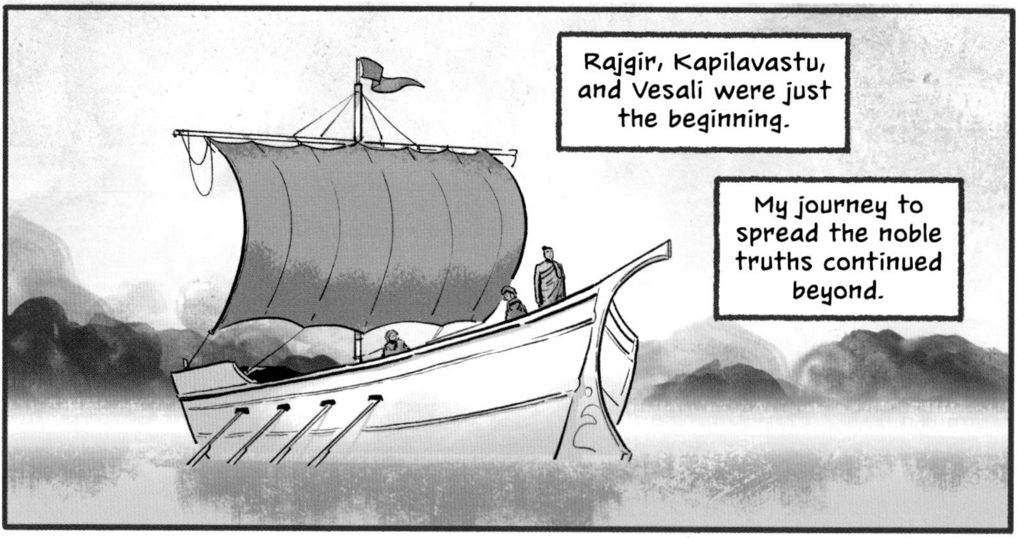
Rajgir, Kapilavastu, and Vesali were just the beginning.
My journey to spread the noble truths continued beyond.

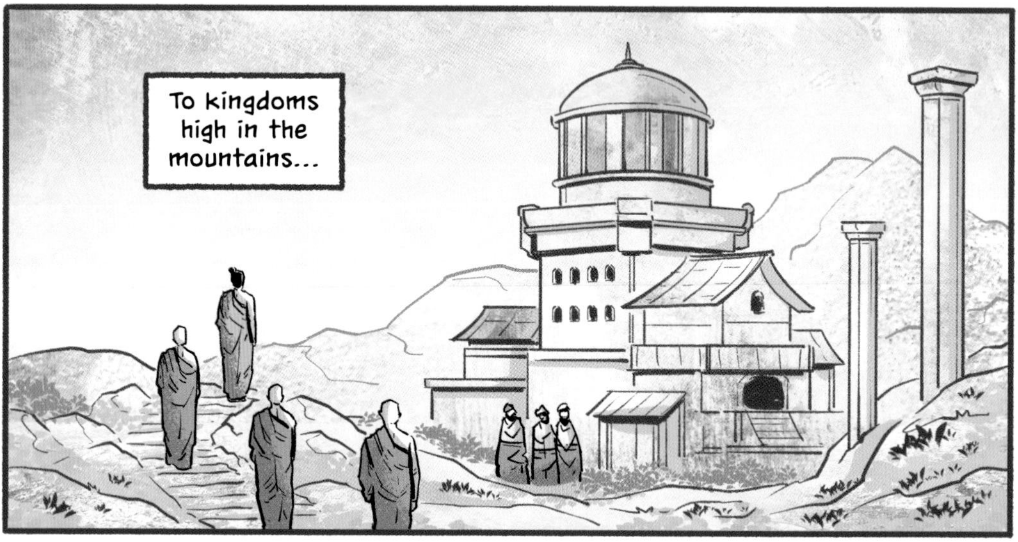
To kingdoms high in the mountains...

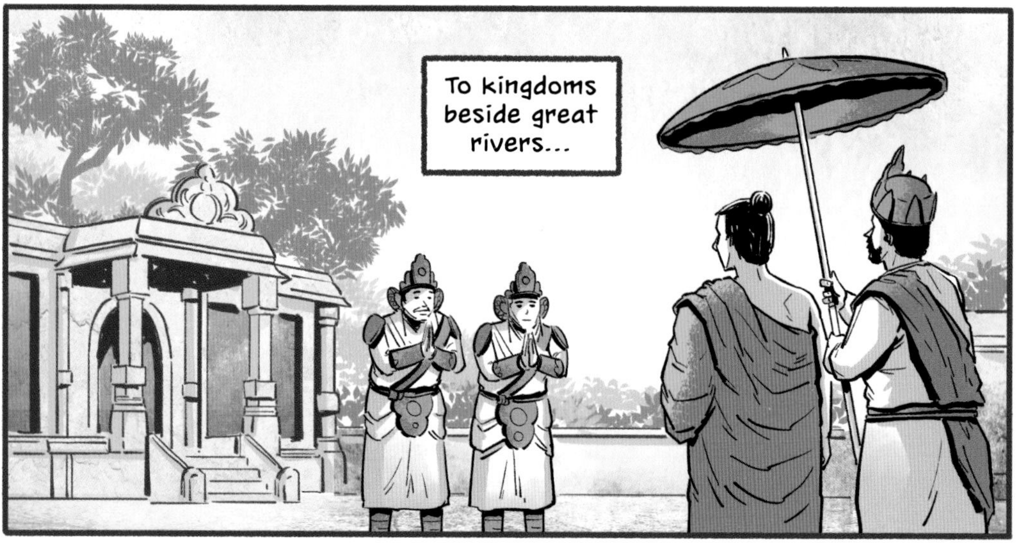
To kingdoms beside great rivers...

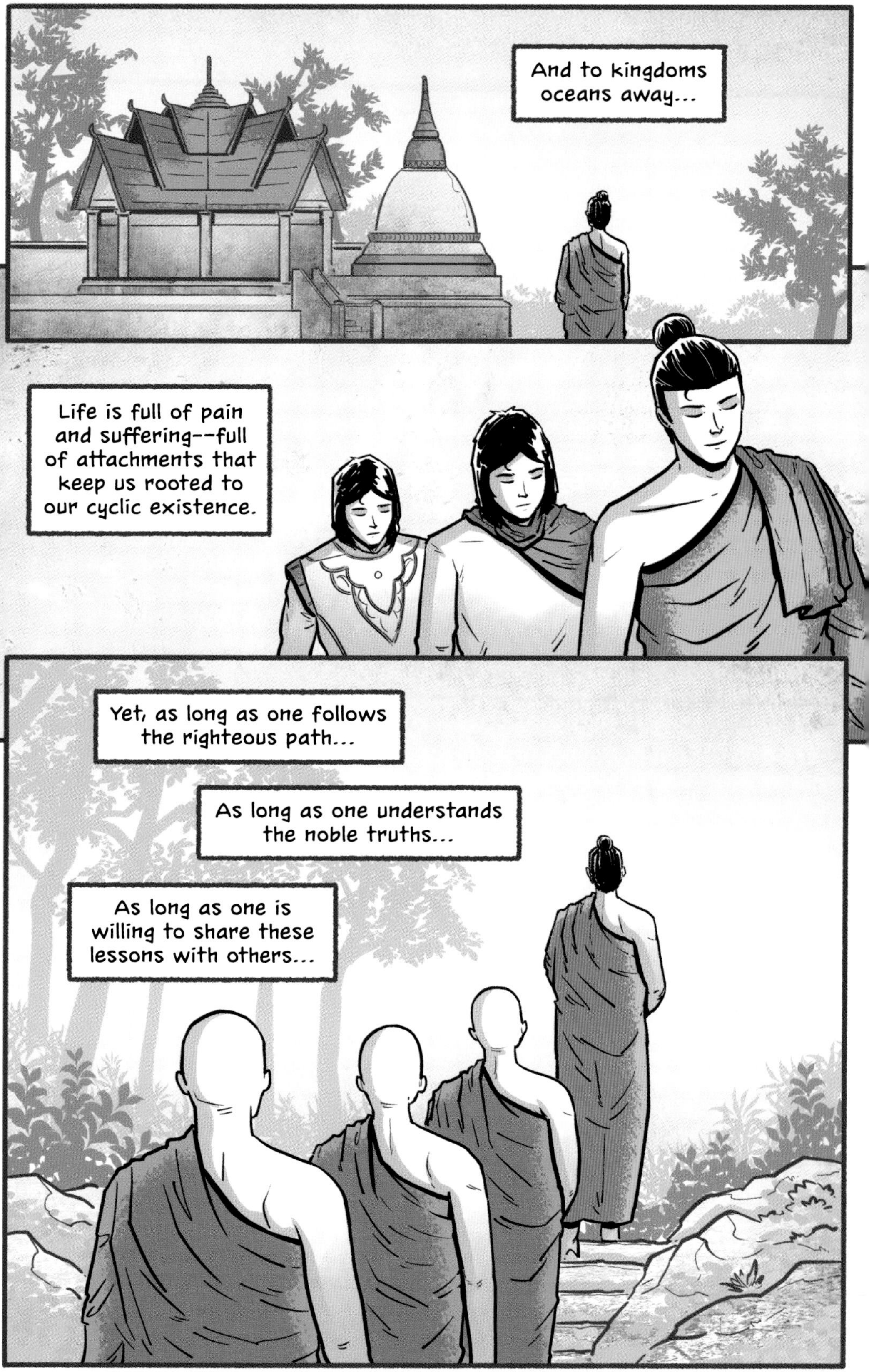
And to kingdoms oceans away...
Life is full of pain and suffering--full of attachments that keep us rooted to our cyclic existence.
Yet, as long as one follows the righteous path...
As long as one understands the noble truths...
As long as one is willing to share these lessons with others...

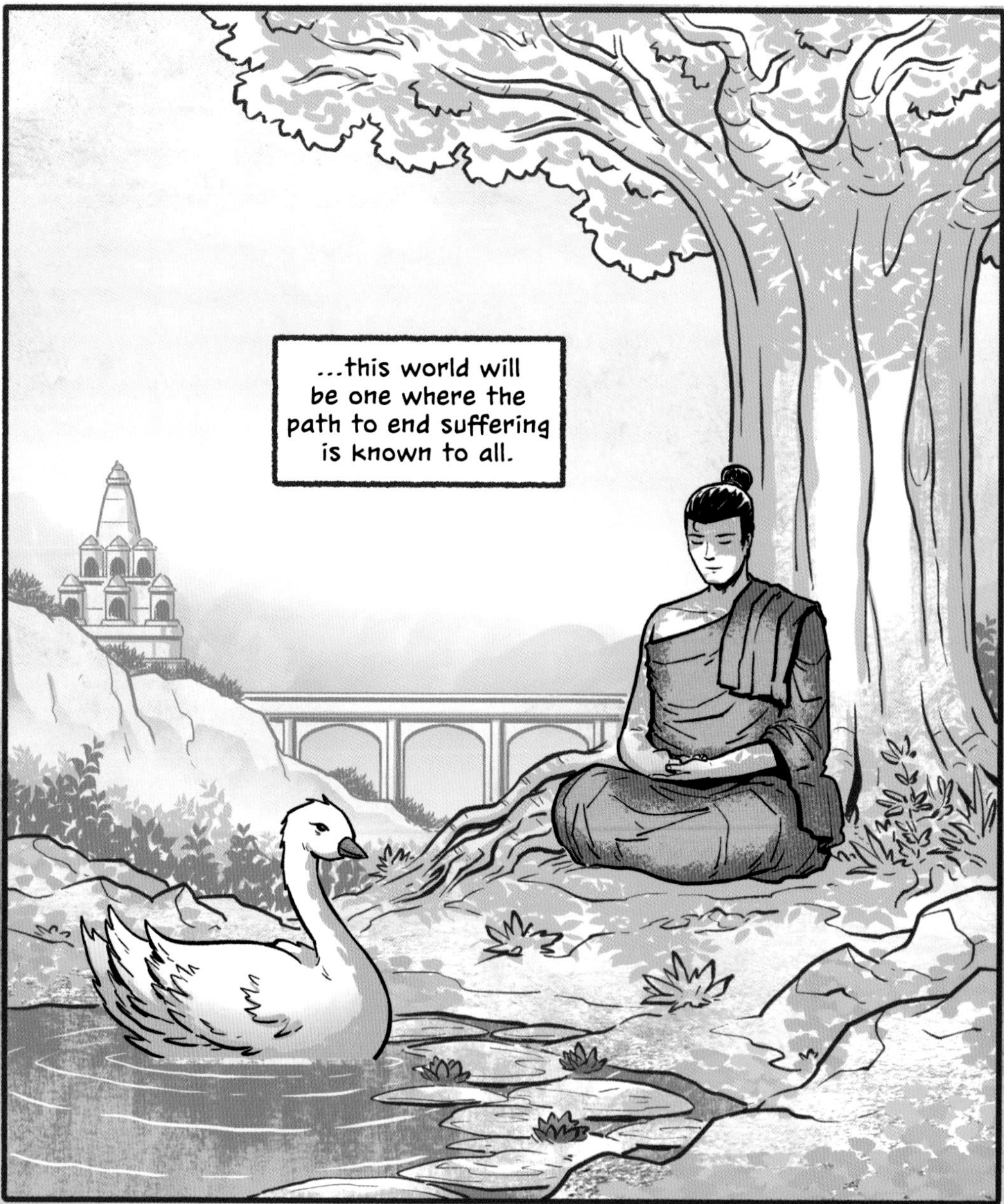
...this world will be one where the path to end suffering is known to all.

End.

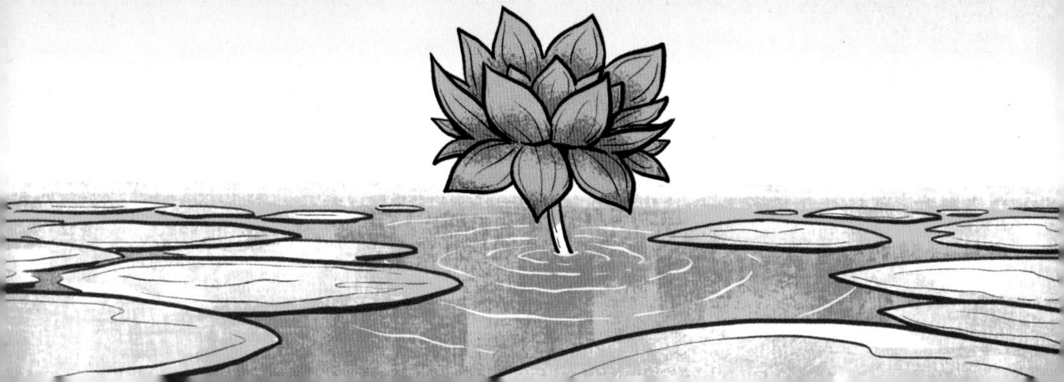

Acknowledgments

Like many Sri Lankan children, my first encounter with the Buddha's teachings was at a Sunday school held in a temple. I confess, I didn't enjoy it much. I wasn't happy that I had to wake up early every weekend when I could've been at home watching cartoons—but I wasn't in a position to protest.

Our lessons usually centered around a story about the Buddha and ended with a Sanskrit verse that we had to memorize for our final exams. I spent a good chunk of these classes daydreaming, and eventually, I began daydreaming about the lessons themselves. The image of a rebellious prince trying to find answers to life's suffering, the image of a wandering sage teaching life lessons intrigued me. As time went by, it became the only reason I continued attending Sunday school.

The idea of turning the Buddha's story into a graphic novel was a result of the world coming to a halt during the early pandemic. My scheduled convention appearances were cancelled. Sri Lanka suddenly closed its borders, and I was stuck in Dubai where my advertising job had just gone fully remote. I needed something to keep me busy in my apartment. Something to keep me from thinking about everything that was going wrong. I began reminiscing about my childhood, the beautiful shores of Hikkaduwa, the untold histories of Anuradhapura, the cool breeze under the mango trees that grew around the temple where I first learned about the Buddha. I was daydreaming again.

The first written words about the Buddha appeared approximately four hundred years after his death. These scripts have since formed the foundation of many cultures and a way of life for millions of Buddhists around the world. As I was outlining this book, my goal was to tell the Buddha's story in a way that had not been done before—by making it a grounded character exploration of a cheerful prince, a loving husband, a father who leaves all his wealth and privilege behind to search for a higher truth. But how could I re-adapt a story that has been told hundreds of times elsewhere? How could I turn this mythos, familiar to so many, into something revelatory? What had I gotten myself into?

While the core of the story I wanted to tell was locked in fairly early on, it still went through multiple iterations until I landed on the version I was happy with—something the younger, daydreaming version of me would've enjoyed too. I never considered myself deeply religious, but I was glad that in making this book, I was able to find peace in the intersection of religion and art.

I'm incredibly grateful to everyone who helped me on this. A huge thank-you to my friend Hernán Guarderas for his incredible guidance on crafting a proposal deck, Professor Jon Walters for graciously sharing his research and writing about the Buddha's life, and Venerable Nibbuto at the Bodhiyana Monastery in Australia for the guidance about the Buddha's teachings.

A special thank-you to my wonderful editor, Alyza Liu, for your trust and for encouraging me to push the story further, and to Greg Stadnyk for the art direction that helped me nail the visual language of the story I wanted to tell. To the wonderful team at Atheneum, Clare McGlade, Elizabeth Blake-Linn, Alex Kelleher-Nagorski, Reka Simonson, and Justin Chanda—thank you so much for your continuous support. And of course, to my incredible agent, Gordon Warnock at Fuse Literary, who believed in this project from day one, and without whom none of this would exist.

To my parents, Ammi and Thatthi, thank you for everything. To my lovely wife, Mahee, thank you for being there during the ups, the downs, and all the immeasurable challenges we faced while I was working on this book. I'm lucky to have you by my side. Finally, you, dear reader, thank you for giving *Enlightened* a chance. The Buddha's life—the mythos this story is based on—is vast, full of interesting characters and countless nuances. There's much more to be discovered outside of this book.

Perhaps even something you might find yourself daydreaming about.

Sachi

Further Reading

Bodhi, Bhikkhu, ed. *In the Buddha's Words: An Anthology of Discourses from the Pali Canon*. Somerville: Wisdom Publications, 2005.

Hanh, Thich Nhat. *The Heart of the Buddha's Teaching: Transforming Suffering into Peace, Joy, and Liberation*. New York: Broadway Books, 1999.

Hecker, Hellmuth, and Nyanaponika Thera. *Great Disciples of the Buddha: Their Lives, Their Works, Their Legacy*. Edited by Bhikkhu Bodhi. Somerville: Wisdom Publications, 2003.

Karetzky, Patricia. *Making Sense of Buddhist Art & Architecture*. London: Thames & Hudson Ltd., 2015.

Rahula, Walpola. *What the Buddha Taught*. New York: Grove Press, 1994.

DEVELOPMENTAL SKETCHES

BUDDHA

SIDDHARTHA AGE 16

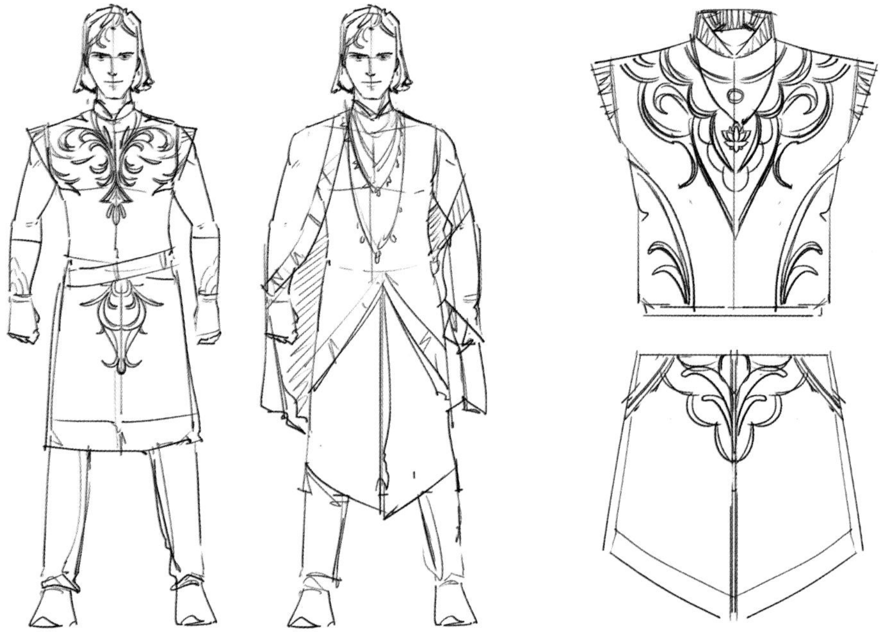

SIDDHARTHA AGE 21

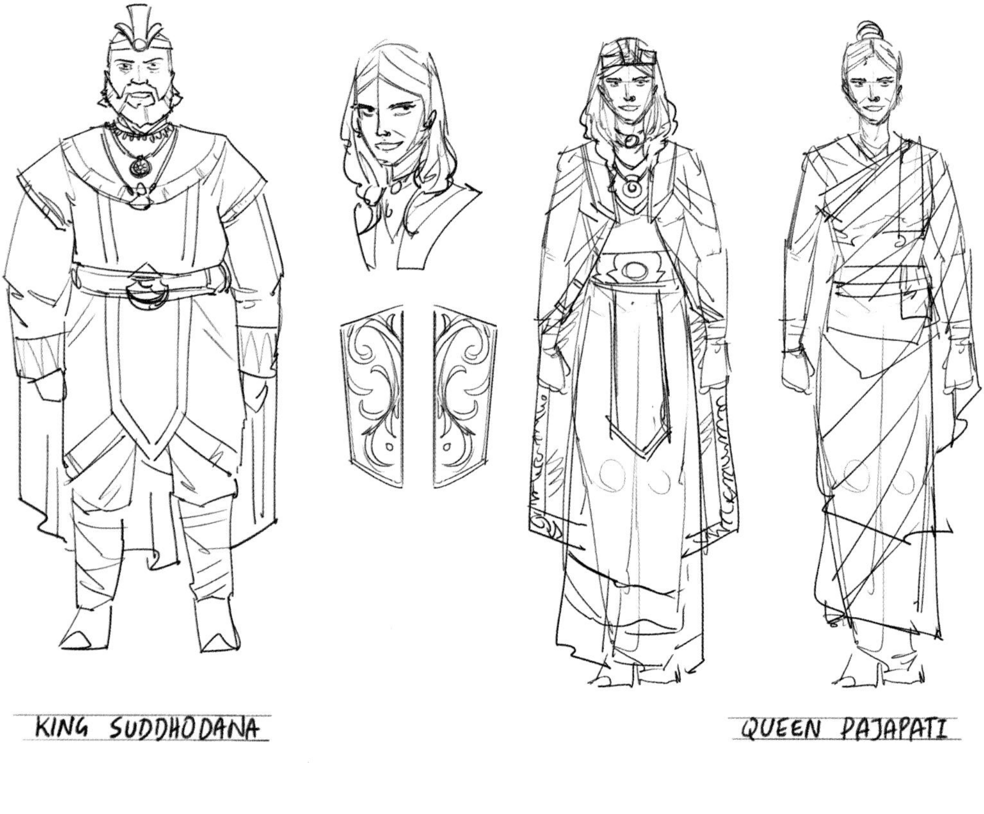

KING SUDDHODANA

QUEEN PAJAPATI

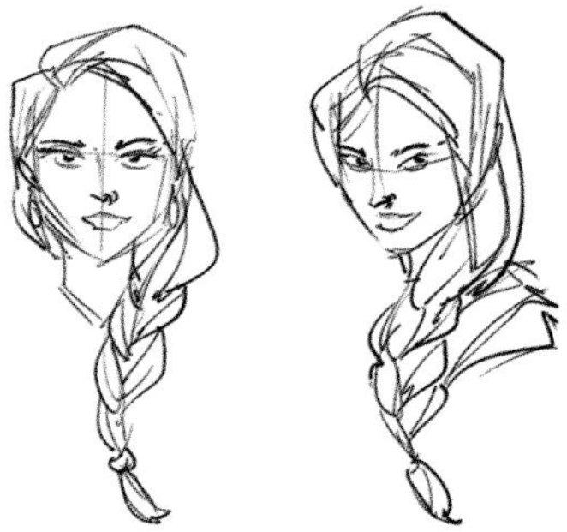

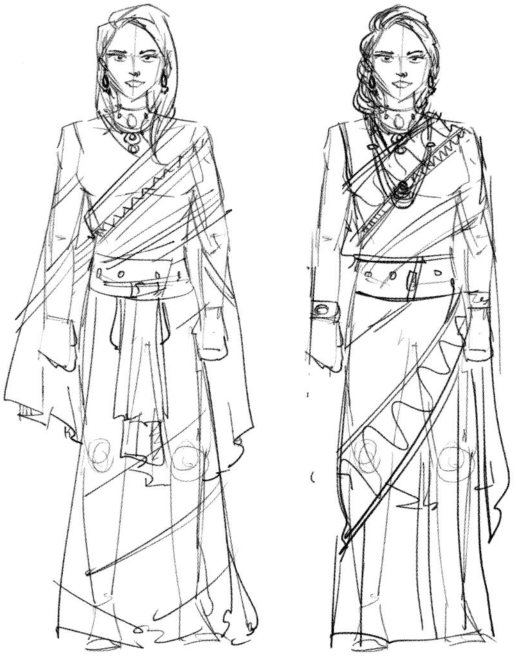

YASHODARA

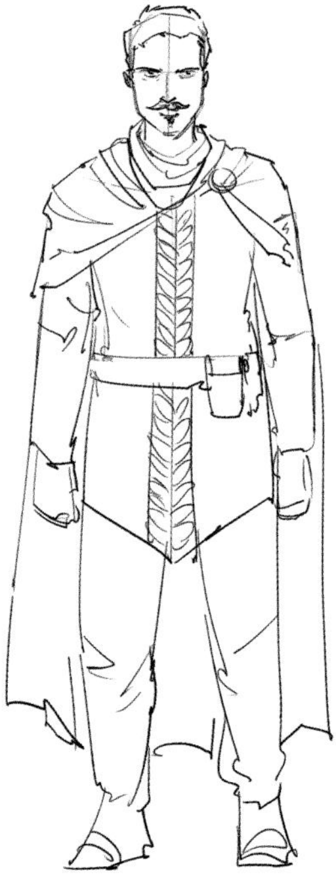

CHANNA

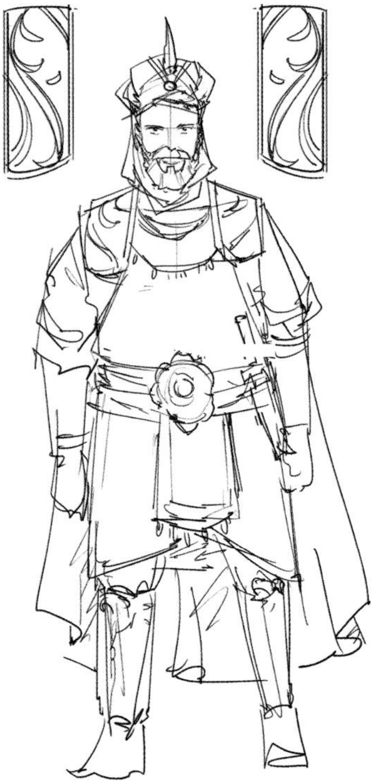

KING BIMBISARA

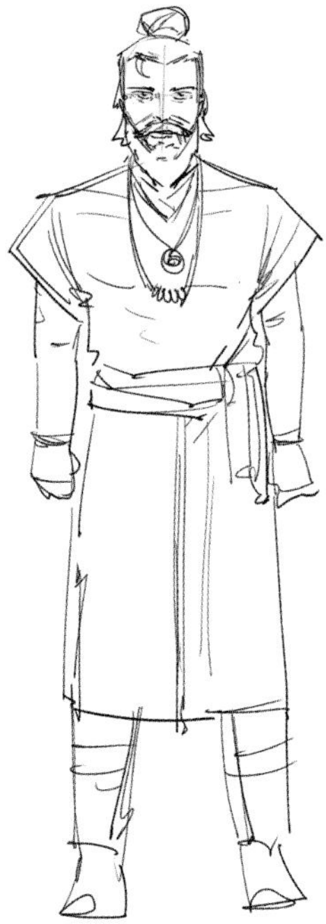

ALARA

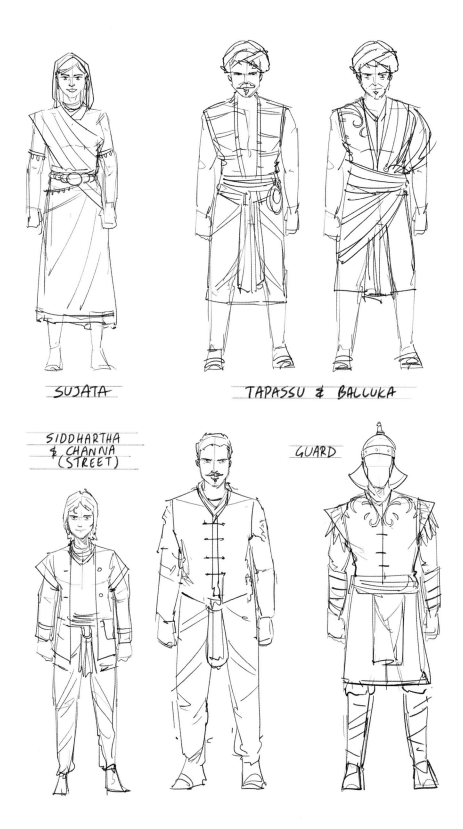

SUJATA

TAPASSU & BALLUKA

SIDDHARTHA
& CHANNA
(STREET)

GUARD

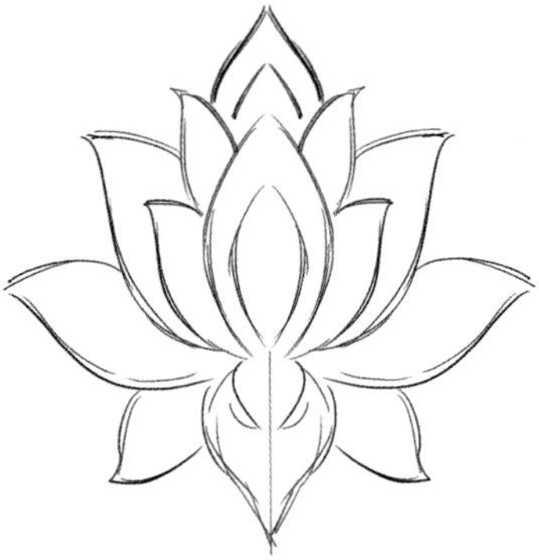

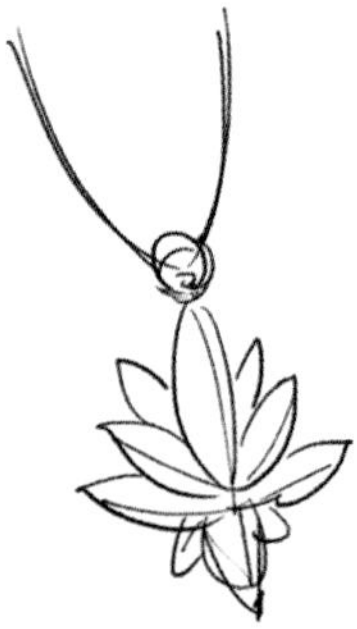

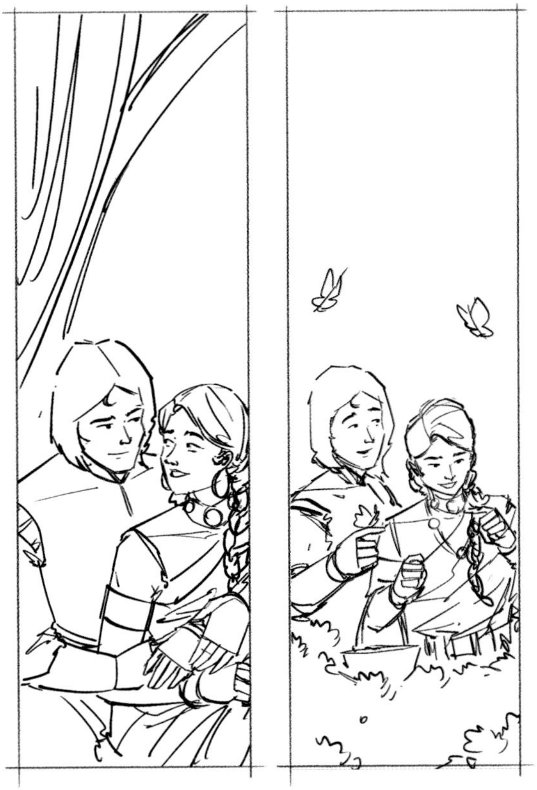

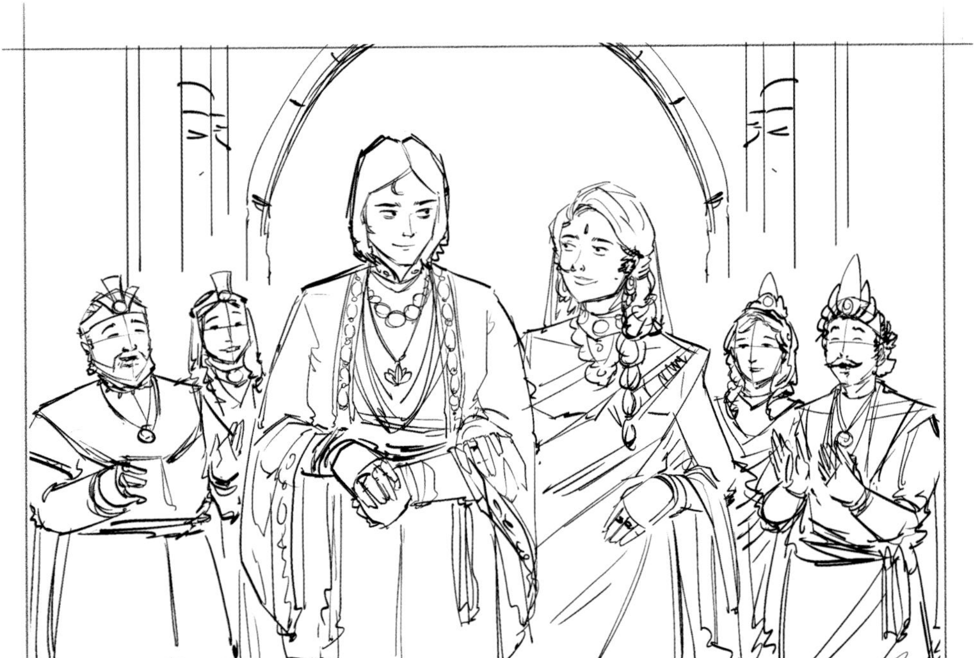

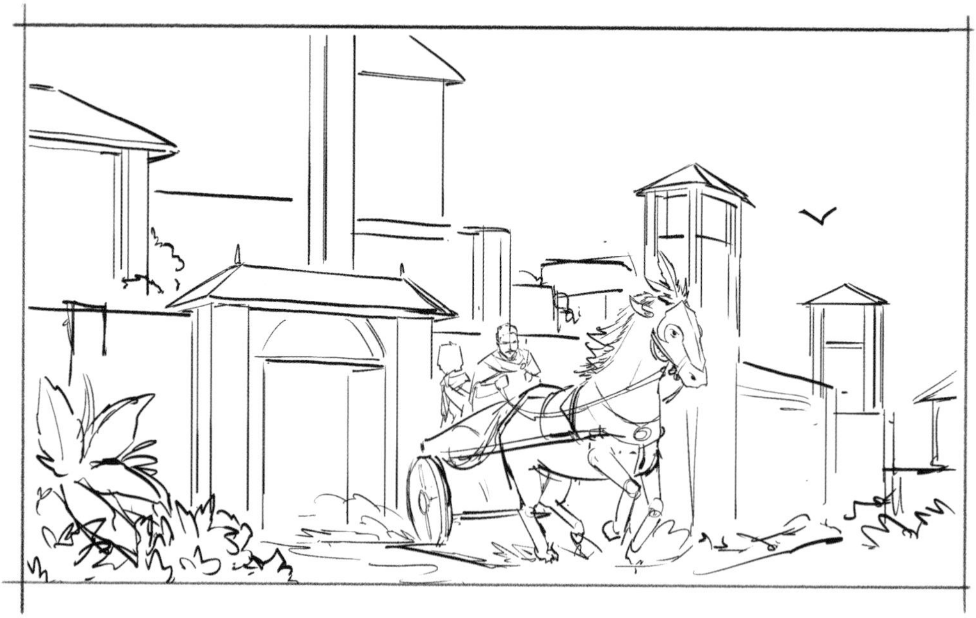

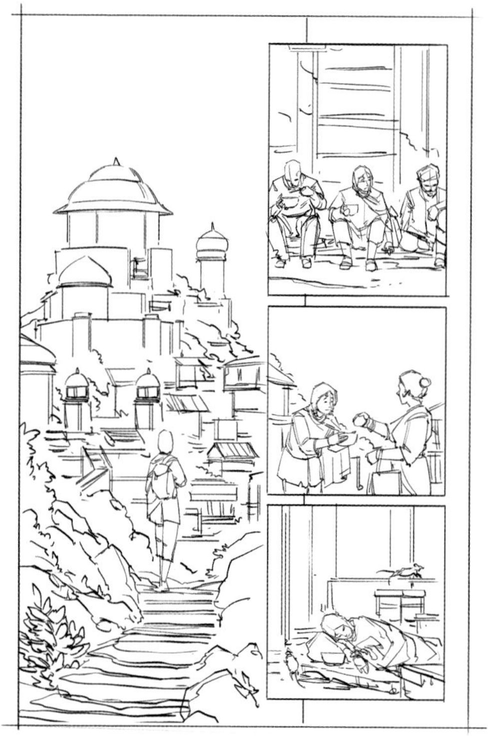

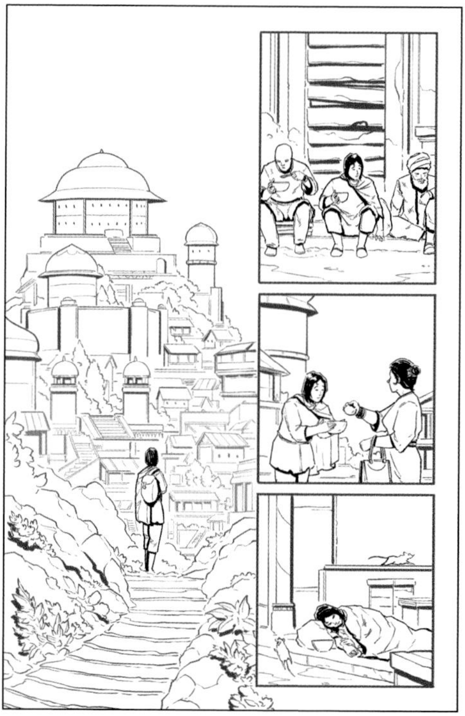

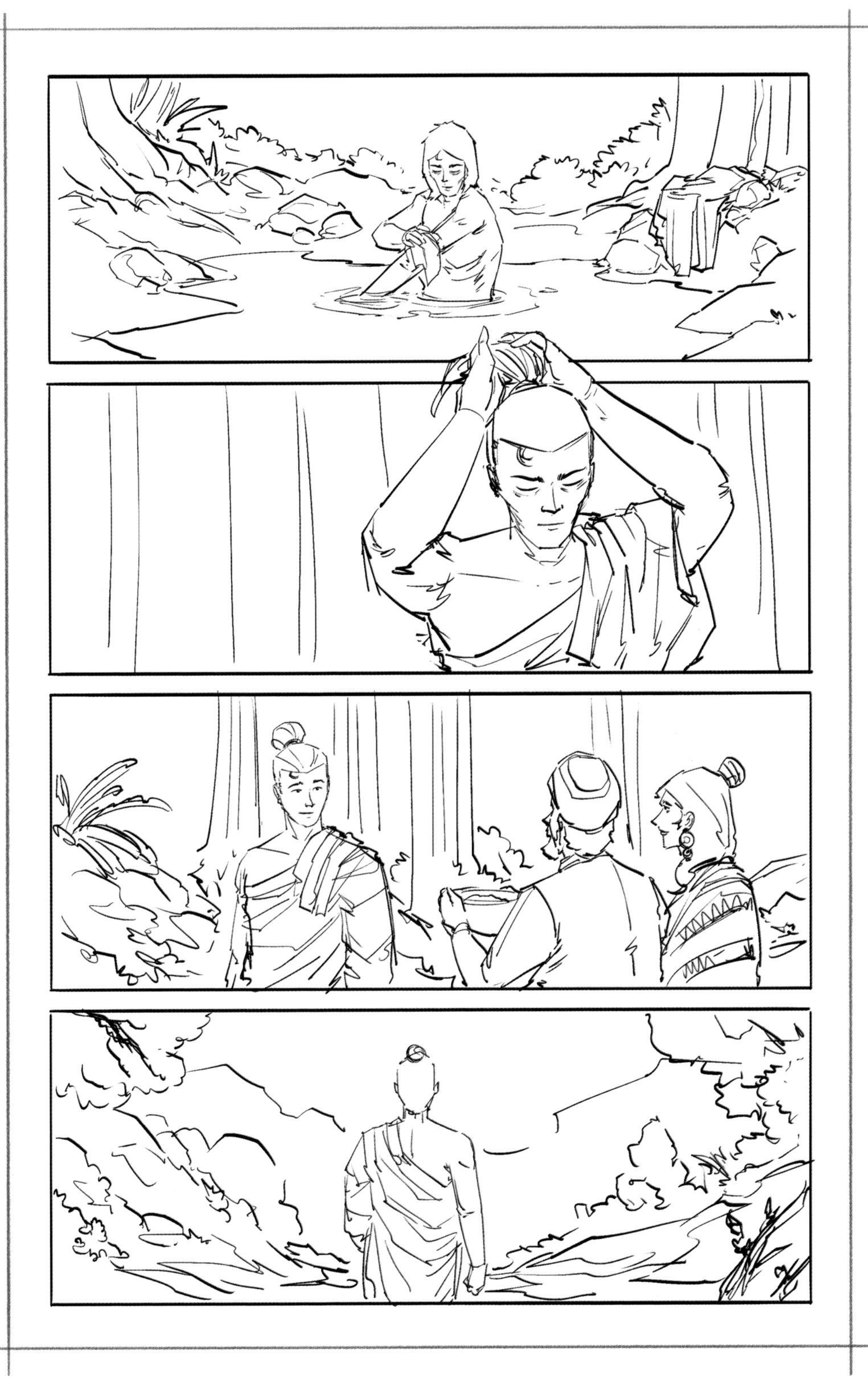

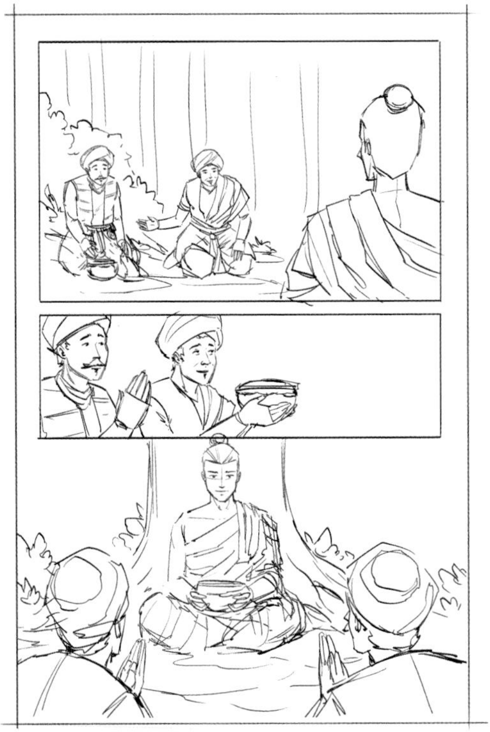
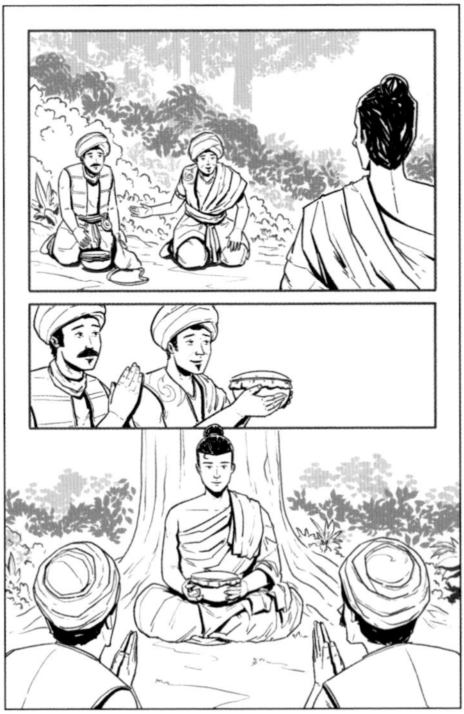
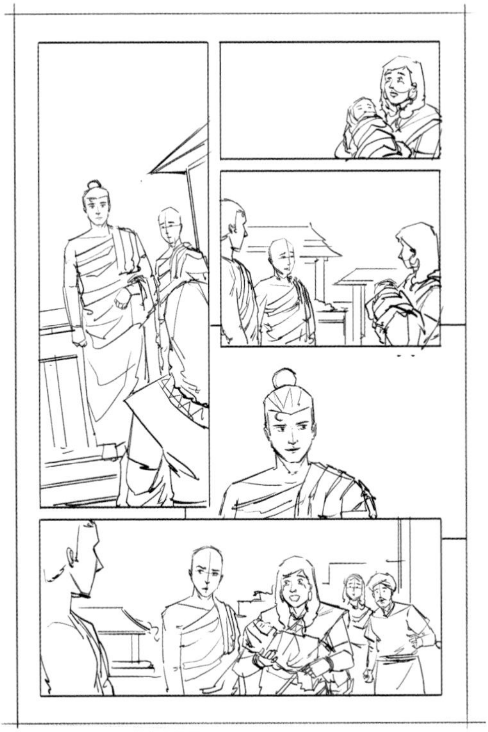
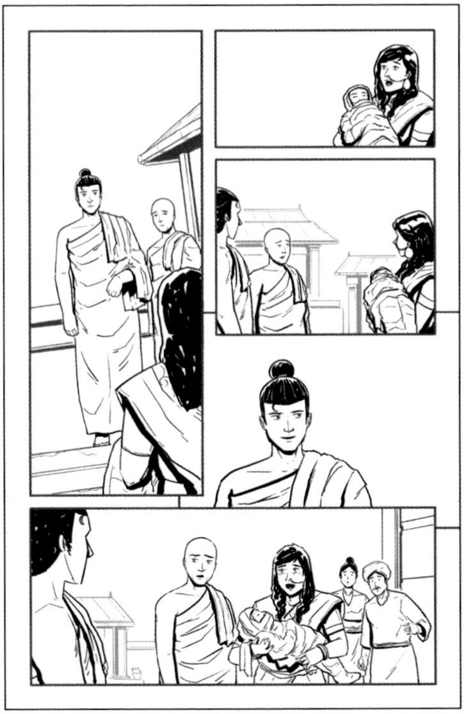

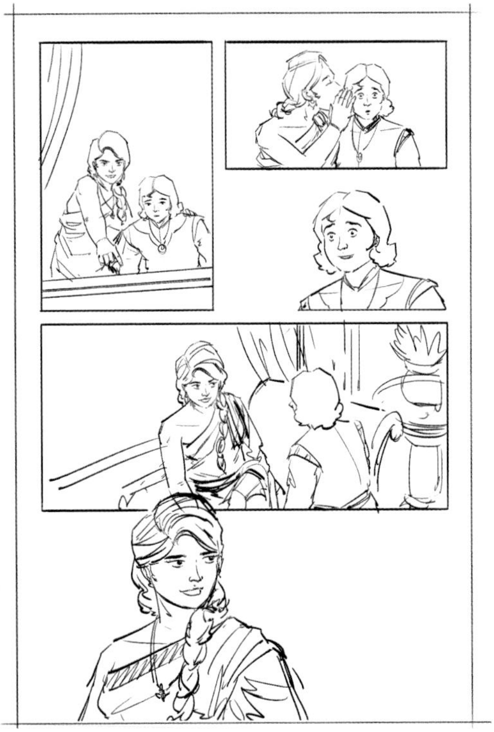

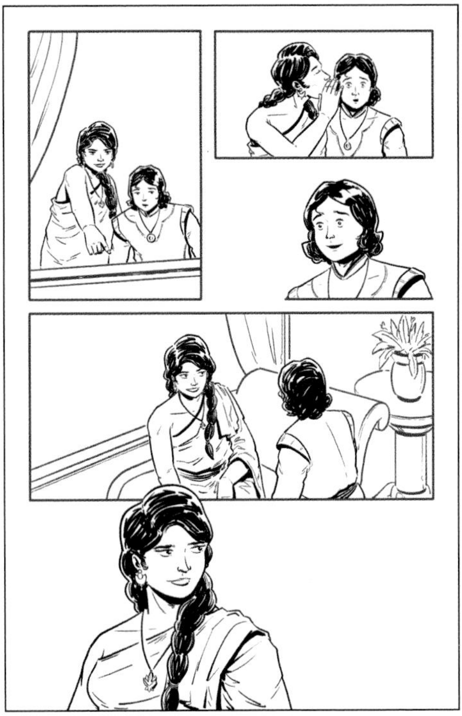

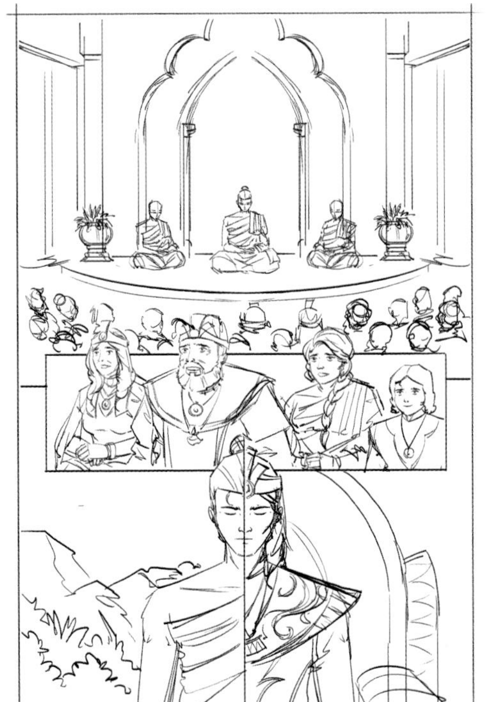

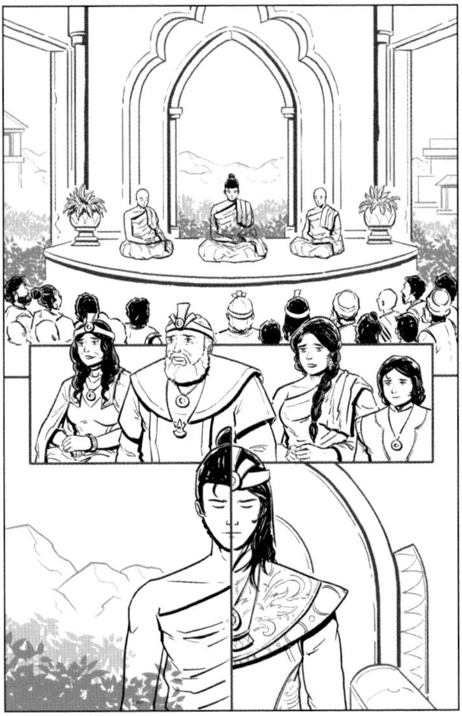